PRAISE FOR THESE
nationally bestselling authors:

Jayne Ann Krentz

"Who writes the best romance fiction today?
No doubt it's Jayne Ann Krentz."
—*Affaire de Coeur*

Tess Gerritsen

"Tess Gerritsen brings us action, adventure
and compelling romance."
—*Romantic Times Magazine*

Stella Cameron

"If you haven't read Stella Cameron,
you haven't read romance."
—*New York Times* bestselling author Elizabeth Lowell

Jayne Ann Krentz is one of today's top contemporary romance writers, with an astounding twelve million copies of her books in print. Her novels regularly appear on the *New York Times,* Waldenbooks and B. Dalton bestseller lists. First published in 1979, Jayne quickly established herself as a prolific and innovative writer. She has delved into psychic elements, intrigue, fantasy, historicals and even futuristic romances. Jayne lives in Seattle with her husband, Frank, an engineer.

Tess Gerritsen is an accomplished woman with an interesting history. Once a practicing physician, she has chosen instead to write full-time. A woman of many talents, she even plays the fiddle in a band! Tess has cowritten *Adrift,* a CBS screenplay, and has several other screenplays optioned by HBO. Having lived in Hawaii, she now resides in Camden, Maine, with her physician husband and two sons.

Stella Cameron is the bestselling author of more than forty books, and possesses the unique talent of being able to switch effortlessly from historical to contemporary fiction. In a one-year period, her titles appeared more than eight times on the *USA Today* bestseller list. This British-born author was working as an editor in London when she met her husband, an officer in the American air force, at a party. He asked her to dance, and they've been together ever since. They now make their home in Seattle, are the parents of three grown children and recently became grandparents.

HARLEQUIN®

TORONTO • NEW YORK • LONDON
AMSTERDAM • PARIS • SYDNEY • HAMBURG
STOCKHOLM • ATHENS • TOKYO • MILAN • MADRID
PRAGUE • WARSAW • BUDAPEST • AUCKLAND

HARLEQUIN BOOKS
225 Duncan Mill Road, Don Mills,
Ontario, Canada M3B 3K9

ISBN 0-373-83477-2

STOLEN MEMORIES

Copyright © 2001 by Harlequin Books S.A.

The publisher acknowledges the copyright holders
of the individual works as follows:

TEST OF TIME
Copyright © 1987 by Jayne Ann Krentz.

THIEF OF HEARTS
Copyright © 1995 by Terry Gerritsen.

MOONTIDE
Copyright © 1985 by Stella Cameron.

This edition published by arrangement with Harlequin Books S.A.

® and TM are trademarks of the publisher. Trademarks indicated with ® are registered in the United States Patent and Trademark Office, the Canadian Trade Marks Office and in other countries.

Visit us at www.eHarlequin.com

Printed in U.S.A.

1/01
BoT

CONTENTS

Test of Time
Jayne Ann Krentz

CHAPTER ONE

THE BRIDE TOOK another shaky sip of champagne and wondered for the thousandth time that day if she was making the biggest mistake of her life.

Katy Randall Coltrane tightened her grip around the glass in her hand in an effort to still the trembling fingers. If she wasn't careful she was going to spill the expensive champagne all over her beautiful gown. That would definitely be a shame, considering the time she had spent selecting the lovely confection of satin and silk.

Bridal jitters, she told herself forcefully. That's all this stupid anxiety amounted to—a bad case of bridal jitters. Surely all brides suffered from such assaults on the nerves. If wedding day jitters weren't a common problem, a label wouldn't have been coined to describe them. Everything was all right. Nothing had changed. There was no reason to develop a frightening sense of doubt at this late stage. All along she had been telling herself she knew what she was doing and that what she was doing was the right thing.

Everything would work out. After all, she was head over heels in love with the man who had just taken his vows alongside her. Furthermore, she was twenty-eight years old. Old enough to know what she was doing.

Of course, it hadn't helped her morale any to accidentally eavesdrop on that conversation taking place out in the hotel gardens a few minutes earlier. Served her right for not asking directions to the rest rooms, Katy told herself. If she had, she would never have taken the wrong turn that had brought her within earshot of two of her mother's acquaintances. The words still burned in her ears.

"The Randalls are certainly sending their one and only daughter off in a first-class manner," Leonora Bates had remarked. "This little bash must have cost Harry and Wilma a fortune."

"They can afford it," her companion had said easily. "If you ask me, they're probably thanking their lucky stars Katy found a husband, any husband at all. Katy's such a quiet, diffident little creature. I didn't think she was interested in anything except managing her father's horse-breeding programs. I wonder how her mother feels about her new son-in-law, though?''

''Wilma accepts Coltrane because her husband approves of him. She trusts Harry's judgment in people. And you know as well as I do that Harry Randall has a habit of judging people on their own merits, not on their background. And Katy didn't exactly find herself a husband,'' Leonora had said meaningfully. ''He found her. In fact, if you want my opinion, Garrett Coltrane took one look at quiet little Katy Randall and decided she was just what he wanted. By marrying her, he marries into several generations' worth of respectability and good social connections. Not to mention money.''

''Coltrane's obviously done well for himself financially in that farm-and-ranch-management consulting business of his,'' the other woman had pointed out. ''He's got money now.''

''True,'' Leonora had agreed, ''but in his own mind that probably doesn't make up for his dirt-poor background, his lack of a classy education and his wild reputation. The man's an ex-rodeo hand, for heaven's sake. Marrying Katy Randall will go a long way toward making people forget just how rough his past is.''

''You know, when that boy left town to join the rodeo, I thought we'd all seen the last of him. Who would have thought he'd come back after all these years and marry the daughter of the man who used to employ him to clean out stables?''

''I wonder if sweet little Katy knows what she's getting into.''

''It makes you think, doesn't it?''

Leonora had chuckled. ''I'll say it does. It makes me think that Garrett Coltrane is one hard, ruthless, shrewd sonova...''

Katy had slipped away before Leonora had finished voicing her opinion of Garrett Coltrane.

Now, sheltered behind a row of leafy plants in the hotel's elegant reception room, Katy nervously glanced down at the band of gold on her left hand. The ancient symbol of her new marriage flashed warmly in the lights of the ballroom chandeliers. She was thinking how very primitive the ring looked, when a laughing voice sliced into her reverie.

"So this is where the new bride is hiding out. What do you think you're doing sneaking around over here behind the potted palms, Katy? This is your day. You're supposed to be the center of attention. You should be out there in the crowd, mingling."

Katy's head snapped up in startled surprise, and she swung around abruptly, the long, heavy skirts of her full gown swirling about her ankles. "Oh, hello, Julie. I wasn't hiding out, I was just—" She broke off as her weak ankle started to give way beneath the combined forces of her sudden off-balance movement and the heavy, swinging weight of her gown.

Automatically she put out a hand to steady herself and succeeded in grabbing the rim of a huge clay pot that held a monstrous fern. Long green fronds bobbed lazily, caressing her face, and champagne spilled from Katy's glass into the rich loam that filled the pot.

"Damn," Katy muttered, righting herself quickly and simultaneously spitting a bit of fern out of her mouth.

"What a way for a bride to talk on her wedding day." Julie Talbot reached out to put a steadying hand under Katy's elbow. "Are you okay?"

"Of course. I'm fine. It's just my ankle. I took it by surprise, and it doesn't handle surprises well. You know that."

Julie grinned with the ease of an old friend. Fair-haired and blue-eyed, Julie was an attractive woman the same age as Katy. A year before, Julie had married the scion of one of the well-to-do families who lived in the local community.

That community, which Katy had called home all her life, was a small enclave of wealthy, established Californians who inhabited a prestigious section of the Southern California Gold Coast. There were wealthier towns in the state but few that boasted as much pedigreed social assurance. The residents of the small, charming, expensively quaint town considered themselves a cut above the glitzy, tacky Los Angeles crowd up the coast, most of whom had made their fortunes in films and limited partnership deals.

The members of the Randalls' social circle enjoyed the self-

confidence and refinement that comes from knowing one's money
and land can be traced back further than one generation. Some of
the locals could trace their heritage all the way back to Spanish
land-grant days. In California, that constituted an impressive heritage.

The Randalls' friends did not get involved in films or limited
partnerships. They invested in land and fabulously expensive horses
and pre-Columbian artifacts. Many enjoyed playing gentleman
farmer. They were shrewd business people who managed their inherited capital with great care.

Such people usually hired folks from Garrett Coltrane's side of
the tracks to work their land, look after their horses and tend their
beautiful gardens. It wasn't often that someone from the working
class segment of the community married into Katy's socioeconomic
class. Katy was well aware that Leonora Bates probably wasn't the
only one commenting on Garrett's coup. She told herself it didn't
matter. She and Garrett were in love, and she sensed instinctively
that Garrett was far too proud to marry for money.

"I wasn't sure if it was the ankle or too much champagne,"
Julie said. "For your ankle's sake, though, I'm glad you had the
sense to stick to flat shoes this afternoon. I was afraid you'd try to
wear a pair of high heels down the aisle."

Katy made a very unbridelike face. "I'm not that idiotic. If I had
tried to wear heels, I would have ended up in a heap at Garrett's
feet. Very embarrassing."

"For you, not for Garrett. I think it would take a lot more than
his bride falling at his feet in the middle of the wedding service to
shake your new husband." Julie sent a thoughtful glance across the
room to where Garrett Coltrane was deep in conversation with a
small group of male wedding guests.

Garrett wasn't doing much of the talking. As usual, he listened
in calm, thoughtful silence while others spoke. But when he finally
said something, everyone else in the group would stop and listen.
Coltrane had that effect on those around him, regardless of his
listeners' financial or social status. It was an inborn talent and one
he had apparently used in recent years to help establish his suc-

cessful consulting firm. He was the kind of man to whom other people automatically paid attention.

Katy followed her friend's gaze, chewing off what remained of her peach-colored lipstick as she studied her new husband with anxious eyes. Julie was right. It would take a lot to shake Garrett's granite-tough self-assurance. He was a man who knew what he wanted, where he was going and how he was going to get there. He was fortified for the tasks he set himself with a vast reservoir of strength that was both physical and emotional.

He was not a tall man; probably a notch or two under six feet in height, which made him slightly shorter than Katy's father. But when he stood in a group, he was the man you noticed first.

There was a supple leanness about him, a smooth, coordinated sense of animal grace that was even more evident when he was in a saddle. There was obvious power in his shoulders and thighs but no dramatic bulge of muscle.

Coltrane's hair was charcoal dark. He wore it short, and when he was outdoors it was usually covered with an expensive Stetson. Coltrane's features were bluntly hewn, and he had a forceful jaw-line. There was nothing delicate or soft about him, but there was, Katy had decided, something very intriguing about his eyes. They were an unusual shade of amber, a warm, golden color that Katy hoped would one day reflect the feelings she felt certain he had for her.

Garrett Coltrane was from an old-fashioned breed of male. The kind of man who was destined to make his own way in life and do it on his own terms. *The strong, silent type,* Katy had told herself time and again. If he were a stallion she would put him into a breeding program in spite of his lack of elegant good looks. She would want to capture his strength, endurance and determination. Such qualities should not be lost in either horses or humans.

Garrett had no talent or inclination to discuss his own emotions, but Katy had been sure all along that he was capable of great depth of feeling. Just because he could not or would not talk about his feelings did not mean he was unemotional. Katy had been sure of her analysis, sure that deep down Garrett loved her in his own strong, silent way.

At least she had been sure when she had accepted his calm, unemotional offer of marriage.

Katy wasn't certain just when during the four weeks since she had accepted Garrett's offer of marriage she had begun to question his real feelings for her. She had pushed the gathering cloud of uncertainties firmly to the back of her mind while she busied herself with the myriad tasks of planning a wedding and the move to Garrett's home.

The soft, hidden, romantic streak in her nature had led Katy into organizing a magnificent wedding. She had wanted everything to be perfect. Her mother had been delighted to help, and together they had produced a beautiful ceremony and reception. Everyone in the community had been invited, and everyone had accepted the invitation. The whole affair had gone off like clockwork.

But today as she had walked carefully down the aisle to join Coltrane at the altar, the storm of doubts and fears had begun to break free inside Katy's mind.

"Bridal jitters," Julie said easily beside her. "Relax."

Katy's mouth curved ruefully. She should have known Julie was bound to detect the attack of nerves. "Did you have them?"

"A small dose," Julie admitted. "Don't worry about it. You'll get over them. Let's see your ring."

Katy obediently held out her hand to allow Julie to examine the plain gold band. "Garrett is the old-fashioned type. He isn't very interested in fancy jewelry."

"Hmm. I see what you mean. But I like it, Katy. There's something fitting about it. It looks right on you, if you know what I mean."

"A plain ring for a plain woman?"

"Don't be silly. You always look attractive, and today you look downright beautiful. You were glowing as you came down the aisle."

"I think that was sweat."

"What on earth are you talking about?"

Katy grinned briefly. "All right—a fine, delicate sheen of perspiration. Does that sound better? That was probably what was causing the glow you think you saw. I was scared to death."

Julie giggled. "Well, you looked terrific. I like your hair down around your shoulders like that." She eyed Katy's dark ash-brown hair with a critical eye. "It looks good down. You should wear it that way more often."

"Maybe," Katy replied noncommittally. Garrett had said nothing about her hair today. Of course, he had never said anything about her usual style—a neat, businesslike twist—either. Garrett wasn't the kind of man who paid much attention to a woman's clothing or her hairstyle.

"Back to this ring," Julie went on determinedly, "I think it's a very appropriate sort of wedding ring." Her blue eyes twinkled. "Did you know that wedding rings are ancient symbols of fertility?"

Katy grimaced. "Trust a horse person to remember that bit of lore."

"Horse people worry a lot about fertility. You of all people should know that. Your family has been breeding those beautiful Arabians since before you were born, and you've been managing the Randall breeding program for the past four years. Very successfully, too, I might add. Makes one wonder if maybe you used your knowledge of breeding selection to pick your husband."

"Julie! For heaven's sake. What a thing to say."

Julie laughed delightedly, drawing the attention of some of the guests who happened to be standing within hearing distance on the other side of the ferns. They smiled as they spotted the bride talking privately to her friend.

"Frankly, I think Garrett will make an excellent stud," Julie went on, undaunted. "Viewed in strictly technical terms, the two of you should make a perfect match. You've got the aristocratic bloodlines and he's got strength and stamina. I can't wait to see the kids. Neither can your parents, if you ask me."

Katy blushed a vivid pink as her friend put into words the very thoughts Katy herself had been thinking. "I'm sure my parents haven't even begun to think about grandchildren."

"That's what you think. Your parents can't wait for a grandchild. It's my guess they'll be counting nine months from the wedding night and marking their calendar."

Katy's mouth tightened, and the brief sense of amusement she had been experiencing faded. "They had better not be holding their breath. I have no intention of being rushed into anything as important as having a baby."

"What about Garrett?" Julie demanded. "Doesn't he have a say in the matter?"

"Garrett and I haven't discussed children," Katy admitted quietly. If the truth were known, it was one of many personal topics they had not yet discussed.

Julie frowned. "No offense, but wouldn't it have been smart to talk about something that basic before you two made wedding plans?"

Katy felt her flush intensify. She glanced away from her friend. "Garrett is a very private person. It isn't always easy to talk to him about...about certain things."

"And you suffer from the same kind of reserve," Julie accused. "Makes me wonder what the two of you do talk about when you're together. But, Katy, you can't be shy about discussing things like children. Good grief, this is your future that's at stake."

"Don't worry about it, Julie. I know what I'm doing."

Julie's eyes narrowed thoughtfully. "I thought you did, but for some reason I'm suddenly not so sure."

"Thanks a lot. I'm twenty-eight years old, I'm considered intelligent and I've had a good education. I'm marrying a man with whom I have business and professional interests in common. It's a very logical thing for me to be marrying Garrett Coltrane. It makes perfect sense. Give me a little credit."

"I don't know." Julie was still obviously doubtful. "You're a woman in love. That wipes out a lot of the benefits of intelligence and education and logic."

Katy groaned at Julie's insight. So much for keeping her own feelings hidden. "Some friend you are."

"Well, I'll take comfort in the knowledge that even if you don't know what you're doing, Garrett probably does."

"He always seems to, doesn't he?" Katy agreed with an uneasy feeling. She covered the prickle of uncertainty with her best smile as her beaming mother came through the crowd in search of her daughter.

On the other side of the room Garrett glanced toward the cluster of huge potted ferns and saw Katy standing amid the greenery. She was talking to her mother and Julie Talbot. Garrett nodded to himself, satisfied that Katy had not managed to retreat to the sidelines at her own wedding.

She was quite capable of doing exactly that, he reflected. It wasn't that she was shy or inhibited. She was simply quiet and restrained. She didn't go around calling attention to herself. A very calm, quiet woman. Not the sort to hold center stage or go all dramatic in front of an audience. She had a sort of subdued, refined classiness. He liked that. It was one of the many small things he liked about Katy Randall.

No, he reminded himself with an unexpected feeling of possessiveness, she wasn't Katy Randall any longer. She was Katy Coltrane as of an hour ago.

There was something very satisfying about having everything in his life falling into place at last. He had a business that was expanding rapidly, a new home that suited the life-style he was carving out for himself, and now he had a wife who would function as both business partner, hostess and, well, as a *wife*.

A wife. His wife.

He now had a woman for his bed as well as an acknowledged expert on equine breeding programs for his high-powered consulting staff. He had someone to share breakfast with as well as someone with whom he could discuss business problems.

Until this past week he hadn't given more than casual thought to what having a wife was actually going to mean in personal, physical terms.

The decision to marry Katy had been almost instantaneous when he had seen her for the first time after all those years. He had paid a visit to the Randall Stud Farm because he knew it was one of the best managed in the state. It was true he was professionally interested in seeing that management firsthand. But a part of him acknowledged he had wanted to show Harry Randall that the wild kid Randall had given a job to when no one else would had eventually turned out all right.

It had been a surprise to learn that the little solemn-faced girl who had spent all her spare time hanging around her father's stables was now the brilliantly intuitive manager of the Randall breeding programs. Somehow it hadn't startled Garrett to learn that Katy had not turned into the sophisticated debutante type. Her whole world as a child had been filled with horses, and apparently nothing much had changed over the years except that she no longer rode.

On some gut level Garrett had known instantly that the grown-up version of Katy Randall would suit him perfectly as a wife. He had briefly tried to analyze his certainty and had come to the conclusion that it was all very simple. He had found himself an intelligent, sensible young woman who would fit right into his business and his life. She would be an asset to the consulting firm, and she would be comfortable with the kind of people he now saw socially.

Garrett was convinced Katy wasn't going to turn temperamental or difficult on him the way a more sophisticated woman might have. She would not grow bored and difficult when the novelty of being married faded. She was not the kind to wander off in search of adventure, amorous or otherwise. She had proved that, when she had come back to her father's stud farm after she had gotten her master's degree and tried working in Los Angeles. Instead of staying to make her future amid the bright lights of the city, she had come running back home and promptly settled down on her father's farm.

Garrett liked the way Katy seemed eager to please him, and he liked the fact that she could talk about the things that were important to him and to his business. She was also attractive in a quiet, refined way. There was no other man in the picture. All things considered, Garrett had seen no reason that he and Katy shouldn't get along very well together. Katy had plainly been of the same opinion.

But tonight was his wedding night and Garrett found himself thinking of other things besides the logical considerations that had led to his marriage. He had a right to enjoy this evening. After all, he had taken on the responsibilities of a husband today. There was a gold ring on his hand to prove it.

Garrett glanced down at the ring. He wouldn't wear it all the time, of course. It was dangerous for a man who worked outdoors a lot to wear rings. Even though he was now called a consultant, Garrett still spent a lot of time in stables, barns, pastures and farm fields. It was all too easy to lose a finger by having a ring catch on a stray nail or a sliver of metal. But he didn't mind wearing the ring for social occasions. And he liked the idea of Katy wearing hers all the time. It was a way of telling other men she was taken.

Garrett shifted slightly, aware of a deep anticipation that was purely physical in nature. His mouth curved ruefully in very private amusement. No doubt about it, he was beginning to think more and more about the rights and privileges he had gained along with his new status as a husband today.

Lifting the glass in his hand to sample the good champagne Harry and Wilma Randall had bought for the occasion, Garrett listened to the conversation going on around him while he surreptitiously studied his bride.

Calm, quiet, serene, gentle, intelligent, comfortable. Those were all adjectives that came to mind whenever he thought of Katy. She wasn't going to drive him crazy by demanding exotic vacations to far-off places or frequent trips to the bright lights of the city. In spite of her background, she was accustomed to a quiet life-style that revolved around the demands of the horse business. She would adapt easily to Garrett's life-style.

But it wasn't her adaptability Garrett was thinking about right then. Instead, he found himself wondering if Katy was going to lose any of that calm, quiet, gentle serenity in bed. He had speculated more than once during the past few weeks on what it would be like to go to bed with Katy. Judging from the gentle, almost shy manner in which she had responded to his kisses, he assumed she would be soft and sweet and very undemanding in bed. He sensed her experience was quite limited, and he told himself that should make things easy on him. She wouldn't be making a lot of awkward comparisons.

But he wanted to please her, Garrett realized. He wanted her to be happy and contented with her lot in life. Tonight he would do his best to bring her pleasure in bed.

He just hoped her natural restraint would not cause her to freeze up completely on him. He was not a Don Juan or a Casanova. He was thirty-five years old and he had known a few women in his life, but the truth was, he'd spent a lot more time with horses and cattle than with females of his own species.

The whole matter of mating was a lot simpler and easier for horses and cattle. They didn't have several thousand years of civilization to contend with, in addition to the basic instincts.

Garrett thought about that as he studied Katy. He tried to imagine her with her dark brown hair fanned out around her on a pillow. Her hair was very soft, he had discovered the first time he'd impulsively thrust his fingers into it.

The action had been unpremeditated. He had been standing beside Katy at a paddock fence, watching a new foal discover the wonders of the great outdoors in the company of its attentive mother when a brisk wind had arisen. Katy's neat hair had been blown into a tangled mane. She had laughingly clutched at it, but before she could control the dark stuff Garrett had caught a handful of it in his fist. He could still remember the silky feel of it between his fingers. He wondered now what her hair would feel like on the naked skin of his chest and thighs.

Tonight when she lay in bed beside him she would be looking up at him with those wide, serious gray eyes of hers. He imagined the feminine curiosity and, perhaps, the eagerness, that would be lighting those eyes and felt his body grow taut at the mental image. He liked Katy's eyes. They reflected honesty and warmth and intelligence. You could tell a lot about a mare by her eyes, Garrett told himself. There was no reason to think you couldn't tell a lot about a woman the same way.

Garrett found himself mentally stripping the full wedding gown from Katy's slender figure and trying to imagine what he would discover underneath the silk and satin. He had already seen enough of her in jeans and snug knit tops to have a fair idea of what to expect.

She was a few inches shorter than he was, somewhere in the

vicinity of five feet, four inches. Her figure had a neat, compact quality to it. If she'd been an Arabian, he would have described her conformation as excellent. Small and delicate, but sound, like a well-built mare. Sound, that is, except for her left ankle.

Her breasts were high and gently curved, her waist small, her hips nicely flared. It was true her slight limp marred the sense of gracefulness that delineated the rest of her body, but Garrett found himself rarely noticing her slightly halting stride. When he did, he found it oddly endearing. It occurred to him that a bad ankle was not going to matter one bit in bed.

Not for the first time today he wondered why he hadn't made an effort to get Katy into bed before the wedding. Realistically speaking, part of the problem had been logistics. After his initial visit to the farm, he hadn't been able to manage a lot of time with Katy. The demands of his own business had kept him occupied at the home office in San Luis Obispo. The courtship of Katy Randall had been conducted in a series of short, hurried weekend visits. In addition to the timing problems, there had been the added complication that Katy lived within shouting distance of her parents. She had a small cottage near the main house, and Garrett wasn't honestly sure how she would feel if her parents knew he had spent the night with their one and only daughter, even if she was twenty-eight. He hadn't wanted to commit any unforgivable social blunders at that stage of the game.

In addition to the logistics of the situation, Garrett had told himself that Katy wasn't the kind of woman who should be rushed.

There had been a lot of good reasons for not rushing off to bed with Katy, Garrett decided. But he was honest enough to admit there had been one final, half-understood explanation for his hesitation.

The truth was that a part of him had worried that Katy might change her mind about marrying him if he didn't perform up to her expectations in bed. The problem was that Garrett hadn't known for certain what sort of expectations a gently bred, possibly inhibited young woman of Katy's background would hold. He had been half afraid of lousing up his chances of marrying her by lousing up the seduction. It was very much out of character for him to have such qualms. Garrett had learned long ago to go after what he wanted and not allow uncertainties or doubts to get in the way.

But courting Katy had been different from pursuing his other goals in life.

His thoughts were interrupted by a familiar masculine chuckle.

"Getting restless, Garrett? I wondered how long you and my daughter would stick around to enjoy the party. I can't blame you for starting to think about leaving. It's nearly nine o'clock, and you've got an hour's drive ahead of you if you're going to get to that hotel over on the coast tonight. Wilma tells me Katy picked the honeymoon spot?"

Garrett nodded briefly at his new father-in-law. "That's right. I told her to handle that end of things along with the wedding plans. Not really my field of expertise."

Harry Randall grinned knowingly. "Definitely women's work."

Garrett liked Harry Randall. When he had first gone to work for him years ago, Randall had been the wealthiest man Garrett had ever met. Since then he had met a number of men who controlled a great deal more money than Randall did, but Garrett hadn't met any he liked or respected as much as he did Harry Randall.

It wasn't just that Randall had given him that all-important job years ago when Garrett had been running wild and looking for trouble. Garrett also respected Randall professionally. He had learned a lot working in the Randall stables. Randall knew most of what there was to know about breeding techniques, auctions and show rings. He was an expert stud-farm manager, and many of the management techniques Garrett had learned back then had been directly applicable to other areas of ranching and farming.

Randall was a strong, raw-boned man whose dark hair had turned gray over the years and whose athletic build was still surprisingly intact.

Harry Randall, was, in fact, an excellent match for his tall, striking wife, Wilma. She, too, had maintained a good figure by dint of daily riding and was still active in the show ring, where she sat regally atop the beautiful Randall Arabians. Wilma was also a brilliant hostess, a skill that had considerable value in a world where people who spent thousands of dollars on horses expected a certain amount of pampering and attention.

"I'm going to miss my daughter, Garrett. Best breeding-program manager I've ever had. She had a real talent for the business. You're getting one heck of a smart business partner."

"I know," Garrett admitted.

Harry smiled genially. "Well, I can hardly complain, can I? After all, I may be losing a manager, but I'm gaining a son-in-law. I was a bit startled to see you when you showed up a few months back, but I wasn't altogether surprised by what you'd done with your life. I always knew you had what it takes to make it on your own."

"You gave me a hand when I needed it, Harry. I won't ever forget that."

"I got my money's worth out of you," Harry said with a chuckle. "You worked harder than any stable boy I've ever had, except maybe my own daughter. I remember how she used to hang around you when you took that job with us. She was just a kid, but I think she was half in love with you then. When I saw the way she looked at you when you walked back into our lives a few months ago, I knew how the wind was blowing. And you weren't trying to run in the opposite direction, were you?"

Garrett's teeth flashed in one of his rare grins. "No, sir, I wasn't doing any running."

"Everything all set at your new place?"

Garrett nodded, his tone turning instantly serious. It was important that Harry Randall knew Garrett would do right by his daughter. "Don't worry. Your daughter will have a proper home. It's a big house, a little like your own. Sits on a bluff with a view of the ocean. Lots of land around it. Used to be a lot more land, but the owner began selling off parcels a few years back. Now there's just a stable and paddock, although the stable building needs some work. I'm having my old quarter horse, Red Dazzle, moved there as soon as it's ready. I've got him on some rental pasture now."

"You said someone's been living on the place?"

Garrett nodded. "There's a caretaker and his wife. They've been living there for years. I gather they were loyal to the original owner

and didn't have anyplace to go when he sold to me. I more or less
inherited them, but that's all right. I need a handyman, and I want
Katy to have a housekeeper. You and Wilma will have to come
visit us soon.''

"Thanks, Garrett, we'll look forward to the visit. But we won't
rush it. Newlyweds need a little time to themselves. Speaking of
time, Katy tells me you've arranged to take a couple of weeks off
for the honeymoon?''

Garrett nodded. "I figured we could both use the time to settle
in to the new house, and I want to get Red's stable in shape. There's
a lot to do. The caretaker has let a few things go. Not much incen-
tive to keep everything in shape, I guess. He wasn't certain the new
owner would even want him to stay on. As far as the house goes,
I haven't spent a night there myself. The interior designer just got
finished last week, and I had my personal belongings moved just
before I came down here for the wedding.''

"I know Katy is looking forward to seeing her new home.''
Harry smiled fondly across the room to where Katy stood talking
to a small group of well-wishers. His eyes darkened into a familiar
seriousness.

"Don't worry about her, Harry,'' Garrett said in response to the
unspoken question. "I'll take good care of her.''

"I know you will, Garrett. But it's still a little strange, you know.
Gives a man a funny feeling to see his little girl get married. Do
me a favor, will you?''

Garrett looked at him. "What's that?''

"Try to get her back in a saddle one of these days.''

"I understood she hasn't ridden in years. Wilma said Katy will
never get on a horse again.''

"Katy used to be beautiful in a saddle,'' Harry Randall said a
bit wistfully. "Even when she was a little girl. Remember? When
she took a horse into the show ring, she dominated the place. Every
eye was on her and the horse she was riding. She had a way of
making that particular animal look like the most important horse in
the entire known world. What's more, she made the horse feel the
same way. She won ribbons on animals I wouldn't bother to take
out on a Sunday walk. Somehow when she was with them, they

turned into champions. An amazing talent, and all of it gone to waste because of what happened the night of that damned barn fire.''

"She was badly hurt, wasn't she?'' Garrett asked, his eyes on his wife. He remembered how much she had loved riding when she was a kid. He'd lost count of the number of times he had tossed her up into the tiny, elegant English saddles she always used. When she'd cantered into a show ring, she almost always came out with more than her share of ribbons. Harry Randall was right—Katy had come alive when she was on a horse.

"Yes, she was badly hurt,'' Harry said softly. "But more than that, she was badly scared. So scared she's refused to ride again.''

"Is Katy's limp a leftover from the injuries she received in that fire?'' Garrett asked. Katy had never talked about what had happened that night. Garrett had picked up bits and pieces of the story from others.

"She was nearly killed trying to get the horses out.'' Harry's voice was suddenly grim. "She was leading the last one to safety when a burning timber fell right in the path of the horse. The animal was already on the verge of panic. The falling timber was the last straw. The blindfold came off and the horse went wild. A big, heavy stallion. Katy didn't have a chance of controlling him. The stallion knocked her down and trampled her in his effort to escape the fire.''

"Who got her out?'' Garrett asked tightly. It was the first time he had heard the full story.

"I did,'' Harry said simply. "I hadn't even realized she was inside the barn until someone told me she was missing. I found her unconscious, lying there in the dirt and the smoke. The flames were starting to explode around her. I found her and carried her out, and when she came to in a hospital bed she told me she would never ride again. The fear and the pain did something to her.''

"She lost her nerve when it came to horses,'' Garrett concluded. "You should have made her get back into a saddle the minute she came out of the hospital.''

Harry shook his head. "I couldn't do it. She wasn't a child. She was twenty years old and she had been severely traumatized. She made up her mind never to ride again and that was that. The fear in her eyes when she even thought about riding after that was more than enough to keep me from trying to force her to do anything. But maybe one of these days you'll be able to convince her to get back on a horse. Husbands can sometimes accomplish things fathers can't.''

''What makes you think I could get her to do something you and her mother haven't been able to get her to do?'' Garrett asked with genuine curiosity.

Harry shrugged. ''I don't know,'' he said softly. ''It's something about the way she looks at you. I think my daughter is very much in love.''

Garrett thought about that. ''Good,'' he said finally. ''That'll make things simpler.''

CHAPTER TWO

THE BIGGEST mistake of her life.

Katy sat staring out the window of Garrett's white Mercedes and tried to tell herself that her fears were groundless. Her bridal jitters would vanish now that the stress of the wedding and reception were behind her. She had worked very hard during the past few weeks to ensure that everything went exactly as planned.

The wedding had been picture perfect, an elaborate, formal ceremony followed by a joyous, no-expense-spared celebration. No bride could have wished for more. But perhaps this particular bride had worked a little too hard and was now paying the price. The stressful part was over. She was alone with her husband at last. She could relax.

But the truth was she could detect no real improvement in her mood. Her nerves felt raw and jumpy, her stomach was tied in knots and she was experiencing a strange sensation that seemed to hover somewhere between fear and wild panic. She had to get a grip on herself. She would not allow herself to have a full-scale anxiety attack on her wedding night.

"Are you okay, Katy?" Garrett slanted his wife a quick, assessing glance as he skillfully steered the car along the coastal highway. The road was shrouded in darkness. An invisible sea pounded on the cliffs below the curving highway. "You look a little tense."

"Getting married turned out to be more stressful than I had imagined," she admitted with a determinedly cheerful smile. "The whole thing doesn't seem to have bothered you much, though. I thought weddings made men nervous, not women."

Garrett shrugged, his shoulders moving easily beneath his expensive white shirt. His jacket had been tossed impatiently onto the back seat earlier when he had climbed behind the wheel, and he had loosened his tie before he'd started the car. It was obvious

Garrett had merely been tolerating the formal clothes he had been obliged to wear. "A wedding is just something a man goes through to get to the other side. No point getting worked up about one. A wedding is nothing more than a formality."

"A very pragmatic thought." Katy wondered if he had heard the underlying sarcasm in her voice. Probably not, she decided. Garrett wouldn't be expecting any sarcasm from her. She was almost never sharp-tongued, least of all with him. She leaned her head back against the headrest and contemplated the hours of planning, preparation and decision making she had put into the elaborate event he had just labeled a mere "formality." The task of arranging the perfect wedding had consumed her for weeks.

"You're tired," Garrett told her, as if that explained her unfamiliar mood to his satisfaction.

"I suppose so." She didn't feel tired, however. She felt keyed up and on edge, as though she were waiting for the other shoe to drop.

"Why don't you try to nap until we reach the hotel?"

"I can't sleep in a car."

"Try."

"I said," she repeated, spacing each word out carefully, "I can't sleep in a car."

"All right," Garrett said calmly, "why don't you talk instead? You haven't said more than a handful of words since we left the reception."

Katy drew a deep, steadying breath and blinked away a hint of painful moisture from her eyes. She was acting like an idiot. Nothing was wrong. She was married to the man she loved and he was trying to conduct a pleasant conversation as they approached the intimacy of their wedding night. She must calm down and relax. Everything was all right.

"It was a lovely reception, wasn't it?" Katy tried to sound relaxed and casual.

"Uh-huh," Garrett replied absently, his mind clearly on other matters. "You know, honey, I'm anxious for you to see your new home. You're going to like it. It fits you."

"I'm looking forward to seeing it," Katy said politely.

Garrett was momentarily reflective, unusual for him. "Maybe I should have let you see the place before I bought it."

"You bought the place before you asked me to marry you," Katy reminded him, mildly amused by his mood of momentary doubt. She knew it wouldn't last long. Garrett was invariably very sure of himself. "In fact, you'd already hired the craftspeople and the interior designer before you even mentioned that you'd bought a house. There wasn't any opportunity for me to get involved in the process."

Garrett frowned, his short flicker of uncertainty vanishing quickly. "I couldn't wait for the deal. When Atwood finally decided to sell, I had to act immediately. I couldn't risk losing the place. As far as the interior design part was concerned, I already knew what I wanted."

"I know." Katy half smiled to herself. "You told me you wanted a home that looked like my parents' home."

Garrett nodded. "I like that Southwestern stuff. It suits me and it suits you. You're going to be happy in your new home."

"I'm sure the designer did a fine job." Katy's brief flash of amusement disappeared. Now she wanted to cry. This was her wedding night. If she and Garrett were going to talk, they should be talking about themselves, not the work the interior designer had done. Normally Garrett's enthusiasm for his new property charmed and delighted her. His desire to create a real home of his own was touching. But tonight she couldn't summon the sense of anticipation she usually felt when she talked about such things with Garrett. She wanted him to talk to her on a more personal level.

"I was telling your dad there's still some work to be done on the stables before I have Red Dazzle delivered, but I don't think it will take too long to get one of the stalls in shape. I've got Bracken, the caretaker who's been living on the place, to help me."

"I'm looking forward to meeting the Brackens." Katy tried to keep her voice neutral. She propped her elbow on the door and leaned her head against her hand. The darkness outside seemed endless.

"Like I told you a few weeks ago, if they don't work out, we can let them go. But I felt more or less obliged to keep them on and give them a chance after I closed the deal with Silas Atwood. Atwood gave me this long story about how they'd been with his family since the year one, and he didn't want to see them dumped on the street.''

"It was nice of him to be concerned."

"It was the only thing he was concerned about," Garrett said. "That and not selling to his neighbor, Royce Hutton. Hutton had been after Atwood for years to sell him the last strip of Atwood land, but old Silas didn't like Hutton."

"Any particular reason?" Katy asked, not really caring.

"Hutton and Atwood's sons were friends. When Atwood's boy was killed in a fall several years ago, Hutton was one of the boys with him. From what I could gather, Atwood never forgave any of the kids who had been with his son that night, even though what happened was an accident."

"I see. Well, I'm anxious to see the place." Katy tried to inject a little more enthusiasm into her voice. What was wrong with her tonight? Most of her conversations with Garrett were about his plans for his consulting business, her role in that business or the land and house he had recently bought outside of San Luis Obispo. She had told herself time and again that Garrett wasn't the type of man who found it easy to talk about more intimate subjects.

During the past couple of months Katy had thought she and Garrett were growing close. Beneath their shared interests lay the promise of another kind of sharing. Katy had been deeply aware of the physical attraction between them almost from the start. The adolescent hero worship she had experienced in her youth was nothing compared to the rush of excitement that had materialized the day Garrett Coltrane had reappeared at the Randall Stud Farm.

It wasn't that she had spent the intervening years missing him. She had been busy showing her father's Arabians until her accident. Then she had become totally involved with her studies at college. Later she had immersed herself in her work. In fact, in recent years, she had only occasionally thought of Garrett and wondered what had become of him. But the day he'd walked back into her life a couple of months ago, it was as if her old, childish emotions had been in hibernation for years. They'd leaped into life, and this time they were no longer adolescent fantasies. They were full-blooded passions of a mature woman.

She had told herself Garrett was as aware of the physical attraction between the two of them as she was. Katy had assured herself he felt the same emotions she did. It was just unfortunate that the logistics of their situation had made it impossible to give full rein to their feelings until tonight. Besides, Garrett was not a man to rush matters. He did things in his own way and in his own time.

The strong silent type. How many times had she privately pinned that label on him, she wondered.

During the past two months she had been the subject of a very proper, very polite courtship conducted under the eyes of her parents and everyone else in town. But it had also been a very definite, very determined courtship. Katy had been happy enough to surrender to the joy of being courted by Garrett Coltrane, but she had once or twice wondered what would have happened if she hadn't been so willing. Somehow she wasn't at all certain the conclusion would have been any different. Garrett had learned how to get what he wanted in recent years.

It had not been a particularly romantic sort of courtship, Katy reflected. Garrett wasn't the kind of man who brought flowers or wrote poetry. He hadn't even tried to take the intimate side of the relationship too far, even though she had offered no resistance. He had kissed her, certainly, but there had been a certain restraint in all his displays of affection.

Katy had told herself that Garrett's physical remoteness was a very admirable, very endearing aspect of his nature. Most men these days were not so concerned about sexual restraint. They wanted to climb all over a woman and feel free to walk away the next morning with no sense of commitment. She had been deeply appreciative of Garrett's approach because she was the shy type herself. Her nature was warm and giving, but she definitely did not want to be pushed too quickly into a physical relationship. She was the kind of woman who needed time.

Well, she'd had time—too much time. Time enough to start developing a few doubts. Now her wedding night was upon her.

Perhaps Garrett had found it easy to restrain himself during the past few weeks for the simple reason that he wasn't all that interested in making love to her.

Perhaps he wasn't in love with her at all.

Katy knew that, objectively speaking, Leonora Bates had been right. Garrett had something to gain from a marriage to Katy Randall, something he hadn't had most of his life. Respectability, acceptance, and social connections were all reasons for a man to marry a particular woman. So, too, was proving something to himself. By marrying Katy, Garrett had made it clear that he really had pulled himself up by his bootstraps. He was now a force to be reckoned with. He had transformed himself from a no-account stable boy into a man who could ask for and get the hand of his former employer's daughter in marriage. Garrett Coltrane had come a long way. Marrying Katy Randall proved that fact to anyone who cared to look.

It gave Katy cold chills now to think that Garrett might have married her as a way of proving something to himself and the world.

She had to be wrong. Her future happiness depended on her fears being totally false.

Just a bad case of bridal jitters, she reassured herself.

But soon she would know the truth, Katy realized. She would know how Garrett really felt when he made love to her. Surely a man wouldn't hide his true feelings from a woman during the intimate act of love.

By dawn all her questions and doubts would be resolved one way or the other.

AN HOUR AND A HALF later Katy lay beneath the fluffy covers of a wide bed in the honeymoon suite she had selected and waited for Garrett to emerge from the bathroom. When she heard the shower stop, she put out a hand and switched off the bedside lamp. The romantic room was immediately concealed in darkness. Katy felt more comfortable in the shadows.

She had chosen this hotel and this suite from a brochure. It was one of many brochures she had collected after Garrett had casually put her in charge of finding a place to spend their wedding night.

The photo in the pamphlet hadn't lied. The suite was indeed all pink and silver and white and frilly and romantic. There was a mirror in the canopy that covered the circular bed, champagne in a silver bucket and a bowl of exotic fruit on the table in front of the window. There was even a fireplace set in one wall. Pink toweling robes labeled His and Hers hung in the bathroom.

Katy had been forced to stifle a nervous giggle when Garrett had first stalked into the room behind the bellboy. He had stood staring in astonishment at the fantasy that surrounded him. The contrast was outrageous. He was hard and dark and utterly male and the room was frothy and pink and quite feminine. He looked like a free-roaming stallion that had somehow found himself locked up in a boudoir.

"How in the hell did you find this place?" he had demanded ruefully as he'd tipped the grinning bellboy and dismissed him.

"It wasn't easy," Katy had assured him. "I went through a lot of brochures before I discovered the one advertising this particular suite."

Garrett had stared at her in chagrined amazement. "You mean you knew it looked like this when you made the reservations?"

Katy's momentary flash of amusement had faltered. "I thought it looked romantic in the picture."

Garrett had looked as if he wanted to say a great deal more on the subject, but something had stopped him. He had gallantly swallowed the rest of his outrage, glanced meaningfully at his watch and suggested gently that Katy use the bathroom first.

When she had come hesitantly out of the bathroom in her expensive new peignoir, she had found Garrett pacing back and forth across the pink carpet. He had stopped abruptly when she appeared, and his eyes had skimmed over her silk-draped figure with a degree of hunger that was startling. Katy realized she was too accustomed to his restraint. Then, with a brief, surprisingly gentle smile, he had vanished into the bathroom.

Now she was waiting for him, and it seemed easier to wait in darkness.

He loved her, Katy thought forcefully. He had to love her. She couldn't have misjudged him completely. The problem was simply that he wasn't the type of man who was good with words of intimacy. But when he came out of the bathroom and made love to her, she would be reassured. Her doubts would be put to rest once and for all.

In the bathroom Garrett dried himself quickly, fiercely aware of the sexual tension that now gripped his entire body. He couldn't remember ever feeling that much throbbing sensual anticipation. The ache in his loins was almost painful. It was as if an invisible barrier that had been in place for the past two months had crumbled completely today.

For the past eight weeks he had been thinking of a hundred different things, of his new home, of the future of his business, of how well Katy would suit him, of how satisfying it was to have Harry Randall's approval. Garrett knew he had been thinking of everything except about what it really meant to be marrying sweet, gentle, tractable Katy Randall.

Tonight he was no longer thinking of anything else except the most personal, intimate side of marriage, and the results of that thinking were evident in the pulsating hardness of his body. He felt as if he were suddenly and without any warning at the edge of his self-control.

His fingers shook slightly as he opened the bathroom door.

Garrett stood for a moment in the doorway, a towel draped loosely around his waist, and blinked to accustom his eyes to the unexpected darkness.

Then he smiled to himself as he realized what the absence of light meant. He should have known Katy was going to be shy at this stage.

"Hey," he said softly as he moved forward into the room. "Are you out there somewhere, honey?" His bare feet sank deeply into the carpeting.

"I'm here," Katy whispered from the bed.

He heard the nervousness in her voice and instantly wanted to soothe her. "I thought maybe you'd been turned into pink candy floss by some mysterious force in this room."

"Not quite. Maybe by morning the transformation will be complete." She sounded a bit more relaxed, as if his small attempt at humor had reassured her. "You'll wake up next to a big wad of sticky cotton candy."

Garrett grinned to himself. At least she hadn't frozen up completely on him. He halted beside the bed and stood looking down at her. He wasn't sure he would have known what to do if her natural shyness had caused her to panic and go ice cold.

She was just a little nervous, he told himself. It was only natural. Hell, he was feeling a bit strange himself. A tense, restless desire was beginning to pour through him. It was as if something in him had recognized that the waiting was over. After all these years, everything was at last over. After all these years, everything was at last in place. He had his business, his home and his woman. His future was waiting for him to claim it.

Slowly he sat down on the edge of the bed and looked at his new wife as she lay waiting for him in the shadows.

Now that his eyes had adjusted to the darkness he could see her more clearly in the pale light filtering through the curtains. Her hair was as he had imagined it would be, a dark, silky fan that framed her face on the pillow. The dim light washed out the color of her eyes but he could see the intense, questioning expression in them as she gazed up at him. There was a small, uncertain smile playing about her mouth. He wanted to soothe her, gentle her, make her relax so that she could fully enjoy the passion that was about to blossom between them. He groped for unfamiliar words.

"You looked good today," he said.

"Thank you. So did you."

So much for compliments. They obviously weren't his forte. He wondered what else a new bride might like to hear. Garrett rummaged around inside his head for something that would be reassuring and encouraging.

"I forgot to ask if you might be hungry. You didn't eat much at the reception. There's fruit over there on the table."

"I'm not hungry," she replied gently.

So much for the topic of food. Maybe he shouldn't be worrying about making reassuring conversation now. After all, they weren't kids. He and Katy both knew what was supposed to happen next. But Garrett still felt an illogical need to wipe away some of the tension he sensed in his new bride. There was still something in her eyes that made him uneasy.

"We could open the champagne," he suggested, glancing at the silver bucket. The ice inside had just about melted.

"If that's what you want," Katy said politely.

Garrett's mouth tightened. "No, I don't want any. Not now." Enough of this nonsense, he told himself. Maybe it would be easier to communicate in a more fundamental manner. Garrett stood up abruptly and let the pink towel drop to the plush carpet. Without a word he pulled back the covers and slid in beside Katy. He could feel the warmth of her slender, gently curved body immediately. His whole body ached to claim that warmth. Without any further hesitation he reached out to take his bride in his arms.

"Katy, you feel good," he grated thickly as she came willingly to him.

"So...so do you," she whispered against his shoulder.

Garrett didn't see any further need for casual conversation. He wasn't much good at it, anyway. His body was throbbing with the force of his need, and he was sure now that Katy wanted him, too. She might be shy but she certainly wasn't fighting him. In fact, she snuggled close, responding to the pressure of his hand on the small of her back.

Garrett fumbled for a few minutes with the nightgown and then lost patience.

"This is worse than trying to get a bridle on a saddle bronc. Why do women wear such complicated things to bed?" he asked as he finally grabbed the hem of the gown and swept the whole, frothy garment up toward Katy's head.

"I thought it looked romantic," she mumbled through the folds of the material.

"It's a nuisance."

"What should I have worn? A horse blanket?"

Garrett frowned in the darkness, wondering if she had taken offense. Instantly he was contrite. "The nightgown's pretty enough, I guess."

"Like me?"

That startled him. "What's that supposed to mean?"

"Am I pretty enough for you?"

"What a crazy thing to say! Of course you're pretty enough." This was getting outrageous. He didn't understand her peculiar mood. She had been acting strangely since the wedding. Garrett leaned over and kissed her, anxious to stop the odd words and the even stranger tone. "Katy, honey, you're all I want tonight. You're beautiful."

As soon as his mouth covered hers, a part of him relaxed. She responded at once, her lips soft and pliant beneath his own. Garrett groaned as he deepened the kiss. His hand slipped eagerly over her nude body, finding and enjoying the sweet curves of hip and thigh.

Katy's arms stole around his neck. He heard her whisper something against his mouth but he didn't catch the words. He urged her lips apart, eager to taste the exciting warmth of her. His body stirred, seeking hers with a swift, consuming hunger. Garrett knew that he wouldn't be able to wait very long before he slaked that hunger in Katy's soft warmth. He couldn't remember ever needing a woman as badly as he needed Katy tonight. Somewhere within him a dam that had been in place for months had burst.

Beneath the covers he stroked Katy and felt a jolt of satisfaction when she moaned softly and pressed against him.

Her small cry sent euphoric tremors through Garrett. She was reacting so beautifully to his touch. It surprised him, but it also pleased him as nothing else ever had. His fingers glided over her breasts and paused briefly when her nipples went taut.

The lure was irresistible. Garrett reluctantly freed Katy's mouth and lowered his head to taste the hard berries he had aroused. Katy shivered when his tongue circled the peaks of her swelling breasts. Garrett was enthralled by the reaction.

"So sweet," he muttered.

His hand went lower as he eagerly searched for the soft, shadowed thicket that shielded Katy's most intimate secrets. She gasped as he found it, stiffening slightly as though afraid he would handle her roughly. She should know him better than that, Garrett thought. He would never hurt her.

"Take it easy, honey," he whispered. "Relax. Just relax and let me touch you. Lord, you're warm. And so soft." He found the tender dampening womanflesh between her legs and closed his hand around her.

Her fingers clenched in his hair, and her body arched beneath him in sudden, wild abandon. She was a sweet, even-tempered well-bred, well-mannered little mare who was suddenly showing him that she had a sensual, spirited side to her nature. Garrett hadn't expected it, and the new knowledge he was gaining about his wife sent the blood pounding through his veins.

He wanted her; wanted her with a hot, sweeping passion that was totally new to him. He couldn't remember ever having felt quite like this. No woman had ever given herself to him this freely, no woman had ever clung to him with so much urgency. He wanted nothing more than to bury himself in the velvet-lined sheath he was preparing. The small cries Katy was making against Garrett's perspiration-damp skin assured him she was as eager as he was.

Unable to wait any longer, Garrett moved onto her, aware that he was trembling with the effort it took to keep from forging into her too quickly. He could feel his muscles bunching in his shoulders and tightening across his stomach as he struggled to keep a grip on the last shreds of his self-control. He was shuddering the way a stallion shuddered in the presence of a mare. Garrett felt the same primitive wildness coursing through himself. It made him light-headed and filled him with a sense of raw masculine power. At the same time he longed to give Katy the same kind of pleasure he was soon going to be feeling.

"Part your legs, honey," he said through his teeth as he came down on top of Katy's soft, welcoming body. "Part your legs for me. Let me come inside. I want you."

Katy's hands tightened around him, her fingernails digging into his skin and setting off new sparks of electric excitement. She shyly opened her thighs for him, and Garrett groaned as he reached down to guide himself into her warmth.

Katy's small intake of breath was accompanied by a tightening of her whole body as Garrett thrust heavily into her. Her muscles constricted as if in protest and Garrett went still, aware of how small and tight she was. He must not hurt her. He must make this good for her. Maybe he'd already ruined things by pushing too fast.

"Garrett, oh, Garrett my darling, I love you so much," Katy murmured, clinging to him as if her life depended on it.

Garrett closed his eyes in an overwhelming sense of relief. It was going to be all right. She still wanted him. Slowly, carefully he began to move inside her, but the instant he sensed her renewed response he felt the last of his control slip rapidly out of reach.

He clamped a possessive hand around Katy's rounded buttocks, bringing her up into the position he wanted so that he could drive as deeply as possible into her.

"I want all of you," he told her hoarsely. "I want every inch of you."

She said nothing, but she cried out again as he stroked into her. Garrett pushed his hand between their bodies, seeking the bold little nubbin of desire that was the center of her sensation. When he discovered it, he was rewarded by Katy's sudden, delicate convulsion.

She seemed to explode beneath him as she found her release. Garrett was sucked into the vortex of passion that spiraled around them both. He felt Katy surge upward, instinctively seeking the fullness of him, and he gave himself to her with a husky shout of satisfaction.

Katy was stunned by the sensation of pleasure bursting deep within her. This was what her body had been seeking for the past few minutes. She had never experienced it before, and the full impact left her breathless. Unable to do anything else, she wrapped herself tightly around Garrett and rode the shifting currents of the storm with him.

It was a long time before she came completely back to reality. She was aware that Garrett hadn't left her body. He was still lying on top of her, the weight of him pushing her into the bedding. She could feel the sheen of dampness on his skin. He felt heavy and replete.

A physically satisfied male.

Well, she could hardly complain about that, she thought. In all honesty, she was forced to admit that physically, she, too, had found satisfaction. The difference was that for Garrett this kind of satisfaction was clearly sufficient.

But as she came slowly back to reality, Katy realized it was not enough for her.

Her own words, spoken in the most intimate moments of passion came back to haunt her. *I love you.*

There had been no answering response from Garrett. Even in the depths of desire he had been unable to speak of his love.

She could no longer tell herself that he was simply the strong, silent type. After all, he had been able to speak of such things as desire and his own need. He had said excitingly rough, urgent things to her that had increased her response to him. He had told her he wanted her.

But there had been no words of love.

Katy slowly opened her eyes and looked up into the dark mirror overhead. She had to accept the truth. Whatever Garrett felt for her, it didn't include love.

She had made a terrible mistake.

Garrett shifted finally. He exhaled deeply, a long, relaxed sigh of contentment and satisfaction and then he raised his head to look down at Katy. In the shadows she could see the possessive gleam in his mouth. He stroked her tangled hair back from her cheek with an absent gesture of affection.

It was the kind of gesture, Katy told herself grimly, that he might have used with a mare who had performed especially well for him.

"You're a little new at this, aren't you?" he asked equably.

In her overly sensitive state of mind, Katy wondered if the comment was meant as a mild insult. Perhaps she hadn't performed all that well. She stiffened slightly beneath him, but Garrett didn't seem to notice.

"A little," she said cautiously.

He nodded, apparently not too put out by the information. "I thought so."

"Was I that bad?"

He looked shocked at the question and at the underlying vehemence. His big hands cradled her face with unexpected urgency. "What the hell are you talking about now? It was great. All of it. I've never felt—" He broke off abruptly. "Forget it. I was completely satisfied and I had the impression you were, too. Don't try to deny it, honey."

"I'm not denying it."

"Good." He appeared relieved. He rolled onto his back, cradling her against him. "I guess a woman like you is bound to be somewhat high-strung on her wedding night."

"Is that right?"

"Sure, and I can understand it." He made a sweeping, magnanimous gesture with one hand. "You're kind of quiet by nature. You always were. You haven't exactly led a wild life since I last saw you, have you, honey?"

"No," she agreed coolly, "I haven't. Compared to your life, I imagine mine must seem rather dull."

"No, it doesn't. It seems warm and safe and comfortable. I'm glad you've been safe and secure all these years. You're not the type to try for the fast lane."

The thought that he found her inability to fit into the fast lane amusing fueled the dangerous mixture of emotions that were beginning to simmer in Katy. "I haven't exactly been living in a locked box, you know. I have plenty of friends and a reasonably active social life."

"Hey, calm down, I didn't say you'd been living in total seclusion."

He tried soothing her with a slow stroking motion that only made Katy think of the techniques he used to soothe horses. She remembered well that Garrett had always been good with horses. He'd handled animals in her father's stables that no one else could control. She stirred against him and tried to pull away. "Please," she whispered, "I want to go clean up."

He held her more tightly. "It's all right, you know. There's nothing to be embarrassed about. It's all natural. Go to sleep, Katy. It's been a long, tiring day and you're still riding on your nerves. Just go to sleep."

She knew she wasn't going to be able to escape the restraint of his arm without causing a major scene, so Katy lay still beside her new husband and waited for him to follow his own advice. She had a horror of scenes.

It didn't take long. Garrett was asleep within minutes.

Katy carefully slipped out from under his arm to go into the bathroom. Once inside, she shut the door and sat down on the edge of the tub to cry.

She didn't cry for long. She wasn't the type. Ten minutes later Katy wiped her eyes and made her decision.

CHAPTER THREE

SOMETIME AFTER one o'clock Katy managed to crawl back into bed without disturbing Garrett and fall into a restless sleep. Garrett had been right about one thing—it had been a long, tiring day and she needed the rest.

She awoke shortly before dawn, coming alert with an unnatural abruptness. She knew a brief sense of disorientation until, with a jolt of adrenaline, she registered the fact that she wasn't alone in the wide bed.

Of course she wasn't alone. Garrett was beside her. She had married a man who didn't love her but who now had the right to sleep with her.

Slowly Katy pushed aside the covers. She sat up carefully, not wanting to awaken her husband. Her beautiful nightgown was in a crumpled heap on the floor beside the bed, a pool of silver on a carpet of pink. Katy reached for the robe of the peignoir and pulled it around herself.

In the light of an approaching dawn the wedding suite appeared frivolous to the point of being ridiculous. Katy winced as she looked around. The place could give a person cavities just from looking at it. It was as phony and full of illusion as her marriage. En route to the bathroom, Katy noticed that there was nothing but water left in the ice bucket. The champagne would be warm. But that hardly mattered. Women such as she did not drink champagne for breakfast. Only fast-living types got to do that sort of thing. Katy barely resisted the urge to pick up the bucket and hurl the contents at Garrett's unsuspecting head.

By the time she had emerged from the bathroom dressed in jeans and a green top, the sun was just barely above the horizon. A glance at the bed showed Garrett still apparently asleep. Katy glared at his motionless figure sprawled beneath the pink-and-white-striped sheet. The man hadn't even noticed that his bride was missing from his side, she thought resentfully. She stalked to the window.

It took her a moment to identify the emotions she was experiencing. Katy had not had a lot of experience with such things as resentment, anger and outrage.

Outside, sunlight played on the Pacific, changing the color of the ocean into an intense blue that stretched to the end of the world. Katy gazed out at the endless vista and wondered at the force of the anger that blazed within her. She had never felt like this before in her life. It was as startling in its own way as the discovery of the depths of her own passionate nature had been last night.

Garrett Coltrane, she reflected furiously, was the cause of both new experiences. For some reason that only made her angrier.

"Morning, honey." Garrett's voice came from behind her, rich and husky with sleep and what sounded suspiciously like remembered satisfaction. "You're up bright and early. Get enough rest?"

"I'm fine, Garrett." Katy kept her eyes on the view outside the window.

"You're already dressed. What's the rush? We've got plenty of time. Why don't you take off those jeans and hop back into bed?"

Katy seethed. "Now, why on earth would I want to do that?" she asked very softly without turning around. "Give me one good reason."

There was a slight pause behind her as if Garrett was finally beginning to sense that all was not quite as he had assumed it would be that morning.

"You want a reason?" he asked blandly, "How about because this is the morning after our wedding and new brides usually want to spend a little extra time in bed. So do grooms." He spoke carefully, obviously feeling his way. The sheets rustled slightly as he pushed them aside.

"What would you know about the behavior of new brides and grooms? Have you been married very many times?"

"No, I haven't been married before and you know it. Katy, what's wrong?" He stood up and started toward her.

Katy could hear him padding barefoot across the carpet. She was afraid to turn around, afraid to see the whole of him in the light of day. He was strong enough and powerful enough to affect her senses in darkness. She didn't want to have to deal with the full force of him in daylight. Not yet.

"Katy?" He sounded impatient now.

"You don't love me." She spoke without moving and she knew her words had halted him, too.

"Hell, Katy, ever since the wedding, you've been saying the damnedest things. What's the problem here?"

"The problem," she repeated as if he were a slow-witted mule, "is that you don't love me."

He took a deep breath, clearly striving for patience and understanding. Both were, apparently, alien. "Katy, I don't know what's gotten into you. You're not making much sense. Nothing has changed between us since yesterday or last week or last month, for that matter. Everything is going just as we planned. I feel the same way about you as I did when I asked you to marry me."

"I know." Her voice was laced with disgust.

"Then why in hell are you so upset?" He sounded honestly confused.

"It's not your fault."

"Well, that's a relief," he retorted. "Mind telling me who is to blame and exactly what he or she is being blamed for?"

Katy's fingers clenched around a fistful of curtain. "It's my fault," she said starkly. "I'm to blame. I misjudged you, your feelings and the whole situation. I thought you loved me. Do you hear me? I was stupid enough to think you loved me. I thought you just had trouble saying the words. I thought the only problem," she added scathingly, "was that you were the strong, silent type. Isn't that a joke?" She spun around to confront him, and her treacherous left ankle collapsed beneath her, pitching her forward.

Instantly Garrett was there, gliding to catch her in his arms before she hit the floor. "Take it easy," he muttered, steadying her. "Calm down, honey. You're going to hurt yourself. Just take it easy." His voice was the familiar, soothing rumble he used to quiet a horse.

Katy shut her eyes in an agony of fury and humiliation. She swore bluntly, using a four-letter word she knew Garrett had never heard her use before in all the time he had known her. As she found her balance, she jerked free of his grasp. She stumbled a little as she righted herself, but she stayed upright when she reached out to catch hold of the edge of the table. Using it as a prop, she faced him once more. Her eyes were brilliant with the force of her emotions.

"It finally dawned on me yesterday that I might have made the biggest mistake of my life. During the past week I got more and more uncertain, but I kept telling myself all brides were nervous. Yesterday I decided I was just suffering a bad case of bridal jitters. But the truth was, I wasn't willing to admit to myself that I had been so wrong about you. But last night I had to face the truth."

Garrett stared at her as if she'd taken leave of her senses. He appeared totally unconcerned with his own nudity. His body was lean and powerful in the morning light as he faced her with his legs braced. His eyes glittered with annoyance and a growing frustration.

"Last night," he said, "the only truth you had to face was the fact that you're a very sensual woman. I fail to see what's so devastating about that. From all outward appearances, you liked what you found in my arms."

Katy's anger leaped into a bright flame. "I'm not talking about sex, I'm talking about love. I did not find love in your arms last night, Garrett. The sex isn't much good without it."

The first traces of real anger appeared in his eyes. "What happened between us last night was damned good. Don't try to deny it."

Katy threw up her hands in a gesture of frustrated fury. "Why am I even bothering to argue with you? You don't understand. You never will understand. You married me because I'm Katy Randall. Because you like my father. Because I'm an expert on breeding programs. Because you had reached the point in your life when you wanted to add a wife to your list of possessions."

Garrett raked his fingers through his dark hair. He was still making a bid for patience. "You're right about one thing; I don't understand you. Katy, during the whole time we've been seeing each other seriously during the past couple of months you've been a reasonable, sensible woman. You and I have a lot in common. We've known each other for years. Your father approves of me. We're physically attracted to each other. What more do you want? No one forced you to marry me. You seemed to want it as much as I did. I just don't understand what's wrong with you this morning."

"Last night I told you I loved you," she said, hating to have to repeat the words.

His expression softened. "I know," he said gently. "You were very sweet last night."

She ignored him. "You didn't bother to respond."

"Not respond! Lady, I made love to you."

"That doesn't count."

It was Garrett's turn to swear. He did so, forcefully. "What did you want from me? Some kind of flowery, mushy love poem in the middle of the night? If that's what you were expecting, then you're more naive than I thought."

"All I wanted," Katy said, "was to be told that you loved me, too. I wanted some reassurance that I had made the right decision."

"You *did* make the right decision. Ours is going to be a good marriage. At least it will be as soon as you settle down and stop carrying on like a filly who's just had a saddle put on her back for the first time."

It was all Katy could do to keep herself from throwing something at him. She lifted her head and pinned him with her eyes. "Are you saying I was wrong? That I'm upset over nothing? Are you saying you do love me?"

He sucked in his breath but his eyes never wavered. "I'm saying that we've got everything going for us. I don't know what the hell's the matter with you this morning, but we're going to make this marriage work."

"Do you love me?"

"I want you, I respect you, I intend to take care of you," he stated with dogged determination. "I've never done anything to make you think otherwise. Christ, I didn't even take you to bed until I put a ring on your finger. I thought you'd appreciate all that gentlemanly restraint, if nothing else."

"But you don't love me."

Garrett's hard face was set in rigid lines. He was obviously fighting an internal battle as he tried to dampen his growing anger. "Don't do this to yourself, Katy. You're tearing yourself apart for no good reason."

"Just answer my question, damn you!"

Something snapped in his self-control. "All right, if you want to hear it spelled out, the answer is no, I don't love you."

Katy felt the last of her naive hope wither and die. She blinked rapidly and swallowed to get rid of the tears that were threatening to overwhelm her. Her fingers were shaking as she clamped her hand around the edge of the table to steady herself.

"I guess it's better to get the facts straight now, even if it is a little late," she whispered.

Garrett watched her through narrowed eyes. Then he took a long step forward and caught her by the arms. His fingers locked around her, and he anchored her in front of him. "You've had your say, Katy, now you're going to listen to me. There's no need to look like a foal who's just had her legs kicked out from under her the first time she tries to stand. It's not my fault you've got some fantasy notion about love and marriage. I thought you were too sensible and down-to-earth to indulge in that kind of idiocy. I thought you understood what was important and what wasn't. Love is just like this screaming pink hotel room—nothing more than a lot of pink-and-white froth that evaporates in the sun or melts in the rain."

"You don't know what you're talking about."

"I do know what I'm talking about," he gritted. "It's easy enough to say the words. Do you think I haven't heard them before? Do you think I don't know how meaningless they are? Words like love don't count, Katy. Commitment counts. Honesty counts. Compatibility counts. Sex counts."

She flinched, her eyes widening. "What do you mean, you've heard words like love before?"

"Katy, I'm thirty-five," he reminded her in exasperation. "I've had a little more experience than you have."

"Oh, I see. I'm not the first woman you've had in your bed who's told you she loves you, is that it?" she snapped.

Garrett looked exasperated. "No, you're not."

"Did you give those other women the same lecture you're giving me? Did you spell out in detail the fact that you didn't love them? Did you call them idiots for wanting all the silly pink-and-white trappings?"

"You talk as if there have been hundreds of women," he retorted gruffly. "Katy, I'm a working man. I always have been. You, of all people, know the kind of life I lead. It doesn't allow a lot of time or opportunity for an endless chain of affairs."

"Okay, forget the numbers," she shot back. "Just tell me how many of those women you loved in return."

His gaze turned very dangerous. "I only made the mistake once, and that was a long time ago. It happened after I left that job at your father's stables and hit the rodeo circuit as a pro. She was the prettiest woman I'd ever seen and she wanted me. Me, a guy who's biggest accomplishment at that point was that he'd managed to stay out of jail. A guy with no respectable family and no respectable future. I couldn't offer her more than a lot of dreams and hopes and plans. But it turned out she didn't care about things like that. She was a spoiled little rich girl who got her kicks sleeping with rodeo cowboys. Some women go for rock stars, some go for race-car drivers and some go for cowboys. Cowboys were her thing. And when she was tired of one, she dropped him and went looking for another. The thought of actually marrying some blue-collar, working-class hick who wore jeans and boots made her laugh."

"Garrett..."

"She said she loved me, but when I asked her to marry me, she laughed in my face. I couldn't blame her, but it taught me a lesson."

"What sort of lesson?" Katy demanded with passionate anger.

"It taught me that next time I wanted to marry a woman I would make damned certain the relationship was based on a more solid foundation than some fairy-tale emotion labeled love!"

"And you thought our relationship was based on something more solid and reliable than love, right?"

"Right." His fingers flexed around her arms. "I thought," he continued pointedly, "that I'd picked the right kind of woman this time, the kind of woman I needed."

"And now you find out her head is filled with just as much pink fluff as any other woman's. We've been so busy planning your future for the past few weeks that we forgot to discuss mine. A bad oversight, Garrett. Rather like buying a mare without first checking her teeth."

"Katy, stop it. You're talking nonsense. Just settle down and listen to me. I've spent all my life learning that you can't trust fancy words. My father trusted the words of the banker who let him put his ranch so deep in debt he never could get back out. The bank wound up with the ranch. My mother believed my father when he told her he was going to get rich raising cattle. My father trusted my mother to stick by him when the going got tough. They were both disappointed. Katy, pretty words don't mean anything. It's what people do that counts."

"You're wrong, Garrett. Some words are important."

"I'll give you the important ones. But I won't give you or any other woman the meaningless ones."

Katy's eyes blazed. "You're just making excuses. Maybe you're so damned macho you're afraid to let yourself fall in love. Maybe you're the kind of man who thinks he makes himself vulnerable if he tells a woman he loves her. That's not like proving yourself against a bull or a saddle bronc, is it? Falling in love means taking a *real* risk—the kind of risk I took by marrying you yesterday."

"Honey, this is crazy. You're my wife. You belong to me now. We've got a future together. It's a future we both want. Why are you trying to rip everything to shreds just because I'm not romantic enough to suit your feminine notions of how a husband is supposed to act?"

Garrett's hands tightened around her arms, and Katy suddenly sensed the physical change in him. Instinctively she glanced down. She nearly choked with fury and another equally dangerous emotion when she realized Garrett was fully, heavily aroused. It was the last straw. Hastily she turned her head to one side and stared fixedly at a picture on the wall.

"Will you please get dressed, for heaven's sake?"

"What's the matter, Katy? Don't you like knowing you have this effect on me?" There was an amused, taunting quality in his words now.

"Not particularly."

Garrett's mouth crooked slightly and he pulled her closer. His voice softened. "I don't believe you. You've been through a lot during the past few days getting ready for the wedding. You're feeling emotional and you're not thinking clearly. Let's go back to bed and start this morning out the way we should have started it in the first place."

Katy stood stiffly in his grasp, appallingly aware of the hard feel of him as he held her close. "Please, Garrett. You said you're not interested in love, well, I'm not interested in sex without it. I married you under a...a misapprehension. It's been a terrible misunderstanding. A horrible mistake. I'm not blaming you. You've never lied to me. I deceived myself. But the deception is over. I know where I stand now."

"Don't look so martyred. You stand with me, dammit. You made a commitment yesterday, and last night you gave yourself to me."

"Well, I'm taking myself back," she retorted, struggling to free herself from his hold.

He didn't release her. "Just what do you think you're going to do?"

"I thought it all out last night after you went to sleep. Since it's too late for an annulment, I'll have to file for divorce. It shouldn't be too complicated. I won't be making any claims on you."

"Divorce! Katy, are you out of your mind? We've got our whole future ahead of us."

"No, you've got your whole future ahead of you. I'm going to find a different future."

"The hell you are. You want everything I want. That's one of the reasons I married you."

"I married you because I loved you, not because I wanted a similar future!" she protested.

"I don't believe you. Don't tell me you aren't interested in the kind of future I intend to build."

"I had a perfectly good future at my father's stud farm. Let go of me. It's obvious I'm wasting my time trying to explain anything to you." She lifted her flaring eyes to his grim face. "I said, let go of me."

Garrett shook his head slowly, his jaw set. "There's something different about you this morning. I've never seen you like this. Ever since I've known you, you've been sweet-natured and reasonable and..."

"And docile and good-tempered and well-mannered and obedient, right? I responded immediately to the leading rein and a little carefully applied pressure," she concluded for him. "Just like a well-bred mare. Well, I've got news for you, Garrett Coltrane— I'm not a horse. I apologize for any inconvenience caused by the confusion. Now go put on some clothes. I have no intention of finishing this argument while you're standing there stark naked looking like a stallion who's just been introduced to the mare he's supposed to impregnate."

Garrett froze. For a moment it seemed as though he might do something drastic, but with an obvious effort he restrained himself. He glowered down into Katy's brilliant eyes and determined face for a long moment, and then he abruptly released her. With a brutal exclamation, he turned and strode toward the bathroom, snagging a pair of jeans on the way.

"All right, I'll go have a shower and get dressed. I think we both need a little time to cool down. This *discussion* has gotten totally out of hand." He paused in the doorway and sent a warming glance back over his shoulder. "But don't get any ideas of leaving while I'm in the shower. Use a few of those brains I always credited you with having and think about what you're doing. You've got my promise we're going to settle this when I get out."

Katy's mouth trembled faintly, but her gaze didn't waver. "I'm not going to run off. I know we have to make some logistical plans. We need to talk about the legal formalities, for one thing. We'll have to consult lawyers, I suppose."

Garrett cut off the remainder of her words with a short, vicious comment. "No, we are not going to consult lawyers. Just make sure you're still here when I get out of the shower. I'll tell you then just what plans we're going to make.'' He closed the door with an unnerving softness, leaving Katy to stare morosely at the silver-and-pink flocked wall.

Inside the bathroom Garrett met the eyes of the man in the mirror. The other guy looked ready for battle.

"Lawyers," Garrett muttered as he wrenched the shower handle. "*Lawyers.* Of all the stupid, crazy, emotional things to say. She's talking about getting a lawyer and we've only been married less than twenty-four hours.''

In his wildest flights of imagination, Garrett knew he could never have envisioned the kind of morning after the wedding night that he had encountered today. Katy was normally a sweet, gentle little creature. To think he had always felt protective of her, even when she was a kid. Hell, this morning he was the one who needed protection. He'd gone to bed with a butterfly and awakened with a wildcat.

Garrett planted his hands on the rim of the sink and glared into the mirror as he waited for the shower water to heat. A pair of dangerous gold eyes stared back at him. He had to admit that the fierce gaze, combined with the dark stubble of his beard and the natural unhandsomeness of his features did not present a particularly endearing appearance. He looked like a somewhat shopworn devil. Hardly the sort of face a new bride expected to see on the first morning after her wedding.

Garrett jerked away from the mirror and stepped into the hot shower. He couldn't do much about the rough beard or the lack of good looks—they were a part of him that his bride was going to have to learn to accept.

But, dammit, he hadn't awakened with that look in his eyes. Katy's strange, irrational behavior had been responsible for it.

To think that for the past two months he'd believed the shy kid he'd once known had grown up into such a nice, levelheaded, sensible young woman. The perfect wife for him.

Garrett groaned silently as he thought about exactly what it was he had felt when he had awakened a short time ago. His body still pulsed with morning arousal. The confrontation with his wife had done nothing to alleviate it. If anything, that had only aggravated matters. Katy was the cause of the problem. Unfortunately, she was also the cure.

Garrett leaned into the hot water, letting it pound over his head and shoulders while he tried to think his way through the wholly unexpected situation in which he found himself. He felt baffled and angry, cheated in ways he couldn't put into words. In the whole time he had known her, Katy had never looked at him the way she had this morning. He realized he had grown accustomed to the seemingly bottomless well of respect and admiration and shy feminine longing he had seen in her clear gray eyes for the past two months. He was completely dumbfounded by the change in her.

Garrett opened his eyes and stared at the swan-headed, chrome-plated shower fixture in front of him. A silly, romantic doodad, that fixture. The whole blasted hotel room was a silly, romantic, flower-scented version of a film-set French boudoir.

The elaborate wedding production had surprised him. He hadn't expected Katy to go in for that kind of hoopla. But her choice of a honeymoon suite had really amazed him. It had surprised the hell out of him, in fact. This didn't seem like Katy's kind of place at all. And all that chatter about love. The woman obviously had an unexpectedly romantic streak in her nature. Garrett felt totally unprepared.

A frivolous, romantic side to Katy was something he had not allowed for when he'd made his plans.

That realization brought him up short as a new, disturbing possibility flashed into his head. Maybe this whole mess was the result of that hidden streak of romanticism in Katy. Maybe that same element in her nature had led her to expect a lot more than what she had gotten last night.

The thought was painful in the extreme. Garrett got out of the shower and reached for a towel. Slowly he began to examine the possibility that he'd really made a mess of things last night. Perhaps he'd moved too quickly. He had wanted her so badly. She had been shy but apparently willing, and she had responded beautifully. He knew from the way she had reacted that she had never experienced that kind of sensual satisfaction before in her life.

She had given herself to him wholeheartedly.

But just maybe it had all been something of a letdown for her, Garrett acknowledged uneasily.

Just maybe Katy's romanticism, coupled with her limited amount of experience, had led her to expect nothing less than an aurora borealis flaring across the bedroom ceiling, a full orchestra playing in the background and a shimmering, cascading, dazzling display of stars.

Garrett groaned. As he had told himself during the reception, he wasn't any Don Juan or Casanova. He'd hoped gentle, intelligent, even-tempered Katy would be satisfied with what she had gotten for a bedmate, but maybe she wasn't.

He shouldn't have fallen asleep right after making love to her last night. Bad mistake. Katy had apparently spent the remainder of the night wide awake telling herself she'd been shortchanged in the husband department. By morning she had worked herself into a real fit of hysterics.

But underneath the strange display of feminine emotion, Garrett knew the real Katy still lurked. The woman he had gotten to know during the past two months must still be there somewhere. He had to find a way to reach through the fireworks and retrieve the good-natured, rational, hard-working woman behind them. Desperately he tried to think of the best approach. He had to find the key to calming her down and making her see sense again.

Garrett sucked in his breath as the answer leaped to mind. It was obvious now that he'd thought of it. The key to handling Katy was to remind her of her obligations. She was fundamentally honest, a woman of integrity. It was always a mistake to use brute force on a creature as sensitive as Katy, but a little judiciously applied guilt might work wonders. All he needed was time. She was bound to return to normal sooner or later.

He hung the towel on the rack, not noticing the entwined hearts that had been embroidered on the thick terry cloth. His mind was focused on the problem at hand. He needed to buy time. He'd try for six months.

In the other room Katy sat sipping the tea she had just ordered from room service. The minutes ticked slowly past while she tried to think of the best way to make her exit from the hotel. It would probably be best to rent a car, she decided. She wouldn't go straight home. She needed to find a place to be by herself for a while. She needed time to recover from the disaster.

Twenty minutes after he'd disappeared into the bathroom, Garrett reappeared, fastening his jeans with a quick, impatient gesture. He looked up abruptly, eyes narrowed and curiously thoughtful as he spotted Katy seated near the window. Her fingers clenched around the delicate handle of the cup, but she refused to let him see how nervous she was. He hadn't put on a shirt yet, and the morning sunlight gleamed on his broad shoulders.

In spite of herself, Katy succumbed automatically to good manners. Old habits died hard, and her mother had drilled manners into her at an early age. "Would you like a cup of tea? I ordered a pot for two."

Garrett scowled briefly at the gleaming silver pot and then shrugged. "Pour me a cup. I want to talk to you."

"There's not much more to be said." Katy manipulated the pot carefully. Her fingers were still trembling, and the last thing she wanted to do was spill the hot tea all over the beveled-glass surface of the delicate white wrought-iron table.

Garrett reached down to grasp the back of one of the little pink-cushioned chairs. He spun it around and straddled it. Then he reached for the cup Katy had just finished pouring. "There's a lot more to be said, Katy. The sooner we get it said, the better."

"Such as?" Her chin came up aggressively.

"You seem to think you've been cheated by this marriage. For some reason you've decided you aren't going to get out of it what you want. I think you're wrong. I think that when you calm down you'll realize you want the same things I do. But in the meantime we've got a problem."

"That's putting it mildly."

He ignored that, plowing grimly onward. "I had a few expectations, too, you know. As of today I expected to have a wife who would help me develop a comprehensive breeding-consultation department within my company. I expected to be marrying a partner, a woman who was willing to work as hard as I was."

Katy bit her lip as the first twinges of guilt struck her. He was right. He had been cheated, too. He had gone into this marriage with his own set of expectations, and she had given him little or no warning of hers. "I know, Garrett."

He took a long swallow of tea and continued. "If you walk out on me now, you'll be leaving me in a real bind, Katy. I was counting on you. I wanted to get that department up and running during the next six months."

She stirred uneasily. "I know. But, Garrett, don't you see—"

"All I see," he said, interrupting her ruthlessly, "is that I'm left with a serious problem."

Katy was silent. Privately she thought him more than capable of handling any serious problems that came down the road, but there was no denying she was shaking up his plans. There was also no denying that in a way he was totally innocent of any accusations of cheating or manipulation. He had never pretended to be other than he was, and he had never offered more than what he intended to provide. She was the one who had built castles of sand and fallen under the spell of her own imagination.

"I was counting on having you around, Katy." Garrett's voice was rough and bleak now. "I had a lot of plans."

"Yes, but…"

"It would help if you could stay with me for a while," he said gently.

Katy risked a questioning glance. His tone of voice was very disturbing. "For a while?"

"Six months, Katy. That's all I'm asking. Hell, the damage is done. You're already married to me and we've spent a night together. Nothing worse can happen, right? Just stick around and give me a hand for the next few months. You can think of it as just another job. You'll be doing the same kind of work you did for your father. We'll make it official. I'll pay you a salary."

Katy's eyes widened in astonished dismay. "Six months! But, Garrett…"

"All right," he said wearily, as if she had just driven a terrifically hard bargain. "You win. Make it three months."

CHAPTER FOUR

THREE MONTHS!

As she sat curled into her corner of the Mercedes, staring at the curving coastal highway unwinding ahead of her, Katy still couldn't believe she'd allowed herself to get talked into the deal. Three months of living with Garrett. Three months of living with the illusion of being his wife. The time stretched out ahead of her, an endless sentence. It was going to be sheer torture.

So why was a part of her unaccountably relieved, she asked herself with wry self-honesty. She knew the answer to that question. She loved Garrett, and even as she had told him she wanted out of the ill-starred marriage, she had been breaking up inside. Now she had a three-month reprieve. Garrett had tried to coerce her into accepting that reprieve, but the truth was, she had allowed herself to be pushed into the arrangement.

Guilt was a powerful motivator, but it wasn't strong enough to keep her with Garrett unless that was where she wanted to be. Katy knew that. Dreams were even more powerful than guilt when it came to motivation, and a part of her did not want to let go of her fantasy.

It was stupid to allow herself to start dreaming again. Nothing would change in three months. Garrett would be the same man at the end of that time as he was now: hard, determined, his eyes fixed on his own vision of a future that was run according to his rules. Under those rules he got what he wanted without having to risk himself emotionally. He was a man with no room in his life for anything as soft as love. He admitted it.

But Katy knew that in spite of her best efforts to stop it, a thread of hope was once more coiling itself into a glittering skein that could easily blind her to reality. Three months was a long time. A lot could happen in three months.

If she was very lucky.

Katy slanted a covert glance at Garrett, who was driving with his usual relaxed concentration. He had said very little since they had checked out of the hotel. He'd slipped back into his strong, silent act, Katy decided derisively. But then, she hadn't had a whole lot to say, either. The truth was, she was still feeling rather stunned by the unnerving events that had taken place last night.

"Hungry?" Garrett broke the long silence to ask.

Katy had a difficult time refocusing her thoughts. When she did so, she was astonished to discover that she actually was hungry. "A little."

"Hardly a surprise after that poor excuse for a breakfast you ate. I told you to have something more filling than a slice of toast."

"Yes, you told me. I wasn't hungry then." Katy stared sightlessly out the window.

"You mean you didn't feel like doing anything I suggested," Garrett countered with more insight than Katy had expected him to demonstrate.

Katy's mouth tilted ruefully. "That was probably a factor."

"Well, at least you admit it. Are you going to spend the next three months acting as if your whole life has been put on hold?" It was the first hint of irritation Garrett had shown since he'd won the battle in the hotel room.

"Isn't that exactly what's happened?"

"I don't see where you're any worse off now than you were working for your father. You'll be doing the same kind of job." He paused as something crossed his mind. "Almost the same kind of job," he amended.

Katy had a strong hunch Garrett had qualified the statement because he had just remembered that she was married to him and that his status as husband still carried certain marital privileges. She felt the warmth in her cheeks as memories of her wedding night returned. Garrett had a one-track mind where anything involving his future plans were concerned, but he had also proved last night that he was more than capable of focusing his attention on at least one form of short-term gratification. He had been a sensual and powerful lover during that time when he was thinking of nothing else except his new bride.

During that brief, perfect time she had spent in his arms, Katy knew herself to be enthralled. Garrett's attention had been focused entirely on her in a way it had never been before, and she had gloried in it until the magic had ended and she had faced reality. But it was obvious that Garrett saw no jolting problem with the situation that had been created. It did not faze him in the least that his actions in bed were chillingly at odds with his convictions that he had no interest in falling in love. Katy, on the other hand, was both angry and resentful that he could be such a wonderful lover to her but have no real love in his heart for her.

Now, with typical male arrogance, Garrett was assuming that she would accept her job responsibilities in the bedroom as well as in the offices of Coltrane and Company. As far as he was concerned, he had a wife and a new equine breeding-program consultant for the next three months. She hadn't found a way to set him straight yet. Her emotions were too unsettled.

Katy stole a glance at her wedding band and wondered when she would get the nerve to actually remove it. She had a hunch Garrett would hit the roof when she did. A surreptitious glance told her he was still wearing his ring.

"You think I'm behaving like an emotional idiot, don't you?" Katy asked.

He shot her an assessing look, as if judging whether or not she could handle the truth. "I don't think you're an idiot. I know you too well to believe that. You're smart, organized and efficient."

"Gosh, thanks."

He paid no attention to her sarcasm. Maybe he was getting more accustomed to it. Either that or he thought he could squelch it by ignoring it. "But you are going off the deep end over all this. You're letting a case of bridal jitters turn into a full-scale emotional circus. We both went into this marriage with our eyes open. I let you know exactly what I wanted and expected from a wife. You've admitted I never lied to you or tried to mislead you."

"What about my expectations and needs?" she asked with soft passion. "What about what I wanted from marriage?"

"I thought," he said forcefully, "that I knew what you wanted from a husband. You never gave me an inkling that I wasn't satisfactory."

"We should have talked more, I guess," Katy said, her gaze wistful.

"We did a hell of a lot of talking during the past couple of months."

"We talked about horses and breeding programs and Red Dazzle and your plans for the future. We talked about my new job in your consulting firm. We talked about your new home. But we never really talked about us—you and me. I see that now."

"When we talked about plans for the future we were talking about you and me."

"If that's so, then we have a serious communication problem, don't we?" she tossed back.

"Nothing that can't be straightened out, given time." The words came softly between his teeth.

"I don't think three months is enough time to solve the problem we have, Garrett."

"We'll get a start on it during the next couple of weeks."

"There's no need for you to pretend we're on a honeymoon for the next two weeks. As far as I'm concerned, what we have now is a business arrangement, not a marriage." Katy was rather surprised by her own assertiveness. It was as if she were actually trying to provoke him, and that was completely out of character for her. She never deliberately caused scenes, and the only time she was really assertive was when she was talking about horses. It was odd to think that her marriage might actually have changed her personality. She had always believed such things were immutable once one became an adult.

"Does it occur to you, Katy, that I have something more at stake here than just a business deal?"

Katy flashed him a look of intense curiosity. "Such as?"

"My pride, for one thing," Garrett retorted tightly.

"Oh, that." Katy lost interest in the subject.

Garrett's temper gleamed for an instant in his eyes as he slid a sidelong glance in her direction. "You may not give a damn about my pride, lady, but I sure as hell do. I do not want all my employees and friends aware of the fact that my wife changed her mind about the marriage on her wedding night. We will take the next two weeks off, just as I originally planned, and we will spent the time trying to act like newlyweds, at least when we're in front of others. Besides, I've got some work I want to do around the house and stables. I need the time. I haven't taken more than an occasional weekend off in five years.''

"If you want to waste the next two weeks, that's your business." Katy leaned forward, determined to put a halt to the conversation. "Look, there's a fast-food place coming up. We can grab a meal there.''

THEY ARRIVED at Garrett's new home sometime after dark. A fitful cloud cover obscured the moonlight and made it almost impossible to see any details of the property. But Katy sensed Garrett's inner satisfaction as he turned off the main road and drove along a tree-lined road that led toward the sea. He began describing the night-shrouded scene to her.

"The main house is over there on the left behind those trees. You'll see it in a moment. It's near the top of the cliffs. You're going to like it, Katy. Red tile roof, white stucco finish and lots of arched doorways and windows. Plenty of gardens, too. Over there on the right are the stables and paddocks. The setup will house two horses. On that hill above the stables is the Brackens' cottage. Wait until you see it all in the daylight, Katy. This is beautiful land.''

Katy heard the enthusiasm in his voice and tried to ignore it. It wasn't easy because her own curiosity was getting the better of her. Until last night, she had been looking forward to living here. She had thought the place was going to be her home. Well, she reminded herself, it was still to be her home for the next three months.

"Looks like Bracken didn't leave any lights on in the main house. Dammit, I told him I wanted the porch light left on in case we got in after dark.'' Garrett slowed and finally stopped the car in a long, curving drive. He frowned at the darkened two-story house. The headlights picked up a small section of a wide, arched front door and a portion of rockery that enclosed a flower garden.

"Perhaps he forgot about the light," Katy suggested as she slowly opened her door and stepped out onto the drive. On the other side of the vehicle, Garrett's door slammed as he got out.

"Yeah, maybe he forgot," Garrett muttered as he searched for the house key. "Or maybe he started drinking too early in the afternoon."

"He's got an alcohol problem?"

"Atwood implied something of that nature. Didn't go into details. I'll talk to Bracken in the morning. If the man wants to stay on here, he's going to have to learn to follow orders."

Katy wisely said no more, but she privately hoped the unknown Emmett Bracken would learn quickly that his new employer allowed very little slack. As a teenager in her father's stables, he had always given Harry Randall his money's worth. Katy had learned during the past two months that Garrett had not changed in that respect. He worked hard and expected others to do the same.

The front door swung open on silent hinges as Garrett turned the key in the lock. He leaned inside and found the hall switch. An instant later light blazed, revealing a wide foyer with a floor of rich, burnished quarry tile. Katy stepped inside, smiling in spite of herself.

"Oh, this is lovely, Garrett," she whispered as she glanced around. The overhead light fixture, a handsome creation of wrought iron and glass, gleamed. Katy saw herself in an ornately framed mirror that hung above a long, polished table. She was vaguely startled by the woman who looked back at her. Her gray eyes seemed to dominate her face. They reflected a strange combination of caution and fatigue. Her hair was coming loose. Wispy tendrils curled around her nape. Her green blouse was rumpled from the hours she had spent sitting in the car. All in all, she did not look crisp, efficient or businesslike. Katy regretted that.

"I'm glad you like the house. I thought you would. I had you in mind when I told the designer what I wanted." Garrett's eyes were fastened on her as she wandered slowly through the foyer and into the living room.

Katy was deeply aware of Garrett's scrutiny as she turned on lamps and studied the warm glow of expansive hardwood floors. A massive stone fireplace dominated one wall. There was a collection of surprisingly beautiful leather furniture grouped around the fireplace. The large, fringed area rug on the floor was a modern interpretation of a Southwest Indian pattern. Floor-to-ceiling windows lined the wall that looked out over the darkened sea.

"The designer did a wonderful job," Katy admitted, looking around.

There was speculative satisfaction in Garrett's eyes. "I told her I wanted it perfect for my wife."

A twinge of guilt went through Katy as she realized just how much Garrett wanted her to like the place. Then she bracingly reminded herself that he had his own purely pragmatic, practical reasons for wanting her to be pleased. Her impulsive smile of pleasure faded.

"Kitchen's through there," Garrett said quickly as Katy turned around. "It's the old-fashioned type. Huge. Has everything in the way of appliances."

Katy walked through a dining room furnished with a long, elegant pine table and into a huge kitchen that had obviously been outfitted for someone who enjoyed cooking. The overhead light revealed acres of gleaming tile, professional cookware hanging from copper hooks and a round glass-topped kitchen table.

"During the past couple of months I found out you like to cook," Garrett murmured.

Katy glanced at him sharply. Apparently he had paid attention to some things of a personal nature during the past several weeks. She said nothing and opened the doors of the stainless steel refrigerator. The interior was empty.

"Good thing we picked up some groceries a while back," Garrett said briskly as he surveyed the empty shelves. "I'm starving."

Katy wondered if that was a hint that she was now supposed to assume her wifely chores. She shoved her hands into the pockets of her jeans and regarded her husband through thoughtful eyes. He looked as innocently expectant as it was possible for a man with Garrett's blunt, stark features to look.

Katy gave up the small battle before the first skirmish. She was hungry, too. This wasn't the time or place to draw lines. "Why don't you bring in the groceries and I'll see what I can do about dinner."

Garrett's mouth tilted in faintly concealed satisfaction. "Sounds like a good idea."

Forty-five minutes later Katy had put together a salad of tomatoes, cucumbers and feta cheese, rice and a simple shrimp curry. Garrett had spent the time unloading the car. He walked into the kitchen just as she was putting the food on the glass-topped table.

"It's been a long time since lunch," he announced. He sauntered over to the table and studied the neatly arranged salad and curry. He appeared to be pleased. "Smells good. Did you open the wine?"

"No." Katy watched him out of the corner of her eye as she finished the last of her preparations. "I didn't know if you would want a glass with dinner."

Garrett gave her a narrow look. "This is our first meal in our new home. It seems to me that warrants a glass of wine."

"Does it?" She hid her astonishment. It had never occurred to her that Garrett would concern himself with the small, intimate celebrations of life. "Well, given the circumstances of our marriage, I don't think we have to feel obliged to celebrate tonight." She sat down abruptly and reached for the salad bowl.

"This is a special event," Garrett said roughly, "and we are going to treat it with all due respect." He reached the refrigerator with two long, impatient strides and yanked open the door. He reached inside and withdrew the bottle of champagne Katy had last seen languishing in a warm ice bucket.

"I thought we left that behind at the hotel." She stared at Garrett as he took the bottle over to the counter and went to work on the cork.

"If it had been up to you, we would have left it behind. But since we paid through the teeth for that damned cotton-candy room, I thought we ought to get our money's worth out of it. The only thing salvageable this morning was the champagne, so I picked it up when we left.'' He threw Katy a glittering look and then went back to work on the cork.

Katy felt the warmth steal into her face. He didn't have to spell out the fact that he considered everything else about that infamous hotel room a total disaster. So did she. But it struck her as strange that he had packed the champagne. She hadn't given it a thought. She had just wanted to be free of the room and everything that had happened in it.

The cork came off with a contained explosion. None of the bubbling contents of the bottle was lost. It was typical of Garrett that he had maintained control over the champagne, Katy thought with a certain amount of resentment. He was always in control of everything.

Garrett saw her expression as he came back to the table with a couple of long-stemmed glasses he had found in a cupboard. ''Are you going to remember our wedding night every time you drink champagne, honey?''

She did not like the soft, taunting edge in his voice. ''Who knows? A couple of glasses of this stuff and I might even be able to forget all about our wedding night.''

''Not a chance,'' he murmured as he sat down across from her and poured champagne. He put down the bottle, picked up a glass and handed it to her. Golden bubbles glinted between his fingers. Above the rim of the glass, golden eyes met Katy's. ''It might not have been everything you wanted or expected in the way of a wedding night, but it *was* our wedding night, and the last thing I'm going to do is let you forget that fact.''

Katy froze in the act of reaching across the small table to accept the glass of champagne. She sensed the force of his willpower reaching out to envelop her and she boldly tried to resist. ''Some things are better off forgotten, Garrett.''

''Some things,'' he corrected her, ''get better with a little practice.''

Katy drew a slow, steadying breath. She knew exactly what he was saying to her. He was telling her he fully expected to sleep with her.

''What we have is a business arrangement.'' Katy struggled to keep her voice neutral. She took the champagne from his hand and forced herself to take a sip. It struck her for the first time just what it meant to be totally alone with Garrett. She had spent very little time completely alone with him during the past two months, she realized. And on most of those few occasions, he had spent most of the time talking about his plans for the future. He had never focused on her the way he was doing tonight. It was, Katy discovered, unnerving to be the center of his complete, undivided attention. "You were the one who wanted that kind of arrangement, if you'll recall."

Garrett gave her a long look and then he took a swallow from his own glass. "I wasn't given much choice in the matter."

Katy stared at him pleadingly. "I don't think this is going to work, Garrett. I think we should cut our losses now, tonight, without trying to make a business arrangement out of what was meant to be a marriage."

"It's one thing for you to suggest we cut our losses," he retorted, putting down his champagne and picking up a fork. "You've got a lot less to lose than I do. Or so you've apparently concluded. But maybe you'll change your mind. Three months is a long time."

Three months was beginning to look like forever, Katy thought.

TWO HOURS LATER Katy climbed into bed. She glanced around the room just before switching off the bedside lamp. It was, she suspected, a guest bedroom, done in pleasant earth tones. This bedroom was smaller than the master suite down the hall, which Katy had discreetly left for the new master of the house.

As she curled up alone beneath the covers, she experienced a flash of resentment that mingled with a deep, underlying sadness. She didn't want to acknowledge the unhappiness, so she concentrated on the resentment. It was an emotion less likely to bring tears to her eyes.

Meanwhile, down the hall, the new master of the house emerged from the bathroom wearing only a pair of jeans and discovered what he had half expected to find. He was alone in the beautiful suite.

It was, Garrett knew, too much to hope that Katy would quietly acquiesce to sharing a bedroom for the next three months. But that hadn't stopped him from hoping, anyway. It would have made things so much easier. Somehow, Garrett told himself, if he could just persuade Katy to sleep with him on a normal basis, he knew he could gradually overcome her irrational reaction to the whole mess. Under ordinary circumstances she was such a sweet, soft, compliant creature. In addition, whether she wanted to acknowledge it or not, she was also a very sensual woman. Surely if he tapped into that sweetness and that softness and that sensuality over a long enough period of time he could convince her that what they had together was more than enough for both of them.

She had taken him by surprise with her unexpected flight into romantic fantasy land, but underneath it all she was still the realistic, gentle, undemanding woman he had come to know during the past couple of months. Once she'd looked up at him with the hero-worshiping eyes of a child. Last night he knew that expression of shy hero worship had been replaced with a woman's look of passion. Given time and propinquity, he was sure he could teach her to be contented with him.

Well, he had bought himself the time, but Katy seemed intent on denying him the element of propinquity where it counted most—in the bedroom.

Garrett stood in the middle of the room and eyed the closed door for a long moment, his brows in a rigid, determined line. Katy was just down the hall in one of the other three bedrooms. It was a cinch she wasn't going to come to him.

If anything was going to be done about the untenable situation, he would have to do it.

With a low oath, Garrett strode to the door, opened it and started down the long hall. He opened doors as he went along.

He found her in the last room and decided to take heart from the fact that the door wasn't locked. He twisted the knob and stepped inside. A startled movement from the bed drew his eyes instantly. In the shadows he could see her pale face and the deliciously tangled dark cloud of hair that framed her features. She looked very alone and very vulnerable in the double bed.

"Garrett!"

"Who were you expecting? The fairy-tale prince you thought you had married? Sorry, honey, you're stuck with the frog." He folded his arms and leaned one shoulder against the doorframe. He knew he was backlit by the hall light. All Katy could see of him was his silhouette. She wouldn't be able to read the expression on his face. Maybe that was just as well.

She propped herself up on her elbows, trying to see him more clearly. "Maybe it wasn't such a good idea for you to finish off the last of that champagne by yourself."

"I had to finish it off by myself. I didn't hear you offering to help. You quit after one glass."

"I didn't feel like drinking champagne."

"Why not?" he challenged, feeling put upon. "It's supposed to be so damned romantic." He'd salvaged that stupid bottle for her and she hadn't had more than half a glass. That fact had been annoying him all evening. Saving their wedding-night champagne had struck him as a brilliantly romantic move that morning when he'd first thought of it. Just the sort of move that would appeal to the new, unexpected and unpredictable side of Katy that he was discovering.

"Garrett, please. The only way we're going to get through the next three months together is if you make some effort to be civil."

"A man can't be civil all the time."

"You can," she retorted. "You've been perfectly civil to me since I met you. At least, you were perfectly civil until..."

"Never mind, I don't want to hear about the exact moment when you began to realize that I wasn't your knight in shining armor. I already know the big revelation struck you when I demonstrated that I was fully capable of making love to you without giving you a mushy, meaningless declaration of undying love."

"That's enough, Garrett." Her voice was quiet but laced with stubbornness. "More than enough. I don't have to listen to any more of this."

"The hell you don't. You're my *wife*."

"I'm your employee," she shot back. "Now close the door and go back to your own room before I charge you with sexual harassment.'' She lay back down, turned her face toward the wall and pulled the quilt up over her shoulder.

Garrett stared at the curve of her shoulder and decided he now knew how the expression ''cold shoulder'' had originated. He wondered if the man who had first coined it had ever figured out a way of thawing out a frozen wife. If so, he had not been generous enough to pass along the information to posterity. Every man, it seemed, was fated to have to discover the trick on his own.

''Just tell me one thing, Katy.''

''What do you want to know?''

''I want you to tell me if I was really such a clumsy lover last night that now you can't stand the thought of me touching you.''

There was a fraught silence from the bed before Katy said stiffly, ''You know the answer to that.''

''No, I don't know the answer. If I did, I wouldn't be asking.''

''For heaven's sake, Garrett.''

''Just tell me the truth.''

''All right,'' she stormed, pulling the covers up over her head, ''I'll tell you the truth. As far as the physical side of things went, everything was...was perfect. There. Are you satisfied? I have no complaints in that department. Now get out of here.''

Garrett started to back quietly out of the bedroom. He stopped when he saw Katy lower the covers to her chin. She glared at him in the shadows.

''Garrett?''

Hope soared in him. ''What is it, honey?''

''Was she very beautiful?''

He looked at her blankly. ''Was who very beautiful?''

''That woman you thought you loved all those years ago.''

Hope turned into exasperation. ''That's a damned fool question, Katy, I don't even remember what she looked like. I said I learned a lesson from her, I didn't say I carried her picture around in my wallet.''

''I just wondered.''

''You mean you wondered if I was carrying a torch for her,'' he snapped, thoroughly irritated. ''The answer is no.''

''But how do you know?'' Katy persisted.

"Because five years ago I ran into her again," Garrett said, feeling goaded. "I could have had her then. Instead I took one look at her and thanked my lucky stars I'd escaped the first time. She was one cold, calculating little bitch. Satisfied?"

"I guess so."

"You'd better be. The subject is now closed." Garrett swung away from the door and stalked back the hall to his lonely room. His body was painfully taut with unreleased desire. He took one look at the empty bed waiting for him and then went on into the bathroom to acquaint himself with the therapeutic effects of a cold shower.

CHAPTER FIVE

KATY WAS IN THE MIDDLE of grilling corn cakes the next morning when the knock sounded on the kitchen door. She had told herself during the long, restless night that she would feed Garrett cold cereal for breakfast or maybe even leave him to fend for himself. But somehow she couldn't bring herself to do it.

It was undoubtedly some bizarre form of wifely guilt that was prompting her, she decided in irritation. She was going to have to learn how to overcome that. Perhaps she should learn how to concentrate more on her newfound temper. There was something liberating about discovering one had a temper.

Startled by the knock, she hastily flicked the last corn cake off the griddle and onto a warming plate. Then she headed for the door. She wondered if she should call Garrett. He was still in the shower as far as she knew. He seemed to have taken a lot of showers in the past twenty-four hours.

Katy opened the door to find a wiry, withered man on the step. The man could have been anywhere between fifty and seventy. It was hard to tell because a lifetime of outdoor work had marked him with a deep tan and a network of sun-induced lines on his lean face. He was wearing an ancient pair of jeans, worn boots, a faded plaid shirt and a battered cap. He tipped the brim of the cap briefly and studied her with rheumy blue eyes that were as faded as his shirt. Years of drinking had left their mark, but he was obviously not drunk this morning.

"Morning, ma'am. I'm Emmett Bracken. You must be Mrs. Coltrane. Coltrane said he was going to bring a wife back with him."

"How do you do?" She decided not to clarify her exact status in the household. It was too hard to explain, especially while she was wearing a wedding ring. She made a mental note to remember to remove the ring later. "It's nice to meet you, Emmett. I understand you've been holding things together around here since the owner more or less abandoned the place a couple of years ago.''

"Never thought I'd see the day anyone except an Atwood lived on this hill. Could have knocked me and my wife over with a feather the day we heard the place had been sold. Been real sad watching Atwood get rid of the land bit by bit these past few years. We thought he'd stay here till he died. Who'd have thought he'd up and move to Palm Springs?''

"Yes, well, I'm sure it was a surprise to a lot of local people,'' Katy said diplomatically.

"You can say that again,'' Bracken said in his slow drawl. "Royce Hutton had himself a real fit when he found out the house and this last piece of property was going to a new owner.''

"Royce Hutton?''

"Yeah, owns a few acres on down the road. Breeds fancy cattle. Sells his stock all over the world to folks trying to improve their breeding programs. He's had his eye on this piece of land for years. Tried for the past couple of years to get Atwood to sell to him, but Atwood got real stubborn. Hutton was with Atwood's boy the night young Brent died. Atwood never wanted anything to do with Hutton after that. Didn't want anything to do with any of the kids who were involved that night.''

"I see,'' Katy said, vaguely remembering Garrett's telling her the story. She wished Garrett would appear. She wasn't quite sure what to say to Emmett Bracken. "Won't you come in for coffee, Emmett?''

"No thanks. Just had some of my wife's coffee. It'll hold me. I stopped by because Coltrane told me he'd want to start work early on those stables. Says he's bringing his horse here in a few days.''

"I'm sure he will want to get to work early, but he hasn't had a chance to eat breakfast yet. He'll be out as soon as he's finished.''

Bracken nodded, accepting that. "Okay. Tell him I'll be in the stables.''

"I'll tell him.''

Bracken hesitated, glancing past her into the kitchen. "This place has sure been changed around. Doesn't even look like the same house. Sure seems strange not having any Atwoods here.'' He shook his head. "After all these years. Me and the missus were sure the boy would take over one day."

"I can understand that."

"He had a thing going with my daughter, Felice, you know." There was a touch of pride in the man's voice.

Katy cleared her throat. "No, I didn't know."

"My Felice is a real beauty. They were gonna get married. She and Brent were seein' each other real regular. Then the accident happened. Everything sort of fell apart after that. Silas's wife died and gradually Silas just seemed to lose interest in the place. My wife took it hard. Never quite got over it. Had her heart set on Felice marrying young Brent."

"Life doesn't always go as planned," Katy said, feeling very wise from recent experience.

"No, it sure don't."

"What happened to your daughter?" Katy couldn't resist asking.

"She went off to college and got herself a job workin' for a big company that makes things like stereos and those gadgets that let you record TV shows. She seems happy enough. It's the missus who never quite forgot what might have happened if young Brent hadn't gone and broke his neck that night." Bracken tipped his old hat again. "Well, see you later, Mrs. Coltrane. My wife'll be by in a while to say hello. Tell your man I'm getting started."

"I will," Katy promised. She closed the door slowly, sensing Garrett's presence behind her.

"Was that Bracken?" Garrett asked crisply as he strode into the kitchen. He was rolling back the cuffs of his long-sleeved blue work shirt. There was a faint frown of concentration on his face as he attended to the small task.

"Yes." Katy stood looking at him, both hands behind her on the doorknob. She felt a flash of wistfulness. As she had told Emmett Bracken, life didn't always go as planned. This was her first morning in her new home. Things should have been different. "He said to tell you he'll be starting work in the stables."

Garrett nodded perfunctorily. "Good. What's for breakfast?" He glanced toward the stove.

"Corn cakes and maple syrup. The coffee's ready." Instantly

she made herself sound more brisk. Dammit, she could be as efficient and businesslike as he was. It had been her idea in the first place to be efficient and businesslike. Katy launched herself away from the door and aimed for the stove. "Sit down and I'll get you a cup. Emmett was just telling me about Royce Hutton wanting this house and the land around it."

"Hutton will learn to live with the disappointment of not getting what he wanted," Garrett said laconically. "We all have to learn that lesson sooner or later, don't we?"

Katy wondered if there was a message in that remark intended for her. She carried the hot platter of corn cakes over to the table. "Yes, we all have to learn that." She sat down. "When do you think you'll have the stall and paddock ready for Red Dazzle?"

"Not long. A couple of days' work should get one of the stalls in order. I'll arrange for a hay and grain delivery as soon as possible."

Katy nodded, determined to maintain the businesslike atmosphere that seemed to have established itself. "Mrs. Bracken is coming by later this morning to go through the house with me."

"Fine," Garrett murmured coolly. There was a pause as he bit into the corn cakes. "Sure am glad you can cook," he finally said with grudging appreciation. "Bracken's wife can take care of the house during the day, but I'd just as soon have you doing the cooking. I don't like having people underfoot first thing in the morning or during dinner. I like my privacy."

"Does that mean I should add cooking to my new job description?" Katy tried to speak lightly, but she knew there was a sting in the words.

Garrett slanted her a chilling look. "You've got my reasons for marrying you all figured out, don't you?"

"I figured them out a little late, but, yes, I finally did figure them out."

Garrett forked up another bite of corn cakes. "You are one stubborn female. I don't know why I didn't see that before I married you."

"Maybe you didn't see it because you weren't really looking at me," Katy said quietly. "All you saw were the trappings that surrounded me. Good social connections, a good pedigree, a useful education. All the things you lacked while you were growing up. On top of everything else I seemed good-natured, undemanding and biddable. What more could a man want in a wife?''

Garrett looked at her, amber eyes glinting with an emotion that might have been anger, annoyance or warning. "Do you really want me to answer that?"

Katy flushed and speared a piece of corn cake. "No."

"I didn't think so. Katy, things are tense enough between us. For both our sakes, I suggest you don't spend a lot of time baiting me."

Katy wasn't certain how to take that so she kept quiet.

To her surprise, matters seemed to stabilize during the next two days. She went out of her way to be polite and businesslike when she was with Garrett, and he reciprocated with a remote civility that didn't quite mask his dissatisfaction. Katy got the feeling he was determined to give the situation time. She thought about telling him that time wasn't going to make any difference but thought better of it. He was right—baiting him might be a dangerous pastime.

Nadine Bracken, a dour-faced woman who appeared to be in the same age range as her husband proved helpful, if not particularly talkative. When Katy praised her for taking such excellent care of the main house she just shrugged.

"Been takin' care of this house for as long as I can remember. I've always had a feeling for this place," she had said. "I went to work for the Atwoods when I was in high school. Emmett did, too. The Atwoods always made us feel like we were family, if you know what I mean. I even thought we might be family, one day." She'd favored Katy with a strange look. "Emmett and I thought our girl, Felice, would wind up livin' here in this house."

Katy hadn't quite known what to say to that, so she'd changed the subject. "I gather the interior designer Garrett hired made several changes."

Nadine had stared balefully at the new furniture in the living room. "She did. Acted as if no one important had ever lived here.

Had no respect. Just came through and tore the place up from one end to the other.''

"It looks lovely now," Katy had said, feeling an odd need to defend Garrett's choice of interior designers. Garrett had given the orders to redo the place because he had wanted to please his new wife. Katy felt a familiar twinge of emotion at the thought. She was going to have to try harder to avoid those guilt pangs.

ROYCE HUTTON dropped by to introduce himself on Katy's third morning in her new home. Garrett was out taking a look at the final preparations for Red Dazzle at the time, and it was Katy who answered the door to find a tall, rangy, good-looking man in his late thirties on the doorstep. His grin was infectious.

"You must be the new Mrs. Coltrane. I'm your neighbor, Royce Hutton. Came by to introduce myself properly and then kick myself one more time around the block for missing out on this piece of property. Hope you're enjoying your new home.''

Katy was unable to resist the humor in Royce Hutton's hazel eyes. After the tension of living with Garrett's grim, remote mood, she found it was a relief to speak to someone who was obviously intent on being charming. "Please come in, Royce. I heard you wanted the house and land. It is a beautiful setting, isn't it?''

"You can say that again." Royce followed her into the living room, his eyes sweeping over the furnishings. "Hey, Coltrane really went first-class in here, didn't he? I heard he spent a fortune having this place redone. Looks like something out of a magazine.''

"Yes, it does, doesn't it? Garrett wanted it to be polished and perfect. Can I offer you a cup of coffee?''

"Sounds great.''

Nadine Bracken materialized silently behind them, wiping her hands on a dish towel. "I'll get the coffee, Mrs. Coltrane.''

Katy smiled gratefully. "Thanks, Nadine.''

Royce raised an eyebrow as the unsmiling woman disappeared. "The Brackens have been here forever, you know," he murmured. "They took it hard when old Silas got rid of the place. Is Garrett going to keep them on?''

"As far as I know," Katy said carefully. "Garrett hasn't said anything one way or the other, but things seem to be working out. Please sit down.''

"Thanks." Royce threw himself casually into a white leather chair. The action revealed the fine tooling on a pair of handmade boots. "Heard your last name was Randall up until a couple of days ago and that your people breed Arabians. Would that be the Randall Stud Farm people?"

"News travels, doesn't it?"

Royce chuckled. "Coltrane didn't go out of his way to keep it a secret. I got the impression he was very proud to be bringing you home as his wife."

Proud to be bringing a *Randall* home for a wife, Katy thought. That sounded like Garrett. She was saved from having to make a response by the appearance of Mrs. Bracken. "Oh, here's the coffee. Thanks, Nadine."

Nadine nodded once, saying nothing, set down the tray and disappeared again. Katy began to pour.

"I did some business with your father a while back," Royce continued easily as he accepted his cup. "Sent one of my best mares down to Randall Farm to be bred to Silver Moon. Got a terrific little colt out of it."

"What was the mare's name?"

"Morning Mist."

Katy smiled. "I remember her. I was managing my father's breeding operation until recently. Silver Moon is a beautiful stallion. His offspring always get his intelligence as well as his conformation. You'll win some championships with that colt."

Royce grinned. "Guess I should have come along with the mare. I could have met you before Coltrane did."

A boot step sounded on the polished wood floor, and Garrett's voice cut into the conversation with the lethal swiftness of a razor blade.

"It wouldn't have done you any good to meet Katy a year ago, Hutton. You were married at the time." Garrett strode into the room, his eyes skimming briefly over his wife and settling on Royce Hutton.

"Just another example of my bad timing," Royce said dryly.

"Win some, lose some." Garrett sat down on the couch beside Katy. He seemed totally unconcerned about the possibility of transferring the dust from his jeans to the immaculate leather. He was apparently far more concerned about staking a quiet claim on Katy. "Any coffee left?"

"I'll have Nadine bring another cup." Katy began to grow uneasy as she quietly arranged for the coffee. Garrett was radiating a new variety of tension, a version she had never before detected in him. For an instant she wondered if it was jealousy, then she told herself it was more likely a form of possessiveness. As she surreptitiously studied her husband's hard face, it occurred to her that he was the kind of man who had learned the hard way how to hang on to what he considered his, even if the possession in question did not care to be possessed.

Royce Hutton's easygoing manner defused the potentially awkward situation. He seemed willing enough to respect Garrett's obvious claim to both the house and the woman. Katy wasn't sure she liked being written off as another man's property, but she was grateful there wasn't going to be a scene.

"I didn't drop by just to introduce myself and allow Coltrane here to gloat." Royce smiled at Katy a few minutes later as he finished his coffee. "I wanted to invite you both over for a few drinks with the neighbors this evening. I know it's short notice, but I figured what with you two being on your honeymoon, you probably weren't booked solid with social engagements."

"I'd love to meet the neighbors," Katy said quickly, even as Garrett's heavy dark brows came together over his narrowed eyes. She was not certain if she was accepting because she didn't want to face another long evening alone with her husband or if she was subtly and only half-consciously trying to challenge him in some way. There were moments lately when she didn't understand herself.

Garrett gave her a slow, speculative glance, but he finally nodded without much enthusiasm. "We'll be there," he said calmly to Royce Hutton.

"Mission accomplished," Royce announced, getting to his feet.

"I'd better be on my way. I've got some Australians arriving this afternoon to look at my Charolais-Angus crosses."

"Thanks for dropping by," Katy said warmly as she opened the front door. "Garrett and I will be looking forward to this evening."

"Right. See you later." Royce walked out to his BMW, climbed inside, turned the key and backed out of the driveway.

"You don't have to stand in the doorway staring after him," Garrett muttered.

Katy blinked in surprise at the harsh tone. "I wasn't staring after him."

"I hope not. I wouldn't want you getting any ideas about Hutton. And I sure as hell don't want him getting any ideas about you."

Katy's eyes widened. "That's not likely," she retorted.

"Think not? The man's only been divorced a few months. He's out to prove he's still got what it takes. Lately he's been chasing anything shaped like a female."

"Garrett, you're being ridiculous."

"I'm being careful."

"I don't know what you're so upset about," Katy said through her teeth. She was suddenly furious. "After all, Royce knew all about my father's farm. He knew I was Harry Randall's daughter, and I'm certain he'll make sure everyone at the cocktail party tonight also knows who I am. That's one of the reasons you married me, wasn't it? So that you could get some mileage out of my family connections? You wanted to prove to yourself and everyone else that you were rich enough and successful enough now to marry the daughter of the man whose stables you had once cleaned. Thanks to Royce's invitation you'll be able to show off your new acquisition this evening."

Something sharp and violent flared in Garrett's eyes. "You don't know what the hell you're saying."

"I'm only saying what several other people were saying at the wedding."

He stared at her. "And you believed it?"

"Not then. I didn't believe it until later when I realized you didn't love me. Then I had to look for other reasons why you married me. The fact that I was Harry Randall's daughter explained a lot of your interest in me. I was too stupid to look for the real reasons for our marriage before I found myself walking down the aisle.''

''Dammit, Katy, the only thing you've been looking for lately is trouble, and if you're not careful, you're going to find it. I did not marry you just to prove to the world that I was now in the position to marry my former employer's daughter. For God's sake, use your head. Do you honestly think I'd tie myself to a woman I didn't want just to prove I could marry her? I'm not a masochist.''

The sound of a truck engine out in the driveway halted Garrett. Grateful for the diversion, Katy glanced through the open door. A truck pulling a horse trailer was approaching.

''I think Red Dazzle is here,'' Katy said stiffly.

Garrett shoved his hat down low over his eyes and stepped outside. ''About time.'' He walked away with long, impatient strides, heading toward the truck and trailer.

Katy stood in the doorway wishing she had kept her mouth shut. She didn't move until a faint tingle down her spine told her she was not alone. She swung around a little nervously and saw Nadine Bracken standing in the arched doorway that opened onto the dining room. The woman was just standing there, staring. Katy wondered how much she had overheard.

''You gave me a start,'' Katy said, summoning a smile.

''I just wondered if you wanted me to change the beds.''

Katy winced at the realization that Nadine Bracken knew her new employers were not sleeping together. ''No, that can wait until tomorrow. You can go now. I think everything's under control for today. Garrett and I are going out this evening.''

''All right.'' Nadine moved soundlessly out of sight.

Katy turned back to watch the scene outside the door. Garrett was deep in conversation with the young driver of the truck. Katy walked outside and slowly strolled toward the horse trailer. She was curious about Red Dazzle. Memories of a stolen day at the county fair rodeo when she was fifteen drifted through her head. She'd had eyes only for Garrett that day, but she did have a vague recollection of a sleepy-looking chestnut quarter horse built like a bulldog. She also remembered the way that same lethargic-looking creature had exploded out of a chute in hot pursuit of a calf. The memory made Katy smile. Garrett had won big that day.

Red Dazzle must be getting on in years, Katy realized. The gelding was probably seventeen or eighteen by now. That was old age for a horse. It said something about Garrett that he had taken care of Red Dazzle all these years after leaving the rodeo circuit. Something softened within Katy as she thought about that.

Red Dazzle was in the process of being unloaded from the trailer by the time Katy reached the vehicle. Katy smiled slightly as she watched the animal back down the ramp. Garrett was at the horse's head, guiding him. It was clear Red Dazzle did not need any assistance. This business of being untrailered was an old routine for him. The horse made a soft, woofling sound against Garrett's hand by way of greeting. Then he absently swished his tail. He looked patiently bored.

"He doesn't look any more wide awake now than he did the last time I saw him," Katy said, wanting to break the new barrier of unpleasantness she had just succeeded in erecting between herself and her husband. She wished she'd had the sense to control her tongue a few minutes earlier.

Garrett glanced at her, as if trying to identify the unexpected note of friendliness in her voice. Red Dazzle's ears twitched at the sound of her voice, and he turned his large head to give the stranger a sleepy-eyed glance.

"Old Red here looked this way the day he was born. Dozed off about five minutes after he'd finally got up on his feet for the first time, and he's been busy conserving his energy ever since. He's not like those high strung Arabians your father raises, all nerves and delicate breeding."

Katy had the impression the comment about nerves and delicate breeding was meant to include her as well as her father's horses. "No," she agreed smoothly, "there's nothing delicate about Red Dazzle." Or about his owner, she added silently.

Garrett stroked the dark chestnut neck with brusque affection. But his expression was curious as he looked at Katy. "When did you see Red before today?"

"At a fair rodeo when I was fifteen. I snuck away from school because I'd heard you—'' Katy bit off the revealing confession. She tried to cover it with a shrug. ''Some friends and I decided to skip school and go to the rodeo at the county fair. It seemed exciting at the time. I had never cut school in my life. A big event for me. You and Red Dazzle were riding, as I recall.''

''Is that right?'' Garrett spoke reflectively, but there was an alert gleam in his golden eyes. ''What was the attraction? I thought you were into fancy hunting and performance classes in those days. Itsy-bitsy English saddles, little nipped-in jackets, riding breeches and knee-high boots.'' A trace of humor crept into his voice. ''Why would you want to go to a dusty, dirty rodeo and watch a bunch of guys in old jeans take a lot of falls in the mud?''

Katy's chin came up. Damned if she was going to let him goad her like this. ''It made a change of pace.''

''I'll just bet it did. Did you enjoy watching me fall in the mud?''

Katy bit her lip and then admitted in a soft rush, ''It occurred to me at the time that you'd eventually break every bone in your body if you kept on with the rodeo circuit.''

''You were right. It's a young man's game. No future in it. That's why I got out of it when I did.'' Garrett stared at her, his hand still moving idly over Red Dazzle's neck. ''Did you think I'd broken a few bones that day?''

''Yes.'' Her voice was stark as she recalled the tremor of fear that had gone through her when she'd watched him come out of the chute on top of a huge bull. Garrett had hung on for a high-scoring ride, but when he'd finally hit the dirt the bull had turned on him. Things had been close for a while. Garrett had dodged horns and the crowd had roared its approval until the bull had been distracted. Katy had been shaking in her seat by the time the whole thing was over. A short time later Garrett was scoring points in the calf-roping competition just as if he hadn't been facing death or serious injury half an hour earlier.

''But as it turns out you were the one who eventually got hurt so badly you couldn't bring yourself to ride again,'' Garrett pointed out quietly.

''Life has its little ironies, doesn't it?'' Katy started to turn away.

''Katy.''

Unwillingly she halted and glanced back at Garrett. "What is it?"

"That day you skipped school to go to the rodeo..."

"What about it?"

"Did you do it just to see me ride?" Garrett asked softly.

He knew, she thought. He'd noticed her small slip earlier and he'd put two and two together. She tried for a serenely haughty smile. "That was a long time ago, Garrett. I've forgotten now exactly why I thought going to the rodeo was worth the risk of skipping school." Katy headed determinedly toward the house.

Garrett watched her go, silently appreciating the curve of her derriere which was very nicely outlined by her jeans. He could still remember the feel of that particular curve and the memory produced an uncomfortably strained sensation in the front of his own jeans. A side glance at the driver of the truck showed that Garrett wasn't the only one enjoying the scenery. It seemed to Garrett that every man in the vicinity was eyeing his wife today. First Royce Hutton and now the young man standing nearby.

"I'm going to put Red in his stall," Garrett said roughly. There was enough of an edge to his voice to capture the younger man's attention. "I'll be back in a few minutes."

"Sure," the young man said. There was a faint flush under his tan. "I can wait."

Red Dazzle woofled again and experimentally lipped the sleeve of Garrett's shirt.

Garrett tugged gently on the gelding's halter. "Let's go, pal. You know something? She was lying. I could see it in her eyes. She has a terrible time when it comes to lying. The truth is, she skipped school that day just so she could watch you and me be heroes for a few minutes. I do believe we were the objects of a teenage crush. Her parents would have flipped in those days if they'd known their daughter had stars in her eyes for a low-class, blue-collar rodeo cowboy who was sure-fired guaranteed never going to amount to anything."

Red Dazzle sighed gustily, but it was difficult to tell if he was responding to the remark or simply expressing mild boredom. Garrett led him toward the roomy stall and paddock that had been prepared.

"You know, Red, back in our glory days, you used to be able to make me look real good in front of a crowd," Garrett told the horse as he opened the stall door. "Too bad I can't just climb on board and look like a knight in shining armor again."

Red Dazzle wasn't paying any attention. He had spotted the hay in the corner of his new stall. He bestirred himself into a slightly speedier pace and entered his new home. Garrett closed the door and was in the process of securing it carefully when Emmett Bracken walked into the stable.

"So that's the critter we've been waiting for, huh?" Emmett shoved his hat back on his head and surveyed Red Dazzle's large, muscular rear quarters.

"That's him." Garrett leaned on the stall door. "You know, Emmett, I think it's time I started looking for a good-tempered little mare for my wife."

"She ride?" Emmett asked.

"She got hurt a few years back and hasn't ridden since. Got spooked. But I think it's time she got back in the saddle."

"What does she think about the idea?" Emmett asked. "Folks that get spooked by a horse often don't want to get back on one." There was clear skepticism in his faded eyes. "And the more time that passes, the less they want to try."

"Now, Emmett, you know better than to ask a woman for her opinion. Especially when it's a subject she's already made up her mind about."

"Meaning she isn't going to think much of the idea of getting back in the saddle," Emmett concluded.

"We'll see," Garrett said.

He left Red Dazzle in the stall and went to talk to the man who had transported the horse to his new home. The more he thought about getting Katy back into the saddle, the more Garrett liked the idea. Riding would establish a bond between himself and his wife, he decided. It was something the two of them could do together. It would be one more thing they had in common.

In addition, he told himself, Katy was bound to feel some sense of gratitude toward him if he helped her overcome the traumatic fear that had plagued her since that barn fire. A man could do a lot with a woman's gratitude.

He might even be able to turn it back into love.

CHAPTER SIX

SEVERAL HOURS LATER Garrett stood quietly near a door that opened onto a patio at Royce Hutton's home. The evening was warm, but there was a storm moving in from the sea. It would reach the coast soon. Garrett glanced at his watch and decided he and Katy would probably wind up driving home in the rain.

Hutton had gathered most of the neighborhood for his informal cocktail party. The people filling his living room were casually dressed, but there was no mistaking the fact that they were a successful, affluent group. Garrett recognized many of them. There were a couple of professors from the nearby college, as well as a variety of other people ranging from software entrepreneurs to wine makers. Several of those present considered themselves gentleman farmers with strong interests in Thoroughbreds, pedigrees and expensive stallions.

It was a collection of people, Garrett knew, who wouldn't have given him a second glance ten years ago, but today they accepted him as their equal. They also accepted his wife. Her background allowed her to slip right into the community, just as he had known it would.

That thought brought back memories of the accusation Katy had made that afternoon. Dammit, he hadn't married her to gain an entrée into this world. The image of her accusing eyes made him set his back teeth. He had known she was a soft, gentle little thing, but her vulnerability surprised him. Just because he hadn't reassured her with a melodramatic declaration of undying love, she had jumped to a whole truckload of wrong-headed conclusions.

As he listened to the cheerful chatter around him, Garrett sipped a beer and watched his wife deal gracefully with a talkative older man who was deep into a discussion about bloodlines. Katy was at ease with the topic, and she was obviously charming her new ac-

quaintance as well as impressing him with the extent of her knowledge on the subject. Her eyes were alive with interest, and her smile
was enough to make Garrett want to throw her over his shoulder
and carry her off to the nearest bed. Now that he knew about the
blazing sensuality hidden deep within her, he couldn't stop himself
from dwelling on his condition of enforced celibacy. Three long
months of temptation and an aching need loomed ahead of him. It
made him groan to think of all the time he had wasted before the
wedding.

On the other hand, Garrett thought gloomily, if he'd taken Katy
to bed before the wedding she might have made her devastating
"discovery" that much sooner and canceled the marriage plans. At
least this way he had a tenuous hold on her for three months.

The only problem was that it was going to drive him crazy holding on to something he couldn't have.

Then he remembered the look in her eyes when she had confessed to the skipped day of school all those years ago. She'd had
a crush on him back then—there was no doubt about it. And two
months ago when he had come back into her life, she had convinced
herself she was in love with him. On their wedding night she had
given herself to him wholeheartedly.

Surely that kind of emotion didn't just dry up and disappear in
a matter of hours, even if he had botched the wedding night. Garrett
studied the disintegrating foam in his glass as his mind worked
through the problem. He needed to find a way past the barriers she
had erected between them. He wished he knew as much about ro-
mancing a woman as he did about handling a horse or terrorizing
a banker who was threatening to foreclose on a Coltrane and Company client.

"So how's married life, Coltrane?"

Garrett inclined his head briefly at the sound of the familiar masculine voice, but he kept his eyes on Katy. "Interesting, Dan."

Dan Barton, a neatly dressed, well-groomed man about Garrett's
age, grinned. His gaze followed Garrett's. "I can see you're still
in the adjustment stage."

"What stage is that?"

"The stage where you're discovering you can't always tell what she's thinking. Women are strange creatures, my friend. Fascinating but strange.''

''I'll buy that.'' Garrett took another sip of his beer. He liked Dan. He had met him when the two of them had been invited to do some guest lectures for some college extension courses. Dan was an accountant. His talk on farming finances had neatly dovetailed with Garrett's discussion of farm management. Since that first set of classes, he and Dan had frequently appeared together in similar situations.

''Glad to see you had the sense to pick a lady who knows something about your business. I talked to her earlier. She's an expert in her own right, isn't she?''

''Her family has been breeding Arabian show horses since before she was born,'' Garrett said. ''She won a hell of a lot of ribbons when she was younger. Katy has been managing her father's stud farm for the past couple of years.''

''She'll be an asset to your consulting business.''

''I thought so,'' Garrett responded moodily.

''Sounds like a perfect marriage to me.''

''It's going to be,'' Garrett vowed quietly. Then he noticed Royce Hutton making his way through the crowd toward Katy. Garrett moved away from the wall. ''Excuse me, Dan. I'd better be getting back to my wife.''

Dan's eyebrows rose as he gave Garrett a knowing look. ''I understand completely. Hutton's been on the prowl lately. A divorce will do that to a man. Makes him act a little crazy for a while.''

Katy saw Garrett approaching at the same moment she noticed Royce Hutton making his way toward her. She wondered if it was coincidence or if Garrett was just feeling possessive and protective. Deciding to think positive, she greeted her husband with a demure smile. When he put his hand around her waist she made no effort to pull away. Hutton reached her side a moment later and stood grinning down at her.

''Looks like Coltrane still remembers a few tricks from his rodeo days. He's got you on a short rope, Katy.''

Katy flushed as several people nearby laughed. She felt Garrett's hand tighten at her waist and looked up to find him regarding her with a faint smile. His eyes were gleaming.

"We live in a dangerous age," Garrett said blandly. "A man has to take care of his valuables." He glanced at his watch. "I think it's about time we headed for home, honey," he said to Katy.

"There speaks the newly married man," someone remarked with a chuckle. "Can't wait to get home after a party."

"I remember those days well," another man said with a theatrical sigh. His wife poked him. There was a round of good-natured comments and best wishes for the newlyweds.

Katy felt an uncomfortable warmth spread up into her cheeks. She thought about the two separate beds waiting at home. This sort of teasing would have been bad enough if the marriage had been for real. Given her present state of détente with Garrett, however, it was almost unbearable. She wanted nothing more than to escape. When Garrett applied a little mild pressure in the direction of the door she went with him willingly.

"Good night, Royce. Thank you for having us over. It was a pleasure to meet everyone." Katy spoke quickly, trying to get the formalities concluded before Garrett had whisked her out the door.

"My pleasure, Katy." Royce grinned wickedly. "We'll see you again soon."

The rain was coming down in sheets as the door closed behind Garrett and Katy. Lightning crackled in the distance.

"Stay here," Garrett ordered, depositing Katy beneath the shelter of the porch. "I'll get the car."

"It's not that far away," Katy protested. "We can both make a dash for it."

"Dammit, Katy, I said, stay where you are. There's no need for both of us to get soaked. I'll be right back." He left her on the top step and moved out into the rain.

Katy stifled a sigh and stayed where she was. So much for trying to be helpful. The last thing she wanted to be was a nuisance. Garrett had married a *partner*, she reminded herself. She was determined to act like one.

But he seemed determined to treat her like a wife.

The unbidden thought danced through her head, creating all sorts of wistful, hopeful feelings. She had been contending with those treacherous feelings for three days now, and she didn't know how much longer she could push them aside.

The truth was, she was very much in love with her husband and she was woman enough to know he wanted her. On top of that, they were living under the same roof. That combination of emotions and circumstances was enough to undermine even the most stubbornly held decision. Only the heat of her recently discovered temper had kept her going this long. Katy was astute enough to recognize that she wouldn't be able to rely on it much longer. Living in a state of high dudgeon was totally alien to her nature.

Katy gazed out through the pouring rain and saw her immediate future with devastating clarity. She was never going to make it through three months playing the role of Garrett's business associate and roommate when the role she longed to play was that of wife.

She was still dealing with that realization when the lights of the white Mercedes sliced through the rain. A few seconds later the vehicle was in front of her and the passenger door was being thrust open.

"Hurry, Katy, or you'll get drenched."

Katy went down the steps as quickly as she dared. The last thing she wanted to endure was a fall in the mud caused by her weak ankle.

But she made it safely into the dry warmth of the car with only a few splashes of rain on her coat.

"This storm certainly came in quickly," she said, striving for a neutral comment as she buckled her seat belt.

"Yeah."

So much for neutral conversation. Silence descended inside the car. It was similar to the silence that had accompanied the drive from Garrett's home to Hutton's earlier that evening.

Well, there was no denying the drive back was going to require a great deal of concentration on Garrett's part. The rain was descending in torrents, obscuring the road a few feet ahead. Minutes passed.

"Did you enjoy yourself?" Garrett finally asked.

"It was a pleasant evening."

There was another tense pause, and then Garrett said coolly, "I've met most of those people at one time or another during the past few years while I've been building up the consulting business."

"So I gathered." Katy wondered what he was trying to say. She sensed there was a message hidden somewhere in the words. "They seem nice, for the most part."

Garrett shrugged. "They are. Hutton's running a little wild these days because of the divorce, and a few of the others have a tendency to think the official poverty line is anything below an income of a hundred thousand a year, but they're decent people."

"I believe you." She still felt she was missing something. Apparently Garrett did, too, because the next time he spoke, his low, rough voice sounded almost explosive.

"Katy, I've been accepted by that crowd for the past five years. I didn't need your family name to get them to issue invitations. All I needed was an income level equivalent to theirs and the ability to talk their language."

Katy sucked in her breath. So that was it. He was trying to prove he hadn't married her just because she was a Randall. In the darkness Katy studied her folded hands. "I'm sorry about what I said this afternoon, Garrett. I had no right to accuse you of marrying me just to use my family connections."

"You may not like all the reasons I had for marrying you, but I want it clear that I never had any intention of using you as bait to attract important clients or to get myself into certain social circles."

She knew then just how deeply she had offended him. Her hands twisted together. "I know that, Garrett. You're much too proud to use a woman in that way. I was angry this afternoon. Angry and upset. Both of us have been under a lot of stress during the past few days."

"Unnecessary stress," Garrett said bluntly.

"We're living in a very difficult situation," Katy said carefully.

"We're living in a damned unnatural situation. A stupid situation. A crazy mixed-up totally idiotic situation. It's enough to drive a sane man over the edge."

Katy studied him with a sidelong glance. Garrett's face was set in stern lines. His hands gripped the wheel so tightly that she thought he might crack it.

"It isn't going to work, is it, Garrett?" Katy finally asked in a very quiet voice.

"What isn't going to work? Three months of living together like buddies who are sharing an apartment? No, it isn't going to work."

Katy drew a deep breath. She had to make a decision. She couldn't go on like this and neither could Garrett.

"Perhaps," Katy began with exquisite caution, "perhaps we could try again. If you want to, that is."

"Katy." Garrett sounded stunned.

"Maybe you're right," she said slowly, trying to sort out the thoughts that had been plaguing her for the past few days. "Maybe I went into this looking for the wrong things. Maybe I did expect too much. I let myself get tangled up in a lot of old, juvenile emotions that I should have discarded a long time ago."

"Katy..."

She ignored him, frowning intently in the darkness as she worked through her shaky logic. Slowly the spinning chaos that had invaded her mind on the night of her wedding settled, allowing her to view her situation more rationally for the first time. "You're right about a lot of things, Garrett. We could be a good team. We have common interests and mutual respect and, until our wedding night, we had what I thought was a good friendship."

"Katy, honey, we do have all those things—that's what I've been trying to tell you for the past few days." Garrett's voice sounded unnaturally husky in the darkness. His big hands flexed on the wheel and then regripped it more tightly than before. "I'm sorry your wedding night didn't live up to your expectations. It was my fault. I was tired, and by the time we got into bed I was aching for you. It had been a long time since I had, well, been with a woman." He brushed that subject aside. "At any rate, I moved too fast. I know that now. I should have taken more time to make it good for you. And then I fell asleep on you. That was stupid. It was just that I got the impression you didn't want any more, uh, lovemaking, that night and I... Never mind. Let's just say I know I didn't handle things well and I'm sorry. If you'll give me another chance I'll do my best to make it good for you—I swear it.''

Katy stared at his shadowed profile. Her own embarrassment was overcome by a realization of what he had been thinking for several days. ''Garrett, what on earth are you talking about? It *was* good for me. I told you that. In fact, it was unbelievable. I had no idea I could feel such sensations. You're a...a fantastic lover.'' Flushing furiously now, Katy stared fixedly out the window.

Garrett took his eyes off the road long enough to pin her with a glittering glance. ''If I were all that fantastic, we would never have gotten into this mess. You wouldn't have had so many doubts and uncertainties. You wouldn't have awakened hating me.''

''Garrett, I don't hate you.'' Katy stared at him, shocked that he could have come to such a conclusion.

''Do you have any idea what I've been going through since our wedding night?''

''I know, Garrett.'' She stared into the rain.

''For God's sake, honey, I—''

Whatever he was going to say next was lost forever as Garrett hit the brakes with lightning-swift reflexes.

Katy saw the huge, dark shape lunge from the gully out into the middle of the road in the same instant that Garrett saw it and reacted. For a few blinding seconds the headlights illuminated a very wide-awake-looking Red Dazzle.

The horse stood, trembling and tense in the center of the narrow road as the Mercedes slammed to a halt less than a couple of feet away. Lightning flashed. The frightened animal shuddered, gathered himself and dashed toward the opposite side of the pavement. An instant later he bounded up the short incline and vanished in the blinding rain.

''It's Red,'' Katy whispered, horrified. ''We almost hit him.''

''If we'd been going any faster, we would have hit him.''

''All three of us would have wound up in the emergency room,'' Katy murmured.

''Or the morgue. Thirteen hundred pounds of horseflesh and a

Mercedes don't mix well." Garrett's voice was savage as he pulled the car to the side of the road and switched off the engine. "How the hell did he get out? I checked the stall door myself before we left tonight."

"We'll have to go after him. He's scared and he's lost. He could wander out in front of another car."

"I'll go after him," Garrett said. He reached into the back seat and picked up a length of rope. "You drive the car back to the house."

"I'll help you find him first." Katy shoved the handle on the car door. "In his present condition it might take two of us to round him up and get a rope attached."

"Stop it, Katy, you'll ruin your clothes. I can handle this."

But Katy was already out of the car, and she was rapidly getting drenched. "Too late. My clothes are already ruined. Lucky I wear flat shoes, isn't it? Imagine having to tromp around in this mud in a pair of heels."

"Katy, so help me…"

But Katy was already starting across the road, following the direction Red Dazzle had taken. With a muttered oath, Garrett grabbed a flashlight and went after her.

Katy heard him give a low, piercing whistle in the darkness as they scrambled up the small incline.

"Does this trick pony of yours come when you call?" she asked as they plowed through a cluster of wet bushes.

"If he feels like it."

"Maybe his normal dormant state will overtake him before he gets very far. I must admit, he didn't look particularly sleepy a minute ago, though."

"No," Garrett said thoughtfully, "he looked downright spooked. It takes a heck of a lot to spook old Red."

"The lightning storm might have done it."

"Yeah. The question is, what was he doing out in the first place?"

"Vandals? Pranksters?" Katy suggested. "Or a broken lock on the stall door?"

"Damned if I know," Garrett muttered as he swung the arc of

the light through the rainy darkness. "But I sure intend to find out." He gave the low whistle again.

"I don't hear the thundering hooves of a big red horse returning to his master's call," Katy noted.

"He's not Trigger."

A moving shadow caught Katy's eye. A low, questioning wicker came through the darkness.

"Over there, Garrett."

"I saw him. You go left and circle slowly in from the other side. Don't make any sudden moves. Just ease in on him."

"I know how to handle a spooked horse."

Garrett grinned briefly. "Sorry. Guess I forgot who I had married. Go get 'em, cowgirl."

Katy wrinkled her nose but said nothing as she moved off into the rain.

The process didn't take long. Red Dazzle seemed relieved more than anything else once he realized who had come after him. His ears came to attention as he identified his old rodeo pal, and after a few muffled snorts and assorted irritated comments he ambled toward Garrett and allowed the rope to be attached to the halter.

Katy's flanking movement proved unnecessary. By the time she emerged beside Garrett and the horse, it was clear Red Dazzle was disgusted with his night out in the rain and longed only to get home.

"I know the feeling," Garrett said as Red Dazzle prodded his shoulder. "It's time we all went home."

He abruptly reached out and clamped a hand around the nape of Katy's neck. Her wet hair spilled over his fingers. Pulling her toward him, he kissed her soundly on the mouth and then vaulted lightly up on his horse's back. "I'll ride him back. You bring the car. As soon as you get home, hop into a hot shower."

"All right."

Garrett saw her safely behind the wheel. As she started to close the door he leaned down. "Drive carefully, Katy. We're not far from the house but this road is dangerous on a night like this."

"Yes, Garrett." It was sweet of him to be protective, Katy decided. From now on she would take comfort from such things.

"I'll see you in a few minutes."

Katy gave one last obedient nod and closed the car door. She sat silently for a moment, savoring the taste of Garrett's kiss as she watched Red Dazzle move off down the road. The horse was responding to the invisible pressure signals Garrett gave with his knees. Old Red might appear to be half asleep most of the time, but he was, in fact, beautifully trained. Garrett didn't even need a bridle to guide him.

Man and horse vanished into the rain, taking a shortcut back to the barn, and Katy reached out to switch on the ignition. She drove slowly back to the big house, her mind filled with the import of the decision she had made.

In a way it was like deciding to get married all over again, she thought. Then she smiled wryly. Not quite. This time around, it had been harder to make the decision. She knew she was allowing her love for Garrett to guide her, and the logical part of her brain warned that such guidance might be suspect.

She was stepping willingly back into an intimate relationship with a man who did not love her. This time around, she knew the facts, yet she was making the same decision.

She was going to take the risk because a part of her refused to give up on Garrett Coltrane.

He might not know how to love, but there was great depth to the man. It was, Katy decided with jubilant anticipation, entirely possible that he could learn how to love.

And who better to teach him than a wife, she asked herself as she parked in the driveway. Irrational optimism surged through her as she bounded out of the car and dashed for the front steps.

There was a light on down at the stable, she noted. Garrett and Red Dazzle had arrived. It would be a while before Garrett got back to the house. The horse had to be dried off and settled for the night. Katy decided to follow orders.

It seemed very bold and adventurous to walk into the master bedroom and strip off her wet clothes. During the past few days she had come to think of this room as Garrett's. She glanced around as she walked nude into the adjoining bath. In the few days he had been occupying the bedroom, Garrett had somehow managed to put his stamp on it. She could see the two contrasting sides of the man as she studied the room.

The closet contained both faded jeans and expensively cut business suits. Scuffed boots were lined up next to fine dress shoes that had been polished to a high gloss. Hanging from a hook were several belts of thin, supple leather designed to go with the suits. Dangling alongside was a wide, gaudily tooled strip of leather that ended in a huge flashy silver buckle. The big buckle was engraved with words that immortalized Garrett's championship status as a rodeo cowboy.

Garrett Coltrane had come a long way since the days he had cleaned out her father's stables, Katy acknowledged. He'd learned a lot but he'd never learned how to love. A lot of factors had been working against him, she told herself charitably. For one thing he'd had poor teachers in his parents and a bad experience with a woman who used an artificial form of love to satisfy her craving for excitement. In addition to those factors, vaulting up several rungs on the ladder of success and respectability was bound to have taken a tremendous amount of drive and energy. There would have been very little left over for the softer things in life. But maybe it was not too late for Garrett to learn about love.

Katy walked on into the bath, turned on the shower and stepped under the hot spray.

She was just beginning to relax under the warm water when a change in the atmosphere warned her that someone had opened the bathroom door. Her fingers tightened nervously around the bar of soap she was holding.

"Garrett?"

The shower door opened abruptly, and Katy gave a small squeak. Garrett stood there, his eyes drinking in the sight of her as she stood beneath the cascading water. He had undressed, and he seemed to fill the shower entrance. He was already fully, magnificently aroused. When he stepped inside and closed the door behind him, muscle rippled smoothly under the hard planes of his shoulders and flanks.

"This is supposed to be romantic," Garrett said, still staring at her.

"What is?" Instinctively she held the washcloth over her breasts and then realized how little she was hiding. She smiled tremulously.

"Taking a shower together." His mouth curved slightly as he put his hands behind her neck and tipped up her chin with his thumbs. "I think I could get used to some of this romantic stuff."

"I have great faith in your adaptability." Katy's eyes were luminous. She splayed her fingers on his wet chest, enjoying the rough texture of the hair that covered him there. She could feel and see him responding to her, and the knowledge that she had such an effect on him made her light-headed. Her shyness melted quickly, just as it had the first time Garrett had taken her in his arms.

Garrett let his hands slide down to cup her shoulders. His eyes were brilliant and intense as he looked at her. "Katy, honey, you won't regret giving us another chance, I swear it. We belong together. We're right for each other. We've got everything going for us, and we're going to make it work."

"You seem very sure of that."

"I wouldn't have married you if I wasn't sure. I know what I want, and I'm willing to work to get it. You're a hard worker, too. I know you are. All I'm asking is that you put in some effort to make our marriage work."

She cradled his face between her soft palms. "It seems little enough to ask, doesn't it?" She urged his head down to hers and parted her lips invitingly.

"Katy, my sweet Katy." His voice was a muffled groan of desire as his mouth closed hungrily over hers.

Katy felt the trembling in Garrett's muscles as he sought to hold himself in check. She was touched by his obvious effort not to rush matters.

"This time I want a chance to explore you," she whispered against his wet chest.

"Yes, Katy, honey, anything you want. Anything. Take your time. I want you to touch every part of me." His hands slipped heavily down her back to her hips. He cupped her in his palms, squeezing gently. "I want you to know me. I want you to be comfortable with me. I want you to learn me so well you'll never want to go to a stranger." The words came in a deep, aching, husky tone.

Now that he was holding her again, Katy admitted to herself that she couldn't imagine going to any other man. "You're the only one I want to touch. There's no one else I could possibly want. No one." Her fingertips moved over his water-slick shoulders.

"Ah, Katy, that feels so good." He shuddered heavily and urged her closer. His fingers tightened under her rounded buttocks, and he lifted her up against him. "Look what you do to me."

"I can feel what I'm doing to you." She clung to him, her arms around his neck and gloried in the strength of his body. He was hard and strong and tight with his need.

His fingers flexed strongly. Katy cried out softly as a wave of excitement swept through her. She buried her face in the curve of his shoulder, tasting him with the tip of her tongue as the water poured over both of them.

"Slow down, honey. I want to do this right." Garrett groaned as Katy wriggled against him. His body throbbed against hers in response.

"Stop worrying about doing it right. You're doing just fine." She laughed softly.

"What's so funny?" he demanded.

"Nothing," she said quickly and then smiled as she dipped her head to nip his shoulder. Her small white teeth tantalized him.

"*Katy.*"

"I was just thinking that it seems strange for me to be reassuring you. You always seem to know what you're doing and how you're going to do it."

"Not with you, apparently. I think I've made some mistakes with you, sweetheart."

She laughed up at him with her eyes. "Not in this department, you didn't."

His smile was slow and infinitely sexy as he eased her down the length of him until she was standing on her feet again. Then he reached around her to turn off the shower.

"If this is the one thing I'm good at," he murmured as he led her out of the shower and reached for a towel, "then I'd better concentrate on doing it well."

Katy closed her eyes, enjoying a deep, sensual pleasure that was still new to her as Garrett caressed her slowly and thoroughly with the towel. He used the rough side of the terry cloth to tease her nipples, and when he was satisfied with their tight, budlike appearance, he leaned down and kissed each with great care.

"Do you like that, Katy?"

"Yes," she said, her voice husky with desire. "Yes, I like it very much."

"Tell me what else you like. Please, Katy. Tell me what you want me to do."

"Everything you do feels right." She slid her hand down to his flat stomach and then went lower, cupping him intimately.

Garrett's breath hissed between his teeth. "Oh, God, Katy."

"I'm doing all right?"

"You're doing perfectly. Too perfectly. I'm about to explode."

"So am I."

Garrett finished drying both of them, taking as much time as he could with the process. He lingered over every curve and valley. When he was finished Katy could hardly stand. She wrapped her arms around him.

"Hold me," she pleaded.

"I'll hold you, Katy." He picked her up and carried her into the other room, setting her down on the bed he had turned back on his way into the bathroom. "I'll hold you so tight and so close that you'll never want to leave."

He came down beside her, parting her legs with his own so he could sink his fingers into her silken, liquid warmth. Katy twisted at the intimate touch, reaching out to pull him closer.

Garrett resisted, using his hands and lips to coax the response he wanted from her. He was so intent on pleasuring her, Katy thought bemusedly. It seemed to be the only thing he cared about in the whole world. Once again he was focused completely on her, and the sensation was dazzling.

In the end both of them were shivering in each other's arms, feverish with the passionate need that drove them. Katy surrendered willingly once more to the strong, primitive storm that swept into existence just long enough to catch man and woman and bind them together for a split-second glimpse of eternity.

CHAPTER SEVEN

THE NEXT MORNING Red Dazzle looked none the worse for his adventure during the night. Garrett lounged against the bottom half of the stall door and watched the stocky horse contentedly munch hay. The red tail swished idly, and the surprisingly sensitive ears rotated with mild curiosity as Garrett spoke a few soft words. The powerful jaws never ceased their steady chewing action as Red Dazzle worked his way through breakfast. Red had set his priorities early in life. Food was at the top of the list, closely followed by napping.

"I reckon we both had ourselves one heck of an exciting night last night, didn't we, Red?" Garrett's mouth curved into a wickedly complacent grin as he recalled his own private adventures in bed. "On the whole, though, I'll bet I had a better time than you did."

Red Dazzle favored Garrett with a brief, sidelong glance but didn't stop eating.

Garrett was feeling extraordinarily good that morning. He hadn't felt so good in a long time. "I've got me one sweet, sexy little wife, Red. You'd never know it to look at her. On the surface she's calm and polite and serious and just a little shy. But in bed she turns into a waterfall made out of fire. Soft as a kitten, wild as a filly who's never had a saddle on her. You never saw anything like it."

Red twitched his tail again and used his mobile lips to tug free a particularly tasty clump of hay. He was obviously not impressed with human sexuality.

Garrett shrugged, not offended by Red's lack of interest in the wonders of married life. "There are times when I feel sorry for you, Red. Being a gelding has its drawbacks."

Garrett went back to work, whistling softly between his teeth as he examined the stall door closure. The metal mechanism appeared to be in perfect condition. There was no obvious explanation for how the door had accidentally opened last night.

The sun was shining crisp and clear. All traces of the storm had vanished, leaving behind a fresh, glistening fall morning. The day felt new and full of promise.

Just like his marriage.

Garrett experienced a sense of deep satisfaction at the thought. The brief, astonishing, totally unexpected storm that had erupted the morning after the wedding appeared to be over as quickly as it had begun. Katy was back to normal. Everything was going to be all right. It was going to work out just the way he had originally planned. Better than he had planned, Garrett decided cheerfully. When he had first decided to marry Katy, he hadn't realized just how much of a woman he would be getting. He hadn't known how lucky he was going to be.

"You're fortunate you don't have to worry about the female psyche, Red. I'm telling you, it's a maze. Even the intelligent, sensible-looking ones can surprise you. Who would have thought sweet, gentle little Katy would have gone all stubborn and temperamental the way she did the day after we got married? Bridal jitters, they call it, but I'll tell you, for the past few days I felt like I was the one walking through a mine field. But it's all over now. Things are back to normal."

Red sighed gustily in agreement and reached for more hay.

"I'm going to have to keep an eye on her, though," Garrett confided to the gelding. "I saw the way Hutton and a few of the others looked at her last night. Every time she opened her mouth about breeding programs, she had a male audience hanging on every word. I don't think she realized just how sexy she is when she starts talking about confirmation, pedigrees and fertility. She gets so serious and intent and the nearest males start thinking of themselves as studs. When she launched into a discussion of the advantages of natural breeding over artificial insemination, I thought I was going to have to hog tie her and carry her out of the room. Every man listening to her was salivating. The funny part is, I don't think she even realized it."

Red Dazzle, who saved his salivating for his feed, twitched his ears and went on chewing energetically. Garrett went back to whistling while he played with the stall door lock. It was Emmett Bracken's sour, hung-over greeting that made him glance up a few minutes later. The man had obviously tied one on the night before.

"Morning, Mr. Coltrane." Emmett came into the small stable carrying a pitchfork. "How's it going?"

Garrett nodded, a brief, casual greeting. "There was a problem with this stall door last night."

Emmett frowned, his leathery features seaming into countless small lines. His faded eyes narrowed. "What kind of problem?"

"Old Red here got out. I nearly hit him on the road coming back from Hutton's party."

"He was on the road?"

"Yeah. Spooked by the storm. Or something. I almost didn't see him in time."

Emmett pursed his lips and gazed thoughtfully at Red Dazzle. "Is the hardware on the door okay?"

"The door's fine."

"He's one smart old horse. Been around. Any chance he figured out how to open that latch himself?" Emmett asked slowly.

"No," Garrett said bluntly. "There's no chance he got it open himself. He's smart but he doesn't have hands. It took a pair of hands to get this door open."

"Or a pair of hands to forget to close it properly last night," Emmett pointed out in a neutral-sounding voice.

"I checked it myself around six o'clock."

There was a long silence. Emmett stood holding the pitchfork, staring at the latch on the stall door. "You figure someone opened it deliberately?"

"The thought had crossed my mind." Garrett watched Emmett closely.

The old man shook his head and straightened his worn cap so the brim of the hat came down low over his eyes and shielded his gaze. "I guess it could have happened that way."

"What way?" Garrett prodded.

Emmett shrugged. "Could have been deliberate."

"You know something I don't know, Bracken?" Garrett asked very softly.

"I know that horse means a lot to you. Anyone who's been around you very long knows that much," Emmett said cryptically.

Garrett folded his arms and leaned back against the stall door. "What are you trying to say, Bracken?"

"Just that someone with a grudge against you might have decided to go after old Red." Emmett started to turn away.

"Bracken." Garrett didn't move, but Emmett stopped as if he'd been jerked to a halt.

"I don't know anything you don't know, Coltrane." Emmett rubbed the back of his neck in a nervous fashion.

"Meaning?"

"Meaning that you know the people who got grudges against you better than I do."

"Maybe," Garrett said dryly, "But I'd like to hear you name a few, just the same."

Emmett gave a grim snort, and his hand clenched around the handle of the pitchfork. "If I were you, I'd start with the females on the list. A woman who feels she'd been wronged will do some mighty strange things. Or haven't you lived long enough to know that fact of life yet?" Emmett walked out of the stable.

Katy heard Emmett's voice as she was just about to step into the stable. She moved aside as he strode past her.

"'Scuse me, ma'am. Didn't see you." Bracken kept moving, not pausing to greet her.

Katy smiled fleetingly at the man's back. She was growing accustomed to Emmett Bracken's morose ways. Then she went toward Garrett who was regarding her with a curious expression. "Hi. I came to see how Red Dazzle looks this morning."

"He's fine." Garrett continued to study her thoughtfully.

Katy swallowed, suddenly uncomfortable under that steady gaze. Her heart plunged. She had spent most of the night convincing herself that she was doing the right thing by agreeing to make the marriage a real one. Now, with a single unreadable glance from her husband, she was forced to wonder if she'd made another mistake.

Garrett looked grim and aloof this morning. Not at all the way he had looked during the night.

"Is something wrong, Garrett?"

"Emmett and I were just discussing the fact that the only way Red could have gotten free last night was with a little human help."

"What?" Katy was startled. "Someone let him out?"

"Looks that way."

"But who?"

"That," Garrett said quietly, "is the interesting part of the question."

"Kids playing dangerous pranks? Or some vagrant who wanted to spend the night in a warm stable?"

"Emmett suggested a woman might have done it," Garrett said. "He implied that trying to hurt Red was the kind of revenge a woman might take against a man she felt had wronged her."

Katy caught her breath and reached out to brace herself against the wall of the stable. The full import of what he had just said struck her with the impact of a slap. Instinctively she recoiled.

"You think I had something to do with this?" Katy whispered. "You think I would do such a thing? After...after what happened between us last night?"

Garrett studied her a moment longer. "Red was set free several hours before you and I went to bed. There's no telling exactly when he did get out."

"Garrett!"

"He could have been killed. He could have blundered over the cliffs during that storm. Or he could have been hit by a truck. Hell, I almost killed him myself. That would have been a rather vicious piece of revenge, wouldn't it?"

"Garrett, for heaven's sake." Katy's nails were biting into the palm of her hand. She couldn't believe this was happening. "Do you really think I would do such a thing just because I didn't like the way my marriage turned out? Do you think I would take my revenge out on a horse?"

Garrett straightened and took a step toward her. His big hands closed around her shoulders as he looked down at her with an intensity that made Katy shiver. It was obvious he had come to some inner decision.

"No," he said roughly, "I don't believe you would use old Red to take revenge against me. Bracken's wrong. A woman who feels she'd got a right to a grudge might do some strange things, but one thing's for certain: I know a few things about you, and one of those things is that you love horses. You would never put one at risk the way Red was put at risk last night. You wouldn't use a horse to get even with me. You're an honest woman, Katy. You fight your own battles."

Katy went limp under his hands. "Well, thank you for that much, at least."

Garrett groaned and pulled her against him. He wrapped his arms around her and spoke into her hair. "I'm sorry, Katy. For a few minutes there, after Emmett implied it could have been a woman, all I could think of was how upset you've been since the wedding. For days I didn't know what you were thinking or feeling. You seemed different from the Katy I thought I knew. All that foolishness about living together as if we were roommates or business partners or something was enough to make a man feel as if he'd just stepped down the rabbit hole in *Alice in Wonderland*. I didn't know what was going on."

Some of Katy's immediate sense of relief began to fade. "Obviously it doesn't take much to completely baffle the male brain."

"We're simple, straightforward creatures, Katy. Just ask any man." He was smiling.

Katy put her arms around his waist and leaned her head against his broad chest. The tension seeped slowly out of her. "All right. If we're agreed that it wasn't me who let Red out last night, who is the culprit?"

Garrett shook his head. "Damned if I know. Probably a prankster, like you said. Or some kid who just wanted to pet the nice horsey or take a joy ride. In any event, I'm going to see it doesn't happen again."

Katy lifted her head to look up at him. "How?"

"I'm going to put an alarm system on the stable this afternoon. Nothing complicated. Just something that will set off some bells in the house if someone decides to open the stable door after it's been closed for the night. That should be enough to take care of any kids or troublemakers who come nosing around."

Katy nodded. "I'm sorry you thought it might have been me, even for a moment, Garrett."

He hugged her fiercely and then stepped back. He left one arm draped possessively around her shoulders. "You've had me so confused for the past few days I haven't known which end was up, lady. But everything's back to normal now." He looked down at her, eyes gleaming with memories of the night. "Isn't it?"

Katy smiled tremulously, her own memories making her blush warmly. "I'm not sure what normal is supposed to feel like, Garrett."

"As long as it feels like last night, we'll do fine." Amusement and satisfaction were heavy in his voice. He was a man who was back in complete charge of his own private universe. "You know, I've been thinking, Katy."

"I understand that's a dangerous thing for a man to attempt."

He gave her an affectionate shake. "Don't get sassy. I'm serious. You and I have a lot in common, and we should take advantage of that fact. It's good for a marriage."

"Since when did you become such an expert on marriage?" Katy leaned into the stall to survey Red Dazzle, who took a few seconds out from his busy schedule to blow into her palm. Katy smiled and glanced up at Garrett out of the corner of her eye. To her surprise he was taking the question seriously.

"I'll admit I'm learning as I go along. But it makes good sense to share things, Katy. One of the reasons we got married was because we have a lot of mutual interests."

"I suppose it was." She concentrated on Red Dazzle, wondering what was coming next. She might have succeeded in baffling Garrett on a few occasions lately, but that was nothing compared to what he was capable of doing to her.

"We should take advantage of those mutual interests."

"Okay, I'll buy that," Katy said agreeably.

"I think it's time somebody threw you back up on a horse, Katy."

Katy went rigid. She clung to the stall door, staring blindly at the red horse inside. "Forget it."

"Now, Katy, honey, it's time you were reasonable about this." Garrett's voice took on a rich, soothing quality. He gentled Katy with his hand, stroking her the way he would a nervous mare. "I know all about what happened to you during that barn fire. I know about how long you spent getting well. But that's all in the past. I talked to your father at the wedding about it and we agreed. Riding used to be a big part of your life. It's wrong to just abandon it because you had a bad experience."

"A bad experience! Garrett, I nearly died." Katy swung around. "You can't even imagine what it was like that night. The smoke and the flames and the terrified animals. And the pain. Garrett, do you have any idea how much I hurt afterward? Can't you understand?"

"Honey, I understand. But if you'd had a car accident, you would have had to learn to get back into a car sooner or later. This is no different."

"This is different. I have a choice and I've chosen not to ride ever again. Don't lecture me, Garrett. I made my decision a long time ago. I'm an adult and I have a right to make my own decisions."

"You've let yourself develop a phobia about it. But riding was something special to you," Garrett persisted. "I remember how you looked when you were in a saddle. You came alive on a horse, the same way you do when you're in my arms."

Katy flushed. "For heaven's sake, Garrett, that's a ridiculous analogy. How would you remember how I looked? I was just a kid when you knew me all those years ago."

He smiled whimsically, his fingers toying with a tendril of her hair. "I remember, Katy. I remember how much you liked the blue ribbons and the excitement of the show ring. I remember how intense and serious you were during a show and how elated you were afterward. I remember all the hours you spent getting a horse ready for the ring. And I remember how gutsy you were. Riding was the most important thing in your life in those days. You were very, very good."

"People change, Garrett. You should know that as well as any-one."

"I agree. People change. But some things don't change. You love horses and you were a beautiful rider once upon a time. Riding is something you and I can do together. It's something we have in common. It's time you got back on a horse. You've spent too many years building up the fear in your mind until it's way out of pro-portion." Garrett smiled warmly. "I'm going to help you get over that old fear."

"Don't push me, Garrett."

"You'll thank me for it later, honey."

Katy's eyes widened in anger and exasperation. "Don't you dare patronize me. Garrett, so help me, if you don't—"

"Hush," he said, leaning down to kiss her lightly on the mouth. "Take it easy, honey. I'm not going to rush you into anything. We'll take our time, I promise. Just like we took our time last night." Deliberately he deepened the kiss. "You taste good," he muttered against her parted lips.

"You're trying to distract me," Katy accused, her fear and ex-asperation dissolving beneath the warmth of his kiss. Her mouth opened instinctively for his sensual invasion. The night before she had decided that if this was the one area in which they could truly communicate, then her only option lay in trying to facilitate that communication. The problem with that decision was that she faced many moments such as this, moments in which she was afraid she surrendered too much of herself into the hands of a man who had not yet learned to love her. The risk she ran was enormous and she knew it.

"I like distracting you." He eased her back against the stable wall, planting his hands on either side of her and caging her with his body. He moved his knee between her legs, and when she gave way to the insistent pressure he thrust his thigh intimately between hers. "That's it, honey. Tighten your legs around me the same way you would around a stallion. Ride me."

Katy was torn between a surge of desire and a surge of panic. "Garrett! Someone will see us. Emmett is nearby. He could come back at any time."

"Not if he knows what's good for him," Garrett muttered. "But since you're still such a shy little thing, I guess I better ensure some privacy."

"What are you going to do?"

"Guess." He scooped her up and tossed her lightly over his shoulder.

"We can't! Not here. Put me down, Garrett. Do you hear me?"

"I hear you." Garrett was carrying her into the empty stall where straw and hay were stored. He closed the stall door firmly behind them. They were instantly in shadow. Golden sunlight seeped through the cracks in the wooden walls. Garrett lowered Katy slowly into the straw. "Your problem is that you still haven't gotten accustomed to being a wife yet."

"Is that right?" She looked up at him from beneath her lashes as he loomed over her. She could feel the gathering sexual tension in him, and it thrilled her to know she had this effect on him. "I suppose you figure it's your job to help me get accustomed to my role?"

"My solemn duty and responsibility," he assured her as he came down on top of her. His eyes were brilliant in the gloom of the shadowed stall, as brilliant as they had been during the long night.

Katy sighed softly and put her arms around him, drawing him down to her. When he looked at her like that, she let her hopes and dreams sweep through her and take command of her senses.

Garrett dealt impatiently with their clothing, flinging jeans and shirts into a careless pile. Then he moved onto his back, nestling against the discarded clothing and grasped Katy by the waist. His aroused body was taut with desire, and she was suddenly, violently ready for him. He touched her lingeringly, testing the moist warmth between her legs, and when she moaned, he growled his pleasure.

Slowly, he eased Katy down on top of him, sheathing himself within her. Katy gasped and trembled in his hands.

"Show me how good a rider you are," he said in a dark, husky voice.

Then he laughed with soft triumph as her fingers bit into the hard, muscled skin of his shoulders. A few minutes later he was no longer laughing.

The passion captured them both.

A LONG TIME LATER Katy felt Garrett stir beneath her. With a sigh, she reluctantly eased herself off him. He swore with great depth of feeling and winced as he sat up beside her.

"Remind me to think twice before I try this again." Garrett brushed straw off himself and handed Katy her clothes. "A man could do himself permanent injury making love on straw."

Katy pulled a piece of straw out of her hair and smiled wistfully. "I thought it was kind of romantic."

Garrett stepped into his jeans and fastened them quickly. "That's because you were on top."

"Don't blame me. It was your idea." Katy concentrated on doing up her shirt.

"Hey." Garrett reached down and tipped up her chin. "I was just teasing you." He searched her face, his expression intently curious. "Did you really think it was romantic?"

Katy hesitated and then nodded once, briefly.

Garrett grinned suddenly, obviously pleased with himself. "Well, how about that? I never would have thought... Never mind. You thought it was romantic, huh?"

"Umm-hmm." Katy wondered at his look of pride.

"In that case, maybe we will try it again sometime. A man has to be prepared to make certain sacrifices for his woman."

Katy smiled in spite of herself. "Is that right?"

"Damned right." Garrett finished buttoning his shirt and watched with lazy, possessive interest as Katy pulled on her clothing more slowly. Then his grin faded and his expression grew more serious again.

"Is something wrong?" Katy eyed him warily.

"I was just thinking about Bracken's suggestion that a woman might have let Red out last night."

Katy's head came up abruptly. Pain and fear knifed through her. "Are we back to that again? What is this? Now that you've had your morning fling in the straw, you've decided to start wondering if I might be the guilty party, after all?"

Garrett's eyes narrowed warningly. "Calm down. You sure are

jumpy lately. Downright temperamental. I wasn't thinking it might have been you who opened the door. I know damned well it wasn't. It was something else that was bothering me.''

"What?''

"I was just wondering where Bracken got the idea that it might have been you who did it. He said something about a woman feeling wronged.''

Katy stared at him for a moment. Then her eyes slid away. "I can guess where he got the idea.''

"Yeah? Suppose you share your guesses with me.'' There was a soft challenge in Garret's words.

Katy sighed. "Nadine has noticed our...our sleeping arrangements. She's been working in the house with me, getting things organized. She knows we've been using separate bedrooms. That's a bit odd for two people who are on their honeymoon. She also overheard our argument yesterday after Royce Hutton left. I suspect she drew her own conclusions about the state of our marriage and passed them along to her husband.''

"I see.'' Garrett opened the stall door. "It makes sense. You have been acting like a woman wronged lately, haven't you?''

Katy glared at him. "I hadn't noticed.''

Garrett's mouth curved humorously, and he reached out to ruffle her hair. "So that's where Bracken got his ideas this morning. But that's all over, isn't it, Katy? We've got this marriage back on course, and it's going to stay there. No more emotional storms or tantrums. No more cases of extended bridal jitters.''

Katy raised her eyebrows and pitched her voice into tones of artificially sweet docility. "Whatever you say, Garrett.'' It gave her an odd feeling to tease him.

Garrett laughed, hugged her fiercely and kissed the top of her head. "Come on, lady, let's go get a cup of coffee and something to eat. Any of those muffins left over from breakfast?''

"You just ate an hour ago.''

"I seem to have worked up an appetite.''

But the phone was ringing when they walked into the kitchen. Garrett gave an impatient exclamation and reached for it. Katy listened to the one-sided conversation and knew that something serious had happened at the Fresno office at Coltrane and Company, something that had Garrett's instant attention. As he spoke into the receiver, he watched Katy bustle around the kitchen.

"All right, Carson, calm down. Is Layton there? What the hell do you mean, he's on vacation? Get hold of him and tell him to get back to the office." There was a pause and then Garrett swore softly. "Okay, okay, I hear you. He can't be reached. Damn. Next time the man takes a week off, make sure he goes someplace where they have telephones. Sounds like I'll have to come on over." He glanced at his watch. "I can be there by late afternoon. Tell Bisby to sit tight. The bank can't move as fast as we can. He's not going to lose his land in the next forty-eight hours. He'll get his loan. See you by three o'clock. Now pay attention, Carson. Here's what I want you to do while you're waiting for me."

Katy listened to Garrett rattle off a terse list of instructions that displayed a fine knowledge of how bankers and accountants worked and thought. Then he hung up the phone with a loud, irritated clatter. He reached for the cup of coffee Katy had set in front of him.

"You heard?" he asked.

"You're going to drive to Fresno this afternoon?" Katy sat down across from him and wrapped her hands around her own mug. She delicately blew on the hot brew.

"Afraid so. They're short staffed this month, and the head of the office, Layton, is on vacation somewhere in the wilds of Mexico. Can't be reached. One of our clients is in trouble with the IRS and the bank. Everyone's running around screaming foreclosure. Normally I wouldn't have to get involved in something like this unless it got a lot worse, but in this case it looks like I'd better go on over and get things calmed down."

Katy nodded. "It will be a good opportunity for me to see the inner workings of one of your offices. Will we be staying overnight?"

Garrett blinked at her over the rim of the coffee cup. Then he shook his head firmly. "I'll be staying overnight. You'll be staying here. There's no reason for you to come with me. I'll be back tomorrow. We're still on our honeymoon, remember?"

Katy smiled tentatively. "Yes, I know, but this marriage is supposed to be a working partnership. You made that very clear right from the beginning. This is a perfect opportunity for me to start learning my new job."

He shot her a glowering look. "There'll be plenty of opportunity for you to learn the ins and outs of Coltrane and Company after we've had our honeymoon."

"Why postpone the learning session, Garrett? It makes sense for me to go with you today. I'll get a chance to meet the people in the Fresno office, and I'll see how things function in a crisis."

"A crisis is no time to learn a new job." Garrett's tone had a hard edge. He picked up a muffin and took a savage bite out of it. "You'd just be in the way."

Katy bit her lip, a little hurt and a little angry. "I'll stay out of your way."

"You'll stay here," he exploded. "Dammit, you're supposed to be a new bride. You're not supposed to have to start worrying about a new job at this stage."

"Why not?" Katy shot back, her temper fracturing. "It's the reason you hired me, isn't it? To go to work for Coltrane and Company?"

"*Hired you.*" Garrett's coffee cup came down with a crash. He stared at her. "Hired you? What the hell are you talking about? I didn't hire you, I married you, woman!"

Katy winced. "Sorry, it was just a slip of the tongue."

"A slip of the tongue?" Garrett was incredulous. "You get the word 'hire' mixed up with the word 'marry' and you call it a slip of the tongue?"

"Calm down, Garrett. I told you, it was a simple mistake." One she was rapidly regretting, Katy thought dismally.

"Like hell." He got to his feet, his face thunderous. "Let's get one thing clear, Katy Coltrane—that wasn't an employment application you filled out a couple of weeks ago, it was a marriage license application. This isn't a probationary training period you're in at the moment, it's a honeymoon. You're my wife, not my employee. Try to figure out just what that means during the next twenty-four hours, will you?"

"Garrett…"

"I'm going to get hold of a guy I know who does home security work. I want something installed on that stable this afternoon."

He stalked out of the kitchen, leaving Katy feeling as though she had just tangled with a tornado. Her fingers were trembling as she lifted her cup of coffee again.

Slowly she took a long, soothing sip. When she set down her cup again, she was smiling very slightly to herself. If she had looked in a mirror, her eyes would have sparkled back at her.

Teaching Garrett Coltrane how to love was a risky business, but she thought she had prepared herself for most of the hazards involved.

What she hadn't prepared herself for was the discovery of her own spirited, unexpectedly bold nature. There was something exhilarating about challenging Garrett, even when she lost. Just as there was something very exhilarating about making love to him.

One way or another, the man was finally beginning to notice her.

She hadn't felt like this since the last time she had ridden one of her father's Arabians to a blue ribbon.

CHAPTER EIGHT

THE BIG HOUSE felt empty and lonely that night. Katy poured herself a glass of wine and cooked a light dinner, which she ate in the kitchen. She turned the television on for the evening news but turned it off again later when it became annoying. She read for a while and finally treated herself to a nightcap of brandy. It was going to be a long night.

The master bedroom at the end of the hall seemed very large and forbiddingly formal when she finally wandered into it around ten o'clock. The room needed Garrett's earthy, masculine presence to counteract its designer perfection, Katy decided as she undressed slowly and crawled into bed. Garrett had a way of making a room his when he was in it.

He also had a way of dominating a bed when he was in it. Katy felt very much alone as she curled up on her side of the huge bed. It was strange, she thought. She had only spent one night in this bed with her husband, but apparently she had gotten addicted to his presence in it already. It seemed very empty without him sprawled beside her like a lazily sensual lion. She wondered if Garrett would take some satisfaction from knowing that she missed him. She hoped he was missing her tonight.

It didn't take any great amount of intuition to figure out the real reason he hadn't wanted to take her with him to Fresno. Katy sensed that in his own, very male, very chauvinistic and rather convoluted fashion, he was trying to turn her into a wife before he turned her into a business associate. It was touching, in a way. He was nervous about allowing her to get involved in her new job while certain matters were still unresolved in their relationship.

She wasn't sure if Garrett himself realized exactly how his logic was working, but Katy took heart from the muddle-headed approach he was using. She smiled to herself. On some level he recognized that their relationship was more important than their business association, and he wanted it firmly established.

One of these days Garrett might even realize he was in love.

As if on cue, the phone on the nightstand burbled plaintively. Katy picked it up.

"Hello?"

"Hi, Katy." Garrett sounded alert. It was obvious he wasn't just about to crawl into bed. "Thought I'd check in and see how things were going with you."

Katy sat up against the pillows and switched on the light. "I'm fine. I just got into bed. How are things there?"

"Fresno is Fresno. But the client's going to survive. Barely. I saw the bankers personally this afternoon and got a reprieve. Tomorrow we'll work on getting the IRS to back off for a while. I'll be home tomorrow afternoon."

"Good." She said nothing more, waiting. Katy swallowed a silent grin when she heard Garrett's next question.

"Miss me?"

"Yes, as a matter of fact, I do," she said demurely.

There was a pause and then Garrett said roughly, "I miss you, too. I'd much rather be climbing into bed with you than sitting here at this desk."

There was a voice in the background. It was a man's voice, and Katy listened attentively. "I take it you're not alone?"

"No, some of the staff are staying late with me. Did you and Emmett test that alarm system before the installer left? I couldn't hang around to check it out myself."

"Yes, we tested it. Works fine. We checked it out from both our house and the Brackens' place. Garrett, did you know Emmett keeps a gun in a cigar box right on top of the fireplace mantle? Emmett showed it to me this afternoon when we tested the alarm system."

"No, I didn't know, but it doesn't surprise me." There was a moment's silence. "Considering his drinking problem, I think the idea of him having a gun close at hand is not exactly reassuring, is it?"

"No, it isn't," Katy admitted. She wrapped her arms around her drawn-up knees. "I get the feeling he's the kind of drunk who just nods off to sleep, though, not the kind who gets violent."

"I don't know about those two, Katy. I hate to kick them out, but I'm not sure I want to keep them on forever, either. They were Atwood's concern, not ours."

"I know what you mean."

"Well, we'll talk about it when I get back. I've got enough on my mind this evening. Get some sleep, honey. I'll see you tomorrow."

Katy sighed as she hung up the phone. They hadn't exactly said good-night like lovers, but she had heard the rough affection in his voice. Garrett did care for her. She was sure of it. She had to be sure of it because she'd staked her happiness on that assumption.

It was when she reached up to turn out the bedside lamp that Katy saw the glint of gold in the small ceramic bowl on the dressing table. For a moment she stared at it, wondering if she'd accidentally left some of her jewelry out. Then she realized what it was.

Garrett had left his wedding ring behind before taking off for the Fresno office.

The optimism Katy had been feeling when she'd climbed into bed a few minutes earlier faded. She got up and walked slowly over to the dressing table. She picked up the gold band and studied it with a feeling of growing depression. The symbol of their marriage meant so little to Garrett that he could casually take it off and forget to put it back on.

Anger began to simmer in her. It seemed that every time she thought she might be making progress in the task of teaching Garrett how to love, something happened to puncture her balloon.

She thought of Garrett working late with his staff in the Fresno office. He would be sitting at that desk, a newly married man who wasn't even bothering to wear a wedding ring.

Katy tugged the ring off her own finger and tossed it down into the ceramic bowl beside Garrett's band.

The small gesture of getting even did little to make her feel better.

THREE HOURS later Katy awoke with a surge of adrenaline. She sat bolt upright, aware of damp palms and a trickle of perspiration under her arms. It took her a few seconds to identify the shrill clamor that had awakened her so suddenly.

It was the new alarm system that had been rigged up on Red Dazzle's stall that afternoon.

Katy didn't stop to think. She threw off the covers and scrambled for her slippers. Grabbing her robe, she hurried down the hall, turning on lights as she went. She scurried downstairs, the robe flapping around her ankles. With any luck, whoever was fooling around the stables would soon realize he had awakened the inhabitants of the main house. The knowledge should send him scurrying.

Katy felt her ankle give way just as she reached the front steps. She grabbed the wrought-iron railing for support but knew it was too late. She had managed to twist the joint at its weak point. Pain shot through her. She set her teeth and forced herself to keep going. She would worry about the injury later.

Her slowed pace was maddening. With every step Katy bit back a groan. But she managed to half run, half hobble to the stable. A shadow loomed out of the darkness just as she reached the structure. Somehow Katy turned her scream into a shout. It was only a kid, she told herself. Only a troublemaking kid. Belatedly she realized how unarmed and vulnerable she was. She tried to compensate by putting as much authority as possible into her voice.

"Hey, you! Get away from there! Go on, get out of here before I call the police! This is private property!"

"Take it easy, Mrs. Coltrane—it's just me, Emmett Bracken."

Relief poured through Katy as the looming shadow took form and substance in the starlight. Emmett's voice was a little slurred, but he was obviously in control of himself.

"Emmett! Good grief, you gave me a scare. The new alarm went off up at the house. I thought someone was down here messing around with Red's stall door again." Katy sagged against a post, gasping for breath. Her ankle was throbbing violently.

"I woke up and couldn't get back to sleep. Thought I'd get some air to see if that would help. Came down to check on old Red, and I guess I set off the alarm by mistake. I promised your husband I'd keep an extra close eye on things while he was gone. I sure am sorry to upset you. Should have paid better attention this afternoon when that security man explained the alarm system. Are you all right, Mrs. Coltrane?'' Emmett came toward her.

"I'm fine," Katy said through set teeth. "I may have sprained my ankle, but it will be okay." She looked around. The stable seemed peaceful enough. Limping painfully, she went inside and turned on the light.

Red Dazzle stirred sleepily and stuck his large head out over the stall door. He blinked owlishly at Katy, silently questioning the late-night ruckus.

Katy smiled and hobbled forward to stroke his neck. "Sorry about the rude awakening, Red. Go back to sleep."

The horse woofled grumpily and retreated into the dark shadows of his stall. A munching noise a few seconds later indicated he had decided that as long as he was up, he might as well have a midnight snack.

"Everything's fine," Emmett Bracken said, peering over Katy's shoulder into the stall. "Just a false alarm. Sure am sorry about all the excitement."

"That's okay, Emmett. I guess it takes a while to get accustomed to new alarm systems." Katy limped outside and turned out the stable light. "I'll see you in the morning."

"You want some help getting back to the house? That ankle of yours seems mighty weak."

"I can manage. This isn't the first time I've twisted it. Don't worry, I know exactly what to do for it." What she would do for it was suffer, Katy thought. She swore silently to herself and made her way slowly back to the main house.

So much for middle-of-the-night heroics. Something told her Garrett was going to blow his stack when he found out what had happened.

GARRETT DROVE back from Fresno with a feeling of pleasant anticipation. It took him a while to identify the unfamiliar sensation. He was accustomed to going back to an empty apartment. The idea of having a home of his own and a woman waiting for him seemed slightly unreal.

Not just a woman—a wife. His wife, Katy.

Garrett savored the notion of Katy waiting for him on the front steps with a welcoming drink in hand. It would be getting close to dinnertime, so she would probably have something interesting cooking in the kitchen. All in all, a man could do a whole lot worse.

After all his years of instability and change and uncertainty, permanence was amazingly good to think about.

The word *permanence* clanked loudly inside his head, striking a discordant note. A flicker of uneasiness invaded his pleasant sense of anticipation.

It suddenly occurred to him that even though things seemed to have settled down between himself and Katy, there was one issue that had not been discussed.

Neither of them had brought up the unpleasant matter of her initial agreement to stay with him for only three months.

Garrett's mouth tightened thoughtfully. Surely that nonsense was behind them now. Katy had capitulated completely two nights ago, after Hutton's party. She had given herself to him with all the sweet, sensual generosity of her spirit that night. She wasn't the type of woman who could surrender in that way unless she was totally committed, Garrett told himself.

But he had to face the fact that he was learning a lot of new things about Katy. She was a far more complex creature than he had originally thought. There was more to her, including a temper and a stubborn feminine will, than he had initially believed. He could no longer be completely certain of just what was going on inside her head.

His mind drifted back over the things she had said to him that night on the drive back from Hutton's cocktail party. There had been no mention of the three-month time limit. She had suggested only that they start sleeping together again because sleeping apart was too hard on both of them.

It was just barely conceivable that she had convinced herself she could have what amounted to nothing more than an affair with him for the remainder of the three months, Garrett realized.

His mood turned abruptly grim, and a cold wash of anger went through him. There were still some important matters to be resolved between himself and Katy. Garrett wanted everything crystal clear between the two of them. Most of all, he wanted to be certain of her commitment to the marriage.

He remembered her flare of temper yesterday when he had informed her he was going to Fresno alone. Perhaps he should have taken her with him. But the truth was, he hadn't liked the idea of her talking about the business side of marriage when the honeymoon had just barely gotten off the ground. He had wanted her to accept her role as his wife before she got involved in her new job.

But he hadn't been able to think of a way to explain that to her, hadn't been at all sure she would accept the explanation, even if he had found the right words. So he had practically issued an order for her to stay behind while he went to Fresno.

Garrett swore. He had probably handled that scene all wrong yesterday. There was a hell of a lot to learn about handling a woman like Katy.

An hour later he turned into the long, tree-lined drive with a feeling of relief. He was home at last and Katy would be waiting. Tonight they would settle the last uncertainties that surrounded their marriage.

But Katy was not waiting on the front steps when Garrett finally parked the Mercedes and climbed out. Nor did she appear when he opened the front door and walked into the wide foyer. The house was very silent. Garrett felt himself tighten instinctively, as if he were preparing for a physical confrontation as he stalked up the stairs to the master bedroom. Deep in his guts, he sensed something was wrong.

The first thing that caught his eye as he threw open the bedroom door was the glint of gold in the ceramic dish on the dressing table. He flexed his left hand, belatedly realizing he had forgotten to put on his wedding ring yesterday morning after working around Red Dazzle's stall. He still wasn't accustomed to wearing the thing.

Then he saw the smaller, more delicate band of gold lying in the bowl alongside his own ring, and Garrett felt as if he'd been kicked in the stomach.

KATY SAT DOWN on a convenient boulder overlooking the ocean and absently rubbed her ankle. The breeze off the sea was turning from crisp and invigorating to blustery and threatening. Another storm was on the way.

Experimentally she rotated her foot. It was stiff but only mildly painful. Apparently she hadn't done as much damage as she had feared last night. Still, she admitted she probably shouldn't have attempted to walk along the cliffs after lunch. It had taken far longer than she had anticipated.

But she had gotten extremely bored sitting in Garrett's home waiting for his return. The decision to limp down to the cliffs overlooking the ocean had been an impulsive one that she was now regretting. She had justified it by telling herself she needed to work the ankle in order to keep it from stiffening up, but now she suspected she should have given it a full day of rest.

A month ago she wouldn't have been so impulsive, Katy acknowledged. Marriage to Garrett Coltrane was definitely having an effect on her normally placid, cautious, quiet ways. She wasn't certain if that effect was good or bad. The only thing she felt reasonably sure of was that the change was permanent. She didn't see herself ever sinking back into that quiet, serene, limited way of life she had lived for the past few years.

For better or worse, marriage had changed her. She could only hope Garrett was going through some changes, too.

The wind began to whine through the short, scruffy bushes that clung to the rocks along the cliffs. A dark, forbidding curtain stretched across the horizon, a herald of the storm to come. Katy clutched her jacket more tightly around her and got to her feet. It was time to start back to the house. At the rate she was moving today, it would take a while to make the journey.

Katy was in the process of turning back toward the path that led to the house when she spotted the dark figure standing some distance away, forlornly looking out to sea. At first she didn't recognize the person huddled into the old dark coat—then she saw the wind-tossed gray hair.

"Nadine!"

Katy started slowly toward the woman. There was no response, and she assumed Nadine hadn't heard her. The wind was getting forceful enough to obliterate the sound of a voice. Katy almost shrugged and gave up the attempt to call a greeting, but something stopped her. There was a look of such pathetic unhappiness about the dark figure on the cliffs that Katy couldn't bring herself to turn away. She moved laboriously closer to Nadine Bracken.

"Hi," she tried again as she approached the older woman. "That's some storm coming in, isn't it? It's getting cold and I think the first of the rain is about to hit. Want to walk back to the house together?"

At first Katy thought there was not going to be a response, but Nadine eventually turned her head. Katy was shocked by the expression she saw in the woman's eyes. The woman was staring at her as if Katy were a total stranger.

"Are you all right, Nadine?"

"Of course I'm all right." Nadine looked down at the water foaming at the base of the cliffs. "What are you doing out here?"

"Just thought I'd take a walk." Katy tried to keep her voice light and cheerful. She wasn't at all sure of Nadine Bracken's mood. Perhaps she was intruding. "I hurt my weak ankle last night, and I thought walking today might keep it from stiffening."

"What's wrong with your ankle?" Nadine seemed only remotely interested.

"I injured it badly a few years ago. If I push it too far these days, I'm asking for trouble. Last night I apparently overdid it when I went chasing down to Red Dazzle's stall."

Nadine looked at her with an unreadable gaze. "Emmett said the alarm went off accidentally."

Katy nodded. "I guess that's a problem with security systems. You have to learn to tolerate a few false alarms. They sure get the blood pumping, though."

There was silence on the cliffs for a few minutes. Again Katy almost made the decision to leave, but something held her. "It really is getting chilly out here, Nadine," she said gently. "Why don't you walk back with me? A cup of hot tea would taste great about now."

Nadine shook her head. "This is where it happened, you know," she said after a moment.

Katy eyed her curiously. "Where what happened?"

"This is where the boy was killed."

Katy glanced down at the treacherous cliff. "Silas Atwood's son? He died here?"

"That's right. He was down there on the beach, drinking with his friends. They had a party that night. Just a bunch of young kids. Big bonfire and too much alcohol. You know how teenagers are. No common sense. They started daring each other to climb up the cliff instead of using the path."

"In the dark?" Katy shivered as she looked down to the beach far below. The rock face was almost sheer. There were very few toeholds or clumps of weeds to grasp.

"Two of them made it. But when Brent Atwood tried it, he slipped on the rocks. Broke his neck."

"How terrible."

"It changed everything," Nadine whispered. "Everything. It wasn't right."

After a moment Nadine simply turned away without another word and started walking heavily back toward her cottage. Katy opened her mouth to call out to her but changed her mind when she saw the ramrod-stiff carriage of Nadine's chunky figure. The woman would not welcome any more conversation or companionship today. Katy felt a rush of sympathy, but she knew there was nothing she could do. Nadine had obviously been very attached to the Atwood family.

Slowly Katy made her way back toward the house. The rain reached land just as she was opening the kitchen door. The cup of tea she had offered Nadine sounded too good to pass up.

She was filling the tea kettle at the sink when she glanced outside and saw Garrett's car in the drive. He was home.

"Garrett?"

A mixture of emotions shot through her; chief among them was excitement. Katy put down the kettle and went into the living room. There was no sign of him. "Garrett? Where are you?" Perhaps he had gone to the stable to look in on Red Dazzle. She started up the stairs to see if his overnight case was in the bedroom.

She saw him standing beside the dressing table as she walked through the bedroom door. His eyes went to her face instantly as she came into the room. His right hand was closed in a fist. Katy had a rash impulse to throw herself into his arms. She risked a smile instead.

"Hello, Garrett. I didn't realize you were back. I was out on the cliffs, taking a walk. How was the drive?"

"The drive was fine." His voice sounded slightly hoarse and a little rusty, as if he wasn't quite certain how to use it. His amber eyes were glittering with an emotion Katy couldn't define. "There wasn't any problem until I got home and found this." He opened his hand, revealing the wedding rings.

Katy glanced warily at the gold bands cradled in his palm and suddenly realized she was on dangerous ground. Well, he had started this, she told herself. She kept her smile pinned firmly in place.

"Is something wrong, Garrett?"

"When I found your ring a minute ago, it crossed my mind that you had walked out on me while I was gone," he told her harshly.

Katy forced her smile up another notch. "As you can see, I haven't gone anywhere." She went forward and stood on tiptoe. Her mouth brushed lightly across his. Without giving him a chance to respond, she stepped back. "Are you hungry? I was going to put dinner on in a few minutes. How about a drink?"

"Dammit, Katy, I'm trying to talk to you."

"About what?" She looked at him innocently.

"About the fact that your wedding ring was sitting here on the dressing table," he retorted. "Mind explaining that?"

"What's to explain? Your ring was also sitting there. Why are you so upset, Garrett?"

"I told you why I'm upset. I thought you'd left."

"I haven't left," she repeated patiently.

"I can see that," he gritted. "What I want to know is why you took off your ring and put it here."

"It's simple enough, Garrett. I put my ring there because yours was there. Excuse me, I've got to go wash some lettuce for the salad."

He caught her before she got through the door. His hand closed around her shoulder and he spun her around to face him. "Katy, what kind of game are you playing with me?"

She shook her head. "I don't know what you're talking about."

"The hell you don't. Are you telling me you took off your wedding ring because you saw that I'd left mine behind?"

Katy summoned up another smile. "We both want this marriage to be on a totally equal footing, don't we?"

Sheer, unadulterated masculine outrage blazed in his eyes. "Now you listen to me, lady, and you listen good. I took off my ring to work around the stables yesterday morning. It's dangerous to wear a ring when you're working with tools. When I set out for Fresno, I was in a hurry, as you well know. I'd been busy until the last minute with the alarm system guy, remember? I threw some clothes in a bag and went. I forgot to put the ring back on, that's all."

"Maybe next time you'll remember," Katy murmured. She ducked out from under his hand and tried once more to escape.

"Why, you little witch." He caught her again, this time anchoring her with both hands on her shoulders as he forced her to confront him. "What the devil did you think you were going to accomplish?" His eyes narrowed as he glowered down at her. And then realization dawned in his eyes. "You were trying to teach me a lesson, weren't you?"

"Actually," Katy admitted judiciously, "when I first saw your ring lying there last night, I had just hung up the phone from talking to you. I realized you were over there in beautiful downtown Fresno, working late with your staff and that you would probably have a drink with everyone later when the job was done. They would all know about your recent marriage, of course, and they would all probably look for your new ring. I wondered what they would be thinking when they realized you weren't wearing it."

"Nobody but a woman would put together a scenario like that!" Garrett roared.

"In case it's escaped your notice, I am a woman."

Garrett's expression turned even more fierce. "Don't get sassy with me, Katy."

"I'm not being sassy. I'm being assertive." Katy tried to step clear of him. His hands didn't give an inch. She was locked in place.

"I think I'm finally beginning to put this all together. You were really upset, weren't you? You thought I had left my ring behind deliberately and you decided to get even."

Katy considered that carefully. "Let's just say I was annoyed that you found it so easy to forget to wear your ring. It made me wonder just how casually you regarded our marriage."

Garrett gave her a slight shake, but to her amazement he was no longer glaring at her. Instead there was the suspicious hint of a smile in his eyes. His mouth curved faintly as he studied her face.

"You know damned well I don't regard it in a casual light," he said.

"Well, you can't blame me for getting that impression," she retorted.

"Sure I can and I do. You know me better than that, Katy. I'm a married man, whether I remember to wear my ring or not." There was an undertone of unyielding pride in the words. "I don't take my responsibilities as a husband lightly."

Katy sensed the strength of that unbending, arrogant pride, and something in her relaxed. She drew a deep breath. "I believe you. If it makes you feel any better, I consider myself thoroughly married, too, even if I happen not to be wearing my ring."

They stared at each other for a long moment, each clearly sizing up the other. Then Garrett pulled Katy abruptly against him. His arms went around her in a tight, compelling embrace.

"I'm glad you consider yourself thoroughly married because you are thoroughly married. So am I."

Katy swallowed back the wave of emotion that poured through her. She put her arms around Garrett's waist and leaned heavily into his strength. "Welcome home, Garrett."

He chuckled into her hair. "Thanks. But do me a favor the next time I come home after a business trip. Don't spring any surprises on me like this one. I'm not sure I can take the shock."

Katy lifted her head. "Was it really a shock to see my ring lying there beside yours?"

He tangled his hands in her hair and kissed her with rough passion. "Let's just say you made your point. I'm not likely to forget to put my ring on next time when I leave the house."

"Good."

Garrett laughed at the depth of satisfaction in her voice. He tumbled her down onto the bed and sprawled on top of her. Very deliberately he caught her hand and slipped her wedding ring back on her finger. "You are turning out to be one surprise after another, Katy Coltrane. Who would have thought you had such a streak of primitive female pride in you? You always seemed so...so..."

"Sensible? Calm? Rational? Demure? Levelheaded?"

Garrett grinned wickedly, putting on his own ring. Then his fingers went to the buttons of Katy's shirt. "Yeah. Something like that."

"Garrett, what about dinner?"

"We can eat later. Right now I've got other things on my mind."

"I noticed." Katy sighed happily and started to work on the buttons of his shirt.

CHAPTER NINE

"SPEAKING OF SHOCKS," Katy began an hour and a half later as she and Garrett finally sat down to dinner, "I had a mild one myself last night around midnight."

Garrett looked up from his salmon and fettucine. His eyes, which had been full of lazy contentment since the lovemaking in the bedroom, suddenly gleamed with alertness. "What happened?"

"Emmett accidentally tripped the new alarm on Red Dazzle's stall. I went down to check it out." Katy went on to explain the events of the night. "It seems to be a very sensitive system," she concluded.

"It's supposed to be sensitive." Garrett dismissed that fact impatiently and glared at Katy. "What the devil did you think you were doing dashing off in response to it, though? It was the middle of the night. It could have been anyone down there at the stable, a young punk, a dangerous vagrant, *anyone*."

Katy sighed inwardly and picked up her wineglass. She had been afraid of this. "Calm down, Garrett. Nothing happened. I told you, it was just an accident."

Garrett was not so easily placated. "That was a stupid thing to do, Katy. You should have called Emmett's cottage or called the cops, but you sure as hell had no business chasing down to the stable by yourself."

"Garrett—"

"I'm not through yet," he informed her. He planted both elbows on the table and proceeded to chew her out thoroughly for another five minutes on the subject of reckless, impulsive behavior. The salmon and fettucine got cold.

Her husband had a distinct talent for making his feelings known on such matters, Katy decided. He might not be able to tell her that he loved her, but he certainly had no problem telling her he was annoyed with her. Katy waited until he finally wound down and then she smiled hopefully. "Now are you through?"

"You're not taking me seriously, are you?"

Katy nodded quickly. "Yes, I am, I promise. I know I reacted hastily last night, but everything turned out all right and I really don't need the lecture today. Tell me about your trip to Fresno, instead."

Garrett muttered a dark warning about never doing such a thing again and then gave up the thankless job of taking his wife to task for her foolishness. He poured himself another glass of wine.

"The trip was reasonably successful. We salvaged the Bisbys for a while, at any rate. A classic case of hard work and bad management. All the back-breaking, dawn-to-dusk work in the world won't do a farmer or a rancher a damned bit of good if he doesn't have a handle on the management and accounting end of things. Management and planning are everything. In this day and age, the only ones that are going to make it are the ones who know how to run cattle and crops like a real business. The Bisbys of this world are just like my father. They pour everything they have into the land but nothing into learning about the business of managing it."

"Your father didn't have Coltrane and Company to call on for advice and assistance," Katy pointed out softly.

"Knowing my father, I'd say he probably wouldn't have listened, even if help had been offered. He was an old-fashioned rancher who thought he knew all there was to know about cattle. It wouldn't have occurred to him that he could have used some management consulting. So he wound up losing the two things that mattered the most to him—his land and his woman. After that he didn't have much to live for, I guess." Garrett stabbed at his food with subdued violence.

Katy ate slowly, thinking about what that loss had meant. Garrett's father had died in a senseless one-car accident on a county road when Garrett was in his teens. Some had suspected suicide. Some had suspected drunk driving. It was shortly after that Harry Randall, who had known the Coltrane family for years, had given Garrett the stable job.

The only steady thing in Garrett's life had been his part-time job in the Randall stables. Later, when he had learned he could make a lot more money on the rodeo circuit, Garrett had quit his job. Harry Randall had understood and wished him well.

Garrett was finishing the last of his meal when he surprised Katy with an announcement.

"I thought I'd invite some friends over next Friday evening." He watched Katy's face as he spoke. "Bob and Diane Greeley. Bob's an old rodeo hand. He and I used to hang out together on the circuit. Roped as a team. You'll like Diane."

Katy nodded acquiescently. "Is Bob still on the circuit?"

"Nope. Like me, he got smart and got out before he broke every bone in his body. He went back to college and got a degree in computer science, of all things."

Katy smiled. "Hard to imagine a rodeo cowboy becoming a computer expert."

Garrett didn't return the smile. "I know what you classy show-ring types think about cowboys. It's probably hard for you to believe they're capable of thinking about anything more refined than bulls, beer and broads."

Katy raised her eyebrows. "If I ever did have such limited notions, you've certainly set me straight, haven't you? You've come a long way from the rodeo circuit."

Garrett relaxed, his mouth crooking ruefully. "Sorry. Didn't mean to jump all over you. Sometimes the old feelings resurface."

And sometimes, the old feelings never quite fade away, Katy thought with a flash of insight.

"Get Nadine to help you with dinner on Friday night," Garrett said. "No reason you should knock yourself out. I want you to enjoy the evening. I think you and Diane will hit it off."

Katy nodded, realizing from the way he said it that he really wanted her and the unknown Diane to be friends. Garrett was trying to provide her with a friend in the area, one more inducement to settle down and be contented with her lot as his wife. It was a touching thought.

INVOLVING Nadine Bracken in the Friday-evening dinner preparations proved unexpectedly difficult. Katy sat down with the older woman on Thursday to go over the menu. She went through her plans for paella, salad and sourdough bread.

"I thought we could have cheese wafers, smoked oysters in pastry and fresh vegetables together with a sour cream dip, for hors d'oeuvres," Katy concluded. "None of this is too complicated. The preparation can all be taken care of ahead of time."

Nadine glared at the menu for a long moment and then finally announced, "Mrs. Atwood never served anything like this paella to her guests. She always served the best cut of steaks. Mr. Atwood cooked them on the barbecue out back. He enjoyed doing that."

Katy blinked. "Ah, yes, well, I prefer seafood to steaks so I think we'll go with the paella. I'd also like to have a cheesecake for dessert."

"It just won't be the same," Nadine warned.

Katy smiled coolly. "No," she agreed, "it won't be the same."

"I don't know why things have to keep changing," Nadine muttered as she got to her feet. "I just don't know why."

Katy sighed and wondered privately if it wouldn't be easier to take care of the Friday-night dinner preparations by herself. She liked to cook and the truth was, she was only involving Nadine because Garrett had wanted her to do so.

The next three days passed without incident. Garrett busied himself with small chores around the stables and the house. As far as business went, he contented himself with daily phone calls to his office. He took Katy to San Luis Obispo for shopping and sightseeing, and they stopped by the college campus to visit one of Garrett's friends on the faculty.

During the days, Katy was aware of Garrett watching her closely. She felt as if everything she said or did was being monitored to see if she showed evidence of settling down permanently into the role of wife. At times it was very unnerving. At other times Katy tried to assure herself it was a good sign.

At night Garrett made love to her with a passion and urgency that left no doubt that he was not above using sex to try to bind her to him. He would hold back, keeping himself savagely in check until she cried out and convulsed gently in his arms. Only then would he sink himself into her completely and take his own satisfaction.

On Thursday morning Katy surprised Garrett in his study in the act of concluding a phone call. She had just opened the door to see if he was around, and his reaction startled her. He had finished the call with a brusque farewell.

"You know what I want. Everything's arranged on this end. Just be sure everything's taken care of at your end. I'll talk to you later." Garrett had replaced the phone abruptly, swiveling around in his chair to confront Katy. He scowled at her. "What is it, Katy?"

"Nothing. I was going to go for a walk on the cliffs. I wondered if you wanted to join me. But if you're busy we'll make it later."

"No." He got to his feet, reaching for his Stetson. "I could use a little exercise. Let's go." He had hustled her out of the room as if anxious to get her away from the scene of the phone call.

Katy toyed with the idea of demanding an explanation but something stopped her. She sensed instinctively Garrett would not appreciate being pinned down about the mysterious phone call. She decided to let it ride. There were still many areas in which she felt obliged to tread cautiously around her new husband.

She took consolation in the fact that he still apparently felt obliged to walk carefully around her, too. It was an interesting, if occasionally unsettling, situation. She wondered frequently if it would lead to love.

Friday evening arrived and began to unfold without incident, in spite of Nadine Bracken's reluctance to condone paella as a fitting meal to be served in the old Atwood home.

Garrett had been secretly amused by the small domestic confrontation between his wife and Nadine. If Nadine had thought she could dominate the new young lady of the house, she'd learned the truth now. Katy might come across initially as gentle and sweet and shy and manipulable but the fact was, there was a stubborn will buried under all that softness. Garrett himself had recently had a few lessons on the subject, and it gave him a certain amount of satisfaction to see someone else undergoing the same education.

It also pleased him to see Katy asserting herself in her own house. It meant she might be finally starting to think of it as her real home.

For the past few days he had been watching Katy intently for signs of progress. She was everything he could want in bed, and during the day she seemed happy to be a wife.

But the raw fact he kept chewing on was that the three-month deadline she had originally set on the marriage had never been officially lifted. The knowledge that Katy might still be thinking of leaving after three short months was a constant goad. More than once Garrett had been strongly tempted to bring the subject out into the open and demand that Katy admit she was no longer thinking of their marriage as a three-month-long affair. But inevitably he'd talked himself out of the showdown.

It wasn't like him to let something this serious stay under wraps. He was a man accustomed to facing life and forcing it into the path he wanted. But he wasn't altogether certain how to go about forcing Katy into the role of committed wife.

At five o'clock Katy came into the master bedroom to dress. Garrett was just finishing his shower. He saw her as he came out of the bathroom.

"Everything all set for dinner?" he asked.

"I think so. We'll eat around seven-thirty." Katy started into the still-steamy bathroom, unbuttoning her blouse as she went. She was still shy around him, and Garrett knew she would finish undressing behind the closed door of the bathroom. It was ridiculous. This same woman would catch fire in his arms later that night when he made love to her. She wouldn't be at all shy then. She would be hungry and exciting and full of soft, feminine, passionate demand. She would ride him the way she had once ridden her father's magnificent Arabians and he would lose himself in her.

And if she thought she could give him that for three months and then call it quits, she had another think coming. With sudden resolve, Garrett took a step forward.

"Katy."

The rough edge in his voice stopped her abruptly. She glanced back inquiringly over her shoulder. "Yes, Garrett?"

He folded his arms and leaned against the closet door, studying her. His whole body was throbbing with an urgent need to nail down his future with Katy.

"I want to talk to you," he said in a voice that was as neutral as he could manage.

"About what?"

"About your plans for the future."

"My plans?" She tilted her head and regarded him curiously. "What about them?"

"I have a right to know what you think you're going to do at the end of three months, Katy. I want to know if you still plan to walk away from our marriage."

She stared at him, her gray eyes unfathomable. It was rare that she could succeed in hiding her thoughts from him, Garrett realized. Usually he could read what she was thinking just by looking into those huge cloud-colored pools. But not tonight.

"Garrett, this is hardly the time to discuss our marriage. We've got guests coming in less than an hour and I'm not even dressed."

"You're still thinking of running away from me after three months, aren't you?" he challenged.

She edged toward the bathroom door, clutching her unbuttoned blouse across her breasts. "You make me sound like a teenage bride who's planning on running home to mama. That's hardly the case. If things end after three months I'm sure we'll both handle the…the dissolution of our marriage in a mature, adult, businesslike manner. Neither of us is a child."

Garrett felt a violent tension ripple through his whole body. She was still thinking of leaving him.

He could hardly believe it. She had appeared to be settling down. She was looking forward to starting work in his office, and he knew he was satisfying her at night. What more could a woman want, he demanded silently of the universe. Instantly his mind shied away from the answer she had given him the morning after the wedding. Instead he opted for the approach that had always served him well in a world that was constantly shifting underfoot. It was time to flex a little muscle.

Garrett didn't move. He stayed where he was against the closet door and pinned Katy with his eyes. "What makes you think I'll let you act as if you're involved in nothing more than an affair for three months, Katy?"

She took another step toward the bathroom. "Calm down, Garrett. There's no need to become irrational about this."

"I'm not the one who's behaving irrationally. You're the fluff-headed little fool who thinks she's got a legitimate gripe just because marriage didn't prove to be the romantic hearts-and-flowers arrangement she'd fantasized about."

"Take it easy, Garrett. Your guests will be here soon, and I've got a lot to do." She was safely over the bathroom threshold now, reaching for the door.

Garrett came away from the closet. He started forward with slow, deliberate strides. It was like dealing with a fractious little mare, he told himself. If he moved too quickly, she would turn tail and run. If he didn't move at all, she would think she had won the encounter and she would be even more difficult to handle later.

"I don't know where you got your notions of what marriage is supposed to be all about, Katy, but I think it's time somebody set you straight. Who better to do that than your husband? I'll tell you what marriage is about. It's about sticking it out when the going gets tough or the money gets short. It's about honoring the promises you made in front of witnesses. It's about building something lasting. It's about commitment. If you think I'm going to let you run away from that commitment, you'd better think again. I'm putting you on notice, lady. There's no place on this earth where you can hide that I can't find you. If it comes down to the crunch, I'm a lot stronger, tougher and meaner than you'll ever be. Remember that."

"I don't need lectures on the subject of marriage from you, dammit!"

Katy jumped back and slammed the bathroom door in Garrett's face. A split second later he heard the lock click. Swearing softly, he slammed the wooden door frame with his open palm, turned around and went back to the closet to finish dressing. He winced as he yanked his trousers off the hanger. His hand hurt.

GARRETT had been right about one thing, Katy decided later that evening—she did, indeed, like Diane Greeley. The other woman was small, petite and blond. She was not a raving beauty, but she had a lovely smile and warm blue eyes. Diane was also very pregnant.

"Seven months," Diane confided as she followed Katy on a tour of the house. "Bob and I can hardly wait. We put it off so long while Bob went back to college that we both began to worry." She glanced around at the interior of the huge home. "Looks like you and Garrett had better get busy, too, if you want to fill this place up with kids."

Katy smiled whimsically, seeing the house through Diane's eyes. She decided not to mention the fact that Garrett had never brought up the subject of children. "It really is a lot of house, isn't it?"

Diane chuckled. "I knew that when he finally bought a home of his own, Garrett would do it in a big way. He always makes his plans very carefully, like a good general going into battle. And he never acts until he's absolutely sure of what he's doing. Garrett always seems to have everything under control, doesn't he?"

Everything except me, Katy thought, remembering the short, fiery exchange in the bedroom before Diane and Bob arrived. She felt a twinge of unease when she realized that in a few more hours she would be alone with Garrett once more. It didn't take any great amount of wifely intuition to know that he did not consider the argument concluded.

"Have you known Garrett a long time?" Diane asked as the two women walked slowly toward the staircase.

"I knew him when I was a kid. But he left town when I was twelve, and I didn't see much of him again until a few months ago," Katy said.

Diane nodded. "Bob told me something about Garrett's background once. Sounds like it was rather rough."

"It was."

"I heard his parents lost the family ranch and that Garrett's mother left." Diane slanted Katy a curious glance. "Garrett grew up more or less on his own after that, I gather?"

"More or less. He started out on the rodeo circuit when he left high school."

Diane laughed, shaking her head. "Talk about replacing one insecure life-style with another equally uncertain one. That rodeo business is enough to drive any person to drink. A man is constantly on the move to the next town. His family life is usually a disaster. He has no financial security at all and he never knows whether the next fall he takes is going to kill him or just break a couple of bones." Diane shuddered. "There's never any security. I can't tell you how glad I am that Bob got out when he did. I know you must be equally glad Garrett had the intelligence and the determination to do the same. So many of those cowboys don't. Of course that left both Bob and Garrett with the job of building whole new careers."

Never any security.

Something clicked in Katy's mind as Diane's words sank in. For most of his life Garrett had never known any stability or security except that which he had forged for himself. He had learned long ago not to rely on anyone. She had known that all along, but it was only now that the full implications of the knowledge struck home. She stopped at the top of the stairs and turned to stare at her new friend.

"Is something wrong?" Diane asked, alarmed.

"No." Katy shook her head slowly. "No. Nothing's wrong. I just realized I've been looking at something backward."

It was Diane's turn to stare. "Backward?"

"Yes. Upside down and backward."

"Uh, was it something I said?" Diane asked warily.

Katy laughed softly. "Yes, as a matter of fact, it was. I should have seen it for myself but I've been paying too much attention to my own feelings. I didn't stop to realize—" She broke off. "Never mind. I must sound like my mind is wandering. Let's go downstairs and join the men. They're probably nearing starvation."

Garrett looked up from Bob Greeley, who had been talking, just as Katy came down the stairs alongside Diane. His eyes met hers, and Katy trembled for an instant at the expression she saw in his golden gaze. He wanted her. He would do whatever he had to do in order to hold on to her. For Garrett, that constituted love.

She should have understood, Katy told herself. She should have realized she was making a gigantic mistake when she had threatened to pull the rug out from under Garrett. He was accustomed to having it pulled out from under him. By holding the three-month time limit over his head she had been doing to him what everything and everyone had always done to him. She had been telling him he couldn't count on her or her love.

It was suddenly very important that Garrett realize he could depend on her love.

Then Bob moved forward to hand his wife a glass of fruit juice and the small spell was broken. Bob was a tall, rangy man with laughing brown eyes and a ready smile. "Quite a house, isn't it, honey?" he asked. "I was just telling Garrett here that he's come a long way from those fleabag motels on the rodeo circuit."

"So have you," Diane pointed out affectionately. She smiled at Katy. "I was just saying to Katy that she and Garrett were going to have to get busy and fill up this place with kids. A big house like this needs a family."

Aware that Garrett was watching her more closely than ever, Katy felt a rush of color sweep into her cheeks. "If you'll excuse me, I'll go check with Nadine. The paella should be about ready." Katy was glad to be able to make even a temporary escape. She had a lot to think about.

Three hours later Katy again found herself alone with her husband. Ever since the conversation with Diane she had been thinking of ways to handle the coming scene with Garrett. But her mind felt jumbled and unclear. She didn't know whether to blurt out her intention to stay and make the marriage work or to lead up to it in a more mature, sophisticated, subtle fashion. She wasn't at all sure there was a more mature, sophisticated or subtle way to do it. It all seemed fairly raw and basic. She decided to try for the middle ground.

"Things went well, didn't they?" Katy remarked on the way up the stairs. "I enjoyed meeting Diane and Bob."

Garrett said nothing. He unfastened the cuffs of his shirt as he climbed the stairs beside Katy. All his attention appeared focused on the task.

"I was worried Nadine might decide to sabotage the paella, but she didn't," Katy went on with determined cheerfulness. "Everything came through just fine, including the cheesecake."

Garrett still said nothing. They were walking down the hall to the bedroom now. Katy began to grow more nervous. She took a deep breath as she stepped through the bedroom door. "Garrett..."

He closed the door with a soft finality and leaned back against it, facing her. His expression was harsh.

"Have you considered the fact that you might be pregnant?" he asked.

Katy nearly choked. She thought of the little pills she had been taking for a few weeks. "Uh, no, I haven't. It's not possible. I went to the doctor before we were married. I've been taking the pill."

"I see." He continued to regard her in silence.

Katy grew flustered. This wasn't going at all the way she had planned. "Garrett, I would like to talk to you about, well, about what we were, uh, discussing earlier this evening."

He ignored that, his eyes gravely serious. "I would be a good father, Katy. I know you probably don't think so because of the way my own father was, but that's just the reason why I would be a good one. Do you understand? I'd take care of my family. You don't have to be afraid that I'd leave you and the kid alone. You could trust me, Katy."

Emotion nearly overwhelmed her. "I do trust you," she whispered. "If you say you'll stick around, I'll believe you."

"I've already said I'll stick around. I said that much on our wedding day when I took those vows, remember?"

"I remember."

"You're the one who's been waffling, lady. Not me."

"I know. I'm sorry." She walked slowly toward him, her smile tremulous. "I had it all wrong."

He scowled at her. "Had what all wrong?"

"Never mind. It's time you knew that I plan to stick around, too. I won't be going anywhere after three months, Garrett. Not unless you ask me to leave." She laced her arms around his neck.

Incredulous relief and satisfaction flared in his eyes. "*Katy*. It's about time, you admitted that. It's about time."

He picked her up and carried her to the bed. He began to undress her with such tenderness, such exquisite care, that Katy almost cried. Instead she reached for him and drew him down on her. Her fingers trembled as she began undoing the buttons of his shirt.

"Katy, my sweet little Katy." Garrett's voice was husky with emotion. "Everything's going to be all right now."

"Yes, Garrett. Everything's going to be all right."

He finished undressing her and when she was lying nude beside him, Garrett lifted himself up on one elbow to gaze hungrily down at Katy. His hand moved over her with gentle possession. He touched her breasts, drawing tiny, exciting circles around each nipple until both responded by forming small, hard peaks.

Garrett leaned down to taste the tips of Katy's breasts. As he did so he caught one of her questioning hands and guided her fingers to his strong, thrusting shaft. When her palm closed around him he groaned with an aching pleasure.

Katy teased him gently, delighting in the sweet, feminine power she had over him. Then she felt his fingers in the silken hair between her legs and she cried out softly.

Garrett's dark head bent over her as he worked a string of kisses slowly down the length of her body. When he parted her with his fingers and kissed the soft, vulnerable flesh of her inner thighs, Katy gasped.

And then her fingers were digging into him and Garrett was settling himself within the cradle of her legs. She clung to him as he pushed powerfully forward, entering her with a harsh exclamation of satisfaction.

"Hold me," Garret whispered thickly. "Hold me, Katy."

She held him as if her whole future depended on it.

CHAPTER TEN

GARRETT spent the weekend basking in the many and assorted pleasures of being a happily married man. There were, he was discovering, a host of advantages, not the least of which was a comfortable feeling of rightness.

"You don't know what you're missing, Red," he told the gelding on Monday morning.

Red Dazzle, who had been attempting to take his morning nap, blinked sleepily and ambled over to the paddock fence. Garrett laughed softly and patted the horse's neck. Red dozed contentedly in the morning sunshine.

"She's finally settled down," Garrett told the horse. "No more talk about three-month deadlines and no more nasty cracks about our 'business partnership.' It's been a rough honeymoon, but I think we've finally got everything ironed out. Who would have thought one little female would have packed so much sheer cussed stubbornness?"

Red Dazzle declined to answer.

"She loves me, you know," Garrett explained. "She had a crush on me when she was just a kid, and now she's a full-grown woman and she's in love with me. She told me on our wedding night."

But she hadn't repeated the confession since that disastrous evening, Garrett admitted silently. It was the only thing that was still bothering him. Katy had surrendered all her bristling defenses except the last one.

It hadn't even dawned on Garrett that there was still one more barrier to demolish, until he had awakened that morning and realized Katy had not repeated her wedding night confession of love.

It shouldn't bother him. He had everything else he wanted and needed from her, he told himself. She had committed herself to the marriage at last. She had even told him she would trust him to be a good father for their children.

That admission had shaken him. It wasn't until she had made it that he had realized how important it was to him to hear her talk about children. When he had seen how pregnant Diane Greeley was on Friday night, all Garrett had been able to think about was what Katy would look like carrying his child. He had spent most of the evening envisioning her all soft and round with his baby.

Then he had acknowledged that Katy might have several reservations about making a baby with a man who had grown up with a very limited home life. The thought that she might not want his child had sent a cold chill through Garrett. It was a subject he had not even thought about before the wedding except in the vaguest of terms. He took it for granted that eventually there would be children. Children were pieces of the future, and he fully intended to ensure that part of his future. But on Friday night the subject was no longer a vague, distant one. It had suddenly dominated his whole world. He could still feel the incredible relief he had experienced when Katy had assured him she would trust him to be a father.

That relief coupled with her willingness to abandon the three-month time limit on the marriage had satisfied him for the remainder of the weekend. He and Katy had spent much of the time playing like the lovers they were.

It was only this morning that Garrett realized there was one more small, niggling, but surprisingly important hurdle left. He wanted to hear Katy tell him she loved him again. He wanted to hear the soft, sweet words he had heard on his wedding night.

"No doubt about it, Red, I've turned into a greedy man." Garrett gave the gelding one last affectionate slap. "Well, I'd better check your new roommate's quarters. Wouldn't want the little lady to be shocked. You know how these gently bred, cosseted females are. They don't take kindly to the idea of roughing it. Got to handle 'em with kid gloves."

The way he had been handling Katy, Garrett told himself as he strode into the stables. Katy had a lot in common with the delicate Arabian mare that would be arriving that afternoon. Spirited but gentle. Both needed a light hand on the reins. The last thing Garrett wanted to do was bruise either one of them. But he also had no intention of losing either one.

The mare was going to be a surprise for Katy, a surprise Garrett was realistic enough to admit she might not be exactly thrilled with at the start. But he was complacently optimistic. Some people didn't know what was good for them at first sight, but they could learn. He was convinced that eventually Katy would thank him for what he was about to do. He was going to get her back into riding and when she rediscovered the joy she had once known, she would turn to him with gratitude in her eyes.

Gratitude and love.

He had ordered the three-year-old Arabian from Harry Randall last week and finalized the arrangements in a phone call that Katy had unwittingly interrupted. The animal was due to be delivered today.

KATY WAS FINALLY beginning to enjoy her honeymoon. It had been a strange period of time, filled with highs and lows and unexpected curves, but she was feeling more serene now than she had at any point since her wedding day. As honeymoons went, this one had hardly been idyllic, but there was no doubt that she had learned a great deal about her new husband.

She had also learned something about herself.

As she walked from the house to the stables, Katy thought about those personal discoveries. She had never dreamed she would turn out to be the type of woman who could be overcome with passion, for example. She had a hunch Garrett had been equally astonished, though he'd been far too gallant to comment on the subject.

She had also never thought of herself as stubborn, temperamental or demanding, either. But during the past several days she had learned she was capable of indulging all those interesting human traits and a few others, as well.

Katy was smiling secretly when she reached the stables.

"Garrett? Where are you?"

"In here."

She followed the sound of his voice through the stable door. He was checking the hardware on the empty stall next to Red Dazzle's. "What are you doing?"

"Just going over a few things," he explained cryptically.

"Oh. You've been spending a lot of time down here at the stables lately. Is everything all right with the alarm system?"

"Everything's fine," he assured her. He emerged from the stall, a lazy, affectionate grin on his face. He shoved his hat back on his head. "I could use a cup of coffee, though. How about you?" He reached out to snag her hand and hold on to it.

"Sure. We really should do some grocery shopping today. I wouldn't mind investigating a few of those little dress shops you pointed out the other day. Diane gave me some names of the ones she likes. And it's about time you showed me your main offices."

"We've got plenty of time for you to learn about Coltrane and Company," Garrett said dismissively. "Let's not rush things. I'm still enjoying the honeymoon."

"Is that right?" she teased. "What about that talk you have to give this evening to that group of cattlemen? Is that any way to spend one of your honeymoon evenings?"

Garrett groaned. "Don't remind me. I made that commitment a couple of months ago and there's no way I can get out of it. I'll only be gone a few hours. I should be home by nine o'clock at the latest."

"I could go with you," Katy suggested.

"I've told you, honey, this is an all-male group. You'd feel out of place, and I'd spend the whole evening fighting off lecherous cattlemen."

"Bunch of chauvinists, I take it?"

"When you're talking ranchers and farmers, you're talking old-fashioned, unenlightened males," Garrett agreed blandly.

"What about you?" Katy laughed up at him with her eyes. "Are you in that old-fashioned, unenlightened category?"

"Of course not." Garrett's tone was one of lofty arrogance. "I'm one of the new breed—haven't you noticed? Hell, I'm even going to make my wife a partner in my business. What more proof do you need of my enlightened ways?"

"I'm not so sure making me a partner qualifies as an example of your advanced thinking and attitudes. It could be just a way of getting free work out of me.''

Garrett contrived to look hurt. ''I'm crushed.''

''Uh-huh.'' Katy was humorously skeptical. ''You know what I think? I think that deep down you are one very old-fashioned—'' She broke off at the sound of a vehicle in the driveway. ''Were we expecting anyone?'' she asked as she turned to glance behind her.

Garrett stopped and draped his arm around her shoulders. He watched the truck and horse trailer approaching, his expression one of quiet expectation. ''We,'' he announced cheerfully, ''are expecting a new stablemate for Red Dazzle. You're going to love her.''

''What on earth are you talking about?'' Katy stared at the horse trailer as the truck came to a halt. ''Did you buy another horse for yourself?''

''Not for me, although I'll admit I've got my eye on a good-looking young stallion your father is trying to sell me. But this little lady is for you.'' Garrett started forward, dragging Katy easily along with him. ''Her name is Shadow Silk. Remember her?''

''Shadow Silk! That's one of my father's mares!'' Katy groped for an explanation, panicked by the one that was taking shape. ''What do you mean, she's for me? Garrett, what have you done?''

''I bought her for you,'' he said simply. His arm tightened slightly around her shoulders as if he expected her to pull away. ''Relax, honey. We'll take it slow and easy.''

''Take what slow and easy?'' Katy felt a flame of wild anger spring to life within her as she realized just what Garrett had in mind. ''If you think you can force me back on a horse, you're out of your mind. How dare you pull a trick like this! How dare you? Who do you think you are, Garrett Coltrane?''

''Calm down. Just take it easy, honey. Everything's going to be okay.''

''Don't talk to me as if I were a horse, dammit!'' Katy felt her voice crawling up the scale toward hysteria. Frantically she struggled for self-control. Her throat was suddenly tight with intense emotion. ''Garrett, you had no right to spring this on me. You can send Shadow Silk back to my father right now, do you hear me?''

"I hear you. So does the driver of the truck and anyone else within shouting distance." Garrett's tone lost a measure of its soothing quality. It was replaced by an implacable firmness. "I hate to have to be the one to point this out to you, but you're making a scene and you know how you hate scenes. Now why don't you just calm down and let me see about getting your new mare unloaded and into her stall."

Tears of fury and frustration were stinging Katy's eyes. Her hands clenched into small fists. Her breath felt tight in her chest. She wanted to scream and couldn't get the words out. "You don't understand," she managed in a strangled whisper. "You just don't understand. No one does. Even my parents and my friends never understood, not really. Why can't any of you just accept my right to make my own decisions? I don't ever want to ride a horse again as long as I live. How much clearer can I make it?"

Garrett frowned, catching her face between rough palms. "Honey, it's time you got over your fear. Riding was once the most important thing in your life. You loved it. You're going to love it again. We're going to ride together a lot, you and I. It's going to be one of the things we share."

Despairingly Katy shook her head, knowing she did not have the words to make him comprehend her fear. "You just don't understand."

"I know what it's like to be afraid, honey," he surprised her by saying. "I also know that the only solution is to face the fear. You should have gotten back up on a horse years ago."

"I chose not to ride again!"

"Well, someone should have overridden your decision."

"Is that what you think you're going to succeed in doing now?" she challenged.

"It's what I know I'm going to succeed in doing."

"Not a chance, Garrett. Do you hear me? Not a chance!" Katy turned and started toward the house. She refused to look back. The anger in her was unlike anything she had ever known.

It was, amazingly enough, even stronger than the fear.

A few minutes later she watched through the kitchen window as Shadow Silk was untrailered and led into the stable. Katy remembered the small, delicate mare well. Shadow Silk was a lovely creature, full of grace and equine power. The mare was a dappled gray with a dark, high-arched tail and a dark mane. Her conformation was excellent, a good, deep chest, a refined head, a short back. The mare was a fine example of the excellent breeding program at Randall Farm. She had a fine pedigree. Katy could recite that pedigree back for generations. She also knew that the mare was beautifully trained, with a soft mouth and a good disposition. All her father's animals were trained with patience and gentleness.

But even the most even-tempered horse turned dangerous when it was panicked, and even the most perfectly trained animal became a lunging, thirteen-hundred-pound juggernaut of flashing hooves when it was caught in the grip of terror. A 115-pound human being was no match for such a creature. Katy shivered as memories swept through her.

Those memories had been sufficiently unnerving to keep Katy from getting back on a horse for several years. For a while her parents and others had urged her to try riding again, but in the end her quiet resistance had defeated them. No one had wanted to pressure her too much. No one had wanted to take the responsibility of forcing her back into a saddle.

No one, that is, except Garrett Coltrane.

Katy's mouth tightened ominously, and she turned away from the kitchen window. She had surrendered on every front to that man. Damned if she would let him win in this arena, too.

But she knew, even as she swore to fight him, that it was going to be a difficult, never ending battle. Garrett would be steady and insistent and relentless.

Katy looked around herself, feeling trapped inside the big, beautifully furnished house. Garrett would be coming for her soon, urging her to go down to the stable and look at Shadow Silk. Katy decided she needed some breathing time. She picked up the keys to the Mercedes, grabbed her purse and went outside to where the car was parked in the driveway.

Garrett came out of the stable when he heard the car's engine being switched on.

"Katy!"

Resentfully she rolled down the window and waited as he strode briskly toward her. When he reached the vehicle, he shoved the Stetson back on his head, planted both hands on the roof and leaned down to talk to her.

"Just where in hell do you think you're going?" he asked softly.

"Shopping."

"We'll do the grocery shopping later. It can wait."

"I'm sure you'll be much too busy getting your new mare settled in," Katy told him. "So I'll go by myself." She put the car in gear and slammed her foot down on the gas pedal.

"Now, Katy, you listen to me. You're acting like a child." The Mercedes leaped forward, and Garrett hastily stepped back out of the way.

Katy glanced back only once in the rearview mirror as she raced down the tree-lined driveway. Garrett stood with his feet apart, his big hands on his hips, his expression grim as she drove out of sight.

Garrett watched until the Mercedes vanished, and then he walked slowly back toward the stable. He had been through a lot since his wedding day; he had learned a great deal about his surprisingly unpredictable wife. But he had never seen her in this mood.

"She'll calm down," he informed Shadow Silk a few minutes later. "Just give her a little time. She's a bit high-strung these days, but she'll settle."

Shadow Silk nickered politely and ambled over to investigate her new feeding arrangements.

By five o'clock that evening Garrett was wondering seriously about his own feeding arrangements. Katy had not returned from town, and he was due to leave for the cattlemen's meeting in another hour. He had assumed Katy would cook an early dinner. When she didn't show up by five-thirty, he opened the refrigerator and morosely examined the contents.

At five forty-five, Garret finally admitted to himself that he was worried. Regardless of her mood, Katy should have been home by now. For the first time he faced the fact that she might not be returning.

She couldn't do that to him. She wouldn't do that to him. She loved him.

But she hadn't said that since the wedding night. Garrett realized he was pacing the large kitchen, his hands flexing in restless movements the way they used to back in the days when he was sitting in a rodeo arena chute, waiting to explode through the gate on the back of a Brahma bull.

It had been a long time since he had felt that same mixture of tension and adrenaline. It was an unpleasant sensation at best, and this time around it was worse than in the old days because it was laced with raw fear.

The sound of the Mercedes in the driveway had an instant effect on the fear. It was converted almost magically into a blazing fury. Vaguely Garrett realized it was the first time that he had ever completely lost his temper with Katy. He launched himself toward the door and flung it open just as Katy came slowly, warily, up the steps. She was carrying a sack of groceries. She stopped short when she saw the look on his face.

"Hello, Garrett." Her voice was very soft. She didn't move.

"Just where in hell have you been?" The words were much too low and dangerous. Garrett knew it, but he couldn't do anything about it. He was feeling dangerous. In fact, he'd never felt quite like this in his whole life.

"I told you, I went shopping." She took a cautious step forward and stopped again when he showed no signs of moving. "Groceries." She indicated the sack in her arms.

Garrett's eyes flicked to the sack. He saw the way she was clutching it as though it were a shield. "You've been gone for hours."

"Sorry. Was I supposed to sign out when I left? Am I under a curfew?"

"Katy, don't push your luck. I've got almost nothing left in the way of patience. What you did this afternoon was silly, emotional and infantile. Did it occur to you I might be worried?"

"No." She risked another step and stopped again. "I figured you'd be too busy with your new horse."

"The mare belongs to you, Katy," he said through his teeth. "She's all yours, whether or not you ever put a saddle on her."

"I don't want her."

"That's too bad, because you've got her." Garrett stepped back, allowing Katy to cross the threshold. She did so slowly, reluctantly, and her obvious hesitation fanned the fires of his anger. "Katy, don't ever pull a stunt like this again."

Something flickered in her eyes, a combination of resentment and anguish. "Don't give me orders, Garrett. I've had it. You've won every battle since the day we were married, and I'm tired of being the loser, do you hear me?"

He stared at her. Was that really the way she saw things, he wondered. "Is that what our honeymoon has been to you? A series of battles?"

Her mouth tightened and her eyes slid away from his. She started toward the kitchen. "At times it seemed like that. I'm sick of it, Garrett. What you did this afternoon was the last straw."

He was outraged. He was also getting scared again. He handled his fear the way he always had, by fighting back. "The last straw?" He loomed in the kitchen door behind her. "I buy you the most beautiful little mare in the whole world and you tell me it's the last straw?"

Katy slammed the sack of groceries down onto the tiled counter and spun around. Her face was tight with emotion. "Why do you keep pushing me? I've given it to you all the way down the line. How much more do you want from me, dammit?"

The expression in her eyes pushed him over the edge. "Everything," he exploded. "I want everything."

"What gives you that right?"

"You're my wife, that's what gives me the right. Whether you'll admit it or not, you love me. One of these days you'll say it again, just the way you said it on our wedding night."

"And have you throw the words back in my face the way you did then?" she raged.

"I'd never do that. I didn't do it then and I won't do it this time, either. If you're really convinced that I threw your words of love back in your face, you have no one to blame but yourself. It was your damned female temper that made you see things that way. You went off the deep end because your wedding night didn't quite fit the rosy fantasy you had imagined ahead of time."

"Is that right?" she shot back. "Well, I've learned a few things on this honeymoon, thanks to you. But look who's playing around with rosy little fantasies now. Why do you want me to tell you I love you? What difference does it make to you? You don't even believe in love.''

He took a step forward and halted, not trusting himself to touch her. ''Has it ever occurred to you that you're not the only one who's learned a few things during the course of this crazy honeymoon?'' he shouted.

Katy's eyes widened. ''No.''

''No?'' He was enraged now. ''No? You don't think I'm capable of learning? You think you've got a monopoly?''

Katy chewed on her lower lip. ''Garrett, calm down. Take it easy.''

''Don't talk to me as if I were a horse. I'm your husband.''

''Yes, I know,'' she said very softly. ''You're stubborn, arrogant, proud as the devil and equally infuriating on occasion, but for better or worse, you are my husband.''

He couldn't figure out what she was thinking, but Garrett sensed the change in the atmosphere. ''Katy, listen to me—'' he began, only to be interrupted.

''No, you listen to me. I'm tired of losing battles.''

''We're not fighting a war,'' he protested, suddenly anxious to get her off that subject. It was too close to the truth.

''That's a matter of opinion.'' She put her hands on either side of herself, gripping the edge of the counter behind her. Garrett realized she was bracing herself for something. ''You said you never threw my words of love back in my face.''

''That's the truth, Katy.''

''You claim you've learned a few things during the past few days.''

''I'd have to have been blind, deaf and dumb not to have learned a few things,'' he muttered.

She took a deep breath. ''All right, let's find out just how much you have learned. What happens now if I tell you I love you?''

''That's easy,'' Garrett said without stopping to think. ''I say it back.''

Katy's mouth fell open in amazement. Neither she nor Garrett moved.

"Garrett, I love you," Katy finally whispered.

It was Garrett's turn to take a deep breath. "I know. I love you, too."

He held open his arms and she rushed into them, stumbling a little as her weak ankle gave way slightly. But he caught her safely in his arms and folded her close.

"I love you, Katy. I love you, I love you, I love you." Now that he had learned how to say it, he couldn't seem to stop.

She clung to him, her own words of love spilling from her lips. For a timeless moment they stood locked in each other's arms and let the wonder of what was happening envelop them. Garrett felt a deep sense of peace and an equally joyous sense of release. It was as if his need to love Katy had suddenly been set free to be acknowledged and indulged to the hilt. He felt drunk with reaction.

It was Katy who abruptly broke the embrace. "What about your meeting?" she asked shakily. She glanced at the kitchen clock. "You're going to be late."

"Who cares?" Garrett started to pull her back into his arms.

Katy laughed softly. "Don't be silly. You have to go and you'd better be on your way. We'll have all night to talk."

"Talking isn't what I plan to be doing tonight." He nibbled her ear.

"Too bad. You were just getting good at it, too."

"Don't tease the lion. He's had a rough afternoon."

"Pity the poor lion," Katy whispered, spearing her fingers lovingly through his hair.

"Oh, God, Katy, I love you so. I should have realized days ago exactly what I was feeling. I should have known—"

She shook her head, cutting off his awkward confession. "It's been a very educational honeymoon."

"It's not over yet," he reminded her.

"True. But we're going to have to take a short intermission while you attend that cattlemen's meeting."

"Katy, I don't want to leave you now."

It took her another ten minutes to get him out of the house. As she stood in the doorway and waved, Katy nearly laughed aloud with happiness. She didn't need Garrett's assurances to know that he would be back the instant the meeting was over. They would have the rest of the night to practice telling each other of their love.

Katy closed the door at last, almost giddy with relief and wonder. Garrett loved her. He had admitted it. Together they had battled their way through to the point where she had naively assumed they had started on their wedding day.

The good things in life sometimes take a while to gel, Katy decided as she wandered back into the kitchen and began unpacking groceries. The good things took a little extra work.

She knew what it was like to work at something that was important to her. She had learned those skills years ago when she had trained horses and herself for the show ring.

That thought brought Shadow Silk to mind. For the first time Katy allowed herself to think about Garrett's intentions. He had meant well, she knew. He had wanted to give her back something that had once been very important to her, something that he could share with her.

It was impossible to hold his intentions against him. Katy thought about that while she ate a leisurely meal of cold leftovers. The man was heavy-handed at times, straightforward and determined, even ruthless on occasion, but now that she had calmed down, she couldn't help but be touched by his goal.

Half an hour later, Katy let her dishes go into the sink with a clatter. Then she walked out to the hall closet and grabbed a windbreaker to put on over her jeans and long-sleeved pullover.

There was no reason not to go down to the stable and take a look at Shadow Silk, Katy told herself. She might have no intention of ever riding the mare, but she still loved horses, and Garrett had said that Shadow Silk was now hers.

A few minutes later Katy opened the stable door to find Shadow Silk safely ensconced in her new stall, knee-deep in golden straw.

It was Red Dazzle who was missing.

CHAPTER ELEVEN

KATY HOPED desperately that Red Dazzle had simply found his way out of the back of his closed stall into the paddock, but even as she hurried outside to double-check, something told her she was wasting her time. There was no hulking four-legged shape dozing peacefully in the cold moonlight. The gelding was gone.

As Katy went back inside the stable to check the lock on the stall door, she told herself firmly to calm down. Red Dazzle was an energy-conserving creature. He wouldn't have wandered far. There was no storm to spook him tonight.

A soft, inquisitive whicker announced Shadow Silk's interest in the unexpected activity. A beautifully shaped equine head appeared over the stall door. Katy held out her hand and let the mare nuzzle her palm.

"What's going on around here, Silk? What have you done with your stablemate?" Katy frowned as she fingered the closure on Red Dazzle's stall. "I know he's not the most handsome male in the world. Not particularly refined or well-bred. Definitely a working-class background and proud of it. But he's got heart, you know? And guts. Actually, he's got quite a few things in common with his owner." Katy thought about that for a moment and then added with a fleeting grin, "There is one major difference, of course. Garrett is no gelding."

Shadow Silk snorted in a ladylike fashion.

Katy gave up on the stall door. It wasn't going to tell her whether the closure had been opened manually or by a particularly clever equine mouth. Then she remembered the alarm system.

"It should have gone off, regardless of how the stall door got opened," Katy muttered to Shadow Silk. Anxiously she made her way into the tack room where the alarm system wiring had been installed.

The instant she opened the door and turned on the light, Katy saw the open cover of the control panel box. Someone had switched off the system.

Real anxiety set in now. Red Dazzle wasn't simply wandering around loose somewhere nearby. Someone had deliberately taken him out of his stall.

For the second time?

Katy couldn't imagine why anyone would be playing games with an aging quarter horse, but she didn't spend any more time speculating on the matter. She left the stable and started quickly up the hill toward the Brackens' cottage.

The night air was chilly, but the moonlight provided enough illumination to see the path that led toward the small house. Lamplight glowed through the windows. Nadine hadn't yet lowered the shades against the night.

Breathing quickly from the exertion of her rapid walk up the hill, Katy pounded sharply on the front door of the cottage. When there was no immediate answer, she tried again.

"Emmett? Nadine? It's Katy. Something's happened to Red Dazzle. You've got to help me find him."

Silence was the only answer. Katy stepped back, glancing toward the side of the house. Emmett's old pickup truck was parked there in the shadows. The Brackens had to be home.

Katy tried pounding on the door once more and when that proved useless, she stepped off the front step and went around to the living room window. Feeling as if she was doing something slightly illegal, she peered through the uncovered window.

Emmett Bracken was sprawled on the sofa in front of the fireplace, obviously asleep. A half-empty bottle of whiskey sat on the floor beside him. Emmett had gotten an early start on his evening drinking. Katy frowned to herself as she scanned the room. Everything was as she remembered it from her one visit the afternoon they had tested the new alarm system. There was the pair of old, expensive silver candlesticks on the mantle. Nadine had proudly told Katy they had been a gift from the Atwoods. They framed the old cigar box that sat in the middle of the wooden shelf.

The lid of the box was open.

Memory returned in a rush. Emmett had told Katy he kept a gun in that box. But the colorful box was empty now. Katy wondered if Nadine removed the weapon as a precaution when Emmett got drunk.

Disgusted, Katy turned away. She wasn't going to get any help from that source. Then she started worrying about what had happened to Nadine. Perhaps Emmett had gone into a drunken rage and frightened his wife into leaving for a while.

But the real question was how that scenario fitted in with the missing gelding. A prickle of apprehension went through Katy. The fact that Nadine Bracken and Red Dazzle were both missing began to seem like too much of a coincidence.

Katy stood in front of the cottage and used the vantage point to survey the moonlit stables below. Nothing moved in the shadows. Slowly she made her way around the house, peering into the darkness and wishing badly that she had a flashlight.

It wasn't until Katy reached the back of the cottage that she saw the moving figures silhouetted against the night sky. A horse was being led along the top of the cliffs. It had to be Red Dazzle.

Even as Katy watched in astonishment, horse and human dipped momentarily from sight behind a large outcropping.

"Oh, my God." Katy broke into a ragged, unsteady run. Every step sent a jolt of pain up through her weak ankle.

It had to be Nadine Bracken leading Garrett's horse along the cliffs, but it made no sense. Katy couldn't begin to imagine what Nadine wanted with Red Dazzle. Not being able to guess only made the situation more nerve-racking, however. Whatever Nadine was up to, Katy knew in her bones it was nothing good.

Memories of Nadine's dour, unhappy attitude flooded Katy's brain as she struggled to move as quickly as possible over the uneven ground. There was an old, twisted bitterness in Nadine. The woman felt she had been dealt a raw deal by fate. She saw her whole life as having been ruined when Silas Atwood's son died in that freak climbing accident.

For the first time Katy began to wonder just how warped Nadine Bracken's emotions really were.

The roar of the ocean on the beach below the cliffs concealed any sound Red Dazzle's hooves might have made. Katy anxiously scanned the moonlit shadows ahead, trying to catch fleeting glimpses of her quarry.

Fortunately, Red Dazzle was never in a hurry to get anywhere, and he seemed to have no inclination to speed up for the sake of the stranger who was tugging on the halter lead. Katy prayed the gelding would continue his slow, stubborn ways. She was having trouble catching up with the horse as it was. Her ankle was getting worse by the minute.

Still, she was closing the gap, and Katy was on the point of calling out to Nadine when intuition suddenly warned her just where the older woman was taking Red Dazzle.

Real fear crawled down Katy's spine as she finally began to understand where the horse was being led. Nadine was taking him to the same point on the cliffs where the Atwood heir had died years before.

Katy gasped and bit back what would surely have been a useless yell. Instead she concentrated on using all her energy to catch up with Nadine.

Katy was panting heavily by the time she came around the last clump of trees that lay between her and Nadine's goal. She stumbled in the sand and grabbed for the side of a boulder to steady herself. Nadine still hadn't heard her. The older woman was wholly intent on what she was doing. Katy stared in horror, trying to see clearly in the pale light.

Nadine had come to a halt at the top of the cliffs. She had positioned the gelding between herself and the sheer rock wall that fell to the beach. Then she took something out of her coat pocket and put it down on a nearby rock. She was still holding on to the halter lead. For the first time Katy saw clearly what the other woman was holding in her left hand. It was a pitchfork.

"Go on, get back," Nadine hissed to a disinterested Red Dazzle. "Get back, I say." She jabbed at the horse with a pitch fork.

Red Dazzle snorted as the wicked weapon came toward him. For the first time he began to show some interest in his precarious situation. He backed away from the fork, flinging his head up in irritation. Nadine lifted her arm and started to make another pass with the pitchfork.

"Nadine! Stop it! *Stop it!*" Katy threw herself forward, feeling her ankle give way completely. She was flung awkwardly down onto the sand.

"What are you doing here?" Nadine demanded as she whirled to confront Katy. "You're not supposed to be here. Get out of here. I won't let you stop me."

Katy clambered unsteadily to her feet. There were still several yards between her and Nadine. She had to move carefully. Nadine could use the pitchfork on Red Dazzle long before Katy could get to her.

"What's going on here?" Katy asked. "What do you think you're doing?"

"I'm going to punish him," Nadine explained. She still held Red Dazzle's lead. The horse was beginning to move restlessly on the end of the rein.

"Punish the horse? Nadine, that's ridiculous. Why would you want to hurt Red Dazzle?" Katy tried to keep her voice calm and reasonable. Slowly she edged forward, ignoring the pain in her ankle.

"Stay back," Nadine warned. She waved the pitchfork at Katy. "Don't come near me."

Katy halted. "Just tell me what you have against the gelding."

"It's not the horse," Nadine shouted, clearly goaded by Katy's denseness. "It's *him*."

"Who?"

"Your husband. The new owner." Nadine was breathing heavily. She kept the fork aimed at Katy. "It's your husband who has to be punished. He had no right, don't you see? No right to buy this place. This was Atwood land. As far as the eye can see, it was Atwood property. And it should have stayed that way. Don't you understand? My girl should have been an Atwood. This land should have become ours. Garrett Coltrane has no right here. No right at all. I'm an old woman and he's a strong man in his prime. There's not much I can do to Coltrane himself, but I can destroy something he loves. I can destroy this horse. Coltrane needs to be punished!''

"Nadine, it was Atwood's decision to sell the property. Garrett just happens to be the man who came along and bought it. He had nothing to do with Atwood's original decision. Nothing to do with what happened all those years ago when Atwood's son fell and broke his neck.''

"Coltrane shouldn't be here!'' Nadine shouted hoarsely. "He has no right to be here.''

"Nadine, listen to me...''

Nadine ignored her. "I thought at first it might be you I should destroy. I thought about that a lot. A man in love would be crushed to lose his new young wife, I told myself. Then I saw right away how it was between you and Coltrane. You two weren't even sleeping together. Some honeymoon, I said to myself. There's something wrong here. Coltrane doesn't love her. I overheard that argument you two had the day Royce Hutton came over here, you know. I heard you say that Coltrane had married you because of your social connections. There was no love lost between the two of you, was there?''

Katy felt a wave of panic. She tried edging a few steps closer. Nadine didn't seem to notice. The woman was too caught up in her strange, convoluted fantasy world. "Nadine, put down the pitchfork and let me talk to you. Let me explain things to you.''

The response was another menacing movement of the pitchfork. Nadine must have yanked on Red Dazzle's lead at the same time, because the horse stamped one foot and tossed his head. His ears flickered warningly. His rear hooves were getting dangerously close to the cliff edge.

"You don't have to explain anything to me,'' Nadine said. "I saw how it was between the two of you and then I decided I could punish Coltrane by making him realize he'd married a woman he not only couldn't love, but one he couldn't trust. I could convince him to divorce you. The new family he wanted to start here on Atwood land would be destroyed before it even began. I was sure he'd think you'd let Red Dazzle out of his stall the night the two of you went to Hutton's party. If the horse got himself hurt or

killed, Coltrane would be furious with you. He'd hate you. I had a
plan, you see. I was going to start doing all sorts of things to make
him wonder about you. I wanted to put doubts in his mind, make
him worry and sweat until he finally came to the conclusion he had
to divorce you.''

"But your plan never got off the ground because Garrett never
believed I was the one who had let Red Dazzle out of his stall."

"After that things seemed to get better instead of worse between
the two of you. You even started using the same bed. You got
smart, didn't you? It was obvious you'd decided to seduce him,
and like any man he was willing to take advantage of the situation.
But I can still punish him. I can still turn him against you. Just
because he's sleeping with you doesn't mean he can't be made to
see things the way I want him to see them. Coltrane cares about
this horse, you know. He has a real sentimental attachment to this
old gelding. And when Coltrane finds him dead at the bottom of
this cliff he's going to have to wonder if you were responsible.''

"Why would he think that? He loves me, Nadine.''

Nadine's face twisted in a dark scowl. "Loves you? That's a
laugh. You and him had another big fight today, didn't you? You
were mad as hell when you found out he'd bought that fancy little
mare for you. When he finds Red Dazzle dead, Coltrane is going
to think you killed his horse to get even with him for trying to
make you ride again.''

Katy went cold. "Garrett's not that stupid. He knows I'd never
do anything like that.''

"We'll see." Nadine lifted her chin with arrogant fury. "We'll
just see what happens. I've got this all planned out. I even got
Emmett started early on his whiskey tonight just so's he'd be out
of the way. He stopped me last time, you know. The old fool. All
his drinking has made him softheaded. He doesn't understand this
is the only way.''

Katy sucked in her breath. "The night the alarm went off in the
stables? That was you?''

"Coltrane was out of town. I was going to take the gelding that
night and force him off this cliff. Earlier I'd made Emmett show
me how to work the alarm system. But Emmett followed me and

stopped me that night. Then he accidentally set off the system himself. He was half drunk, as usual. He made me go back to the house just as you arrived. But I waited for another chance, and tonight I've got it. Coltrane is gone again and this time when he gets back, his favorite horse will be dead and you'll be the one he blames. You'll see.''

''I'll tell him you did it,'' Katy cried.

''It'll be your word against mine, won't it? And he knows you were angry with him. You're the only one with a reason to want to hurt him. He knows you've got a temper and that you're high-strung.''

''I am not temperamental and high-strung!'' Katy shouted, beginning to feel both.

''He told Emmett you were,'' Nadine retorted triumphantly.

Katy abandoned that angle of attack. She went back to edging cautiously closer. ''Nadine, stop this foolishness. Put down the pitchfork and give me Red's lead. I'll take him back to his stall where he belongs.''

''No!'' Nadine whirled around to confront Red Dazzle with the pitchfork. She jabbed fiercely at the horse. This time the tines of the fork scraped the chestnut colt.

Red Dazzle danced backward, his front hooves leaving the ground. He screamed his fear and rage.

Katy realized there was only a foot or two between Red's hind legs and the edge of the cliff. ''Red,'' she called frantically and then she tried the low, sharp whistle Garrett had used the night they had found Red in the storm. The gelding's ears pricked forward in response, and he voiced his disapproval of the entire situation. He moved about in agitation.

''Go on, you stupid horse.'' Nadine dropped the lead and hefted the pitchfork with both hands.

Nadine couldn't jab at the horse and defend herself from Katy at the same time. Katy used the few seconds of advantage to lunge at the woman.

In the last instant, Nadine realized she was being attacked. She swung around, bringing the pitchfork through the air in a lethal arc.

Katy sprawled flat to avoid the tines of the fork. Her hand groped for and found Nadine's ankle. She yanked hard.

Nadine screamed as she tumbled to the ground and began to thrash around. Katy gasped for air as she struggled to her feet. The surge of adrenaline in her bloodstream made it possible to temporarily ignore the agony in her ankle. Her toe struck the handle of the pitchfork and she leaned down to pick it up. She hurled it over the edge of the cliff.

Red Dazzle whinnied nervously and pranced as Katy started toward him.

"Hey, take it easy," Katy murmured, reaching for the trailing rein. "Take it easy, Red. It's just me. I know you've had a hell of a night, but it's all over now. We're going to take you back to your stall and tuck you in. This will all seem like a bad dream in the morning."

She kept up the low, soothing patter as she gently urged the horse away from the edge of the cliffs. Red Dazzle snorted and made low, irritating woofling noises, but he came forward obediently when Katy tugged the rein.

Behind her, Katy heard Nadine lumbering painfully to her feet, but she didn't turn around. She had her hands full with Red Dazzle at the moment and besides, the woman was now unarmed.

"I won't let you stop me," Nadine said fiercely. "Do you hear me? I won't let you stop me."

The new hysteria in the woman's voice finally caught Katy's attention. She glanced back over her shoulder in time to see Nadine reach for the small dark object she had taken out of her pocket earlier and placed on the boulder.

Belatedly an image of the empty cigar box on the Bracken mantle went through Katy's head. The gun Emmett kept there was gone. Katy had a sudden premonition about where it was now.

"I didn't want to use this," Nadine sobbed as she scrabbled about for the gun. "I didn't want to do it this way, but you're forcing me..."

Katy waited no longer. There was no way she could reach the gun ahead of Nadine, not with her weak, throbbing ankle. There was only one hope for both herself and Red Dazzle.

"Okay, Red," Katy said between her teeth as she used her good right leg to hop up onto a nearby rock, "dazzle me." Holding on to the long lead, Katy grabbed a fistful of mane and flung herself onto Red Dazzle's back.

It wasn't the most graceful of mountings, but Red Dazzle was apparently too surprised to complain.

"Let's get out of here." Katy leaned forward and dug her heels into Red's sides. She hung on for dear life because she had seen Red in action years ago. When they finally did move, good rodeo horses were like good sports cars. Very fast and very quick.

And then Red Dazzle showed Katy just what had made him one of the best quarter horses on the pro rodeo circuit. He went from a standing start to full gallop in less time than it took to blink an eye. Katy clung to the horse with both arms and tightened her thighs. The night wind whipped Red's mane into her face and tangled her own hair.

Katy heard the crack of sound behind her and knew Nadine had used the gun. But since Red didn't slow and Katy felt nothing, she assumed they were both all right. A few more seconds would take them well out of range.

The Mercedes headlights coming up the long driveway announced Garrett's return just as Red Dazzle came pounding around the corner of the big house. Katy tugged on the flying mane and the leading rein she still held in one hand.

"Whoa, Red," she murmured. "We're okay now. Take it easy."

The gelding responded almost too quickly. Sudden stops were his specialty. Katy nearly went flying from his back as he plowed to a halt almost directly in front of the Mercedes. She managed to cling to her perch, however, as Garrett slammed open the door of the car. He stood staring at horse and rider for an astounded second, and then he strode quickly forward to grab Red Dazzle's halter. The gelding blew heavily and dropped almost instantly back into his normal, relaxed state. Only his still-heaving sides gave evidence of his recent exertion.

"What the hell is going on here?" Garrett looked up at Katy.

"It's Nadine. She tried to kill Red Dazzle by forcing him over a cliff."

"She *what*?"

"Garrett, she's got a gun. The woman is insane."

"Where is she?" Garrett demanded.

"The last I saw of her, she was back on the cliffs with the gun. Red got both of us out of there just in time."

"Are you all right?"

Katy nodded breathlessly. "I'm fine. I'm worried about Red, though. He probably hasn't had that much exercise in ages."

"Red's okay," Garrett said with an absentminded slap on the chestnut's neck. "I keep him in good shape. Leave him here and get into the house. Lock the door and call the cops."

"Where are you going?" Katy asked anxiously.

"I'm going to find Nadine and put a stop to this nonsense."

"Garrett, I don't think you should go out on the cliffs. Nadine is crazy and she's got Emmett's gun."

"Just get into the house and call the cops." Garrett reached up and hauled her down from Red's back. When she stumbled against him and clutched him for support, he groaned. "What have you done to your ankle?"

"It's all right—really it is."

That wasn't exactly true, but there was no point going into specifics. The ankle hurt badly, but Katy knew perfectly well that she wasn't going to die from the injury. A quick look into her husband's face told her she wasn't going to succeed in stopping him from going after Nadine, either.

"Just promise me you'll be careful, Garrett."

"I'll be careful." He opened the front door of the house and thrust her into the safety of the hallway.

Katy hobbled painfully toward the telephone.

Garrett looped Red Dazzle's lead rein around a convenient bush and then went to look for Nadine Bracken. He didn't have to search very hard to find the defeated woman. As he neared the cliffs the sound of racking sobs guided him to where she sat hunched on a boulder. Without a word he reached down and removed the gun from her hand.

"It wasn't right that everything should change the way it did," Nadine said sadly.

A LONG TIME LATER that night Katy lay back against the pillows of the bed and waited impatiently for Garrett to come out of the bathroom. Her ankle was carefully bound in an elastic bandage, and she knew from experience that it would recover in a day or two.

In the meantime, she and Garrett had a lot to talk about. Between answering the questions the police asked, dealing with a drunken Emmett Bracken and restoring Red Dazzle to the peace and tranquility of his stall, there had been very little time to talk. On top of everything else, Garrett had fussed endlessly about Katy's ankle, until she had finally convinced him she could take care of it as well as any doctor. Katy smiled at the memory of his scowling expression as he'd watched her wrap the bandage herself, and in that moment the bathroom door opened.

Garrett stood in the doorway, a towel draped around his lean waist. "Well, I'm glad someone is finding this evening amusing," he muttered as he switched off the light and came toward the bed. "Personally, I've about had it. Me and old Red are getting too old for this kind of excitement."

"Oh, I don't know about that," Katy said. "You and old Red both seemed to hold up pretty well under the circumstances."

Garrett tossed back the covers, dropped his towel and came down onto the bed beside Katy. He cradled her in his arms, his hand moving idly in her hair. In the shadows his eyes gleamed behind his lashes.

"You," he announced, "have been one surprise after another since our wedding day."

"Variety is the spice of life," she reminded him.

"Yeah? Well, I've had enough for a while. It's about time this marriage finally settled down and ran itself the way it's supposed to."

"How's that?"

Garrett chuckled and dropped a quick kiss on her parted lips. "Beats me. When I married you, I thought I knew how marriage between us would work. It would be pleasant, predictable and reliable. You'd be undemanding and easy to manage. You didn't seem to be the temperamental type. We'd have professional interests in common, and we both seemed to find each other attractive enough to share a bed.''

"Hah. That's putting it mildly, and you know it. You know perfectly well that I found you more than just attractive enough to go to bed with. I was head over heels in love with you. On top of that, you were the sexiest man I had ever met. I couldn't wait to go to bed with you. In fact, we would have wound up in bed together a lot sooner than our wedding night if you had shown a little more interest in the matter.''

"I was an idiot," Garrett freely admitted.

"True."

"You don't have to agree with everything I say."

"I'm practicing being undemanding and easy to manage. Agreeing with everything one's husband says is part of the process," Katy explained seriously.

Garrett gave her a small, affectionate shake. "Undemanding, easy-to-manage wives do not spend all their time finding ways to bait their husbands.''

"Is that right? What do they spend their time doing?''

"I'll be happy to demonstrate," Garrett said, starting to roll Katy over onto her back.

"Wait! I've got some questions." Katy held him off, both her hands planted on his broad shoulders. "What about Emmett and Nadine?''

"What about them?" Garrett nuzzled the tip of his wife's nose. "As far as I'm concerned, we've got openings for a new handyman and a new housekeeper.''

"You're going to let Emmett go?''

"He's got his pension from Atwood and he's got Social Security. He won't starve. If he wants to go on working, he can find a job somewhere else.''

"And Nadine?''

"Something tells me Nadine is going to be taken care of by the state for the next few years.''

"Garrett, maybe we should think about this," Katy began earnestly. "After all, they've both lived here for years and—''

Garrett put his hand over her mouth and smiled down into her wide, questioning eyes. "Honey, we gave the Brackens all the rope they wanted, and it was you who almost got hanged. You and Red Dazzle. I'm not about to invite trouble by giving them any second or third chances. I want them off this property and that's final. This particular subject is not open for discussion. You're a little too softhearted about some things."

Katy sighed, knowing she had lost this small battle and knowing, too, that Garrett was probably right. She would never feel easy with either Emmett or his crazy wife around. Katy put out the tip of her tongue and touched Garrett's palm. He laughed and removed his hand.

"No more arguments on that score?" he asked.

"No. I hate to admit it, but I think you're right."

Garrett grinned. "Words like that are music to a husband's ears. Now that we've settled that matter, there's another I think we might as well get out of the way."

"What's that?" Katy eyed him, torn between wariness and laughter.

"This business of your midnight riding habits."

"Oh, that."

"Yes, that." Garrett tightened his hold on her. "I don't suppose you know what a shock it was to see you come flying around the corner of the house the way you did tonight? At full gallop in the moonlight? With no saddle or bridle?"

"It was rather adventurous of me, wasn't it?"

"It took a dozen years off my life," Garrett declared. "But at least now I won't have to listen to any more excuses about how you can't or won't ride again."

Katy thought about that. "Uh, Garrett?"

"Forget it, Katy. You got back on a horse tonight and you didn't collapse in terror, so don't try telling me you can't handle riding."

"It was odd," Katy admitted, remembering the rush of sensation she had experienced on Red Dazzle. "I guess I just didn't have time to think. In any event, there wasn't much choice. It was either ride your horse or face Nadine's gun."

"Sometimes life makes things simple for us," Garrett said with deep satisfaction."

"How's that?"

Garrett smiled down at her as he gathered her close. "I love you," he said. "How much simpler can things get?"

"Sometimes," Katy whispered, "loving someone can be very complicated."

"Only for a woman who lets her imagination get carried away. Now hush, sweetheart, and let me show you just how simple life can be."

Katy smiled up at him as he slipped the nightgown off over her head. "I love you, Garrett."

"I love you, too." He bent his head to brush her mouth with his own.

Katy's fingers slid into his dark hair, and her body twisted sensually beneath his. "I know," she said, "But it's nice to hear the words."

Thief of Hearts
Tess Gerritsen

PROLOGUE

SIMON TROTT stood on the rolling deck of the *Cosima*, and through the velvety blackness of night he saw the flames. They burned just offshore, not a steady fire, but a series of violent bursts of light that cast the distant swells in a hellish glow.

"That's her," the *Cosima*'s captain said to Trott as both men peered across the bow. "The *Max Havelaar*. Judging by those fireworks, she'll be going down fast." He turned and yelled to the helmsman, "Full ahead!"

"Not much chance of survivors," said Trott.

"They're sending off a distress call. So someone's alive."

"Or was alive."

As they neared the sinking vessel, the flames suddenly shot up like a fountain, sending out sparks that seemed to ignite the ocean in puddles of liquid fire.

The captain shouted over the roar of the *Cosima*'s engines, "Slow up! There's fuel in the water!"

"Throttling down," said the helmsman.

"Ahead slowly. Watch for survivors."

Trott moved to the forward rail and stared across the watery inferno. Already the *Max Havelaar* was sliding backward, her stern nearly submerged, her bow tipping toward the moonless sky. A few minutes more and she'd sink forever into the swells. The water was deep, and salvage impractical. Here, two miles off the Spanish coast, was where the *Havelaar* would sink to her eternal rest.

Another explosion spewed out a shower of embers, leafing the ripples with gold. In those few seconds before the sunlike brilliance faded, Trott spotted a hint of movement off in the darkness. A good two hundred yards away from the *Havelaar*, safely beyond the ring of fire, Trott saw a long, low silhouette bobbing in the water. Then he heard the sound of men's voices, calling.

"Here! We are here!"

"It's the lifeboat," said the captain, aiming the searchlight toward the voices. "There, at two o'clock!"

"I see it," said the helmsman, at once adjusting course. He throttled up, guiding the bow through drifts of burning fuel. As they drew closer, Trott could hear the joyous shouts of the survivors, a confusing babble of Italian. How many in the boat? he wondered, straining to see through the murk. Five. Perhaps six. He could almost count them now, their arms waving in the searchlight's beam, their heads bobbing in every direction. They were thrilled to be alive. To be in sight of rescue.

"Looks like most of the *Havelaar*'s crew," said the captain.

"We'll need all hands up here."

The captain turned and barked out the order. Seconds later the *Cosima*'s crew had assembled on deck. As the bow knifed across the remaining expanse of water, the men stood in silence near the bow rail, all eyes focused on the lifeboat just ahead.

By the searchlight's glare Trott could now make out the number of survivors: six. He knew the *Max Havelaar* had sailed from Naples with a crew of eight. Were there two still in the water?

He turned and glanced toward the distant silhouette of shore. With luck and endurance, a man could swim that distance.

The lifeboat was adrift off their starboard side.

Trott shouted, "This is the *Cosima*! Identify yourselves!"

"Max Havelaar!" shouted one of the men in the lifeboat.

"Is this your entire crew?"

"Two are dead!"

"You're certain?"

"The engine, she explodes! One man, he is trapped below."

"And your eighth man?"

"He falls in. Cannot swim!"

Which made the eighth man as good as dead, thought Trott. He glanced at *Cosima*'s crew. They stood watching, waiting for the order.

The lifeboat was gliding almost alongside now.

"A little closer," Trott called down, "and we'll throw you a line."

One of the men in the lifeboat reached up to catch the rope.

Trott turned and gave his men the signal.

The first hail of bullets caught its victim in midreach, arms extended toward his would-be saviors. He had no chance to scream. As the bullets rained down from the *Cosima,* the men fell, helpless before the onslaught. Their cries, the splash of a falling body, were drowned out by the relentless spatter of automatic gunfire.

When it was finished, when the bullets finally ceased, the bodies lay in a coiled embrace in the lifeboat. A silence fell, broken only by the slap of water against the *Cosima*'s hull.

One last explosion spewed a finale of sparks into the air. The bow of the *Max Havelaar*—what remained of her—tilted crazily toward the sky. Then, gently, she slid backward into the deep.

The lifeboat, its hull riddled with bullet holes, was already half submerged. A *Cosima* crewman heaved a loose anchor over the side. It landed with a thud among the bodies. The lifeboat tipped, emptying its cargo of corpses into the sea.

"Our work is done here, Captain," said Trott. Matter-of-factly he turned toward the helm. "I suggest we return to—"

He suddenly halted, his gaze focused on a patch of water a dozen yards away. What was that splash? He could still see the ripples of reflected firelight worrying the water's surface. There it was again. Something silvery gliding out of the swells, then slipping back under the water.

"Over there!" shouted Trott. "Fire!"

His men looked at him, puzzled.

"What did you see?" asked the captain.

"Four o'clock. Something broke the surface."

"I don't see anything."

"Fire at it, anyway."

One of the gunmen obligingly squeezed off a clip. The bullets sprayed into the water, their deadly rain splashing a line across the surface.

They watched for a moment. Nothing appeared. The water smoothed once again into undulating glass.

"I know I saw something," said Trott.

The captain shrugged. "Well, it's not there now." He called to the helmsman, "Return to port!"

Cosima came about, leaving in her wake a spreading circle of ripples.

Trott moved to the stern, his gaze still focused on the suspicious patch of water. As they roared away he thought he spotted another flash of silver bob to the surface. It was there only for an instant. Then, in a twinkling, it was gone.

A fish, he thought. And, satisfied, he turned away.

Yes, that must be what it was. A fish.

CHAPTER ONE

"A SMALL BURGLARY. That's all I'm asking for." Veronica Cairncross gazed up at him, tears shimmering in her sapphire eyes. She was dressed in a fetching off-the-shoulder silk gown, the skirt arranged in lustrous ripples across the Queen Anne love seat. Her hair, a rich russet brown, had been braided with strands of seed pearls and was coiled artfully atop her aristocratic head. At thirty-three she was far more stunning, far more chic than she'd been at the age of twenty-five, when he'd first met her. Through the years she'd acquired, along with her title, an unerring sense of style, poise and a reputation for witty repartee that made her a sought-after guest at the most glittering parties in London. But one thing about her had not changed, would never change.

Veronica Cairncross was still an idiot.

How else could one explain the predicament into which she'd dug herself?

And once again, he thought wearily, it's faithful old chum Jordan Tavistock to the rescue. Not that Veronica didn't need rescuing. Not that he didn't want to help her. It was simply that this request of hers was so bizarre, so fraught with dire possibilities, that his first instinct was to turn her down flat.

He did. "It's out of the question, Veronica," said Jordan. "I won't do it."

"For me, Jordie!" she pleaded. "Think what will happen if you don't. If he shows those letters to Oliver—"

"Poor old Ollie will have a fit. You two will row for a few days, and then he'll forgive you. That's what will happen."

"What if Ollie doesn't forgive me? What if he—what if he wants a..." She swallowed and looked down. "A divorce," she whispered.

"Really, Veronica." Jordan sighed. "You should have thought about this before you had the affair."

She stared down in misery at the folds of her silk gown. "I didn't think. That's the whole problem."

"No, it's obvious you didn't."

"I had no idea Guy would be so difficult. You'd think I broke his heart! It's not as if we were in love or anything. And now he's being such a bastard about it. Threatening to tell all! What gentleman would sink so low?"

"No gentleman would."

"If it weren't for those letters I wrote, I could deny the whole thing. It would be my word against Guy's, then. I'm sure Ollie would give me the benefit of the doubt."

"What, exactly, did you write in those letters?"

Veronica's head drooped unhappily. "Things I shouldn't have."

"Confessions of love? Sweet nothings?"

She groaned. "Much worse."

"More explicit, you mean?"

"Far more explicit."

Jordan gazed at her bent head, at the seed pearls and russet hair glimmering in the lamplight. And he thought, *It's hard to believe I was once attracted to this woman.* But that was years ago, and he'd been only twenty-two and a bit gullible—a condition he sincerely hoped he'd outgrown.

Veronica Dooley had entered his social circle on the arm of an old chum from Cambridge. After the chum bowed out, Jordan had inherited the girl's attentions, and for a few dizzy weeks he'd thought he might be in love. Better sense prevailed. Their parting was amicable, and they'd remained friends over the years. She'd gone on to marry Oliver Cairncross, and although *Sir* Oliver was a good twenty years older than his bride, theirs had been a classic match between money on his side and beauty on hers. Jordan had thought them a contented pair.

How wrong he'd been.

"My advice to you," he said, "is to come clean. Tell Ollie about the affair. He'll most likely forgive you."

"Even if he does, there's still the letters. Guy's just upset enough to send them to all the wrong people. If Fleet Street ever got hold of them, Ollie would be publicly humiliated."

"You think Guy would really stoop so low?"

"I don't doubt it for a minute. I'd offer to pay him off if I thought it would work. But after all that money I lost in Monte Carlo, Ollie's keeping a tight rein on my spending. And I couldn't borrow any money from you. I mean, there are some things one simply *can't* ask of one's friends."

"Burglary, I'd say, lies in that category," noted Jordan dryly.

"But it's not burglary! I wrote those letters. Which makes them *mine*. I'm only retrieving what belongs to me." She leaned forward, her eyes suddenly glittering like blue diamonds. "It wouldn't be difficult, Jordie. I know exactly which drawer he keeps them in. Your sister's engagement party is Saturday night. If you could invite him here—"

"Beryl detests Guy Delancey."

"Invite him anyway! While he's here at Chetwynd, guzzling champagne—"

"I'm burgling his house?" Jordan shook his head. "What if I'm caught?"

"Guy's staff takes Saturday nights off. His house will be empty. Even if you *are* caught, just tell them it's a prank. Bring a—a blow-up doll or something, for insurance. Tell them you're planting it in his bed. They'll believe you. Who'd doubt the word of a Tavistock?"

He frowned. "Is that why you're asking *me* to do this? Because I'm a Tavistock?"

"No. I'm asking you because you're the cleverest man I know. Because you've never, ever betrayed any of my secrets." She raised her chin and met his gaze. It was a look of utter trust. "And because you're the only one in the world I can count on."

Drat. She would have to say that.

"Will you do it for me, Jordie?" she asked softly. Pitifully. "Tell me you will."

Wearily he rubbed his head. "I'll think about it," he said. Then he sank back in the armchair and gazed resignedly at the far wall, at the paintings of his Tavistock ancestors. Distinguished gentlemen, every one of them, he thought. Not a cat burglar in the lot.

Until now.

AT 11:05, THE LIGHTS WENT out in the servants' quarters. Good old Whitmore was right on schedule as usual. At 9:00 he'd made his rounds of the house, checking to see that the windows and doors were locked. At 9:30 he'd tidied up downstairs, fussed a bit in the kitchen, perhaps brewed himself a pot of tea. At 10:00 he'd retired upstairs, to the blue glow of his private telly. At 11:05 he turned off his light.

This had been Whitmore's routine for the past week, and Clea Rice, who'd been watching Guy Delancey's house since the previous Saturday, assumed that this would be his routine until the day he died. Menservants, after all, strived to maintain order in their employers' lives. It wasn't surprising they'd maintain order in their own lives, as well.

Now the question was, how long before he'd fall asleep?

Safely concealed behind the yew hedge, Clea rose to her feet and began to rock from foot to foot, trying to keep the blood moving through her limbs. The grass had been wet, and her stirrup pants were clinging to her thighs. Though the night was warm, she was feeling chilled. It wasn't just the dampness in her clothes; it was the excitement, the anticipation. And, yes, the fear. Not a great deal of fear—she had enough confidence in her own ability to feel certain she wouldn't be caught. Still, there was always that chance.

She danced from foot to foot to keep the adrenaline pumping. She'd give the manservant twenty minutes to fall asleep, no longer. With every minute that passed, her window of opportunity was shrinking. Guy Delancey could return home early from the party tonight, and she wanted to be well away from here when he walked in that front door.

Surely the butler was asleep now.

Clea slipped around the yew hedge and took off at a sprint. She didn't stop running until she'd reached the cover of shrubbery. There she paused to catch her breath, to reevaluate her situation. There was no hue and cry from the house, no signs of movement anywhere in the darkness. Lucky for her, Guy Delancey abhorred dogs; the last thing she needed tonight was some blasted hound baying at her heels.

She slipped around the house and crossed the flagstone terrace to the French doors. As expected, they were locked. Also as expected, it would be an elementary job. A quick glance under her penlight told her this was an antique warded lock, a bit rusty, probably as old as the house itself. When it came to home security, the English had light years of catching up to do. She fished the set of five skeleton keys out of her fanny pack and began trying them, one by one. The first three keys didn't fit. She inserted the fourth, turned it slowly and felt the tooth slide into the bolt notch.

A piece of cake.

She let herself in the door and stepped into the library. By the glow of moonlight through the windows she could see books gleaming in shelves. Now came the hard part—where was the Eye of Kashmir? Surely not in this room, she thought as the beam of her penlight skimmed the walls. It was too accessible to visitors, pathetically unsecured against thieves. Nevertheless, she gave the room a quick search.

No Eye of Kashmir.

She slipped out of the library and into the hallway. Her light traced across burnished wood and antique vases. She prowled through the first-floor parlor and solarium. No Eye of Kashmir. She didn't bother with the kitchen or dining areas—Delancey would never choose a hiding place so accessible to his servants.

That left the upstairs rooms.

Clea ascended the curving stairway, her footsteps silent as a cat's. At the landing she paused, listening for any sounds of discovery. Nothing. To the left she knew was the servants' wing. To the right would be Delancey's bedroom. She turned right and went straight to the room at the end of the hall.

The door was unlocked. She slipped through and closed it softly behind her.

Through the balcony windows moonlight spilled in, illuminating a room of grand proportions. The twelve-foot-high walls were covered with paintings. The bed was a massive four-poster, its mattress

broad enough to sleep an entire harem. There was an equally massive chest of drawers, a double wardrobe, nightstands and a gentleman's writing desk. Near the balcony doors was a sitting area—
two chairs and a tea table arranged around a Persian carpet, probably antique.

Clea let out an audible groan. It would take hours to search this
room.

Fully aware of the minutes ticking by, she started with the writing desk. She searched the drawers, checked for hidden niches. No
Eye of Kashmir. She moved to the dresser, where she probed
through layers of underwear and hankies. No Eye of Kashmir. She
turned next to the wardrobe, which loomed like a monstrous mono-
lith against the wall. She was just about to swing open the wardrobe
door when she heard a noise and she froze.

It was a faint rustling, coming from somewhere outside the
house. There it was again, louder.

She swiveled around to face the balcony windows. Something
bizarre was going on. Outside, on the railing, the wisteria vines
quaked violently. A silhouette suddenly popped up above the tangle
of leaves. Clea caught one glimpse of the man's head, of his blond
hair gleaming in the moonlight, and she ducked back behind the
wardrobe.

This was just wonderful. They'd have to take numbers to see
whose turn it was to break in next. This was one hazard she hadn't
anticipated—an encounter with a rival thief. An incompetent one,
too, she thought in disgust as she heard the sharp clatter of outdoor
pottery, quickly stilled. There was an intervening silence. The burglar was listening for sounds of discovery. Old Whitmore must be
deaf, thought Clea, if he didn't hear *that* racket.

The balcony door squealed open.

Clea retreated farther behind the wardrobe. What if he discovered
her? Would he attack? She'd brought nothing with which to defend
herself.

She winced as she heard a thump, followed by an irritated mutter
of "*Damn* it all!"

Oh, Lord. This guy was more dangerous to himself than to her.

Footsteps creaked closer.

Clea shrank back, pressing hard against the wall. The wardrobe door swung open, coming to a stop just inches from her face. She heard the clink of hangers as clothes were shoved aside, then the hiss of a drawer sliding out. A flashlight flicked on, its glow spilling through the crack of the wardrobe door. The man muttered to himself as he rifled through the drawer, irritated grumblings in the queen's best English.

"Must be mad. That's what I am, stark raving. Don't know how she talked me into this...."

Clea couldn't help it; curiosity got the better of her. She eased forward and peered through the crack between the hinges of the door. The man was frowning down at an open drawer. His profile was sharply cut, cleanly aristocratic. His hair was wheat blond and still a bit ruffled from all that wrestling with the wisteria vine. He wasn't dressed at all like a burglar. In his tuxedo jacket and black bow tie, he looked more like some cocktail-party refugee.

He dug deeper into the drawer and suddenly gave a murmur of satisfaction. She couldn't see what he was removing from the drawer. *Please,* she thought. *Let it not be the Eye of Kashmir.* To have come so close and then to lose it....

She leaned even closer to the crack and strained to see over his shoulder, to find out what he was now sliding into his jacket pocket. So intently was she staring, she scarcely had time to react when he unexpectedly grasped the wardrobe door and swung it shut. She jerked back into the shadows and her shoulder thudded against the wall.

There was a silence. A very long silence.

Slowly the beam of the flashlight slid around the edge of the wardrobe, followed cautiously by the silhouette of the man's head.

Clea blinked as the light focused fully on her face. Against the glare she couldn't see him, but he could see *her.* For an eternity neither of them moved, neither of them made a sound.

Then he said, "Who the hell are *you?*"

The figure coiled up against the wardrobe didn't answer. Slowly Jordan played his torchlight down the length of the intruder, noting the stocking cap pulled low to the eyebrows, the face obscured by camouflage paint, the black turtleneck shirt and pants.

"I'm going to ask you one last time," Jordan said. "Who are you?"

He was answered with a mysterious smile. The sight of it surprised him. That's when the figure in black sprang like a cat. The impact sent Jordan staggering backward against the bedpost. At once the figure scrambled toward the balcony. Jordan lunged and managed to grab a handful of pant leg. They both tumbled to the floor and collided with the writing desk, letting loose a cascade of pens and pencils. His opponent squirmed beneath him and rammed a knee into Jordan's groin. In the onrush of pain and nausea, Jordan almost let go. His opponent got one hand free and was scrabbling about on the floor. Almost too late Jordan saw the pointed tip of a letter opener stabbing toward him.

He grabbed his opponent's wrist and savagely wrestled away the letter opener. The other man struck back just as savagely, arms flailing, body twisting like an eel. As Jordan fought to control those pummeling fists, he snagged his opponent's stocking cap.

A luxurious fountain of blond hair suddenly tumbled out across the floor, to ripple in a shimmering pool under the moonlight. Jordan stared in astonishment.

A woman.

For an endless moment they stared at each other, their breaths coming hard and fast, their hearts thudding against each other's chests.

A woman.

Without warning his body responded in a way that was both automatic and unsuppressibly male. She was too warm, too close. And very, very female. Even through their clothes, those soft curves were all too apparent. Just as the state of his arousal must be firmly apparent to her.

"Get off me," she whispered.

"First tell me who you are."

"Or *what?*"

"Or I'll—I'll—"

She smiled up at him, her mouth so close, so tempting he completely lost his train of thought.

It was the creak of approaching footsteps that made his brain snap back into function. Light suddenly spilled under the doorway and a man's voice called, "What's this, now? Who's in there?"

In a flash both Jordan and the woman were on their feet and dashing to the balcony. The woman was first over the railing. She scrambled like a monkey down the wisteria vine. By the time Jordan hit the ground, she was already sprinting across the lawn.

At the yew hedge he finally caught up with her and pulled her to a halt. "What were you doing in there?" he demanded.

"What were *you* doing in there?" she countered.

Back at the house the bedroom lights came on, and a voice yelled from the balcony, "Thieves! Don't you come back! I've called the police!"

"I'm not hanging around *here*," said the woman, and made a beeline for the woods.

Jordan sighed. "She does have a point." And he took off after her.

For a mile they slogged it out together, dodging brambles, ducking beneath branches. It was rough terrain, but she seemed tireless, moving at the steady pace of someone in superb condition. Only when they'd reached the far edge of the woods did he notice that her breathing had turned ragged.

He was ready to collapse.

They stopped to rest at the edge of a field. The sky was cloudless, the moonlight thick as milk. Wind blew, warm and fragrant with the smell of fallen leaves.

"So tell me," he managed to say between gulps of air, "do you do this sort of thing for a living?"

"I'm not a thief. If that's what you're asking."

"You act like a thief. You dress like a thief."

"I'm not a thief." She sagged back wearily against a tree trunk. "Are you?"

"Of course not!" he snapped.

"What do you mean, *of course not?* Is it beneath your precious dignity or something?"

"Not at all. That is— I mean—" He stopped and shook his head in confusion. "What *do* I mean?"

"I haven't the faintest," she said innocently.

"I'm *not* a thief," he said, more sure of himself now. "I was...playing a bit of a practical joke. That's all."

"I see." She tilted her head up to look at him, and her expression was plainly skeptical in the moonlight. Now that they weren't grappling like savages, he realized she was quite petite. And, without a doubt, female. He remembered how snugly her sweet curves had fit beneath him, and suddenly desire flooded through his body, a desire so intense it left him aching. All he had to do was step close to this woman and those blasted hormones kicked in.

He stepped back and forced himself to focus on her face. He couldn't quite make it out under all that camouflage paint, but it would be easy to remember her voice. It was low and throaty, almost like a cat's growl. Definitely not English, he thought. American?

She was still eyeing him with a skeptical look. "What did you take out of the wardrobe?" she asked. "Was that part of the practical joke?"

"You...saw that?"

"I did." Her chin came up squarely in challenge. "*Now* convince me it was all a prank."

Sighing, he reached under his jacket. At once she jerked back and pivoted around to flee. "No, it's all right!" he assured her. "It's not a gun or anything. It's just this pouch I'm wearing. Sort of a hidden backpack." He unzipped the pouch. She stood a few feet away, watching him warily, ready to sprint off at the first whiff of danger. "It's a bit sophomoric, really," he said, tugging at the pouch. "But it's good for a laugh." The contents suddenly flopped out and the woman gave a little squeak of fright. "See? It's not a weapon." He held it out to her. "It's an inflatable doll. When you blow it up, it turns into a naked woman."

She moved forward, eyeing the limp rubber doll. "Anatomically correct?" she inquired dryly.

"I'm not sure, really. I mean, er..." He glanced at her, and his mind suddenly veered toward *her* anatomy. He cleared his throat. "I haven't checked."

She regarded him the way one might look at an object of pity.

"But it *does* prove I was there on a prank," he said, struggling to stuff the deflated doll back in the pouch.

"All it proves," she said, "is that you had the foresight to bring an excuse should you be caught. Which, in your case, was a distinct possibility."

"And what excuse did *you* bring? Should you be caught?"

"I wasn't planning on getting caught," she said, and started across the field. "Everything was going quite well, as a matter of fact. Until you bumbled in."

"What was going quite well? The burglary?"

"I told you, I'm not a thief."

He followed her through the grass. "So why did *you* break in?"

"To prove a point."

"And that point was?"

"That it could be done. I've just proven to Mr. Delancey that he needs a security system. And my company's the one to install it."

"You work for a *security* company?" He laughed. "Which one?"

"Why do you ask?"

"My future brother-in-law's in that line of work. He might know your firm."

She smiled back at him, her lips immensely kissable, her teeth a bright arc in the night. "I work for Nimrod Associates," she said. Then, turning, she walked away.

"Wait. Miss—"

She waved a gloved hand in farewell, but didn't look back.

"I didn't catch your name!" he said.

"And I didn't catch yours," she said over her shoulder. "Let's keep it that way."

He saw her blond hair gleam faintly in the darkness. And then, in a twinkling, she was gone. Her absence seemed to leave the night colder, the darkness deeper. The only hint that she'd even been there was his residual ache of desire.

I shouldn't have let her go, he thought. *I know bloody well she's a thief.* But what could he have done? Hauled her to the police?

Explained that he'd caught her in Guy Delancey's bedroom, where neither one of them belonged?

With a weary shake of his head, he turned and began the long tramp to his car, parked a half mile away. He'd have to hurry back to Chetwynd. It was getting late and he'd be missed at the party.

At least his mission was accomplished; he'd stolen Veronica's letters back. He'd hand them over to her, let her lavish him with thanks for saving her precious hide. After all, he *had* saved her hide, and he was bloody well going to tell her so.

And then he was going to strangle her.

CHAPTER TWO

THE PARTY AT Chetwynd was still in full swing. Through the ballroom windows came the sounds of laughter and violin music and the cheery clink of champagne glasses. Jordan stood in the driveway and considered his best mode of entry. The back stairs? No, he'd have to walk through the kitchen, and the staff would certainly find *that* suspicious. Up the trellis to Uncle Hugh's bedroom? Definitely not; he'd done enough tangling with vines for the night. He'd simply waltz in the front door and hope the guests were too deep in their cups to notice his disheveled state.

He straightened his bow tie and brushed the twigs off his jacket. Then he let himself in the front door.

To his relief, no one was in the entrance hall. He tiptoed past the ballroom doorway and started up the curving staircase. He was almost to the second-floor landing when a voice called from below.

"Jordie, where on earth have you been?"

Suppressing a groan, Jordan turned and saw his sister, Beryl, standing at the bottom of the stairs. She was looking flushed and lovelier than ever, her black hair swirled elegantly atop her head, her bared shoulders lustrous above the green velvet gown. Being in love certainly agreed with her. Since her engagement to Richard Wolf a month ago, Jordan had seldom seen her without a smile on her face.

At the moment she was not smiling.

She stared at his wrinkled jacket, his soiled trouser legs and muddy shoes. She shook her head. "I'm afraid to ask."

"Then don't."

"I'll ask anyway. What happened to you?"

He turned and continued up the stairs. "I went out for a walk."

"That's all?" She bounded up the steps after him in a rustle of skirts and stockings. "First you make me invite that horrid Guy

Delancey—who, by the way, is drinking like a fish and going 'round pinching ladies' bottoms. Then you simply vanish from the party. And you reappear looking like that.''

He went into his bedroom.

She followed him.

''It was a long walk,'' he said.

''It's been a long party.''

''Beryl.'' He sighed, turning to face her. ''I really *am* sorry about Guy Delancey. But I can't talk about it right now. I'd be betraying a confidence.''

''I see.'' She went to the door, then glanced back. ''I *can* keep a secret, you know.''

''So can I.'' Jordan smiled. ''That's why I'm not saying a thing.''

''Well, you'd best change your clothes, then. Or someone's going to ask why you've been climbing wisteria vines.'' She left, shutting the door behind her.

Jordan looked down at his jacket. Only then did he notice the leaf, poking like a green flag from his buttonhole.

He changed into a fresh tuxedo, combed the twigs from his hair and went downstairs to rejoin the party.

Though it was past midnight, the champagne was still flowing and the scene in the ballroom was as jolly as when he'd left it an hour and a half earlier. He swept up a glass from a passing tray and eased back into circulation. No one mentioned his absence; perhaps no one had noticed it. He worked his way across the room to the buffet table, where a magnificent array of hors d'oeuvres had been laid out, and he helped himself to the Scottish salmon. Breaking and entering was hard work, and he was famished.

A whiff of perfume, a hand brushing his arm, made him turn. It was Veronica Cairncross. ''Well?'' she whispered anxiously. ''How did it go?''

''Not exactly clockwork. You were wrong about the butler's night off. There was a manservant in the house. I could have been caught.''

''Oh, no,'' she moaned softly. ''Then you didn't get them....''

''I got them. They're upstairs.''

"You *did?*" A smile of utter happiness burst across her face. "Oh, Jordie!" She leaned forward and threw her arms around him, smearing salmon on his tuxedo. "You saved my life."

"I know, I know." He suddenly spotted Veronica's husband, Oliver, moving toward them. At once Jordan extricated himself from her embrace. "Ollie's coming this way," he whispered.

"Is he?" Veronica turned and automatically beamed her thousand-watt smile at Sir Oliver. "Darling, there you are! I lost track of you."

"You don't seem to be missing me much," grunted Sir Oliver. He frowned at Jordan, as though trying to divine his real intentions.

Poor fellow, thought Jordan. Any man married to Veronica was deserving of pity. Sir Oliver was a decent enough fellow, a descendant of the excellent Cairncross family, manufacturers of tea biscuits. Though twenty years older than his wife, and bald as a cue ball, he'd managed to win Veronica's hand—and to keep that hand well studded with diamonds.

"It's getting late," said Oliver. "Really, Veronica, shouldn't we be going home?"

"So soon? It's just past midnight."

"I have that meeting in the morning. And I'm quite tired."

"Well, I suppose we'll have to be going, then," Veronica said with a sigh. She smiled slyly at Jordan. "I think I'll sleep well tonight."

Just see that it's with your husband, thought Jordan with a shake of his head.

After the Cairncrosses had departed, Jordan glanced down and saw the greasy sliver of salmon clinging to his lapel. Drat, another tuxedo bites the dust. He wiped away the mess as best he could, picked up his glass of champagne and waded back into the crowd.

He cornered his future brother-in-law, Richard Wolf, near the musicians. Wolf was looking happy and dazed—just the way one expected a prospective bridegroom to look.

"So how's our guest of honor holding up?" asked Jordan.

Richard grinned. "Giving the old handshake a rest."

"Good idea to pace oneself." Jordan's gaze shifted toward the source of particularly raucous laughter. It was Guy Delancey, clearly well soused and leaning close to a buxom young thing. "Unfortunately," Jordan observed, "not everyone here believes in pacing himself."

"No kidding," said Wolf, also looking at Delancey. "You know, that fellow tried to put the make on Beryl tonight. Right under my nose."

"And did you defend her honor?"

"Didn't have to," said Richard with a laugh. "She does a pretty good job of defending herself."

Delancey's hand was now on Miss Buxom's lower back. Slowly that hand began to slide down toward dangerous terrain.

"What do women see in a guy like that, anyway?" asked Richard.

"Sex appeal?" said Jordan. Delancey did, after all, have rather dashing Spanish looks. "Who knows what attracts women to certain men?" Lord only knew what had attracted Veronica Cairncross to Guy. But she was rid of him now. If she was sensible, she'd damn well stay on the straight and narrow.

Jordan looked at Richard. "Tell me, have you ever heard of a security firm called Nimrod Associates?"

"Is that based here or abroad?"

"I don't know. Here, I imagine."

"I haven't heard of it. But I could check for you."

"Would you? I'd appreciate it."

"Why are you interested in this firm?"

"Oh..." Jordan shrugged. "The name came up in the course of the evening."

Richard was looking at him thoughtfully. Damn, it was that intelligence background of his, an aspect of Richard Wolf that could be either a help or a nuisance. Richard's antennae were out now, the questions forming in his head. Jordan would have to be careful.

Luckily, Beryl sauntered up at that moment to bestow a kiss on her intended. Any questions Richard may have entertained were quickly forgotten as he bent to press his lips to his fiancée's upturned mouth. Another kiss, a hungry twining of arms, and poor old Richard was oblivious to the rest of the world.

Ah, young lovers, sizzling in hormones, thought Jordan and polished off his drink. His own hormones were simmering tonight as well, helped along by the pleasant buzz of champagne.

And by thoughts of that woman.

He couldn't seem to get her out of his thick head. Not her voice, nor her laugh, nor the catlike litheness of her body twisting beneath his....

Quickly he set his glass down. No more champagne tonight. The memories were intoxicating enough. He glanced around for the tray of soda water and spotted his uncle Hugh entering the ballroom.

All evening Hugh had played genial host and proud uncle to the future bride. He'd happily guzzled champagne and flirted with ladies young enough to be his granddaughters. But at this particular moment Uncle Hugh was looking vexed.

He crossed the room, straight toward Guy Delancey. The two men exchanged a few words and Delancey's chin shot up. An instant later an obviously upset Delancey strode out of the ballroom, calling loudly for his car.

"Now what's going on?" said Jordan.

Beryl, her cheeks flushed and pretty from Richard's kissing, turned to look as Uncle Hugh wandered in their direction. "He's obviously not happy."

"Dreadful way to finish off the evening," Hugh was muttering.

"What happened?" asked Beryl.

"Guy Delancey's man called to report a burglary at the house. Seems someone climbed up the balcony and walked straight into the master bedroom. Imagine the cheek! And with the butler at home, too."

"Was anything stolen?" asked Richard.

"Don't know yet." Hugh shook his head. "Almost makes one feel a bit guilty, doesn't it?"

"Guilty?" Jordan forced a laugh from his throat. "Why?"

"If we hadn't invited Delancey here tonight, the burglar wouldn't have had his chance."

"That's ridiculous," said Jordan. "The burglar—I mean, if it *was* a burglar—"

"Why wouldn't it be a burglar?" asked Beryl.

"It's just—one shouldn't draw conclusions."

"Of course it's a burglar," said Hugh. "Why else would one break into Guy's house?"

"There could be other...explanations. Couldn't there?"

No one answered.

Smiling, Jordan took a sip of soda water. But the whole time he felt his sister's gaze, watching him closely.

Suspiciously.

THE PHONE WAS RINGING when Clea returned to her hotel room. Before she could answer it, the ringing stopped, but she knew it would start up again. Tony must be anxious. She wasn't ready to talk to him yet. Eventually she would have to, of course, but first she needed a chance to recover from the night's near catastrophe, a chance to figure out what she should do next. What Tony should do next.

She rooted around in her suitcase and found the miniature bottle of brandy she'd picked up on the airplane. She went into the bathroom, poured out a splash into a water glass and stood sipping the drink, staring dejectedly at her reflection in the mirror. In the car she'd managed to wipe away most of the camouflage paint, but there were still smudges of it on her temples and down one side of her nose. She turned on the faucet, wet a facecloth and scrubbed away the rest of the paint.

The phone was ringing again.

Carrying her glass, she went into the bedroom and picked up the receiver. "Hello?"

"Clea?" said Tony. "What happened?"

She sank onto the bed. "I didn't get it."

"Did you get in the house?"

"Of course I got in!" Then, more softly, she said, "I was close. So close. I searched the downstairs, but it wasn't there. I'd just gotten upstairs when I was rudely interrupted."

"By Delancey?"

"No. By another burglar. Believe it or not." She managed a tired laugh. "Delancey's house seems to be quite the popular place to rob."

There was a long silence on the other end of the line. Then Tony asked a question that instantly chilled her. "Are you sure it was just a burglar? Are you sure it wasn't one of Van Weldon's men?"

At the mention of that name, Clea's fingers froze around the glass of brandy. "No," she murmured.

"It's possible, isn't it? They may have figured out what you're up to. Now *they'll* be after the Eye of Kashmir."

"They couldn't have followed me! I was so careful."

"Clea, you don't know these people—"

"The hell I don't!" she retorted. "I know *exactly* who I'm dealing with!"

After a pause Tony said softly, "I'm sorry. Of course you know. You know better than anyone. But I've had my ear to the ground. I've been hearing things."

"What things?"

"Van Weldon's got friends in London. Friends in high places."

"He has friends everywhere."

"I've also heard…" Tony's voice dropped. "They've upped the ante. You're worth a million dollars to them, Clea. Dead."

Her hands were shaking. She took a desperate gulp of brandy. At once her eyes watered, tears of rage and despair. She blinked them away.

"I think you should try the police again," Tony said.

"I'm not repeating that mistake."

"What's the alternative? Running for the rest of your life?"

"The evidence is *there*. All I have to do is get my hands on it. Then they'll *have* to believe me."

"You can't do it on your own, Clea!"

"I can do it. I'm sure I can."

"Delancey will know someone's broken in. Within twenty-four hours he'll have his house burglarproof."

"Then I'll get in some other way."

"How?"

"By walking in his front door. He has a weakness, you know. For women."

Tony groaned. "Clea, no."

"I can handle him."

"You *think* you can—"

"I'm a big girl, Tony. I can deal with a man like Delancey."

"This makes me sick. To think of you and..." He made a sound of disgust. "I'm going to the police."

Firmly Clea set down her glass. "Tony," she said. "There's no other way. I have some breathing space now. A week, maybe more before Van Weldon figures out where I am. I have to make the most of it."

"Delancey may not be so easy."

"To him I'll just be another dimwitted bimbo. A rich one, I think. That should get his attention."

"And if he gives you too much attention?"

Clea paused. The thought of actually making love to that oily Guy Delancey was enough to nauseate her. With any luck, it would never get that far.

She'd see to it it never got that far.

"I'll handle it," she said. "You just keep your ear to the ground. Find out if anything else has come up for sale. And stay out of sight."

After she'd hung up, Clea sat on the bed, thinking about the last time she'd seen Tony. It had been in Brussels. They'd both been happy, so very happy! Tony had had a brand-new wheelchair, a sporty edition, he called it, for upper-body athletes. He had just received a fabulous commission for the sale of four medieval tapestries to an Italian industrialist. Clea had been about to leave for Naples, to finalize the purchase. Together they had celebrated not just their good fortune but the fact they'd finally found their way out of the darkness of their youth. The darkness of their shared past. They'd laughed and drunk wine and talked about the men in her life, the women in his, and about the peculiar hazards of courting from a wheelchair. Then they'd parted.

What a difference a month made.

She reached for her glass and drained the last of the brandy. Then she went to her suitcase and dug around in her clothes until she found what she was looking for: the box of Miss Clairol. She stared at the model's hair on the box, wondering if perhaps she should have chosen something more subtle. No, Guy Delancey wasn't the type to go for subtle. Brazen was more his style.

And "cinnamon red" should do the trick.

"I've CHECKED THE NAME Nimrod Associates," said Richard. "There's no such security firm. At least, not in England."

The three of them were sitting on the terrace, enjoying a late breakfast. As usual, Beryl and Richard were snuggling cheek to cheek, laughing and darting amorous glances at each other. In short, behaving precisely as one would expect a newly engaged couple to behave. Some of that snuggling might be due to the unexpected chill in the air. Summer was definitely over, Jordan thought with regret. But the sun was shining, the gardens still clung stubbornly to their blossoms and a bracing breakfast on the terrace was just the thing to clear the fog of last night's champagne from his head.

Now, after two cups of coffee, Jordan's brain was finally starting to function. It wasn't just the champagne that had left him feeling muddled this morning; it was the lack of sleep. Several times in the night he'd awakened, sweating, from the same dream.

About the woman. Though her face had been obscured by darkness, her hair was a vivid halo of silvery ripples. She had reached up to him, her fingers caressing his face, her flesh hot and welcoming. As their lips had met, as his hands had slid into those silvery coils of hair, he'd felt her body move against his in that sweet and ancient dance. He'd gazed into her eyes. The eyes of a panther.

Now, by the light of morning, the symbolism of that nightmare was all too clear. Panthers. Dangerous women.

He shook off the image and poured himself another cup of coffee.

Beryl took a nibble of toast and marmalade, the whole time watching him. "Tell me, Jordie," she said. "Where did you hear about Nimrod Associates?"

"What?" Jordan glanced guiltily at his sister. "Oh, I don't know. A while ago."

"I thought it came up last night," said Richard.

Jordan reached automatically for a slice of toast. "Yes, I suppose that's when I heard it. Veronica must have mentioned the name."

Beryl was still watching him. This was the downside of being so close to one's sister; she could tell when he was being evasive.

"I notice you're rather chummy with Veronica Cairncross these days," she observed.

"Oh, well." He laughed. "We try to keep up the friendship."

"At one time, I recall, it was more than friendship."

"That was ages ago."

"Yes. Before she was married."

Jordan looked at her with feigned astonishment. "You're not thinking...good Lord, you can't possibly imagine..."

"You've been acting so *odd* lately. I'm just trying to figure out what's wrong with you."

"Nothing. There's nothing wrong with me." *Save for the fact I've recently taken up a life of crime,* he thought.

He took a sip of tepid coffee and almost choked on it when Richard said, "Look. It's the police."

An official car had turned onto Chetwynd's private road. It pulled into the gravel driveway and out stepped Constable Glenn, looking trim and snappy in uniform. He waved to the trio on the terrace.

As the policeman came up the steps, Jordan thought, *This is it, then. I'll be ignominiously hauled off to prison. My face in the papers, my name disgraced...*

"Good morning to you all," said Constable Glenn cheerily. "May I inquire if Lord Lovat's about?"

"You've just missed him," said Beryl. "Uncle Hugh's gone off to London for the week."

"Oh. Well, perhaps I should speak with you, then."

"Do sit down." Beryl smiled and indicated a chair. "Join us for some breakfast."

Oh, lovely, thought Jordan. What would she offer him next? *Tea? Coffee? My brother, the thief?*

Constable Glenn sat down and smiled primly at the cup of coffee set before him. He took a sip, careful not to let his mustache get wet. "I suppose," he said, setting his cup down, "that you know about the robbery at Mr. Delancey's residence."

"We heard about it last night," said Beryl. "Have you any leads?"

"Yes, as a matter of fact. We have a pretty good idea what we're dealing with here." Constable Glenn looked at Jordan and smiled.

Weakly, Jordan smiled back.

"A matter of excellent police work, I'm sure," said Beryl.

"Well, not exactly," admitted the constable. "More a case of carelessness on the burglar's part. You see, she dropped her stocking cap. We found it in Mr. Delancey's bedroom."

"*She?*" said Richard. "You mean the burglar's a woman?"

"We're going on that assumption, though we could be wrong. There was a very long strand of hair in the cap. Blond. It would've reached well below her—or his—shoulders. Does that sound like anyone you might know?" Again he looked at Jordan.

"No one I can think of," Jordan said quickly. "That is—there *are* some blondes in our circle of acquaintances. But not a burglar among them."

"It could be anyone. Anyone at all. It's not the first break-in we've had in this neighborhood. Three just this year. And the culprit might even be someone you know. You'd be surprised, Mr. Tavistock, what sort of misbehavior occurs, even in your social circle."

Jordan cleared his throat. "I can't imagine."

"This woman, whoever she is, is quite bold. She entered through a downstairs locked door. Got upstairs without alarming the butler. Only then did she get careless—caused a bit of a racket. That's when she was chased out."

"Was anything taken?" asked Beryl.

"Not so far as Mr. Delancey knows."

So Guy Delancey didn't report the stolen letters, thought Jordan. Or perhaps he never even noticed they were missing.

"This time she slipped up," said Constable Glenn. "But there's always the chance she'll strike again. That's what I came to warn you about. These things come in waves, you see. A certain neighborhood will be chosen. Delancey's house isn't that far from here, so Chetwynd could be in her target zone." He said it with the authority of one who had expert knowledge of the criminal mind. "A residence as grand as yours would be quite a temptation." Again he looked directly at Jordan.

Again Jordan had that sinking feeling that the good Constable

Glenn knew more than he was letting on. *Or is it just my guilty conscience?*

Constable Glenn rose and addressed Beryl. "You'll let Lord Lovat know of my concerns?"

"Of course," said Beryl. "I'm sure we'll be perfectly all right. After all, we do have a security expert on the premises." She beamed at Richard. "And he's *quite* trustworthy."

"I'll look over the household arrangements," said Richard. "We'll beef up security as necessary."

Constable Glenn nodded in satisfaction. "Good day, then. I'll let you know how things develop."

They watched the constable march smartly back to his car. As it drove away, up the tree-lined road, Richard said, "I wonder why he felt the need to warn us personally."

"As a special favor to Uncle Hugh, I'm sure," said Beryl. "Constable Glenn was employed by MI6 years ago as a 'watcher'—domestic surveillance. I think he still feels like part of the team."

"Still, I get the feeling there's something else going on."

"A woman burglar," said Beryl thoughtfully. "My, we *have* come a long way." Suddenly she burst out laughing. "Lord, what a relief to hear it's a *she!*"

"Why?" asked Richard.

"Oh, it's just too ridiculous to mention."

"Tell me, anyway."

"You see, after last night, I thought—I mean, it occurred to me that—" She laughed harder. She sat back, flush with merriment, and pressed her hand to her mouth. Between giggles she managed to choke out the words. "I thought *Jordie* might be the cat burglar!"

Richard burst out laughing, as well. Like two giddy school kids, he and Beryl collapsed against each other in a fit of the sillies.

Jordan's response was to calmly bite off a corner of his toast. Though his throat had gone dry as chalk, he managed to swallow down a mouthful of crumbs. "I fail to see the humor in all this," he said.

They only laughed harder as he bore the abuse with a look of injured dignity.

CLEA SPOTTED GUY DELANCEY walking toward the refreshment tent. It was the three-minute time-out between the third and fourth chukkers, and a general exodus was under way from the polo viewing stands. Briefly she lost sight of him in the press of people, and she felt a momentary panic that all her detective work would be for nothing. She'd made a few discreet inquiries in the village that morning, had learned that most of the local gentry would almost certainly be headed for the polo field that afternoon. Armed with that tip, she'd called Delancey's house, introduced herself as Lady So-and-So, and asked the butler if Mr. Delancey was still meeting her at the polo game as he'd promised.

The butler assured her that Mr. Delancey would be at the field.

It had taken her the past hour to track him down in the crowd. She wasn't about to lose him now.

She pressed ahead, plunging determinedly into the Savile-Row-and-silk-scarf set. The smell of the polo field, of wet grass and horseflesh, was quickly overpowered by the scent of expensive perfumes. With an air of regal assuredness—pure acting on her part—Clea swept into the green-and-white-striped tent and glanced around at the well-heeled crowd. There were dozens of tables draped in linen, silver buckets overflowing with ice and champagne, fresh-faced girls in starched aprons whisking about with trays and glasses. And the ladies—what hats they wore! What elegant vowels tripped from their tongues! Clea paused, her confidence suddenly wavering. Lord, she'd never pull this off....

She glimpsed Delancey by the bar. He was standing alone, nursing a drink. *Now or never,* she thought.

She swayed over to the counter and edged in close to Delancey. She didn't look at him, but kept her attention strictly focused on the young fellow manning the bar.

"A glass of champagne," she said.

"Champagne, coming up," said the bartender.

As she waited for the drink, she sensed Delancey's gaze. Casually she shifted around so that she was almost, but not quite, looking at him. He was indeed facing her.

The bartender slid across her drink. She took a sip and gave a weary sigh. Then she drew her fingers slowly, sensuously, through her mane of red hair.

"Been a long day, has it?"

Clea glanced sideways at Delancey. He was fashionably tanned and impeccably dressed in autumn-weight cashmere. Though tall and broad shouldered, his once striking good looks had gone soft and a bit jowly, and the hand clutching the whiskey glass had a faint tremor. *What a waste,* she thought, and smiled at him prettily.

"It has been rather a long day." She sighed, and took another sip. "Afraid I'm not very good in airplanes. And now my friends haven't shown up as promised."

"You've just flown in? From where?"

"Paris. Went on holiday for a few weeks, but decided to cut it short. Dreadfully unfriendly there."

"I was there just last month. Didn't feel welcome at all. I recommend you try Provence. Much friendlier."

"Provence? I'll keep that in mind."

He sidled closer. "You're not English, are you?"

She smiled at him coyly. "You can tell?"

"The accent—what, American?"

"My, you're quick," she said, and noted how he puffed up with the compliment. "You're right, I'm American. But I've been living in London for some time. Ever since my husband died."

"Oh." He shook his head sympathetically. "I'm so sorry."

"He was eighty-two." She sipped again, gazing at him over the rim of her glass. "It was his time."

She could read the thoughts going through his transparent little head. *Filthy rich old man, no doubt. Why else would a lovely young thing marry him? Which makes her a rich widow....*

He moved closer. "Did you say your friends were supposed to meet you here?"

"They never showed." Sighing, she gave him a helpless look. "I took the train up from London. We were supposed to drive back together. Now I suppose I'll just have to take the train home."

"There's no need to do that!" Smiling, he edged closer to her. "I know this may sound a bit forward. But if you're at loose ends,

I'd be delighted to show you 'round. It's a lovely village we have here.''

"I couldn't impose—''

"No imposition at all. I'm at loose ends myself today. Thought I'd watch a little polo, and then go off to the club. But this is a far pleasanter prospect.''

She looked him up and down, as though trying to decide if he could be trusted. "I don't even know your name,'' she protested weakly.

He thrust out his hand in greeting. "Guy Delancey. Delighted to make your acquaintance. And you are...''

"Diana,'' she said. Smiling warmly, she shook his hand. "Diana Lamb.''

CHAPTER THREE

IT WAS THREE minutes into the fourth chukker. Oliver Cairncross, mounted on his white-footed roan, swung his mallet on a dead run. The *thwock* sent the ball flying between the goalposts. Another score for the Bucking'shire Boys! Enthusiastic applause broke out in the viewing stands, and Sir Oliver responded by sweeping off his helmet and dipping his bald head in a dramatic bow.

"Just look at him," murmured Veronica. "They're like children out there, swinging their sticks at balls. Will they never grow up?"

Out on the field Sir Oliver strapped his helmet back in place and turned to wave to his wife in the stands. He frowned when he saw that she was leaning toward Jordan.

"Oh, no." Veronica sighed. "He's seen you." At once she rose to her feet, waving and beaming a smile of wifely pride. Sitting back down, she muttered, "He's so bloody suspicious."

Jordan looked at her in astonishment. "Surely he doesn't think that you and I—"

"You *are* my old chum. Naturally he wonders."

Yes, of course he does, thought Jordan. Any man married to Veronica would probably spend his lifetime in a perpetual state of doubt.

The ball was tossed. The thunder of hoofbeats, the whack of a mallet announced the resumption of play.

Veronica leaned close to Jordan. "Did you bring them?" she whispered.

"As requested." He reached into his jacket and withdrew the bundle of letters.

At once she snatched them out of his hand. "You didn't read them, did you?"

"Of course not."

"Such a gentleman!" Playfully she reached up and pinched his cheek. "You promise you won't tell anyone?"

"Not a soul. But this is absolutely the last time, Veronica. From now on, be discreet. Or better yet, honor those marriage vows."

"Oh, I will, I will!" she declared fervently. She stood and moved toward the aisle.

"Where are you going?" he called.

"To flush these down the loo, of course!" She gave him a gay wave of farewell. "I'll call you, Jordie!" As she turned to make her way up the aisle, she brushed past a broad-shouldered man. At once she halted, her gaze slanting up with interest at this new specimen of masculinity.

Jordan shook his head in disgust and turned his attention back to the polo game. Men and horses thundered past, chasing that ridiculous rubber ball across the field. Back and forth they flew, mallets swinging, a tangle of sweating men and horseflesh. Jordan had never been much of a polo fan. The few times he'd played the game he'd come away with more than his share of bruises. He didn't trust horses and horses didn't trust him and in the inevitable struggle for authority, the beasts had a seven-hundred-pound advantage.

There were still four chukkers left to go, but Jordan had had his fill. He left the viewing stands and headed for the refreshment tent.

In the shade of green-and-white-striped awning, he strolled over to the wine bar and ordered a glass of soda water. With so much celebrating this past week, he'd been waking up every morning feeling a bit pickled.

Sipping his glass of soda, Jordan wandered about looking for an unoccupied table. He spotted one off in a corner. As he approached it, he recognized the occupant of the neighboring table. It was Guy Delancey. Seated across from Delancey, her back to Jordan, was a woman with a magnificent mane of red hair. The couple seemed to be intently engaged in intimate conversation. Jordan thought it best not to disturb them. He walked straight past them and was just sitting down at the neighboring table when he caught a snatch of their dialogue.

"Just the spot to forget one's troubles," Guy was saying. "Sun.

Sugary beaches. Waiters catering to your every whim. Do consider joining me there."

The woman laughed. The sound had a throaty, hauntingly familiar ring to it. "It's rather a leap, don't you think, Guy?" she said. "I mean, we've only just met. To run off with you to the Caribbean..."

Slowly Jordan turned in his chair and stared at the woman. Lustrous cinnamon red hair framed her face, softening its angles. She had fair, almost translucent skin with a hint of rouge. Though she was not precisely beautiful, there was a hypnotic quality to those dark eyes, which slanted like a cat's above finely carved cheekbones. *Cat's eyes,* he thought. *Panther's eyes.*

It was her. It had to be her.

As though aware that someone was watching her, she raised her head and looked at Jordan. The instant their gazes met she froze. Even the rouge couldn't conceal the sudden blanching of her skin. He sat staring at her, and she at him, both of them caught in the same shock of mutual recognition.

What now? wondered Jordan. Should he warn Guy Delancey? Confront the woman on the spot? And what would he say? *Guy, old chap, this is the woman I bumped into while burgling your bedroom....*

Guy Delancey swiveled around and said cheerily, "Why, hello, Jordan! Didn't know you were right behind me."

"I...didn't want to intrude." Jordan glanced in the woman's direction. Still white-faced, she reached for her drink and took a desperate swallow.

Guy noted the direction of Jordan's gaze. "Have you two met?" he asked.

Their answer came out in a simultaneous rush.

"Yes," said Jordan.

"No," said the woman.

Guy frowned. "Aren't you two sure?"

"What he means," the woman cut in before Jordan could say a word, "is that we've *seen* each other before. Last week's auction at Sotheby's, wasn't it? But we've never actually been introduced."

She looked Jordan straight in the eye, silently daring him to contradict her.

What a brazen hussy, he thought.

"Let me properly introduce you two," said Guy. "This is Lord Lovat's nephew, Jordan Tavistock. And this—" Guy swept his hand proudly toward the woman "—is Diana Lamb."

The woman extended a slender hand across the table as Jordan turned his chair to join them. "Delighted to make your acquaintance, Mr. Tavistock."

"So you two met at Sotheby's," said Guy.

"Yes. Terribly disappointing collection," she said. "The St. Augustine estate. One would think there'd be *something* worth bidding on, but no. I didn't make a single offer." Again she looked straight at Jordan. "Did you?"

He saw the challenge in her gaze. He saw something else as well: a warning. *You spill the beans,* said those cheerful brown eyes, *and so will I.*

"Well, did you, Jordie?" asked Guy.

"No," muttered Jordan, staring fiercely at the woman. "Not a one."

At his capitulation, the woman's smile broadened to dazzling. He had to concede she'd beaten him this round; next round she'd not be so lucky. He'd have the right words ready, his strategy figured out....

"...dreadful shambles. Pitiful, really. Don't you agree?" said Guy.

Suddenly aware that he was being addressed, Jordan looked at Guy. "Pardon?"

"All the estates that have fallen on hard times. Did you know the Middletons have decided to open Greystones to public tours?"

"I hadn't heard," said Jordan.

"Lord, can you imagine how humiliating that must be? To have all those strangers tramping through one's house, snapping photos of your loo. I'd never sink so low."

"Sometimes one has no choice," said Jordan.

"Certainly one has the choice! You're not saying you'd ever let the tourists into Chetwynd, would you?"

"No, of course not."

"Neither would I let them into Underhill. Plus, there's the problem of security, something I'm acutely tuned in to after that robbery attempt last night. People may *claim* they're tourists. But what if they're really thieves, come to check the layout of the place?"

"I agree with you on that point," said Jordan, looking straight at the woman. "One can't be too careful."

The little thief didn't bat an eyelash. She merely smiled back, those brown eyes wide and innocent.

"One certainly can't," said Guy. "And that goes triply for you. When I think of the fortune in art hanging on your walls..."

"Fortune?" said the woman, her gaze narrowing.

"I wouldn't call it a fortune," Jordan said quickly.

"He's being modest," said Guy. "Chetwynd has a collection any museum would kill for."

"All of it under tight security," said Jordan. "And I mean, *extremely* tight."

The hussy laughed. "I believe you, Mr. Tavistock."

"I certainly hope you do."

"I'd like to see Chetwynd some day."

"Hang around with me, darling," said Guy, "and we might wangle an invitation."

With a last squeeze of the woman's hand, Guy rose to his feet. "I'll have the car sent 'round, how about it? If we leave now, we'll avoid the jam in the parking lot."

"I'll come with you," she offered.

"No, no. Do stay and finish your drink. I'll be back as soon as the car's ready." He turned and disappeared into the crowd.

The woman sat back down. No shrinking violet, this one; brazenly she faced Jordan. And she smiled.

FROM ACROSS the refreshment tent Charles Ogilvie spotted the woman. He knew it had to be her; there was no mistaking the hair color. "Cinnamon red" was precisely how one would describe that glorious mane of hers. A superb job, courtesy of Clairol. Ogilvie had found the discarded hair-color box in the bathroom rubbish can when he'd searched her hotel room this morning, had confirmed its effect when he'd pulled a few silky strands from her hairbrush. Miss Clea Rice, it appeared, had done another quick-change job. She was getting better at this. Twice she'd metamorphosed into a different woman. Twice he'd almost lost her.

But she wasn't good enough to shake him entirely. He still had the advantage of experience. And she had the disadvantage of not knowing what *he* looked like.

Casually he strolled a few feet along the tent perimeter, to get a better look at her profile, to confirm it was indeed Clea Rice. She'd gone heavy with the lipstick and rouge, but he still recognized those superb cheekbones, that ivory skin. He also had no trouble recognizing Guy Delancey, who had just risen to his feet and was now moving away through the crowd, leaving Clea at the table.

It was the other man he didn't recognize.

He was a blond chap, long and lean as a whippet, impeccably attired. The man slid into the chair where Delancey had been sitting and faced the Rice woman across the table. It was apparent, just by the intensity of their gazes, that they were not strangers to each other. This was troubling. Where did this blond man fit in? No mention of him had appeared in the woman's dossier, yet there they were, deep in conversation.

Ogilvie took the lens cap off his telephoto. Moving behind the wine bar, he found a convenient vantage point from which to shoot his photos, unobserved. He focused on the blond man's profile and clicked off a few shots, then took a few shots of Clea Rice, as well. A new partner? he wondered. My, she was resourceful. Three weeks of tailing the woman had left him with a grudging sense of admiration for her cleverness.

But was she clever enough to stay alive?

He reloaded his camera and began to shoot a second roll.

"I LIKE THE HAIR," said Jordan.

"Thank you," the woman answered.

"A bit flashy, though, don't you think? Attracts an awful lot of attention."

"That was the whole idea."

"Ah, I see. Guy Delancey."

She inclined her head. "Some men are *so* predictable."

"It's almost unfair, isn't it? The advantage you have over the poor dumb beasts."

"Why shouldn't I capitalize on my God-given talents?"

"I don't think you're putting those talents quite to the use He intended." Jordan sat back in his chair and returned her steady gaze. "There's no such company as Nimrod Associates. I've checked. Who are you? Is Diana Lamb your real name?"

"Is Jordan Tavistock yours?"

"Yes, and you didn't answer my question."

"Because I find you so much more interesting." She leaned forward, and he couldn't help but glance down at the deeply cut neckline of her flowered dress.

"So you own Chetwynd," she said.

He forced himself to focus on her face. "My uncle Hugh does."

"And that fabulous art collection? Also your uncle's?"

"The family's. Collected over the years."

"Collected?" She smiled. "Obviously I've underestimated you, Mr. Tavistock. Not the rank amateur I thought you were."

"What?"

"Quite the professional. A thief *and* a gentleman."

"I'm nothing of the kind!" He shot forward in his chair and inhaled such an intoxicating whiff of her perfume he felt dizzy. "The art has been in my family for generations!"

"Ah. One in a long line of professionals?"

"This is absurd—"

"Or are you the first in the family?"

Gripping the table in frustration, he counted slowly to five and let out a breath. "I am not, and have never been, a thief."

"But I saw you, remember? Rooting around in the wardrobe. You took something out—papers, I believe. So you *are* a thief."

"Not in the same sense *you* are."

"If your conscience is so clear, why didn't you go to the police?"

"Perhaps I will."

"I don't think so." She flashed him that maddening grin of triumph. "I think when it comes to thievery, *you're* the more despicable one. Because you make victims of your friends."

"Whereas you make friends of your victims?"

"Guy Delancey's not a friend."

"Astonishing how I misinterpreted that scene between you two! So what's the plan, little Miss Lamb? Seduction followed by a bit of larceny?"

"Trade secrets," she answered calmly.

"And why on earth are you so fixated on Delancey? Isn't it a bit risky to stick with the same victim?"

"Who said *he's* the victim?" She lifted the glass to her lips and took a delicate sip. He found her every movement oddly fascinating. The way her lips parted, the way the liquid slid into that moist, red mouth. He found himself swallowing as well, felt his own throat suddenly go parched.

"What is it Delancey has that you want so very badly?" he asked.

"What were those papers you took?" she countered.

"It won't work, you know."

"What won't work?"

"Trying to lump me in your category. *You're* the thief."

"And you're not?"

"What I lifted from that wardrobe has no intrinsic value. It was a personal matter."

"So is this for me," she answered tightly. "A personal matter."

Jordan frowned as a thought suddenly struck him. Guy Delancey had romanced Veronica Cairncross, and then had threatened to use her letters against her. Had he done the same to other women? Was Diana Lamb, or someone close to her, also a victim of Guy's?

Or am I trying to talk myself out of the obvious? he thought. The obvious being, this woman was a garden-variety burglar, out for loot. She'd already proven herself adept at housebreaking. What else could she be?

Such a pity, he thought, eyeing that face with its alabaster cheeks and nut brown eyes. Sooner or later those intelligent eyes would be gazing out of a jail cell.

"Is there any way I can talk you out of this?" he asked.

"Why would you?"

"I just think it's a waste of your apparent...talents. Plus there's the matter of it being morally wrong, to boot."

"Right, wrong." She gave an unconcerned wave of her hand. "Sometimes it isn't clear which is which."

This woman was beyond reform! And the fact he knew she was a thief, knew what she had planned, made him almost as guilty if she succeeded.

Which, he decided, she would not.

He said, "I won't let you, you know. While I'm not particularly fond of Guy Delancey, I won't let him be robbed blind."

"I suppose you're going to tell him how we met?" she asked. Not a flicker of anxiety was in her eyes.

"No. But I'm going to warn him."

"Based on what evidence?"

"Suspicions."

"I'd be careful if I were you." She took another sip of her drink and placidly set the glass down. "Suspicions can go in more than one direction."

She had him there, and they both knew it. He couldn't warn Delancey without implicating himself as a thief. If Delancey chose to raise a fuss about it to the police, not only would Jordan's reputation be irreparably tarnished, Veronica's, too, would suffer.

No, he'd prefer not to take that risk.

He met Diana's calm gaze with one just as steady. "An ounce of prevention is worth a pound of cure," he said, and smiled.

"Meaning what, pray tell?"

"Meaning I plan to make it bloody difficult for you to so much as lift a teaspoon from the man and get away with it."

For the first time he saw a ripple of anxiety in her eyes. Her brightly painted red lips drew tight. "You don't understand. This is not your concern—"

"Of course it is. I plan to watch you like a hawk. I'm going to follow you and Delancey everywhere. Pop up when you least expect it. Make a royal nuisance of myself. In short, Miss Lamb, I've adopted you as my crusade. And if you make one false move, I'm going to cry wolf.'' He sat back, smiling. ''Think about it.''

She *was* thinking about it, and none too happily, judging by her expression.

''You can't do this,'' she whispered.

''I can. I have to.''

''There's too much at stake! I won't let you ruin it—''

''Ruin *what?*''

She was about to answer when a hand closed over her shoulder. She glanced up sharply at Guy Delancey, who'd just returned and now stood behind her.

''Sorry if I startled you,'' he said cheerily. ''Is everything all right?''

''Yes. Yes, everything's fine.'' Though the color had drained from her face, she still managed to smile, to flash Delancey a look of coquettish promise. ''Is the car ready?''

''Waiting at the gate, my lady.'' Guy helped her from her chair. Then he gave Jordan a careless nod of farewell. ''See you around, Jordan.''

Jordan caught a last glimpse of the woman's face, looking back at him in smothered anger. Then, with shoulders squared, she followed Delancey into the crowd.

You've been warned, Diana Lamb, thought Jordan. Now he'd see if she heeded that warning. And just in case she didn't...

Jordan pulled a handkerchief out of his jacket pocket. Gingerly he picked up the woman's champagne glass by the lower stem and peered at the smudge of ruby red lipstick. He smiled. There, crystal clear on the surface of the glass, was what he'd been looking for.

Fingerprints.

OGILVIE FINISHED SHOOTING his third roll of film and clipped the lens cap back on his telephoto. He had more than enough shots of the blond man. By tonight he'd have the images transmitted to London and, with any luck, an ID would be forthcoming. The fact Clea Rice had apparently picked up an unknown associate disturbed him, if only because he'd had no inkling of it. As far as he knew, the woman traveled alone, and always had.

He'd have to find out more about the blond chap.

The woman rose from her chair and departed with Guy Delancey. Ogilvie tucked his camera in his bag and left the tent to follow them. He kept a discreet distance, far enough back so that he would blend in with the crowd. She was an easy subject to tail, with all that red hair shimmering in the sunlight. The worst possible choice for anyone trying to avoid detection. But that was Clea Rice, always doing the unexpected.

The couple headed for the gate.

Ogilvie picked up his pace. He slipped through the gates just in time to see that head of red hair duck into a waiting Bentley.

Frantically Ogilvie glanced around the parking lot and spotted his black MG socked in three rows deep. By the time he could extricate it from that sea of Jaguars and Mercedes, Delancey and the woman could be miles away.

In frustration he watched Delancey's Bentley drive off. So much for following them; he'd have to catch up with her later. No problem. He knew which hotel she was staying at, knew that she'd paid for the next three nights in advance.

He decided to shift his efforts to the blond man.

Fifteen minutes later he spotted the man leaving through the gates. By that time Ogilvie had his car ready and waiting near the parking-lot exit. He saw the man step into a champagne gold Jaguar, and he took note of the license number. The Jaguar pulled out of the parking lot.

So did Ogilvie's MG.

His quarry led him on a long and winding route through rolling fields and trees, leaves already tinted with the fiery glow of autumn. Blueblood country, thought Ogilvie, noting the sleek horses in the pasture. Whoever *was* this fellow, anyway?

The gold Jaguar finally turned off the main road, onto a private roadway flanked by towering elms. From the main road Ogilvie could just glimpse the house that lay beyond those elms. It was magnificent, a stone-and-turret manor surrounded by acres of gardens.

He glanced at the manor name. It was mounted in bronze on the stone pillars marking the roadway entrance.

Chetwynd.

"You've come up in the world, Clea Rice," murmured Ogilvie. Then he turned the car around. It was four o'clock. He'd have just enough time to call in his report to London.

VICTOR VAN WELDON HAD HAD a bad day. The congestion in his lungs was worse, his doctors said, and it was time for the oxygen again. He thought he'd weaned himself from that green tank. But now the tank was back, hooked onto his wheelchair, and the tubes were back in his nostrils. And once again he was feeling his mortality.

What a time for Simon Trott to insist on a meeting.

Van Weldon hated to be seen in such a weak and vulnerable condition. Through the years he had prided himself on his strength. His ruthlessness. Now, to be revealed for what he was—an old and dying man—would grant Simon Trott too much of an advantage. Although Van Weldon had already named Trott his successor, he was not yet ready to hand over the company reins. *Until I draw my last breath,* he thought, *the company is mine to control.*

There was a knock on the door. Van Weldon turned his wheelchair around to face his younger associate as he walked into the room. It was apparent, by the look on Trott's face, that the news he brought was not good.

Trott, as usual, was dressed in a handsomely tailored suit that showed his athletic frame to excellent advantage. He had it all— youth, blond good looks, all the women he could possibly hope to bed. *But he does not yet have the company,* thought Van Weldon. *He is still afraid of me. Afraid of telling me this latest news.*

"What have you learned?" asked Van Weldon.

"I think I know why Clea Rice headed for England," said Trott. "There have been rumors...on the black market..." He paused and cleared his throat.

"What rumors?"

"They say an Englishman has been boasting about a secret purchase he made. He claims he recently acquired..." Trott looked down. Reluctantly he finished. "The Eye of Kashmir."

"*Our* Eye of Kashmir? That is impossible."

"That is the rumor."

"The Eye has not been placed on the market! There is no way anyone could acquire it."

"We have not inventoried the collection since it was moved. There is a possibility…"

The two men exchanged looks. And Van Weldon understood. They both understood. *We have a thief among our ranks. A traitor who has dared to go against us.*

"If Clea Rice has also heard rumors of this sale, it could be disastrous for us," said Van Weldon.

"I'm quite aware of that."

"Who is this Englishman?"

"His name is Guy Delancey. We're trying to locate his residence now."

Van Weldon nodded. He sank back in his wheelchair and for a moment let the oxygen wash through his lungs. "Find Delancey," he said softly. "I have a feeling that when you do, you will also find Clea Rice."

CHAPTER FOUR

"To new friends," said Guy as he handed Clea a glass brimming with champagne.

"To new friends," she murmured and took a sip. The champagne was excellent. It would go to her head if she wasn't careful, and now, more than ever, she needed to keep her head. Such a sticky situation! How on earth was she to case the joint while this slobbery Casanova was all over her? She'd planned to let him make only a few preliminary moves, but it was clear Delancey had far more than just a harmless flirtation in mind.

He sat down beside her on the flowered settee, close enough for her to get a good look at his face. For a man in his late forties, he was still reasonably attractive, his skin relatively unlined, his hair still jet black. But the watery eyes and the sagging jowls were testimony to a dissipated life.

He leaned closer, and she had to force herself not to pull back in repulsion as those eyes swam toward her. To her relief, he didn't kiss her—yet. The trick was to hold him off while she dragged as much information as she could out of him.

She smiled coyly. "I love your house."

"Thank you."

"And the art! Quite a collection. All originals, I take it?"

"Naturally." Guy waved proudly at the paintings on the walls. "I haunt the auction houses. At Sotheby's, if they see me coming, they rub their hands together in glee. Of course, this isn't the best of my collection."

"It isn't?"

"No, I keep the finer pieces in my London town house. That's where I do most of my entertaining. Plus, it has far better security."

Clea felt her heart sink. Darn, was that where he kept it, then?

His London town house? Then she'd wasted the week here in Buckinghamshire.

"It's a major concern of mine these days," he murmured, leaning even closer toward her. "Security."

"Against theft, you mean?" she inquired innocently.

"I mean security in general. The wolf at the door. The chill of a lonely bed." He bent toward her and pressed his sodden lips to hers. She shuddered. "I've been searching so long for the right woman," he whispered. "A soul mate..."

Do women actually fall for this line? she wondered.

"And when I looked in your eyes today—in that tent—I thought perhaps I'd found her."

Clea fought the urge to burst out laughing and managed—barely—to return his gaze with one just as steady. Just as smoldering. "But one must be careful," she murmured.

"I agree."

"Hearts are so very fragile. Especially mine."

"Yes, yes! I know." He kissed her again, more deeply. This was more than she could bear.

She pulled back, rage making her breath come hard and fast. Guy didn't seem at all disturbed by it; if anything, he took her heavy breathing as a sign of passion.

"It's too soon, too fast," she panted.

"It's the way it was meant to be."

"I'm not ready—"

"I'll *make* you ready." Without warning he grasped her breast and began to knead it vigorously like a lump of bread dough.

Clea sprang to her feet and moved away. It was either that or slug him in the mouth. At the moment she was all in favor of the latter. In a shaky voice she said, "Please, Guy. Maybe later. When we know each other better. When I feel I know *you*. As a person, I mean."

"A person?" He shook his head in frustration. "What, exactly, do you need to know?"

"Just the small things that tell me about you. For instance..." She turned and gestured to the paintings. "I know you collect art. But all I know is what I see on these walls. I have no idea what moves you, what appeals to you. Whether you collect other things. Besides paintings, I mean." She gave him a questioning look.

He shrugged. "I collect antique weapons."

"There now, you see?" Smiling, she came toward him. "I find that fascinating! It tells me you have a masculine streak of adventure."

"It does?" He looked pleased. "Yes, I suppose it does."

"What sort of weapons?"

"Antique swords. Pistols. A few daggers."

Her heart gave an extra thump at that last word. *Daggers.* She moved closer to him. "Ancient weaponry," she murmured, "is wonderfully erotic, I think."

"You do?"

"Yes, it—it conjures up knights in armor, ladies in castle towers." She clasped her hands and gave a visible shiver of excitement. "It gives me goose bumps just to think of it."

"I had no idea it had that effect on women," he said in wonder. With sudden enthusiasm he rose from the couch. "Come with me, my lady," he said, taking her hand. "And I'll show you a collection that'll send shivers down your spine. I've just picked up a new treasure—something I purchased on the sly from a very private source."

"You mean the black market?"

"Even more private than that."

She let him guide her into the hallway and up the stairs. *So he keeps it on the second floor,* she thought. Probably the bedroom. To think she had gotten so close to it that night.

Somewhere, a phone was ringing. Guy ignored it.

They reached the top of the stairs. He turned right, toward the east wing—the bedroom—and suddenly halted.

"Master Delancey?" called a voice. "You've a telephone call."

Guy glanced back down the stairs at the gray-haired butler who stood on the lower landing. "Take a message," he snapped.

"But it—it's—"

"Yes?"

The butler cleared his throat. "It's Lady Cairncross."

Guy winced. "What does she want?"

"She wishes to see you immediately."

"You mean *now?*"

Guy hurried down the stairs to take the receiver. From the upper landing Clea listened to the conversation below.

"Not a good time, Veronica," Guy said. "Couldn't you...look, I have other things to do right now. You're being unreasonable. No. Veronica, you mustn't! We'll talk about this some other— Hello? Hello?" He frowned at the receiver in dismay, then dropped it back in the cradle.

"Sir?" inquired the butler. "Might I be of service?"

Guy glanced up, suddenly aware of his predicament. "Yes! Yes, you'll have to see that Miss Lamb's brought home."

"Home?"

"Take her to a hotel! In the village."

"You mean—now?"

"Yes, bring the car 'round. Go!"

Guy scampered up the steps, snatched Clea by the arm and began to hustle her down to the front door. "Dreadfully sorry, darling, but something's come up. Business, you understand."

Clea planted her heels stubbornly into the carpet. "Business?"

"Yes, an emergency—client of mine—"

"Client? But I don't even know what you *do* for a living!"

"My chauffeur will find you a hotel room. I'll pick you up at five tomorrow, how about it? We'll make it an evening."

He gave her a quick kiss, then Clea was practically pushed out the front door. The car was already waiting, the chauffeur standing beside the open door. Clea had no choice but to climb in.

"I'll call you tomorrow!" yelled Guy, and waved.

As the chauffeur drove her out through the gates, Clea clutched the leather armrest in frustration. *I was so damn close, too,* she thought. He'd been about to show her the dagger. She could have had her hands on it, were it not for the phone call from that woman.

Just who the hell *was* Veronica?

VERONICA CAIRNCROSS turned from the telephone and looked inquiringly at Jordan. "Well? Do you think that call did the trick?"

"If it didn't," he said, "then your visit will."

"Oh, must I really go see him? I told you, I want nothing to do with the man."

"It's one sure way to flush that woman out of the house before she does any damage."

"There must be some other way to stop her! We could call the police—"

"And have it all come out? My late-night foray into Guy's house? Those stolen letters?" He paused. "Your affair with Delancey?"

Veronica gave a vigorous shake of her head. "We certainly can't tell them *that*."

"That's what I thought you'd say."

Resignedly, Veronica picked up her purse and started for the door. "Oh, all right. I got you into this. I suppose I owe you the favor."

"Plus, it's your civic duty," observed Jordan. "The woman's a thief. No matter what bitter feelings you have for Guy, you can't let him be robbed blind."

"Guy?" Veronica laughed. "I don't give a damn what happens to *him*. It's your lady burglar I'm thinking of. If she gets caught and talks to the police…"

"Then my reputation is mud," admitted Jordan.

Veronica nodded. "And so, I'm afraid, is mine."

CLEA KICKED OFF her high heels, tossed her purse in a chair and flung herself with a groan across the hotel bed. What a ghastly day. She hated polo, she despised Guy Delancey and she detested this red hair. All she wanted to do was go to sleep, to forget the Eye of Kashmir, to forget everything. But whenever she closed her eyes, whenever she tried to sleep, the old nightmares would return, the sights and sounds of terror so vivid she thought she was reliving it.

She fought the memories, tried to push them aside with more pleasant images. She thought of the summer of '72, when she was eight and Tony was ten, and they'd posed together for that photo that later graced Uncle Walter's mantelpiece. They'd been dressed in identical tans and bib overalls, and Tony had draped his skinny arm over her scrawny shoulder. They'd grinned at the camera like a pair of shysters in training, which they were. They had the world's best teacher, too: Uncle Walter, con man *extraordinaire,* damn his larcenous heart of gold. How was the old fellow faring in prison these days? she wondered. Uncle Walter would be up for parole soon. Maybe—just maybe—prison had changed him, the way it had changed Tony.

The way it had changed her.

Maybe Uncle Walter would walk out of those prison gates and into a straight life, sans con games and grifters.

Maybe pigs could fly.

She jerked as the phone rang. At once she reached for the receiver. "Hello?"

"Diana, darling! It's me!"

She rolled her eyes. "Hello, Guy."

"Dreadfully sorry about what happened this afternoon. Forgive me?"

"I'm thinking about it."

"My chauffeur said you're planning to stay in the village for a few days. Perhaps you'll give me a chance to make it up to you? Tomorrow night, say? Supper and a musicale at an old friend's house. And the rest of the evening at mine."

"I don't know."

"I'll show you my collection of antique weapons." His voice dropped to an intimate murmur. "Think of all those knights in shining armor. Damsels in distress…"

She sighed. "Oh, all right."

"I'll be by at five. Pick you up at the Village Inn."

"Right. See you at five." She hung up and realized she had a splitting headache. Ha! It was her just punishment for playing Mata Hari.

No, her *real* punishment would come if she actually had to bed that dissolute wretch.

Moaning, she rose to her feet and headed toward the bathroom to wash off the smell of polo ponies and the greasy touch of Guy Delancey.

DELANCEY WAS SCARCELY sober when he came to fetch her the next evening. She debated the wisdom of climbing into the car with him behind the wheel, but decided she had no choice—not if she wanted to see this through. All things considered, the dangers of riding with a tipsy driver seemed almost insignificant. Risk was a relative thing and this was the night for taking risks.

"Should be a jolly bunch tonight," said Guy, dodging traffic along the winding road. High hedgerows obscured the view of the road ahead; Clea could only hope that some car wasn't zooming toward them from the opposite direction. "I don't go for the music, really. It's more for the conversation afterward. The laughs."

And the drinks, she thought, clutching the armrest as they whizzed past a tree with inches to spare.

"Thought it'd be my chance to introduce you," said Guy. "Show you off to my friends."

"Will Veronica be there?"

He shot her a startled glance. "What?"

"Veronica. The one who called yesterday. You know, your client."

"Oh. Oh, *her.*" His laugh was patently forced. "No, she's not a music fan. I mean, she's fond of rock and roll, that sort of rubbish, but not classical music. No, she won't be there." He paused, then added under his breath, "Lord, I hope not, anyway."

Twenty minutes later his hopes were dashed when they walked into the Forresters' music room. Clea heard Guy suck in a startled breath and mutter, "I don't believe it" as a russet-haired woman approached them from across the room. She was dressed in a stunning gown of cream lawn, and around her neck hung a magnificent strand of pearls. But it wasn't the woman whom Clea focused on.

It was the woman's companion, a man who was now regarding Clea with a look of calm amusement. Or was it triumph she saw in Jordan Tavistock's sherry brown eyes?

Guy cleared his throat. "Hello, Veronica," he managed to say.

"I'd heard there was a new lady in your life."

"Yes, well…" Guy managed a weak smile.

Veronica turned her gaze to Clea, and offered an outstretched hand. "I'm Veronica Cairncross."

Clea returned the handshake. "Diana Lamb."

"We're old friends, Guy and I," Veronica explained. "*Very* old friends. And yet he does manage to surprise me sometimes."

"I surprise *you?*" Guy snorted. "Since when did you become a fan of musicales?"

"Since Jordan invited me."

"Oliver is so trusting."

"Who's Oliver?" Clea ventured to ask.

Guy laughed. "Oh, no one. Just her husband. A minor inconvenience."

"You are an *ass,*" hissed Veronica, and she turned and stalked away.

"Takes one to know one!" Guy retorted and followed her out of the room.

Jordan and Clea, equally cast adrift, looked at each other.

Jordan sighed. "Isn't love grand?"

"*Are* they in love?"

"I think it's obvious they still are."

"Is that why you brought her here? To sabotage my evening?"

Jordan picked up two glasses of white wine from a passing butler and handed a glass to Clea. "As I once said to you, Miss Lamb—or is it Miss Lamb?—I've taken on your reformation as my personal crusade. I'm going to save you from a life of crime. At least, while you're in my neighborhood."

"Territorial, aren't you?"

"Very."

"What if I gave you my solemn oath not to cut into your territory? I'll let you keep your hunting grounds."

"And you'll quietly leave the area?"

"Provided you carry out your side of the bargain."

He eyed her suspiciously. "What are you proposing?"

Clea paused, studying him, wondering what made him tick. She'd thought Jordan Tavistock attractive from the very beginning. Now she realized he was far more than just a pretty face and a pair of broad shoulders. It was what she saw in his eyes that held her interest. Intelligence. Humor. And more than a touch of determination. He might be an incompetent burglar, but he had class, he had contacts and he had an insider's familiarity with this neighborhood. By the looks of him, he was an independent, not a man who'd work for someone else. But she might be able to work *with* him.

She might even enjoy it.

She glanced around at the crowded room and motioned Jordan into a quiet corner. "Here's my proposition," she said. "I help you, you help me."

"Help you do what?"

"One itty-bitty job. Nothing, really."

"Just a small burglary?" He rolled his eyes. "Where have I heard that line before?"

"What?"

"Never mind." He sighed and took a sip of wine. "What, may I ask, would I get in return?"

"What would you like?"

His gaze focused with instant clarity on hers. And she knew by the sudden ruddiness of his cheeks that the same lascivious thought had flickered in both their brains.

"I'm not going to answer that," he said.

"Actually, I was thinking of offering up my expert advice in exchange," she said. "I think you could use it."

"Private tutelage in the art of burglary? That *is* a difficult offer to turn down."

"I won't actually help you do it, of course. But I'll give you tips."

"From personal experience?"

She smiled at him blandly over the wineglass. *Time to inflate the old résumé,* she thought. While burgling had never actually been her occupation, she did have a knack for it, and she'd rubbed shoulders with the best in the business, Uncle Walter among them. "I'm good enough to make a decent living," she said simply.

"A tempting proposition. But I'll have to decline."

"I can do wonders for your career."

"I'm not in your line of work."

"Well, what line of work *are* you in?" she blurted in frustration. There was a long silence. "I'm a gentleman," he said.

"And what else?"

"Just a gentleman."

"That's an occupation?"

"Yes." He smiled sheepishly. "Full time, as a matter of fact. Still, it leaves me enough leisure for other pursuits. Such as local crime prevention."

"All right." She sighed. "What *can* I offer you just to stay out of my way? And not pop up at inconvenient times?"

"So that you can finish the job on poor old Guy Delancey?"

"Then I'll be out of here for good. Promise."

"What does he own that's so tempting to you, anyway?"

She stared down at her wineglass, refusing to meet his gaze. No, she wouldn't tell him. She couldn't tell him. For one thing, she didn't trust him. If he heard about the Eye of Kashmir, he might want it for himself, and then where would that leave her? No evidence, no proof. She'd be left twisting in the wind.

And Victor Van Weldon would go unpunished.

"It must be quite a valuable item," he said.

"No, its value is rather more…" She hesitated, searching for a believable note. "Sentimental."

He frowned. "I don't understand."

"Guy has something that belongs to my family. Something that's been ours for generations. It was stolen from us a month ago. We want it back."

"If it's stolen property, why not go to the police?"

"Delancey knew it was hot when he purchased it. You think he'd admit to its ownership?"

"So you're going to steal it back?"

"I haven't any choice." Meekly she met his gaze, and she saw a flicker of uncertainty in his eyes. Just a flicker. Was he actually buying this story? She was surprised how rotten that made her feel. She'd been telling a lot of lies lately, had justified each and every one of them by reminding herself this was what she had to do to stay alive. But lying to Jordan Tavistock felt somehow, well…*criminal.* Which made no sense at all, because that's exactly what *he* was. A thief and a gentleman, she thought, gazing up at him. He had the most penetrating brown eyes she'd ever seen. A face made up of intriguing angles. And a smile that could make her knees weak.

In wonder she glanced down at her drink. What was *in* this wine, anyway? The room was starting to feel warm and she was having trouble catching her breath.

The return of Guy Delancey was like an unwelcome slap of cold air. "It's starting," said Guy.

"What is?" murmured Clea.

"The music. Come on, let's sit down."

She focused at last on Guy and saw that he was looking positively grim. "What about Veronica?"

"Don't mention the name to me," he growled.

Now Veronica entered the room, and she came toward them, her gaze pointedly avoiding Guy. "Jordie, *darling,*" she purred, snatching Jordan's arm with ruthless possession. "Let's sit down, shall we?"

With a look of resignation, Jordan allowed himself to be led away to the performance room.

The musicians, a visiting string quartet from London, were already tuning up, and the audience was settled in their seats. Clea and Guy sat on the opposite end of the room from Jordan and Veronica, but the two couples might as well have been seated side by side, for all the barbed looks flying between Guy and Veronica. All during the performance Clea could almost hear the zing of arrows soaring back and forth.

Dvorak was followed by Bartok, Quartet no. 6, and then Debussy. Through it all, Clea was busy plotting out the evening, wondering how close she could get to the Eye of Kashmir. Hoping that this would be the last evening she'd have to put up with Guy Delancey, with the lies, and with this hideous red hair. She scarcely heard the music. It was only when applause broke out that she realized the program had come to an end.

Refreshments followed, an elegant display of cakes and canapés and wine. A lot of wine. Guy, who'd been barely on the edge of sobriety when he entered the house, now proceeded to drink himself into outright intoxication. It was Veronica's presence that did it.

The sight of a lost love flirting with her new escort was just too much for Guy.

Clea watched him reach for yet another glass of wine and decided that things had gone far enough. But how to stop him without making a scene? He was already talking too loudly, laughing too heartily.

That's when Jordan stepped in. She hadn't asked him to, but she'd seen him frowning at Guy, counting the glasses of wine he'd consumed. Now he slipped in beside Guy and said quietly, "Perhaps you should slow down a bit, chap?"

"Slow down what?" demanded Guy.

"That's your sixth, I believe. And you'll be driving the lady home."

"I can handle it."

"Come on, Delancey," Jordan urged. "A little self-control."

"Self-*control?* Who the hell're you to be talking about self-control?" Guy's voice had risen to a bellow, and all around them, conversations ceased. "You take up with another man's wife and you point at *me?*"

"No one's taken up with anyone's wife—"

"At least when I did it, I had the decency to be discreet about it!"

Veronica gave a startled gasp of dismay and ran out of the room.

"Coward!" Guy yelled after her.

"Delancey, please," murmured Jordan. "This isn't the time or place—"

"Veronica!" Guy broke away and pushed his way toward the door. "Why don't you face the bloody music for once! Veronica!"

Jordan looked at Clea. "He's pickled. You can't drive home with him tonight."

"I'll handle him."

"Well, take his keys, at least. Insist on driving yourself."

That was exactly what she'd planned to do. But when she followed Guy outside, she found that he and Veronica were still wrangling away, and loudly, too. Guy was so drunk he was weaving, barely able to stay on his feet. Lying bitch, he kept saying, couldn't trust her, could never trust her. She'd rip your heart in pieces, that's what she'd do, damn her, and he didn't need that. He could find another woman with just the snap of his fingers.

"Then why don't you?" Veronica lashed back.

"I will! I have." Guy swiveled around and focused, bleary-eyed, on Clea. He grabbed her hand. "Come on, let's go!"

"Not in your condition," Clea said, pulling back.

"There's nothing wrong with my condition!"

"Give me the car keys, Guy."

"I can drive."

"No, you can't." She pulled out of his grasp. "Give me the keys."

In disgust he waved her off. "Go on, then. Find your own way home! To hell with both of you! To hell with women!" He stumbled away to his car. With difficulty he managed to open the door and climb in.

"Bloody idiot," muttered Veronica. "He's going to get himself killed."

She's right, thought Clea. She ran to Guy's car and yanked open the door. "Come on, get out."

"Go away."

"You're not driving. I am."

"Go away!"

Clea grabbed his arm. "I'll take you home. You get into the back seat and lie down."

"I don't take orders from any bloody *woman!*" he roared and viciously shoved her away.

Tottering on high heels, Clea stumbled backward and landed in the shrubbery. Stupid man, he was too damn drunk to listen to reason. Even as she struggled to disentangle her necklace from the branches, she could hear him cranking the engine, could hear him muttering about parasitic women. He cursed and slapped the steering wheel as the motor died. Again he cranked the ignition. Just as Clea managed to free her necklace from the shrub, just as she started to sit up, the car's engine roared to life. Without even a farewell glance at her, Guy pulled away.

Idiot, she thought, and rose to her feet.

The explosion slammed her backward. She flew clear over the

shrub and landed flat on her back under a tree. She was too stunned to feel the pain of the impact. What she registered first were the sounds: the screams and shouts, the clatter of flying metal hitting the road and then the crackle of flames. Still she felt no pain, just a vague awareness that it was surely to come. She got to her knees and began to crawl like a baby—toward what, she didn't know. Just away from the tree, from the damn bushes. Her brain was starting to work now and it was telling her things she didn't want to know. Her head was starting to hurt, too. Pain and awareness in a simultaneous rush. She thought she was crying, but she wasn't sure; she couldn't even hear her own voice through the roar of noises. She couldn't tell if the warmth streaming down her cheek was blood or tears or both. She kept crawling, thinking, *I'm dead if I don't get away. I'm dead.*

A pair of shoes stood in her way. She looked up and saw a man staring down at her. A man who seemed vaguely familiar, only she couldn't quite figure out why.

He smiled and said, "Let me get you to a hospital."

"No—"

"Come on, you're hurt." He grabbed her arm. "You need to see a doctor."

"No!"

Suddenly the man's hand evaporated and he was gone.

Clea huddled on the ground, the night twirling around her in a carousel of flames and darkness. She heard another voice now—this one familiar. Hands grasped her by the shoulders.

"Diana? *Diana?*"

Why was he calling her that? It wasn't her name. She squinted up into the face of Jordan Tavistock.

And she fainted.

CHAPTER FIVE

THE DOCTOR switched off the ophthalmoscope and turned on the hospital room light. "Everything appears neurologically intact. But she has had a concussion, and that brief loss of consciousness concerns me. I recommend at least one night in hospital. For observation."

Jordan looked at the pitiful creature lying in bed. Her red hair was tangled with grass and leaves, and her face was caked with dried blood. He said, "I wholeheartedly agree, Doctor."

"Very good. I don't expect there'll be any problems, but we'll watch for danger signs. In the meantime, we'll keep her comfortable and—"

"I can't stay," the woman said.

"Of course you're staying," said Jordan.

"No, I have to get out of here!" She sat up and swung her legs over the side of the bed.

Jordan quickly moved to restrain her. "What the blazes are you doing, Diana?"

"Have to… Have to…" She paused, obviously dizzy, and gave her head a shake.

"You can't leave. Not after a concussion. Now then, let's get back into bed, all right?" Gently but firmly he urged her back under the covers. That attempt to sit up had drained all the color from her face. She seemed as fragile as tissue paper, and so insubstantial she might float away without the weight of the blankets to hold her down. Yet her eyes were bright and alive and feverish with…what? Fear? Grief? Surely she didn't harbor any real feelings for Guy Delancey?

"I'll have a nurse in to help you straightaway," said the doctor. "You just rest, Miss Lamb. Everything will be fine."

Jordan gave her hand a squeeze. It felt like a lump of ice in his grasp. Then, reluctantly, he followed the doctor out of the room.

Down the hall, out of the woman's earshot, Jordan asked, "What about Mr. Delancey? Do you know his condition?"

"Still in surgery. You'd have to inquire upstairs. I'm afraid it doesn't sound hopeful."

"I'm surprised he's alive at all, considering the force of that blast."

"You really think it was a bomb?"

"I'm sure it was."

The doctor glanced at the nurses' station, where a policeman stood waiting for a chance to question the woman. Two cops had grilled her already, and they hadn't been very considerate of her condition. The doctor shook his head. "God, what's the world coming to? Terrorist bombs going off in *our* corner of the world now...."

Terrorists? thought Jordan. Yes, of course it *would* be blamed on some shadowy villain, some ill-defined evil. Who but a terrorist would plant a bomb in a gentleman's car? It was a miracle that only one person had been seriously hurt tonight. A half dozen other musicale guests had suffered minor injuries—glass cuts, abrasions—and the police were calling this a lucky escape.

For everyone but Delancey.

Jordan rode the lift upstairs to the surgical floor. The waiting room was aswarm with police, none of whom would tell him a thing. He hung around for a while, hoping to hear some news, any news, but all he could learn was that Delancey was still alive and on the operating table. As for whether he would live, that was a matter for God and the surgeons.

He returned to the woman's floor. The policeman was still standing in the nurses' station, sipping coffee and chatting up the pretty clerk. Jordan walked right past them and opened the door to Diana's room.

Her bed was empty.

At once he felt a flicker of alarm. He crossed to the bathroom door and knocked. "Diana?" he called. There was no answer. Cautiously he opened the door and peeked inside.

She wasn't there, either, but her hospital gown was. It lay in a heap on the linoleum.

He yanked open the closet door. The shelves were empty; the woman's street clothes and purse had vanished.

What the hell are you thinking? he wondered. Why would she crawl out of her hospital bed, get dressed and steal away like a thief into the night?

Because she is a thief, you bloody fool.

He ran out of the room and glanced up and down the hall. No sign of her. The idiot cop was still flirting with the clerk and was oblivious to anything but the buzz of his own hormones. Jordan hurried down the hall, toward the emergency stairs. If the woman was running from the police, then she'd probably avoid the lift, which opened into the lobby. She'd go for the side exit, which led straight to the parking lot.

He pushed into the stairwell. He was on the third floor. When last he'd seen Diana, she'd looked scarcely strong enough to stand, much less run down two flights of stairs. Could she make it? Was she even now lying in a dead faint on some lower landing?

Terrified of what he might find, Jordan started down the stairs.

HER HEAD WAS POUNDING mercilessly, the high heels were killing her, but she kept marching like a good soldier down the road. That was how she managed to keep going, left-right-left, some inner drill sergeant screaming commands in her brain. Don't stop, don't stop. The enemy approaches. March or die.

And so she marched, stumbling along on her high heels, her head aching so badly she could scream. Twice she heard a car approaching and had to scramble off the road to hide in the bushes. Both times the cars passed without seeing her, and she crawled back to the road and resumed her painful march. She had only a vague plan of what came next. The nearest village couldn't be more than a few miles away. If she could just get to a train station, she could get out of Buckinghamshire. Out of England.

And then where do I go?

No, she couldn't think that far ahead. All she knew was that she'd failed miserably, that there'd be no more chances and that she was at the very top of Van Weldon's hit list. With new desperation she pushed on, but her feet didn't seem to be working, and the road was weaving before her eyes. *Can't stop,* she thought. *Have to keep going.* But shadows were puddling her vision now, creeping in from the sides. Suddenly nauseated, she dropped to her knees and lowered her head, waiting for the dizziness to pass. Crouching there in the darkness, she vaguely sensed the vibrations through the asphalt. Little by little the sound penetrated the fog clouding her brain.

It was a car, approaching from behind.

Her gaze shot back up the road and she saw the headlights gliding toward her. With a spurt of panic she stumbled to her feet, ready to dash into the bushes, but the dizziness at once assailed her. The headlights danced, blurred into a haze. She discovered she was on her knees, and that the asphalt was biting into her palms. The slam of a car door, the hurried crunch of shoes over gravel told her it was too late. She'd been spotted.

"No," she said as arms closed around her body. "Please, no!"

"It's all right—"

"*No!*" she screamed. Or thought she had. Her face was wedged against someone's chest, and her cry came out no louder than a strangled whisper. She began to flail at her captor, her fists connecting with his back, his shoulders. The arms only closed in tighter.

"Stop it, Diana! I won't hurt you. *Stop it!*"

Sobbing, she raised her head, and through a mist of tears and confusion she saw Jordan gazing down at her. Her fists melted as her hands reached out to clutch at his jacket. The wool felt so warm, so substantial. Like the man. They stared at each other, her face upturned to his, her body feeling numb and weightless in his arms.

All at once his mouth was on hers, and the numbness gave way to a flood of glorious sensations. With that one kiss he offered his warmth, his strength, and she drank from it, felt its nourishment revive her battered soul. She wanted more, more, and she returned his kiss with the desperate need of a woman who's finally found, in a man's arms, what she'd long been seeking. Not desire, not passion, but comfort. Protection. She clung to him, relinquishing all control of her fate to the only man who'd ever made her feel safe.

Neither of them heard the sound of the approaching car.

It was the distant glare of headlights that forced them to pull apart. Clea turned to look up the road and registered the twin lights burning closer. Instantly she panicked. She jerked out of Jordan's arms and plunged headlong into the bushes.

"Wait!" called Jordan. "Diana?"

Blindly she thrashed through the branches, desperate to flee, but her legs still weren't working right. She heard Jordan right behind her, his footsteps snapping across twigs as he ran to catch up. He snagged her arm.

"Diana—"

"They'll see me!"

"Who?"

"Let me go!"

On the road, the car braked to a stop. They heard the door swing open. At once Clea dropped to the ground and cowered in the shadows.

"Halloa!" called a man's voice. "Everything all right?"

Please, Jordan, Clea prayed. *Cover for me! Don't tell him I'm here....*

There was a pause, then she heard Jordan call back, "Everything's fine!"

"Saw your car had pulled off. Just wanted to check," said the man.

"I'm, er..." Jordan gave a convincingly sheepish laugh. "Answering the call of nature."

"Oh. Well. Carry on, then." The car door slammed shut, and the taillights glided away down the road.

Clea, still shaking, gave a sob of relief. "Thank you," she whispered.

For a moment he stood watching her in silence. Then he reached down and pulled her to her feet. She swayed unsteadily against him.

"Come on," he said gently. "I'll take you back to the hospital."

"No."

"Now see here, Diana. You're in no condition to be wandering around at night."

"I can't go back."

"What are you afraid of, anyway? The police?"

"Just let me *go!*"

"They won't arrest you. You haven't done anything." He paused. Softly he asked, "Have you?"

She wrenched herself free. That one effort cost her what little strength she had left. Suddenly her head was swimming and the darkness seemed to whirl around her like black water. She didn't remember sinking to the ground, didn't remember how she got into his arms, but suddenly she was there, and he was carrying her to the car. She was too tired to struggle, too weak to care anymore what happened to her. She was thrust into the front seat, where she sagged with her head against the door, trying not to faint, fighting the nausea that was beginning to roil her stomach again. *Can't throw up in this nice car,* she thought. *What a shame it would be to ruin his leather upholstery.* She vaguely registered the fact that he was sitting beside her, that the car was now moving. That was enough to nudge fear back into her addled brain.

She reached for his arm, her fingers clutching at his jacket sleeve. "Please," she begged. "Don't take me back to the hospital."

"Relax. I won't force you to go back."

She struggled to focus. Through the darkness of the car, she saw his profile, lean and tense as he stared ahead at the road.

"If you insist, I'll take you to your hotel," he offered. "But you need someone to look after you."

"I can't go there, either."

He frowned at her. Her fear, her desperation, must have registered on her face. "All right, Diana." He sighed. "Just tell me where you want to go."

"The train station."

He shook his head. "You're in no condition to travel."

"I can do it."

"You can scarcely stand up on your own two feet!"

"I have no choice!" she cried. Then, with a desperate sob, she whispered, "I have no choice."

He studied her in silence. "You're not getting on the train," he said at last. "I won't allow it."

"Won't *allow* it?" Sudden rage made her raise her head in defiance. "You have no right. You don't have any idea what I'm facing—"

"Listen to me! I'm taking you to a safe place. You have to trust me on this." He looked at her, a gaze so direct it defied her not to believe him. How simple it would be to hand over her fate to this man, and hope for the best. She wanted to trust him. She *did* trust him. Which meant it was all over for her, because no one who made a mistake that stupid would live long enough to regret it.

I don't have a choice, she thought as another wave of dizziness sent her head lolling to her knees. She might as well wave the white flag. Her future was now out of her hands.

And firmly in the grasp of Jordan Tavistock.

"How is she doing?" asked Richard.

Drained and exhausted, Jordan joined Richard in the library and poured himself a generous shot of brandy. "Obviously scared out of her wits," he said. "But otherwise she seems all right. Beryl's putting her to bed now. Maybe we'll get more out of her in the morning." He drained the brandy in a few gulps, then proceeded to pour himself a well-deserved second shot. He could feel Richard's doubtful gaze on him as he took another sip and sank into the easy chair by the fireplace. Sobriety was normally one of Jordan's virtues. It was unlike him to guzzle a triple brandy in one sitting.

It was certainly not like him to drag home stray females.

Yet that's exactly what he had upstairs at this moment, bundled away in the guest bedroom. Thank God Beryl hadn't bombarded him right off with questions. His sister was good that way; in a crisis she simply did what needed to be done. For the moment the bruised little waif would be well taken care of.

Questions, however, were sure to follow, and Jordan didn't know how to answer them because he himself didn't have the answers. He didn't even know why he'd brought Diana home. All he knew was that she was terrified, and that he couldn't turn his back on her. For some insane reason he felt responsible for the woman.

Even more insane, he *wanted* to feel responsible for her.

He leaned back and rubbed his face with both hands. "What a night," he groaned.

"You've been a very busy fellow," Richard observed. "Car bombs. Runaway females. Why didn't you tell us all this was cooking?"

"I had no idea bombs *would* be going off! I thought all I was dealing with was a cat burglar. Or is it burglaress?" He gave his head a shake to clear away the pleasant fog of brandy. "Theft is one thing. But she never mentioned anything about mad bombers."

Richard moved closer. "My question is," he said quietly, "who was the intended victim?"

"What?" Jordan looked up. He had great respect for his future brother-in-law. Years of working in the intelligence business had taught Richard that one should never accept evidence at face value. One had to examine around it, under it, looking for the twists and turns that might lead to completely different conclusions. Richard was doing that now.

"The bomb was planted in Guy Delancey's car," said Richard. "It could have been a random attack. It could have been aimed specifically at Delancey. Or..."

Jordan frowned at Richard. He saw that they were both considering the same possibility. "Or the target wasn't Delancey at all," Jordan finished softly.

"She was supposed to be riding in the car with him," said Richard. "She would have been killed, as well."

"There's no doubt Diana's terrified. But she hasn't told me what she's afraid of."

"What *do* you know about the woman?"

Jordan shook his head. "All I know is her name is Diana Lamb. Other than that I can't tell you much. I'm not even sure what her real hair color is! One day she's blond, then the next day she transforms into a redhead."

"What about the fingerprints? The ones you got off her glass?"

"I had Uncle Hugh's friend run them through the Scotland Yard computer. No match. Not a surprise, really. Since I'm sure she's a Yank.''

"You *have* been busy, haven't you? Why the hell didn't you let me in on this earlier? I could've sent the fingerprints off to American authorities by now.''

"I wasn't at liberty to say a thing. I'd promised Veronica, you see.''

Richard laughed. "And a gentleman always keeps his promises.''

"Well, yes. Except under certain circumstances. Such as car bombs.'' Jordan stared at his empty brandy snifter and considered pouring another. No, better not. Just look at what drink had done to Guy Delancey. Drink and women—the sole purpose of Delancey's life. And now he lay deprived of both.

Jordan set down the glass. "Motive,'' he said. "That's what I don't know. Why would someone kill Diana?''

"Or Delancey.''

"That,'' said Jordan, "isn't too difficult to answer. God only knows how many women he's gone through in the past year. Add to that a few angry husbands, and you've probably got a slew of people who'd love to knock him off.''

"Including your friend Veronica and her husband.''

That possibility made Jordan pause. "I hardly think either one of them would ever—''

"Nevertheless, we have to consider them. Everyone's a suspect.''

The sound of footsteps made both men turn. Beryl walked into the library and frowned at her brother and her fiancé. "Who's a suspect?'' she demanded.

"Richard wants to include anyone who's had an affair with Guy Delancey,'' said Jordan.

Beryl laughed. "It'd be easier to start off with who *hasn't* had an affair with the man.'' She caught Richard's inquiring glance and she snapped, "No, I never have.''

"Did I say anything?'' asked Richard.

"I saw the look in your eye.''

"On that note,'' cut in Jordan, rising to his feet, "I think I'll make my escape. Good night all.''

"Jordan!" called Beryl. "What about Diana?"

"What about her?"

"Aren't you going to tell me what's going on?"

"No."

"Why not?"

"Because," he said wearily, "I haven't the faintest idea." He walked out of the library. He knew he owed Beryl an explanation, but he was too exhausted to repeat the story a second time. Richard would fill her in on the details.

Jordan climbed the stairs and started up the hall toward his bedroom. Halfway there, he stopped. Some compulsion made him turn around and walk, instead, to the bedroom where Diana was staying. He lingered outside the closed door, debating whether he should walk away.

He couldn't help himself; he tapped on the door. "Diana?" he called.

There was no answer. Quietly he entered the room.

A corner lamp had been left on, and the glow spilled softly over the bed, illuminating its sleeping occupant. She lay curled up on her side, her arms wrapped protectively around her chest, her hair rippling in red-gold waves across the pillow. The linen nightgown she wore was Beryl's, and a few sizes too big; the billowing sleeves almost engulfed her hands. He knew he should leave, but he found himself sinking into the chair beside the bed. There he watched her sleep and thought how very small she looked, how defenseless she truly was.

"My little thief," he murmured.

A sigh suddenly escaped her throat and she stirred awake. She looked at him with unfocused eyes, then slowly seemed to comprehend where she was.

"I'm sorry," he said, and rose from the chair. "I didn't mean to wake you. Go back to sleep." He turned to leave.

"Jordan?"

He glanced back at her. She seemed to be lost in a sea of white sheets and goose-down pillows and puffy nightgown linen, and he had the ridiculous urge to pull her out of there before she drowned.

"I...have to tell you something," she whispered.

"It can wait till tomorrow."

"No, I have to tell you now. It's not fair of me, pulling you into this. When you could get hurt."

Frowning, he moved back to the bed. "The bomb. In the car. *Was* it meant for Guy?"

"I don't know." She blinked, and he saw the sparkle of tears on her lashes. "Maybe. Or maybe it was meant for me. I can't be sure. That—that's what makes this so confusing. Not knowing if I'm the one who was supposed to die. I keep thinking…" She looked at him, her eyes full of torment. "I keep thinking it's my fault, what happened to Guy. He never really did anything wrong. I mean, not *seriously* wrong. He just got caught up in a bit of greed. But he didn't deserve…" She swallowed and looked down at the sheets. "He didn't deserve to die," she whispered.

"There's a chance he might live."

"You saw the explosion! Do you really think anyone could survive it?"

After a pause Jordan admitted, "No. To be honest, I don't think he'll survive."

They fell silent for a moment. *Had she cared at all for Delancey?* he wondered. *Or are her tears purely from guilt?* He couldn't help but feel a little guilty himself. After all, he'd invaded the man's house. He'd never really liked Delancey, had thought him laughable. But now the man was at death's door. No one, not even Guy Delancey, deserved such a terrible end.

"Why do you think *you* might have been the target?" he asked.

"Because…" She let out a deep breath. "Because it's happened before."

"Bombs?"

"No. Other things. Accidents."

"When?"

"A few weeks ago, in London, I was almost run down by a taxi."

"In London," he noted dryly, "that could happen to anyone."

"It wasn't the only time."

"You mean there was another accident?"

She nodded. "In the Underground. I was standing on the train platform. And someone pushed me."

He stared at her skeptically. "Are you positive, Diana? Isn't it more likely that someone just bumped into you?"

"Do you think I'm *stupid?*" she cried. "Wouldn't I know it if someone *pushed* me?" With a sob of frustration she buried her face in her hands.

Her unexpected outburst left him stunned. For a moment he could think of nothing to say. Then, gently, he reached for her shoulder. With that one touch, something seemed to leap between them. A longing. Through the flimsy nightgown fabric he felt the warmth of her skin, and with sudden vividness he remembered the taste of her mouth, the sweetness of her kisses earlier that night.

Ruthlessly he suppressed all those inconvenient urges now threatening to overwhelm his sense of reason. He sat beside her on the bed. "Tell me," he said. "Tell me again what happened in the Underground."

"You won't believe me."

"Give me a chance. Please."

She raised her head and looked at him, her gaze moist and uncertain. "I—I fell onto the tracks. The train was just pulling in. If it hadn't been for a man who saw me..."

"A man? Then someone pulled you out?"

She nodded. "I never even learned his name. All I remember is that he reached down and yanked me back onto the platform. I tried to thank him, but he just—just told me to be more careful. And then he was gone." She shook her head in bewilderment. "My guardian angel."

He looked into those glistening brown eyes and wondered if any of this was possible. Wondered how anyone could be cold-blooded enough to push this woman under a train.

"Why would anyone want you dead?" he asked. "Is it something you've done?"

Instantly she stiffened, as though he'd struck her. "What do you mean, is it something I've done?"

"I'm just trying to understand—"

"Do you think I deserve this somehow? That I must be guilty of something?"

"Diana, I'm not accusing you of anything. It's just that murder—attempted murder—generally involves a motive. And you haven't told me what it is."

He waited for an answer, but he realized that he'd somehow lost her. She was huddled in a self-protective embrace, as though to ward off any further attacks he might launch against her.

"Diana," he said gently, "you have to trust me."

"I don't have to trust anyone."

"It would make it easier. If I'm to help you at all—"

"You've already helped me. I can't really ask you for anything more."

"The least you can do is tell me what I've gotten involved in. If bombs are going to be blowing up around here, I'd like to know why."

She sat stubbornly huddled, not responding. In frustration he rose from the bed, paced to the door, then paced back. Damn it all, she *was* going to tell him. Even if he had to use the threat of last resort.

"If you don't tell me," he said, "I really shall have to call the police."

She looked up in astonishment and gave a disbelieving laugh. "The *police?* I'd think they're the last people you'd want to call. Considering."

"Considering what?"

"Delancey's bedroom. The minor matter of a little burglary."

Sighing, he clawed his hair back. "The time has come to set you straight on that. The truth is, I broke into Guy's house as a favor to a lady."

"What favor?"

"She'd written a few…indiscreet letters to him. She wanted the letters back."

"You're saying it was all a gentleman's errand?"

"You could call it that."

"You didn't mention any lady before."

"That's because I'd promised her I'd stay silent. For the sake of her rather tenuous marriage. But now Delancey's been hurt and

bombs are exploding. I think it's time to start telling the truth."
He gave her a pointed look. "Don't you agree?"

She thought it over for a moment. Then her gaze slid away from
his and she said, "All right. I guess it's confession time." She took
a deep breath. "I'm not a thief, either."

"Why were you in Delancey's bedroom?"

"I was doing my job. We're trying to collect evidence. An insurance fraud case."

This time Jordan burst out laughing. "You're claiming to be with
the police?"

Red faced, she looked up defiantly. "Why is that funny?"

"Which branch do you work for? The local constabulary? Scotland Yard? Interpol, perhaps?"

"I...I work for a private investigator. Not the police."

"Which investigator?"

"You wouldn't know the company."

"I see. And who, may I ask, is the subject of your investigation?"

"He's not English. His name's not important to you."

"How does Guy Delancey fit in?"

Wearily she ran her hand through her hair. In a voice drained of
emotion, she said, "A few weeks ago Guy purchased an antique
dagger known as the Eye of Kashmir. It was one of several art
pieces reportedly carried aboard the *Max Havelaar* last month. That
ship later sank off the coast of Spain. Nothing was recovered. The
man who owned the vessel—a Belgian—filed a thirty-two-million-
dollar insurance claim for the loss of the ship. And for the artwork.
He owned it all."

Jordan frowned. "But you say Delancey recently acquired this
dagger. When?"

"Three weeks ago. *After* the boat sank."

"Then...the dagger was never aboard the vessel."

"Obviously not. Since Delancey was able to buy it from some
private seller."

"And that's the case you're trying to build? Against the owner
of the boat? This Belgian fellow?"

She nodded. "He gets reimbursed by the insurance company for the losses. And he keeps the art to resell. It works out as a sort of double indemnity.''

"How did you know Delancey'd acquired the dagger?''

Drained, she sank back against the pillows. "People brag." She sighed. "Delancey did, anyway. He told friends about a seven-teenth-century dagger he'd bought from a private source. A dagger with a star corundum—a sapphire—mounted in the hilt. Word got around in the antiques community. From the description, we knew it was the Eye of Kashmir.''

"And that's what you were trying to steal from Delancey?''

"Not steal. Confirm its whereabouts. So it can later be confis-cated as evidence.''

Silently he mulled over this rush of new information. Or was it new fabrication? "You told me earlier tonight that you were steal-ing something once owned by your family.''

She gave a regretful shrug. "I lied.''

"Really?"

"I didn't know if I could trust you.''

"And you trust me now?''

"You've given me no reason not to." She studied his face, as though looking for some betraying sign that he was not to be trusted, that she'd made a fatal mistake. Slowly she smiled. A coy, almost seductive smile. "And you've been so awfully kind to me. A true gentleman.''

Kind? he thought with a silent groan. Was there anything that could dash a man's hopes more brutally than to be called *kind?*

"I *can* trust you," she asked, "can't I?''

He began to pace again, feeling irritated at her, at himself, at how much he wanted to believe this latest outlandish story. He'd been gazing too long into those doe eyes of hers. It was turning his brain into gullible mush. "Why not trust me?" he muttered in exasperation. "Since I've been so awfully *kind.*''

"Why are you angry? Is it because I lied to you before?''

"Shouldn't I be angry?''

"Well, yes. I suppose so. But now that I've come clean—''

"Have you?''

Her jaw squared. It made her even prettier, damn it. He could kick himself for being so susceptible to this creature.

"Yes," she said, her gaze steady. "The Belgian, the *Max Havelaar,* the dagger—it's all *completely* on the level." She paused, then added quietly, "So is the danger."

The bomb is proof enough of that, he thought.

That, and the sight of her curled up in that bed, gazing at him with those liquid brown eyes, was enough to make him accept everything she'd told him. Which meant he was either going out of his mind or he was too exhausted to think straight.

They both needed to sleep.

He knew he should simply say good-night and walk out of the room. But some irresistible compulsion made him lean down and place a kiss on her forehead. The scent of her hair, the sweetness of soap, was intoxicating.

At once he backed away. "You'll be absolutely safe here," he said.

"I believe you," she said. "And I don't know why I should."

"Of course you should. It's the solemn word of a gentleman." Smiling, he turned off the lamp and left the room.

An hour later he still lay awake in bed, thinking about what she'd told him. All that babbling about insurance fraud and undercover investigations was rubbish and he knew it. But he did believe she was in danger. That much he could see in her eyes: the fear.

He considered just how safe she was here. He knew the house was up-to-date when it came to locks and alarm systems. During the years Uncle Hugh had worked with British Intelligence, security had been a priority here at Chetwynd. The grounds had been monitored, the personnel screened, the rooms regularly swept for listening devices. But since his uncle's retirement a few months ago, those precautions had gradually fallen by the wayside. Civilians, after all, did not need the trappings of a fortress. While Chetwynd was still fairly secure, anyone determined to break in could probably find a way.

But first they'd have to learn that the woman was here.

That last thought eased Jordan's fears. No one outside this house could possibly know the woman's location. As long as that fact remained a secret, she was safe.

CHAPTER SIX

CLEA WAITED until the house had fallen completely silent before she climbed out of bed. Her head still pounded, and the floor seemed to wobble under her bare feet, but she forced herself to cross the room and crack open the door.

The hallway was deserted. At the far end a small lamp burned, casting its glow across the carpet runner. Next to the lamp was a telephone.

Noiselessly Clea crept down the hall and picked up the receiver. Shaking off a twinge of guilt, she punched in Tony's number in Brussels. All right, so it was a long-distance call. This was an emergency, and the Tavistocks could surely afford the phone bill.

Four rings and Tony answered. "Clea?"

"I'm in trouble," she whispered. "Somehow they've tracked me down."

"Where are you?"

"Safe for the moment. Tony, Delancey's been hurt. He's in a hospital, not expected to live."

"What? How..."

"A bomb went off in his car. Look, I don't think I can reach the Eye. Not for a while. There'll be hordes of police watching his house."

He didn't answer. She thought for a moment the call had been cut off. Then Tony said, "What do you plan to do?"

"I don't know." She glanced around at the sound of a creak, but saw no one. Just old house noises, she thought, her heart still hammering. She said softly, "If they found me, they could find you, too. Get out of Brussels. Go somewhere else."

"Clea, there's something I have to tell you—"

She spun around at another noise. It came from one of the bedrooms. Someone was awake! She hung up the phone and scurried away up the hall.

Back in her room she stood by the door, listening. To her relief, she heard nothing more. At least she'd had a chance to warn Tony. Now it was time to think about herself. She locked the door and wedged a chair against it for good measure. Then she climbed back into bed.

Her headache was starting to fade; perhaps by morning she'd be as good as new. In which case she'd leave Chetwynd and get the hell away before Van Weldon's people tracked her down again. She'd been lucky up till now, but luck couldn't hold, not against the sort of people she was facing. Another change of appearance was called for. A haircut and a reincarnation as a brunette. Glasses. Yes, that might do it, might allow her to slip unnoticed into the London crowd. Once she got out of England, Van Weldon might lose interest in her. She might have a chance of surviving to a ripe old age.

Might.

TONY DROPPED THE RECEIVER back in the cradle. "She hung up on me," he said, and turned to the other man. "I couldn't keep her on the line."

"It may have been long enough."

"Christ, she sounded scared out of her wits. Can't you people call this off?"

"Not yet. We don't have enough. But we're getting close."

"How do you know?"

"Because Van Weldon's getting close to her. He'll be making another move soon."

Tony watched the other man pull out a cigarette and tap it against his lighter. *Why do people do that, tap their cigarettes?* Just another annoying habit of this fellow. In the past week Tony had gotten to know Archie MacLeod's every tic, every quirk, and he was well-nigh sick of the man. If only there was some other way.

But there wasn't. MacLeod knew all about Tony's past, knew about the years he'd spent in prison. If Tony didn't cooperate, MacLeod and Interpol would have that information broadcast to every antiques buyer in Europe. They'd ruin him. Tony had no choice but to go along with this crazy scheme. And pray that Clea didn't get killed in the process.

"You let Van Weldon get too close this time," Tony observed. "Clea could've been blown up in that car."

"But she wasn't."

"Your man slipped up. Admit it!"

MacLeod exhaled a puff of cigarette smoke. "All right, so we were taken by surprise. But your cousin's alive, isn't she? We're keeping an eye on her."

Tony laughed. "You don't even know where she is!"

MacLeod's cellular phone rang. He picked it up, listened a moment, then hung up. He looked at Tony. "We know exactly where she is."

"The phone call?"

"Traced to a private residence. A Hugh Tavistock in Buckinghamshire."

Tony shook his head. "Who's that?"

"We're running the check now. In the meantime, she'll be safe. Our field man's been notified of her whereabouts."

Tony sat on the bed and clutched his head. "When Clea finds out about this, she's bloody well going to kill me."

"From what we've seen of your cousin," said MacLeod with a laugh, "she very likely will."

"THEY HAVE LOST HER," said Simon Trott.

Victor Van Weldon allowed no trace of alarm to show on his face as he received the news, but he could feel the rage tightening its grip on his chest. In a moment it would pass. In a moment he'd let his displeasure be known. But he must not lose control, not in front of Simon Trott.

"How did it happen?" asked Van Weldon, his voice icy calm.

"It happened at the hospital. She was taken there after the bombing. Somehow she slipped away from our man."

"She was injured?"

"A concussion."

"Then she can't have gotten very far. Track her down."

"They're trying to. They're afraid, though, that..."

"What?"

"She may have enlisted the help of authorities."

Again, that giant fist seemed to close around Van Weldon's chest. He paused for a moment, struggling for air, counting the seconds for the spell to pass. This was a bad one, he thought, and all because of that woman. She'd be the death of him. He took out his bottle of nitroglycerin and slipped two tablets under his tongue. Slowly the discomfort began to fade. I'm not ready to die, he thought. Not yet.

He looked at Trott. "Have we any proof she's contacted the authorities?"

"She's escaped too many times. She must be getting help. From the police. Or Interpol."

"Not Clea Rice. She'd never trust the police." He slipped the nitroglycerin bottle back in his pocket and took a deep breath. The pain was gone.

"She has been lucky, that's all," said Van Weldon. He gave a careless wave of his hand. "Her luck will run out."

SHE HAD NOT MEANT to sleep so late, but the concussion had left her groggy and the bed was so comfortable and she felt safe in this house—the safest she'd felt in weeks. By the time she finally crawled out of bed, the sun was shining straight through her window and her headache had faded to only a dull soreness.

I'm still alive, she thought in wonder.

From various parts of the house came the sounds of morning stirrings: creaking floorboards, water running through the pipes. Too late to make an escape unnoticed. She would simply have to play the guest for a few hours. Later she'd slip away, make it on foot to the village train station. How far was it, a few miles? She could do it. After all, she'd once trudged ten miles along the Spanish coast. And that was in the dead of night, while sopping wet. But then, she hadn't been wearing high heels.

She surveyed her clothes. Her dress, torn and dirt stained, was draped over a chair. Her stockings were in shreds. Her shoes, those wretched instruments of torture, sat mocking her with their three-inch spike heels. No, she'd rather go barefoot. Or perhaps in bedroom slippers? She spied a pair by the dresser, comfy-looking pink slippers edged with fluff. Wouldn't *that* blend in with the crowd?

She pulled on a silk bathrobe she found in the closet, slid her feet into the pink slippers and pulled away the chair she'd wedged against the door. Then she ventured out of the room.

The rest of the household was already up and about. She went downstairs and spied them through the French doors. They were outside, assembled around a breakfast table on the terrace. It looked like a photo straight from the pages of some stylish magazine, the iron railings traced by climbing roses, the dew-kissed autumn garden, the table with its linen and china. And the people sitting around that table! There was Beryl with her model's cheekbones and glossy black hair. There was Richard Wolf, lean and relaxed, his arm slung possessively around Beryl's shoulders.

And there was Jordan.

If last night had been a trial for him, it certainly didn't show this morning. He was looking unruffled and elegant as ever, his fair hair almost silvery in the morning light, his tweed jacket perfectly molded to his shoulders. As Clea watched them through the glass, she thought how perfect they looked, like thoroughbreds reared on bluegrass. It wasn't envy she felt, but a sense of wonder, as though she were observing some alien species. She could move among them, could even act the part, but the wrong blood would always run in her veins. Tainted blood. Like Uncle Walter's blood.

Too timid to intrude on that perfect tableau, she turned to retreat upstairs. But as she backed away from the French doors she heard Jordan call her name and she knew she'd been spotted. He was waving to her, beckoning her to join them. No chance of escape now; she'd simply have to brazen it out.

She smoothed out the silk robe, ran her fingers through her hair and stepped out onto the terrace. Only then did she remember the pink slippers. The soles made painfully distinct scuffing sounds across the flagstones.

Jordan rose and pulled out a chair for her. "I was about to check on you. Feeling better this morning?"

Uneasily she tugged the edges of the robe together. "I'm really not dressed for breakfast. My clothes are a mess and I didn't know what else—''

"Don't give it a thought. We're a casual bunch here.''

Clea glanced at Beryl, flawlessly pulled together in cashmere and jodhpurs, at Jordan in his wool tweed. A casual bunch. Right. Resignedly she sat down in the offered chair and felt like some sort of zoo specimen with fluffy pink feet. While Jordan poured her coffee and dished out a serving of eggs and sausages, she found herself focusing on his hands, on his long fingers, on the golden hairs glittering on the backs of his wrists. An aristocrat's hands, she thought, and remembered with sudden clarity the gentle strength with which those hands had reached for her in the road last night.

"Don't you care for eggs?''

She blinked at her plate. Eggs. Yes. Automatically she picked up the fork and felt all eyes watching her as she took her first bite.

"I did try to leave you some fresh clothes this morning,'' Beryl explained. "But I couldn't seem to get in your door.''

"I had a chair in front of it,'' said Clea.

"Oh.'' Beryl gave a sheepish smile, as though to say, *Well, of course. Doesn't everybody barricade their door?*

No one seemed to know how to respond, so they simply watched Clea eat. Their gazes were not unfriendly, merely...puzzled.

"It's just a habit I picked up,'' Clea said as she poured cream in her coffee. "I don't trust locks, you see. It's so easy to get past them.''

"Is it?'' said Beryl.

"Especially bedroom doors. One can bypass your typical bedroom lock in five seconds. Even the newer ones with the disk tumblers.''

"How very useful to know that,'' Beryl murmured.

Clea looked up and saw that everyone was watching her with fascination. Face flushing, she quickly dropped her gaze back to the eggs. *I'm babbling like an idiot,* she thought.

She flinched when Jordan reached for her hand.

"Diana, I've told them.''

She stared at him. "Told them? You mean...about...''

"Everything. The way we met. The attempts on your life. I *had* to tell them. If they're to help you, then they need to know it all."

"Believe me, we *do* want to help," said Beryl. "You can trust us. Every bit as much as you trust Jordie."

Clea's hands were unsteady. She dropped them to her lap. *They're asking me to trust them,* she thought in misery. *But I'm the one who hasn't been telling the truth.*

"We have resources that might prove useful," said Jordan. "Connections with Intelligence. And Richard's firm specializes in security. If you need any help at all..."

The offer was almost too tempting to resist. For weeks she'd been on her own, had hopscotched from hotel to hotel, never sure whom she could trust, or where she would go next. She was so very tired of running.

And yet she wasn't ready to put her life in anyone's hands. Not even Jordan's.

"The only favor I ask," she said quietly, "is a ride to the train station. And perhaps..." She glanced down at the pink slippers and gave a laugh. "A change of clothes?"

Beryl rose to her feet. "That I can certainly arrange." She tugged on her fiancé's arm. "Come on, Richard. Let's go rummage around in my closet."

Clea was left sitting alone with Jordan. For a moment they sat in silence. Up in the trees, doves cooed a lament to the passing of summer. The clouds drifted across the sun, tarnishing the morning to gray.

"Then you'll be leaving us," said Jordan.

"Yes." She folded her napkin and carefully laid it on the table. Though she remained focused on that small square of cream linen, she couldn't shut out her awareness of the man. She could almost feel the warmth of his gaze. All her senses were conspiring against her efforts at indifference. Last night, with that first kiss, they'd crossed some invisible threshold, had wandered into territory with no boundaries, where the possibilities seemed limitless.

That's all they are, she reminded herself. *Possibilities.* Fantasies winking in the murk of half-truths. She had told him so many lies, had changed her story so many times. She still hadn't told him the worst truth of all. Who she was, what she was.

What she had been.

Better to leave him with the fantasy, she thought. Let him assume the best about me. And not know the worst.

She looked up and found he was watching her with a gaze both puzzled and thoughtful. "Where will you go next?" he asked.

"London. It's clear I can't handle this alone. My...associates at the agency will carry on the investigation."

"And what will you do?"

She gave a shrug, a smile. "Take an easier case. Something that doesn't involve exploding cars."

"Diana, if you ever need my help—anything at all—"

Their gazes met and she saw in his eyes the offer of more than just assistance. She had to fight off the temptation to confess everything, to draw him into this dangerous mess.

She shook her head. "I have some very capable colleagues. They'll see I'm taken care of. But thanks for the offer."

He gave a curt nod of the head and said no more about it.

SEATED ON A BENCH on the train platform, a gray-suited man read his newspapers and watched the passengers gather for the twelve-fifteen to London. It was the fourth train of the day, and so far he hadn't spotted Clea Rice. The bench was occupied by three other women and a bouncy child who kept knocking at the newspaper, and the man was ready to give the brat a whack out of frustration. He'd been so sure Clea Rice would choose the train; now it looked as if she'd managed to sneak out of town some other way. Yes, she was definitely getting better at the game—a quick study at doing the unexpected. He still didn't know how she'd managed to slip away from the hospital last night. That would have been a far easier place to finish it, a private room, the patient under sedation. He had passed for a doctor once before, on a previous job. He certainly could have repeated the ruse.

A pity she hadn't cooperated.

Now he'd have to track her down again, before she vanished into the teeming masses of London.

"Other people 'ere could use the bench, y'know," said a woman.

He looked sideways and saw a steel-haired lady toting a shopping bag. "It's occupied," he said, and snapped his newspaper taut.

"Decent man'd leave it to folks wi' difficulties," said the woman.

He kept reading his newspaper, his fingers suddenly itching for the automatic in his shoulder holster. A hole right between the old biddy's eyes, that's what he'd like to do, just to shut her up. She was nattering on and on now about the dearth of gentlemen in this world, saying it to no one in particular, but loudly enough to draw the attention of people standing nearby. This was not good.

He stood, shot a poisonous look at the old hag, and surrendered his spot on the bench. She claimed it with a grunt of satisfaction. Folding up his newspaper, he wandered to the other end of the platform.

That's when he spotted Clea Rice.

She'd just emerged from the loo. She was wearing a houndstooth skirt and jacket, both a few sizes too large. Her hair was almost completely concealed by a scarf, but a few tendrils of red bangs peeked out. That, plus the way she moved—her gaze darting around, her circuitous route keeping her well away from the platform's edge—told him it was her.

This was not the place to do it.

He decided he'd let her board and would follow her onto the train. There he could keep an eye on her. Perhaps when she got off again...

He had his ticket ready. He stepped forward and joined the crowd of passengers waiting to board.

SO CLEA RICE WAS TAKING the twelve-fifteen to London. Not the wisest move she could make, thought Charles Ogilvie as he stood in line behind her at the ticket office. He'd had no trouble tailing her from Chetwynd. Jordan Tavistock's champagne gold Jaguar wasn't exactly easy to miss. If he had been able to stay on their trail, surely someone else could do it, as well.

And now the woman was about to board a train in broad daylight. Ogilvie reached the head of the line and quickly purchased his ticket. Then he followed the woman onto the platform. She vanished into the women's loo. He waited. Only as the train approached the station did she reemerge. There were about two dozen people standing on the platform, a mingling of business types and housewives, any one of whom could prove lethal. Ogilvie allowed his gaze to drift casually across the faces, trying to match one of them with a face he might have seen before.

At the far edge of the crowd he spotted someone who seemed familiar, a man in a gray suit and carrying a newspaper. His face, while not in any way distinctive, still struck a memory chord. Where had he seen him before?

The hospital. Last night, in the lobby. The man had been buying a paper from the hall newsstand.

Now he was boarding the twelve fifteen to London. Right behind Clea Rice.

A surge of adrenaline pumped through Ogilvie's veins. If something was going to happen, it'd be soon. Perhaps not here in the crowd, but on the train, or at the next stop. All it took was a gun barrel to the back of the head. Clea Rice would never see it coming.

The man in the gray suit was edging closer to the woman.

Ogilvie pushed forward. Already he had his jacket unbuttoned, his shoulder holster within easy reach. His gaze stayed focused on Mr. Gray Suit. At the first sign of attack, he'd bloody well better be ready. He was Clea Rice's only lifeline.

And there'd be no second chances.

ALMOST THERE. Almost there.

Clea clutched the ticket like a good-luck charm as she waited for the train to glide to a stop. She hung back a bit, allowing everyone else to press forward first. The memory of that incident in the London Underground was still too fresh; never again would she stand at any platform edge while a train pulled in. All it took was one push from behind. No, it was better to hang back where she could see trouble coming.

The train had pulled to a stop. Passengers were starting to board.

Clea eased into the gathering. Her headache had come throbbing back with a vengeance, and she longed for the relative privacy of a train compartment. A few more steps, and she'd be on her way back to London. To anonymity. It was the best choice, after all— to simply drop out of sight. She'd been insane to think she could match wits with Van Weldon, an opponent who'd met her every thrust with a deadlier parry, who had every reason, and every resource, to crush her. Call it surrender, but she was ready to yield. Anything to stay alive.

She was so focused on getting aboard that she didn't notice the disturbance behind her. Just as she climbed onto the first step, a hand gripped her by the arm and tugged her back onto the platform.

She spun around, every nerve instantly wired for attack, her fingers arcing to claw across her assailant's face. An instant before striking flesh, she froze.

"Jordan?" she said in astonishment.

He grabbed her wrist. "Let's get out of here."

"What are you doing?"

"I'll explain later. Come on."

"But I'm leaving—"

He tugged her away, out of the line of passengers. She tried to yank free but he caught her by the shoulders and pulled her close to him. "Listen to me," he whispered. "Someone's followed us here, from Chetwynd. You can't get on the train."

Instantly she stiffened. His breath felt hot in her hair, and her awareness of his scent, his warmth, had never been more acute. Even through the tweed jacket she could feel the thudding of his heart, the tension in his arms. Without a word she nodded, and the arms encircling her relaxed their hold. Together they turned away from the train and took a step back up the platform.

A man seemed to appear from nowhere. He materialized directly in their path, a man in a gray suit. His face was scarcely worth noting; it was the gun in his hand that drew Clea's stunned gaze.

She was already pivoting away to the left when the first shot rang out. Something slammed into her shoulder, shoving her away. Jordan. In what seemed like slow motion she caught a flash of Jordan's tweed jacket as he lunged against her, and then she was stumbling sideways, falling to her knees onto the platform. The impact of the pavement sent a shock wave straight up her spine. The pain in her head was almost blinding.

Screams erupted all around her. She scrambled back to her feet, at the same time twisting around to locate the attacker. The platform was a melee of panicked bodies scattering in every direction. Jordan still shielded her from a clear view, but over his shoulder she caught a glimpse of the gunman.

Just as he caught a glimpse of her. He raised his pistol.

The shot was like a thunderclap. Clea flinched, but she felt no pain, no impact, nothing but astonishment that she was still alive.

On the gunman's face was registered equal astonishment. He stared down at his chest, where the crimson stain of blood was rapidly blossoming across his shirt. He wobbled, dropped to his knees.

"Get out of here!" barked a voice somewhere off to the side.

Clea turned and saw a second man with a gun standing a few yards away. Frantically he waved at her to get moving.

The man in the gray suit was crawling on hands and knees now, gurgling, cursing, still refusing to drop his pistol. It took a firm push from Jordan to propel Clea forward. Suddenly her legs were working again. She began to run along the edge of the platform, every pounding footstep like another nail being driven into her aching head. She could hear Jordan right behind her, could hear the shouts of confusion echoing in their wake. They reached the rear of the train, leapt off onto the tracks and dashed across to the opposite platform.

Clea scrambled up first. Jordan seemed to be lagging behind. She paused to grab his hand and haul him up from the tracks.

"Don't wait for me," he gasped as they sprinted for the steps. "Just go—the parking lot—"

"I have to wait for you! You have the bloody car keys!"

The Jaguar was double-parked near the station gate. Jordan tossed Clea his keys. "You'd better drive," he said.

She didn't stop to argue. She slid in behind the wheel and threw the car into gear. They screeched out of the lot.

Farther up the road the sound of sirens drew close. The police were headed for the station, thought Clea; they weren't interested in *her*.

She was right. Two police cars sped right past them and kept going.

Clea glanced in the rearview mirror and saw that the road behind them was empty. "No one seems to be following us. I think we're all right."

"For now."

"You said we were tailed from Chetwynd. How did you know?"

"I wasn't sure at first. I kept seeing a black MG on the road behind us. Then it dropped out of sight. That's why I didn't mention it. I thought it was gone."

"But you came back to get me."

"On the way out of the gate I saw the MG again. It was pulling in to a parking space. That's when I realized..." Grimacing, he shifted in his seat. "Are you going to tell me what the hell's going on?"

"Someone just tried to kill us."

"That I think I knew. Who was the gunman?"

"You mean his name?" She shook her head. Just that movement brought the throbbing back to her skull. "No idea."

"And the other man? The one who just saved our lives?"

"I don't know his name, either. But..." She paused. "I think I've seen him before. In London. The Underground."

"Your guardian angel?"

"But this time *you* saw him. So I guess he's not an angel at all." She glanced in the mirror. Still no one following them. Breathing more easily, she thought ahead to what came next. Chetwynd?

As if he'd read her mind, he said, "We can't go back to Chetwynd. They'll be expecting that."

"*You* could go back."

"I'm not so sure."

"You're not the one they want."

"Are you going to tell me who *they* are?"

"The same people who blew up Guy Delancey's car."

"These people—are they connected with this mysterious Belgian? Or was that just another fable?"

"It's the truth. Sort of."

He groaned. "Sort of?"

She glanced sideways and she noticed that his jaw was tightly squared. *He must be as terrified as I am,* she thought.

"I think I have the right to know the whole truth," he said.

"Later. When I've carved us out some breathing space." She nudged the accelerator. The Jaguar responded with a quiet purr and a burst of speed. "Right now, I just want to get the hell out of this county. When we hit London—"

"London?" He shook his head. "You think it'll be that easy? Just cruise down the highway? If they're as dangerous as you say, they'll have the main roads covered."

And a pale gold Jaguar wasn't a car they'd be likely to miss, she realized. She'd have to ditch the Jag. And maybe the man, as well. He'd be better off without her. Trouble seemed to attach itself to her like iron filings to a magnet, and when the next crisis hit, she didn't want Jordan caught in the cross fire. She owed him that much.

"There's a turnoff coming up," he said. "Take it."

"Where does it go?"

"Back road."

"To London?"

"No. It'll take us to an inn. I know the proprietors. There's a barn where we can hide the car."

"And how do I get to London?"

"We don't. We stay put for a while and get our bearings. Then we figure out our next move."

"I say our next move is to keep going! On foot if we have to! I won't hang around this neighborhood any longer than—"

"But I'm afraid I'll have to," he murmured.

She glanced sideways again. What she saw almost made her swerve off the road in horror.

He had pulled back the edge of his jacket and was staring down at his shirt. Bright splotches of blood stained the fine linen.

CHAPTER SEVEN

"OH, MY GOD," said Clea. "Why didn't you tell me?"

"It's not serious."

"How the hell can you tell?"

"I'm still breathing, aren't I?"

"Oh, that's just *wonderful*." She spun the wheel and sent the Jag in a dizzying U-turn. "We're going to a hospital."

"No." He reached over and grabbed her hand. "They'd be on you in a flash."

"What am I supposed to do? Let you bleed to death?"

"I'm all right. I think it's stopped." He looked down again at his shirt. The stains didn't seem to be spreading. "What's the cliché? 'It's only a flesh wound'?"

"What if it isn't? What if you're bleeding internally?"

"I'll be the first to beg for help. Believe me," he added with a pained smile, "I'm truly a coward at heart."

A coward? she thought. Not this man. He was the least cowardly man she knew.

"Go to the inn," he insisted. "If this is really serious, I can call for help."

Reluctantly she made another U-turn and headed back the way they'd been going. The turnoff brought them onto a narrow road lined by hedgerows. Through gaps in the foliage she spied a patchwork of fields and stone walls. The hedgerows gave way to a graveled driveway, and they pulled up at last in front of the Munstead Inn. A cottage garden, its blossoms fading into autumn, lined the front walk.

Clea scrambled out of the car to help Jordan to his feet.

"Let me walk on my own," he said. "Best to pretend nothing's wrong."

"You might faint."

"I'd never do anything so embarrassing." Grunting, he managed to slide out of the car and stand without her assistance. He made it on his own power through the garden and up the front steps.

Their knock on the door was answered by an elderly gentleman whose peat-colored trousers hung limp on his bony frame. He peered at them through bifocals, then exclaimed in pleasure, "Why, if it isn't young Mr. Tavistock!"

Jordan smiled. "Hello, Munstead. Any rooms available?"

"For friends o' yours, anytime!" The old man stepped aside and waved them into the front hall. "Chetwynd's full up, then?" he asked. "No room for guests?"

"Actually, this room would be for me and the lady."

"You and..." Munstead turned and regarded Jordan with surprise. A sly grin spread across his face. "Ah, it's a bit of a hush thing, is it?"

"Just between us."

Munstead winked. "Gotcha, sir."

Clea didn't know how Jordan managed to hold up his end of the banter. As the old man rummaged for a key, Jordan politely inquired as to Mrs. Munstead's health, asked how the garden was this summer and were the children coming to visit at Christmas? At last they were led upstairs to the second floor. Under better circumstances Clea might have appreciated the romantic touches to the place, the flocked wallpaper, the lace curtains. Now her only focus was to get Jordan into a bed and his wound checked.

When they were safely behind closed doors, Clea practically forced Jordan down onto the mattress. He sat there, his face screwed up in discomfort, as she pulled off the tweed jacket. The droplets of blood staining his shirt led a trail under his right arm.

She unbuttoned the shirt. The blood had dried, adhering the fabric to his skin. Slowly, gently she peeled the shirt off, revealing a broad chest with tawny hair, some of it caked with blood. What she saw looked more like a slash than a bullet wound, as though a knife blade had caught him just in front of the armpit and sliced straight back along his right side.

She gave a sigh of relief. "It looks like just a graze. Caught you in passing. It could just as easily have gone straight through your chest. You're lucky."

He stared down at his wound and frowned. "Maybe it's more a case of divine intervention than luck."

"What?"

"Hand me my coat."

Perplexed, she passed him the tweed jacket. The bullet's entry was easy to locate. It cut a hole through the fabric over the right chest. Jordan reached inside the inner pocket and pulled out a handsome watch attached to a chain. Clearly stamped on the gold watch cover was an ugly dent.

"A helping hand from beyond the grave," he said, and handed Clea the watch.

She flipped open the dented cover. Inside was engraved the name Bernard Tavistock.

"My father's," said Jordan. "I inherited it on his death. It seems he's still watching out for me."

"Then you'd better keep it close by," she said, handing it back. "So it can ward off the next bullet."

"I sincerely hope there won't *be* a next bullet. This one's bloody uncomfortable as it is."

She went into the bathroom, soaked a towel in warm water and wrung it out. When she came back to the bed, he was looking almost sheepish about all the fuss. As she bent to clean the wound, their heads brushed, and she inhaled a disturbingly primal mingling of scents. Blood and sweat and after-shave. His breath warmed her hair, and that warmth seemed to seep into her cheeks. Desperately trying to ignore his effect on her, she kept her gaze focused on his wound.

"I had no idea you'd been hurt," she said softly.

"It was the first shot. I sort of stumbled into it."

"Stumbled, hell! You pushed me away, you idiot."

He laughed. "Chivalry goes unappreciated."

Without warning she planted both hands on either side of his face and lowered her mouth to his in a fierce kiss. She knew at once it was a mistake. Her stomach seemed to drop away inside her. She felt his lips press hard against hers, heard his growl of both longing and satisfaction. Before he could tug her against him, she pulled away.

"You see, you're wrong," she whispered. "Chivalry is most definitely appreciated."

"If that's my reward, I may just do it again."

"Well, don't. Once is chivalry. Twice is stupidity."

Breathing hard, she focused her attention back on his wound. She could feel him watching her, could still taste the tang of his lips on hers, but she stubbornly refused to meet his gaze. If she did, they'd only kiss again.

She wiped up the last dried flecks of blood and straightened. "How are we going to dress it?"

"I've a first aid kit in the car. Bandages and such."

"I'll get it."

"Park the car in the barn, while you're at it. Get it out of sight."

With almost a sense of relief, she fled the room and hurried down the stairs. Once outside, she felt she could breathe again, felt she was back in control.

She walked deliberately to the Jaguar, started the engine and parked it inside the barn. After fetching the first aid kit out of the trunk, she stood by the car for a moment, taking deep, calming breaths of hay-scented air. At last her headache was all but gone and she could think clearly again. *Must concentrate,* she thought. *Remember what it is I'm facing. I can't afford to be distracted. Even by someone as distracting as Jordan.*

With first aid kit in hand, she returned to the room. The instant she stepped inside she felt her hard-won composure begin to crack around the edges. Jordan was standing at the window, his broad back turned to her, his gaze focused somewhere on the garden outside. She suppressed the impulse to go to him, to slide her hands down that expanse of naked skin.

"I hid the car," she said.

She thought he nodded, but he didn't answer.

After a pause she asked, "Is something wrong?"

He turned to look at her. "I called Chetwynd."

She frowned, trying to understand why, with that one call, his whole demeanor should change. "You called? Why?"

"To tell them what's happened. We're going to need help."

"It's better if they don't know. Safer if we don't—"

"Safer for whom?"

"For everyone. They might talk to the wrong people. Reveal things they shouldn't—"

She couldn't read his expression against the glare of the window. But she could hear the anger in his voice. "If I can't count on my own family, who *can* I count on?"

Stung by his tone, she sat on the bed and stared dully at the first aid kit in her lap. "I envy you your blind faith," she said softly. She opened the kit. Inside were bandages, adhesive tape, a bottle of antiseptic. "Come here. I'd better dress that wound."

He came to the bed and sat beside her. Neither of them spoke as she opened packets of gauze and snipped off lengths of tape. She heard him suck in a startled gasp of air when she dabbed on the antiseptic, but he said nothing. His silence frightened her. Something had changed between them since she'd left the room, something about that phone call to Chetwynd. She was afraid to ask about it, afraid to cut what few threads of connection still remained between them. So she said nothing, but simply finished the task, the whole time fighting off a sense of panic that she'd lost him. Or even worse, that he'd turned against her.

Her worst suspicions seemed confirmed when he said, as she was pressing the last strip of tape to his chest, "Richard's on his way."

She sat back and stared at him. "You told him where we are?"

"I had to."

"Couldn't you just say you're alive and well? Leave it at that?"

"He has something to tell me."

"He could have said everything over the phone."

"It has to be face-to-face." Jordan paused, then he added quietly, "It has to do with you."

She sat clutching the roll of tape, her gaze frozen on his face. *He knows,* she thought. She felt sick to her stomach, sick of herself and her sorry past. Whatever attraction Jordan had felt for her was obviously gone now, destroyed by some revelation gleaned from a phone call.

She swallowed and looked away. "What did he tell you?"

"Only that you haven't been entirely honest about who you are."

"And..." She cleared her throat. "How did he find out?"

"Your fingerprints."

"What fingerprints?"

"The polo field. You left them on your glass in the refreshment tent."

It took her a moment for the implications to sink in. "Then you—*you're* the one who—"

He nodded. "I picked up your glass. Your fingerprints weren't on record at Scotland Yard. So I asked Richard to check with American authorities. And they had the prints on file."

She shot to her feet and backed away from the bed. "I trusted you!"

"I never meant to hurt you."

"No, you just prowled around behind my back."

"I knew you weren't being straight with me. How else could I find out? I had to know."

"Why? What difference would it make to you?" she cried.

"I wanted to believe you. I wanted to be absolutely sure of you."

"So you set out to prove I'm a fraud."

"Is that what I've proved?"

She shook her head and laughed. "What else would I be but a fraud? It's what you looked for. It's what you expected to find."

"I don't know what I expected to find."

"Maybe that I'd be some—some princess in disguise? Instead you learn the truth. A frog instead of a princess. Oh, but you must be *so* disappointed! *I* find it disappointing that I can't ever outrun my past. No matter how hard I try, it follows me around like one of those little cartoon rain clouds over my head." She looked down at the flowered rug. For a moment she studied the pattern of its weave. Then, wearily, she sighed. "Well, I do thank you for your help. You've been more of a gentleman than any man has ever been to me. I wish...I'd hoped..." She shook her head and turned to the door.

"Where are you going?"

"It's a long walk to London. I think I'll get started."

In an instant he was on his feet and crossing toward her. "You can't go."

"I have a life to get on with."

"And how long will it last? What happens at the next train station?"

"Are you volunteering to take another bullet?"

He caught her arm and pulled her against him. As she collided with his chest, she felt her whole body turn liquid against his heat.

"I'm not sure what I'm volunteering for," he murmured. "But I think I've already signed up..."

The kiss caught them both off-balance. The instant their lips met, Clea felt herself swaying, tilting. He pressed her to the wall, his lips on hers, his body a warm and breathing barrier to escape. Their breaths were coming so loud and fast, their sighs so needy, that she didn't hear the footsteps creaking on the stairs, didn't hear them approach their room.

The knock on the door made them both jerk apart. They stared at each other, faces flushed with passion, hair equally tousled.

"Who is it?" Jordan called.

"It's me."

Jordan opened the door.

Richard Wolf stood in the hall. He glanced at Clea's reddened cheeks, then looked at Jordan's bare chest. Without comment he stepped into the room and locked the door behind him. Clea noticed he had a file folder stuffed with papers.

"You weren't followed?" asked Jordan.

"No." Richard looked at Clea, and she almost felt like slinking away, so cool was that gaze of his. *So now the truth will be spilled. He knows all, of course.* That must be what he had in that folder— the proof of her identity. Who and what she'd been. He would lay it all out for Jordan, and she wouldn't be able to deny it. And how would Jordan react? With anger, disgust?

Feeling defeated beyond words, she went to the bed and sat down. She wouldn't look at either one of the men; she didn't want to see their faces as they shared the facts about Clea Rice. She would just sit here and passively confirm it all. Then she would leave. Surely Jordan wouldn't bother to stop her this time. Surely he'd be happy to see her go.

She waited on the bed and listened as the truth was finally told. "Her name isn't Diana Lamb," said Richard. "It's Clea Rice."

Jordan looked at the woman, half expecting a protest, a denial, *some* sort of response, but she said nothing. She only sat with her shoulders hunched forward, her head drooping with what looked like profound weariness. It was almost painful to look at her. This was not at all the brash Diana—correction, Clea—he knew. But then, he'd never really known her, had he?

Richard handed the folder to Jordan. "That was faxed to me just an hour ago from Washington."

"From Niki?"

Richard nodded. Nikolai Sakaroff was his partner in Sakaroff and Wolf, Security Consultants. Formerly a colonel with the KGB and now an enthusiastic advocate of capitalism, Sakaroff had turned his talents for intelligence gathering to more profitable uses. If anyone could dig up obscure information, it was Niki.

"Her fingerprints were on file with the Massachusetts police," said Richard. "Once that fact was established, the rest of it came easy."

Jordan opened the folder. The first page he saw was a grainy reproduction of a mug shot, a frontal and two profiles. The faxing process had blurred the details, but he could still tell it was a younger version of Clea. The subject gazed unsmiling at the camera, her dark eyes wide and bewildered, her lips pressed tightly together. Her hair, free flowing about her shoulders, appeared to be blond. Jordan glanced once again at the live woman. She hadn't moved.

He turned to the next page.

"Three years ago she was convicted of harboring a felon and destruction of evidence," said Richard. "She served ten months in the Massachusetts State Penitentiary, with time off for good behavior."

Jordan turned to Clea. "Is this true?"

She gave a low and bitter laugh. "Yes. In prison I was *very* well behaved."

"And the rest of it? The conviction? The ten months served?"

"You have it all there. Why are you asking me?"

"Because I want to know if it's true."

"It's true," she whispered, and her head seemed to droop even lower. She seemed in no mood to elaborate, so Jordan turned back to Richard. "Who was the felon? The one she aided?"

"His name's Walter Rice. He's still serving time in Massachusetts."

"Rice? Is he a relative?"

"He's my uncle Walter," said Clea dully.

"What crime did this uncle Walter commit?"

"Burglary. Fraud. Trafficking in stolen goods." She shrugged. "Take your pick. Uncle Walter had a long and varied career."

"Of which Clea was a part," said Richard.

Clea's chin shot up. It was the first spark of anger she'd displayed. "That's not true!"

"No? What about your juvenile record?"

"Those were supposed to be sealed!"

"Sealed doesn't mean nonexistent. At age twelve, you were caught trying to pawn stolen jewelry. At age fourteen, you and your cousin burglarized half a dozen homes on Beacon Hill."

"I was only a child! I didn't know what I was doing!"

"What did you *think* you were doing?"

"Whatever Uncle Walter told us to do!"

"Did Uncle Walter have such power over you that you didn't know right from wrong?"

She looked away. "Uncle Walter was…he was the one I looked up to. You see, I grew up in his house. It was just the three of us. My cousin Tony and my uncle and me. I know what we did was wrong. But the burglaries—they didn't seem real to me, you know. It was more of a…a game. Uncle Walter used to dare us. He'd say, 'Who's clever enough to beat *that* house?' And we'd feel cowardly if we didn't take him up on the dare. It wasn't the money. It was never the money." She looked up. "It was the challenge."

"And what about that issue of right and wrong?"

"That's why I stopped. I was eighteen when I moved out of

Uncle Walter's house. For eight years I stayed on the straight and narrow. I swear it.''

"In the meantime, your uncle went right on robbing houses. The police say he was responsible for dozens of burglaries in Boston's wealthiest neighborhoods. Luckily, no one was ever hurt.''

"He'd never hurt anyone! Uncle Walter didn't even own a gun.''

"No, he was just a virtuous thief.''

"He swore he never took from people who couldn't afford it.''

"Of course not. He went where the money was. Like any smart burglar.''

She stared down again at her knotted hands. A convicted criminal, thought Jordan. She hardly looked the part. But she had managed to deceive him from the start, and he knew now he couldn't trust his own eyes, his own instincts. Not where she was concerned.

He refocused his attention on the file. There were a few pages of notes written in Niki Sakaroff's precise hand, dates of arrest, conviction, imprisonment. There was a copy of a news article about the career of Walter Rice, whose exploits had earned legendary status in the Boston area. As Clea had said, old Walter never actually hurt anyone. He just robbed and he did it with style. He was known as the Red Rose Thief, for his habit of always leaving behind his calling card: a single rose, his gesture of apology to the victims.

Even the most skillful thief, however, eventually meets with bad luck. In Walter's case it took the form of an alert homeowner with a loaded pistol. Caught in the act, with a bullet in his arm, Walter found himself scrambling out the window for his life.

Two days later he was arrested in his niece's apartment, where he'd sought refuge and first aid.

No wonder she did such a good job of dressing my wound, thought Jordan. *She's had practice.*

"It seems to be a Rice family trait,'' observed Richard. "Trouble with the law.''

Clea didn't refute the statement.

"What about this cousin Tony?'' asked Jordan.

"He served six years. Burglary,'' said Richard. "Niki hears through the grapevine that Tony Rice is somewhere in Europe, working as a fence in black market antiques. Am I right, Miss Rice?''

Clea looked up. ''Leave Tony out of this. He's clean now.''

''Is he the one you're working with?''

''I'm not working with anyone.''

''Then how were you planning to fence the loot?''

''What loot?''

''The items you planned to steal from Guy Delancey?''

She reacted with a look of hopeless frustration. ''Why do I bother to answer your questions?'' she said. ''You've already tried and convicted me. There's nothing left to say.''

''There's plenty left for you to say,'' said Jordan. ''Who's trying to kill you? And maybe pop me off in the process?''

''He won't bother with you, once I'm gone.''

''*Who* won't?''

''The man I told you about.'' She sighed. ''The Belgian.''

''You mean that part of the story was true?''

''Yes. Absolutely true. So was the part about the *Max Havelaar.*''

''What Belgian?'' asked Richard.

''His name is Van Weldon,'' said Clea. ''He has people working for him everywhere. Guy was just an accidental victim. *I'm* the one Van Weldon wants dead.''

There was a long silence. Richard said slowly, ''Victor Van Weldon?''

A glint of fear suddenly appeared in Clea's eyes. She was staring at Richard. ''You...know him?''

''No. I just heard the name. A short time ago, in fact.'' He was frowning at Clea, as though seeing some new aspect to her face. ''I spoke to one of the constables about the man shot at the railway station.''

''The one who tried to kill us?'' said Jordan.

Richard nodded. ''He's been identified as a George Fraser. English, with a London address. They tried to track down his next of kin, but all they came up with was the name of his employer. He's a service rep for the Van Weldon Shipping Company.''

At the mention of the company's name, Jordan saw Clea give

an involuntary shudder, as though she'd just been touched by the chill hand of evil. Nervously she rose to her feet and went to the window, where she stood hugging herself, staring out at the after-noon sunlight.

"What about the other gunman?" asked Jordan.

"No sign of him. It seems he managed to slip away."

"My guardian angel," murmured Clea. "Why?"

"You tell us," said Richard.

"I know why someone's trying to kill me. But not why anyone wants to keep me *alive*."

"Let's start with what you do know," said Jordan. He went to her, placed his hand gently on her shoulder. She felt so small, so insubstantial to his touch. "Why does Victor Van Weldon want you dead?"

"Because I know what happened to the *Max Havelaar*."

"Why it sank, you mean?"

She nodded. "There was nothing valuable aboard that boat. Those insurance claims were false. And the crew was considered expendable."

"How do you know all this?"

"Because I was there." She turned and looked at him, her eyes haunted by some vision of horror only she could see. "I was aboard the *Max Havelaar* the night it went down."

CHAPTER EIGHT

"IT WAS MY FIRST trip to Naples," she said. "My first year ever in Europe. I was desperate to escape all those bad memories from prison. So when Tony wrote, inviting me to Brussels, I leapt at the chance."

"That's your cousin?" asked Richard.

Clea nodded. "He's been in a wheelchair since his accident on the autobahn last year. He needed someone he could trust to serve as his business representative. Someone who'd round up buyers for the antiques he sells. It's a completely legitimate business. Tony's no longer dealing in the black market."

"And that's why you were in Naples? On your cousin's behalf?"

"Yes. And that's where I met my two Italian sailors." She looked away again, out the window. "Carlo and Giovanni..."

They were the first mate and navigator aboard a boat docked in the harbor. Both men had liquid brown eyes and ridiculously long lashes and a penchant for innocent mischief. Both adored blondes. And although they'd flirted and made eyes at her, Clea had known on some instinctive level that they were absolutely harmless. Besides, Giovanni was a good friend of Tony's, and in Italy the bond of trust between male friends overrode even the Italian's finely honed mating instinct. Much as they might be tempted, neither man would dream of crossing the line with Clea.

"We spent seven evenings together, the three of us," murmured Clea. "Eating in cafés. Splashing in fountains. They were so sweet to me. So polite." She gave a soft laugh. "I thought of them as younger brothers. And when they came up with this wild idea of taking me to Brussels aboard their ship, I never thought to be afraid."

"You mean as a passenger?" asked Jordan.

"More as an honored stowaway. It was a little escapade we

hatched over Campari and pasta. Their ship was sailing in a few days, and they thought, wouldn't it be fun if I came along? Their captain had no objections, as long as I stayed below and out of sight until they left the harbor. He didn't want any flack from the ship's owner. I could come out on deck once we were at sea. And in Brussels they'd sneak me off again.''

"You trusted them?"

"Yes. It sounds crazy now, but I did. They were so...harmless.'' Clea smiled at the memory. "Maybe it was all that Campari. Maybe I was just hungry for a bit of adventure. We had it all planned out, you see. The wine we'd bring aboard. The meals I'd whip up for everyone. They told me it was a large boat, and the only cargo was a few crates of artwork bound for an auction house in Brussels. There'd be plenty of room for a crew of eight. And me.

"So that night I was brought aboard. While the men got ready to leave, I waited below in the cargo hold. Giovanni brought me hot tea and chocolate biscuits. He was such a nice boy...."

"It was the *Max Havelaar* you boarded?" asked Richard softly.

She swallowed. "Yes. It was the *Max Havelaar*." She took a deep breath, mustering the strength to continue. "She was an old boat. Everything was rusted. Everything seemed to creak. I thought it odd that a vessel that large would carry as its only cargo a few crates of artwork.

"I saw a manifest sheet hanging on one of the crates in the hold. I looked it over. And that's when I realized there was a fortune's worth of antique art in those crates.''

"Was the owner listed?"

"Yes. It was the Van Weldon company. They were the shipping agent, as well."

"What did you do then?"

"I was curious, of course. I wanted to take a peek, but all the crates were nailed shut. I looked around for a bit, and finally found a knothole in one of the boards. It was big enough to shine a penlight through. What I saw inside didn't make sense.''

"What was there?"

"Stones. The bottom of the crate was lined with stones."

She turned from the window. The two men were staring at her in bewilderment. No wonder. She, too, had been just as bewildered.

"Did you speak to the crew about this?" asked Richard.

"I waited until we'd left the dock. Then I found Giovanni. I asked him if he realized they were carrying crates of rocks. He only laughed. Said I must be seeing things. He'd been told the crates were valuable. He'd seen them loaded aboard himself."

"Who loaded them?"

"The Van Weldon company. They came in a truck directly from their warehouse."

"What did you do then?"

"I insisted we speak to Vicenzo. The captain. He laughed at me, too. Why would a company ship rocks, he kept asking me. And he had other concerns at the time. The southern coast of Sardinia was coming up, and he had to keep a watch out for other ships. He told me he'd check the cargo later.

"It wasn't until we'd passed Sardinia that I was able to drag them below decks to look. They finally pried open one of the crates. There was a layer of wood shavings on top. Typical packing material. I told them to keep digging. They went through the shavings, then through a layer of newspapers. They kept going deeper and deeper, expecting to find the artwork that was on the manifest. All they found were stones."

"The captain must have believed you then?"

"Of course. He had no choice. He decided to radio Naples, to find out what was going on. So we climbed up the steps to the bridge. Just as we got there, the engine room exploded."

Richard and Jordan said nothing. They only watched her in grim silence as she told them about the last moments of the *Max Havelaar*.

In the panic that followed the explosion, as Giovanni radioed his last SOS, as the crew—what remained of the crew—scrambled to lower the lifeboat, the rocks in the cargo hold were forgotten. Survival was all that mattered. The flames were spreading rapidly; the *Max Havelaar* would be a floating inferno.

They lowered the lifeboat onto the swells. There was no time to climb down the ladder; with the flames licking at their backs, they leapt into the dark Mediterranean.

"The water was so cold," she said. "When I surfaced, I could see the *Havelaar* was all in flames. The lifeboat was drifting about a dozen yards away. Carlo and the second mate had already managed to crawl in, and they were leaning over the gunwale, trying to haul aboard Vicenzo. Giovanni was still in the water, struggling just to keep his head up.

"I've always been a strong swimmer. I can stay afloat for hours if I have to. So I yelled to the men that they should get the others to climb aboard first. And I treaded water...." She'd felt strangely calm, she remembered. Almost detached from the crisis. Perhaps it was the rhythmic motion of her limbs stroking the liquid darkness. Perhaps it was the sense of dreamlike unreality. She hadn't been afraid. Not yet.

"I knew the Spanish coast was only two miles or so to the north. By morning we could've paddled the lifeboat to land. Finally, all the men were hauled aboard. I was the only one left in the water. I swam over to the lifeboat and had just reached up for a hand when we all heard the sound of an engine."

"Another boat?" asked Jordan.

"Yes. A speedboat of some kind. Suddenly the men all were shouting, waving like crazy. The lifeboat was rocking back and forth. I was behind the gunwale and couldn't see the other boat as it came toward us. They had a searchlight. And I heard a voice calling to us in English. Some sort of accent—I'm not sure what kind. He identified their boat as the *Cosima*.

"Giovanni reached down to help me climb aboard. He'd just grabbed my hand when..." She paused. "When the *Cosima* began to fire on us."

"On the *lifeboat?*" asked Jordan, appalled.

"At first I didn't understand what was happening. I could hear the men crying out. And my hand slid away from Giovanni's. I saw that he was crumpled against the gunwale, staring down at me. I didn't understand that the sound was gunfire. Until a body fell into the water. It was Vicenzo's," she whispered, and looked away.

"How did you escape?" asked Jordan, gently.

Clea took an unsteady breath. "I dove," she said softly. "I swam underwater as far as my lungs would carry me. As fast as I could stroke away from that searchlight. I came up for air, then dove again and kept swimming. I thought I heard bullets hitting the water around me, but *Cosima* didn't chase after me. I just kept swimming and swimming. All night. Until I reached the coast of Spain."

She stood for a moment with bowed head. Neither man spoke. Neither man broke the silence.

"They killed them all," she whispered. "Giovanni. The captain. Six helpless men in a lifeboat. They never knew there was a witness."

Jordan and Richard stood watching her. They were both too shocked by her story to say a word. She didn't know if they believed any of it; all she knew was that it felt good to finally tell it, to share the burden of horror.

"I reached the coast around dawn," she continued. "I was cold. Exhausted. But mostly I was desperate to reach the police." She shook her head. "That was my mistake, of course. Going to the police."

"Why?" asked Jordan gently.

"I ended up in some village police station, trying to explain what had happened. They made me wait in a back room while they checked the story. It turns out they called the Van Weldon company, to confirm their boat was missing. It made sense, I suppose. I can't blame the police for checking. So I waited three hours in that room for some representative from Van Weldon to arrive. Finally he did. I heard his voice through the door. I recognized it." She trembled at the memory. "It was the voice from the *Cosima*."

"You mean the killers were working for Van Weldon?" said Jordan.

Clea nodded. "I was climbing out that window so fast I must have left scorch marks. I've been running ever since. I found out later that *Cosima*'s registered owner is the Van Weldon Shipping Company. They sabotaged the *Havelaar*. They murdered its crew."

"And then claimed it as a giant loss," said Richard. "Artwork and all."

"Only there *wasn't* any artwork aboard," said Clea. "It was a dummy shipment, meant to go down on a boat they didn't need anymore. The real art's being stored somewhere. I'm sure it will be sold, piece by piece, on the black market. A double profit, counting the insurance.''

''Who carried the policy?''

''Lloyd's of London.''

''Have you contacted them?''

''Yes. They were skeptical of my story. Kept asking me what I wanted out of this, whether I had a grudge against the Van Weldon company. Then they learned about my prison record. After that, they didn't believe anything I said.'' Sighing, she went to the bed and sat down. ''I told my cousin Tony to drop out of sight—he's the obvious person they'd use to track me down. He's in a wheelchair. Vulnerable. He's hiding out somewhere in Brussels. I can't really expect much help from him. So I'm floundering around on my own.''

A long silence passed. When at last she found the courage to look up, she saw that Jordan was frowning at the wall, and that Richard Wolf was obviously not convinced of her story.

''You don't believe me, do you, Mr. Wolf?'' she said.

''I'll reserve judgment for later. When I've had a chance to check the facts.'' He turned to Jordan. ''Can we talk outside?''

Jordan nodded and followed Richard out of the room.

From the window Clea watched the two men standing in the garden below. She couldn't hear what they were saying, but she could read their body language—the nods, the grim set of Jordan's face. After a few moments Richard climbed in his car and drove away. Jordan reentered the building.

Clea stood waiting for him. She was afraid to face him, afraid to confront his skepticism. Why should he believe her? She was an ex-con. In the past month she had told so many lies she could scarcely keep them all straight. It was too much to ask that he would take her word for it this time.

The door opened and Jordan entered, his expression unreadable. He studied her for a moment, as though not certain just what to do with her. Then he let out a deep breath.

''You certainly know how to throw a fellow for a loop,'' he said.

"I'm sorry" was all she could think of saying.

"Sorry?"

"I never meant to drag you into this. Or your family either. It would be easier all around if you just go home. Somehow I'll get to London."

"It's a little late in the game, isn't it? To be casting me off?"

"You'll have no problems. Van Weldon isn't interested in *you*."

"But he is."

"What?"

"That's what Richard wanted to tell me. On his way to meet us, he was followed. Someone's watching Chetwynd, monitoring everyone's comings and goings."

Clea stiffened with alarm. "They followed him here?"

"No, he lost them."

"How can he be sure?"

"Believe me, Richard's an old hand at this. He'd know if he was followed."

Heart racing, she began to pace the room. She didn't care how skilled Richard Wolf might be—the chances were, he would underestimate Van Weldon's power, his resources. She'd spent the past month fighting for her life. She'd made it her business to learn everything she could about Van Weldon, and she knew, better than anyone, how far his tentacles reached. He had already discovered the link between her and the Tavistocks. It was just a matter of time before he used that knowledge to track her down.

She stopped pacing and looked at Jordan. "What next? What does your Mr. Wolf have in mind?"

"A fact-finding mission. Some discreet inquiries, a chat with Lloyd's of London."

"What do we do in the meantime?"

"We sit tight and wait right here. He'll call us in the morning."

She nodded and turned away. *In the morning,* she thought, *I'll be gone.*

VICTOR VAN WELDON WAS having another attack, and this was a severe one, judging by the pallor of his face and the tinge of blue around his lips. Van Weldon was not long for this world, thought

Simon Trott—a few months at the most. And then he'd be gone and the path would be clear for his appointed successor—Trott himself.

If Van Weldon didn't sack him first, a possibility that was beginning to seem likely since the latest news had broken.

"How can this be?" Van Weldon wheezed. "You said it was under control. You said the woman was ours."

"A third party stepped in at the last moment. He ruined everything. And we lost a man."

"What about this family you mentioned—the Tavistocks?"

"The Tavistocks are a distraction, nothing more. It's not them I'm worried about."

"Who, then?"

Trott paused, reluctant to broach the possibility. "Interpol," he said at last. "It seems the woman has attracted their attention."

Van Weldon reacted with a violent spasm of coughing. When at last he'd caught his breath again, he turned his malevolent gaze to Trott. "You have brought us to disaster."

"I'm sure it can be remedied."

"You left the task to fools. And so," he added ironically, "did I."

"The police have nothing. Our man is dead. He can't talk."

"Clea Rice can."

"We'll find her again."

"How? Every day she grows more and more clever. Every day we seem to grow more and more stupid."

"Eventually we'll have a lead. Our contact in Buckinghamshire—"

Van Weldon gave a snort. "That contact is a liability! I want the connection severed. And there must be a consequence. I will not tolerate such treachery."

Trott nodded. Consequences. Penalties. Yes, he understood their necessity.

He only hoped that he would not someday be on the receiving end.

IT WAS WELL AFTER DARK when Richard Wolf finally drove in through the gates of Chetwynd. As he passed between the stone pillars his gaze swept the road, searching for a telltale silhouette, a movement in the bushes. He knew he was being watched, just as he knew he'd been followed earlier today. Even if he didn't quite believe Clea Rice's story, he did believe that she was in real danger. Her fear had infected him as well, had notched up his alertness to the point he was watching every shadow. He was glad Beryl had gone off to London for a few days. He'd call her later and suggest she stay longer—anything to keep her well away from this Clea Rice mess.

A car he didn't recognize was parked in the driveway.

Richard pulled up beside it. Cautiously he got out and circled around the Saab, glanced through the window at the interior. Inside were a few folded newspapers, nothing to identify the driver.

He went up the steps to the house.

Davis greeted him at the front door and helped him off with his raincoat. "You have a visitor, Mr. Wolf."

"So I've noticed. Who is it?"

"A Mr. Archibald MacLeod. He's in the library."

"Did he mention the purpose of his visit?"

"Some sort of police business."

At once Richard crossed the hall to the library. A man—brown haired, short but athletic build—stood beside the far bookcase, examining a leather-bound volume. He looked up as Richard entered.

"Mr. MacLeod? I'm Richard Wolf."

"Yes, I know. I've made inquiries. I've just spoken to an old colleague of yours—Claude Daumier, French Intelligence. He assures me I can have complete confidence in you." MacLeod closed the book and slid it back on the shelf. "I'm from Interpol."

"And I'm afraid I'm quite in the dark."

"We believe you and Mr. Tavistock have stumbled into a somewhat hazardous situation. I'm anxious to see that no one gets hurt. That's why I'm here to ask for your cooperation."

"In what matter?"

"Tell me where I can find Clea Rice."

Richard hoped his alarm didn't show on his face. "Clea Rice?" he asked blankly.

"I know you're familiar with the name. Since you requested an ID of her fingerprints. And a copy of her criminal record. The American authorities alerted us to that fact."

The man really must be with the police, Richard concluded. Nevertheless, he decided to proceed cautiously. Just because MacLeod was a cop didn't mean he could be trusted.

Richard crossed to the fireplace and sat down. "Before I tell you anything," he said, "I'd like to hear the facts."

"You mean about Clea Rice?"

"No. About Victor Van Weldon."

"Then will you tell me how to find Miss Rice?"

"Why do you want her?"

"We've decided it's time to move on her. As soon as possible."

Richard frowned. "You mean—you're arresting her?"

"Not at all." MacLeod faced him squarely. "We've used Miss Rice long enough. It's time to bring her into protective custody."

A SOFT DRIZZLE WAS falling as Clea stepped out the front door of the Munstead Inn. It was past midnight and all was dark inside, the other occupants having long since retired. For a full hour she had lain awake beside Jordan, waiting until she was certain he was asleep. Since the revelations of that afternoon, mistrust seemed to loom between them, and they had staked out opposite sides of the bed. They'd scarcely spoken to each other, much less touched.

Now she was leaving, and it was all for the better. The break was cleaner this way—no sloppy emotions, no uneasy farewells. He was the gentleman. She was the ex-con. Never the twain could meet.

The back gate squealed as she opened it. She froze, listening, but all she heard was the whisper of drizzle on tree leaves and, in the distance, the barking of a dog. She pulled her jacket tightly against the moist chill and began to trudge down the road.

It would be an all-night walk; by daybreak she could be miles from here. If her feet held out. If she wasn't spotted by the enemy.

Ahead stretched the twin hedgerows lining both sides of the road. She debated whether or not to walk on the far side of the hedge, where she would be hidden from the road, but after a few steps in the mud she decided the pavement was worth the risk. She wouldn't get far in this sucking mire. Chances were, no one would be driving this late at night, anyway. She slogged back around the hedge and clambered onto the road. There she froze.

The silhouette of a man was standing before her.

"You could have told me you were leaving," said Jordan.

Relieved it was him, she found her breath again. "I could have."

"Why didn't you?"

"You would have stopped me. And I can't afford any more delays. Not when I know they're one step behind."

"You'll be safer with me than without me."

"No, I'm safer on my own. I'm getting good at this, you know. I may actually survive to see the ripe old age of thirty-one."

"As what, a fugitive? What kind of life is that?"

"At least it's a life."

"What about Van Weldon? He gets off with murder?"

"I can't do anything about that. I've tried. All it's earned me is a bunch of thugs on my tail and a head of peroxide-damaged hair. I give up, okay? He wins. And I'm out of here." She turned and began to walk away, down the road.

"Why did you come to England, anyway? Was it really the dagger you were after?"

"Yes. I thought, if I could steal it back, I'd have my evidence. I could prove to everyone that Van Weldon was lying. That he'd filed a false claim. And maybe—maybe someone would believe me."

"If what you're saying is true—"

"*If* it's true?" She turned in disgust and continued walking up the road. Away from him. "I suppose I made up the guy with the gun, too."

He followed her. "You can't keep running. You're the only witness to what happened to the *Havelaar*. The only one who can nail Van Weldon in court."

"If he doesn't nail me first."

"The police need your testimony."

"They don't believe me. And they won't without solid evidence. I wouldn't trust the police, anyway. You think Van Weldon got rich playing by the rules? Hell, no. I've checked into him. He has a hundred lawyers who'll pull strings to get him off. And probably a hundred cops in his pocket. He owns a dozen ships, fourteen hotels and three casinos in Monaco. Okay, so last year he didn't do so well. He got overextended and lost a bundle. That's why he ditched the *Havelaar,* to—pardon the pun—keep his head above water. He's a little desperate and a little paranoid. And he'll squash anyone who gets in his way."

"I'll get you help, Clea."

"You have a nice mansion and a CIA-in-law. That's not enough."

"My uncle worked for MI6. British Intelligence."

"I suppose your uncle's chummy with a few members of Parliament?"

"Yes, he is."

"So is Van Weldon. He makes friends everywhere. Or he buys them."

He grabbed her arm and pulled her around to face him. "Clea, eight men died on the *Havelaar.* You saw it happen. How can you walk away from that?"

"You think it's easy?" she cried. "I try to sleep at night, and all I see is poor Giovanni slumping over the lifeboat. I hear gunfire. And Vicenzo moaning. And I hear the voice of that man. The one on the *Cosima.* The one who ordered them all killed...." She swallowed back an unexpected swell of tears. Angrily she wiped them away. "So, no, it ain't easy. But it's what I have to do if I want—"

Jordan cut her off with a sharp tug on her arm. Only at that instant did Clea notice the flicker of light reflected in his face. She spun around to face the road.

In the distance a car was approaching. As it rounded a curve, its headlights flitted through the hedgerow branches.

At once Jordan and Clea were dashing back the way they'd come. The hedges were too high and thick to cross; their only escape route was along the road. Rain had left the pavement slippery, and Clea's every step was bogged down by the mud still clinging to her shoes. Any second they'd be spotted.

Jordan yanked her sideways, through a gap in the hedge.

They tumbled through and landed together in a bed of wet grass. Seconds later the car drove past and continued on, toward the Munstead Inn. Through the stillness of the night they heard the engine's growl fade away. Then there was nothing. No car doors slamming, no voices.

"Do you think they've gone on?" whispered Clea.

"No. It's a dead-end road. There's only the inn."

"Then what are they doing?"

"Watching. Waiting for something."

For us, she thought.

Suddenly she was frantic to get away, to escape the threat of that car and its faceless occupants. This time she didn't dare use the road. Instead she headed across the field, not knowing where she was going, knowing only that she had to get as far away from the Munstead Inn as she could. The mud sucked at her shoes, slowing every step, making her stumble again and again, until she felt as if she was trapped in that familiar nightmare of pursuit, her legs refusing to work. She was panting so hard she didn't hear Jordan following at her heels. Only when she fell to her knees and he reached down for her did she realize he was right beside her.

He pulled her back to her feet. She stood swaying, her legs shaky, her breath coming in gasps. Around them stretched the dark vastness of the field. Overhead the sky was silvery with mist and rain.

"We're all right," he panted, struggling to catch his breath, as well. "They're not following us."

"How did they know where to look for us?"

"It couldn't have been the Munsteads."

"Then it was Richard Wolf."

"No," said Jordan firmly. "It wasn't Richard."

"They could've followed him—"

"He said he wasn't followed."

"Then he was wrong!" She pulled away. "I should never have trusted you. Any of you. Now it's going to get me killed." She turned and struggled on through the mire.

"Clea, wait."

"Go home, Jordan. Go back to being a gentleman."

"Can you keep on running?"

"Damn right I can! I'm getting as far away as possible. I yanked on the tiger's tail. I was lucky to live through it."

"You think Van Weldon will let you go? He'll hunt you down, Clea. Wherever you run, you'll be looking over your shoulder. You're a constant threat to him. The one person who could destroy him. Unless he destroys you first."

She turned. In the darkness of the field his face was a black oval against the silver of the night clouds. "What do you want me to do? Fight back? Surrender?" She gave a sob of desperation. "Either way, Jordan, I'm lost. And I'm scared." She hugged herself in the rain. "And I'm freezing to death."

At once his arms came around her, pulling her into his embrace. They were both damp and shivering, yet even through their soaked clothes she felt his warmth seep toward her. He took her face in his hands, and the kiss he pressed to her lips was enough to sweep away, just for a moment, her discomfort. Her fear. As the rain began to beat down on the fields and the clouds swept across the moon, she was aware only of him, the salty heat of his mouth, the way his body molded itself around hers.

When at last she'd caught her breath again, and they stood gazing at each other in the darkness, she found she was no longer shaking from fear, but from longing.

For him.

He said softly, "I know a place we can go tonight. It's a long walk. But it will be warm there, and dry."

"And safe?"

"And safe." Again he framed her face in his hands and kissed her. "Trust me."

I have no choice, she thought. *I'm too tired to think of what I should do. Where I should go.*

He took her hand. "We cross this field, then follow the roads," he said. "On pavement, so they won't be able to track our footprints."

"And then?"

"It's a three-, four-mile walk. Think you can make it?"

She thought about the men in the car, waiting outside the Munstead Inn. She wondered if somewhere, in the cylinder of one of their guns, there lurked a bullet with her name on it.

"I can make it," she said, her pace quickening. "I'll do anything," she added under her breath, "to stay alive."

CHAPTER NINE

A FEW TAPS of a rock and the window shattered.

Jordan broke away the jagged edges and climbed in. A moment later he reappeared at the cottage's front door and motioned for Clea to enter.

She stepped inside and found herself standing in a quaint room furnished with rough-hewn antiques and pewter lamps. Massive ceiling beams, centuries old, ran the length of the room, and all around her, burnished wainscoting gleamed against the white-washed walls. It would have been a cozy room were it not so cold and drafty. The English, thought Clea, must have thermally insulated hides.

Jordan, soaked as he was, looked scarcely discomfited as he moved about the room, closing shutters. "I'll have to make it up to old Monty, that broken window. He'll understand. Doesn't much use this cottage except in the summer. In fact, I believe he's in Moritz at the moment. Trying to land the next Mrs. Montgomery Dearborn."

How many Mrs. Dearborns are there? Clea wanted to ask, but she couldn't get out the question; her teeth were chattering too hard. What feeling she had left in her limbs was quickly fading to numbness. She knew she should strip off her wet clothes, should try to start a fire in the hearth, but she couldn't seem to make her body move. She could only stand there, water dripping from her clothes onto the wood floor.

Jordan turned on a lamp. By the light's glow he caught his first real look at her. "Good Lord," he said, touching her face. "You're like an ice cube."

"Fire," she whispered. "Please, start a fire."

"That'll take too long. You need to get warmed up now." He pulled her down a hall and into the bathroom. Quickly he turned on the shower spigot. As water hissed out in a sputtering stream he began to peel off her sopping wool jacket.

"Electric coil heater," said Jordan. "It'll warm up in a minute." He tossed her jacket aside and unzipped her skirt. She was too cold to care about anything so trivial as modesty; she let him pull her skirt off, let the fabric drop in a pile on the floor. The water was steaming now; he tested the temperature, then thrust her, underwear and all, into the shower.

Even with hot water streaming over her body, it seemed to take forever for her to stop shaking. She huddled, dazed, under the spigot. Slowly the heat penetrated her numbness and she could feel her blood start to circulate again, could feel the flush of warmth at last seeping toward her core.

"Clea?" she heard Jordan say.

She didn't answer. She was too caught up in the pleasure of being warm again. Sighing, she shifted around to let the stream roll down her back. Vaguely, through the rattle of water, she heard Jordan call.

"Are you all right?"

Before she could answer, the shower curtain was abruptly pushed aside. She found herself gazing up at Jordan's face.

As he was gazing at hers.

For a moment they said nothing. The only sound was the pounding of the shower. And the pulsing of her heartbeat in her ears. Though she was barely clothed, though her transparent undergarments clung to her skin, Jordan's gaze never wavered from her face. He seemed mesmerized by what he saw there. Drawn by the longing he surely recognized in her eyes.

She reached out and touched his face. His cheek felt rough and chilled under her hot fingertips. Just that one contact, that brush of her skin against his, seemed to melt all the barriers between them. She felt another kind of heat ignite within her. She pulled his face down to hers and met his lips in a kiss.

At once they were both clinging to each other. Whimpering. Hot water streamed across their shoulders, hers bare, his still clothed in the shirt. Through the curls of steam, she saw in his face the long-suppressed desire that had been throbbing between them since the night they'd met.

She pressed even more eagerly against him and gave a soft sigh of pleasure, of triumph, at the burgeoning response of his body.

"Your clothes," she murmured, and reached up feverishly to pull off his shirt. He shrugged it off onto the bathroom floor, baring his chest, so recently bandaged. The golden hairs were damp and matted from the shower. They were both breathing in gasps now, both working frantically at his belt.

Somehow they got the water shut off. Somehow they managed to find their way out of the shower, out of the bathroom with its obstacle course of wet clothes littering the tiles. They left a trail of still more wet clothes, lying where they'd dropped, his trousers near the bathroom door, her bra in the hallway, his undershorts at the threshold of the bedroom. By the time they reached the bed, there were no more clothes to shed. There was only damp flesh and murmurs and the yearning to be joined.

The bedroom was cold and they slid, shivering, beneath the goose-down duvet. As they lay with limbs intertwined, mouths exploring, tasting, the heat of their bodies warmed the bed. Her shivering ceased. The room's chill was forgotten in the rush of sensations now flooding through her, the sweet ache between her thighs, the sharp darts of pleasure as his mouth found her breasts, drawing her nipples to almost agonizing tautness.

She rose above him and returned the torment with a vengeance. Her mouth traced down the plane of his chest, grazed his belly, seeking ever more sensitive flesh. Groaning, he gripped her shoulders, and his body twisted off the mattress, rolling her onto the pillow. Suddenly she was lying beneath him, his body hard atop hers, his hands cupping her face.

Their gazes met, held. They never stopped looking at each other, even as he slid inside her, filled her. Even as she cried out with the pleasure of his penetration.

He moved slowly, gently. Their gazes held.

His breaths came faster, his hands clutching more tightly at her face. Still they looked at each other, joined in a bond that went deeper than flesh.

Only when she felt that exquisite ache build to the first ripples of release did she close her eyes and surrender to the sensations flooding through her. A soft cry floated from her throat, a sound both foreign and wonderful. It was matched, seconds later, by his groan. Through the ebbing waves of her own pleasure she felt his last frantic thrusts, and then he pulsed deep within her. With a shuddering sigh his spent body came to rest and fell still.

She cradled his head against her shoulder. As she pressed a kiss to his damp hair, she felt a wave of tenderness so overpowering it frightened her.

We made love. What does it mean?

They'd enjoyed each other's bodies. They'd given each other satisfaction and, for a few moments, even happiness.

But what does it mean?

She pressed another kiss to the damp tendrils and felt again that twinge of affection, so intense this time it brought tears to her eyes. Blinking them away, she turned her face from him, only to feel his hand cradle her cheek and nudge her gaze back to his.

"You are the most surprising woman I've ever met," he said.

She swallowed. And laughed. "That's me. Full of surprises."

"And delights. I never know what to expect from you. And it's starting to drive me quite mad." He lowered his mouth and tenderly brushed his lips against hers, tasting, nibbling. Enjoying. Already she could feel the rekindling of his arousal, could feel his heaviness stirring against her thigh.

She slid her hand between their hips and with a few silken strokes she had him hard and throbbing again. "You're full of surprises yourself," she murmured.

"No, I'm quite..." he gave a sigh of delight "—conventional."

"Are you?" She lowered her mouth to his nipple and traced a circle of wetness with her tongue.

"Some would even call me—" he dropped his head back and groaned "—damned predictable."

"Sometimes," she whispered, "predictable is good."

With her tongue she began to trace a wet line across his chest to his other nipple. He was breathing hard, struggling to check his rising tide of passion.

"Wait. Clea…" He caught her face. Gently he tilted it up toward him and looked at her. "I have to know. Why were you crying?"

"I wasn't."

"You were. A moment ago."

She studied him, hungrily devouring every detail. The way the light played on his ruffled hair. The crescent shadows cast by his eyelashes. The way he looked at *her,* so quietly, intently. As though she was some strange, unknowable creature.

"I was thinking," she said, "how different you are from any man I've known."

"Ah. No wonder you were crying."

She laughed and gave him a playful slap. "No, silly. What I meant was, the men I've known were always…after something. Wanting something. Planning the next take."

"You mean, like your uncle Walter?"

"Yes. Like my uncle Walter."

The mention of her past, her flawed childhood, suddenly dampened her desire. She pulled away from him. Sitting up, she hugged her knees. If only she could make that part of her life drop away. If only she could be born anew. Without shame.

"I'm embarrassed to admit he's my relative," she said.

He laughed. "I'm embarrassed by my relatives all the time."

"But none of yours are in prison…are they?"

"Not as of this moment, no."

"Uncle Walter is. So was my cousin Tony." She paused and added softly, "So was I."

He reached for her hand. He didn't say anything. He just watched her, and listened.

"It was so ironic, really. For eight years I went perfectly straight. And suddenly Uncle Walter pops up outside my apartment. Bleeding all over my front porch. I couldn't turn him in. And he wouldn't let me take him to the hospital. So there I was, stuck with him. I burned his clothes. Tossed his lock picks in a Dumpster across town. And then the police showed up." She gave a shrug, as though that last detail was scarcely worth mentioning. "The funny thing is," she said, "I don't hate him for it. Not a bit. You can't hate

Uncle Walter. He's so damn..." She gave a sheepish shrug. "Lovable."

Laughing, he pressed her palm to his lips. "You have a most unique take on life. Like no other woman I've known."

"How many ex-cons have you slept with?"

"You, I must admit, are my first."

"Yes, I imagine you'd normally prefer a proper lady."

He frowned at her. "What's this rubbish about *proper* ladies, anyway?"

"Well, I don't exactly qualify."

"*Proper* is dull. And you, my dear Miss Rice, are not dull."

She tossed her head back and laughed. "Thank you, Mr. Tavistock, for the compliment."

He tugged her toward him. "And as for your notorious uncle Walter," he whispered, pulling her down on top of him, "if he's related to you, he must have some redeeming features."

She smiled down at him. "He *is* charming."

He cupped her face and kissed her. "I'm sure."

"And clever."

"I can imagine."

"And the ladies say he's quite irresistible...."

Again Jordan's mouth found hers. His kiss, deeper, harder, swept all thoughts of Uncle Walter from her mind.

"Quite irresistible," murmured Jordan, and he slid his hand between her thighs.

At once she was lost, needing him, crying out for him. She bared her warmth and he took it tenderly. And when it was over, when exhaustion finally claimed him, he fell asleep with his head on her breast.

She smiled down at his tousled hair. "You will remember me fondly some day, won't you, Jordan?" she whispered.

And she knew it was the best she could hope for.

It was all she dared hope for.

HE AWAKENED to the subtle perfume of a woman's scent, to the tickle of hair against his face. He opened his eyes and by the gray light slanting in through the shutters he saw Clea asleep beside him.

Without a trace of makeup, and her hair lushly tangled across the pillow, she looked like some fairy princess over whom a spell of deathless repose had been cast. Unarousable, untouchable. Not altogether real.

How real she'd felt to him last night! Not a princess at all, but a temptress, full of sweet mischief and even sweeter fire.

Even now he couldn't resist her. He reached for her and kissed her on the mouth.

Her reaction was abrupt and startling. She gave a shudder of alarm and jerked up from the pillow.

"It's all right," he soothed. "It's only me."

She stared for a moment, as though not recognizing him. Then she gave a soft gasp and shook her head. "I—I haven't been sleeping very well. Needless to say."

He watched her huddle beneath the duvet and wondered how she had maintained her sanity through these weeks of running and hiding. He couldn't help but feel a rush of pity for her. It was mingled with admiration for her strength. Her will to live.

She glanced at the window and saw daylight gleaming through the closed shutters. "They'll be searching for us. We can't stay here much longer."

"We can't exactly stroll away, either. Not without help."

"Oh, no. No more calling on friends and family. I'm sure that's how they found us last night. Your Richard Wolf must have told someone."

"He'd never do that."

"Then they followed him. Or they've tapped your phone. Something." Abruptly she climbed out of bed and snatched up her underwear. Finding it still damp, she tossed it in disgust onto a chair. "I'm going to have to leave naked."

"Then you'll most certainly catch someone's eye."

"You're not much help. Can't you get out of bed, at least?"

"I'm thinking. I think best in bed."

"Bed is where most men don't think at all." She picked up her bra. It, too, was damp. She looped it over the doorknob and glanced around the room in frustration. "You say the man who owns this place is a bachelor?"

"In between states of wedded bliss."

"Does he have any women's clothes?"

"I've never thought to ask Monty such a personal question."

"You know what I mean."

He rose from the bed and went to open the wardrobe door. Inside hung two summer suits, a raincoat and a few neatly pressed shirts. On Jordan they'd all fit nicely. On Clea they'd look ridiculous. He took out a bathrobe and tossed it to her.

"Unless we can turn you into a six-foot man," he said, "this wardrobe won't work. And even if we did find women's clothes in here, there's still the matter of your hair. That flaming red isn't the most subtle color."

She snatched a lock of her hair and frowned at it. "I hate it, anyway. Let's cut it off."

He eyed those lustrous waves and was forced to give a regretful nod. "Monty always keeps a bottle of hair dye around to touch up his graying temples. We could darken what's left of your hair."

"I'll find some scissors."

"Wait. Clea," he said. "We have to talk."

She turned to him, her jaw set with the determination of what had to be done. "About what?"

"Even if we do change your appearance, running may not be your best option."

"I think it's my only option."

"There's still the authorities."

"They didn't believe me before. Why should they believe me now? My word's nothing against Van Weldon's."

"The Eye of Kashmir would change that."

"I don't have it."

"Delancey does."

She shook her head. "By now, Van Weldon must have realized what a mistake it was to sell the Eye so soon. His people will be trying to get it back."

"What if they haven't? It may still be in Delancey's house, waiting to be snatched. By us."

She went very still. "Us?" she asked quietly.

"Yes, us." He smiled at her, a smile that did not seem to inspire much confidence, judging by her expression. "Congratulations. Meet your new partner in crime," he said.

"That's supposed to make me feel better?"

"Doesn't it?"

"I'm just thinking about your last burglary attempt. And how close you came to getting us both handcuffed."

"That was inexperience. I'm now fully seasoned."

"Right. And ready for the frying pan."

"What is this, a crisis of confidence? You told me you used to burglarize houses just for the challenge of it."

"I didn't know better then. I was a kid."

"And now you're experienced. Better at the art."

Letting out a breath, she began to pace a line back and forth in the carpet. "I know I could break in again. I'm *sure* I could. But I don't know where to look. The dagger could be anywhere upstairs. The bedroom, the guest rooms. I'd need time."

"Together, we could do it in half the time."

"Or get caught twice as fast," she muttered. And she left the room.

He followed her into the kitchen, where he found her rummaging through drawers for the scissors. "There's always the other option," he said. "The logical one. The reasonable one. We go to the police."

"Where they'll laugh in my face, the way they did before. And Van Weldon will know exactly where to find me."

"You'll be under protection. I promise."

"The safest place for me, Jordan, is out where I can run. A moving target's not so easy to hit." She found the scissors and handed them to him. "Especially when the target keeps changing its appearance. Go ahead, do it."

He looked down at the scissors, then looked at that beautiful mane of hair. The task was almost too painful, but he had no choice. Regretfully he took a handful of cinnamon red hair. Just the scent of those silky strands was enough to reawaken all the memories of last night. The way her body had fitted against his. The way she'd moved beneath him, not a docile release but the joyous shudders of a wild creature.

That's what she was. A wild thing. Sensuous. Unpredictable. In time she would drive him crazy.

Already he was losing his long-practiced sense of self-control. All it took was a few whiffs of her hair, the touch of silk in his palm, and he was ready to drag her back to bed.

He gave his head a shake to clear away those inconvenient images. Then he lifted the scissors and calmly, deliberately, began to snip off her hair.

BY THE GRAY MORNING LIGHT, they followed the footprints in the mud—a pair of them, one large set, one smaller set, veering away from the road. The prints headed west across the field. It had rained heavily last night, and the tracks were easy to follow for about three hundred yards or so, until they connected up with another road. Then, after a few muddy imprints on the pavement, the footprints faded.

They could be anywhere by now.

Archie MacLeod gazed out over the field and cursed. "I should've known she'd do this. Probably got one inkling we were on her trail and off she goes. Like a bloody she-fox, that one."

"You can hardly blame her," said Richard. "Of course she'd expect the worst. How did your people fumble this one? They were supposed to bring her into custody. Instead they managed to chase her underground."

"Their orders were to do it quietly. Somehow she got wind of them."

"Or Jordan did," said Richard. "I should have contacted him last night. Told him what was coming down. Now he'll wonder."

"You don't think he doubts *you?*"

"No. But he'll be cautious now. He'll assume Van Weldon's got me covered, that it won't be safe to contact me. That's what I'd assume in his place."

"So how do we find them now?"

"We don't." Richard turned to his car and slid in behind the wheel. "And we hope Van Weldon doesn't, either."

"I'm not so confident of that."

"Jordan's clever. So is Clea Rice. Together they may do all right."

MacLeod leaned in the car window. "Guy Delancey died this morning."

"I know," said Richard.

"And we've just heard rumors that Victor Van Weldon's upped the price on Clea Rice to two million. Within twenty-four hours this area will be swarming with contract men. If they get anywhere near Clea Rice, she won't stand a chance. Neither will Tavistock."

Richard stared at him. "Why the hell did you wait so long to bring her into custody? You should have locked her under guard weeks ago."

"We didn't know whether to believe her."

"So you waited for Van Weldon to make a move, was that the strategy? If he tried to kill her, she must be telling the truth?"

MacLeod slapped the car door in frustration. "I'm not defending what we've done. I'm just saying we're now convinced she's told the truth." He leaned forward. "Jordan Tavistock is your friend. You must have an idea where he'd go."

"I'm not even sure he's the one calling the shots right now. It might be the woman."

"You let me know if you come up with any ideas. Anything at all about where they might go next."

Richard started the car. "I know where *I'd* go if I were them. I'd get away from here. I'd run as fast as I could. And I'd damn well get lost in a crowd."

"London?"

Richard nodded. "Can you think of a better place to hide?"

"THAT WOMAN MUST HAVE nine lives. And she's used up only three of them," said Victor Van Weldon. He was wheezing again. His breathing, which was normally labored even on the best of days, had the moist rattle of hopelessly congested lungs.

Soon, thought Simon Trott. Victor was a dying man. What a relief it would be when it was over. No more of these distasteful audiences, these grotesque scenes of a virtual corpse fighting to hang on. If only the old man would just get it over with and die.

Until then, he'd have to stay in the old man's good graces. And for that, he'd have to take care of this Clea Rice problem.

"You should have seen to this yourself," said Victor. "Now we've lost our chance."

"We'll find her again. We know she's still with Tavistock."

"Has he surfaced yet?"

"No. But eventually he'll turn to his family. And we'll be ready."

Van Weldon exhaled a deep sigh. His breathing seemed clearer, as though the assurances had eased the congestion in his lungs. "I want you to see to it personally."

Trott nodded. "I'll leave for London this evening."

CROUCHED BEHIND THE YEW hedge of Guy Delancey's yard, Jordan and Clea waited in the darkness for the house lights to go out. Whitmore's nightly habit was as it had always been, the checking of the windows and doors at nine o'clock, the pause in the kitchen to brew a pot of tea, then the retreat upstairs to his room in the servants' wing. *How many years has the fellow clung to that petrified routine of his?* Clea wondered. What a shock it must be to him, to know that all would soon change.

Clea and Jordan had heard it on the radio that morning: Guy Delancey was dead.

Soon others would come to claim this house. And old Whitmore, a relic from the dinosaur age, would be forced to evolve.

The lights in the servants' wing went out.

"Give him half an hour," whispered Jordan. "Just to make sure he's asleep."

Half an hour, thought Clea, shivering. She'd freeze by then. She was dressed in Monty's black turtleneck and a baggy pair of jeans, which she'd shortened with a few snips of the scissors. It wasn't enough protection against this chill autumn night.

"Which way do we enter?" asked Jordan.

Clea scanned the house. The French door leading from the terrace was how she'd broken in the last time. No doubt that particular lock had since been replaced. So, undoubtedly, had the locks on all the ground-floor doors and windows.

"The second floor," she said. "Balcony off the master bed-room."

"That's how I got in the last time."

"And if *you* managed to do it," she said dryly, "it must have been a piece of cake."

"Oh, right, insult your partner. See where it gets you."

She glanced at him. His blond hair was concealed under a watch cap, and his face was blackened with grease. In the darkness only the white arc of his teeth showed in a Cheshire-cat grin.

"You're sure you're up to this?" she asked. "It could get sticky in there."

"Clea, if things do go wrong, promise me."

"Promise you what?"

"You'll run. Don't wait for me. And don't look back."

"Trying to be chivalrous again? Something silly like that?"

"I just want to get things straight now. Before things go awry."

"Don't say that. It's bad luck."

"Then this is for good luck." He took her arm, pulled her against him and kissed her. She floundered in his embrace, torn between wanting desperately to get kissed again, and wanting to stay focused on the task that lay ahead. When he finally released her, they stared at each other for a moment. Only the gleam of his eyes and teeth were visible in the darkness.

That was a farewell kiss, she realized. In case things went wrong. In case they got separated and never saw each other again. A chill wind blew and the trees creaked overhead. As the moments passed, and the night grew colder, she tried to commit every detail to memory. Because she knew, as he did, that every step they took could end in disaster. She had not counted on this complication, had not wanted this attraction. But here it was, shimmering between them. The fact it couldn't last, that any feelings they had for each other were doomed by who she was, and who he was, only made those feelings all the sweeter. *Will you miss me someday, Jordan Tavistock?* she wondered. *As much as I'll miss you?*

At last he turned and looked at the house. "I think it's time," he said softly.

She, too, turned to face the house. The wind swept the lawn, bringing with it the smell of dead leaves and chill earth. The scent of autumn, she thought. Too soon, winter would be upon them....

She eased away from the hedge and began to move through the shadows. Jordan was right behind her.

They crossed the lawn, their shoes sinking into wet grass. Beneath the bedroom balcony they crouched to reassess the situation. They heard only the wind and the rustle of leaves.

"I'll go first," he said.

Before she could protest, he was scrambling up the wisteria vine. She winced at the rattle of branches, expecting at any moment that the balcony doors would fly open, that Whitmore would appear waving a shotgun. Lucky for them, old Whitmore still seemed to be a sound sleeper. Jordan made it all the way up without a hitch.

Clea followed and dropped noiselessly onto the balcony.

"Locked," said Jordan, trying the doorknob.

"Expected as much," she whispered. "Move away."

He stepped aside and watched in respectful silence as she shone a penlight on the lock. "This should be even easier than the one downstairs," she whispered and gently inserted the makeshift L-pick she'd fashioned that afternoon using a wire hanger and a pair of pliers. "Circa 1920. Probably came with the house. Let's hope it's not so rusty that it bends my..." She gave a soft chuckle of satisfaction as the lock clicked open. Glancing at Jordan she said wryly, "There's nothing like a good stiff tool."

He answered, just as wryly, "I'll remember to keep one on me."

The room was as she'd remembered it, the medieval curtained bed, the wardrobe and antique dresser, the desk and tea table near the balcony doors. She'd searched the desk and dresser before; now she'd take up where she had left off.

"You search the wardrobe," she whispered. "I'll do the nightstands."

They set to work. By the thin beam of her penlight she examined the contents of the first nightstand. In the drawers she found magazines, cigarettes and various other items that told her Guy Delancey had used this bed for activities beyond mere sleeping. A flicker of movement overhead made her aim the penlight at the ceiling. There was a mirror mounted above the bed. To think she had actually considered a romp in this bachelor playpen! Turning her attention back to the nightstand, she saw that the magazines featured naked ladies galore, and not very attractive ones. Entertainment, no doubt, for the nights Guy couldn't find female companionship.

She searched the second nightstand and found a similar collection of reading material. So intent was she on poking for hidden drawers, she didn't notice the creak of floorboards in the hallway. Her only warning was a sharp hiss from Jordan, and then the bedroom door flew open.

The lights sprang on overhead.

Clea, caught in midcrouch beside the bed, could only blink in surprise at the shotgun barrel pointed at her head.

CHAPTER TEN

THE GUN WAS wavering ominously in Whitmore's unsteady grasp.
The old butler looked most undignified in his ratty pajamas, but
there was no mistaking the glint of triumph in his eyes.

"Gotcha!" he barked. "Thinkin' to rob a dead man, are you?
Think you can get away with it again? Well, I'm not such an old
fool!"

"Apparently not," said Clea. She didn't dare glance in Jordan's
direction, but off in her peripheral field of vision she spied him
crouched beside the wardrobe, out of Whitmore's view. The old
man hadn't yet realized there were two burglars in the room.

"Come on, come on! Out from behind that bed! Where I can
see you!" ordered Whitmore.

Slowly Clea rose to her feet, praying that the man's trigger finger
wasn't as unsteady as his grip. As she straightened to her full
height, Whitmore's gaze widened. He focused on her chest, on the
unmistakable swell of breasts.

"Ye're only a woman," he marveled.

"Only?" She gave him a wounded look. "How insulting."

At the sound of her voice, his eyes narrowed. He scanned her
grease-blackened face. "You sound familiar. Do I know you?"

She shook her head.

"Of course! You come to the house with poor Master Delancey!
One of his lady friends!" The grip on the shotgun steadied. "Come
'ere, then! Away from the bed, you!"

"You're not going to shoot me, are you?"

"We're going to wait for the police. They'll be here any minute."

The police. There wasn't much time. Somehow they had to get
that gun away from the old fool.

She caught a glimpse of Jordan, signaling to her, urging her to shift the butler's gaze toward the left.

"Come on, move out from behind the bed!" ordered Whitmore. "Out where I can get a clear shot if I have to!"

Obediently she crawled across the mattress and climbed off. Then she took a sideways step, causing Whitmore to turn leftward. His back was now squarely turned to Jordan.

"I'm not what you think," she said.

"Denying you're a common thief, are you?"

"Certainly not a *common* one, anyway."

Jordan was approaching from the rear. Clea forced herself not to stare at him, not to give Whitmore any clue of what was about to happen....

What *was* about to happen? Surely Jordan wouldn't bop the old codger on the head? It might kill him.

Jordan raised his arms. He was clutching a pair of Guy Delancey's boxer shorts, was going to pull them like a hood over old Whitmore's head. Somehow Clea had to get that gun pointed in another direction. If startled, Whitmore might automatically let fly a round.

She gave a pitiful sob and fell to her knees on the floor. "You can't let them arrest me!" she wailed. "I'm afraid of prison!"

"Should've thought of that before you broke in," said Whitmore.

"I was desperate! I had to feed my children. There was no other way...." She began to sob wretchedly.

Whitmore was staring down at her, astonished by this bizarre display. The shotgun barrel was no longer pointed at her head.

That's when Jordan yanked the boxer shorts over Whitmore's face.

Clea dived sideways, just as the gun exploded. Pellets whizzed past. She scrambled frantically back to her feet and saw that Jordan already had Whitmore's arms restrained, and that the gun had fallen from the old man's grasp. Clea scooped it up and shoved it in the wardrobe.

"Don't hurt me!" pleaded Whitmore, his voice muffled by the makeshift hood. The boxer shorts had little red hearts. Had Delancey really pranced around in little red hearts? "Please!" moaned Whitmore.

"We're just going to keep you out of trouble," said Clea. Quickly she bound the butler's hands and feet with Delancey's silk ties and left him trussed on the bed. "Now you lie there and be a good boy."

"I promise!"

"And maybe we'll let you live."

There was a pause. Then Whitmore asked fearfully, "What do you mean by *maybe?*"

"Tell us where Delancey keeps his weapons collection."

"What weapons?"

"Antique swords. Knives. Where are they?"

"There's not much time!" hissed Jordan. "Let's get out of here."

Clea ignored him. *"Where are they?"* she repeated.

The butler whimpered. "Under the bed. That's where he keeps them!"

Clea and Jordan dropped to their knees. They saw nothing beneath the rosewood frame but carpet and a few dust balls.

Somewhere in the night, a siren was wailing.

"Time to go," muttered Jordan.

"No. Wait!" Clea focused on an almost imperceptible crack running the length of the bed frame. A seam in the wood. She reached underneath and tugged.

A hidden drawer glided out.

At her first glimpse of the contents, she gave an involuntary gasp of wonder. Jewels glittered in hammered-gold scabbards. Sword blades of finely tempered Spanish steel lay in gleaming display. In the deepest corner were stored the daggers. There were six of them, all exquisitely crafted. She knew at once which dagger was the Eye of Kashmir. The star sapphire mounted in the hilt gave it away.

"They were his pride and joy," moaned Whitmore. "And now you're stealing them."

"I'm only taking one," said Clea, snatching up the Eye of Kashmir. "And it didn't belong to him, anyway."

The siren was louder now and closing in.

"Let's *go!*" said Jordan.

Clea jumped to her feet and started toward the balcony. "Cheerio!" she called over her shoulder. "No hard feelings, right?"

"Bloody unlikely!" came the growl from under the boxer shorts.

She and Jordan scrambled down the wisteria vine and took off across the lawn, headed at a mad dash for the woods fringing the property. Just as they reached the cover of trees, a police car careened around the bend, siren screaming. Any second now the police would find Whitmore tied up on the bed and then all hell would break loose. The threat of pursuit was enough to send Jordan and Clea scrambling deep into the woods. Replay of the night we met, thought Clea. Hanging around Jordan Tavistock must be bad luck; it always seemed to bring the police on her tail.

The sting of branches whipping her face, the ache of her muscles, didn't slow her pace. She kept running, listening for sounds of pursuit. A moment later she heard distant shouting, and she knew the chase had begun.

"Damn," she muttered, stumbling over a tree root.

"Can you make it?"

"Do I have a choice?"

He glanced back toward the house, toward their pursuers. "I have an idea." He grabbed her hand and tugged her through a thinning copse of trees. They stumbled into a clearing. Just ahead, they could see the lights of a cottage.

"Let's hope they don't keep any dogs about," he said and started toward the cottage.

"What are you doing?" she whispered.

"Just a small theft. Which, I'm sorry to say, seems to be getting routine for me."

"What are you stealing? A car?"

"Not exactly." Through the darkness his teeth gleamed at her in a smile. "Bicycles."

IN THE LAUGHING MAN PUB, Simon Trott stood alone at the bar, nursing a mug of Guinness. No one bothered him, and he bothered no one, and that was the way he liked it. None of the usual poking and prodding of a stranger by the curious locals. The villagers here, it seemed, valued a man's privacy, which was all to the better, as Trott had no tolerance tonight for even minor annoyances. He was not in a good mood. That meant he was dangerous.

He took another sip of stout and glanced at his watch. Almost midnight. The pub owner, anxious to close up, was already stacking up glasses and darting impatient looks at his customers. Trott was about to call it a night when the pub door opened.

A young policeman walked in. He sauntered to the bar where Trott stood and called for an ale. A few moments went by, no one saying a word. Then the policeman spoke.

"Been some excitement around 'ere tonight," he said to no one in particular.

"What sort?" asked the bartender.

"'Nother robbery, over at Under'ill. Guy Delancey's."

"Thieves gettin' bloody cheeky these days, if you ask me," the bartender said. "Goin' for the same 'ouse twice."

"Aren't they, though?" The policeman shook his head. "Makes you wonder what's become of society these days." He drained his mug. "Well, I best be gettin' 'ome. 'Fore the missus gets to worryin'." He paid the tab and walked out of the pub.

Trott left, as well.

Outside, in the road, the two men met. They walked across the village green, stepping in and out of shadows.

"Anything stolen from Underhill tonight?" asked Trott.

"The butler says just one item was taken. Antique weapon of some sort."

Trott's head lifted in sudden interest. "A dagger?"

"That's right. Part of a collection. Other things weren't touched."

"And the thieves?"

"There were two of them. Butler only saw the woman."

"What did she look like?"

"Couldn't really tell us. Had some sort of black grease on 'er face. No fingerprints, either."

"Where were they last seen?"

"Escaped through the trees. Could've gone in any direction. I'm afraid we lost 'em."

Then Clea Rice had not left Buckinghamshire, thought Trott. Perhaps she was right now in this very village.

"If I 'ear more, I'll let you know," said the policeman.

Their conversation had come to an end. Trott reached into his jacket and produced an envelope stuffed with five-pound notes. Not a lot of money, but enough to help keep a young cop's family clothed and fed.

The policeman took the envelope with an odd reluctance. "It's only information you'll be wantin', right? You won't be expecting more?"

"Only information," Trott reassured him.

"Times are...difficult, you see. Still, there are things I don't—won't—do."

"I understand." And Trott did. He understood that even upright cops could be tempted. And that for this one, the downhill slide had already begun.

After the two men parted, Trott returned to his room in the inn and called Victor Van Weldon.

"As of a few hours ago, they were still in the area," said Trott. "They broke into Delancey's house."

"Did they get the dagger?"

"Yes. Which means they've no reason to hang around here any longer. They'll probably be heading for London next."

Even now, he thought, Clea Rice must be wending her way along the back roads to the city. She'll be feeling a touch of triumph tonight. Perhaps she's thinking her ordeal will soon end. She'll sense hope, even victory whenever she looks at that dagger. The dagger she calls the Eye of Kashmir.

How wrong she will be.

THE SOUNDS OF LONDON traffic awakened Clea from a sleep so heavy she felt drugged. She rolled onto her back and peered through slitted lids at the daylight shining in through the ratty curtains. How long had they slept? Judging by her grogginess it might have been days.

They'd checked in to this seedy hotel around six in the morning. Both of them had stripped off their clothes and collapsed on the bed, and that was the last she remembered. Now, as her brain began to function again, the events of last night came back to her. The endless wait at the station for the 4:00 a.m. train out of Wolverton. The fear that, lurking among the shadows on the platform, was someone who'd been watching for them. And then, during the train ride to London, the anxiety that they'd be robbed, that they'd lose their precious cargo.

She reached under the bed and felt the wrapped bundle. The Eye of Kashmir was still there. With a sigh of relief she settled back on the bed, next to Jordan.

He was asleep. He lay with his face turned toward her, his bare shoulder tanned a warm gold against the linen, his wheat-colored hair boyishly tousled. Even in sleep he looked every inch the aristocrat. Smiling, she stroked his hair. *My darling gentleman,* she thought. *How lucky I am to have known you. Someday, when you're married to some proper young lady, when your life has settled in according to plan, will you still remember your Clea Rice?*

Sitting up, she stared at her own reflection in the dresser mirror. Right, she thought.

Suddenly depressed, she left the bed and went to take a shower. Later, as she inspected her latest hair color—this time a nut brown, courtesy of Monty's bottle of hair dye—she felt resentment knot up in her stomach. She was not a lady, nor was she proper, but she damn well had her assets. She was bright, she could think fast on her feet and, most important, she could take care of herself. What possible use did *she* have for a gentleman? He'd be a nuisance, really, dragging her off all the time to soirees. Whatever those were. She'd never fit into his world. He'd never fit into hers.

But here, in this room with the mangy carpet and mildewed towels, they could share a temporary world. A world of their own making. She was going to enjoy it while it lasted.

She went back to the bed and climbed in next to Jordan.

At the touch of her damp body, he stirred and murmured, "Is this my wake-up call?"

She answered his question by sliding her hand under the covers and stroking slowly down the length of his torso. He sucked in a startled gasp as she found exquisitely tender flesh and evoked the hoped-for response.

"If that was my wake-up call," he groaned, "I think it worked."

"Maybe now you'll get up, sleepyhead," she said, laughing, and rolled away.

He caught her arm and hauled her right back. "What about this?"

"What about what?"

"This."

Her gaze traveled to the distinct bulge under the sheets. "Shall I take care of that for you?" she whispered.

"Seeing as you're the reason it's there in the first place…"

She rolled on top of him, fitting her hips to his. He was at her mercy now, and she intended to make him beg for his pleasure. But as their bodies moved together, as she felt him grasp her hips in both hands and pull her down against him, it was she who was at his mercy, she who was begging for release. He gave it to her, in wave after glorious wave, and through the roar of her pulse in her ears she heard him say her name aloud. Once, twice, in a murmur of delight.

Yes, I'm the one he's making love to, she thought. *Me. Only me.* For these few sweet moments, it was enough.

ANTHONY VAUXHALL WAS a starched little prig of a man with a nose that always seemed to be tilted up in distaste of mere mortals. Jordan had met him several times before, on matters relating to his late parents' estate. Their conversations had been cordial, and he hadn't formed much of an opinion of the man either way.

He was forming an opinion of Anthony Vauxhall now, and it wasn't a good one.

It was nearly 4:00 p.m., and they were seated in Vauxhall's office in the Lloyd's of London building on Leadenhall Street. In the past hour and a half Jordan and Clea had managed to purchase decent clothes, grab a bite to eat and scurry downtown to Lloyd's before the offices closed. Now it appeared that their efforts might prove futile. Vauxhall's response to Clea's story was one of obvious skepticism.

"You must understand, Miss Rice," said Vauxhall, "Van Weldon Shipping is one of our most distinguished clients. One of our oldest clients. Our relationship goes back three generations. For us to accuse Mr. Van Weldon of fraud is, well..." He cleared his throat.

"Perhaps you weren't listening to Miss Rice's story," said Jordan. "She was *there*. She was a witness. The loss of the *Max Havelaar* wasn't an accidental sinking. It was sabotage."

"Even so, how can we assume Van Weldon is responsible? It could have been another party. Pirates of some kind."

"Doesn't a multimillion-dollar claim concern your firm?"

"Well, naturally."

"Wouldn't your underwriters want to know if they've paid out to a company that staged its own losses?"

"Of course, but—"

"Then why aren't you taking these accusations seriously?"

"Because—" Vauxhall took a deep breath. "I spoke to Colin Hammersmith about this very matter. Right after I got your call earlier today. He's in charge of our investigations branch. He'd heard this rumor a few weeks back and his advice was, well..." Vauxhall shifted uneasily. "To consider the source," he said at last.

The source. Meaning Clea Rice, ex-con.

Jordan didn't need to look at her; he could feel her pain, as surely as if the blow had landed on his own shoulders. But when he did look at her, he was impressed by how well she was taking it, her chin held high, her expression calm and focused.

Ever since that long red hair had been cut away, her face had seemed even more striking to him, her sculpted cheeks feathered by wisps of brown hair, the dark eyes wide and gamine. He had known Clea Rice as a blonde, then a redhead and now a brunette. Though he'd found each and every version of her fascinating, of all her incarnations, this one he liked the best. Perhaps it was the fact he could actually focus on her face now, without the distraction of all that hair. Perhaps it matched her personality, those elfin tendrils wisping around her forehead.

Perhaps he was beyond caring about details as inconsequential as hair because he was falling in love with her.

That's why this insult by Vauxhall so enraged him.

He said, none too civilly, "Are you questioning Miss Rice's integrity?"

"Not...not exactly," said Vauxhall. "That is—"

"What *are* you questioning, then?"

Vauxhall looked miserable. "The story, it just appears— Oh, let's be frank, Mr. Tavistock. A slaughter at sea? Sabotage of one's own vessel? It's so shocking as to be—"

"Unbelievable."

"Yes. And when the accused is Victor Van Weldon, the story seems even more farfetched."

"But I saw it," insisted Clea. "I was there. Why won't you believe me?"

"We've already looked into it. Or rather, Mr. Hammersmith's department did. They spoke to the Spanish police, who assert that it was most probably an accident. An engine explosion. No bodies were ever found. Nor did they find evidence of murder."

"They wouldn't," said Clea. "Van Weldon's people are too clever."

"And as for the wreckage of the *Havelaar,* it went down in deep water. It's not easily salvageable. So we have nothing on which to base an accusation of sabotage."

Throughout Vauxhall's almost disdainful rebuttal, Clea had maintained her composure. She had regarded the man with almost regal calm. Jordan had watched in fascination as she took it all without batting an eyelash. Now he recognized the glimmer of triumph in her eyes. She was going to unveil the evidence.

Clea reached into her purse and withdrew the cloth-wrapped bundle that she'd so carefully guarded for the past sixteen hours. "You may find it difficult to take my word," she said, laying the bundle on his desk. "I understand that. After all, who am I to walk in off the street and tell you some fantastic tale? But perhaps this will change your mind."

Vauxhall frowned at the bundle. "What is that?"

"Evidence." Clea removed the cloth wrapping. As the last layer fell away, Vauxhall sucked in an audible gasp of wonder. A jeweled scabbard lay gleaming in its undistinguished bed of muslin cloth.

Clea slid the dagger out of the scabbard and laid it down, razor tip pointed toward Vauxhall. "It's called the Eye of Kashmir. Seventeenth century. The jewel in the hilt is a blue star sapphire from India. You'll find a description of it in your files. It was part of Victor Van Weldon's collection, insured by your company. A month ago it was being transported from Naples to Brussels aboard a vessel which, coincidentally, was also insured by your company. The *Max Havelaar*."

Vauxhall glanced at Jordan, then back at Clea. "But that would mean..."

"This dagger should be on the ocean floor right now. But it isn't. Because it was never aboard the *Havelaar*. It was kept safely in storage somewhere, then sold on the black market to an Englishman."

"How did *you* get it?"

"I stole it."

Vauxhall stared at her for a moment, as though not certain she was being serious. Slowly he reached for his intercom button. "Miss Barrows," he murmured, "could you ring Mr. Jacobs, down in appraisals? Tell him to come up to my office. And have him bring his loupe or whatever it is he uses to examine gems."

"I'll ring him at once."

"Also, could you fetch the Van Weldon company's file for me? I want the papers for an antique dagger known as the Eye of Kashmir." Vauxhall sat back in his chair and regarded Clea with a troubled look. "This puts a new complexion on things. Mr. Van Weldon's claims, if I recall correctly, were in the neighborhood of fifteen million pounds for the art collection alone. This—" he waved at the dagger "—would call his claims into question."

Jordan looked at Clea and recognized her look of relief. *It's over,* he read in her eyes. *This nightmare is finally over.*

He took her hand. It was clammy, shaking, as though in fear. Of all the frightening events this past week, this moment must have been one of the most harrowing, because she had traveled so long and hard to reach it. She was too tense to smile at him, but he felt her fingers tighten around his. When this is over, he thought, well and truly over, we're going to celebrate. We're going to check in to a hotel suite and have all our meals delivered. And we're going to make love day and night until we're too exhausted to move. Then we'll sleep and start all over again....

They continued to cast knowing looks back and forth even as Vauxhall's secretary entered to deliver Van Weldon's files, even as Mr. Jacobs arrived from appraisals to examine the dagger. He was a distinguished-looking gentleman with a full mane of silver hair. He studied the Eye for what seemed like an eternity. At last he looked up and said to Vauxhall, "May I see the policy appraisal?"

Vauxhall handed it over. "There's a photo, as well. It seems to be identical."

"Yes. It does." Mr. Jacobs squinted at the photo, then regarded the dagger again. This time he focused his attention on the star sapphire. "Quite excellent work," he murmured, peering through the jeweler's loupe. "Exquisite craftsmanship."

"Don't you think it's time to call the authorities?" asked Jordan.

Vauxhall nodded and reached for the telephone. "Even Victor Van Weldon can't argue away the Eye of Kashmir, can he?"

Mr. Jacobs looked up. "But this isn't the Eye of Kashmir," he said.

The room went absolutely silent. Three pairs of eyes stared at the elderly appraiser.

"What do you mean, it's not?" demanded Vauxhall.

"It's a reproduction. A synthetic corundum. An excellent one, probably made using the Verneuil method. But as you'll see, the star is rather more pronounced than you'd find in a natural stone. It's worth perhaps two, three hundred pounds, so it's not entirely without value. But it's not a true star sapphire, either." Mr. Jacobs regarded them with a calm, bespectacled gaze. "This is not the Eye of Kashmir."

Clea's face had drained of color. She sat staring at the dagger. "I don't...don't understand...."

"Couldn't you be mistaken?" asked Jordan.

"No," said Mr. Jacobs. "I assure you, it's a reproduction."

"I demand a second opinion."

"Certainly. I'll recommend a number of gemologists—"

"No, we'll make our own arrangements," said Jordan.

Mr. Jacobs reacted with a look of injured dignity. He slid the dagger to Jordan. "Take it to whomever you wish," he said, and rose to leave.

"Mr. Jacobs?" called Vauxhall. "We hold the policy on the Eye of Kashmir. Shouldn't we retain this dagger until this matter is cleared up?"

"I see no reason to," snapped Mr. Jacobs. "Let them keep the thing. After all, it's nothing but a fake."

CHAPTER ELEVEN

NOTHING BUT A FAKE.

Clea clutched the wrapped bundle in both hands as she and Jordan rode the elevator to the first floor. They walked out into the fading sunlight of late afternoon.

Nothing but a fake.

How could she have been so wrong?

She tried to reason out the possibilities, but her brain wouldn't function. She was operating on autopilot, her feet moving mechanically, her body numb. She had no evidence now, nothing to back up her story. And Van Weldon was still in pursuit. She could change her name a hundred times, dye her hair a hundred different shades, and still she'd be looking over her shoulder, wondering who might be moving in for the kill.

Victor Van Weldon had won.

It would almost be easier just to walk into his office, meet him face-to-face and tell him, "I give up. Just get it over with quick." She wouldn't last much longer, anyway. Even now she was scarcely aware of the faces on the street, much less able to watch for signs of danger. Only the firm guidance of Jordan's hand kept her moving in any sort of purposeful direction.

He pulled her into a taxi and directed the driver to Brook Street.

Gazing out dully at the passing traffic, she asked, "Where are we going?"

"To get that second opinion. There's a chap I know, has a shop in the area. He's done some appraisals for Uncle Hugh in the past."

"Do you think Mr. Jacobs could be wrong?"

"Wrong. Or lying. At this point, I don't trust anyone."

Does he trust me? she wondered. *The dagger's a fake. Maybe he thinks I am, as well.*

The taxi dropped them off at a shop in the heart of Mayfair.

From the exterior it did not look like the sort of establishment any family as lofty as the Tavistocks would patronize. A sign in the window said, Clocks and Jewellery—Bought and Sold. Behind the dusty plate glass was arranged a selection of rings and necklaces that were obviously paste.

"This is the place?" asked Clea.

"Don't be fooled by appearances. If I want a straight answer, this is the man I ask."

They stepped inside, into a dark little cave of a room. On the walls were hung dozens of wooden cuckoo clocks, all of them ticking away. The counter was deserted.

"Hello?" called Jordan. "Herr Schuster?"

A door creaked open and an elderly gnome of a man shuffled out from a back room. At his first glimpse of Jordan, the man gave a cackle of delight.

"It's young Mr. Tavistock! How many years has it been?"

"A few," admitted Jordan as he shook the man's hand. "You're looking very well."

"Me? Bah! I am twenty years on borrowed time. To be alive is enough. And your uncle, he is retired now?"

"As of a few months ago. He's enjoying it immensely." Jordan slid an arm around Clea's shoulders. "I'd like you to meet Miss Clea Rice. A good friend of mine. We've come to ask you for some help."

Herr Schuster shot a sly glance at Clea. "Would this perhaps be for an engagement ring?"

Jordan cleared his throat. "It's rather…your expert opinion we need at the moment."

"On what matter?"

"This," said Clea. She unwrapped the bundle and handed him the dagger.

"The star sapphire in the hilt," said Jordan. "Is it natural or man-made?"

Gingerly Herr Schuster took the dagger and weighed it in his hands, as though trying to divine the answer by its touch. He said, "This will require some time."

"We'll wait," said Jordan.

The old jeweler retreated into the back room and shut the door behind him.

Clea looked doubtfully at Jordan. "Can we trust his opinion?"

"Absolutely."

"You're that sure of him?"

"He used to be the leading authority on gemstones in East Berlin. In the days before the wall came down. He also happened to work as a double agent for MI6. You'd be amazed how much one can learn from chats with the wives of high Communist officials. When things got dangerous, Uncle Hugh helped him cross over."

"So that's why you trust him."

"It's a debt he owes my uncle." Jordan glanced at the door to the back room. "Old Schuster's been keeping a low profile here in London ever since. Touch of paranoia, I suspect."

"Paranoia," said Clea softly. "Yes, I know exactly how he's lived." She turned to the window and stared out through the dusty glass at Brook Street. A bus rumbled past, spewing exhaust. It was early evening now, and the afternoon crowd had thinned out to a few shop girls straggling home for the night and a man waiting at the bus stop.

"If it is a fake," she said, "will you...still believe me, Jordan?"

He didn't answer at first. That brief silence was enough to send despair knifing through her. He said at last, "Too much has happened for me *not* to believe you."

"But you have doubts."

"I have questions."

She laughed softly. Bitterly. "That makes two of us."

"Why, for instance, would Delancey have bought a replica? He certainly had the money to spend. He would have insisted on the genuine item."

"He might have been misled. Believed it was the real Eye of Kashmir."

"No, Guy was a discerning collector. He'd get an expert's advice before he bought it. You saw how easily Mr. Jacobs identified that stone as man-made. Guy would have learned that fact just as easily."

She gave a sigh of frustration. "You're right, of course. He would have had it looked at. Which means whoever appraised it was either crooked or incompetent or..." Suddenly she turned to him. "Or he was right on the money."

"I told you, Guy would never buy a reproduction."

"Of course he wouldn't. He bought the real Eye of Kashmir."

"Then how did he wind up with a fake?"

"Someone switched it for the real one. *After* Guy bought it." She was moving around the room now, her mind racing. "Think about it, Jordan. Before you buy a painting or antique, aren't you very careful to confirm it's genuine?"

"Naturally."

"But after you've bought it—say, a painting—and you've had it hanging on your wall for a while, you don't bother to have it reauthenticated."

Slowly Jordan nodded. "I think I'm beginning to understand. The dagger was replaced sometime after Guy bought it."

"And he didn't realize! He has so many collectibles in that house. He'd never notice that one little dagger wasn't quite the same."

"All right, time for a reality check here. You're saying that our theoretical thief commissioned an exact replica. And then he managed to switch daggers without Guy's knowledge? That would require a hell of a lot of inside knowledge. Remember how much trouble we had, locating the Eye? Without Whitmore's help, we never would've found that hiding place."

"You're right, of course," she admitted with a sigh. "A thief would have to know exactly where it was hidden. Which means it had to be someone very close to Delancey."

"And that would eliminate an outside thug. Van Weldon's or otherwise." He shook his head. "I don't want to say 'the butler did it.' But I think the list of suspects is rather short."

"What about Guy's family?"

"Estranged. None of them even live in the neighborhood."

"One of his lovers, then?"

"He did have a few." He aimed an inquiring glance her way.

"I wasn't one of them," she snapped. "So who *has* Guy romanced in the last month?"

"Only one woman I'm aware of. Veronica Cairncross."

There was a long silence. "You're the one who knows her, Jordan," said Clea. "You two are friends...."

He frowned, troubled by the possibilities. "I've always considered her a bit wild. Impulsive. And not altogether moral. But a thief..."

"She's someone to consider. There's the household staff, as well. Come to think of it, anyone could've slipped into that bedroom. I got in. So did you. If it hadn't been for old Whitmore, we would have slipped out without anyone being the wiser."

Jordan went very still. "Whitmore," he said.

"What about him?"

"I'm thinking."

She watched in bewilderment as he muttered the name again, more softly. With sudden comprehension he looked at her. "Yes, Whitmore's the key."

She laughed. "You're not back to saying the butler did it?"

"No, it's the fact he was *home* that night! Veronica assured me it was Whitmore's night off. That the house would be empty. But when I broke in, he was right there. All this time I assumed she'd made a mistake. But what if it wasn't a mistake? What if she *wanted* the butler home?"

"Why on earth would she?"

"To raise the alarm. And notify the police."

"What would be the point?"

"There'd be an official record of a break-in. If Guy ever discovered the real Eye of Kashmir was gone, he'd assume the theft occurred that night. The night Whitmore raised the alarm."

"A night Veronica had an airtight alibi. Your sister's engagement party."

Jordan nodded. "It'd never occur to him that the switch was made earlier. *Before* that night. By an acquaintance so intimate she knew exactly where the Eye was hidden. An acquaintance who'd been in and out of that bedroom." Jordan slapped his temple in frustration. "All this time I thought *she* was the thick one. *I'm* the idiot."

Clea shook her head. "You're giving Veronica an awful lot of credit. How would she manage to commission such an accurate replica? It would take time. The forger would need to work from the original. I hardly think Guy would let her borrow it for a week. So where would this replica come from?''

''There's always the previous owner,'' said Jordan.

Clea's mouth went dry. *Van Weldon. The previous owner was Van Weldon.*

She went to stand beside him, close enough to lean her cheek against the fine wool of his jacket. Softly she said, ''Veronica. Van Weldon. Could there be a link?''

''I don't know. She's never mentioned Van Weldon's name.''

''He has connections everywhere. People who owe him. People who are afraid of him.''

''It seems unlikely.''

''But how well do you really *know* her, Jordan? How well do we really know anyone?''

He said nothing. He stood very still, not reaching for her, not even looking at her. Aching, she thought, *Oh, Jordan. How well do I really know you? And what little you know of me is the very worst....*

They stood just inches apart, yet she felt cold and alone as they both gazed out at that street where the shadows crept toward dusk. She reached out to him. His shoulder was rigid. Unresponsive to her touch.

''Clea,'' he said softly. ''I want you to go into the back room. Ask Herr Schuster if there's a rear door.''

''What?''

''There's a man standing at the bus stop. See him?''

She focused on the street. And on the man standing there. He wore a brown suit and carried a black umbrella, and every so often he glanced at his watch, as though late for some appointment. No wonder. He'd been waiting for his bus a long time now.

Slowly Clea backed away from the window.

Jordan didn't move, but continued to gaze out calmly at the street. ''He's let two go past now,'' he said. ''I don't think he's waiting for a bus.''

She fought the impulse to run headlong through that rear door.

She had no idea if the man could see them through those dusty front windows. She managed to stroll casually to the rear of the shop, then she pushed through the door, into the workshop.

Herr Schuster was at his jeweler's bench. "I am afraid the news is disappointing. The star sapphire—"

"Is there a back way out?" she asked.

"Excuse me?"

"Another exit?"

Jordan stepped in behind Clea. "There's a man following us."

Herr Schuster rose to his feet in alarm. "I have a back door." At a frantic shuffle, he led them through the workshop's clutter and opened the door to what looked like a closet. Dusty coats hung inside. He shoved the old garments aside. "There is a latch at the rear. The door leads to the alley. Around the corner is South Molton. You wish me to call the police?"

"No, don't. We'll be fine," said Jordan.

"The man—he is dangerous?"

"We don't know."

"The dagger—do you want it back?"

"It's not genuine?"

Regretfully Herr Schuster shook his head. "The sapphire is synthetic corundum."

"Then keep it as a souvenir. But don't show it to anyone."

A buzzer suddenly rang in the workshop. Herr Schuster glanced toward the front room. "Someone has come in the door. Hurry, go!"

Jordan grabbed Clea's hand and pulled her into the closet. Instantly the coats were slid back in place and the door shut on them. In the sudden darkness they blindly fumbled along the rear door for the latch and pushed.

They stumbled out into an alley. At once they tore around the corner onto South Molton Street. They didn't stop running until they'd reached the Bond Street Underground.

Aboard the train to Tottenham Court Road, Clea sat in stunned silence as the blackness of the tunnel swept past her window. Only when Jordan had taken her hand in his did she realize how chilled her fingers were, like icicles in the warmth of his grasp.

"He won't give up," she said. "He'll never give up."

"Then we have to stay one step ahead."

Not we, she thought. *I'm the one Van Weldon wants. The one he'll kill.*

She stared down at the hand now holding hers. A hand with all the strength a woman could ever need, could ever want. In a few short days she'd come to trust Jordan in a way she'd never trusted anyone. And she understood him well enough by now to know the gentleman's code of honor by which he operated—an absurd concept under these brutal circumstances. He would never abandon a woman in need.

So she would have to abandon him.

She chose her words carefully. Painfully. "I think it would be better if..." The words caught in her throat. She forced herself to stare ahead. Anywhere but at Jordan. "I think I would be better off on my own. I can move faster that way."

"You mean without me."

"That's right." Her chin slanted up as she found the courage to keep talking. "I can't afford to spend my time worrying about you. You'll be fine holed up in Chetwynd."

"And where will you go?"

She smiled nonchalantly. "Some place warm. The south of France, maybe. Or Sicily. Anywhere I can be on a beach."

"If you live long enough to climb into a bathing suit."

The train pulled in to the next stop. Abruptly he pulled her to her feet and snapped, "We're getting off."

She followed him off the train and up the station steps to Oxford Street. He was silent, his shoulders squared in anger. So much for self-sacrifice, she thought. All she'd managed to do was turn him against her. And why the hell was he mad at her, anyway? It wasn't as if she'd rejected him. She'd simply offered him the chance to leave.

The chance to live.

"I was only thinking of *you,* you know," she said.

"I'm quite aware of that."

"Then why are you ticked off at me?"

"You don't give me much credit."

"There's nothing more you can do for me. You have to admit, it doesn't make sense for both of us to get our heads blown off. If we split up, they'll forget all about you."

"Will *you* forget all about me?"

She halted on the sidewalk. "Does it matter?"

"Doesn't it?" He turned to face her. They stood looking at each other, an obstruction to all the pedestrians moving along the sidewalk.

"I don't know what you're getting at," she said. "I'm sorry it has to end this way, Jordan. But I have to look out for number one. Which means I can't have you around. I don't *want* you around."

"You don't know what the hell you want."

"All right, maybe I don't. But I do know what's best for *you.*"

"So do I," he said, and reached for her. His arms went around her back and his mouth came down on hers in a branding kiss that held no gentleness, brooked no resistance.

Far from protesting, she welcomed the assault, thrilled to the surge of his tongue into her mouth, the hungry roving of his hands up and down her back. She could not hide her desire from him, nor could he from her. They were both helpless and hopeless, lost to the crazy yearnings that always burst forth whenever they touched. It had been this way from the start. It would always be this way. A look, a touch, and suddenly the tension would be sizzling between them.

His lips slid to her cheek, then her ear, and the tickle of his hot breath sent a tremor of delight down her spine. "Have I made myself clear?" he whispered.

She moaned. "About what?"

"About staying together."

The need was still too strong between them. She pulled away and took a step back, fighting the urge to touch him again. *You and your crazy sense of honor,* she thought, staring up at his face. *It will get you killed. And I couldn't stand that.*

"I'm not exactly helpless, you know," she said.

He smiled. "Still, you have to admit I've come in handy on occasion."

"On occasion," she agreed.

"You need me, Clea. To beat Van Weldon."

She shook her head. "I've already tried. Now there's nothing else I can do."

"Yes, there is."

"The dagger's gone. I have no evidence. I can't see any way to get at him."

"There is a way." He moved closer. "Veronica Cairncross."

"What about her?"

"I've been trying to piece it all together. And I think you're right. She could be the key to all this. I've known Ronnie for years. She's a jolly girl, great fun to be around. But she's a gambler. And a big spender. Over the last few years she's run up a fortune in debts. A scam like this could've saved her skin."

"But now we're back to the problem of how she commissioned that reproduction," said Clea. "How'd she get her hands on the original? It belonged to Van Weldon. Did she buy it from him? Borrow it from him?"

"Or steal it from him?"

Clea shuddered at the thought. "No one's stupid enough to cross Van Weldon."

"Somehow, though, that dagger found its way from Van Weldon into Delancey's hands. Veronica could be the link between them. That's what we have to find out." Jordan paused, thinking. "She and Oliver have a town house here in London. They spend their weekdays here. Which means they'd be in town now."

Clea frowned at him. She didn't like this new shift of conversation. "What, exactly, are you thinking?"

He eyed her hair. "I'm thinking," he said, "that it's time for you to try a wig."

ARCHIE MACLEOD HUNG UP the phone and looked at Richard Wolf and Hugh Tavistock. "They're in London. My man just spoke to an official from Lloyd's. Jordan and Clea Rice paid a visit there around four o'clock today. Unfortunately the man they met with—an Anthony Vauxhall—wasn't aware of the investigation. He just happened to mention their visit to his superior. By the time we found out, Jordan and Clea Rice had already left."

"So we know they're still alive," said Hugh.

"As of this afternoon, anyway."

They were sitting in Chetwynd's library, the room they'd turned into a crisis headquarters. Hugh had hurried back to Chetwynd that morning, and all day the three of them had sat waiting for word from their police contacts.

This last news was good. Jordan had made it safely to London.

Not that Richard was surprised. In the few months he'd known his future brother-in-law, he'd come to appreciate Jordan's resourcefulness. In a pinch there were few men Richard would rather have at his side.

Clea Rice, too, was a survivor. Together, they might just stay alive.

Richard looked at Hugh. The older man was looking drained and weary. The worry showed plainly in Hugh's round face. "That price on Clea Rice's head will be drawing every contract man in Europe," said Richard.

"Surely, Lord Lovat," said MacLeod, "you can marshal some help from your intelligence contacts. We have to find them."

Hugh shook his head. "My Jordan was reared in the lap of the intelligence business. All these years he's been listening. Learning. He's probably picked up a trick or two. Even with help, it won't be easy to track him down. Which means it won't be easy for Van Weldon to track him down, either."

"You don't know Victor Van Weldon the way I do," said MacLeod. "At this point, he'll be willing to pay a fortune to get rid of Clea Rice. I'm afraid money is the world's best motivator."

"Not money," said Richard. "Fear. That's what will keep Jordan alive."

"Blast it all," said Hugh. "Why do we know so little about this Victor Van Weldon, anyway? Is he so untouchable?"

"I'm afraid he is," admitted MacLeod. He sank into a chair by the fireplace. "Victor Van Weldon has always operated on the fringes of international law. Never quite crossing the boundaries into illegality. At least, never leaving any evidence of it. He hides behind a regiment of lawyers. Keeps homes in Gstaad, Brussels and probably a few places we haven't found out about. He's like some rare bird, almost never sighted, but very much alive.''

"You can't dredge up any evidence against him?''

"We know he's involved in international arms shipments. Dabbles in the drug trade. But every time we think we have hard evidence, it disintegrates in our hands. Or a witness dies. Or documents vanish. For years it's been a source of frustration for me, how he manages to elude me. Only recently did I realize how many friends in high places he has, keeping him apprised of my every move. That's when I changed tactics. I picked out my own team of men. An independent team. We've spent the past six months gathering information on Van Weldon, ferreting out his Achilles' heel. We know he's sick—emphysema and heart failure. He hasn't much longer to live. Before he dies, I want him to face a little earthly justice.''

"You sound like a man on crusade,'' said Richard.

"I've lost...people. Van Weldon's work.'' MacLeod looked at him. "It's something one doesn't forget. The face of a dying friend.''

"How close are you now to building a case?''

"We have the foundations. We know Van Weldon took big losses last year. The European economy—it's affected even him. With his empire on the brink of ruin, he was bound to try something desperate. That's when the *Havelaar* went down. Eight men dead, a fortune lost at sea—all of it fully insured. I couldn't convince the Spanish authorities to foot the bill for a proper investigation. It would've required a salvage crew, ships and equipment. Van Weldon, we thought, had slipped away again. Then we heard about Clea Rice.'' MacLeod sighed. "Unfortunately, Miss Rice is not the sort of witness to base any prosecution on. Prison record. Family of thieves. Here we finally find a weapon against Van Weldon, and it's one that could backfire in court.''

"So you can't use her as the basis of any legal case,'' said Hugh.

"No. We need something tangible. For instance, the artwork listed on the *Havelaar*'s manifest. We know bloody well it didn't go down with the ship. Van Weldon's stashed it somewhere. He's waiting for an opportunity to sell it off piece by piece. If we just knew where he's hidden it.''

"It was supposedly shipped from Naples.''

"We searched his Naples warehouse. We also searched—not always legally, mind you—every building we know he owns. We're talking about large items, not things you can just hide in a closet. Tapestries and oil paintings and even a few statues. Wherever he's keeping it, it's a large space.''

"There must be a warehouse you don't know about yet.''

"Undoubtedly.''

"Interpol's not authorized to handle this alone,'' said Hugh. "You're going to need assistance.'' He reached for the telephone and began to dial. "It's not the customary way of doing things. But with Jordan's life at stake…''

Richard listened as Hugh made the contacts, called in old favors from Scotland Yard's Special Branch, as well as MI5—domestic intelligence. After he hung up, Hugh looked at Richard.

"Now I suggest we get to work ourselves,'' said Hugh.

"London?''

"Jordan's there. He may try to reach us. I want to be ready to respond.''

"What I don't understand,'' said MacLeod, "is why he hasn't called you already.''

"He's cautious,'' said Richard. "He knows the one thing Van Weldon expects him to do is contact us for help. Under the circumstances, Jordan's best strategy is to keep doing the *unexpected*.''

"Precisely the way Clea Rice has operated all these weeks,'' observed MacLeod. "By doing the unexpected.''

VAN WELDON WAS WAITING for the call. He picked up the receiver. "Well?''

"They're here,'' said Simon Trott. "They were spotted leaving Lloyd's of London, as you predicted.''

"Is the matter concluded?''

There was a pause. "Unfortunately, no. They vanished off Brook Street—a jewelry store. The proprietor claims ignorance.''

The news made Van Weldon's chest ache. He paused a moment

to catch his breath, the whole time silently cursing Clea Rice. In all his years he'd never known such a tenacious opponent. She was like a thorn that couldn't be plucked out, and she seemed to keep burrowing ever deeper.

When he'd managed to catch his breath again, he said, "So she did go to Lloyd's. Did she take the dagger?"

"Yes. She must have been rather peeved to learn it was a fake."

"And the real Eye of Kashmir?"

"Safely back where it belongs. Or so I've been assured."

"The Cairncross woman brought us to the brink of disaster. She cannot go unpunished."

"I quite agree. What do you have in mind?"

"Something unpleasant," said Van Weldon. Veronica Cairncross was an opportunistic bitch. And a fool as well to think she could slip one over on them. Her greed had taken her too far this time, and she was going to regret it.

"Shall I see to Mrs. Cairncross myself?" asked Trott.

"Wait. First confirm the collection is safe. It must go on the market within the month."

"So soon after the *Havelaar?* Is that wise?"

Trott raised a good point. It was risky to release the artwork onto the market. To think of all those assets bundled away, untouchable, just when he needed them most! Last year he had overextended himself, had made a few too many commitments to a few too many cartels. Now he needed cash. Lots of it.

"I cannot wait," said Van Weldon. "It must be sold. In Hong Kong or Tokyo, we could fetch excellent prices, and without much notice. Buyers are discreet in Tokyo. See that the collection is moved."

"When?"

"The *Villafjord* is scheduled to dock in Portsmouth tomorrow. I will be on board."

"You...are coming here?" There was an undertone of dismay in Trott's voice. He *should* be dismayed. What had started as a minor difficulty had ballooned into a crisis, and Van Weldon was disgusted with his heir apparent. If Trott could not handle such simple matters as Veronica Cairncross and Clea Rice, how could he hope to assume the company's helm?

"I will see to the shipment myself," said Van Weldon. "In the meantime, I expect you to find Clea Rice."

"We have the Tavistocks under surveillance. Sooner or later, Jordan and the woman will surface."

Perhaps not, thought Van Weldon as he hung up. By now Clea Rice would be weary, demoralized. Her instinct would be to run as far and as fast as she could. That would take care of the problem—temporarily, at least.

Van Weldon felt better. He decided there was really no need to worry about Clea Rice. By now she'd be long gone from London.

It's what any sensible woman would do.

CHAPTER TWELVE

AT TWELVE-FIFTEEN Veronica Cairncross left her London flat, climbed into a taxi and was driven to Sloane Street where she had lunch at a trendy little café. Afterward she strolled on foot toward Brompton Road, in the general direction of Harrods. She took her sweet time in one shop to purchase lingerie, and in another shop to try on a half-dozen pairs of shoes.

A disguised Clea observed all of this from a distance and with a growing sense of exasperation. Not only did this exercise seem more and more pointless, but also her long black wig was itchy, her sunglasses kept slipping down the bridge of her nose and her new short-heeled pumps were killing her. Perhaps she should have slipped into that same shoe shop where Veronica had spent so much time and picked up a pair of sneakers for herself. Not that she could have afforded anything in there. Veronica clearly frequented only the priciest establishments. *What is it like to be so idle and so rich?* Clea wondered as she trailed the elegant figure up Brompton Road. *Doesn't the woman ever get tired of constant partying and shopping?*

Oh, sure. The poor thing must be bored to tears.

She followed Veronica into Harrods. Inside she lingered a discreet distance away and watched Veronica sample perfumes, browse among scarves and handbags. Two hours later, loaded down with purchases, Veronica strolled out and hailed a taxi.

Clea scurried out after her and after a few frantic glances, spotted another taxi, this one with tinted windows. She climbed in.

Jordan was waiting in the back seat.

"There she goes," said Clea. "Stay with her."

Their driver, a grinning Sikh whom Jordan had hired for the day, expertly threaded the taxi into traffic and maintained a comfortable two-car distance behind Veronica's vehicle.

"Anything interesting happen?" asked Jordan.

"Not a thing. Lord, that woman can shop. She's way out of my league. Any trouble staying with me?"

"We were right behind you."

"I don't think she noticed a thing. Not me or the taxi." Sighing, Clea sat back and pulled off the wig. "This is getting us nowhere. So far all we've found out is that she has time and money on her hands. And a lot of both."

"Be patient. I know Ronnie, and when she gets nervous, she spends money like water. It's her way of blowing off stress. Judging by all the packages she was carrying, she's under a lot of stress right now."

Veronica's taxi had turned onto Kensington. They followed, skirting Kensington Gardens, and headed southwest.

"Now where's she going?" Clea sighed.

"Odd. She's not headed back to the flat."

Veronica's taxi led them out of the shopping district, into a neighborhood of business and office buildings. Only when the taxi stopped and let Veronica off at the curb did Jordan give a murmur of comprehension.

"Of course," he said. "Biscuits."

"What?"

"It's Oliver's company. Cairncross Biscuits." Jordan nodded at the sign on the building. "She's here to see her husband."

"Hardly a suspicious thing to do."

"Yes, it seems quite innocent, doesn't it?"

"Are you implying otherwise?"

"I'm just thinking about Oliver Cairncross. The firm's been in his family for generations. Appointment to the queen and all that...."

She studied Jordan's finely chiseled face as he mulled it over. *Such eyelashes he has,* she thought. No man had a right to such long eyelashes. Or such a kissable mouth. She could watch him for hours and never tire of the way his face crooked up on one side when he was thinking hard. *Oh, Jordan. How I'm going to miss you when this is over....*

"Cairncross biscuits are internationally known," said Jordan. "They're shipped all over the world."

"So?"

"So I wonder which firm is used to transport all those cookie crates. And what's really inside them."

"Uzis, you mean?" Clea shook her head. "I thought Oliver was supposed to be the innocent party. The cuckolded husband. Now you're saying *he's* the one in league with Van Weldon? Not Veronica?"

"Why not both of them?"

"She comes out again," said their driver.

Sure enough, Veronica had reappeared. She climbed back into her taxi.

"You wish me to follow her?" asked the Sikh.

"Yes. Don't lose her."

They didn't. They stayed on Veronica's tail all the way to Regent's Park. There Veronica alighted from the taxi and began to walk across Chester Terrace, toward the Tea House.

"Back into action." Clea sighed. "I hope it's not another two-hour hike." She pulled on a new wig—this one shoulder length and brown—and climbed out of the cab. "How do I look?"

"Irresistible."

She leaned inside and kissed him on the mouth. "You, too."

"Be careful."

"I always am."

"No, I mean it." He pulled her around by the wrist. His grip was insistent, reluctant to let go. "If there was any other way I could do it instead of you, I would—"

"She knows you too well, Jordan. She'd spot you in a second. Me, she'd scarcely recognize."

"Just don't let your guard down. Promise me."

She gave him a breezy grin that masked all the fears she had rattling inside. "And you promise not to vanish."

"I'll keep you right in view."

Still grinning, Clea turned and crossed Chester Terrace.

Veronica was well ahead of her. She seemed to be merely wandering, strolling toward Queen Mary's Rose Garden, its season of bloom now past. There she lingered, every so often glancing at her watch. Oh, Lord, not waiting for another lover, Clea thought.

Without warning Veronica turned and began walking in Clea's direction.

Clea ducked under an arbor and pretended to inspect the label on the climbing rose. Veronica didn't even glance her way, but headed toward the Tea House.

After a moment Clea followed her.

Veronica had seated herself at a table, and she had a menu propped open in front of her. Clea took a seat two tables behind Veronica and sat facing the other way. At this hour the Tea House was relatively quiet, and she could hear Veronica's whiney voice ordering a pot of Darjeeling and iced cakes. *Now I'll waste another hour,* thought Clea, *waiting for that silly woman to have her tea.*

She glanced toward Cumberland Terrace. Sure enough, there was Jordan sitting on a bench, his face hidden behind a newspaper.

The waiter approached. Clea ordered a pot of Earl Grey and watercress sandwiches. Her tea had just arrived when a man crossed the dining terrace toward Veronica.

Clea caught only a glimpse of him as he moved past her table. He was fair haired, blonder than Jordan, with wide shoulders and a powerful frame—just the sort of hunk Veronica would probably go gaga over. Clea felt a spurt of irritation that yet another hour would be wasted while Veronica made cow eyes at her latest admirer.

"Mr. Trott," Veronica said crossly. "You're late. I've already ordered."

Clea heard the man's voice, speaking behind her, and in the midst of pouring tea, her hand froze.

"I have no time for tea," he said. "I came only to confirm the arrangements."

That was all he said, but his tone of command, the English coarsened by some unidentifiable accent, was enough to make Clea suck in a breath in panic. She didn't dare glance back over her shoulder; she didn't dare let him see her face.

She didn't need to see *his;* his voice was all she needed to recognize him.

She'd heard it before, floating above the sound of lapping Mediterranean waves and the growl of a boat's engine. She remembered how that same voice had cut through the darkness. Just before the bullets began to fly.

All her instincts were screaming at her to lurch from this table and flee. *But I can't,* she thought. *I can't do anything to draw his attention.*

So she sat unmoving, her hands gripping the tablecloth. So acutely did she sense the man's presence behind her, she was surprised that he didn't seem at all aware of *her*.

Her heartbeat thudding, she sat motionless at the table.

TROTT WATCHED VERONICA light a cigarette and take in an unhurried drag of smoke. She seemed not in the least bit worried, which only proved what a stupid bitch she was, he decided. She thinks she's untouchable. She thinks her husband's too important to our operations. What she doesn't know is that we've already found a replacement for Oliver Cairncross.

Casually she exhaled a cloud of smoke. "The cargo's all there. Nothing missing. I told you it would be, didn't I?"

"Mr. Van Weldon is not pleased."

"Why, because I borrowed one of his precious little trinkets? It was only for a few weeks." Calmly she exhaled another cloud of smoke. "We've been stuck with your bloody crates for months now—at no small risk to ourselves. Why shouldn't I borrow what's in them? I got the dagger back, didn't I?"

"This is not the time or place to speak of it," cut in Trott. He passed a newspaper across the table to Veronica. "The information is circled. We'll expect it to be ready and waiting."

"At your beck and call, your highness," said Veronica, her voice dripping with mockery.

Trott pushed his chair back, preparing to leave. "What about compensation?" asked Veronica. "For all our trouble?"

"You'll have it. After all items are accounted for."

"Of course they will be," said Veronica. She blew out another cloud of smoke. "We're not fools, you know."

CLEA HEARD the man's chair scrape back. He was rising to his feet. Instinctively she huddled closer to the table, afraid to be noticed.

She forced herself to take a sip of tea, to pretend no interest whatsoever in the monster standing behind her.

When she heard him walk away, she went almost limp with relief. She glanced back.

Veronica was still sitting at the table, gazing down at a newspaper. After a moment she ripped off half a page, folded it and stuffed it in her purse. Then she, too, rose and left.

It took a while before Clea's nerves steadied enough for her to stand. Veronica was already walking out of the park. Clea started to follow, but her legs were shaking too hard. She took a few steps, faltered and stopped.

By then Jordan had realized something was wrong. She heard his footsteps, and then his arm was around her waist, supporting her, steadying her.

"We can't stay here," she whispered. "Have to hide—"

"What happened?"

"It was him—"

"Who?"

"The man from the *Cosima!*" Wildly she glanced around, her gaze sweeping the park for sight of the blond man.

"Clea, what man?"

She focused at last on Jordan. His gaze seemed to steady her. He held her face in his hand, the pressure of his fingers warming through her numbness.

"Tell me," he said.

She swallowed. "I've heard his voice before. The night the *Havelaar* went down. I was in the water, swimming alongside the lifeboat. He was the one who—the one who—" She blinked, and tears spilled down her face. Softly she finished, "The one who ordered his men to shoot."

Jordan stared at her. "The man with Veronica? You're absolutely certain?"

"He passed by my table. I recognized his voice. I'm sure it was him."

Jordan gave a quick glance around the park. Then he pulled Clea close, wrapping his arm protectively around her shoulder. "Let's get into the car."

"Wait." She went back to Veronica's table and snatched up the discarded newspaper.

"What's that for?" asked Jordan.

"Veronica left it. I want to see what she tore out."

Their taxi was waiting. As soon as they climbed in the back seat, Jordan ordered, "Move. See that we're not followed."

The Sikh driver grinned at them in the mirror. "A most interesting day," he declared, and sent the cab screeching into traffic.

Jordan draped his jacket over Clea's shoulders and took her hands in his. "All right," he coaxed gently. "Tell me what happened."

Clea took a shaky breath and sank back against the seat. No one was following them. Jordan's hand, warm and steady, seemed to radiate enough courage for them both.

"Did you hear what they were saying?"

"No. They were speaking too softly. And I was afraid to get any closer. After I realized who he was..." She shuddered, thinking of the man's voice. In her nightmares she'd heard that same voice drifting across the black Mediterranean waters. She'd remember the explosion of gunfire. And she'd remember Giovanni, slumping across the lifeboat....

Her head came up. "I do remember something. Veronica called him by name. Mr. Trott."

"You're sure that was it? Trott?"

She nodded. "I'm sure."

Jordan's grip tightened around hers. "Veronica. If I ever get my hands around her elegant little neck..."

"At least now we know. She's the link to Van Weldon. Delancey paid for the Eye. She stole it back. Someone earned a nice profit. And the only loser was Guy Delancey."

"What about the newspaper?"

Clea looked down at the folded pages. "I saw Veronica tear something out."

Jordan glanced at the newspaper's date, then tapped their taxi driver on the shoulder. "Excuse me. You wouldn't happen to have a copy of today's *Times?*"

"But of course. And the *Daily Mail,* as well."

"Just the *Times* will do."

The driver reached over and pulled out a slightly mangled newspaper from the glove compartment. He handed it back to Jordan.

"The top of page thirty-five and six," said Clea. "That's what she's torn out."

"I'm looking for it." Jordan thumbed quickly through the driver's copy. "Here it is. Top of page thirty-five. Article about the Manchester slums. Building renovations. Another about horse breeding in Ireland."

"Try the other side."

Jordan flipped the page. "Let's see. Scandal in some ad agency. Drop-off in the fishing harvest. And..." He paused. "Today's shipping schedule for Portsmouth." He looked at Clea.

"That's it! That has to be it. One of their ships must be arriving in port."

"Or leaving." He sat back, deep in thought. "If Van Weldon has a vessel in Portsmouth, then it's here for either a delivery..."

"Or a pickup," she finished for him.

They looked at each other, both struck by the same startling thought.

"It's taking on cargo," she said. "It must be."

"It could be purely legitimate cargo."

"But there's the chance..." She glanced up as they pulled in front of their hotel. At once she was climbing out the door. "We have to call Portsmouth. Check which vessels are Van Weldon's."

"Clea, wait—"

But she was already hurrying into the building.

By the time he'd settled with their driver and followed her up to the room, Clea was already on the phone. A moment later she hung up and turned to Jordan in triumph.

"There's a *Villafjord* scheduled to dock at five this afternoon. She sails again at midnight. And she's registered to the Van Weldon company."

For a moment he stared at her without speaking. Then he said flatly, "I'm going to call the police." He reached for the phone.

She grabbed his hand. "Don't! Jordan."

"We have to alert the authorities. It could be the best chance they'll have to nail Van Weldon."

"That's why we can't blow it! What if we're wrong? What if his ship's here to take on a cargo of—of undies or something? We'll look like a pair of idiots. So will the police." She shook her head. "We can't tell them until we know *exactly* what's on board."

"But the only way to learn that is..." He froze in the midst of that thought. "Don't you even dare suggest it."

"Just one little tiny peek inside."

"*No.* This is the perfect time to call in Richard. Let him—or someone else—handle it."

"But I don't trust anyone else!"

Again he reached for the phone.

Again she grabbed his hand and held on tightly. "If we let too many people in on this," she said, "I guarantee there'll be a leak. Van Weldon will hear about it, and that'll be it for our big chance. Jordan, we have to wait till the last minute. And we have to be sure of what they'll find."

"You don't really think you can stroll aboard that ship and have a look around, do you?"

"When it comes to making unauthorized entries, I had the world's best teacher."

"Uncle Walter? He got caught, remember?"

"*I* won't get caught."

"Because you're not going anywhere *near* the *Villafjord.*" He shook off her hand and began to dial the telephone.

Desperately she snatched away the receiver. "You're not doing this!" she cried.

"Clea." He heaved a sigh of frustration. "Clea, you have to trust me on this."

"No, you have to trust *me.* Trust *my* judgment. *I'm* the one with everything to lose!"

"I know that. But we're both tired. We're going to make mistakes. Now's the time to call the police and put an end to all this. To get back to our lives—our *real* lives. Don't you see?''

She looked into his eyes. *Yes, I see,* she thought. *You've had enough of running. Enough of me. You want your own life back, and I don't blame you.*

Defiantly she raised her chin. "I want to go home, too. I'm sick of hotels and strange beds and dyed hair. I want this all to be over with just as much as you do. That's why I say we do it *my* way.''

"Your way's too bloody risky. The police—''

"I told you, I don't trust them!'' Agitated, she paced over to the window, paced back. "I've survived this long only because I didn't trust anyone. *I'm* the only one I can count on.''

"You can count on me,'' he said quietly.

She shook her head and laughed. "In the real world, darling, it's every man for himself. Remember that. You can't trust anyone.'' She turned and looked at him. "Not even me.''

"But I do.''

"Then you're crazy.''

"Why? Because you're an ex-con? Because you've made a few mistakes in your life?'' He moved toward her and took her by the shoulders. "Are you *afraid* to have me believe in you?''

She gave a nonchalant toss of her head. "I'd hate to disappoint anyone.''

He cupped her face in his hands and lowered his mouth to hers. "I have complete faith,'' he whispered. "And so should you.''

His kiss was sweet enough to break her heart. And that frightened her, because she knew now there could be no clean parting between them, no easy goodbyes. The break would be painful and haunting and bitter.

And inevitable.

He pulled back. "I'm going to have to trust you now, Clea. To do as I ask. To stay in this room and let me take care of this.''

"But I—''

He silenced her by pressing a finger to her lips. "No arguments. I'm going to assert a little male authority here. Something I damn well should have done ages ago. You're going to wait for me. Here, in this room. Understood?''

She looked at his unyielding expression. Then she gave a sigh. "Understood," she said meekly.

He smiled and kissed her.

She smiled, too, as he walked out of the room. But when she went to the window and watched him leave the building, her smile faded. *What makes you think I'm so damn trustworthy?* she thought.

Turning, she saw Jordan's jacket, which she'd left draped over a chair. Impulsively she thrust her hand in the pocket and pulled out the gold watch. She flipped open the dented cover and looked at the name engraved inside: Bernard Tavistock.

And she thought, This will end it. Here and now. It's going to end anyway, and I might as well do it sooner than later. If I take this watch, something he treasures, I'll cut the ties. Cleanly. Decisively. After all, that's what I am. A thief. An ex-con. He'll be relieved to see me go.

She thrust the watch into her own pocket. Maybe she'd mail it back to him someday. When she was good and ready. When she could think of him without feeling that painful twist of her heart.

Glancing out the window, she saw that Jordan was nowhere in sight. *Goodbye,* she thought. *Goodbye, my darling gentleman.*

A moment later she, too, left the room.

CHAPTER THIRTEEN

RICHARD WOLF was on the telephone to Brussels when the doorbell rang. He paid it no attention—the butler would see to any visitors. Only when he heard Davis's polite knock on the study door did Richard break off his conversation.

The butler, looking oddly uncertain, stood in the doorway. It was something Richard hadn't gotten the hang of, dealing with all these servants. His Yankee sense of privacy was always being violated by all the maids and butlers and underbutlers whom the Tavistocks insisted upon keeping underfoot.

"Pardon the interruption, Mr. Wolf," said Davis. "But there's a foreign gentleman at the door. He insists upon speaking to you at once."

"Foreign?"

"A, er, Sikh, I believe." Davis made a whirling gesture over his head. "Judging by the turban."

"Did he say what his business was?"

"He said he would speak only to you."

Richard cut the call short and followed Davis to the front door.

There was indeed a Sikh waiting on the front step, a short, pleasant-looking fellow with a trim beard and a gold tooth. "Mr. Wolf?" he inquired.

"I'm Richard Wolf."

"You called for a taxi."

"I'm afraid I didn't."

Without a word the Sikh handed an envelope to Richard.

Richard glanced in the envelope. Inside was a single gold cuff link. It was inscribed with the initials J.C.T.

Jordan's.

Calmly Richard nodded and said, "Oh, right. Of course. I'd forgotten all about that appointment. Let me get my briefcase."

While the Sikh waited on the doorstep, Richard ducked back into the study, slid a 9 mm automatic into his shoulder holster and reemerged carrying an empty briefcase.

The Sikh directed him to a taxi at the curb.

Neither of them said a thing as the car moved through traffic. The Sikh drove exactly the way one expected of a cab driver—calmly. Recklessly.

"Are we going some place in particular?" asked Richard.

"Harrods. You will stay there half an hour. Visit all the floors. Perhaps make a purchase. Then you'll return to my taxi. You will recognize it by the number—twenty-three. I will wait for you at the curb."

"What am I to expect?"

The Sikh grinned in the rearview mirror. "I do not know. I am only the driver." He paused. "We are being followed."

"I know," said Richard.

At Harrods Richard got out and entered the store. Inside he did as instructed, wandering about the various departments. He bought a silk scarf for Beryl and a tie for his father back in Connecticut. He was aware of two men lingering nearby, a short man and a blond man. They were good—it was a full five minutes before he noticed them, and only because he'd glimpsed them in a mirror as he tried on top hats. He lost them briefly in the gourmet foods section, but picked them up again in housewares. If Jordan hoped to make contact, it was going to be difficult. Richard knew he could shake these guys if he wanted to. But then he'd probably shake Jordan, as well.

A half hour later he walked out of Harrods. He spotted taxi number twenty-three parked across the street, the Sikh driver still sitting patiently behind the wheel.

He crossed the street and climbed in the back seat of the taxi. "No luck," he said. "I was watched the whole time. Is there a backup plan?"

"This *is* the plan," said a familiar voice.

Richard glanced up in surprise at the rearview mirror, at the face of the bearded, turbaned driver. Jordan's brown eye winked back at him.

"Gotcha," said Jordan, and pulled the taxi into traffic.

"What the hell's going on?"

"Little game of wits. How am I doing so far?"

"Splendidly. You outsmarted me." Richard glanced back and spotted the same car following them.

"I see them," said Jordan.

"Where's Clea Rice?"

"A safe place. But things are coming to a head. We need help."

"Jordan, Interpol's already stepped in. They want Van Weldon's head. They'll arrange for the woman's safety."

"How do I know we can trust them?"

"They'd been watching over her for weeks. Until you two shook them off."

"Veronica's working for Van Weldon. Oliver may be, as well."

Richard, stunned, fell momentarily silent.

"You see, it reaches all levels," said Jordan. "It's like an octopus. Tentacles everywhere. The only people I can really count on are you, Beryl and Uncle Hugh. And you may regret hearing from me at all."

"We've been waiting for you to contact us. Hugh's calling in old favors. You'll be in good hands, I'll see to it myself. MacLeod's just waiting for the chance to move on Van Weldon."

"MacLeod?"

"Interpol. That was his man on the train platform. The one who saved your lives."

Jordan chewed on that piece of information for a moment. "If we come in, how will it be arranged?"

"Through your uncle. Scotland Yard will oversee. Whenever you're ready."

Jordan was silent as he dodged around a tight knot of traffic. "I'm ready," he said at last.

"And the woman?"

"Clea'll take some convincing. But she's tired. I think she's ready to come in, too."

"How shall we do it, then?"

"Sloane Square, the Underground. Make it an hour from now—eight-thirty."

"I'll let Hugh know."

They were coming up on the Tavistocks' London residence, one in a row of elegant Georgian town houses. The car was still following them.

Jordan pulled over to the curb. "One more thing, Richard."

"Yes?"

"There's a ship docking this afternoon in Portsmouth. The *Villafjord*."

"Van Weldon's?"

"Yes. My guess is, she'll be taking on cargo tonight. I suggest the police perform a little unannounced inspection before she leaves port."

"What's the cargo?"

"It'll be a surprise."

Richard stepped out and made a conspicuous point of paying for the ride. Then he walked up the steps and entered the house. As Jordan drove off, Richard saw that the car that had followed them remained parked outside the Tavistock residence. It was just as he'd expected. The men were assigned to watch him; they had no interest in any Sikh driver.

All the tension suddenly left his body. Only then did he realize how edgy he'd been.

And how close to the precipice they'd been dancing.

BACK AT THE HOTEL, Jordan parked the taxi a block away, and sat for a moment in the driver's seat, watching to see if any cars had followed him. When he saw nothing suspicious, he stripped off his beard and turban, got out and headed for the building.

Trust me, he thought as he climbed the stairs. *You have to learn to trust me.* He knew it would be a long, slow process, one that might take a lifetime. Perhaps it was too late. Perhaps all the damage done in childhood had robbed Clea forever of her faith in other people. Could they live with that?

Could she?

Only then did he realize that, lately, all his thoughts of the future seemed to include *her.*

Sometime in the past week, the shift had occurred. Where once he would have thought *I,* now he thought *we.* That's what came of sharing so much, so intensely. It was both the reward and the consequence, this link between them.

Trust me, he thought, and opened the door.

The room was empty.

He stood staring at the bed, suddenly, painfully aware of the silence. He went into the bathroom; it was empty, as well. He paced back to the bedroom and saw that her purse was gone. And he saw his jacket, lying draped across a chair.

He picked up the jacket and noticed at once that it was lighter than usual. That something was missing. Reaching into the pocket, he discovered that his father's gold watch was missing.

In its place was a note.

"It was fun while it lasted. Clea."

With a groan of frustration, he crumpled the paper in his fist. Blast the woman! She'd picked his pockets! And then she'd headed for...where?

The answer was only too frightening.

It was eight o'clock. She'd had a solid three hours' head start.

He ran back down the stairs to the taxi. First he'd swing past Sloane Square, to pick up some Scotland Yard assistance. And then it'd be on to Portsmouth, where a certain little burglar was, at this moment, probably sneaking up the gangplank of a ship.

If she wasn't already dead.

THE FENCE WAS HIGHER than she'd expected. Clea crouched in the thickening gloom outside the Cairncross Biscuits complex and stared up in dismay at the barbed wire lacing the top of the chain link. This was not the usual penny ante security one expected for a biscuit warehouse. What were they afraid of? An attack by the Cookie Monster? The fence ringed the entire complex, interrupted only by the main gate, which was padlocked for the night. Floodlights shone down on the perimeter, leaving only intermittent patches of shadow. Judging by the fortune invested in security, there was more than just biscuits being stored in that warehouse.

Right on the money, she thought. *Something else is going on in there besides the manufacture of teatime treats.*

It had required only a small leap of logic to lead her to the Cairncross warehouse on the outskirts of London. If Van Weldon's ship was taking on illicit cargo tonight, then here was the obvious holding place for that cargo. Legitimate trucks were probably in and out of here all the time, pulling up to that handy warehouse platform. If a truck showed up tonight to pick up a load of crates, no one in the neighborhood would bat an eyelash.

Very clever, Van Weldon, she thought. *But this time I'm one step ahead of you.*

She'd be ahead of the authorities, as well. By the time Jordan and his precious police converged on that Portsmouth dock, there'd be no telling how many people would know about the forthcoming raid. Or how much warning Van Weldon would have. Now was the time to view the evidence—before Van Weldon had a chance to change plans.

The sound of someone whistling sent Clea scrambling for the cover of bushes. From her hiding place she watched a security guard stroll past, inside the fence. He had a gun strapped to his hip. He moved at a leisurely pace, pausing to flick away a cigarette and crush the butt with his shoe. Then, lighting up another, he continued his circuit.

Clea timed the gap between his appearances. Seven minutes. She waited, let him go around again. This time it was six minutes. Six minutes, max, to get through the fence and into the building. The fence was no problem; a few snips of the wire cutter she'd brought and she'd be in the complex. It was the warehouse that worried her. Those locks might take a while to bypass, and if the guard circled around too early, she'd be trapped.

She had to take the chance.

She snipped a few links in the fence, then hid as the guard came around. The instant he vanished around the corner she cut the last link, scrambled under with her knapsack and dashed across the expanse of pavement to the warehouse side door.

One glance at the lock told her she was in for some trouble. It was a brand-new pin tumbler, and six minutes might not be enough to bypass it. She set her watch alarm for five minutes. Holding a penlight in her teeth, she set to work.

First she inserted an L-shaped tension wrench and gently applied pressure to slide apart the plug and cylinder plates. Next she inserted a lifter pick, with which she gingerly lifted the first lock pin. It slid up with a soft click.

One down, six pins to go.

The next five pins were a piece of cake. It was the seventh one— the last—that kept tripping her up. She felt the minutes tick by, felt the sweat beading on her upper lip as she struggled to lift that seventh pin. Just one more click and she'd be in the door. Interrupt the effort now, and she'd be back to square one.

Her watch alarm gave a beep.

She kept working, gambling on the chance she'd conquer that last pin in the seconds that remained. She was so close, so close.

Too late, she heard the sound of whistling again. The guard was approaching her corner of the building!

She'd never make it back under the fence in time. Neither was there any cover along the building. She had only one route of escape.

Straight up.

Sheer panic sent her clambering like a monkey up a flimsy-looking drainpipe, seeking the cover of the shadows above.

As the guard rounded the corner, she pressed herself to the wall, afraid to move a muscle, afraid even to breathe. A few feet below, the guard stopped. Pulse hammering, Clea watched as he lighted a fresh cigarette and inhaled deeply. Then, with a satisfied sigh, he continued his circuit. He rounded the next corner without a backward glance.

Clea had to make a quick choice: should she try that bloody lock again or keep climbing? Glancing up, she traced the course of the drainpipe to the three-story-high roofline. There might be another way in from there. Though the drainpipe looked flimsy, so far it had supported her weight.

She began to climb.

Seconds later she scrambled up over the edge and dropped onto the rooftop.

A shadowy expanse of asphalt tile lay before her. She started across it, moving past the whirring fans of vents. At last she came to a rooftop door—locked, of course. Another pin tumbler. She set to work with her tension wrench and lifter pick.

In two minutes flat she had the door open.

At her feet a narrow stairway dropped away into the darkness. She descended the stairs, pushed through another door and entered the vast cavern of the warehouse. Here the area was lighted, and she could see rows of crates. All of them were stamped Cairncross Biscuits, London.

She grabbed a crowbar from a tool bin and pried open one of the crates, releasing the fragrant waft of cookies. Inside she found tins with the distinctive red-and-yellow Cairncross logo. The crate did, indeed, contain biscuits.

Frustrated, she glanced around at the other crates. She'd never be able to search them all! Only then did she spot the closed double doors in the far wall.

With mounting excitement she approached the doors. They were locked. There were no windows, so it was unlikely there was an office beyond.

She picked the lock.

A rush of cooled air spilled out the open door. Air-conditioned, she thought. Climate control? She found the light switch and flicked it on.

The room was filled with crates, each stamped with the Cairncross Biscuits logo. These crates, however, were a variety of sizes. Several were huge enough to house a standing man.

With the crowbar she pried off one of the lids and discovered a fluffy mound of wood shavings. Plunging both arms into the packing, she encountered something solid buried within. She dug into the shavings and the top of the object emerged, its marble surface smooth and gleaming under the lights.

It was the head of a statue, a noble youth with a crown of olive leaves.

Clea, her hands shaking with excitement, pulled a camera from her knapsack and began to snap photos. She took three shots of the statue, then reclosed the lid. She pried open a second crate.

Somewhere in the building, metal clanged.

She froze, listening, and heard the growl of a truck, the protesting squeal of a bay door being shoved open along its tracks. At once she killed the room lights. Opening the door a crack, she peered out into the warehouse.

The loading gate was wide open. A truck had backed up to the platform, and the driver was swinging open the rear doors.

Veronica and the blond man were walking in Clea's direction.

Clea jerked back and shut the door. Frantically she waved her penlight around the room. No other exit. No place to hide except...

Voices were speaking right outside the door.

She grabbed her knapsack, scrambled into the open crate and pulled the lid over her head.

Through the cracks in the wood she saw the room's lights come on.

"It's all here, as you can see," said Veronica. "Would you care to check the crates yourself, Mr. Trott? Or do you trust me now?"

"I have no time for that. They must be moved immediately."

"I hope Mr. Van Weldon appreciates the trouble we've gone to, keeping these safe. He did promise there'd be compensation."

"You've already taken yours."

"What do you mean?"

"Your profit from selling the Eye. That should suffice."

"That was *my* idea! *My* profit. Just because I borrowed the bloody thing for a few weeks..."

There was a momentary pause. Then Clea heard Veronica suck in a sharp breath. "Put the gun away, Mr. Trott."

"Move away from the crates."

"You can't—you wouldn't—" Suddenly Veronica laughed, a shrill, hysterical sound. "You *need* us!"

"Not any longer," said Trott.

Clea flinched at the sound of a gun firing. Three bullets in rapid succession. She pressed her hand to her mouth, clamped it there to stifle the cry that rose up in her throat. She felt as if all the air had been sucked out of the crate and she was suffocating in her fear, choking on silent tears.

Then she heard the sounds of terrified sobbing. Veronica's. She was still alive.

"Just a warning, Mrs. Cairncross," said Trott. "Next time, I'll hit my target."

Trott crossed to the doorway and called out, "In here! Get these crates in the truck!"

More footsteps approached—two men and a squeaky loading cart.

"The large one first," said Trott.

Clea heard the cart move closer, then the men grunted in unison. She braced herself as the crate tilted. She found herself wedged between the side of the crate and something cold and metallic: the bronze torso of a man.

"Christ, this one's heavy. What's in here, anyway?"

"That's not your concern. Just get it moved."

Every little bump seemed to squash Clea into a tighter and tighter space. Only when the crate at last thumped to a rest in the truck was she able to take in a deep breath. And take stock of her predicament.

She was trapped. With the men constantly shuttling back and forth, loading in the rest of the crates, she couldn't exactly stroll out unseen.

The scrape of a second crate being slid on top of hers settled the issue. For the moment she was boxed in.

By the glow of her watch she saw it was 8:10.

At 8:25, the truck pulled away from the warehouse. By now, Clea's calves were cramping, the wood shavings had worked their way into her clothes and she was battling an attack of claustrophobia. Reaching up, she strained to push off the lid, but the crate on top was too heavy.

She pressed her face to a small knothole and took in a few slow, deep breaths. The taste of fresh air took the edge off her panic. *Better,* she thought. *Yes, that's better.*

Something hard was biting into her thigh. She managed to worm her hand into her hip pocket and found what it was: Jordan's watch. The one she'd stolen.

By now he knew she'd taken it. By now he'd be hating her and glad she was out of his life. That's what she'd wanted him to think.

What he should think. He was a gentleman and she was a thief. Nothing could close that gap between them.

Yet, as she huddled in that coffin of a space and clutched Jordan's pocket watch in her fist, her longing for him brought tears to her eyes.

I did it for you, she thought. *To make it easier for you. And me, as well. Because I know, as well as you do, that I'm not the woman for you.*

She pressed the watch to her lips and kissed it, the way she longed to kiss *him,* and never would again. She wanted to curse her larcenous past, her transgressions, her childhood. Even Uncle Walter. All the things that would forever keep Jordan out of her reach. But she was too weary and too frightened.

So she cried instead.

By the time the truck wheezed to a stop, Clea was numb in both spirit and body. Her legs felt dead and useless.

The other crates were unloaded first. Then her crate was tipped onto a cart and began a roller coaster ride, down a truck ramp, up another ramp. She knew there were men about—she heard their voices. An elevator ride brought her to the final destination. The crate hit the floor with a thump.

After a while she heard nothing. Only the faint rumbling of an engine.

Cautiously she pushed up on the lid. The weight of the other crate had redriven the nails into the wood. Luckily she still had the crowbar. It took some tight maneuvering, but she managed to work the tip under the lid and yanked on the bar.

The lid popped open.

She raised her head and inhaled a whiff of diesel-scented air. She was in a storage bay. Beside her were stacked the other crates from the warehouse annex. No one was around.

It took her a few moments to crawl out. By the time she dropped onto the floor, her calves were beginning to prickle with renewed circulation. She hobbled over to the steel door and opened it a crack.

Outside was a narrow corridor. Beyond the corner, two men were laughing, joking in that foul language sailors employ when they're away from the polite company of women. Something about the whores in Naples.

The floor lurched beneath Clea's feet and she swayed sideways. The engine sounds were grinding louder now.

Only then did she focus on the emergency fire kit mounted on the corridor wall. It was stamped with the name *Villafjord*.

I'm on his ship, she thought. *I'm trapped on Van Weldon's ship.*

The floor swayed again, a rolling motion that made her reach out to the walls for support. She heard the engine's accelerating whine, sensed the gentle rocking of the hull through the swells, and she understood.

The *Villafjord* was heading out to sea.

CHAPTER FOURTEEN

HUGH TAVISTOCK'S limousine was waiting at the side of the road just outside Guildford. The instant Jordan and his two Scotland Yard escorts pulled up in a Mercedes, the limousine door swung open. Jordan stepped out of the Mercedes and slid into the limousine's rear seat.

He found himself confronting his uncle Hugh's critical gaze. "It seems," said Hugh, "that I retired from intelligence simply to devote my life to rescuing *you*."

"And a fond hello to you, too," answered Jordan. "Where's Richard?"

"Present and accounted for," answered a voice from the driver's seat. Dressed in a chauffeur's uniform, Richard turned and grinned at him. "I picked up this trick from a certain relative-to-be. Where's Clea Rice?"

"I don't know," said Jordan. "But I have a very good idea. Did you confirm the shipping schedule for Portsmouth?"

"There is a vessel named *Villafjord* due to sail at midnight tonight. That gives us plenty of time to stop the departure."

"Why all this interest in the *Villafjord?*" asked Hugh. "What's she carrying?"

"Wild guess? A fortune in art." Jordan added, under his breath, "And a certain little cat burglar."

Richard pulled onto the highway for Portsmouth. "She'll jeopardize the whole operation. You should have stopped her."

"Ha! As if I could!" said Jordan. "As you may have surmised, she doesn't take to instruction well."

"Yes, I've heard about Miss Rice," said Hugh. "Uncooperative, is she?"

"She doesn't trust anyone. Not Richard, not the authorities."

"Surely she trusts *you* by now?"

Jordan gazed ahead at the dark road. Softly he said, "I thought she did...."

But she didn't. When it came down to the wire, she chose to work alone. Without me.

He didn't understand her. She was like some forest creature, always poised for flight, never trusting of a human hand. She wouldn't *let* herself believe in him.

That lifting of his pocket watch—oh, he understood the meaning of that gesture. It was part defiance and part desperation. She was trying to push him away, to test him. She was crazy enough to put him to this test. And vulnerable enough to be hurt if he failed her.

I should have known. I should have seen this coming.

Now he was angry at himself, at her, at all the circumstances that kept wrenching them apart. Her past. Her mistrust of him.

His mistrust of *her*.

Perhaps Clea had it right from the start. Perhaps there was nothing he could do, nothing she could do, that would get them beyond all this.

With renewed anxiety he glanced outside at a passing road sign. They were still thirty miles from Portsmouth.

MacLeod AND THE POLICE were already waiting at the dock.

"We're too late," said MacLeod as Hugh and Jordan stepped out of the limousine.

"What do you mean, too late?" demanded Jordan.

"This, I take it, is young Tavistock?" asked MacLeod.

"My nephew Jordan," said Hugh. "What's happening here?"

"We arrived a few minutes ago. The *Villafjord* was scheduled to sail at midnight from this dock."

"Where is she, then?"

"That's the problem. It seems she sailed twenty minutes ago."

"But it's only nine-thirty."

MacLeod shook his head. "Obviously they changed plans."

Jordan stared out over the dark harbor. A chill wind blew in from the water, whipping his shirt and stinging his face with the tang of salt. *She's out there. I feel it. And she's alone.*

He turned to MacLeod. "You have to intercept them."

"At sea? You're talking a major operation! We have no firm evidence yet. Nothing solid to authorize that sort of thing."

"You'll find your evidence on the *Villafjord.*"

"I can't take that chance. If I move on Van Weldon without cause, his lawyers will shut down my investigation for good. We have to wait until she docks in Naples. Convince the Italian police to board her."

"By then it may be too late! MacLeod, this could be your best chance. Your only chance. If you want Van Weldon, move *now.*"

MacLeod looked at Hugh. "What do you think, Lord Lovat?"

"We'd need help from the Royal Navy. A chopper or two. Oh, we could do it, all right. But if the evidence isn't aboard, if it turns out we're chasing nothing but a cargo of biscuits, there's going to be enough red faces all around to fill a bloody circus ring."

"I'm telling you, the evidence *is* on board," said Jordan. "So is Clea."

"Is that what you're really chasing?" asked Hugh. "The woman?"

"What if it is?"

"We don't launch an operation this big just because some— some stray female has gotten herself into trouble," said MacLeod. "We move prematurely and we'll lose our chance at Van Weldon."

"He's right," said Hugh. "There are too many factors to weigh here. The woman can't be our first concern."

"Don't give me any bloody lecture about who's dispensable and who isn't!" retorted Jordan. "She's not one of your agents. She never took any oath to protect queen and country. She's a civilian, and you can't leave her out there. *I* won't leave her out there!"

Hugh stared at his nephew in surprise. "She means that much to you?"

Jordan met his uncle's gaze. The answer had never been clearer than at this very moment, with the wind whipping their faces and the night growing ever deeper, ever colder.

"Yes," said Jordan firmly. "She means that much to me."

His uncle glanced up at the sky. "Looks like some nasty weather coming up—it will complicate things."

"But...they'll be miles at sea by the time we reach them," said

MacLeod. "Beyond English waters. There's no legal way to demand a search."

"No *legal* way," said Jordan.

"What, you think they'll just invite us aboard to comb the ship?"

"They're not going to know there *is* a search." Jordan turned to his uncle. "I'll need a navy helicopter. And a crew of volunteers for the boarding party."

Troubled, Hugh regarded his nephew for a moment. "You'll have no authority to back you up on this. You understand that?"

"Yes."

"If anything goes wrong—"

"The navy will deny my existence. I know that, too."

Hugh shook his head, agonizing over the decision. "Jordan, you're my only nephew...."

"And with a bloodline like ours, we can't possibly fail. Can we?" Smiling, Jordan gave his uncle's shoulder a squeeze of confidence.

Hugh sighed. "This woman must be quite extraordinary."

"I'll introduce you," said Jordan, and his gaze shifted back to the water. "As soon as I get her off that bloody ship."

THE MEN'S VOICES MOVED ON and faded down the corridor.

Clea remained frozen by the door, debating whether to risk leaving the storage area. Before they docked again, she'd have to find a new hiding place. Eventually someone would check the cargo, and when that happened, the last place Clea wanted to be was trapped in a crate.

The coast looked clear.

She slipped out of the storeroom and headed in the opposite direction the men had taken. The below-decks area was a confusing maze of corridors and hatches. Which way next?

The question was settled by the sound of footsteps. In panic, she ducked through the nearest door.

To her dismay she discovered she was in the crew's quarters—and the footsteps were moving closer. She scrambled across to the row of lockers, opened a door and squeezed inside.

It was even a tighter fit than the crate had been. She was crammed against a bundle of foul-smelling shirts and an even fouler pair of tennis shoes. Through the ventilation slits she saw two men step into the room. One of them crossed toward the lockers. Clea almost let out a squeak of relief when he swung open the door right beside hers.

"Hear there's rough weather comin' up," the man said, pulling on a slicker.

"Hell, she's blowin' twenty-five knots already."

The men, now garbed in foul-weather gear, left the quarters.

Clea emerged from the locker. She couldn't keep ducking in and out of rooms; she'd have to find a more permanent hiding place. Some spot she'd be left undisturbed...

The lifeboats. She'd seen it used as a hiding place in the movies. Unless there was a ship's emergency, she'd be safe waiting it out there until they docked.

She scavenged among the lockers and pulled out a sailor's pea coat and a black cap. Then, her head covered, her petite frame almost swallowed up in the coat, she crept out of the crew's quarters and started up a stairway to the deck.

It was blowing outside, the night swirling with wind and spray. Through the darkness she could make out several men moving about on deck. Two were securing a cargo hatch, a third was peering through binoculars over the port rail. None of them glanced in her direction.

She spotted two lifeboats secured near the starboard gunwale. Both were covered with tarps. Not only would she be concealed in there, she'd be dry. Once the *Villafjord* reached Naples, she could sneak ashore.

She pulled the pea coat tighter around her shoulders. Calmly, deliberately, she began to stroll toward the lifeboats.

SIMON TROTT STOOD on the bridge and eyed the increasingly foul weather from behind the viewing windows. Though the captain had assured him the passage would present no difficulties for the *Villafjord*, Trott still couldn't shake off his growing sense of uneasiness.

Obviously, Victor Van Weldon didn't share Trott's sense of foreboding. The old man sat calmly beside him on the bridge, oxygen hissing softly through his nasal tube. Van Weldon would not be anxious about something so trivial as a storm at sea. At his age, with his failing health, what was there left for him to fear?

Trott asked the captain, "Will it get much rougher?"

"Not by much, I expect," said the captain. "She'll handle it fine. But if you're that concerned, we can turn back to Portsmouth."

"No," spoke up Van Weldon. "We cannot return." Suddenly he began to cough. Everyone on the bridge looked away in distaste as the old man spat into a handkerchief.

Trott, too, averted his gaze and focused on the main deck below, where three men were working hunched against the wind. That's when Trott noticed the fourth figure moving along the starboard gunwale. It passed, briefly, under the glow of a decklight, then slipped into the shadows.

At the first lifeboat the figure paused, glanced around and began to untie the covering tarp.

"Who is that?" Trott asked sharply. "That man by the lifeboat?"

The captain frowned. "I don't recognize that one."

At once Trott turned for the exit.

"Mr. Trott?" called the captain.

"I'll take care of this."

By the time Trott reached the deck, he had his automatic drawn and ready. The figure had vanished. Draped free over the lifeboat was an unfastened corner of tarp. Trott prowled closer. With a jerk he yanked off the tarp and pointed his gun at the shadow cowering inside.

"Out!" snapped Trott. "Come on, *out.*"

Slowly the figure unfolded itself and raised its head. By the glow of a decklight Trott saw the terror in that startlingly familiar face.

"If it isn't the elusive Miss Clea Rice," said Trott.

And he smiled.

THE CABIN WAS LARGE, plushly furnished and equipped with all the luxuries one would expect in a well-appointed living room. Only the swaying of the crystal chandelier overhead betrayed the fact it was a shipboard residence.

The chair Clea was tied to was upholstered in green velvet and the armrests were carved mahogany. *Surely they won't kill me here,* she thought. *They wouldn't want me to bleed all over this pricey antique.*

Trott emptied the contents of her pockets and her knapsack onto a table and eyed the collection of lock picks. "I see you came well prepared," he commented dryly. "How did you get on board?"

"Trade secret."

"Are you alone?"

"You think I'd tell you?"

With two swift steps he crossed to her and slapped her across the face, so hard her head snapped back. For a moment she was too stunned by the force of the blow to speak.

"Surely, Miss Rice," wheezed Victor Van Weldon, "you don't wish to anger Mr. Trott more than you already have. He can be most unpleasant when annoyed."

"So I've noticed," groaned Clea. She squinted, focusing her blurred gaze on Van Weldon. He was frailer than she'd expected. And old, so old. Oxygen tubing snaked from his nostrils to a green tank hooked behind his wheelchair. His hands were bruised, the skin thin as paper. This was a man barely clinging to life. What could he possibly lose by killing her?

"I'll ask you again," said Trott. "Are you alone?"

"I brought a team of navy SEALs with me."

Trott hit her again. A thousand shards of light seemed to explode in her head.

"Where is Jordan Tavistock?" asked Trott.

"I don't know."

"Is he with you?"

"No."

Trott picked up Jordan's gold pocket watch and flipped open the lid. He read aloud the inscription. "Bernard Tavistock." He looked at her. "You have no idea where he is?"

"I told you I don't."

He held up the watch. "Then what are you doing with this?"

"I stole it."

Though she steeled herself for the coming blow, the impact of his fist still took her breath away. Blood trickled down her chin. In dazed wonder she watched the red droplets soak into the lush carpet at her feet. *How ironic,* she thought. *I finally tell the truth and he doesn't believe me.*

"He is still working with you, isn't he?" said Trott.

"He wants nothing more to do with me. I left him."

Trott turned to Van Weldon. "I think Tavistock is still a threat. Keep the contract on him alive."

Clea's head shot up. "No. No, he's got nothing to do with this!"

"He's been with you this past week."

"His misfortune."

"Why were you together?"

She gave a shrug. "Lust?"

"You think I'd believe that?"

"Why not?" Rebelliously she cocked up her head. "I've been known to tweak the hormones of more than a few men."

"This gets us nowhere!" said Van Weldon. "Throw her overboard."

"I want to know what she's learned. What Tavistock's learned. Otherwise we'll be operating blind. If Interpol—" He suddenly turned.

The intercom was buzzing.

Trott crossed the room and pressed the speaker button. "Yes, Captain?"

"We've a situation up here, Mr. Trott. There's a Royal Navy ship hard on our stern. They've requested permission to come aboard."

"Why?"

"They say they're checking all outbound vessels from Portsmouth for some IRA terrorist. They think he may have passed himself off as crew."

"Request denied," said Van Weldon calmly.

"They have helicopter backup," said the captain. "And another ship on the way."

"We are beyond the twelve-mile limit," said Van Weldon. "They have no right to board us."

"Sir, might I advise cooperation?" said the captain. "It sounds like a routine matter. You know how it is—the Brits are always hunting down IRA. They'll probably just want to eyeball our crew. If we refuse, it will only rouse their suspicions."

Trott and Van Weldon exchanged glances. At last Van Weldon nodded.

"Assemble all men on deck," said Trott into the intercom. "Let the Brits have a good look at them. But it stops there."

"Yes, sir."

Trott turned to Van Weldon. "We'd both better be on deck to meet them. As for Miss Rice..." He looked at Clea.

"She will have to wait," said Van Weldon, and wheeled his chair across the room to a private elevator. "See that she's well secured. I will meet you on the bridge." He maneuvered into the elevator and slid the gate shut. With a hydraulic whine, the lift carried him away.

Trott turned his attention to Clea's bonds. He yanked the ropes around her wrists so tightly she gave a cry of pain. Then quickly, efficiently he taped her mouth.

"That should keep you," he said with a grunt of satisfaction, and he left the room.

The instant the door shut behind him, Clea began straining at her bonds. It took only a few painful twists of her wrists to tell her that it was hopeless. She wasn't going to get loose.

Shedding tears of frustration, she slumped back against the chair. Up on deck, the Royal Navy would soon be landing. They would never know, would never guess, that just below their feet was a victim in need of rescue.

So close and yet so far.

She gritted her teeth and began to strain again at the ropes.

"YOU'RE CERTAIN YOU WANT to go in with us?"

Jordan peered through the chopper windows at the deck of the *Villafjord* below. It would be a bumpy landing into enemy territory, but with all this wind and darkness as cover, there was a reasonable chance no one down there would recognize him.

"I'm going in," Jordan said.

"You'll have twenty minutes at the most," said the naval officer seated across from him. "And then we're out of there. With or without you."

"I understand."

"We're on shaky legal ground already. If Van Weldon lodges a complaint to the high command, we'll be explaining ourselves till doomsday."

"Twenty minutes. Just give me that much." Jordan tugged the black watch cap lower on his brow. The borrowed Royal Navy uniform was a bit snug around his shoulders, and the automatic felt uncomfortably foreign holstered against his chest, but both were absolutely necessary if he was to participate in this masquerade. Unfortunately the other seven men in the boarding party—all naval officers—were plainly doubtful about having some amateur along for the ride. They kept watching him with expressions bordering on disdain.

Jordan ignored them and focused on the broad deck of the *Villafjord,* now directly beneath the skids. A little tricky maneuvering by the pilot brought them to a touchdown. At once the men began to pile out, Jordan among them.

The pilot, mindful of the hazards of a rolling deck, took off again, leaving the crew temporarily stranded aboard the *Villafjord.*

A man with blond hair was crossing to greet them.

Jordan slipped behind the other men in his party and averted his face. It would be bloody inconvenient to be recognized right off the bat.

The ranking officer of the naval team stepped forward and met the blond man. "Lieutenant Commander Tobias, Royal Navy."

"Simon Trott. VP operations, the Van Weldon company. How can we help you, Commander?"

"We'd like to inspect your crew."

"Certainly. They've already been assembled." Trott pointed to the knot of men huddled near the bridge stairway.

"Is everyone on deck?"

"All except the captain and Mr. Van Weldon. They're up on the bridge."

"There's no one below decks?"

"No, sir."

Commander Tobias nodded. "Then let's get started."

Trott turned to lead the way. As the rest of the boarding party followed Trott, Jordan hung behind, waiting for a chance to slip away.

No one noticed him duck down the midship stairway.

With all the crew up top, he'd have the below-decks area to himself. There wasn't much time to search. Slipping quickly down the first corridor, he poked his head into every doorway, calling Clea's name. He passed crew's quarters and officers' quarters, the mess hall, the galley.

No sign of Clea.

Heading farther astern, he came across what appeared to be a storage bay. Inside the room were a dozen crates of various sizes. The lid was ajar on one of them. He lifted it off and glanced inside.

Swathed in fluffy packing was the bronze head of a statue. And a black glove—a woman's, size five.

Jordan glanced sharply around the room. "Clea?" he called out.

Ten minutes had already passed.

With a surging sense of panic he continued down the corridor, throwing open doors, scanning each compartment. So little time left, and he still had the engine room, the cargo bays and Lord knew what else might lie astern.

Overhead he heard the sound of rumbling, growing louder now. The helicopter was about to land again.

A mahogany door with a sign Private was just ahead. Captain's quarters? Jordan tried the knob and found it was locked. He pounded on it a few times and called out, "Clea?"

There was no answer.

She heard the pounding on the door, then Jordan's voice calling her name.

She tried to answer, tried to shout, but the tape over her mouth muffled all but the faintest whimper. Frantic to reach him, she thrashed like a madwoman against her bonds. The ropes held. Her hands and feet had gone numb, useless.

Don't leave me! she wanted to shriek. *Don't leave me!*

But she knew he had already turned from the door.

In despair, she jerked her body sideways. The chair tipped, carrying her down with it. Her head slammed against an end table. The pain was like a bolt of lightning through her skull; it left her stunned on the floor. Blackness swam before her eyes. She fought the slide toward unconsciousness, fought it savagely with every ounce of will she possessed. And still she could not clear the blackness from her vision.

Faintly she heard a thumping. Again and again, like a drumbeat in the darkness.

She struggled to see. The blackness was lifting. She could make out the outlines of furniture now. And she realized that the thumping was coming from the door.

In a shower of splinters the wood suddenly split open, breached by the bright red blade of a fire ax. Another blow tore a gaping hole in the door. An arm thrust in, to fumble at the lock.

Jordan shoved into the room.

He took one look at Clea and murmured, "My God..."

At once he was kneeling at her side. Her hands were so numb she scarcely felt it when he cut the cords binding her wrists.

But she did feel his kiss. He pulled the tape from her mouth, lifted her from the floor and pressed his lips to hers. As she lay sobbing in his arms he kissed her hair, her face, murmuring her name again and again, as though he could not say it enough, could never say it enough.

A soft beeping made his head suddenly lift from hers. He silenced the pager hung on his belt. "That's our one-minute warning," he said. "We have to get out of here. Can you walk?"

"I—I don't think so. My legs..."

"Then I'll carry you." He swept her up into his arms. Stepping across the wood-littered carpet, he bore her out of the room and into the corridor.

"How do we get off the ship?" she asked.

"The same way I got on. Navy chopper." He rounded a corner.

And halted.

"I am afraid, Mr. Tavistock," said Simon Trott, standing in their path, "that you are going to miss your flight."

CHAPTER FIFTEEN

CLEA FELT Jordan's arms tighten around her. In the momentary silence she could almost hear the thudding of his heart against his chest.

Trott raised the barrel of his automatic. "Put her down."

"She can't walk," said Jordan. "She hit her head."

"Very well, then. You'll have to carry her."

"Where?"

Trott waved the gun toward the far end of the corridor. "The cargo bay."

That gun left Jordan no choice. With Clea in his arms he headed up the corridor and stepped through a doorway, into a cargo bay crammed full with packing crates.

"The landing party knows I'm on board," said Jordan. "They won't leave without me."

"Won't they?" Trott glanced upward toward the rumble of the chopper rotors. "They're about to do just that."

They heard the roar of the helicopter as it suddenly lifted away.

"Too late," said Trott with a regretful shake of his head. "You've now entered the gray world of deniability, Mr. Tavistock. We'll claim you never came aboard. And the Royal Navy will have a sticky time admitting otherwise." Again he waved the gun, indicating one of the crates. "It's large enough for you both. A cozy end, I'd say."

He's going to shut us inside, thought Clea. And then what?

A ditching at sea, of course. She and Jordan would drown together, their bodies locked forever in an undersea casket. Suddenly she found it hard to breathe. Sheer terror had drained her of the ability to think, to act.

When Jordan spoke, his voice was astonishingly calm.

"They'll be waiting for you in Naples," said Jordan. "Interpol and the Italian police. You don't really think it's as simple as toss-ing one crate overboard?''

"We've bought our way into Naples for years."

"Then your luck is about to change. Do you like dark, enclosed places? Because that's where *you're* going to find yourself. For the rest of your life."

"I've had enough," Trott snapped. "Put her down. Pry the lid off the crate." He picked up a crowbar and slid it across the floor to Jordan. "Do it. And no sudden moves."

Jordan set Clea down on her feet. At once she slid to her knees, her legs still numb and useless. Dropping down beside her, Jordan looked her in the eye. Something in his gaze caught her attention. He was trying to tell her something. He bent close to her and the flap of his jacket sagged open. That's when she caught a glimpse of his shoulder holster.

He had a gun!

Trott's view was blocked by Jordan's back. Quickly she slipped her hand beneath Jordan's jacket, grabbed the pistol from the hol-ster and hugged it against her chest.

"Leave her on the floor!" ordered Trott. "Just get the bloody crate open!"

Jordan leaned close, his mouth grazing her ear. "Use me as a shield," he whispered. "Aim for his chest."

She stared at him in horror. "No—"

He gripped her shoulder with painful insistence. *"Do it."*

Their gazes locked. It was something she'd remember for as long as she lived, that message she saw in his eyes. *You have to live, Clea. For both of us.*

He gave her shoulder another squeeze, this one gentler. And he smiled.

"Come on, get the lid off!" barked Trott.

Clea hooked her finger around the pistol trigger. She had never shot anyone before. If she missed, if she was even slightly off target, Trott would have time to squeeze off his entire clip into Jordan's body. She had to be accurate. She had to be lethal.

For his sake.

His lips brushed her forehead and she savored their warmth,

knowing full well that the next time she touched them they might carry the chill of death.

"It seems you need a jump start," said Trott. He raised his pistol and fired.

Clea felt Jordan shudder in pain, heard him groan as he clutched his thigh. In horror Clea saw bright red droplets spatter the floor. The sight of Jordan's blood seemed to cloud her vision with rage. All her hesitation was swept away by a roaring wave of fury.

With both hands she aimed the pistol at Trott and fired.

The bullet's impact punched Trott squarely in the chest. He stumbled backward, his face frozen in surprise. He weaved on his feet like a drunken man. The gun slipped from his grasp and clanged to the floor. He dropped to his knees beside it, made a clumsy attempt to pick it up again, but his hands wouldn't function. As he sank to the floor, his fingers were still clawing uselessly for the gun. Then they fell still.

"Get out of here," gasped Jordan.

"I won't leave you."

"I can't leave, period. My leg—"

"Hush!" she cried. On unsteady legs she stumbled over to Trott's body and snatched up his gun. "There's no getting off this ship, anyway! They've heard the shots. They'll be down here any minute, the whole lot of them. We might as well stick together." She tottered back to his side.

He sat huddled in a pool of his own blood. Tenderly she took his face in her hands and pressed a kiss to his mouth.

His lips were already chilled.

Sobbing, despairing, she cradled his head in her lap. *It's over,* she thought as she heard footsteps pounding toward them along the corridor. *All we can do now is fight till the bitter end. And hope death comes quickly.* She bent down to him and whispered, "I love you."

The footsteps were almost at the cargo door.

With a strange sense of calmness she raised the gun and took aim at the doorway....

And held her fire. A man in a Royal Navy uniform stood blinking at her in surprise. Behind him stood three other men, also in uniform. One of them was Richard Wolf.

Richard shoved through into the room and saw Jordan and the growing pool of blood. Turning, he yelled, "Call back the chopper again! Have the Medevac team standing by!"

"Yes, sir!" One of the naval officers headed for the intercom.

Clea was still clutching the pistol. Slowly she let the barrel drop, but she did not release the grip. She was almost afraid to let go of the one solid thing she could count on. Afraid that if she did let go, she would drop away into some dimensionless space.

"Here. I'll take it."

Dazed, she looked up at Richard. He regarded her with an almost kindly smile and held out his hand. Wordlessly she gave him the pistol. He nodded and said softly, "That's a good girl."

Within fifteen minutes a team of medics had appeared, helicoptered in from the nearby Royal Navy ship. By then, Clea's legs had regained their circulation and she was able to stand, albeit unsteadily. Her head was aching worse than ever, and a medic tried to pull her aside to examine the bruises on her temple, but she shrugged him away.

All her attention was focused on Jordan. She watched as IV lines were threaded into Jordan's veins, as he was lifted and strapped onto a stretcher. In numb silence she squeezed onto the elevator that carried his stretcher up to the deck.

Only when one of the officers held her back as they lifted Jordan into the chopper did she understand they were taking him from her. Suddenly she panicked, terrified that if she lost sight of him now, she would never see him again.

She shoved forward, elbowing aside the naval officer, and would have run all the way to the chopper were it not for a grip that firmly closed around her arm.

Richard Wolf's.

"Let me go!" she sobbed, trying to fight him off.

"He's being transported to a hospital. They'll take care of him."

"I want to be with him! He needs me!"

Richard took her firmly by the shoulders. "You'll see him soon,

I promise! But now *we* need you, Clea. You have to tell us things. About Van Weldon. About this ship.''

The roar of the rotor engine drowned out any other words. With despairing eyes, Clea saw the chopper lift away into the wind-buffeted darkness. *Please take care of him,* she prayed. *That's all I ask. Please keep him safe.*

She watched the taillights wink into the night. A moment later the rumble had faded, leaving only the sounds of the wind and the sea.

''Miss Rice?'' Richard prodded gently.

Through tears Clea looked at him. ''I'll tell you everything, Mr. Wolf,'' she said. And an anguished laugh suddenly escaped her throat. ''Even the truth.''

IT WAS TWO DAYS before she saw Jordan again.

She was told that Jordan had lost a great deal of blood, but that the surgery had gone well, without complications. She could learn no more.

Richard Wolf installed her in an MI6 safe house outside London. It was a sweet little stone cottage with a white fence and a garden. She considered it a prison. The three men guarding the entrances did nothing to dispel that impression.

Richard had told her the men were a necessity. The contract on her life might still be active, he'd explained. It was dangerous to move her. Until Van Weldon's topple from power became general knowledge, Clea would have to be kept out of sight.

And away from Jordan.

She understood the real purpose of the separation. It did not surprise her that his aristocratic family would, in the end, prevail. Clea was not the sort of woman one allowed into one's family. Not if one had a reputation to uphold. No matter how much Jordan cared about her—and he *did* care, she knew that now—her past would come between them.

The Tavistocks had only Jordan's well-being in mind. For that she could not fault them.

But she did resent them for the way they had taken control of her freedom. For two days she tolerated her pleasant little prison.

She paced in the garden, stared at the TV, leafed without interest through magazines.

By the second day in captivity, she'd bloody well had enough.

She picked up her knapsack, marched outside and announced to the guard posted in the front yard, "I want out."

"Afraid that's quite impossible," he said.

"What're you going to do about it, Buster, shoot me in the back?"

"My orders are to ensure your safety. You can't leave."

"Watch me." She slung the knapsack over her shoulder and was pushing through the gate when a black limousine rolled into the driveway. It came to a stop right in front of her. In amazement she watched as the chauffeur emerged, circled around and opened the rear door.

An elderly man stepped out. He was portly and balding, but he wore his finely tailored suit with comfortable elegance. For a moment he regarded Clea in silence.

"So you are the woman in question," he said at last.

Coolly she looked him up and down. "And the man in question?"

He held out his hand in greeting. "I'm Hugh Tavistock. Jordan's uncle."

Clea momentarily lost her voice. Wordlessly she accepted his handshake and found the man's grip firm, his gaze steady. *Like Jordan's.*

"We have much to talk about, Miss Rice," said Hugh. "Will you step into the car?"

"Actually, I was just leaving."

"You don't wish to see him?"

"You mean...Jordan?"

Hugh nodded. "It's a long drive to the hospital. I thought it would give us a chance to get acquainted."

She studied him, searching for some hint of what was to come. His expression was unreadable, his face a cipher.

She climbed into the limousine.

They sat side by side, not speaking for a while. Outside the window, the countryside glided past. The brilliant hues of fall were tingeing the trees. *What do we possibly have to say to each other?* she wondered. *I'm a stranger to his world, as he is to mine.*

"It seems my nephew has formed an attachment to you," said Hugh.

"Your nephew is a good man," she said. She stared out the window and added softly, "A very fine man."

"I've always thought so."

"He deserves…" She paused and swallowed back tears. "He deserves the very best there is."

"True."

"So…" She raised her chin and looked at him. "I'll not be difficult. You must understand, Lord Lovat, I have no demands. No expectations. I only want…" She looked away. "I only want him to be happy. I'll do whatever it takes. Even if it means vanishing."

"You love him." It was not a question but a statement.

This time she couldn't keep the tears at bay. They began to fall slowly, silently.

Sighing, he sat back in the seat. "Well, it's certainly not without precedent."

"What do you mean?"

"A number of women have fallen for my nephew."

"I can see why."

"But none of them were quite like you. You do realize, don't you, that you are almost single-handedly responsible for bringing down Victor Van Weldon? For smashing an arms shipment empire?"

She shrugged, as if none of it mattered. And at the moment, it didn't. It all seemed irrelevant. She scarcely listened as Hugh outlined the ripple of developments since the *Villafjord* was boarded. The arrests of Oliver and Veronica Cairncross. The new investigation into the *Max Havelaar*'s sinking. The cache of surface-to-air missiles found in the Cairncross Biscuits warehouse. Unfortunately, Victor Van Weldon would probably not live long enough to go to trial. But he had, in some measure, met justice. The final rendering would have to come from his Maker.

When Hugh had finished speaking, he looked at Clea and said,

"You have performed a service for us all, Miss Rice. You're to be congratulated."

She said nothing.

To her surprise he chuckled. "I've met many heroes in my time. But none so uninterested in praise."

She shook her head. "I'm tired, Lord Lovat. I just want to go home."

"To America?"

Again she shrugged. "I suppose that *is* my home. I...I don't know anymore...."

"What about Jordan? I thought you loved him."

"You yourself said it's not without precedent. Women have always been falling in love with your nephew."

"But Jordan's never fallen in love with them. Until now."

There was a silence. She frowned at him.

"For the past two days," said Hugh, "my normally good-natured nephew has been insufferable. Belligerent. He has badgered the doctors and nurses, twice pulled out his intravenous lines and commandeered another patient's wheelchair. We explained to him it wasn't the right time to bring you for a visit. That contract on your life, you know—it made every transfer risky. But now the contract's off—"

"It is?"

"And it's finally time to fetch you. And see if you can't restore his good humor."

"You think I'm the one who can do that?"

"Richard Wolf thought so."

"And what does Jordan say?"

"Bloody little. But then, he's always been closemouthed." Hugh regarded her with his mild blue eyes. "He's waiting to speak to you first."

Clea gave a bitter laugh. "How distressing it must be for you! A woman like me. And your nephew. You'd have to hide me in the family closet."

"If I did," he said dryly, "you'd find half my ancestors lurking in there with you."

She shook her head. "I don't understand."

"We Tavistocks have a grand tradition of choosing mates who are most...unsuitable. Over the centuries we've wed Gypsies, courtesans and even a stray Yank or two." He smiled. For the first time she recognized the warmth in his eyes. "You would scarcely raise an eyebrow."

"You'd...allow someone like me in your family?"

"It's not my decision, Miss Rice. The choice is Jordan's. Whatever will make him happy."

How can we predict what will make him happy? she thought. *For a month, or a year, he might find contentment in my arms. But then it will dawn on him who I was. Who I am...*

She clutched her knapsack in her lap and suddenly longed for escape, longed to be on the road to somewhere else, anywhere else. That was how she'd survived these past few weeks—the quick escape, the shadowy exit. That, too, was how she'd always resolved her romantic relationships. But now there was no avoiding the encounter that lay ahead.

She'd simply have to be straight about this. Lay her cards on the table and be brutally honest. She owed it to Jordan; it was the kindest thing she could do.

By the time they reached the hospital, she had talked herself into a benumbed sense of inevitability. She stood stiff and silent as they rode up the service elevator. When they got off on the seventh floor and walked toward Jordan's hospital room, she was composed and prepared for what she knew would be a goodbye. Calmly she stepped into the room.

And lost all sense of resolve.

Jordan was standing by the window, a pair of crutches propped under his arms. He was fully dressed in gray trousers and a white shirt, no tie—casual for a Tavistock. At the sound of the door's opening, he turned clumsily around to face her. The crutches were new to him, and he wobbled a bit, struggling to find his balance. But his gaze was steady on her face.

Her escorts left the room.

She stood just inside the door, longing to go to Jordan, yet afraid to approach. "I see you came through it" was all she said.

He searched her face, seeking, but not finding, what he wanted. "I've been trying to see you."

"Your uncle told me. They were afraid to move either one of us." She smiled. "But now Van Weldon's gone. And we can go back to our lives."

"And will you?"

"What else would I do?"

"Stay with me."

He stood very still, watching her. Waiting for a response.

She was the first to look away. "Stay? You mean...in England?"

"I mean with *me*. Wherever that may happen to be."

She laughed. "That sounds like a rather vague proposition."

"I'm not being vague at all. You're just refusing to recognize the obvious."

"The obvious?"

"That we've been through bloody hell together. That we care about each other. At least, I care about *you*. And I'm not about to let you run."

She shook her head and laughed—not a real laugh. No, it felt as though her heart had gotten caught in her throat. "How can you possibly care about me? You're not even sure who I am."

"I know who you are."

"I've lied to you. Again and again."

"I know."

"Big lies. Whoppers!"

"You also told me the truth."

"Only when I had to! I'm an ex-con, Jordan! I come from a family of cons. I'll probably have kids who'll be cons."

"So...it will be a parenting challenge."

"And what about *this?*" She reached into her knapsack and took out the pocket watch. She dangled it in front of his face. "I *stole* this. I took something I knew you cared about. I did it to prove a point, Jordan. To show you what an idiot you are to trust me!"

"No, Clea," he said quietly. "That's not why you stole it."

"No? Then why did I take it?"

"Because you're afraid of me."

"I'm afraid? *I'm* afraid?"

"You're afraid I'll love you. Afraid you'll love *me*. Afraid it'll all fall apart when I decide you're hopelessly flawed."

"Okay," she retorted. "Maybe you've got it figured out. But it does make a certain amount of sense, doesn't it? To get the disillusionment over with right at the start? You can put a nice romantic spin on all of this, but sooner or later you'll realize what I am."

"I know what you are. And I know just how lucky I am to have found you."

"Lucky?" She shook her head and laughed bitterly. "Lucky?" Holding up the pocket watch, she let it swing in front of his face. "I'm a thief, remember? I steal things. I stole this!"

He grabbed her wrist, trapping it in his grip. "The only thing you stole," he said softly, "was my heart."

Wordlessly she stared at him. Though she wanted to pull away, to turn from his face, she found that her gaze was every bit as trapped as her hand.

"No, Clea," he said. "This time you don't run away. You don't retreat. Maybe it's the way you've always done things. When life gets rough, you want to run away. But don't you see? This time I'm offering you something different. I'm giving you a home to run *to*."

She stopped struggling to free herself and went very still. Only then did he release her wrist. Slowly. They stood looking at each other, not touching, not speaking. His gaze was all that held her now.

That and her heart.

So many times I've tried to run away from you, she thought. *And it was really myself I was running from. Not you. Never you.*

Tenderly he stroked her face and caught the first tear as it slid down her cheek. "I'm not going to force you to stay, Clea. I couldn't, even if I wanted to. But I've already made a decision. Now it's time you made one, too."

Through the veil of tears blurring her vision, she saw his look of uncertainty. Of hope.

"I...want to believe," she whispered.

"You will. Maybe not now, or next year, or even ten years from now. But one of these days, Clea, you will believe." He edged his crutches forward and pressed his lips to hers. "And that, Miss Rice," he whispered, "is when your running-away days will finally be over."

She looked at him in wonder through her tears. *Oh, Jordan, I think they already are.*

She threw her arms around his neck and pulled him close for another kiss. A sealing kiss. When she pulled away, she found he was smiling.

It was the smile of the thief who had stolen *her* heart. And would forever keep it.

Moontide
Stella Cameron

PROLOGUE

BLUE LIGHT PULSED across the darkened corridor from windows high in the wall. The wailing siren slurred to an echo and died. Andrew stood still for a moment and rubbed his eyes. God, he was tired. Emergency must be busy tonight. Summer always brought visitors streaming from the industrial regions of England to the south coast. With them came an increased rash of accidents. He'd heard the familiar sounds of controlled drama again and again while he worked on the Beckett baby.

Why? The question swirled in his head. Damn it all, why hadn't he been able to save her? For three weeks the tiny child had hung on, and just when he thought success was only a matter of time, she gave up. Andrew sat on the edge of a chair just inside the double doors leading out of the premature-infant unit.

The usual response to learning he was a pediatrician often ran along the lines of "It must be fun dealing with kids. I don't think I could stand all the misery of older people and dying every day." He slid back and rested his head against the wall. Did they think one had to be old to die? Or was it supposed to be easier to watch eyes close for the last time if they had never seen much? Once he had thought there could be only joy in helping children, and it was true, except when he failed.

It was almost midnight. Greer Beckett would be asleep by now. Andrew pressed his lips together and felt the muscles in his jaw quiver. Hadn't it been enough for a twenty-four-year-old to watch her husband die in a car crash that had also left her with a smashed hip? A few hours after the accident Greer went into labor and her condition demanded immediate cesarean section. Any fetus delivered two months prematurely was a high risk. But this one had been a fighter, and she had almost made it.

Earlier in the day he had visited the young American woman to give a good report on little Colleen. He flinched. When Greer said what name she'd chosen for her daughter, even the blasé nurse in the room sniffled. Colin had been the husband's name. Now Andrew supposed Colleen would be buried close to her father in an English churchyard, thousands of miles from the Beckett's Seattle home.

Andrew wanted to see Greer. Unfamiliar smarting in his eyes made him blink. All the study and training, the years of practice, hadn't been able to stop him from losing Greer Beckett's child. It was no one's fault, yet he felt responsible.

You care about the woman. Andrew stood and swept through the doors. The impact of metal pressure plates against his thrusting wrists stung. *You wish this was another time and place, and that you were in it with her. The rule, Monthaven, remember the golden rule—never become personally involved with a patient.*

He turned the corner and punched a button on the elevator panel. Exhaustion was making him rummy. Greer Beckett was alone in a foreign country. It was natural for him to feel sympathetic and drawn to her. The elevator doors slid open and he stepped inside. Glaring white light made him squint. Andrew didn't remember why the Becketts were in Dorset County. Must simply have been on vacation. Each one's passport had borne the other's name as an emergency contact. Greer insisted that neither had any family to be notified. She said she did have a younger sister in the States, but wouldn't allow the hospital to call her. "Casey would try to come. We'll manage. By the time we get back the worst will be over." "We" had meant she and the baby.

Greer had written one letter that Andrew offered to mail. She commented that it was business. Sent to a Josh Field, the envelope showed no return address. She was strong, determined to get through this ordeal alone. He prayed silently that she would prove strong enough after tonight.

The elevator ground slightly before it jolted to a stop on the third floor of the Dorchester Medical Center. Andrew headed for the nurses' station, then hesitated, staring at a sign on the desk that read Surgical Unit. She was bound to be asleep. Better wait until tomorrow.

"Hello, Dr. Monthaven. You're off your beaten track tonight."

Andrew stared. "Yes." He fingered the stethoscope that still hung around his neck and smiled back at a student nurse whose face he didn't recall. Just a kid. Bright. All pink and white and optimistic.

The girl tucked a wisp of blond hair behind her ear. "Dr. Monthaven...?" A puzzled frown clouded earnest blue eyes.

"It's okay, nurse. Carry on. I don't need any assistance." He strode purposefully past, catching her bemused expression. During her next coffee break, "that dishy Dr. Monthaven" would be the main topic. Andrew grimaced. At some point, being eligible, single and, as he knew he was frequently described by the female staff, a dish had lost appeal. Tonight he felt closer to a hundred than thirty-three. And the only woman he wished would look at him with even a spark of interest was recovering from surgery in one of the rooms ahead. *Was he losing his mind?*

Certainly his behavior was irrational. Coming up here in the middle of the night proved that. What did he intend to do? Leave a note beside her while she slept? *Dear Mrs. Beckett. I didn't want to wake you, but I thought you'd like to know that your little girl died at 11:07 P.M.* We did our best. Very sorry—

Andrew halted. He tried to take a breath and felt it lodge at the top of his lungs. Down the hall, a pale wedge of light painted the tiled floor outside her door. Greer must be awake.

In the seconds that followed he felt his blood drain away, then rush back to pound in his ears. This *was* personal, and he knew it. He'd been in practice too long, watched people die too often, to react so passionately for any other reason.

The first time he saw Greer Beckett he'd been struck by her smallness. He was accustomed to towering over most women, and many men, and Greer had been lying down. But when he came to talk to her about Colleen, a few hours after delivery, the almost boyish figure outlined through the sheets had made him feel like a giant. A tangle of dark red curls tumbled over the pillow, and huge blue eyes contrasted brilliantly with her pallid, bruised face. And despite the contusions and the anguish in those lovely eyes, something about her had touched Andrew in a way he had never thought possible. He had wished she was his, that Colleen was his and that he could insulate them both from any more pain.

That had been three weeks ago. Three weeks that almost made him forget what his world was like before Greer Beckett became part of it. He had invented reasons to visit her frequently. And every moment they spent together intensified his protective urge. Her strength seemed to keep pace with her baby's valiant fight for survival, as if they unknowingly spurred each other on toward life.

He walked forward slowly, concentrating on his own footfalls. The fleeting temptation to turn back came and went. There would never be a good time to do what must be done. The tenth step brought him into the slice of light from Greer's room. Andrew grasped the doorknob in one broad hand and looked into the room.

Rather than being in bed as he expected, she sat in a chair by the window, gazing into the blackness outside. Her right leg stretched out, she balanced most of her slight weight on her left hip. For several days she had been walking with the aid of crutches but she still tired quickly. The surgeon whose care Greer was under had mentioned how determined she was, but that he would prefer her not to push too hard.

She raised her head and Andrew saw her jump. He glanced up at the window and realized she had seen his reflection in the glass.

"Didn't mean to startle you, Mrs. Beckett." He thought of her as Greer, but had never spoken her first name aloud.

She turned her head. "Hi. Fellow insomniac, or are you so dedicated you never go home?" Her gentle smile revealed even white teeth. Americans always seemed to have marvelous teeth, he thought irrelevantly.

"Neither," he said, "just busy." That wasn't what he should have said. It wouldn't help to fence.

"Up here?"

"No. I came to see you. I just got off duty."

She cleared her throat and smiled again. "You've been very good to me, Dr. Monthaven. Come and sit down."

He went to stand in front of her. His every nerve, every muscle was tightly coiled. Suddenly he felt so awake that the air seemed to sing about him. Andrew couldn't sit. He studied Greer, ignoring the question in her glistening eyes.

Her russet hair was no longer matted, but brushed into glossy waves and curls that reached her shoulders. Color had returned to her perfect, softly bowed mouth, and her skin was creamy, dotted with a fine sprinkling of freckles across her cheeks and nose. Livid suture marks emphasized a small scar above her right eyebrow, but the bruising below the eye had faded, and all the swelling had disappeared. She wore only a hospital gown and her small firm breasts rose and fell beneath the thin fabric. Her right leg and hip were immobilized in a walking cast but the left leg, which was amply revealed, confirmed she was indeed slender and finely boned.

Tinkling music snapped his mind into sharp focus. She held the music box he'd given her for Colleen, and must have turned the base unconsciously as she waited for him to speak. "Brahms Lullaby." Flowers would have been too obvious. The Hummel box had been a perfect solution, apparently intended for the mother to wind up for her child: secretly designed to be touched by the woman and, perhaps, to remind her of the giver.

Andrew drove his long fingers into his dark hair and kept them there. He pivoted away sharply. "I've got to tell you this."

"Yes." The single word was almost inaudible.

"Colleen." Andrew faced Greer and for a ghastly instant he thought he might cry before he could finish. "She didn't make it. Her heart just stopped. We tried to start it again for over an hour, but..." He paused, horrified by the slow transformation in the woman's features. Then he rushed on. "This happens sometimes, and we're never a hundred percent sure why. The lungs are bound to be immature, and the circulatory system. But she'd been off support for over a week—totally on her own. Everything looked so good. Seven months is the most critical time where the respiratory system's concerned. And the strain can catch up with the baby's heart, even when you think you're home free." Andrew only had to look at Greer to know nothing he could say would help now.

Her pupils had dilated and the skin on her face had stretched taut and shiny over the bones. With exaggerated care she set the music box on the windowsill and started to push herself upright.

"Sit still. Please." Andrew went to touch her but she instantly rejected him. "Please," he repeated, crossing his arms to restrain the urge to hold her.

She dragged and shoved until she stood, the top of her head not even level with his shoulders. Then she met his eyes. "You said she was fine." Her voice was as stretched taut as the rest of her. "This afternoon, you told me Colleen was thriving. You said that."

"She was, Greer, she was. I can't explain what happened, but it's always a possibility, even when the child seems to be gaining strength. She didn't suffer—just slipped away. You'll have other children." The platitudes, like her first name, rolled out thoughtlessly.

"And that will put everything right? Will I find another man to replace Colin, too? Well, for your information Dr...Monthaven, I don't want anyone else. I want to be where they are. I want to die."

Before Andrew could react, she lunged at the bedside table, sweeping a water carafe to the floor. The glass exploded, fragments and clear liquid sparkling like a million tears. Greer's hand closed convulsively around a small vase of yellow carnations. He expected her to throw it. Instead she squeezed it tightly, and crumpled the flowers in her fist.

"Greer, please."

She jerked to face him and overbalanced. Her short fingernails scratched the skin at the open neck of his shirt and dragged at the hair. The stethoscope dug into his flesh before it slithered down among the glass. He supported her waist, felt how his fingers almost met around her. For an instant they stood there, Greer's breathing coming in short gasps before the last of her frail energy ebbed and she sagged, clutching the lapels of his white jacket.

Andrew wrapped his arms around her, his hands touching satiny flesh where the gown gaped at the back. Trembling shook her body in violent waves and all he could do was hold on, crooning meaningless words into her hair. She smelled like the roses in his own gardens when the breeze off the ocean moved their lush petals. Each tiny move she made, deepened his awakened longing for her.

But she would never be his—the fragile hope he'd nurtured had dissolved in the past five minutes.

Effortlessly he lifted her, carefully cradled her right hip and leg until he could lay her on the bed. He pulled the gown around her, covering bare skin, although she appeared oblivious to her near nakedness.

Greer closed her eyes, but Andrew knew she didn't sleep. He waited.

"Give me the music box," she said clearly, without looking at him.

Andrew did as she asked.

With one twist of the base, familiar, soft notes filled the room. And as they faded to a last, few, punctuated sounds, silence seemed to expand around Andrew. The mid-August night was humid and sweat coursed between his shoulder blades.

"Here." Greer held the music box toward him. "I don't need this. I'll be going home to my sister soon and I like to travel light."

"Of course." She was already thinking of getting away from England. Why wouldn't she? It had been her hell on earth. "Sleep now. I'll sit with you until you do, if you like."

"That won't be necessary."

"I want to. Then I'll come back tomorrow."

"No, no. Thank you. I'd prefer it if you didn't. I'll be fine. I'm not your patient and I'm sure you've got plenty to do."

"Greer, Mrs. Beckett. Won't you let me do something for you?"

She rolled her head toward him. All light had left her eyes. "You've done enough, Dr. Monthaven. Allowing my baby to die was quite enough."

TWO DAYS LATER Andrew stood beside a tiny grave at the base of a much larger but still fresh mound of earth. He was the only mourner for Colleen Beckett, daughter of Colin and Greer Beckett.

"Colleen will rest close to her father," the minister said in a reedy monotone. He clutched a closed Bible to his chest and stared skyward.

Andrew only half heard the rest of the odd little eulogy, about a human who had barely existed. It was delivered solely for his benefit, and he wondered if it would have been spoken at all had he not come. A single grave digger had retreated to pour tea from a Thermos and drag on a skinny cigarette that he'd rolled himself.

When the minister finished his homily, he held out his hand. "So sad. So very sad," he said.

Andrew shook the man's thin fingers. "So pointless," he replied. Then he knelt and filled one hand with earth. Slowly he let the hardened clumps fall.

Before the last hollow drum of soil on white wood sounded, he stood and walked briskly toward the green metal gate leading out of the churchyard. As he climbed into his car he wondered again why Greer had chosen to bury her family in an obscure village like Ferndale. If she didn't want to fly them to the States, it would have seemed more logical to use a cemetery in Dorchester, close to the hospital. He'd thought about it when a staff member told him that Colin Beckett had been interred in Ferndale. But Greer hadn't mentioned the subject, and there had never been an appropriate time to ask her the reason.

The accident happened late on the night when she and her husband arrived in Dorset. They'd driven from London and, as far as Andrew knew, could never have visited the isolated hamlet. Ferndale *was* a peaceful spot. Perhaps one of the nurses had suggested it. He dismissed the question.

Three more weeks passed before Greer Beckett was discharged. The days and nights became a tormented blur for Andrew while he battled his desire to go to her. He ached to see her, but knew he was part of a nightmare she must long to forget.

On the evening of September 28, he broke a late-blooming rose from a trellis on the grounds of his house. The night air was intoxicating, and Andrew wasn't tired. He walked down a double flight of stone steps leading to the cliff path, and moved on until he stood above the ocean.

Could it have been four days since he watched from a hospital window as Greer was helped into a taxi? She had glanced over her shoulder at the medical center just once, before disappearing into the back seat. His last thought as the cab rounded the corner was that she was wrong to blame him for the baby's death, but in the same instant he knew he could never be angry because she did.

One day, when the pain faded, she'd stop hating him. Eventually another man would help her forget what she had lost. Andrew frowned. It made no sense to be jealous of someone he would never know—but he was.

Andrew rested the rose against his lips and looked out over the sea. The tide was coming in. Across the water a full moon spread a silvered path that transformed obsidian into burnished indigo: the color and quality of Greer Beckett's eyes when she'd first seen him on the night Colleen died. For a few minutes they'd been as vibrantly alive and welcoming as this moontide.

CHAPTER ONE

GREER BECKETT breathed deeply, filling her lungs with the same air that caressed her upturned face. Indian summer. She had once heard Seattle's weather described as "perpetual drizzle interrupted by occasional rain." The remark was fairly accurate much of the time, but she doubted if any city could be more spectacular on a balmy, mid-September day like this.

She glanced at her adoptive sister who sat beside her on a bench. A breeze ruffled Casey Wyatt's short, blond curls. Her pert features were arranged into a distant expression.

"What are you thinking about, Case?"

Casey stirred. "How much I like being here, with you. I've been very lucky."

"Not half as lucky as me," Greer replied. She touched Casey's hand lightly and concentrated on the familiar scene around them. "I'm still grateful I managed to salvage enough out of the business to open Britmania. I've also never regretted deciding to have the shop down here. This place always feels so alive."

Pioneer Square was crammed with its usual assortment of humanity. Tourists and local workers rubbed shoulders with shambling street people amid a jumble of small, offbeat shops and restaurants bordering the cobblestone plaza. The city hugged the square on three sides. Towering modern buildings in the central business district loomed immediately north, like a painted backdrop against a cerulean sky. To the west a warren of narrow streets led beneath a viaduct to Elliot Bay and the awesome vista of Puget Sound and the snowcapped Olympic mountains beyond.

On a bench across from Casey and Greer, an old man lay outstretched, his bare ankles pale between ragged polyester pants and the tops of new army boots. A yellowed newspaper shaded his face from the early afternoon sun, and his crossed hands rose and fell atop a protruding belly that jiggled with each breath. Greer eyed the brown paper sack wedged between his body and the back of the bench, noting that the wine was probably the only possession he had in the world. She began to wonder where the man came from and who missed him. Dozens of transients roamed the area day and night, but she could never think of them as faceless and forgotten. Everyone had a past.

Casey had hooked her elbows over the seat back and crossed her long legs. Her pink T-shirt, which read, Seattleites Don't Tan, They Rust, was hiked up to show an inch of smooth midriff.

"Sis," she said, peering sideways at Greer. "Let's be irresponsible."

"What did you have in mind?" Greer asked cautiously.

Casey's eyes closed like a lazy cat. "Taking the afternoon off."

Greer chuckled and brushed sandwich crumbs from the lap of her beige cotton jump suit. "Lunch break's over for me. Time to get back to the grind. You can fritter away the rest of the day if you want to. But if we're going to keep on paying the rent and covering my expensive whims, someone had better tend the shop."

"Don't start that again." Casey put an arm around Greer's shoulders and squeezed. "This trip back to England isn't a whim. It's something you've got to do. And it'll be good for the store, too. Where better to dredge up some oddball British memorabilia?" She tugged her hair theatrically, stopping with her elbows pointing to the sky. "The mind boggles. I can see the newspapers. 'Glamorous proprietor of Seattle's trendiest shop does it again. Import store becomes the only American establishment to stock genuine imitation crown jewels. Orders are being taken at Britmania by—'"

Greer placed a finger to Casey's lips. "You're wonderful. I love you. But you talk too much. Stay and soak up the sun for a while. I'll start back." She stood, threw the remnants of her lunch into a garbage can and adjusted the corded belt around her tiny waist.

"Okay, slave driver. You win." In one smooth motion Casey was beside her sister. "I was only trying to make you take it easy for once. You push yourself too hard. Remember what the doctor said? It hasn't been two months since the hysterectomy and he told you to give yourself at least three before returning to full activity."

"I don't want to discuss that."

"Why?" Casey shook her head impatiently at a grizzled man who approached from a doorway, his hand held out. "Why don't you want to discuss it, Greer? It's unnatural for you to avoid something so traumatic as if it never happened."

While Casey marched ahead Greer dug in her purse for some coins. "Here, Charlie," she said to the white-haired man, who gave a courtly, slightly wobbly bow. "Something to eat this time, okay?" She handed him the money. He closed his grimy fingers around the money and displayed a mouthful of stained teeth.

"I wish you wouldn't do that," Casey said when Greer caught up to her. "You shouldn't encourage these people. They know you're a soft touch."

Greer shrugged, grateful for the change of subject. "It doesn't hurt anything. And I've seen you do the same thing. Want to go to Takara for dinner tonight?"

"Maybe. Is it four weeks or five before you leave?"

"Five. October 21."

"I worry about you going alone. Why don't we hire someone to run the shop and I'll come with you?"

Familiar threads of anxiety started to wind through Greer. "No. Even if we could afford it. This is one thing I want to do by myself. And there's nothing to worry about. Anyone listening to you would think you were the one who was four years older instead of me. I know what's best for me."

"Josh would help us out..."

"No!" Greer snapped. Somehow she must make Casey understand without hurting her. Josh Field had been Colin's partner and, since she became a widow, Greer's close friend—too close for Greer. Lately she sensed his growing impatience for more than a platonic attachment. She wanted to gently discourage the relationship, not encourage it.

Casey caught Greer's elbow and pulled her to a halt. "Look at me," she said. "Your behavior isn't normal."

Two couples passed, glancing curiously at the women. "This isn't the time or place for this," Greer muttered, feeling her color rise.

"There never is a time or place. But at least out in the open, you can't hide. Please, Greer, don't stay clammed up like this. I've waited weeks for you to let your feelings out."

"I don't feel anything," Greer insisted. At five-foot-one, Greer had to crane her neck to meet her tall sister's eyes. "What difference does a hysterectomy make to me now? We're late."

"Fine," Casey said as she released Greer's arm. "Keep on pretending you don't give a damn. When you said you were going back to England, I thought you'd decided to stop pretending you don't care about all that's happened to you. You're only twenty-six. And you're gorgeous. You ought to marry again and we both know who'd be only too happy to oblige."

Greer walked faster, but Casey hardly lengthened her stride to stay alongside. They crossed Occidental Square and headed for Post Street where they had rented space in the basement of a renovated building.

"Listen, Greer," Casey began, before having to dodge a wild-eyed teenager in a headset who practiced a dance that took up the width of the sidewalk. "Listen," she repeated as they fell into step again.

A panicky sensation invaded Greer's stomach. She smiled, knowing the effort was obviously phony. "If you're still planning to palm me off on poor Josh Field, forget it. Just because he used to be Colin's partner, and he's been good to me, it doesn't mean he wants to get permanently saddled with a cripple."

"Give me a break," Casey exploded. "You limp a bit. Since when did that make you a cripple? And if you're worried about not being able to have children, big deal. Mom and dad adopted you. They felt exactly the same about both of us, and if you adopted kids you'd love them, too. Anyway, I don't think Josh even likes children that much. You'd be perfect for each other."

The panicky sensation spread to Greer's legs. Why would Casey choose now to bring all this up? There was nothing to say that hadn't already been said a hundred times. She slowed down, forcing herself to take deep breaths. "Don't get mad, Case. Let's drop it," she managed to say.

A garish poster flapped away from a wall as they passed and

Casey batted it with a fist. "I'm not mad, just frustrated. Josh isn't good to you, as you put it. The guy's crazy about you and all he gets is the runaround."

"That's not true."

"It is, sis. He wants you to be his wife."

They reached the flight of stairs leading down to Britmania. "I've been a wife. And I had the best husband in the world. That's enough, more than most women ever have," she said, favoring her right leg slightly as she walked down.

Casey's backless sandals slapped the concrete when she loped past, taking two steps at a time. She fumbled in her jeans' pocket and produced a key. "Colin was a good man. But he wasn't a saint." She unlocked the door and went inside. Quickly she flipped the sign on the door to read *open*. "I understood that the main reason for you going to England again was to make another attempt to find your biological family. And I thought that was great. But I'm beginning to suspect the real reason. What you want to do most is be where you last were with Colin, isn't it? You're going to his and Colleen's graves, aren't you?"

"Yes," Greer muttered. She took a comb from her purse and started to drag it through her hair. "Is that so strange?"

"I suppose not," Casey said. China wine decanters—each shaped like one of the wives of Henry VIII—clattered as she pushed them to the end of a shelf. "Maybe there you'll finally cry the tears that must be waterlogging your brain by now. Put the ghosts to rest and get on with your life." She twisted a ceramic head sharply on its cork neck.

"Look, Casey," Greer said laying the comb on the counter. "I'm not falling apart. When I first got back here I was pretty broken up. Destroyed would be a better description, but who wouldn't be? If I didn't cry then it was because I was too numb, and later there wasn't time."

"Greer..."

"No, Case. You wanted me to spill all this, so let me finish."

Taking several deliberate steps, Greer reached the door, locked it and turned the sign around to read *closed*. She paced in front of her sister. "I want to trace my original family very much. And I do intend to search for them. But I never faced up to Colin and Colleen dying. They say you have to go through a bunch of phases to grieve properly, and I missed just about all of them. I thought about it a lot while I was in the hospital for the hysterectomy and decided I'd like to try and catch up. Does that make sense?"

"Yes. I'm glad. You know I didn't mean to criticize you, don't you, sis?" Casey inquired gently.

"Yes, I know, but it's important to get things straight between us," Greer answered just as gently. "Before the accident, Josh had already signed the papers to buy Colin out. I took what money was left after—after everything—and made it work for me. You make it sound as if I've sat around for two years feeling sorry for myself."

"I never said that..."

"Pretty close. I know Colin would approve, of Britmania and of what I've done. He'd be proud of me. And I thought you enjoyed all this—this crazy stuff we deal in. It works, and it uses my only real talent—imagination. I love selling ashtrays with coats of arms to people named Smith. It's a kick to watch customers cart away bits of the white cliffs of Dover in plastic bags or key rings with Wimbledon locker-room numbers. Oh, sure, they pretend the whole thing's a big spoof but they enjoy every minute of it. And we make a good living. As far as I'm concerned that's success, and I made it." Greer paused. Her blood pumped hard and it felt good.

Casey massaged her temples. "Every word you say is true. You've done marvelously well. I love being a part of it all, and you know that. But I still say you're avoiding the point."

"I don't know what you mean."

"You do." The younger woman grasped Greer's shoulders and backed her to a chair. "Sit there and listen. All you're talking about is the business. There's no question that it's a success. But I'm worried about you—Greer Beckett, the woman. If Josh twists your arm you go out to dinner or the theater. By eleven you're home and he's fortunate if you allow him in for coffee. The guy wants you. If you gave him one little word of encouragement he'd whisk you down the aisle so fast our heads would spin."

To her horror Greer felt moisture well in her eyes. She tipped her head back, but the tears sprang free and coursed down her cheeks. "Do you think I don't know that?" she whispered. "And feel like a creep about it?"

Casey dropped to her knees, cradling Greer's head against her shoulder. "I don't know how you feel. You never tell me."

"I don't want to marry Josh. I don't want to marry anyone. If I live to be a hundred I'll always miss Colin. I haven't cried becuase I'm afraid that if I do I'll never stop." She felt herself begin to tremble and took a deep, controlling breath. "If you just relax Casey, everything will be fine. Josh will find someone else and, hopefully, still be my friend. I have all I want. Forget the idea I'm yearning for new beginnings."

"Oh, Greer," Casey said in a wobbly voice, "I want you to be happy."

"I am. Please let it go at that."

Casey sat back on her heels and sniffed. "Okay. I guess I'll have to—for now. Need a tissue?"

Greer swiped her cheeks with the backs of her hands. "Yup. But I'll get it. Turn that sign over, kid. I'm going to unpack the stuff that was delivered this morning. Then I'll make us some coffee." Before she went through the door to the storeroom she looked over her shoulder. Casey was still on her knees, staring through the window. "You didn't say yes or no to Takara's for dinner," Greer said, deftly smoothing over the awkward moment. "Sushi's healthy, you know. Then we could go upstairs to the ice-cream place and have seven-layer mocha cake—just to keep up our energy."

"You're on," Casey said, not turning around. Her voice was muffled.

Greer went into the sloping space under the stairs of the business behind Britmania. A naked electric bulb hung from a long wire that could be looped over various hooks in the wall, depending on where light was needed. How could she explain feelings that were a mystery even to her? Greer started the coffee maker and went to work opening boxes.

"Hey, Greer," Casey said as she stuck her head around the door.

"Josh just called. He sounded lonely, so I invited him to come with us for dinner. You don't mind, do you?"

Yes, I mind. I mind. "Of course not."

"Great. I told him to meet us here at six."

The door closed and Greer stared hard at it. Maybe if she stayed in England long enough, Josh would lose interest or meet someone else. He was handsome, charming and well-off. Too bad he wasn't ten years younger so she could encourage a liaison with Casey—maybe she still should. She wrinkled her nose. Josh wasn't Casey's type. He was basically a quiet man, with brown hair and liquid hazel eyes. Casey went for the flamboyant Nordic types, just as Greer had...

Greer attacked the boxes with fresh ardor. After weeks of not really thinking about him, the familiar picture of Colin sprang to mind. It was always the same. He was asleep beside her, his sun-streaked hair tousled against the pillow, his slender tanned face turned toward her. Then he opened eyes so blue they seemed to burn and smiled as he reached for her.

Sweat broke out on Greer's upper lip. She filled her arms with crackly packages but they kept slipping. The second she straightened, the mental picture of Colin changed. A lattice of blood wove across his forehead, staining the pillow, his eyes became dull and puzzled. Greer squeezed her eyelids shut and leaned against the wall. The scene had always faded there, but this time it only blurred.

Musical notes tapped like ice spicules across her brain. Colin's image dimmed, to be replaced by the stricken features of a tall, dark man whose honey-colored eyes stared pleadingly into hers. The music persisted. Greer twisted her head, pressing it against the cool brick. She heard the man's deep voice from a long way off, unclear. Then his lips formed a single word and she knew what he said, "Colleen."

Greer felt hollow. She'd made Andrew Monthaven the target of all her hate. No one could know for sure why her baby had died—or if it was anyone's fault. Yet she had blamed him and still did in the times when it hurt, and she ached for what she could never have. But he had been kind—he cared. If she'd just said Thank-

you, it might have helped them both. Please let her have the courage
to go to him and say those two words.

Greer opened her eyes, but the music still played.

"Brahms Lullaby."

CHAPTER TWO

WHAT A FANTASTIC evening, Andrew Monthaven thought. October in Dorset. Perfect. Too bad everything else in his life wasn't equally satisfying. He stood at the edge of a bluff behind his house with his friend, Bob Wilson, staring toward the English Channel. Below them, fog bumped in soft heaps against sheer chalk cliffs. Where the vaporous mass thinned, steely water glistened in the dusk like fine pewter.

The sound of Bob's impatient intake of breath came as an intrusion. Andrew bent to pick up a limestone pebble. Asking Bob's opinion had been a mistake. If one sought advice, one should be prepared to listen. But Andrew's mind was already made up.

He faced Bob and the two men exchanged a long look. Both an inch or so taller than six feet, any physical similarity ended there. Bob was husky and blond, with a studied stylishness, Andrew dark, lean, unconsciously elegant.

"What do you want me to say?" Bob said at last.

"Nothing." Andrew leaned back and shied the rock high into the air, then listened, hand outstretched, until it plopped into veiled waters. He faced Bob. "I shouldn't have laid this on you. It was wrong to involve you in my problems. But we've known each other so long it's instinctive to ask your advice."

Bob began to pace slowly. He stopped, puffed out his cheeks, then let air slip past his teeth in a hissing whistle. "You're not thinking, Andy. Only reacting. Drop this thing with Coover. If you don't, he'll have your head on a platter."

It took three sharp tugs for Andrew to loosen his burgundy silk tie. "Winston Coover is senior pediatric consultant for Dorset County, and he's my boss," he said. "But his incompetence caused the death of one of my patients and I'm going to prove it."

"The only thing you'll prove is that you can't fight the system."

Bob's light blue eyes shifted slightly. "Coover's powerful. He's got everyone who counts in his hip pocket. They'll crucify you."

Moisture had made Andrew's sable hair curl over his forehead. He raked it back. "So toe the line, right? Michael Drake's dead and there's no point in causing trouble now. It'll probably never happen again. Come on, Bob. You know me better than that. I can't take the risk."

Bob patted the pockets of his tan suit until he located a pack of cigarettes. "Your conscience is admirable," he muttered, cupping his lighter to protect its flame from the breeze. For a moment he dragged thoughtfully on a cigarette. "It's also going to ruin you," he continued. "The bottom line is that you can't win. The surgeon who operated on young Drake will back Coover and so will the pathologist. They already have."

"There's no record of blood work in Michael's files," Andrew said. "If nothing else, with his symptoms, a white-cell count should have been routine."

"What if they say you removed the lab sheets?" Bob challenged him.

Resolve glittered in Andrew's golden-brown eyes. "Hell, I don't know. But that boy was my patient, and he was something special. Sensitive. He was fifteen, Bob. Remember when you and I were fifteen? We were dreamers and planners and nothing was ever going to stop us. Michael was like that."

"You knew him pretty well, didn't you?"

"He'd been my patient since I first took the job in Dorchester. Six years. One of those intense kids who run into a lot of abdominal pain. I checked him out for appendicitis several times. If he hadn't chosen my weekend off to pull the real thing, he'd be alive now."

The tip of Bob's cigarette glowed briefly. "You were in London, weren't you?"

"Yes. You know I usually go up when I get a couple of free days. It's a good idea to keep the flat lived in as much as possible."

Bob bit a thumbnail, then examined it closely. "Were you alone again?"

"Yes—what about it?" Andrew spread his hands on his hips

beneath the jacket of his navy suit. "Why should you care how I spend my spare time—or who I spend it with?"

"Forget it. I worry about you, that's all. You're alone too much. Some steady female company would do you good."

"Somehow we got from Michael Drake to my love life. What's the connection?"

Bob turned up his collar. "Coover's bound to be looking for something to nail you with."

Irritation mounted in Andrew. "Great. And I repeat. What point are you making?"

"How long is it since you took a woman to bed?"

Andrew dropped his hands to his sides. "I didn't hear what I just thought I heard, did I?"

Ruddy streaks blazed across Bob's flat cheekbones, but Andrew sensed something other than embarrassment was the cause. He felt his scalp tighten as an invisible screen seemed to separate him from the man who had been closer than a brother since they were children.

"Bob," Andrew persisted. "What is this?"

"Okay. You might as well hear it from me as from a disciplinary board." Bob threw down the cigarette and ground it underfoot. "You're thirty-five and unmarried. You may not be filthy rich, but you're not a pauper, either. There isn't an unattached nurse on the staff of the medical center who hasn't made a play for you, but you don't even seem to notice."

Andrew began to laugh. "Who's keeping track?" Bob wasn't making any sense.

"This isn't funny," Bob said. "Damn it, Andy. Do I have to spell it out word for word? I haven't been keeping track. But someone has. And when one or two comments were dropped, I couldn't defend you because I had nothing to defend you with."

"Defend me?" Andrew turned back toward the sea and tried to concentrate on the fuzzy panorama. "I don't understand."

When Bob answered, his tone held a softness that was menacing. "The last time I remember you with a woman was when you and Lauren and I went to Stratford to see a play. You took Chris Hardy—nice and safe—one of the girls we both knew from medical school. That was over two years ago—two years last July to be precise. Since then, apart from occasional dinners at our house, when you come alone, your private life has been just that—totally private. Andy, are you gay?''

Disbelief seeped into Andrew's brain, followed almost immediately by rage. He grabbed Bob's sleeve, then let go as if it burned. ''This is madness. Gay? Is that what Coover and his cronies are going to suggest. Are they spreading nasty little rumors to muddy up my reputation and hoping that'll be enough to keep me quiet?''

''Something like that. Yes.''

''And you couldn't defend me? Bob Wilson who grew up on one of my father's farms right here in Dorset? The kid who spent as much time at my home as he did at his own? You listened to that obvious fabrication and didn't stand up for me?'' Andrew said, wanting to retch.

''It wasn't like that.'' With one fist Bob slowly pounded his other palm. ''I listened so that I could tell you what was in the wind. Then I thought it through and realized they might be able to make their accusations stick. The only thing to do now is back off and hope things die down,'' he concluded.

''By that you mean that if I shut up, I won't be dragged before a board on a charge of possible misconduct. What am I supposed to do? Start carving a notch on my stethoscope for every nurse I take to bed?''

Bob kicked loose gravel over the edge of the cliff. ''You're being irrational,'' he snapped. ''It wasn't easy to tell you any of this. I probably shouldn't have.'' He started up the path.

''Wait. Good Lord, man, wait.'' Andrew caught up. ''This is too much to take in. I wouldn't have been surprised if you'd said Coover might make a thing out of my opening Ringstead Hall to the public.'' He nodded toward his Jacobian mansion atop a rise of smooth lawn. ''It struck me that he could suggest I was after his job because I was short of money. But homosexuality? You floored me.''

''I'm not surprised. It didn't do much for my equilibrium when I heard the rumor.''

Bob's lapse into a hint of a Dorset accent alerted Andrew to the depth of his friend's agitation. He squinted at the driveway beside his house. A straggling line of visitors steadily disappeared aboard an orange-and-white bus that already belched a murky cloud from its exhaust pipe.

"Monday's last load of eager sightseers appears about to depart," he said. "Join me for a drink?"

Bob's expression was enigmatic. "Thanks, but Lauren will have dinner ready. Pick you up in the morning?"

"Pass, Bob. I'm going in late tomorrow—and Wednesday."

"To avoid me?"

"Of course not. My morning clinics have been canceled this week. Not enough patients." Andrew blew into his cupped hands, then rubbed them together. "Maybe my reputation's already catching up with me," he said lightly even though he could not smile.

"And maybe you'd be wise to take this very seriously," Bob replied quietly. "You're important to me, Andy. That's why I'm so worried." He hurried toward a flight of crumbling steps that led to the back of the house. A cobalt sky silhouetted the impressive, gray stone structure on its grassy knoll.

"Bob," Andrew called out to the other man. "Trust me. Whatever happens, I'll make sure it doesn't touch you."

When he faced Andrew, Bob's expression was unreadable. "You may not be able to."

Andrew flinched. "What exactly does that mean?" he asked tightly.

"That's something I don't think I have to explain." Bob said. "See you sometime tomorrow. In the meantime...think."

CHAPTER THREE

THE TEA in the bottom of her cup was tepid. Greer took another swallow and grimaced at the bitter taste. Tea as the English obviously preferred it—strong enough to stand a spoon in—would never take the place of her beloved black coffee.

She should be more tired than she felt. Less than forty-eight hours ago she'd still been in Seattle. Excitement had made sleep impossible both the night before she left and on the plane. The long flight to London and then a three-hour train journey had brought her to Weymouth in Dorset County the previous evening. The seaside town would be headquarters for her stay. She'd settled gratefully into her ocean-front boardinghouse but had again been too wound up to relax. After a restless night she was up at five, watching a gray dawn, impatient to explore the town that had been her home when she was too young to remember. Armed with a map, she'd set off on foot immediately after breakfast.

Greer looked around the tiny second-floor tea shop. It was lunch time and every table was occupied—mostly by fresh-faced women engrossed in animated conversation. Their voices all seemed to have a similar high, clear quality, and the speed with which they drank tea and ordered more told Greer they wouldn't appreciate her opinion of England's national brew.

Bumble's. The name of the shop had caught her attention from the other side of the street. The ground floor was a charmingly cluttered retail showroom that reminded Greer of Britmania. Every shelf was jammed with locally made pottery, unusual kitchen tools, beaten copper jewelry and a profusion of wooden bowls and ornaments. Racks displayed greeting cards and gift wrappings. Boxes of chocolates were stacked on the counter amid piles of partially unpacked merchandise. Greer had browsed, noting one or two possible ideas for her own stock, before climbing a short flight of stairs to the restaurant. Small original paintings of local scenes dotted the walls on her way up. The pictures were for sale and she immediately thought of approaching the artist to see if he'd be interested in exporting some of his work.

The spinach quiche she'd ordered was excellent, but too much. She speared a forkful and pushed it around her plate. It was time to take her next step. To make peace with her past she must return to the unfinished business of two years ago. And Dr. Andrew Monthaven was the first loose end to be tied.

She had looked for his name in the telephone book as soon as her suitcases were unpacked. She'd found only one listing: "A. Monthaven, M.D., Ringstead Hall." Twice she dialed the number and listened to the grinding rings, so different from those she was accustomed to. An hour later she again inserted coins in the hallway phone. Still no answer. Then she lost her nerve. She should have tried the Dorchester Medical Center as she had planned, but even the idea of making contact with that place had wrapped ribbons of tension around her heart.

Dorchester was only eight miles northeast of Weymouth. It would be easy to catch a bus or train and go to see him.

At breakfast her landlady had hovered while Greer spread marmalade on toast. "Not much to see here but hills and a lot of wild seas at this time of year," the woman had said, crossing her arms over a wraparound floral apron. "If you like old places, there's Thomas Hardy's cottage—muddy to get to. Or Athelhampton Hall in Puddletown. They say parts of the house are more than five hundred years old. Crumbling and drafty I'd call it—probably—never been there. Then there's Ringstead Hall. Some of my people have liked that. You could go to Lawrence of Arabia's house..."

Ringstead Hall—Andrew Monthaven's home? Greer had only half heard the rest of the woman's words. "Ringstead?" Mrs. Findlay had sniffed at her interest. "It's open to the public for tours twice a week. Mondays and Tuesdays. I'm not much for that sort of thing myself, but foreigners seem to like it."

Tomorrow would be Tuesday. Impulsively Greer had decided to visit the tour offices in the center of Weymouth and make a reservation. She'd already made up her mind to see Andrew as soon as possible, say what she should have said years ago, then put the episode behind her. If Ringstead Hall was his house, she might be lucky enough to run into him. Not likely, but possible. One way or another she must get the meeting with Andrew Monthaven over. Glancing around Bumble's once more, her only regret was she couldn't stay here forever. Maybe she'd just have one more cup of tea before she went to make a reservation.

WHAT HAS SHE expected? Andrew Monthaven playing the gracious host to a bevy of tourists? And if he had appeared, what would she have said to him in front of several dozen strangers?

Good grief, her feet hurt. Greer hung back until she was the last of her sightseeing group in the room, then slumped into a stiffly upholstered chair. This was the ninth bedroom she had been ushered through, each one crammed with what the tour guide pompously described as "priceless pieces." Stuffy was the only adjective that came to Greer's mind. She smiled a little wistfully. Colin would have loved every inch of Ringstead Hall. European antiques had been his passion and his area of expertise. Too bad she'd never been interested enough to learn more from him.

The guide's voice came from the corridor, "Ringstead Hall is one of the best examples of Jacobean architecture in the country. Very early sixteen hundreds. Please don't touch the wall hangings." His words gradually ebbed beneath the sound of many clumping feet on the stairs.

Greer unzipped her boots and slid them off. She wiggled her toes. The guide had promised "a quick peek" at the wine cellars before they left and she ought to hurry or everyone else would get too far ahead. But how her feet ached. She yawned. Delayed jet lag had her in its grip.

The house reminded her of a museum. All spectacular, but remote. The information pamphlet confirmed that the owner was still in residence, but Greer saw no sign of life. And any occupant of such a house should be Lord or Sir something, not an unassuming young doctor.

There must be two Andrew Monthavens in southern Dorset. The one she knew was surely married with a gaggle of happy children.

His home would be tasteful, yet comfortable, not a repository for curios. But she had found only one listing for Monthaven in the telephone directory.

She'd better move. If the guide noticed she was missing, he would come searching for her and she'd feel like a fool. She tugged on her rust suede boots with difficulty. Why did feet always choose the most inconvenient times to swell?

Greer left the bedroom and made her way along a narrow hallway lined with grim portraits—mostly of men in armor or elaborate, military uniforms. Expressions were dour; long, austere features, carefully posed to convey the serious nature of each subject. She slowed down. Scattered between the men were likenesses of a few women, heavy jewels prominent on curved bosoms, soft hands folded around a small book, a flower, a delicate piece of needlework. Greer began to wonder about the people in the pictures. What had the young girl with pale ringlets and luminous gray eyes thought a century earlier? Next to the shy-looking girl was a painting of a young man dressed in dark green velvet with a froth of white lace at neck and cuff.

Slowly she backed away, studying each plane and angle of the face intently. The features were finely chiseled, yet intensely masculine. Dark brows arched above the golden-brown eyes that held a flicker of mirth in their depths. The bridge of the straight nose was narrow, balanced perfectly by high cheekbones and an angular jaw. Unlike most of his silent companions he wore no hat, and his curly black hair appeared damp. Greer found herself smiling as if the man who had sat for the artist so long ago was inviting her to share his own secret joke.

It was him. The smile slipped from Greer's lips. Not really Andrew Monthaven, of course, but a man so like him that he could have been Andrew dressed in the clothing of another era.

The distant sound of a large engine bursting to life broke into her thoughts. The bus couldn't be leaving, not without her. She had no idea how she would get back to Weymouth if it did. She ran to the top of the stairs and started down before she saw the vehicle bumping away. Distorted through the stained-glass windows of the great entry hall, the bus moved steadily out of sight. When the guide had said "a quick peek" at the wine cellars, he must have meant exactly that.

For several seconds Greer stood immobile, then she sank onto a step and cupped her chin in both hands. What a nitwit. She tried to remember how far they had traveled from the main road, down a winding lane to the driveway of Ringstead Hall. Greer had never thumbed a ride in her life, but there was a first time for everything, and if she could reach a thoroughfare she'd take whatever help she could get.

Uncertainty crowded in. It was already getting dark. She would probably have to walk a couple of miles over rough ground—far more stress than she had put on her hip since the injury. There must be a telephone somewhere. Of course there was. She'd found the number herself, yesterday.

Deepening gloom at the foot of the stairs intimidated her. Greer retraced her path along the upper hallway, peering hopefully into alcoves, but finding only an endless array of marble statues.

Not sure what to do next, she hesitated. Then she realized she was a few feet from the portrait that resembled Andrew Monthaven. She went to stand in front of it once more. This time, so close, she could make out brush strokes, cracked with age.

Tentatively she touched a shaded area beneath one cheekbone, followed it to the hint of a groove beside the mouth. A beautiful mouth. Andrew's had been like that, wide and mobile. How strange that she only realized how handsome he was in retrospect.

With the tip of one forefinger she outlined the sharply defined lips in the painting. Would Andrew want to see her again after the way she had treated him? Perhaps he'd forgotten about her and she should leave the past alone. She shook her head impatiently. *Looking for an easy out again.* Tomorrow she'd call him in Dorchester.

At the sound of a door clicking shut to her left, Greer froze, her finger still resting on the portrait. The footsteps that approached so slowly were soft. She looked over her shoulder and clutched the rolled neck of her raincoat. Her heart soared upward to jam in her throat.

The man who approached was in shadow, until he stopped a few feet away, in the light from the bedroom where Greer had lingered too long. "Good Lord," he said. "Greer Beckett? It can't be."

Greer couldn't answer. Her heart plummeted like a runaway elevator. Andrew Monthaven looked so much like the portrait that she felt suddenly disoriented. Instead of green velvet, he wore a brown terry robe, loosely tied at the waist. But his hair *was* wet. It glistened dark and curly about his forehead and ears, and on his muscular chest where the robe gaped. Greer glanced downward. His bare feet accounted for the muffled footsteps.

He came closer until she could see the soft gold of his eyes, and the expression of shocked disbelief she saw there made her knees weak.

"What are you doing here?" he asked quietly.

"I looked you up—" Greer's voice broke and she cleared her throat. For some inexplicable reason she felt like crying. The sensation that engulfed her at the sight of him threatened to destroy every shred of her composure, but she held herself erect. No way was she going to fall apart. He'd pity her again—something she didn't need—from anyone.

"How? I mean..." Andrew took another step, then stopped and ran his fingers through the hair at his temples.

The way he did that night, Greer thought. She'd hurt him then and now all she could possibly do was remind them both of those terrible moments. Fool.

His lips moved, but he made no sound. Finally he raised his chin and Greer saw him swallow. "I don't understand any of this."

"Your address was in the phone book," she said, keeping her voice level. "Then I found out about the house tours. I came on a bus."

"The bus left."

She hooked a thumb into each pocket. "I know. This is a wonderful house. I got too interested in one of the rooms and didn't realize everyone else was gone." At least she didn't sound as garbled as she felt.

"You were hoping you'd see me? That's why you came?"

He wouldn't have to be very bright to figure that out. Greer turned to face the painting. "Yes—no. I'm not sure why I came now." *I'm babbling like an idiot.*

She felt him move close to her shoulder, felt his height and breadth overpower her. He smelled of soap and fresh air.

"Why didn't you call me?" he asked. "Instead of coming on a tour bus, for pity's sake?"

"I did call. You weren't in." Heat suffused Greer's cheeks. What else could she say that would make sense? "I like this painting. It reminds me of you..." Her voice faded.

"He was Giles Monthaven, my great-great-grandfather. A bit of a rake I'm told." An almost palpable tension underlay Andrew's words.

Greer couldn't get enough oxygen. "He was a very handsome man," she blurted. Why had she said that?

They both became silent, but Greer was acutely aware of the man behind her.

"Your hair's longer," Andrew said at last. "It always reminded me of autumn oak leaves."

Greer heard a soft breath escape his lungs and then felt his fingertips pass lightly over her hair from crown to the curling ends at her shoulder blades. The contact made her throat squeeze and her brain refuse to operate.

"How are you, Greer?"

"Fine," she said, vaguely surprised at the steadiness of her voice. "Never better."

"And your sister? I don't remember her name."

"Casey. She's terrific." Greer wanted to bolt. This was miserable—for both of them.

Andrew touched her shoulder. "Look at me. I keep expecting you to disappear."

She faced him and found herself close enough to see the rapid pulse in his neck. "This was a bad idea, Dr. Monthaven," she began, avoiding his eyes. "I'm sorry for barging in on you. I didn't want to visit the area without at least saying hi...you were very good to me and I was rotten." She finished in a rush.

"It's been two years," Andrew said extremely quietly. "Two years exactly. If you knew how often I've thought of you and wondered how you were. I almost wrote a couple of times. But I knew how you felt.'' He waited until she met his gaze.

''I almost wrote, too. I should have.'' Greer took a step backward and her heel scraped the wall. *He had thought of her.* ''Anyway. You're probably tired. I'm sorry I disturbed you.''

His hand on her elbow stopped her retreat. ''You aren't disturbing me. Could you manage to call me Andrew?''

The unmistakable tingling in Greer's belly frightened her. ''Andrew,'' she said. ''It was great to see you again. But I'd better go.''

He continued to hold her arm. ''Where are you staying?''

The man was magnetic. ''In Weymouth. A boardinghouse in St. John's Terrace. It's near an old church, by the ocean.'' She was bound to be affected by him, but so strongly?

''I know St. John's Terrace. I hope you have a view of the bay from your room,'' he said, studying her intently. When he ran two fingers along the scar above her eyebrow, Greer almost jumped. ''This has healed beautifully,'' he said. ''Have you had any trouble with the hip?''

The quivering in her belly made it difficult to speak. ''It's a bit weak, that's all,'' she answered. She pushed her hair behind one shoulder. There was no way he wouldn't notice her nervousness.

''Maybe you don't exercise enough.'' Andrew was absorbed in thought. ''You can't be giving it what it needs or you'd be able to do anything by now.''

''I do what I want to do, Andrew.'' In her agitation, she'd pulled the house-tour pamphlet from her pocket. When she tried to stuff it back, it slipped through her fingers.

Andrew dropped to one knee to retrieve the paper, then sat back on his heels and looked up at her. ''Sorry,'' he said, grinning, deepening the grooves beside his mouth. ''I didn't mean to lecture. Habit, I suppose. Did I ever tell you that you have the bluest eyes I've ever seen?''

''No,'' Greer muttered. And she wished he wouldn't now.

''With that hair they ought to be green, but blue is definitely more interesting on you. I'd forgotten those marvelous freckles.''

He was too close, too masculine. His robe fell away from one thigh, revealing a well-toned muscle, finely covered with dark hair.

Beneath the carefully belted terry cloth he must be naked. The realization jolted Greer. "It was good to see you. But I really must run," she said once again, painfully aware she was beginning to sound like a recording.

Andrew stood immediately. "Come and have a drink while I dress. Then I'll drive you back."

Greer straightened her shoulders. What was it that made everyone she met want to take care of her? "No," she said quickly. "Thanks anyway. I'll manage." There had to be public transportation, even in such a remote spot. She lowered her eyes and ducked around Andrew to head for the stairs.

"It's dark. And I don't think you'll be able to—"

"Don't worry," she said, cutting him off. "I'll catch one of those green buses, or something." What the "or something" might be she had no idea, but the sensation Andrew Monthaven aroused in her was an element she did not want to deal with.

Her booted feet thudded rapidly on the wide, curving staircase to the ground floor. At least he wasn't following. Powerful attraction had come Greer's way once before in the person of Colin Beckett. The result had been to love him with all that she had, only to lose him. It was outrageous to compare anything about her marriage with the encounter she'd just experienced. Nevertheless, she had felt the same kind of sexual attraction to Andrew as she had to Colin, and it upset her. That element in her response to men must be cut off, had been since Colin died. And nothing could be allowed to change that.

She tried to visualize Colin, but for the first time couldn't see his face in her mind. When they met, Greer was only eighteen and they married before her nineteenth birthday. Colin was eleven years older, an odd mixture of sophistication and boyishness that had swept Greer's heart and soul away. He had made her feel safe and special, and she wished he were with her now.

The empty hallway echoed as she crossed to the double front doors. She turned one heavy, brass knob and pulled, grateful for the rush of cool breeze, accompanied by the heady scent of autumn roses and sea salt. There had been a suggestion of the ocean's pungent fragrance about Andrew...

Greer closed the door behind her with more force than she intended to, and her right leg gave out. She stumbled, then regained her balance. That hadn't happened for ages. She must have done too much in the past few days. Or had seeing Andrew Monthaven upset her even more than she realized?

She didn't go far. Rough stone steps led down to a gravel drive that wound between a tunnel of yews toward the main gate. With no moon the darkness was complete, and the whispering grove of trees seemed to swallow her. A white wrought-iron bench glowed a few feet ahead, and she hurried to reach it and sit until she could decide what to do next.

No public transportation came out there. Why should it? There were no houses but this one. Andrew had been trying to tell her as much when she interrupted him, and now he was assuredly waiting for her to come back and ask for help. *Damn it.*

Greer wrapped her black raincoat more tightly around her slim body. This mess was the result of her own foolishness. She should have stuck to her original intention and made an appointment with Andrew. Their interview would have been brief and dignified, the misunderstandings of two years before neatly straightened out. As it was, she felt unsettled and defensive.

More reluctant than ever to return to the plainly aristocratic owner of Ringstead Hall, Greer sank farther into her collar. He knew who he was, where he came from; there were no holes in his family tree. He had probably never experienced an insecure moment in his life.

It wasn't important to see her great-grandfathers' pedigrees—or portraits. Simply discovering the story of the first two years of her own life would be enough. And somewhere among Dorset's gentle hills, contrasted by its wild shores and fickle weather, she intended to find that story.

Tom and Dianne Wyatt adopted Greer out of a foster home in Weymouth when she was two years old. The American couple were on a work exchange with a British aircraft company. When Greer was four, a year after their return to the States, Casey was born—the child the Wyatts could supposedly never conceive.

Greer grew up surrounded by love and security, and hid a curiosity about her shadowy beginnings that made her feel traitorous, even now. But although Tom and Dianne were open with her, Greer always felt there were bits and pieces of her past that they knew, but didn't divulge. She and Colin had discussed the possibility that, if this was true, it was probably more for her sake than theirs. Greer resolved to ask them the questions that plagued her, but never did. They both died the year before her visit to England with Colin.

It had been Colin's idea that they make the trip. He often attended European antique auctions as a buyer. But his short absences were confined to well-publicized offerings, usually in London or Paris. This time, he said, he'd stay a month and look for the unexpected finds that sometimes surfaced in private estate sales far from major cities. Colin planned to concentrate his efforts on the south of England, particularly Dorset, so that Greer could look for her original family while he worked.

Almost seven months pregnant at the time, Greer was reluctant at first, but her enthusiasm grew with Colin's persuasive arguments, "The doctor says it's fine for you to travel. You've never stopped wondering about your past. If you decide you don't want to pursue it once you get started—then stop. But I want you with me, especially now." He'd stroked her expanding belly possessively and kissed her. And Greer had acquiesced.

The crash occurred three days after they left Seattle. If only she hadn't agreed to go. Colin had wanted to please her because he loved her. His love had killed him and it was her fault.

She blinked and tilted her head up. The motives for being here again had become distorted. Casey had guessed correctly that Greer wanted to return to the last place she and Colin had been together, to visit his grave—and Colleen's. But she would also never rest unless she at least tried to find out something of her ancestry. Then there was the opportunity to come up with new ideas for Britmania. And Andrew Monthaven...

Gnarled branches scraped together above her head and goose bumps raced across Greer's skin. The temperature was dropping steadily and she wasn't dressed warmly enough. There was no choice. She would have to take Andrew up on his offer of a ride to Weymouth. Even if it was possible to call a taxi out here, she certainly didn't have enough cash to pay for one. A cabbie was likely to frown on traveler's checks, particularly in large denominations.

Greer started back slowly. By the time she cleared the trees, she discerned the open front door and the silhouette of a tall man with dim light behind him. Andrew must have thrown on some clothes and come downstairs to wait for her. He stood with feet apart, hands in his pockets as he stared into the night. In her dark clothing she was probably invisible to him.

"Hi," she called in a falsely cheerful voice, wondering uncomfortably what he thought of her. Empty-headed or flighty no doubt. Unflattering and untrue, but he couldn't know what she was really like. And he never would. How could she have been careless enough to miss the bus? "Hi," she repeated, drawing closer. "This is awful. I'm a pest and I know it. But there's obviously no way for me to get to Weymouth under my own steam—unless I walk. And I wouldn't know where to start." She still chattered as she mounted the steps. Why didn't he say something?

Greer didn't look at his face until she felt his hand under her elbow. Andrew's smile wasn't patronizing. His expression showed no annoyance, only what she thought for a moment might be relief. She was crazy, of course. He had to wish she'd never come, but she returned his smile with a great deal of gratitude.

"I almost came after you," he said casually. "But I was afraid of giving you a shock in the dark. You were so determined to leave, I didn't have the heart to embarrass you by saying you were marooned here." He shut the front doors and led her upstairs.

You are so gentle, she wanted to say. *Confident enough of your own masculinity to be comfortable displaying sensitivity. Forgive me for the way I treated you before.* But the words remained locked in her heart.

Andrew steered Greer to the upper passageway and through the door at the end. "Come and get warm, then I'll run you in to Weymouth." His hand found her waist. "Don't feel badly. You've brightened up a lonely man's dull evening. By the way, although I love every inch of this house, I only live in a very small part of it. The rest I share with the National Trust. This is my wing."

Greer moved with him, conscious of his proximity, the virility
he so subtly exuded. She couldn't believe that the handsome Andrew was ever lonely unless he chose to be. But why shouldn't she
enjoy his charming company, just for a little while? Wasn't that
what she'd hoped for, without admitting it until this moment?

"You must think me naïve," she said in a thin voice. "It was
silly to take the tour at all. I should have kept calling until I reached
you. I really did start a letter once, but I've never been good at
putting my thoughts on paper. And there are things I ought to...I
should have..." She couldn't finish.

Andrew seemed not to notice the uncompleted sentence. "In
here." He showed her into a room that appeared untidy at first
glance. "Give me your coat."

Greer allowed him to help her out of the black raincoat with its
rust knitted collar. She hoped her simple dress, of matching knit
fabric, didn't look the way it felt—baggy and rumpled.

A fire crackled in the fireplace. "This is lovely," she said more
brightly than she felt. "Was it a music room once?"

The impression of untidiness was created by piles of books, folders, papers and magazines heaped on every available space, jammed
in floor-to-ceiling bookcases and stacked on the floor. But it was
an ornate cornice above the bookcase that had prompted Greer's
question. Cherubs, trailing wisps of fabric, cavorted among harps,
cellos and other less recognizable instruments.

Andrew glanced from Greer to the molded cornice she studied.
"Not in my family's time." He waved her into an enormous brown
leather chair and turned to poke the fire to brighter life. "We've
only had the house for two hundred years, but the original owners
may have planned this as a small music salon. In fact I think I was
once told as much by my father. I'm surprised you noticed or made
the connection."

Greer tried not to be irritated. He did think she was empty-
headed. "European antiques were my husband's business. I know
very little on the subject, but I went through some of his books
occasionally. I remember reading that ceiling decoration often suggested the original purpose of the room. Several examples were
shown and one was a bit like this."

"Interesting," he said, punctuating his comment with a smile. Greer lost interest in the ceiling. "Now. A drink, or would you prefer coffee?"

"I think I'd like a glass of dry vermouth. If you have it," she said as her mind focused on something more important. Surely he didn't live here alone.

Andrew went to a desk in the recess of a bay window and sorted among some bottles on a silver tray. He selected one, uncapped it and poured vermouth into a tall glass. "Probably not cold enough for your taste," he said, handing it to her. "But it'll relax you. Shall I get you some ice?"

Greer shook her head and took a sip. He wore a ring on his left hand but it was on the little finger. Not that it mattered to her whether or not he was single. She glanced at her own platinum wedding band that had never been removed since her wedding day.

"Tell me what's been happening to you," Andrew said as he fixed his own drink. "What made you decide to come back? Seems an odd time of year for a holiday. Particularly in a place like this. England can be pretty grim once winter sets in."

The invisible doors started to close inside Greer. "I'm here on business," she said, more shortly than she intended.

He wasn't deterred. "What sort of business?"

"Buying." Please let him leave it alone. Go back to the weather. The English are supposed to love discussing their climate.

Andrew settled himself in a wing chair facing her own. He wore a V-neck black sweater over well-worn jeans that hugged every line of his lean hips and powerful legs. Absently switching his glass from hand to hand, he pushed up his sleeves, revealing muscular forearms covered in the same sprinkling of dark hair she had noticed on his thigh. The unwelcome heavy warmth invaded Greer's body again.

For a few seconds he was silent. Firelight glinted on strands of silver at his temple that hadn't been there when she last saw him. The planes beneath his high cheekbones were accented, as was the hollow under his full lower lip and the slight cleft of his chin. Two years had only made him more attractive. She riveted her attention on the strong hands that slowly rolled a stubby goblet of glowing, amber liquid back and forth. A thin, white scar showed from the base of his left thumb to a point beneath his black watchband.

Greer crossed and uncrossed her legs. He must be searching as frantically as she for a way to bring up the past. They both knew she wouldn't be in his house for any other reason.

He leaned forward to throw another log on the fire, and the sweater tightened over his broad shoulders. "How complicated is importing?" he asked suddenly.

She swallowed too much vermouth and smothered a cough. "Not complicated on the scale we do it. In fact importing, or even buying, is stretching it a bit. I probably should have said I was fishing for ideas rather than buying." Greer met his eyes squarely. Bending the truth had never been her strong suit. If Andrew Monthaven was less impressed when he found out exactly what her business was—too bad.

"'Curiouser and curiouser,' as Alice in Wonderland said." Again his brilliant grin worked its magic.

"Not really. I run a small store. We specialize in the unusual. Everything has a British flavor, although not everything is actually made here. Americans tend to deny it, but they have a tremendous interest in Britain." She hesitated, running a fingernail around the rim of her glass. "A lot of us have roots here. Most people are drawn to their original homelands. Have you noticed that?"

"I suppose so," he said noncommittally. "Who's minding the shop while you're away?"

"My sister. Casey works with me." Greer drank some more vermouth. She felt foolish. How could she expect him to relate to what she was talking about? Andrew Monthaven may have been born in the same country as Greer Beckett, but their worlds were as different as the moon and the earth.

"When you say that you deal in the unusual, what do you mean? Seems you'd run out of unusual British products fairly quickly."

"The shop's called Britmania," she said, as if that might somehow answer his question without her having to elaborate.

"Britmania? Catchy. Sounds like a disease."

Greer became immediately defensive. Regardless of what she

sold, Britmania was a success, and it was hers. She'd salvaged her life with it and helped Casey in the process.

"Greer? Are you all right? You're pale."

"I'm just fine, thanks. Fine. When I chose the name of the store it was intended to suggest a disease as you put it. An addiction to anything British," she said, pausing to breathe deeply. "We sell a lot of heraldic stuff. Coats of arms on transfers for windows or car doors. Plaques, ashtrays, glasses and so on."

One of Andrew's long fingers rubbed at the area between his raised brows. "Doormats, too, I suppose."

He was laughing at her. "Absolutely," she said a little too eagerly. "Doormats are big. Nothing like having people wipe their feet on one's family emblem. But we have something for everyone. This year kits have been very successful. Assemble your own Tower of London or Buckingham Palace. All to scale, of course. Complete with lifelike figures of beefeaters, or the royal family, depending upon the kit."

Andrew sank back into his chair and stared at her with what appeared to be fascinated disbelief.

Greer felt shaky but defiant. "We've also had luck with spittoons, cuspidors I think you call them here," she added, unable to stop herself.

"I know what a spittoon is," Andrew assured her.

"Ours are shaped like the royal coach and come complete with a bag of barroom sawdust to use inside."

"I hope it's genuine sawdust. Nothing that's been cleaned up," he teased.

"We guarantee that it's been used in a London pub," she said seriously.

Andrew began to laugh. He set his glass on the hearth and covered his face with both hands.

Greer waited, trying to keep a serious face, but she wanted to laugh, too. Not because she found her business amusing, but because it would be a relief.

A snort punctuated Andrew's attempt to control himself. Finally he straightened and laced his fingers behind his head. "You're marvelous. You turn up in my house like a specter and scare me half to death. Then you barrel out into the night while I can only wait for you to come back. Now you sit in an Englishman's study, telling him that you make a living by apparently poking fun at anything British. And I thought this was going to be another run-of-the-mill evening at Ringstead Hall, the disgustingly ostentatious little manor I call home.''

The flush that crept from beneath Greer's collar swept over her cheeks, dull and throbbing. She'd overdone it. He thought she was deliberately trying to insult him. "Sorry," she muttered.

"Why should you be? I've been highly entertained. Now I'd better get you home so you can rest that active brain of yours. Tomorrow's another day. Who knows what new and lucrative ideas you'll come up with once you get started?"

Greer felt she had been dismissed. He was a busy man and must have other things to do. Perhaps he had a date. As she put on the coat Andrew held for her, Greer struggled with an irrational sense of disappointment.

This time they left through a side door and walked behind the house to a ramshackle outbuilding. She waited silently while he backed a car from its unlighted shelter.

The decrepit appearance of the tiny vehicle appalled her. It was an Austin Mini and resembled a chipped, black bread box with strategically placed dents. Her own secondhand Chevy was elegant by comparison.

"You were expecting a Rolls?" Andrew said, startling Greer.

He had slipped from the car and come to open the passenger door without breaking her reverie. "What makes you think you can second-guess my thoughts?" she asked, amused.

He laughed. "It doesn't take much effort. They're written all over that gorgeous face of yours. Wait," he said as if he'd just been struck with a dazzling insight. "I've got it. You can sell me a couple of your car decals—something classy. They'll improve the image no end."

"Touché. I asked for that," Greer answered as she moved quietly past him and got into the car. He didn't see her smiling in the dark.

They took the coast road leading southwest to Weymouth. Andrew insisted it was more interesting, particularly since the moon had decided to appear and paint a wide swath of unpolished silver over an inky English Channel. As Greer looked at the glittering path it seemed encrusted with shifting sapphire flecks.

"Have you planned every minute of your stay?" Andrew asked, just when she thought the silence would split her head.

He's as uncomfortable as I am, she thought. "Tomorrow morning I'm going to a market in Dorchester. My landlady told me it's a good one."

"I'm not sure what it's like now," Andrew answered. "That market's been held every Wednesday for as long as I remember. I used to go with my father. He enjoyed the animals. But it'll be the stalls you want to see. Maybe you can buy a supply of miniature chamber pots from some local concern. Perfectly authentic, just a little undersized. People could use them as planters."

"Wonderful," Greer said, determined not to be baited. "I'll remember the idea. Silk flowers might look good in them."

"Then what?"

"After the market, you mean?"

Andrew changed gears to go up a steep hill. "Yes. It's all over by early afternoon." They crested the rise and the lights of Weymouth spread before them. The curve of the bay was outlined by a continuous, looped strand of brilliant lights along the promenade.

"I'm going to the village of Ferndale. There's a church I want to visit." Greer hadn't intended to mention Ferndale. She held her breath, expecting a question from Andrew, but surprisingly he made no comment.

It was time to close one segment of her life and try to open another. Ferndale was more than a burial place for her husband and child. Tomorrow she'd see their graves for the first, and maybe the last time. But she also hoped to begin her quest for the family she had never known.

One of the details she had gotten from Tom and Dianne Wyatt was that Ruby Timmons, Greer's biological mother, came from Ferndale. An address in the village was on her own birth certificate, although the Wyatts also mentioned that her mother moved away shortly after her birth. The certificate didn't give her father's name.

As the car swept down toward the town, Andrew remained silent until they neared St. John's Terrace. Then he only inquired in which boardinghouse she was staying.

Ocean Vista was a grandiose name for the narrow, terraced establishment where Greer had rented a bed-sitting room, with breakfast. When they pulled up outside she tried to concentrate on the comforting thought of the nightly hot water bottle Mrs. Findlay had promised.

She forced herself to wait for Andrew to get out and come to her side of the car. They hadn't mentioned what she knew was as much on his mind as hers. But maybe it wasn't necessary. She had botched their conversation, but surely he sensed that she no longer blamed him for her baby's death.

"Thank you very much for being so kind," she said. He had cupped her elbow as they walked to the steps. "And again, I am sorry for being a nuisance." Why did she wish that he would hold her, that he wasn't about to walk back out of her life?

He opened the unlocked front door and pushed it wide. "You aren't a nuisance. Except when you keep apologizing."

An impulse made Greer turn around before going inside. "I'll send those decals."

Andrew was striding around the car. "Thanks," he said, and without pause continued on. "I'll pick you up in the morning. Is nine too early? All the best bargains go first and we wouldn't want to miss any."

"What do you mean?"

"The market. We should be there early. Wear comfortable shoes."

Greer realized her mouth was open. "Andrew," she started to protest.

But the car door slammed. The engine sputtered, then turned over before the little black vehicle circled toward the coast road and Ringstead Hall.

CHAPTER FOUR

WHEN ANDREW got home, he didn't bother to put the Mini away. He strode through the side door and upstairs to his rooms.

Greer had come back. All the way from Weymouth he had silently repeated the phrase. At the top of the lane leading to his gates, he'd rolled down the window, cut the engine and coasted. Wind tore through hedgerows almost bare of foliage, to carry an earthy aroma of gorse into the car. Instead of distracting him, the scents, the sounds, the cold snap around his ears, had made Greer's lovely image more pervasive.

In his study, he threw the car keys on his desk and splashed a shot of whiskey into a glass. He flopped into the chair Greer had used and flexed the cramped muscles in his long legs. The only problem with the Mini was that it didn't fit him.

Andrew stood abruptly and swallowed the Scotch. With the fire out, a draft stole down the chimney, cooling the room. The casement rattled and he smiled. His favorite kind of night. Only holding Greer secure in his arms until dawn would make it more perfect. His fist clenched around the empty glass. He must take one slow step at a time, or he'd lose her before ever having her. Another shower sounded good. That's where he did some of his clearest thinking.

The bedroom was colder than the study. As Andrew stripped, his skin tightened. He liked the invigorating sensation, but someone who wasn't used to it might not. Installing central heating in a house like this would be costly and difficult: as soon as possible he would look into it, though.

Naked, he crossed the hall to the bathroom and jerked a yellowing shower curtain around the tub. Made of enameled metal, the bath stood on high legs and claw feet. Bluish traces of iron showed through where the coating had thinned.

He rotated the faucets and waited, shivering. It took a while for the water to heat. As a boy he had learned to gauge the right moment to enter this same tub by the amount of steam on the black-and-white tiled walls. Rivulets formed on the shiny surface and Andrew climbed behind the billowing shower curtain. Something about the way air slid beneath the door and along the floor always made the rubberized sheet flap against his body.

Greer was accustomed to the modernistic life-style he had experienced when he visited the States. She probably preferred it, and who could blame her? It wasn't out of the question that he'd choose to move there himself one day. He had good contacts and the career opportunities appealed to him. Perhaps, with Greer...he was fantasizing again. He had been thinking of updating his own part of Ringstead, anyway. This would just speed the process. Maybe she would enjoy helping him make decisions, choose styles and colors—she certainly had plenty of ingenuity. He laughed and allowed the water to beat on his face. Her eyes had glittered when she told him about her shop, challenging him, testing. As he knew very well, Greer was a strong, independent woman, but she cared what he thought of her.

He soaped his skin vigorously. Logical planning was essential. There was a lot of ground to cover, old wounds to heal. And he couldn't be certain of her feelings toward him, not yet. But she came back, dammit. And she had engineered a way to see him. Unanswered questions swarmed in his mind, but one fact remained certain: she wouldn't have sought him out simply to say hi, as she put it.

They had avoided mentioning her husband and child. Tomorrow she planned to visit Ferndale. Andrew's thoughts raced and he scrubbed harder. Any normal man or woman would do the same thing. In the morning he'd tell her he knew why she was going to the village and offer to take her. Make everything open between them. Suffering could push people apart, but it could also bring them together. Greer's loss had already done both. The next move should be his.

He had been the one to suggest taking her back to Weymouth. What would she have said if he'd asked her to stay with him tonight? Would she have agreed? The intense rush of desire that spread through his loins made him arch his back and grit his teeth.

Greer was beautiful. Fragile, like a titian-haired, porcelain doll—so totally feminine that she aroused an overwhelming combination of sensuality and protectiveness. No other woman had reached him in the same way. He wanted her. But it was too soon to make love to her, despite his countless dreams of doing so since he last saw her. In the seething dark of many nights he had mentally undressed and carried her to bed. He imagined her softness beneath him, around him, her blue eyes glazed with passion as he entered her. Each time the fantasy ended, he awoke bathed in sweat. And always as his eyes closed again, he felt her lying in the hollow of his shoulder, her hair spread across his chest. Then, while she slept, he kissed her eyelids, her pliant lips, and bent his head to her breast...

His legs were rubbery. Andrew turned off the water, then dropped his head forward and pressed his palms against the tile to support his weight. He didn't even know how long she intended to stay in Dorset. Their exchanges had been awkward, general, avoiding anything too personal. But it didn't matter. It took time to wear down barriers and he hadn't begun to work at them.

If there were another permanent man in her life she wouldn't be using the name Beckett or wearing the same wedding band he remembered. The only rival he had to contend with was dead, Andrew was sure of that. He was sorry that Colin Beckett had died a violent, senseless death, but there was no reason for Greer to remain a widow indefinitely. She was ready to love again, ready for him.

Andrew stepped onto the linoleum floor and reached for a towel. He hadn't lived the celibate existence his peers apparently suspected, but his liaisons had become infrequent, bringing only fleeting, physical satisfaction. All the time, the woman he hopelessly desired lingered, partially hidden in his subconscious. Two years ago there had been no choice but to let her go. Now there could be no question of losing her again.

Distant ringing jarred his concentration. The phone. Immediately he made a mental check of his hospitalized patients. Francine Stevens was still in the guarded phase with meningitis. Everyone else should be comfortable.

Hitching the towel around his waist, he went to grab the phone in his bedroom. "Monthaven," he said sharply. A steady buzzing told him the caller had hung up.

Andrew depressed the cradle and started to dial the medical-center number, then changed his mind and softly replaced the receiver. It could have been Greer. When he failed to answer, she would assume he'd gone somewhere other than home after he left her. He could get the boardinghouse number and call her. No, he couldn't. All those houses had one phone—in the hallway. He'd disturb everyone and embarrass Greer. Please, he thought, let her call back. He lay on the bed and stared at the ceiling.

When the phone rang again he almost knocked it off the bedside table in his hurry to answer. "Hello—Greer?"

There was a short silence before Bob Wilson asked, "Who's Greer?"

Andrew felt himself redden. "It's late, Bob. Problems?"

"You didn't answer my question, Andy. Who's Greer?"

"A friend. No one you know."

"I'm glad your friend is female. You may need her."

Andrew bit back a sharp retort before answering. "I thought we'd covered that topic. If Coover's looking for a way to shut me up, he's going to have to come up with something better than a question about my sexual preference." He paused, but Bob made no comment. "I'm beat, Bob. Is this important?"

When the other man finally spoke, Andrew had to strain to hear. "Neil called."

"You mean Neil Jones?" Andrew said, frowning.

"Yes, Neil Jones. He said you two had dinner in London a couple of weeks ago."

"So what?" Andrew was getting irritated. "I was eating alone at Simpsons. He asked if he could join me. What could I say? He called to tell you that?" he said, sitting up.

"The man's homosexual," Bob said flatly.

A sliver of cold worked its way up Andrew's spine. "I know what Neil is. It was never a secret, even in school."

Bob's voice dropped to an angry rasp. "Last night he had a visitor, you fool. Lewis Kingsly. He practices dermatology in Harley Street and uses Neil's supply house. His excuse for dropping by Neil's was thin—they only know each other professionally. But Kinglsy's one of Coover's buddies and he asked questions about you. He found out you shared rooms with Neil at Oxford.''

''A lot of people know where I lived in Oxford—and with whom. I've never attempted to hide it,'' Andrew answered.

He heard the familiar sound of Bob inhaling on a cigarette. ''Andy. I care what happens to you. We've been friends too long for me to allow you to destroy yourself over a point of—of—you know, I'm not even sure what is making you persist with this—vendetta. Honor, I suppose. Honor won't pay the bills, friend. Or stop you from dying inside if they take your license away. You've got too much to lose. Please, see Coover personally, tomorrow. Say whatever it takes to stop this thing. Tell him you were too hasty about the Michael Drake case and you'll call off the inquiry.''

''Like hell I will,'' Andrew exploded. ''I've got nothing to hide.'' The moisture on his skin had turned icy. ''Sure, I lived in a house with Neil, the same as you did,'' he said sharply. ''But that's all. He wasn't my type any more than he was yours. Still isn't. I just can't bring myself to ignore the guy when I see him. He's lonely. It can't be easy for him and it isn't up to you, or me or anyone to judge him.'' Andrew paused to gain control. ''And I'm not launching a vendetta. Simply trying to protect potential victims from Winston Coover.''

''Okay,'' Bob said stiffly as he tapped his fingernail against the mouthpiece. ''All true. All admirable sentiments. But. Neil told Kingsly what good friends the three of us still are. Stories are easily distorted. If someone wants to embellish the facts it won't be hard,'' he warned.

''Bob.'' Andrew gripped the telephone cord between his fingers. ''No one could make an accusation like that stick. It won't wash. Thanks for the concern, but stop worrying.''

Muffled laughter skittered across the line. The Wilsons had company. ''I've got to go,'' Bob said shortly. ''Contact Winston Coover and stay away from Neil. Believe me, he can do plenty of damage.''

Andrew continued to stare at the receiver in his hand long after Bob hung up.

CHAPTER FIVE

"HE SAID, 'You won't get anything like it, anywhere else, for less than twice the price.' Roughly," Andrew explained. "Or something pretty close to that. Sometimes I wonder if even a cockney understands what another cockney says."

Greer and Andrew stood in the middle of a throng surrounding open doors at the back of a truck. A thickset man, balanced on the tailgate of the vehicle, held high a red enameled saucepan. He turned it slowly, displaying the utensil as if it was an exquisitely delicate piece of crystal. His sudden loud guffaw at a comment from an onlooker brought an answering ripple of laughter. Then he lowered his head to rub his bulbous nose on a grubby woolen sleeve.

"I love the way he sounds," Greer shouted to make herself heard above the market's cacophony. "Do many people come down from London to sell here?"

Andrew nodded. "Loads. Every week. They make a circuit of markets like this all over the country."

"Now what's going on?" Greer asked. "Is it an auction?" She watched Andrew's profile. His chin was lifted, accenting the sharp angle of his jaw. She noticed the way his hair curled forward behind his ears, and the gold of forgotten summers tipped his thick eyelashes.

He glanced down at her and put a hand on the back of her neck as she was jostled against him. "It's not really an auction. It's a sort of ritual. The seller throws out an inflated price. Then the crowd collectively forces it down to just about what the item's worth. A dozen or so customers buy identical *bargains*, and everyone concerned thinks it's a personal coup. Perfect."

His hand on her neck had been an unconscious gesture. But when their eyes met Greer was sure they both felt drawn together in ways other than totally physical. Carefully, still gazing into her eyes, he rubbed his fingertips up and down, tangling them in her hair. Greer wanted to slip an arm around his waist, to lean against him. Instead she looked away and stood on tiptoe, pretending to be engrossed in the sale until he dropped his hand.

"We'd better move on," he said evenly. "The *collectors'* stalls are on the far side of the yard."

Greer followed in the path he made through straining bodies. A part of her wished she could break free of the reservations that kept her captive. That errant scrap of romantic longing that refused to be snuffed out wanted him to touch her again. Fortunately, he was bound to be more reticent in the future. Although her withdrawal had been subtle, she was sure he'd understood her unspoken message. *Don't come too near.* Her own reactions unsettled Greer. It was as if she'd known him well for a long time. There was a kind of familiarity with him, a closeness. He was gentle, yet masculine in a way that made her guarded femininity come alive. And most disturbing of all, she found him incredibly sexy. The various effects he had on her were threatening, too potent for comfort.

Gravel scrunched under their feet. Spicy scents mingled with the aroma of coffee and warm sugary buns coming from a food vendor's van. Over all hung the earthy smell of farm animals. Myriad rows of clothing dangled from poles wherever Greer looked. She smiled and shook her head each time a garment was held toward her.

"Come on, love. Takes a redhead to wear this color green," a squat man in a checked wool cap cajoled.

Andrew broke his determined stride and turned back to meet her grin. His answering smile did something strange to her insides. They examined the proffered sweater together.

"It would look good on you," Andrew said. Then to the salesman he added, "We'll take it."

"*I'll* take it," Greer corrected firmly, when he reached inside his tweed jacket for his wallet. She shouldn't buy anything she didn't need, but neither could she accept a gift from Andrew.

It was a mistake to be with him again. She should have followed her first instinct this morning and told the landlady that she didn't want to be disturbed—by anyone. But he wouldn't really come, she had assured herself, while she tried to ignore the flicker of hope that he might. The doorbell had rung at exactly nine o'clock and she'd barely stopped herself from grabbing her coat and running to meet him.

While Greer paid for the sweater, she heard Andrew's soft whistle. A tune she'd heard on the radio and liked. Now it grated on her nerves. She received her change and waited for her package to be wrapped. The process took too long. And all the time Andrew whistled. This was pointless. He didn't really want to be here, and she wouldn't be able to concentrate on the merchandise as long as he was.

"Andrew—" she began.

"I know," he said, cutting her off as he tucked the parcel under his arm. "You're sorry. And again, don't be. I'm a man you hardly know and you'd probably be too independent to accept a gift from me if we'd been friends for years. Am I right?" he said, flashing her his winning smile.

I wish you wouldn't smile at me like that. "Yes. Only I couldn't have said it so well. Anyway, I wanted to say something else," she hedged.

"Shoot." He ducked under an empty rack and started away.

Greer fell into step beside him. "It was nice of you to bring me here. I appreciate your kindness. But you must be bored sick and knowing you are embarrasses me." She pressed her lips together and stared ahead with fierce concentration.

They walked in silence for endless moments before Andrew stopped and pushed the parcel into her arms. She almost dropped it.

"Are you trying to tell me to get lost?" he asked bluntly.

Blood rushed to Greer's cheeks. Ugly blushes—the curse of having pale skin. "No," she said, hating the wobble in her voice. "I just know you're a busy man with a job to do. You can't be getting anything out of this, and I don't want you to feel you have to guide me around. You wouldn't spend a morning here by choice. You're being polite. Of course, I think that's very nice, but I also think it's time we both got on with what we should be doing."

A battery of expressions crossed Andrew's features, ending with a smile that made a mockery of Greer's speech.

"Have you finished?" he inquired softly. "Polite. What a laugh. I don't spend time anywhere I don't choose to be just as you didn't come to Ringstead Hall yesterday because you wanted to admire antiques. Greer, you were looking for me, whether you admit it or not. You and I have a past to confront. Before you left England you were hurting too badly to see straight, and I didn't have what it would have taken to help you. The feelings I had for you then were confused. I still don't entirely understand them. But I know I've never forgotten you. And once you started to recover from— once you recovered you remembered me, too..."

"Please..."

Andrew grasped her left wrist. "Admit it."

"You're very sure of yourself," Greer answered evasively. Her nerves felt raw.

People bustled around them but Andrew seemed oblivious. "Not as sure as I'd like to be," he said.

"We shouldn't be having this conversation—not like this. All I wanted was to face up to the things I can't change, then let them go. I needed to apologize to you—and to say thank-you for everything you did for Colleen."

"It wasn't enough." His mouth closed in a bitter line. "And I'm still sorry about that."

"I think we should both try to forget it all," Greer said shakily.

He slid his fingers to her wedding band. "Colin's ring, right? You didn't marry again?"

"No."

"If you're trying to make a fresh start, isn't it time you took this thing off?"

She shook her head. "I never thought about it." *I can't cope with this.*

"You aren't in love with someone else?"

"No!" *Too emphatic.* Her temples throbbed.

"Then why are you so standoffish? Is there something about me that you don't like? If so, tell me and I will get lost." Andrew's voice dropped a fraction.

Greer was disgusted to feel tears well in her eyes. She squinted at an overcast sky. "I'm..."

"*Don't*—say you're sorry."

She tapped the toe of her suede boot against the gravel. Obviously, he would not take no for an answer. The only thing to do was confront him. "I think you're attractive," she began. "Much too attractive. But I can't stay in England indefinitely and I have a lot to accomplish. I don't have time to—to waste." *Or to fall in love.* The air about her took on a crystalline quality. Was she allowing this man to awaken her sexually and emotionally? Had she unknowingly wanted him even when he was merely a memory, separated from her by five thousand miles and a mountain of bitterness? The idea was incredible—out of the question.

A hint of satisfaction in Andrew's eyes irritated her. He'd been pleased rather than angered by her response—gratified by the confusion her face must have betrayed. He retrieved the parcel from her unresisting grasp. "What's the hurry to get back to the States?" he said easily.

"I didn't say there was a hurry. But I do have a business to run. That's how I make a living and I can't afford to be away too long."

Englishmen of Andrew's class were never supposed to discuss money, particularly the lack of it. Greer watched defiantly for his reaction. His expression revealed nothing.

"I understand," he said, sweeping his free hand in a wide gesture. "But all this definitely counts as attending to business. Let's get a cup of coffee and one of those fattening buns. Then we'll track down chamber pots, or whatever other treasures we can find."

At first, Greer's reaction was total frustration. This man was impossible! Ruffling Andrew Monthaven for more than an instant would never be easy. It seemed the only thing to do was to give in gracefully. Summoning a smile, she decided to throw caution to the wind—temporarily, of course. "I'd love some coffee," she enthused. "But hold the bun or I'll lose my girlish figure."

Immediately she regretted the last comment. Her coat was draped around her shoulders. Andrew surveyed the thin, peach silk blouse and camel gabardine skirt she wore, and there was no mistaking his approval.

"Risk the bun," he teased her. "I don't see any reason why you shouldn't."

The glow of pleasure Greer experienced remained while she took the coffee Andrew bought her. She bit into a doughy round cake that sent a shower of powdered sugar down her front. They both laughed as she tried to balance the sticky confection in the same hand as her Styrofoam cup, while she brushed at her skirt.

Andrew's "Messy, messy" was met by Greer's disdainfully raised brows. "Allow me," he said as he dropped to one knee and flicked away the last grains of sugar with his napkin.

The sight of his dark bent head and the clean hair touching his shirt collar tilted her heart. "There," he said, standing and straightening his sleeves at the wrist. "Good as new."

Greer stared at his wrist, suddenly fascinated by the sinew running along the back of his hand. She had never been so totally aware of a man. Not true. There had been Colin. Her attraction to Andrew could be easily explained by the fact that she was so vulnerable right now. But what about Andrew? What was drawing him to her? She drained the last of her coffee, keeping her lashes lowered. He was attracted to her. He'd as good as said so and she could feel it.

"You're very quiet," he said. "Something wrong?"

Greer blinked rapidly and met Andrew's questioning eyes. He was more than attractive. All man, in an elegantly powerful way. Tall and broad, but not clumsy as some big men were. A mental image of him naked shocked her and she looked away. But she'd pictured him anyway—finely toned muscle, slender waist and hips, the strong legs and arms she'd already glimpsed. Thank goodness he couldn't read her mind. The sooner she put distance between them, the better. No point torturing herself with ideas she could do nothing about. Even if she wanted to get involved, a man like Andrew would never be interested in a woman who was no longer whole.

"Greer?"

She tossed her empty cup into a garbage can. "Just taking everything in. It's all so purposeful—and cheerful. People with missions they expect to accomplish. No doubts," she said emphatically. *Don't think aloud. He's astute and he'll make the right connections if you're not careful. He'll figure out how insecure you are.* Quickly Greer covered her thoughts. "It's amazing how the stall owners can say the same things over and over, then keep laughing with all that gusto," she pointed out.

Andrew paused before replying. "They're a unique breed. Doing the best they can with what has to be done. We could all take a lesson from them," he said seriously. He watched her closely for a second longer then threw his empty coffee cup away with both of their napkins stuffed inside.

When he took her hand and tucked it into the crook of his elbow, Greer stiffened. Then she made a deliberate effort to relax, to stroll nonchalantly beside him. The heat of his body made her acutely conscious of her skin that seemed to consist of a million exposed and vibrating nerves.

"Well—" Andrew exclaimed suddenly. He grinned and swerved away from her.

Before Greer could follow, a small girl shot from a crowd in front of a vegetable stand and launched herself into Andrew's outstretched arms. Greer heard the child's high-pitched, "Andy, Andy," then he scooped her up and swung her around.

Unable to help herself, Greer approached slowly, like a moth drawn to a flame. The man and child were the flame, she was the moth. Simply watching them could bruise her newfound wings, but she couldn't resist the urge to see clearly.

"Why aren't you in school, young lady?" Andrew was saying. "And where's your mother?"

The girl was about five or six, thin, with spindly, blond pigtails and bright blue eyes behind pink-rimmed glasses. "Got a cold," she sputtered, swiping at her nose with the back of a tiny hand. "Mummy's buying cabbage. Yuck. Can't you tell her it's bad for kids with colds to eat cabbage? Ple-a-se, Uncle Andy?"

Small and blond. Greer's build, Colin's coloring. Suddenly so cold that goose bumps chased up the backs of her arms, Greer stood a few feet from them. Her legs seemed like concrete. Colleen might have looked...not now, she mustn't do this now. It was time she ought to be able to get within touching distance of a child without coming unglued. *Stay calm.*

Andrew felt his heart expand to see the trust in Simonne Wilson's bright eyes. He hugged her to his neck. "Little girls should eat what their mothers tell them to eat." When Simonne began to object, he said, "No—don't try soft-soaping me." Her small body was angular, her clutching fingers bony. A waft of licorice met his nostrils and he pulled gently on a pigtail to look at her face. A telltale black rim outlined her bowed mouth. "I see kids with colds can still eat their favorite candy." And she laughed. As always, he was struck by the girl's fragility. Bob and Lauren's child should have been a great, muscular specimen, not this delicate will-o'-the-wisp.

Greer. He held Simonne closer and stood still, smiling at Greer. Her clear blue gaze froze his blood. What was she thinking? A couple passed between them, momentarily obscuring her from him. Then he saw her face again, unchanged, a waxen mold. Simonne twisted to sit more comfortably. He studied her face briefly, kissed the end of her pink nose, then took a step toward the beautiful red-haired woman who suddenly seemed totally removed from him.

"Come and meet my friend Simonne Wilson," he called to Greer.

Why was she making no attempt to move or respond? *Colin and Colleen.* She was looking at a man who bore no resemblance to her dead husband with a child years older than her own ever became, yet he knew she was reminded of them both. Tears pricked at his eyes. She wasn't over any of it. The certainty shook him. So he hadn't imagined her confusion when he'd touched her. For two years she'd kept her emotions on hold. Somehow Greer had managed to avoid coming close to anything—anyone who might peel off the thin veneer she'd drawn over the gaping wound of her loss. He could help her if she'd let him. She needed him as much as he wanted her. She should have another baby—and soon. Her catharsis was long overdue. A baby could be that for her; together with a man who would love her. Simonne wriggled and he set her down, shrugging tense muscles in his shoulders.

Greer felt them coming. She looked into the distance and took a deep breath. Of course he loved children, was wonderful with them. That's why he'd become a pediatrician. Her eyes met Andrew's, then the child's. Something was irresistible about the sight of a strong man's tenderness toward little ones. He should have his own children—something she could no longer give any man. Andrew would marry and have a family. It shouldn't freshen her sense of emptiness to recognize that or make her feel—what—jealous? No, no.

"Simonne, this is my American friend, Greer Beckett. She likes markets—and cabbage," Andrew said, giving Greer a knowing look.

He hadn't noticed her hesitation. "Hi, Simonne. It's nice to meet you," Greer said easily. Her face felt stiff, but no one else could know that.

"Hello," Simonne said. Her pointed chin showed above a gray woolen scarf wound several times around her neck. "My friend Stacey's mother went to America. To Phila—Phila—well anyway, she went there."

"Philadelphia." Greer laughed despite herself. "That's in the state of Pennsylvania. Just as hard to say, and more difficult to spell. I come from the other side of the country."

Simonne grunted thoughtfully. Her glasses gave her a wise-elf appearance and made her nose resemble a slightly squished cherry. Greer held her smile in place. Without thinking she brushed away a strand of hair caught in the girl's mouth, then took an involuntary step backward. Soft little face, innocent eyes. This was exactly why she always avoided getting too near children—easier on the heart.

"Hi, Andy. What brings you here?" A pretty blond woman, carrying a shopping bag, joined them. "Don't tell me you've taken up buying your veggies with the rest of us ordinary mortals," she teased.

Andrew snorted. "Hello, Lauren. How are you? Meet Greer Beckett. Does this child have a fever?" he said all in one breath. His hand lay along Simonne's cheek and neck.

"It was up a point this morning. That's why I kept her out of school," Lauren explained impatiently. "Could you stop being a doctor long enough to make proper introductions, please?'' Lauren gave Greer an exasperated nod.

"Why is she dressed like an Eskimo? You'll drive her temperature up," Andrew said, unwinding the scarf from Simonne's neck. The child sighed in relief, sending her wispy bangs off her forehead.

"Thank you, Andrew," Lauren said. "What would I do without you and Bob to tell me how to be a good mum?" The woman was an older, rounder version of her daughter, with the same piercing blue eyes. And her pleasant face was showing signs of irritation.

Andrew reached to pull Greer to his side. "Lauren Wilson. This is Greer Beckett—"

"From America," Simonne interrupted.

"Right." He pretended displeasure by scowling at the girl. "Greer, Lauren Wilson is a friend of mine. Her husband, Bob, and I grew up together. They're also my closest neighbors—three miles east."

Lauren Wilson's appraisal was frankly curious but cheerful. "Pleased to meet you. This is dreadful," she said turning to Andrew, "but I've got to run. I didn't expect to take so long and Bob will fillet me if I get another parking fine. It costs a fortune if you run over the time limit now, and they won't even let you argue. I think the town keeps running on money extracted from harassed drivers. How about dinner tomorrow night?" she said, taking Simonne's hand. "Bring Greer so I can get to know her," she added.

"Will do," Andrew called after Lauren's retreating figure. Simonne, trotting to keep up with her mother, swung back once to wave.

Left alone, Greer and Andrew avoided direct eye contact.

"Do you usually accept dinner invitations on another person's behalf?" Greer asked finally. "I can't go anyway."

"What did you think of them?"

Greer pivoted to face Andrew, only to find him comfortably slouched against the side of an animal pen scratching the ears of a liquid-eyed calf.

"Don't try to buffalo me with avoidance tactics," she said sharply.

He swatted at flies on the animal's head. "This will grow into a cow, not a buffalo. Actually, it'll only grow as far as it takes to become veal, poor little devil."

She wasn't amused, or distracted. "Give my regrets to Lauren. It was nice of her to include a stranger in her invitation, but I've got a couple of busy days ahead. Thanks for the lift."

Before she'd taken two steps, Andrew blocked her path. Greer moved to go around him and the wretched hip locked. She faltered, and immediately his hand was under her forearm, supporting her. His touch provoked a series of reactions. To be held, desired by a man she might be able to care for—the idea sent her into turmoil— but perhaps this attention sprang from pity or the professional concern that must come so naturally to him. Flights of fancy were a dangerous luxury she should avoid.

"I'm fine, Andrew," she said, but his grip only tightened.

A deep line formed between his fine brows. "I'm not sure you are. But that's something we can discuss later," he said, forcing Greer to look into his eyes. "I wasn't being overbearing when I accepted Lauren's invitation for both of us. She was in a hurry and it was a reflex action. Will you come with me, please? They're nice people—the best. I think you'd have a good time."

He was irresistible when his honey eyes darkened like that. She eased her arm free of his fingers.

"Come on, Greer," Andrew said, unwilling to give up. "Get me off the hook. Lauren will make sure I never hear the last of it if you don't show."

"I shouldn't," she said, sighing. "But—okay. Write down their address and I'll meet you there."

"Don't be ridiculous," he scoffed. "How? On horseback? They live miles from anywhere just as I do. I'll pick you up."

Greer opened her mouth to argue, then shut it with a snap. Petty squabbles weren't her style. And he was right. "Thank you," she said perfunctorily. "What time?"

"I'll find out and let you know." There was a gruffness in his tone. "Greer, we have to talk—you know that?"

I can't. "We will—before I go home."

Andrew studied Greer's averted face. Waiting for her to approach him again would be futile. He straightened the parcel beneath his arm, placed a hand at her waist and propelled her toward the exit. "I think it should be now," he said. "We shouldn't hedge about Colin or the baby any longer."

She didn't answer. It wasn't going to be easy, but he'd wear her down. Little invisible thorns protruded from her, trying to put him off every time he approached. But he wasn't about to be deterred. Not when he wanted something, or someone, the way he wanted Greer Beckett.

Twice she stared at him over her shoulder, a wary glimmer in her wonderful deep blue eyes. Her lashes had to be the thickest and darkest he'd ever seen. All last night, while he tried to sleep, he remembered different things about her. The way those lashes formed shadows on her cheeks when she looked down, the way the loose russet curls swished about her shoulders as she tossed them back. And her mouth, full and soft. How would it feel...

Just what he needed while he was trying to cope with impending disaster in his professional life. The return of the one woman with the ability to knock him flat.

A few large drops of rain started to fall. "Wait." He guided Greer beneath a green-and-white-striped awning. "Put your coat on properly or you'll get soaked," he told her. He held the coat while she slid her arms into the sleeves. The temptation to pull her against him made him feel almost disoriented. "Let's make a run for it."

With one arm around her shoulders, he held her close at his side, and they hurried down the steps and out of the market yard. The rain wasn't heavy, but it gave him an excuse to get near her. At the curb the lights changed and they had to wait before they could cross to South Walks Road. He knew every inch of the little town. Dorchester was only eight miles north of Ringstead Hall, about the same as its distance from Weymouth to the southwest. The medical center was also in Dorchester. Damn—the medical center—he was due there before noon. If, as he suspected, she wanted to get away, that would make it easy for her. Unless he could persuade her to wait for him.

Andrew checked his watch. Eleven-thirty. He glanced down at Greer. She felt insubstantial under his arm and he slid it lower across her back. To appear uncertain could be fatal. Understanding but firm should be a good approach. "How hungry are you?" he inquired.

Her face came up—even paler than usual. "Not very," she said, dropping her head.

A gust of wind whipped her hair across his chest. Several strands flew against his face and he closed his eyes. He couldn't let her slip away from him again. "Do you feel like talking?" he asked tentatively.

"If you want to." Her voice was muffled.

"I want to," he said firmly. "We'll have lunch. But first I have to stop in at—at the medical center. You could scout out the town for an hour. The museum's interesting—" The stiffening of her body alerted him. "You don't like museums?" he said.

Something pinched his back. It was her fingers closing on his skin. "Take me with you," she said. She kept walking although his own pace had slowed. "Then we'll have lunch."

He felt slightly sick. "You'd be bored in the visitors' room. Nothing to do but read old magazines."

"Andrew." Abruptly she pulled up and looked directly into his eyes. "The main reason for coming to England was to confront the things I've avoided. If you'll let me, I'll come to the center with you."

The artificially cheerful voice that said, "Nothing I'd like better," didn't sound like his own.

CHAPTER SIX

GREER LEANED her head against the Mini's cool window. Where had it all begun? Was it back in Seattle, when she and Colin had planned to come here? She supposed that could be the real start of her journey to this point. But it wasn't. Her adoption by Tom and Dianne Wyatt was. Now she must discover her true beginnings in this place. A nerve twitched at the corner of her right eye. Work through the stages, then get on with life.

Small shops slid by. On the left they passed a Tudor building, now a restaurant. *Judge Jeffrey's* was the name painted on a swinging sign above the leaded windows. Across the street black metal railings guarded the gray statue of an unsmiling man. Next she saw a museum. Must be the one Andrew had mentioned. Soon they'd be at the medical center. She didn't feel apprehensive. Odd. As soon as she'd made the decision to go, it had seemed inevitable. Later, after lunch, she'd leave Andrew and go to Ferndale.

"Are you sure you want to do this?" he asked quietly. His fingers were outstretched as he shifted gears with the palm.

"Of course. Apart from anything else, it makes more sense than wandering around in the cold," she said. For the rest of whatever time they spent together, she would prove she wasn't an emotional wreck.

Andrew smiled faintly, his eyes on the road. "That's what I like. Practicality. Unfortunately, you may not find the waiting room much warmer than it is out here. But I won't be long," he assured her.

He swung right onto a narrow street lined with terraced houses and Greer sat straighter. She remembered this. Identical bay windows, one above the other, sporting lace curtains. Only drainpipes, painted in different colors to match the trim, separated and distinguished one building from the next. The taxi had brought her past these homes on her way back to Seattle. Greer looked ahead. Titian ribbons wound along the pavement where many wheels had passed over fallen leaves.

After a left turn, then a right, she saw the medical center. Greer's stomach contracted sharply. The same building, the tall gates she'd seen before, and the wide crescent-shaped steps to the front entrance. Why did she feel as if this was the first time she'd been here?

"Here we are," Andrew said, pulling the decrepit Mini in between a Jaguar and a silver Mercedes sports. "Hang on while I get my stuff."

He got out and tipped his seat forward to reach a black leather medical bag. It was scuffed at the corners, scratched around the latches. The man didn't care about things—only people. So special. Greer watched him gather a pile of folders and tuck them under his arm before slamming his door. She glanced at her hands, deliberately relaxing the fists she'd unconsciously made.

A blast of chilly air blew her hair forward when Andrew opened her door. Immediately she tossed her head and swung her feet out. *Hurry, now. This is easy—just one tiny step forward. There's nothing to be afraid of.*

"Okay?" Andrew held the back of her arm while he slammed the door with an elbow.

Greer smiled up at him. "Mmm. This place hasn't changed much. Looks as thoroughly uninviting as I remember. Not travel-brochure material." She sounded bright. The thought gave her confidence.

"I suppose I've never really looked at it," he said, wrinkling his straight nose. "But you're right. It is a bit grim. I'd better get in so we can have that lunch. I'm starving."

Food didn't interest Greer. She concentrated on the sound of their footsteps crunching gravel. The rain had stopped and there was a smell of damp earth. Andrew walked slightly behind her to the steps, his height and bulk a solid reassurance. They started up and she glanced back. Even a step above him, the top of her head was only level with his chin.

He stopped abruptly and Greer sought his eyes, but he wasn't looking at her. "What is it?" she asked. "Did you forget something?"

Andrew didn't answer. The corners of his mouth turned down, then his features became still, graven. She followed his gaze and saw only two men, deep in conversation outside the doors. After a few seconds he moved slowly on, propelling her up with him, although Greer felt he had forgotten her presence.

At the entrance Andrew paused. The men stood to one side and both saw him at the same time.

"Monthaven." The older man acknowledged shortly. His thin white hair was combed from a low part across his pink, domed scalp.

"Coover." Andrew nodded dismissively before turning to a handsome, blond man about his own age. "Hello, Bob," he said casually. "Just ran into Lauren and Simonne at the market. We're invited for dinner tomorrow."

Pale blue eyes slid to meet Greer's before making a swift inventory of the rest of her. "Great. And who's this?"

Greer heard Andrew introduce her and made the appropriate polite noises. This was Bob Wilson, Lauren's husband—the man Andrew had referred to as his friend since childhood. There was a reserve in his response to her, a speculative glimmer in his expression. A sensation of being judged bothered her. She took the hand he offered and felt power in his brief handshake.

"You're an American, Miss—ah—or is it Mrs. Beckett?" the man Andrew had addressed as Coover broke in.

She touched her ring automatically, then shook his pudgy hand. "Mrs. Yes. I'm visiting from Seattle."

"Well," Andrew said with a tightness she doubted anyone missed. "We must get on. Duty calls, y'know."

Coover set his own shiny medical bag down with a thump. "Nonsense, Andrew. It isn't often an old man gets to meet a beautiful American redhead. The least you can do is share her a moment longer." He turned his shoulder, giving her his full attention. "How long have you been here, my dear?"

Fine hairs on the back of Greer's neck prickled. "A few days," she said briefly, hoping to discourage conversation. There was an undercurrent in the atmosphere she wanted no part of.

"You and Dr. Monthaven just met?"

She hesitated for an instant, feeling Andrew's eyes on her. "No, Dr. Coover. Andrew and I are old friends. We met on my first visit to England."

"I see. Is your husband with you?"

Greer flinched and noticed Bob's face at the same time. He frowned from behind Coover, not at Greer but at Andrew. "My husband's dead," she said flatly, the muscles along her spine so tense they hurt. Glancing quickly at Bob, she could see he was intent on sending some silent message to Andrew. He must think she was too engrossed to notice.

"I'm sorry," Coover said. "Has it been long?"

"Two years," Greer replied.

The fabric of his check worsted suit had a fine sheen. Expensive. Everything about Coover, from the striped silk tie he fingered over his large belly, to the satiny finish on his brown, tasseled shoes, testified to accustomed affluence. His dark eyes had the sharp intensity of a much younger man. Greer waited silently. His flaccid jowls wobbled at the edge of her vision, but she deliberately held his gaze with her own eyes and forced a smile. Bob was still transmitting his wordless message to Andrew and she was sure, without knowing why, that it was important—to Andrew.

Coover gave her a serious nod before his head jerked up. The sympathetic expression on his face altered to something unreadable. Greer couldn't stop a shiver.

"Did you intend to see me, Monthaven?"

Pressure at her elbow surprised her. Andrew pushing her on. Bob lifted his head, mouthing a silent, yes.

"No, thanks, Coover. I've got rounds to make," Andrew answered brusquely.

Bob shook his head slowly. Greer wanted to see Andrew's face but willed herself not to turn around. She trained her eyes on a brass bell set in the wall.

"Have you given any more thought to what we talked about?" Coover closed the top button of his jacket. His nails shone, the tips very white. Soft hands, Greer thought, professionally manicured. There was no reason to dislike him, but she did. The long gaps in what seemed like a coded exchange were wearing her composure thin.

"I left a message on your service," Coover prodded. "Somehow I expected to hear from you before now."

"Andy's been backed up, Winston." The sudden intrusion of Bob's deep voice startled Greer.

"Yes," Winston Coover murmured. "I'm sure he has. But you didn't answer my question, Monthaven. Have you thought about our—ah—little discussion?"

"Certainly," Andrew said evenly. "Constantly. I rarely think of anything else. I'm sure everything will shape up nicely."

She had to look at him. The sarcastic note in his voice was unmistakable and completely new to Greer. The darkly intense fire in his eyes was also new. There was no doubt what she felt emanating from Andrew was hatred and it shocked her.

Coover's restless shifting suggested he felt it, too. "Meaning?" The word was steady but barely audible.

"Exactly what I say. I don't see any benefit from further discussion now. There'll be an appropriate time and place for that." Andrew was barely civil.

"I see." Coover's purplish lips flattened. "The hearing. I'd hoped you'd come around to my point of view—"

"Never," Andrew interrupted, a dull flush spreading over his cheeks.

"You..." The older man's eyes narrowed on Greer and she saw him struggle for self-control. "Andrew. My main concern is for the department—and you, of course. You know how highly I regard you professionally. If I hadn't thought you were talented I wouldn't have hired you."

"That's good of you—sir. The department's reputation must always be of paramount importance, I agree, to say nothing of that of the head of the department."

"Quite. And with that in mind, I think we should find a way around this hearing. For your sake."

Andrew's breath escaped in a hiss. "I'm grateful for your concern. I think it's unfounded—on my behalf. You, on the other hand..."

"Andy," Bob said loudly. "I'm driving Winston to the Antelope for lunch. Why don't you join us?"

"Afraid not. Thanks anyway. I already have a luncheon date—after rounds. Now, if you'll excuse us...?"

Bob's swift move blocked the door. "With Mrs. Beckett—Greer?"

Andrew grunted. He hooked the pile of folders higher beneath his left arm and placed the other hand at Greer's waist.

"Have you been to the Antelope yet, Greer?" Bob stood his ground, turning the full force of a charming smile on her. "It's not to be missed. One of the oldest pubs in the area. Terrific bar food."

Before she could reply, Andrew let her go and reached around Bob to push wide the door. "Greer will get to the Antelope," he said. "But we have other plans today. We wouldn't want to bore her to death with shoptalk anyway, would we? See you later, Bob. Simonne's got the start of something—let me know if you want me to check her over." His failure to look at Winston Coover again was an obvious insult.

The pressure of Andrew's hand at her back, and the purposeful speed with which he entered the building, forced Greer to trot. The door swung shut with a click.

"There's an office for visiting physicians. You can wait there," Andrew said stiffly.

Everyone had another side. Greer hadn't expected Andrew to be any different. But this thinly disguised fury—the overpowering sensation that he was infused with contempt? He was rigid, a stranger.

There was no time to take in the foyer before he whisked her past a glassed-in reception room where a switchboard operator pushed and pulled the leads on an ancient contraption. The first room off a dismal green corridor proved to be the office Andrew intended her to use.

"Andrew," Greer began, facing him deliberately. "If you need to be with your colleagues for lunch, I understand. I don't want to be a nuisance."

He rotated his shoulders almost imperceptibly. "That sounds suspiciously like another apology.'' His smile was lopsided, an obvious attempt at lightening the mood. ''I assure you, lunch with you is what I need—today of all days.''

She wanted to ask him what was wrong, why he was angry. *None of your business, Greer. Probably all your imagination, anyway.* ''I'll be here. Don't hurry.''

He turned and was gone, leaving her with a clear picture of his preoccupied expression. If she hadn't been with him, would there have been an open argument? Greer crossed her arms, hugging herself tightly. Last night she'd felt defensive because he seemed so secure and untroubled. She'd been wrong. Andrew Monthaven had his own problems. But they didn't concern her. The only reason for her being in this hospital was to chase away a few of the shadows she'd harbored too long.

At one side of the room the central bar of a gas fire glowed orange. It gave off little heat, just occasionally hissed and sputtered. A writing desk stood against the wall beneath a high window that rattled incessantly. Greer wandered to sit in a leather armchair that spilled yellow stuffing from its torn cover. She should feel something stronger, some sense of treading on old and unpleasant ground. But all she could respond to was the memory of three men facing each other on the hospital steps and Andrew's subsequent animosity. She wished she could take away the rage, shield him from whatever threatened him. Once he had comforted her, given his support when there was no one else, and now she felt he was as alone as she had been then. Her eyelids sank wearily, then snapped open. She cared for him—whether she wanted to or not.

A grandfather clock ticked loudly in the corner. On its face was a sun, a moon and a cloud that slipped to and fro. Colin had bought a clock like that on one of his buying trips. When he'd seen her admiring it, he'd wanted to give it to her. Greer smiled wistfully. Perhaps, after the next few weeks, she'd be able to think of all those sweet moments without wanting to cry.

The old magazines Andrew had promised were arranged on a circular rosewood table. She knelt to examine them, smelling a hint of lavender polish from the wood. All the publications were medical or surgical. Greer turned enough pages to decide she would rather not look at the photographs and that she didn't understand much of what was written, then retreated to the chair once more.

Sitting alone with nothing but the old room's percussive noises for distraction made her edgy. She went to the door and peered down the corridor. There must be a coffee machine somewhere. A hot drink would warm her up. If Andrew returned before she did, he'd wait.

Closed oak doors lined the hallway. Greer walked quickly past them and turned the corner to find an identical passage stretching ahead. Shiny paint, chipped and peeling in places, reflected overhead strip lighting. This part of the building seemed unfamiliar—the whole building seemed unfamiliar.

Greer reached an elevator just as the doors squeaked open. Two nurses in purple-and-white-striped uniforms got out. Starched white aprons, cinched tight at the waist and pinned to their bodices, swished with each step.

The same uniform. Greer stared and remembered a voice, *"Mrs. Beckett. Mrs. Beckett. Can you hear me? Don't move your head— you've had a bit of a bang. It's all right."* The woman's tone had been soft, her face blurry. When Greer's brain unfogged, the first thing she had seen clearly was the round gold pin fastened to an apron. Then the pain in her hip had struck down her thigh and the circle of gold faded again.

"You look lost. Where did you want to go?"

Greer's head snapped up. She swallowed, meeting one nurse's kind questioning eyes. For a moment she felt bemused, past and present merging.

"Are you a visitor?" the other nurse asked. They looked at each other, then back at Greer.

She smiled vaguely. "I was hoping to find a coffee machine somewhere. Can you point me in the right direction?"

"One floor up," they spoke in unison and laughed, holding the doors until Greer stepped inside. She heard their cheerful voices recede as she pressed the button for the second floor and stared at the illuminated panel above.

A vibrating bump came a few seconds later. Exiting the elevator, she found herself in a square anteroom flanked on one side by three vending machines, on the other by a row of orange plastic chairs.

Her hand closed around the wallet in her pocket at the same time as a watery sensation invaded her legs. Greer glanced around and took an instinctive step toward the closed elevator. Sweat broke out on her temples and upper lip. Had she been in this room before? *Easy. All the rooms in this place look the same.* Impatiently, she went to study the instructions on the coffee machine and searched for the appropriate coins. She made her selection and watched a cup plop down, wiggle, then settle under the weight of pouring liquid.

The waxed cup rested against her lower lip, steam rising to mist her vision, when the elevator opened again to reveal a young woman in a wheelchair, accompanied by an orderly. Greer gulped coffee, burning her tongue and throat. She coughed, then covered her mouth, but not her tearing eyes.

"They said I could hold him today," the patient said breathlessly. "I can hardly wait. It's only been two days but it feels like forever."

If the orderly replied, Greer didn't hear him. He pushed his charge through double doors that swung gently against each other before closing tightly.

For the first time she noticed a sign on the wall next to the doors. Premature Infant Unit. No Admittance Without Permission.

CHAPTER SEVEN

HOT COFFEE splashed her fingers. Greer shook her head and bent to set the cup on a chair, never taking her eyes from the sign. Why hadn't she seen it immediately?

The room had seemed familiar because she, too, had passed through it by wheelchair—several times. Invisible bonds with those other visits, propelled her on. Slowly she pressed a palm on each door and walked into the dimly lighted area beyond.

Windows, high in one wall, filtered in little of the gray midday outside. Several more orange plastic chairs stood against the opposite wall. Institutionally laundered supplies, antiseptic solution and warm dust from old exposed radiators formed a suffocating cocktail of scents. Greer remembered it all now. A wall of glass faced her, the moving shapes on the other side indistinct from a distance. *Go back. What will it prove? You managed to forget all this. You wiped it out.*

She had suppressed everything. Abruptly Greer sat on the closest chair and clamped her hands together between her knees. All those times when Casey asked her to talk about what had happened in England, and she insisted she couldn't—there had been no deliberate attempt to avoid the truth. A shell had formed around the events that took place in the weeks here, walling them off where she couldn't find them. When she'd made up her mind to come back, the locked part of her mind must have been asking to be opened. Would the openness set her free or simply destroy the fragile peace she'd made with life?

Greer heard voices and shrank back in the chair. If someone saw her and asked what she was doing here, she'd have to leave. She didn't want to stay, but she couldn't go, not yet.

There was a loud clatter followed by the squeak of rubber wheels, then silence. When she'd visited Colleen for the last time, in the early morning of the day she died, Greer had felt Colin's presence all around them. In the nursery the baby had been taken from the incubator and nestled in her arms. So tiny. A rapid pulse had beat through almost transparent skin, and beneath tightly closed lids, Greer saw the side to side movement of sleeping eyes. Legs no bigger around than a man's thumb had wiggled free of their pale blanket to reveal the brilliant plaid diaper each premature infant wore. The jerky, splayed fingers had been tapered and slender, like Colin's.

She stood and turned resolutely toward the glass. The cesarean section had been performed shortly after her admission. It took two days of begging for Colin before she learned he had been killed. From that moment every ounce of her will had turned to Colleen. At least they would have each other. Greer would tell their daughter about the father who had wanted his baby so desperately and, in watching the child, she herself would never completely lose the man who'd been everything to her.

Then Colleen died. That seemed like the last day in this hospital now because the weeks that followed were still a faded series of dawns and dusks with endless hours between.

She lifted her chin and walked on. It had been hell to return to Seattle alone, to face a house where she half expected to see Colin everywhere she looked. For months Casey and Josh Field had cast worried glances at each other whenever they thought she wouldn't notice. Moving into a condominium was supposed to help. It simply increased her pain, made her more aware of the chasm widening from her married existence. Then there'd been the hassle over business; made easier by Josh but still exhausting and unwelcome. But she'd made it through. And she would keep on making it, dammit. She was a survivor.

Seven babies. Greer counted the swathed bundles inside their clear plastic cocoons. She huddled into the corner. From there she could see clearly without being easily noticed by anyone who was engrossed in a task, as all the staff appeared to be. The woman in the wheelchair was talking to a nurse who stood beside an open incubator, swabbing a baby's eyes. Greer looked away to concentrate on two infants immediately in front of her.

With their temperature controlled, they wore only diapers and cotton stocking caps. When Greer had asked about the cap on Colleen, the nurse explained that most heat was lost through the cranium. The hats were hand-embroidered, by the hospital auxiliary, the woman had said. Trains for boys, rosebuds for girls. A band of yellow roses for Colleen's...

Greer shut her eyes and took several measured breaths. She gritted her teeth and looked again. These babies would live. They *must* live. Science and the skilled people who applied it could pull these miniscule humans through. Miracles happened here every day. The same kind of miracle that had almost saved Colleen.

For a moment she thought something moved inside her belly. Both hands moved of their own volition, settling on her stomach. Empty. There would be no more babies. The part of her where Colleen had grown was gone.

While she sat staring, someone came to work on the closest infant. Gloved hands unsnapped the plastic porthole covers to enter the incubator access sleeves. Greer couldn't move. Fingers covered the baby's quivering chest and abdomen, confidently palpating, testing. Blood pumped in her ears, and she gripped a narrow sill beneath the window.

Sterile.

She would always be sterile. Why did it hurt so much to say, even in her head, when she'd known as much for months? Why did it matter anymore?

The hands were rapidly withdrawn from the incubator, and Greer looked up to meet concerned eyes above a green mask. Andrew.

He bent his elbows, holding his hands with palms turned in, as she'd seen him do before in the same room. His gown was too small and pulled across the shoulders. Surgical green also covered his hair, an almost perfect disguise except for the troubled golden eyes she'd know anywhere.

She smiled, but the effort tipped free tears she hadn't known were there. Her throat closed. Andrew nodded toward the nursery door, made a move in that direction, then stopped, staring at her face. Greer shook her head, said "It's okay," although he couldn't hear her. It was okay, or it would be in a little while. With a wave and a broader smile, she backed away, turned and walked blindly out of the unit.

THE WEATHER had brightened. Grubby clouds still scudded over a wind-brushed sky but patches of blue showed, and here and there a rim of gold hinted at struggling sunshine.

Restlessness in the queue alerted Greer to the approaching double-decker bus. Its number and final-destination marker matched the one she'd been given for Ferndale, and she shuffled slowly forward until she could climb aboard and up the wooden-slatted stairs. She'd never ridden on the second floor of a bus before and as it swayed away from the curb her stomach rose, making her wonder if she should have chosen the lower deck. She gripped the chrome bar atop the seat in front and watched the scene they passed from a new and quickly engrossing perspective.

After two more stops and only a few minutes, Dorchester receded, to be replaced by open countryside to the southeast. Greer's mutionous insides adjusted to the swinging motion of the bus and she settled back, scrubbing at the grimy window with a tissue to get a clearer view. Again she had the feeling of being separated from what she was about to do, and intuitively she identified the reaction as self-protective. Fine. Whatever it took to allow her the strength to get this all over with was just fine. This was a good day. It was. Without it she would still be where she'd unconsciously chosen to stay for so long—in emotional hiding. Later she must call Andrew.

Rolling hills stretched away as far as she could see. Meadows, separated by woolly hedgerows, undulated like vast patchwork quilts in shades of green and straw blond. The next time the bus stopped, Greer pressed closer to the window. *Bockhampton*. The tops of several heads moved out below. This was where Thomas Hardy had grown up. Mrs. Findlay had missed few details in her chronicles of local attractions.

Jarring vibration rattled Greer's teeth as the big vehicle accelerated. On some of the closer hills Greer spotted clusters of sheep with black faces, their thick winter coats turning them into softly bloated barrels on spindly legs. She sighed. Her roots were here, and her mother's. The thought was bittersweet, unsettling. How was it possible to want to know more about oneself and not want to—at the same time?

A draft corkscrewed up the spiral stairs. She shivered and made a mental note to dress more warmly from now on. Pants and the fur-lined suede jacket she'd brought with her would be just the thing.

She was deep in thought when she felt the bus turn in a more easterly direction. It crested a shallow rise and headed down toward a village bunched around a square-towered church. Ferndale—and St. Peter's. Greer became light-headed before she realized she'd stopped breathing. Her chest ached. Once more she leaned forward to tighten her fingers around the metal bar.

The first few cottages were widely spaced, their thatched roofs covered in protective wire mesh atop white stone walls. Sweet peas and snapdragons hung on in bravely colorful clumps along short garden paths, while fuchsia bushes still showed speckles of red blossoms.

Closer to the village center, shops lined the narrow streets. Turning a corner, the bus leaned, seeming almost to touch the buildings. Outside a greengrocer's, customers picked fruits and vegetables from bright mounds, placing them in the brass scoop of an antique scale to be weighed. Greer captured each vivid cameo and held it, blocking out the other thoughts that tried to steal in.

"All change!"

The bus stopped a second after the conductor's voice boomed the order. She saw him lope to the sidewalk and disappear in the direction of a nearby shop. Greer waited until the rest of the passengers on the upper deck moved and fell in behind them.

St. Peter's church stood at the far side of a small common square—the village green, Greer supposed. She walked steadily along a sidewalk that skirted velvety grass, edged with knobby old oaks bearing only the occasional flapping leaf. Swooping blackbirds landed in front of her to squabble over a discarded peanut shell, then scattered when she neared them.

A green metal fence surrounded the churchyard. Without pausing, Greer pushed open the gate and went inside. Graves stretched across the grounds on either side of the path. She halted. Where should she start? In her wallet was a card noting the location she wanted, but the numbers meant nothing. The rectory adjoined the church. The vicar could tell her where to find them, but Greer didn't feel like talking to anyone.

Bands of crushed rock wound between headstones and inset markers. Greer began her search, methodically plodding away from the main path, then back, glancing quickly from side to side, stopping only when a name was too faint to read easily. Colin's grave would have a flat marker. He'd preferred the simple and she had ordered a plain stone that should show only his name and Colleen's, together with their birth and death dates.

She almost missed it. Tucked between two large monuments, a small white angel at the base of the grave made her look away, then back again as the end of the name caught her eye.

Carefully, her feet sinking into spongy turf, she made her way to the marble angel, then knelt on the stone rim surrounding the plot. She should have brought flowers. The stone had been engraved exactly as she requested, her own name linked with each of theirs. She hadn't ordered the angel. Perhaps it was a local custom to place one on a child's grave. When she touched it, expecting cold, Greer felt only the softness of the finish. Why or how it came to be there didn't matter, she liked it.

Greer sat on her heels and held the lining inside each coat pocket. She hadn't ordered gravel chips, either, or the two azaleas planted in tubs on top. Someone tended the grave carefully. Perhaps they knew these people of hers were alone here and gave them special attention.

The tears started, as she'd known they would, clogging her throat and blurring her vision. She covered her eyes and bent until her forehead rested on her knees. *I miss you. I miss you. I miss you.*

When she lifted her drenched face she flinched against the sun that had just broken free of cloud. Colin had been an intense man, kind but practical. What had he said after Dianne and Tom Wyatt died within a few months of each other, leaving Greer totally crushed? Grieve, that's what he'd told her, and that she had a right to. If she didn't, getting over the loss would take much longer. But what stuck in her mind were his later words, when he'd said it was time to live again, "Don't forget them, but let go. It's okay to let go now."

If he could speak to her at this moment, he'd say the same thing. And he'd be right. She would never forget him or their baby, but it was time to get on. They would always be where they belonged, in her heart. Her life could never again hold the joy she'd once known, but it could be full and peaceful. Sometimes the pain would flare. But each time it would be less.

For minutes she listened to the birds, watched the shifting sky. This was her turning point. The past must be relegated to its place and she must search out her present. Any living members of her biological family were part of that present, and it was time to look for them.

Greer headed purposefully for the church. Stained-glass windows reflected the sun, their facets turned to glittering gems. Set in a pointed Norman frame, the great oak doors were studded with tarnished brass. The ring handle turned easily and she entered the building, her nose wrinkling at the strong odor of old books and used incense.

Old books were exactly what she hoped to find. Baptismal records. Her own certificate had been issued by a vicar of this church. Ferndale had been her mother's home once. There could be an entry for her, too.

Her heels echoed on irregular flagstones. Three blocks of wooden benches, separated by wide aisles, stretched to a distant brass altar rail. Greer wandered forward beneath lofty stone arches, their pillars crowned with carved shields and cherubic bodies. Dust motes tumbled in shafts of colored light that pierced the windows to slash her path.

"Afternoon, miss. Can I help you?"

Greer jumped. "What?" She swung around in the direction of the voice to see an elderly man kneeling in one of the pews.

"Sorry if I frightened you," he said. He stood, no taller than she, and smoothed wrinkles from his long black cassock.

"No—er—vicar." With any luck that was the right salutation. "I didn't expect to see anyone, that's all."

"I'm Mr. Russel," he said. "The verger, not the rector. Did you want to see him? I think he's in."

A verger was a sort of caretaker, she knew that much. And this man looked old enough to have been here for a long time. "I don't think so, Mr. Russel. I was hoping to look through the church's baptismal records. Could you show me where to find them?"

Piercing gray eyes studied her face carefully. "That depends. Recent entries are open in the vestibule." He nodded a bald head toward the entry. "Past ten years in the sacristy."

"And before that?" Greer prayed silently that the rest weren't sent far away, or even disposed of.

Mr. Russel scratched his chin. "Locked in cupboards—up in the gallery. Just how far back did you want to go?"

Greer craned her neck, locating the gallery behind its low banner-hung walls. "About fifty or so years. Maybe a bit less." By her calculations, that should be her mother's approximate age now.

For a second Greer thought he would refuse. She saw him deciding what to say next.

"They'll take some finding," he announced at last. "Would you mind telling me why you want them?"

The man was kind. Greer knew so instinctively and decided to be honest and trust he would respond. "I'm trying to trace my family. My mother. I know I was baptized in this church and that she lived in Ferndale. I was hoping to find an address—anything that might give me a lead."

"Ah," he said, then added, "I see," although his puzzled expression suggested otherwise.

"Did you know a Ruby Timmons?" Greer pulled out her wallet and began searching for the sheet of paper where she'd noted what few facts she had on Ruby.

He shook his head slowly, looking at the sheet she offered but making no attempt to take it. "Can't say I remember the name, miss. But I've only been here since I retired. That was twelve years ago. Wouldn't some other member of the family know—I mean—? You're not English, are you?"

She'd thoroughly confused the poor man. "I was adopted when I was a baby—by an American couple who took me to the States.

They only knew my mother came from this village. Look, if it's too much trouble, I understand. I probably wouldn't find anything, anyway."

A stubby hand on her arm stopped her from backing away. "Nonsense. No such thing, young lady." His ruddy features turned a shade darker. "You follow me and we'll open up those cupboards. I'll have to leave you to it, but you can ferret around as long as you like, and good luck to you. Good luck to you."

The change in Mr. Russel's manner was startling. He hustled Greer ahead of him and up worn steps to the gallery. In an alcove cluttered with piles of threadbare tapestry kneelers, tattered hymnals, even a battered piano, stood two tall cupboards. Only two. While the verger unlocked their doors, Greer cast relieved eyes at the ceiling. *Thank goodness.* She'd half expected dozens of them.

"There you are, Miss—?"

Greer smiled gratefully. "Greer Beckett. And thank you very much."

"Just leave the key in one of the locks, then." His gentle old face was benevolent. "I'll pick it up after evensong."

GREER'S FINGERNAILS were grimy, her coat smeared with dust. She sat on a miniature chair in the children's corner of the church. The note pad she held listed several names, dates and an address.

Ruby Timmons was born to Mollie and William Timmons of Marsh Cottage, Kelloway Lane, and would now be forty-eight. It was too late to start this afternoon, but Greer would try to locate the cottage tomorrow. Finding Ruby's record had taken more than an hour. The books were dated on each spine, but the older volumes weren't in order and their identifying gold numbers had faded.

Beneath her mother's name on the pad, Greer had written another, with the same address. Kurt William Timmons. *Kurt.* She tried to create an image to fit the name.

Curiosity had prompted Greer to search for the entry of her own baptism. Ferndale was a small village, its population probably not more than a few hundred. The register showing her own oddly impersonal statistics, one page before the last, also contained those for children born in a number of previous years. Flipping backward, another entry for Timmons had leaped at her. Six years before Ruby had Greer, she'd given birth to a boy—Kurt.

Greer stuffed the small book into her pocket and hugged her knees. She wanted to cry again. Just as she'd warned Casey, once they started, tears were hard to stop. The attempt didn't work. After a hiccup, her eyes misted. In one day she'd covered a gamut of emotion enough to exhaust an entire army of people. But these tears weren't from sadness, or confusion—they were happy, happy tears.

Her mother hadn't been married. The absence of a father's name for Kurt or herself made Greer certain of that and it didn't seem important. But she had a brother, or at the very least a half-brother.

Muscles in her arms and legs trembled. Somewhere, if nothing had happened to them, she had not only a mother, but a thirty-two-year-old brother.

CHAPTER EIGHT

ANDREW PARKED NEAR the bus stop in Ferndale and got out without taking time to lock the car. He hurried around to the sidewalk and scanned the waiting passengers. No sign of Greer.

Getting free at the hospital had taken twice as long as he hoped and he'd already gone through this process of scrutinizing bus patrons, in Dorchester. A quick call to her boardinghouse confirmed she hadn't returned there. She couldn't reach Weymouth by any other route, so he'd waited for the next inbound load from the village before setting out to head Greer off at this end. There was only her chance comment of the night before to go on, but it seemed likely she'd come to Ferndale as intended.

Surely, she couldn't still be at the graveside. He chewed his bottom lip and hooked back his jacket to thrust both hands in his pants pockets. Glancing up and down the deserted street, he crossed rapidly and stood for a moment before entering the churchyard. There was no need to leave the main path to see she wasn't there. He'd only been back once since Colleen's funeral, to bring the azaleas and make sure the angel and chips he'd ordered were in place, but he knew the exact location of the grave by heart.

Where the hell was she? If he never actually saw her again, there was no way he'd ever forget the poignant suffering on her face outside the nursery. Damn. How had she found her way there, and why hadn't someone stopped her? No good looking for a way to shift the blame—he should have made sure she was properly settled before he left her alone in that miserable office. If he hadn't been so preoccupied with Coover and his own problems...

He started back toward the street. Better check the shops and cafés. Then, if he had no luck, he'd drive to Weymouth and wait outside her rooms until she turned up.

His hand was on the gate when another possibility struck him.

Was she the type of woman who might go into the church to pray? He didn't know for sure, but if Greer *had* been here, she must be emotionally battered and longing for a calm space by now.

Long strides took him quickly to the church doors. One stood slightly ajar and he pushed it inward tentatively, feeling himself slip backward in time. Familiar dank cold crept out at him, and the musty odor that had always sickened him as a boy. "Please, let me get out of here before I keel over," was the only prayer he could remember clearly from those days. He used to repeat it over and over to ward off the dreaded faintness. Morning prayer with his father was a Sunday ritual until Andrew left to become a boarder at Harrow. The church they'd attended, very like this one, had been near Dorchester.

He smoothed the worn door edge, feeling wistful. Ten years since John Monthaven died. The old man had been something, an unchanging rock amid a constantly shifting tide of progress: "Holding the line, Andrew—that's what a fellow has to be sure of. And doing what's right. No hope of holding on to anything without doing what's right."

Andrew smiled and went inside. The place was Norman, graceful in a cavernous sort of way. Candles burned a red-and-white glow on the distant altar. There was little other light now that the afternoon had begun to wane, and only every other wall sconce had been turned on. Peaceful. Unexpectedly reassuring—but empty.

Somewhere, the sound of wood scraping on stone set his teeth on edge. Sounded like a chair leg dragging. He searched around, peering into shadows that spilled from corners and recesses, until a muffled sniff sent him in the direction of a small area separated from the rest of the church by waist-high bookcases.

Andrew approached slowly until he could see over the cases. He ground his teeth. Greer sat with her back to him on a child's chair. Her forehead rested against her knees and her diminutive size struck him afresh. Not much bigger than some children. She must have heard the clipping of his heels, yet she made no attempt to move. Her shoulders rose and fell slightly, regularly, almost as if she dozed. Mentally exhausted, and who wouldn't be?

He rested one elbow on the other forearm, pulling at the front of his hair. All she needed now was for him to startle her out of her wits. Best to wait in the yard until she came out. Then he could insist on taking her home. He hadn't completely turned around when the sound of movement made him look back. Their eyes met. She showed no surprise. Good Lord. Was she in shock?

"Hello," he said lamely, half-raising a hand, then letting it fall to his side. "Don't let me disturb you."

Her laugh was explosive in the echoing loftiness of the building.

There was something wrong with her. Hysteria about to let loose? Extreme tension brought its own entourage of unpleasant mental and physical ills. "Greer," he said ever so gently. He'd try to ease her out of it. "You probably don't feel like talking after what you've been through today. Just relax and let me take you home. A good night's sleep is what you need."

"You sound like a doctor." She laughed again and covered her mouth. "Silly thing to say. You are one."

Could she be feverish? Her face was flushed, the great eyes unnaturally bright. He smiled with an effort and held out a hand. "Funny lady. Come on, I'll get you to Weymouth."

Her palm slid into his and she stood, close enough now for him to see she'd been crying. He checked the urge to hug her. "Come on," he repeated.

"Uh-uh. I don't want to go home, Andrew. There's no one there."

Tender surges overtook him. "What a lousy day this has been for you," he said. Half expecting a protest, he caught her neck in the crook of an elbow, pressing her face to his chest.

A fragile moment. This fleeting capsule of closeness was all he must expect, Andrew knew. Greer leaned against him, her hands at his waist, while he made little circles over her back. The downward tilt of his head would bring his lips against her hair, instead he stared ahead. One small suggestion of what he really felt could send her skittering for cover and he'd be back to square one.

"You're so kind." When she spoke, her breath warmed his skin through the fine cotton shirt. "I've never done anything for you. But you don't know how to stop feeling responsible for people, do you?"

Oh, he was a pillar of chivalry. If only she knew. "I like you, Greer. I'd feel good if I thought you liked me, too."

"I do, Andrew. Very much." She straightened and pushed back her hair. "Did you ever get lunch?"

The hair spilled through her fingers—alive. "What—oh, lunch? No. How about you?"

"I wasn't hungry. But let me take you somewhere. The least I can do is feed you. I've complicated your whole day and caused you to starve, and it'll be dinnertime in a couple of hours. I think I saw a café up the street."

This wasn't what he'd expected. She hadn't mentioned Colin or the baby and although she'd obviously been crying, he'd swear she was elated rather than crushed. This could always be an initial, unconscious avoidance to delayed reaction.

"Are you still with me?" she said, with eyebrows raised.

"Mmm." He needed to stall, to think. "I'd prefer to wait for dinner now. But how would you like to go for a drive along the coast? The sea's stunning right before it gets dark. Particularly on changeable days like this," he said inanely. She was bound to refuse him.

"Sounds great. But are you sure you don't want to eat first? You aren't expected somewhere else—?"

"No! No. Not at all. Let's go," he said before she could change her mind.

They walked side by side to the car. He only touched her briefly when she got in. Lifting her raincoat clear of the door, he waited until she gathered it around her and their hands brushed. Cool skin. None of this was rational. Single thirty-five-year-old men with enough lovers to their histories to have forgotten one or two were supposed to be blasé about women. Andrew rounded to the driver's side. This must be second adolescence. A glance, an unconscious touch that meant nothing to her, and his body turned to fire. He was in love with a woman he'd never even kissed, and she thought of him only as "responsible." Responsible was about as far from the way he felt as he was ever going to get.

Greer watched the sun's last valiant rays spear an early dusk. Hills to the south of Ferndale were gentler than the ones she'd passed through earlier. She could see the road winding away like a tossed roll of celluloid film. What would Andrew say if she told him what she'd discovered in St. Peter's records? Would he understand her excitement, and the tinge of apprehension mixed with it? He might. He was sensitive and she wanted to share her news with him so badly. Andrew was the only one she wanted to share it with.

She crossed her arms. Of course he was the only one—she didn't know another soul in England. He also knew she was alone here. That's what had brought him after her this afternoon, but she mustn't take advantage of him, or read anyuthing deeper than inbred caring for others into his actions.

"You're edgy, Greer. Want to talk about it?" Andrew said carefully.

Yes. "I'm fine. This is lovely. If I relax much more I'll melt."

"Really?" He looked at her quickly. "If you say so, I suppose. But you might want to uncross your arms before you completely cut off circulation to those white knuckles."

He was right. She laughed and dropped her hands to her lap. "You don't miss much, doctor. I guess that comes from working with a lot of patients too young to answer all the questions you'd like to ask."

"Probably," he said vaguely.

It didn't hurt. For the first time since Colleen died, it didn't hurt to think about children or to talk about them. Greer breathed deeply and the air tasted sweet. Andrew had fallen silent. She'd surprised him as much as herself. From the way she reacted at the medical center he wouldn't expect her to want to discuss his work. But he didn't know what happened since then. She wasn't all the way home, but she'd started back, and she no longer doubted she'd get there in time.

"Hold your hat," Andrew said as he turned off the paved road, onto a rutted lane between tall hedges and bare trees bent inland by winds off the sea.

Greer laughed, grabbing the dash with one hand, Andrew with the other. Limestone rocks bumped beneath the car's wheels, jiggling her from side to side. After an abrupt right turn they ground to a halt on a wide verge atop beetling cliffs.

"Wow," Greer exclaimed, tightening her grip on him. "It's fantastic. If someone painted this it wouldn't look real."

The light had reached a point between dusk and night, where the land and the ocean beyond took on an opalescent glow. No trace of sun remained, but lemon and rose cloud banks cast moving shadows in every direction.

"I think you're impressed."

Andrew's teasing tone caught Greer's attention instantly and she blushed. Goggling and oohing like a schoolgirl. Good grief!

He sat with one wrist hanging languidly over the steering wheel, the other elbow hooked over the back of his seat. He faced her, grinning, and might have bent the closest leg for comfort—if she weren't grasping it.

"Oh dear," she said, when she, too, noticed and sheepishly withdrew the hand.

Andrew tipped back his head, showing flawless white teeth in a delighted laugh. "Oh dear? I'm proud of your cool. Not even coy. If I didn't suspect otherwise, I'd think you were a dyed-in-the-wool 'leg woman' doing what comes naturally."

She couldn't think of a snappy comeback. She couldn't think of anything, but his eyes—serious now—and the memory of her hand on his leg. Widows and divorcées were supposed to crave a man more than a woman who had never married. Could that be what was happening to her? Greer turned to throw open the car door and climb out. This really had been some day. Overwhelming enough without her inventing more complications. Another man was the one thing she had never longed for after losing Colin.

Bending her head, she picked her way to the cliff's edge. Scalloped coves curled on either side, spume-capped waves gushing over rock outcrops to reach sheltered beaches.

Andrew came behind her. "I embarrassed you. Forgive me?" he said.

"Forget it." Changing the subject quickly, she said, "Just look at all this."

"I know every inch of this coast without looking, but it never bores me. Here—put this on or you'll freeze."

Before she could protest he was pushing her arms into the sleeves of a tan sheepskin coat, obviously his own. It easily accommodated her thin raincoat, covered her hands and almost reached her ankles.

"What about you?" she shouted, the wind tearing at her words. "You've only got a jacket on."

Methodically, he buttoned the sheepskin, then held her shoulders. "I'm a warm-blooded animal." He turned her firmly toward the open sea. "Take a good look and then let's go back to my place for something hot. It's only a couple of miles from here."

Too easy, she thought. Too enticing. A fire, a warm room and this incredibly appealing man. Heavy layers of clothing separated his hands from her skin, yet it felt naked and electric beneath his touch. She needed a friend now, someone to confide in, and she wished it could be him. Common sense told her the stirrings she felt were the beginning of something that would make simple friendship impossible.

She moved away. "Would you mind if I went down to the beach to get a closer look? You could wait in the car and I wouldn't be long. I can see the path from here."

"It's rough ground. And slippery," he warned her.

"So what? I can walk perfectly well," she snapped.

"Of course you can. I didn't mean—I'd like to go, too."

He didn't mean anything at all. It was just her built-in touchiness. Greer pressed her lips together, smiling directly at him with her eyes. Andrew seemed about to say something. Instead, he went ahead, taking strides that never faltered. The first time Greer slid on the shingle track, he only glanced back, hesitated, then went on. With the next downward cascade of pebbles from beneath her feet, he reached to catch her hand and steady her until she was beside him.

On the beach, Andrew gripped her shoulders while they scrambled closer to the water. The tide was gaining momentum. All about them lay trails of glistening seaweed and with each pounding wave spray leaped high, misting their faces and hair. Greer tasted salt on her mouth and laughed up at him. His ruffled hair was flattened to one side of his head, a jacket lapel caught carelessly inside out.

"Pretty wild, huh?" he shouted, rubbing her arm. "This coast doesn't have its reputation for nothing."

"What do you mean?"

He bent, bringing his ear closer to her mouth.

"What do you mean?" Greer repeated loudly. "Reputation?"

"Shipwrecks. Hundreds of men have lost their lives along the Dorset coastline. Every headland and ledge you see has claimed its victims—with the help of some of the worst races and tides you'll find anywhere. Then there used to be wreckers to contend with as well as the storms."

Greer shook her head uncomprehendingly. "I don't think I ever heard of wreckers."

"Locals—villagers usually. They set out beacons to make sailors think they were headed for safe harbor. When the poor devils broke up on the rocks, there was always a reception committee waiting to collect their spoils from the ships' holds." At the horrified expression on Greer's face, Andrew hurried on to explain. "It wouldn't be fair not to mention how many people actually risked their lives to save others from drowning. And still do. But there was a lot of the other."

Watching slate-green walls of water rise, shiver glassily, then crash, Greer had no difficulty imagining the doomed seamen's fate. She drew closer to Andrew, unconsciously slipping an arm behind his back. He must be cold.

"Sounds terrifying," she said. "You're getting chilled, Andrew. I shouldn't have made you come down here like this."

"You didn't make me. I volunteered."

Andrew watched Greer covertly. She was wonderful with her hair tossed wildly about her face, her eyes alternately shadowed and bright as she reacted to the surroundings and his stories. And she was more relaxed. It didn't make any sense, but he could feel it.

Keeping himself in check was becoming more impossible by the second. Far from being chilled, he was almost unbearably hot. Blood pumped through his veins in time with the surf and the rapidly wheeling gulls overhead. His awareness of her was freshly sharpened by every scent and sound. Unless he forced a diversion he would kiss her. He might even get away with that much, but he was only human. She excited him from fifty yards, beneath his lips and hands she was likely to blow away any thought of control...

At the light feel of her hand on his sleeve, his stomach muscles contracted as if he'd been kicked.

"Do you feel all right, Andrew?" she said above the noise.

"Of course." He glanced at her quickly. "Why do you ask?"

"I don't know," she hedged. "I guess I thought you seemed tense. You must have gotten my imagination into high gear with your sea tales."

"I'm told I have a wicked way with words." Every time he looked at her she was harder to resist.

His fingers wound between hers and she returned their pressure. She must be totally absorbed. Cold little hands. If he weren't so damn selfish he'd take her home immediately.

Andrew tipped up his jacket collar and watched her. His sheepskin flapped around her ankles, obscured her perfect figure as effectively as a stuffed gunnysack, yet she remained the most desirable thing he'd ever seen. She was driving him mad and didn't even know it—did she?

He wrapped both arms around her. "For warmth," he mouthed into her immediately upturned face. The waves beat relentlessly, their roiling crowns rising in phosphorescent billows. Carefully he leaned to rub his cheek against her hair.

She didn't move.

Her chin was cool satin when he took it between finger and thumb. "Greer, look at me," he urged.

"I feel mixed up," she replied. Her lips remained slightly parted, the expression in her blue eyes veiled. "Don't you ever get mixed up?"

Every nerve in his body was a rubber band stretched to breaking point. "Mixed up?" he nearly shouted. "Just looking at you destroys me. But I know what I intend to do right now. I'm going to kiss you unless you try to stop me."

Greer couldn't stop him—didn't want to. When he framed her

face, threading his fingers through her hair, something inside her turned white-hot. He was lowering his head, closer, slowly closer, until she felt his breath, warm and sweet on her lips.

"Kiss me, Andrew."

His mouth was firm, exquisitely gentle at first, a butterfly's caress. She felt herself sinking into him, melting. His tongue at the corner of her mouth startled her—but only for an instant. Her eyes had flown open to find that his were tightly shut, each handsome feature drawn rigid.

He was cold. Through the haze of desire, she felt his cool fingers at the back of her neck, massaging the little dips beneath her ears. Forcing a hand between them, she struggled with his jacket buttons. Andrew appeared too absorbed in an intense study of her lips to notice. With his tongue he followed their outline, then slid between them to her smooth teeth.

Breath came to her in aching gasps. To touch him, hold him— be held. The jacket was undone at last, and her own, until she could wrap him inside, warming him with her body, and the power of what he had ignited.

Standing on tiptoe, she locked her wrists behind his neck, drowning in the feel of him, his fresh scent so like the wind that tangled her hair with his.

"Greer, Greer," he whispered. A hundred nipping kisses covered her face and throat, missing no millimeter of skin until he reached the exposed V at her neck. Immediately he returned to her mouth, opening it wide with his own, delving far inside. Her hands smoothed the hard muscle through his shirt, caressed the hint of roughness along his jaw. And as she pressed more urgently against him, filling her fingers with his hair, Andrew surrounded her waist, sending burning impulses into every part of her.

His thumbs moved in circles over the soft sides of her breasts and Greer shied. Somewhere in her mind a small warning flare burst, but it was very small, then gone.

Their kisses were feverish now, sweet, desperate punishment that forced their tongues together as if there was no getting enough of each other. A storm of desire swept into the depths of her soul. So long since...

Andrew raised his face to stare at her. "You are beautiful," he said. "Do you know how beautiful you are and what you do to me?"

The pressure of his thigh between her legs obscured her mind for endless seconds. Beside her ear he whispered, but she didn't hear what he said.

She was wrapped in his arms, molded to him, when the flare burst again—brighter this time and strangely intrusive. And the magnificent male body that embraced her sent its own inevitable message. Greer stiffened, trying not to pull away. *Fool. What did you expect?* Another thrust of his pelvis proved what she already knew. He was fully aroused.

"Andrew." She held his face until he opened his eyes. "Listen to me, please."

The amber eyes were glazed, and he shook his head like a man drunk on heady wine.

"No more talk, lovely lady. I'm taking you home. To my home."

"We have to slow down, Andrew," she reasoned. "Be sure what we both want."

One more hard kiss, full on her mouth, and he started for the cliff, pulling her with him.

"I know what you want, Greer. I can feel it. And you know what I want. To make love to you—over and over again."

CHAPTER NINE

"ANDREW. Wait," she said stumbling behind him. "I know how I seem—seemed. This is my fault."

"Right, on point one." Undeterred he forged on, not looking at her. "Wrong on point two," he shouted. "We both know how you seem—present tense—and you aren't pretending, even if it does shock you to admit you're responding to me. But when it comes to fault, no one's to blame. I'm not ashamed of being attracted to you or wanting you. Are you embarrassed because you feel the same way?"

He looked back and Greer met his eyes, then lowered her gaze to his mouth—so sensitive, perfectly formed; so firm and erotic wherever it had touched her. No, she wasn't ashamed of the way she felt. Surprised, but not ashamed. They were both adult and free, weren't they?

He pulled her to his side and held the sheepskin close to her neck. "You didn't answer me, Greer. Is it upsetting you to be attracted to me?"

"No, of course not," she said quickly. She ached to feel his lips again. "But, Andrew, this is pure emotional release. I'm not sure of all the elements that led up to it for you, but I don't think they're so different from mine." At least she sounded logical.

"Fascinating. Are you going to let me in on this analysis of yours?" he gibed.

The sudden, fleeting brush of his lips at one corner of hers made her sway against him. "You're laughing at me, but I'm right," she insisted. "We've both had a day charged with tension—problems and confrontations. It's none of my business and I'm not prying, but you have things on your mind, too." Greer brushed her hair out of her mouth before going on. "Then there was Ferndale. You couldn't know all I faced there, but you absorbed my feelings just as if they were your own. I know you did because it was written on your face. You don't have the first idea of how to ignore someone in need. I'm amazed you've lived this long and stayed sane with the load of other people's trouble you must have carted over the years,'' she said, realizing she was unfortunately finished. As long as she kept talking, she'd be safe.

"You're wonderful,'' he said congenially. "Finished summing me up?'' He kissed a spot in front of her ear this time before lifting his head again.

Greer shuddered. It was too easy to respond to this man. "Don't try to distract me. I haven't finished,'' she warned him. "We came here to the coast. It's wild, intoxicating. Every bit of me gets whipped up by the wind and the ocean. The kisses were natural, I guess. An outlet. Let's leave it at that.''

"I went too fast,'' Andrew asked, bending to study her face. "Is that what you're trying to say?''

"No. Oh, Andrew, I don't know what I'm trying to say.'' She grasped his lapels and buried her face against his chest. Feeling his heartbeat, steady beneath her cheek, made her more acutely aware of his strength and humanness. "I'm not cut out for casual encounters, Andrew,'' she mumbled. "I wouldn't even know where to begin or how to react and it would only be hard on both of us.''

As soon as he stiffened she knew she'd said the wrong thing. In that instant, Greer realized what should have been obvious. Andrew Monthaven wasn't a casual man—about anything. This wasn't a spur of the moment attraction for him; mild interest fanned to a need for sexual release that could be satisfied by any woman. It was only she he wanted—had wanted, for how long? The question paralyzed her reason and she clung more closely.

Gradually Andrew's muscles relaxed and he stroked her back and shoulders. "I don't have the stamina for a parade of one-night stands,'' he said. "And I don't think you really believe that's what I want from you.'' Tilting her head, he looked deep in her eyes. "Listen, Greer, we were together in some tough times. They're over, but there's no way for either of us to forget them completely. I don't want something frivolous with you. I want a relationship,

Greer. You may not be ready, but I can wait—about two minutes.''
His laugh was strained.

You want to make love to me. You said so. I want it too, but...
"I don't know what to say," Greer whispered. "It's all in my head
somewhere, but nothing makes sense when I try to tell you."

Andrew held her away. "Take your time. We've got all night.
Although I am slowly freezing and you may have to borrow a
blowtorch to thaw me out soon."

Even in the almost darkness she saw desire flicker in his eyes.
This could be the one man capable of reaching the part of her she'd
thought—had chosen to believe—was dead.

Once more she slipped into his arms, grateful he seemed to know
her greatest need for the moment was to be held. "Maybe it would
be better for me to go home now, Andrew," she said softly, playing
her fingers along his jaw and down to lay against the pulse in his
neck. "Give us both some breathing space."

"I don't want breathing space," he said simply.

"We can't stay here any longer."

"It's better than letting you go."

Was it even possible for her to satisfy another man? She clenched
her teeth, rolling her forehead to the hollow of his shoulder and
feeling his arms tighten around her. *Another man.* Colin had been
the only one in her life. Perhaps, along with her ability to have
children, she'd also lost that wonderful spark that made a woman
half-magic with a man who aroused her. If that was true, and she
couldn't satisfy Andrew, would it be fair to pile yet another of her
problems on him? He might think it his fault. Virile, mature, everything any woman dreamed of—he was all of these. She'd have
to tell him about the hysterectomy. It seemed unlikely that his ma-
turity and professional experience would allow him to be anything
but understanding. But the risk was too great, and she didn't have
to take it.

"What are you thinking?" he asked finally.

"That I've made a mess of this evening and I'm not sure how
to get out of it." Honesty was supposed to be the best policy.

Andrew found her hand and headed for the path. "If this is what a messy evening is like with you, I can hardly wait for one of your better efforts.''

Don't you make this any easier, will you? "Maybe I should say I'm *not* attracted to you," she suggested lamely.

They reached the cliff top. "You aren't the type to lie."

"How about the fact that we only just met?"

"Nothing doing. We're old friends, remember? You said so yourself this morning—to two of my colleagues."

"I guess I did," she admitted. "But it seemed the right thing to say just then." A gust, carrying sand, whipped around them. Greer rubbed her eyes.

Andrew pulled her close, tipping her head forward to shield her from the wind. "It was the right thing to say. Also pretty close to the truth. More than two years is a long time. Any other excuses for escape?" he joked.

The moon had risen, throwing a silver-white crust around crevices, over piles of stones and tussocks of blowing crabgrass. Greer shook her head and made gratefully for the car, hoping not to have to answer any more of Andrew's probing questions.

He had other ideas. When they were both settled, he leaned back to watch her with no evident intention of starting the engine. "You still haven't convinced me that you would rather go to that grisly boardinghouse than come with me to Ringstead Hall. Just come and have a drink, and talk to me," he said casually. "I get lonely in that rattling old house. Then I'll let you go—Scout's honor." His raised right hand obscured half his face, but that didn't lessen the impact of his persuasive smile.

Her long sigh filled the little vehicle. "You make me feel guilty," she said wearily.

"That's the whole idea."

"Dirty pool, Andrew. I'm responsible for a business five thousand miles away, and there's a sister there who relies on me." Greer realized she was beginning to sound desperate.

"So?"

"Let's not start something we can't enjoy for even a little while," she explained. "You said you weren't interested in a one-night stand—neither am I. But that's about all we could have at that distance. You can't argue with the obvious, no matter how badly you'd like to." How much she wished she could let go and take whatever she could from the next few hours.

Her mouth was quickly covered, then he kissed a line along her jaw and down her neck until his lips burrowed beneath her collar for an instant. "For tonight, I told you all I expect—not want, but expect—is the company of a woman who makes me feel good. After that, we'll see. But your sister isn't a kid, is she?" He waited for the reluctant shake of her head. "No. And the airplane's been invented, right." Again he waited for her to nod. "Also, I hope to do research work in the States on a fairly regular basis at some time. When will be up to me." Grinning happily, he chucked her under the chin. "How am I doing so far?"

Greer ran a fingernail over the edge of his tie. "I don't think you're playing fair. But I'm running out of excuses for not being your friend."

"Terrific." In several quick movements he started the car. "I'm dying for that drink."

"You're making this very difficult," she warned him. She felt his excitement. Whatever he said, once they were in the private comfort of his home, a drink and conversation wouldn't be enough—for either of them.

"What's wrong now?"

"All this sparring. It doesn't change what's real."

"I didn't intend it to," he said.

Greer was quickly running out of patience. The best thing to do was lay it on the line. "There isn't room in my life for you now, Andrew," she said firmly. "And it wouldn't be fair to pretend things could change. Why don't you take me back to Weymouth and forget you ever saw me. I shouldn't have come bursting into your tidy existence again."

His laugh was softly derisive. "There's very little about my existence that's tidy. And your bursting into it again was the best thing that could have happened. I'll take you to Weymouth under protest, but that doesn't mean I'm giving up on you."

"It could take a long time for anything to be different with me," she said halfheartedly. How desperately she wanted him to persist.

Why couldn't she just say, *take me with you*, and stop second guessing the future?

He turned the key in the ignition. "We have as long as it takes, my darling."

Darling suddenly sounded like the most beautiful word she'd ever heard. She was almost certainly courting disaster, but she couldn't make herself tell him to leave her alone.

At a truck stop on the outskirts of a tiny place called Winterborne Monkton, Andrew stopped the car and got out without comment. He went inside, his tall body backlit in the yellow light. She watched his movements, the incline of his head, the slight jerk as he laughed at something the proprietor must have said. Then he ran his hand over the glinting dark curls, mussed by the wind. Here was a man with the confident elegance few men ever achieved. She must be mad to hesitate even for a second. Her eyelids closed like leaden weights. Not mad, only scared. It could work out, if...

The slamming of Andrew's door startled her. She stretched.

"Taking a little snooze?" He bent to peer at her closely. "Yup, thought so. Exhaustion and starvation—bad combination. Here, time for your introduction to the English version of American fast food. Floppy tomato sandwiches, stale current buns and good old tea. We built an empire on fare like this. Should pick you up instantly."

Greer blinked and took the plastic-wrapped food and the cup he offered. His irresistible smile marched straight to her defenseless heart. "With a recommendation like that, it's bound to," Greer assured him. No point telling him what she already thought of the tea. "We'd better keep going, though. I can hold yours while you drive."

His wry grimace left no doubt he knew she was determined not to be swayed in her decision to go to the boardinghouse. Handing him his sandwich and watching the steady munch of his jaw reminded her of other trips, one in particular. Nausea twisted tight from her stomach to her throat. She and Colin had usually traded sips of coffee from the same cup and shared whatever they ate while he drove. "Might as well save a hand. I'll risk the bugs if you will," he'd quipped more times than she would ever remember.

They'd done the same thing the night he was killed. And it couldn't have been more than a few miles from here. Tears prickled at Greer's eyes. She didn't know the exact spot where the accident happened and never intended to find out.

Her heart was pounding by the time they swept along the winding stretch of Ridgeway, a hairpin bend above Weymouth. A glance into the murky depths of her waxed cup surprised her. It was empty, although she hadn't even tasted the tea.

With an absentminded twist she opened the window and lifted her head to catch the first whiff of salt from the bay. Exhaustion didn't come close to what she felt and even the bracing air current did nothing to clear her fuddled brain.

Andrew's cup was also empty, and he'd eaten every scrap of the food he'd so denigrated. With a sidelong glance, she stuffed the bun into her raincoat pocket and mashed her barely touched sandwich between their two cups. When she got out, the evidence of her ingratitude would go with her.

The dash clock read eight-thirty when Andrew pulled up in St. John's Terrace. A distant, interior light shone through the pebble-glass inserts in the front door of Bay Vista. "Home, sweet home," he said lightly, and slid an arm around Greer's shoulders before she could make a move.

"Thanks for everything, Andrew," she said quickly. "We'll talk again."

"Oh, we certainly will, sweet lady."

"Good night, then."

His fingers braced her head in a gentle vise while he studied her eyes, her mouth. If he'd suddenly drawn away, she might have stopped him, but he didn't draw away.

The first kiss grazed her forehead, the second her temple. Then she lost count, dropping the cups on the floor to circle his neck and find his mouth. He parted her lips wide, pulling her tongue hard against his before smoothing the moist lining inside her cheeks. Blood hammered in her eardrums. Every thought, every physical response, made a lie of her earlier protests. He knew it, and they both knew he did, but she didn't care.

"Greer," he said against her throat. "I'm going to take you in now."

Almost, she felt a space where his body had been. He got out and came around to open her door.

The sidewalk absorbed the sound of her footsteps until she stood before him on the step. She held herself rigid to hide the tremors that had started.

Andrew touched her cheek lightly. "Tomorrow night?" he said.

She frowned, puzzled.

"We're going to the Wilsons' for dinner, remember?"

"Of course," she said. Relief filled the emptiness inside. "The Wilsons'."

With an effort she turned away, feeling him do the same. At least they would be together again tomorrow night—even if there would be other people there.

"Wait!"

She spun around at the sound of Andrew's voice. He sprinted to the car, opened his door and rummaged inside until he extricated himself with an indistinct bundle.

"Almost forgot this. Seems like a year ago when you bought it."

He returned to hand her the parcel containing her green, market sweater. She'd completely forgotten the thing.

She stared at it briefly before lifting her face and finding Andrew's mouth a scant millimeter from hers.

Cradling the package, she could do nothing while he wrapped her gently in his arms and delivered a totally soul-stripping kiss.

Greer felt him tremble. The firm grip on her shoulders before he stepped away was to steady them both. "'Night," she whispered.

"'Night." He stuck his hands in his pockets, backing away. "Dinner's at seven. Pick you up at six, okay?"

"Yes—perfect," she answered, watching until he left. Then she went slowly indoors.

The sheepskin. Greer shook her head slowly and tiptoed upstairs. No good trying to catch Andrew with the coat now. The sound of his engine had already faded.

In her room, high at the back of the house, Greer shrugged off the cumbersome garment, but couldn't resist burying her nose in the collar before draping it over a chair. A trace of her own perfume clung there, but it was Andrew she smelled—clean sea air, pine.

It was early, but this had been a draining day and bed sounded great. She peeled off her clothes until she stood shivering in bra and panties. Hardy breed these Britishers. They even seemed to take pride in throwing open windows to the night air—healthy they insisted. Crazy, Greer thought, splashing cold water into a sink atop exposed galvanized plumbing. There was a faucet marked *H*, presumably for *hot*, but it didn't work. Neither did the radiator, although it occasionally thumped loudly and gave an ominous hiss. She checked the bed quickly for the lump that would indicate her hot water bottle and groaned when she didn't feel it beneath the quilt.

With brisk determination, she scoured a frosty washcloth over her protesting skin. "No showers at night," Mrs. Findlay had decreed. "Don't hold with them then, and they wake my lodgers." Greer had met only one other boarder, a pale young man who was "doing some sort of paper on Roman stuff," according to their landlady. He'd passed Greer in the hall twice, dropping his head in a shy nod each time, and she'd never seen him at breakfast. According to the books she'd read on Dorset, the area was rich in Roman history and artifacts, and from the preoccupied expression on the man's face, the sound of a shower should be the last thing to distract him.

Greer chuckled, grabbing a flannel nightgown from the rickety middle drawer of a marble-topped dresser. She was falling in love with this quaint country and its determinedly cheerful people. England was in her blood and she felt a growing closeness to everything around her.

Two dormer windows poked out from one wall of the room. Greer knew the scene below without looking. A narrow, concrete courtyard surrounded by woven wood fences, and double gates leading to an alley behind. Swathed in her fleecy aqua bathrobe, knee-high socks pulled up securely and feet jammed into fur slippers, she opened one drape. Night was kind to the plain scene, disguising rows of garbage cans and an array of potted plants, already yellowed by the first frost. Slate roofs reflected moonlight. The few stars that showed were steady, distant pinpricks of polished steel.

Somewhere to the east, Andrew might also be getting ready for bed. She'd never seen his bedroom—had no idea which way it faced. But if he looked up, perhaps he'd notice the same stars, the inky black camouflage of darkness. Would he also think of her, or was she reading too much into the past few hours?

Sleep beckoned and Greer padded to the bed, winced when she took off the bathrobe and slippers and scuttled beneath the covers. She kept on her cable-knit socks. In the morning her legs would bear their imprint, but she'd wear pants.

Before turning out the lamp, she snuggled deeper and took a last covetous look around the room. Already it felt like home, her retreat. Roses had obviously been the only prerequisite for inclusion in the decorating scheme. Drapes sported a larger and slightly more faded design than the bedspread, and the wallpaper, old as it was, had obviously been chosen for its floppy dog roses. Greer made a mental note to check the rug in the morning. She flipped off the light. In the faint glow from the windows she could see the brilliant white shape of a kitten, pictured on an enameled board used to block off the old fireplace.

What was Andrew's bedroom like? She turned on her stomach, shoved her hands beneath the pillow and pressed it to her face. She tried to control her dangerous thoughts. *Think about tomorrow. Back to Ferndale and Kelloway Lane.* To no avail. His room would be masculine, lots of books, a bit disorganized...

The pillow smelled of mothballs. Greer flipped to her back again and stared straight up. Little colored flecks shifted in front of her eyes. Did he sleep nude? *Good Lord, Greer.*

Her nose was cold. She pulled the sheet over her eyes and promptly sneezed. She turned on her side, curling into a tight ball. Immediately, her fingers went to the long scar from hip to thigh, hardly definable through the thick nightgown. Reluctantly she covered her flat abdomen. The cesarean section was a thin, almost invisible line now, but a parallel incision had left a ridge that would take a year or more to flatten and pale. Tightness squeezed her chest. No one could have foreseen the pelvic inflammatory disease that left no choice but hysterectomy. The surgeon who operated on her had waited until any further delay would threaten her life.

Only this recent scar would be new to Andrew—if he even noticed it—he already knew about the others. And all he'd offered was a liaison, not his heart and soul on a platter. She'd told herself she wanted to lead a normal life again. Sex was a healthy, natural part of any human existence. If there was one man likely to help her forget her reservations, it was Andrew Monthaven.

Believing the latest surgery or some mental injury left over from losing Colin had made her incapable of responding to a man was probably a cop-out. Probably...

Dammit! She would never hurt Andrew. But she *would* take whatever happiness she could find with him for as long as they were able to be together.

CHAPTER TEN

GREER WAITED. Finding Reverend Alec Colyer in the pretty village of Chaldon Herring had taken all morning and part of the afternoon. She was increasingly conscious of time passing and the need to be back in Weymouth and dressed for dinner by six.

The reverend sat in a matching chintz chair opposite her own, staring thoughtfully through rain-streaked windows. The temptation to prompt him made her grip the cup and saucer in her hands tightly. He was walking the old paths of his life slowly, feeling the way. Trying to rush him would do no good.

"Ruby you said? Mmm." His light blue eyes returned to her face. "She was an only child, I remember."

"Yes," Greer said, although she hadn't known. She mustn't break his concentration.

He sipped his tea loudly, wrinkling his snub nose. Always tea. Greer suppressed a little smile and drank some of her own. In time she could start to like the stuff. Carefully she set the cup in its saucer, trying not to rattle the china.

"I was vicar of St. Peter's for thirty-five years, young lady. Knew everyone who came and went in the village."

Greer mumbled that she was impressed, which seemed to satisfy him. He shifted his short bulk to a more comfortable position and put his cup on the delicate Chippendale table beside his chair.

"I'd be there yet if the rheumatism hadn't slowed me down."

"Miserable," she commiserated. *Please, get on with it.*

"Didn't mind moving out of the rectory so much, but I wish I could have found a suitable place to live in Ferndale. Knew everyone," he said with regret.

"You have a very nice place here, reverend."

Greer already knew some of the ex-vicar of St. Peter's pet concerns. She also knew almost every street, lane and alley in Ferndale, and most of the shops. Esther Lyle ran the combination post office and variety store. Alf Gleed was the only police constable, and monitored law and order from the kitchen of his four-room cottage. The closest medical or dental care was in Dorchester.

The villagers had been anxious to talk—about weather and crops, and what it was like in Seattle. Did it rain as much there as it did here? Greer's emphatic yes brought laughs all around. They'd been eager to predict bad winter in Dorset—crows nesting low gave a sure sign. But each time she brought up Ruby Timmons, or Kurt, her questions were met with blank expressions, slowly shaken heads and yet another suggestion for some local monument she ought not to miss.

In Kelloway Lane—her first stop—she had walked back and forth in front of Marsh Cottage until she felt too conspicuous to pass it again. Then she'd stood across the lane to watch, and just as she gathered enough courage to start for the front door, it opened. A flustered young woman shouldering a baby emerged and plopped down two empty milk bottles.

Hopeless. No point even asking someone who clearly could have no connection to Ruby. Greer had headed for the village center once more, dismissing the notion that she was almost grateful not to have to go inside the cottage. Later, when she had been ready to give up altogether, the police constable's suggestion that she talk to the rector had paid off.

The present vicar of St. Peter's dealt with her inquiries briskly. A busy middle-aged man, he showed little enthusiasm for his ten-year appointment in Ferndale. No, he had no present parishioners named Timmons. Probably meant the family had left the area. But his retired predecessor, Alec Colyer, who now lived in Chaldon Herring, might be able to help her. Then she'd been favored with a smile she sensed was rare and a warning, "If you can keep him off his favorite subjects. Missing Ferndale, taxation and his rheumatism."

So far she wasn't doing a very good job. Taxes would probably be next.

"Bill Timmons was a good man. Fine stonemason. He did some repairs around the church. Lived in London as a young man, so he said—had a hand in building St. Paul's Cathedral. Quiet though. He and Mollie came south for the peace, I think, and to get their little girl out of the city.''

Greer's cup almost slid from the saucer. She steadied it quickly. Who did he mean? Her grandfather? "What was their little girl's name?''

The old man looked at her sharply. "Ruby. Ruby, of course. I thought that's who we were talking about.''

"We were, are. Did you know her, too—and Kurt?'' Her lips began to quiver. She mustn't cry. He wouldn't understand.

Reverend Colyer blinked several times while he rubbed his swollen knuckles. "Did a bit of carpentry myself before this. Decorative stuff,'' he added, pausing thoughtfully. "Ruby used to come with her mother. Mollie helped clean the church. The girl was a quiet thing with a lot of red hair.''

Greer tipped her head and closed her stinging eyes. *Red hair.* She's already said Ruby was her mother, but he seemed to have forgotten.

"She left Ferndale the year she finished school. Must have been coming up to sixteen then, I suppose. Wasn't a year later she was back and the little boy was born.''

"Kurt?''

"That's what he was christened. They called him Rusty. Killed Bill, though,'' he said, clucking his tongue noisily.

She could stop it now. Colin had told her to stop if she changed her mind. Greer placed the cup on the windowsill and half rose. There had once been heartache in that nondescript cottage she'd walked away from this morning. People had suffered—her people. Did she want to know how much?

"More tea, Miss...?''

"No, thank you,'' she said wearily. She'd come this far. She couldn't run away now. Gathering all her self-control, Greer sat back down. "Please go on, Reverend Colyer.''

"Not much more to tell,'' he said, staring into his teacup. "Ruby's dad died a couple of years after she went away again. She'd left the baby with her folks.'' Now his balding head wobbled sadly. "Mollie took Rusty around like he was her son instead of her grandson. Then Ruby came with the new baby and Mollie would have done the same for that one, too, if she hadn't been ill by then.''

Greer felt her blood run cold. Now he was talking about her. ''Do you know where Ruby went afterward?'' she whispered.

With a wheezy sigh, he stood and moved to peer at the sky. ''More rain coming. Beats the plants down.'' He pulled at the stretched hem of his blue cardigan. ''I don't remember all the details, but after Mollie Timmons died, I think Rusty was put into a school for homeless boys. I never knew what happened to Ruby and the baby.''

''But you do know something about Rusty?''

''And you're the baby. Funny world,'' he said, taking Greer by surprise. Until that moment she had not been sure he was making all the obvious connections. When he turned, his eyes were startlingly clear. ''Rusty was a good boy, levelheaded and resourceful. I heard he went into the merchant navy. He probably decided it was best to get away and let go of the past. Maybe he was right.''

Maybe he was, but Greer had made a distant sighting of her goal. What could it hurt to at least try contacting the brother she'd never met, never even guessed existed before yesterday? And Rusty could very well know where their mother was. The problem that seemed insurmountable was deciding what to do next.

''You've been very helpful, reverend. Thank you.'' Greer said as she stood. ''I don't suppose you know how a person joins the merchant navy?''

He rocked onto his toes, smiling faintly. ''Not really. But if I were a young woman determined to find someone who had, I'd probably contact the Seamen's Union in Southampton. Rusty would have to belong if he went to sea, and they keep each man's work record—the ships he'd signed on with in the past, and his present vessel, if there is one,'' he said, scratching his head absently.

Another step forward. If Rusty had gone to sea, she could very well close the gap between them a little more. ''Thanks again, very much,'' she said, impulsively grabbing the reverend's hand. ''I'll think about everything you've told me.'' Her heart flipped about giddily. Silly. She might find out nothing.

At the door the old man waved. Greer raised a hand, then almost ran down the paved path to the gate. Closer and closer. And in a couple of hours she'd see Andrew again. He would understand how she felt. She knew he would. As soon as they had some time alone she'd explain everything to him. Without someone to share her hopes—and reservations—she'd burst.

Greer stopped and lifted her face to the rain. Even if there were a dozen people she could turn to, here and now, people she liked and trusted, she'd still choose Andrew.

ONE DAY SHE'D have her colors done. Greer surveyed the pile of clothing on the bed critically. She liked simple styles, natural fabrics and usually felt confident of her choices. So why was she having so much trouble choosing something to wear to an informal dinner?

Ridiculous. She was behaving like a teenager going on her first date. Too bad the outfits she'd packed were all so practical though....

Greer checked her watch. Five-thirty, and she was standing in a camisole and panties. *Good Lord.* She eyed the blue-and-black-striped blouse—silk always felt good—black angora vest and black worsted pants. Fine. She dressed quickly, hung the rest of her things again and searched for the black pumps she'd bought but had never yet worn.

The shoes were too high. Knowing how poor her balance could be, why had she selected something she'd probably break her neck in?

Her hair had gotten wet on the way to the bus in Chaldon Herring and then there'd been no time for shampooing. She brushed it hard and succeeded only in creating a springy mass of unruly curls. At least it shone.

This condition was known as panic. Greer sat on the edge of an upright chair and took a deep breath. *Twenty-six-year-old widows don't panic over dinner dates.* What little makeup she wore looked just right, the outfit flattered her and the shoes made the most of small feet and narrow ankles. *Andrew Monthaven, you're a lucky devil.* She grinned. When all else failed, she still had her sense of humor, and life was full of promise now. Later she'd share her new discoveries with Andrew.

The distant jangle of the doorbell sobered her instantly. Murmuring voices followed, then the slow clump, clump, of Mrs. Findlay's sturdy leather brogues on the stairs.

At the expected knock, Greer's heart almost stopped.

"Gentleman for you, Mrs. Beckett. He'll be in the lounge," Mrs. Findlay called through the door.

Greer's weak thank-you was lost beneath even, retreating thuds.

She grabbed her beige fur-lined jacket. Didn't match, but it was that or the raincoat, which wasn't warm enough. The only purse she had was the one she used for travel. Brown with a heavy strap. Out of the question. A lipstick, comb and some money fitted easily into the jacket pockets.

Taking Andrew's sheepskin coat, Greer picked her way carefully downstairs. The thought of making a dashing entry appealed, falling flat on her face didn't.

"Something wrong, Greer?" the deep voice said from the bottom of the stairs.

She jumped. "Andrew! No. Nothing's wrong." *Except you caught me creeping along, staring at my feet like a senior citizen.* "Mrs. Findlay said you were in the lounge," she said as pleasantly as possible.

He smiled and her insides melted. "How much time...?" He leaned to peer down the hall then whispered, "How much time have you spent in the lounge?"

"You mean you don't like the decor?" Greer took the hand he offered and made herself walk confidently at his side. "If I could smuggle out that collection of antimacassars and plaster shepherdesses, I'd be able to auction them to the highest bidder," she said in a conspiratorial voice.

"You're kidding."

"Yep. I sure am."

They both smothered laughs.

"But," Greer said archly. "I like this place, it's comfortable. And I like Mrs. Findlay." Having made her point, Greer quickly changed the subject. "Here's your coat," she said. "Thanks."

Andrew took the sheepskin and opened the front door. "Beautiful, and loyal, too. A paragon." He ignored her narrowed eyes. "The Wilsons's place is even more remote than mine. We'd better get going."

Everyone here drove faster than at home. Greer fidgeted, trying not to look each time a car passed on the narrow two-lane highway. "It's a prettier night than I expected," she said conversationally. She would watch Andrew instead of the traffic.

"I was inside most of the day."

"You didn't miss a thing," she replied.

Andrew was concentrating on the road, his brows drawn together while he checked the rearview mirror before passing a cumbersome builder's truck. He maneuvered back into place and his expression cleared. An intriguing face—not good at hiding the slightest emotion. He glanced at her and smiled. His pearl-gray turtleneck, beneath a charcoal suede jacket, contrasted sharply with the dark hair. Casual but elegant, and she had the feeling he didn't have to try hard to achieve the effect. Fortunately her own outfit seemed appropriate.

He braked to round a bend and even in the failing light Greer's attention was drawn to the movement of his thigh. She turned to the window. Maybe she was becoming what he'd laughingly accused her of being—a leg woman. Her stomach tingled. This was no joke. She was falling for the man and there was no point pretending she didn't want him as more than a friend. His kisses last night, her own in return—the response of her flesh to his touch. The memories were vivid. She wanted to make love with Andrew. The admission thrilled and frightened her.

Minutes slipped by with rows of houses, red telephone booths, tiny shops and the inevitable corner pubs. Greer settled deeper in the seat when the town was behind them and only hills shrouded by approaching night lay ahead. Her hills, her mother and brother's—where were they now?

Andrew drove past the gates of Ringstead Hall and turned south on a paved lane. "Be prepared for chaos," he warned. "Wonderful hospitality, but bedlam. Lauren believes in houses being homes. Nothing in its place and no place for it, anyway."

"Sounds like fun," she answered. A dip jerked her against the seat belt and she hooked a finger through an overhead strap. "I've always envied people who could relax...ouch."

The glove compartment flapped open, sending a shower of books into Greer's lap.

"Damn," Andrew said, slowing the car. "That thing's always doing that. Did you get hurt?"

"No, I'm fine," she assured him. "Just surprised. Keep going. I'll put these back."

She bundled the books into a pile, reaching for several that had slipped to the floor. Children's titles. Inside the cover of the top one she found a library sticker.

"Manage?" Andrew asked. "Slam the compartment hard or it'll happen again."

"These are for children," she said. "Are they Simonne's?"

Andrew shook his head. "No. I like to keep a fresh supply of something interesting in the waiting room at the hospital. The stuff they provide looks as if it arrived with William the Conqueror."

"You go to the library to get them?"

"Mmm. That way I can change them every couple of weeks."

Greer's eyes grew moist. Stupid reaction. She already knew he was crazy about children. Why else would he be a pediatrician? "I doubt if many of your colleagues are so conscientious," she said seriously.

"I enjoy the books as much as the kids do. This is it. What do you think?"

A modernistic house faced them across a bridged ravine. "Wow. It's the last thing I expected," she admitted. "You had me visualizing a Victorian manor, with multiple bad additions."

Andrew hugged his elbows and laughed. "Wait until you see inside."

The front door flew open before Greer and Andrew could get to the steps. Simonne launched herself into his arms. Her cheeks were flushed and long, sparkling earrings waggled from her ears. "I've got a new fish pond, Uncle Andy. Daddy built it up by the rockery. Come and see."

"Simonne. Enough. You can show off the pond later." Bob Wilson disentangled his daughter and set her firmly inside the door. "Come in. Come in," he said to both of them. "She's been watching out the window ever since she got home from school."

Attractive man, Greer thought. Rugged. The child looked too fragile to be his, yet the clear blue eyes, high foreheads and unruly blond hair were the same.

Bob moved to Greer's shoulder. "Let me take your coat, Greer. Lauren and I are delighted you could make it."

She shrugged out of the jacket. He was charming, relaxed. Very different from the anxious impression he'd given on the hospital steps. "Thank you," she said.

"Where is Lauren?" Andrew put one hand at Greer's waist, the other on Simonne's neck.

"In the kitchen. She'll be out in a minute." Bob raised his eyebrows at Andrew and grinned. "You know how she is? Company means we try a new dish, and I'm not sure how this one's going."

He loves her. They're happy. Greer quelled a tinge of envy and felt ashamed.

She was guided from a cathedral-ceilinged hall, topped with skylights, into an extraordinary living room. Black and white, and stainless steel. It was spectacular in its stark design, or it would have been without the clutter Andrew had mentioned. Fabric had been hastily bunched on top of an open sewing cabinet. Spools of thread were scattered all over the plush white carpet. Evidence of Simonne's attempts to entertain herself dotted the ultramodern furniture.

Simonne bounded into the room demanding the spotlight. "The pond's down there," she said eagerly, pressing her face to the glass overlooking the grounds behind the house. "You *have* to come and see," she insisted.

"There you are Andrew—and Greer." Lauren hustled into the room, swathed in a navy-and-white-striped cook's apron. "Simonne, calm down," she said firmly. "And take off those dreadful earrings. Andrew, look at her. Do you think we've created a monster?"

He appeared to consider, rubbing his chin while Simonne came to stare innocently up into his face. "I'm not sure. There may still be time to save her," he said dramatically. "But I don't think we'll get much peace until I look at these fish. Who's coming with us? Greer?"

Greer shook her head. "I'll help the cook," she answered evenly, hoping Andrew wouldn't notice the slight tremor in her voice. She wasn't as ready to get close to the world of children as she'd hoped earlier.

"Wait until you see this, Andy." Bob was already heading for the hall with Simonne. "They've got this ready-mix concrete stuff now. It's a snap. I even managed a bit of a waterfall."

Andrew hesitated, looking down at Greer. "Sure you don't mind?"

"Of course not," she said.

His expression brightened. "Won't be long." He brushed an errant curl away from her temple, then followed Bob and Simonne.

Greer's fingers went to her face. The sensation of his touch remained. A long sigh startled her and she coughed self-consciously. Lauren Wilson was smiling like an approving mother of the bride. *Bride.* Imagination could be a dangerous, painful thing.

"Is there something I can do?" she asked pleasantly.

Lauren's kitchen was like its owner, bright, busy and cheerfully disorganized. But delicious smells told Greer her hostess was a good cook, even if she was an inveterate culinary gambler.

"Do you like to cook?" Lauren asked, skillfully deveining shrimp.

Greer started drying a pile of draining pots. "I used to."

Lauren's knife slipped briefly.

"Of course," she said. "Silly of me. Bob mentioned you'd been widowed. It can't be the same on your own, I suppose. I'm sorry."

"Don't be. I still miss Colin, but it doesn't hurt like it used to." She chewed her bottom lip thoughtfully as she set down a skillet. It *didn't* hurt the same anymore.

Lauren came to stand beside her at the sink. "I'm glad," she said softly. "Andrew's obviously smitten—something we've waited a long time for. How did you two meet?"

Greer began to panic. She couldn't, wouldn't resurrect all the memories again. "Just by chance when I was visiting England once before." At least she wasn't lying.

"And you kept in touch?"

"In a way...something's burning."

Lauren rushed to the stove to retrieve a singed potholder and plunge it into the sink. "I think my timing's a bit off." She smiled rather tremulously. "Just like when I was pregnant with Simonne. We're finally going to have another baby."

Tears in the woman's eyes were from pure joy and Greer smiled. "Congratulations. I envy you..." She hadn't meant to say that.

"You don't have any children?"

"No."

"I hope you will. You obviously get along with them. Simonne was very taken with you yesterday," Lauren confessed.

Greer knew she had to change the subject. "Did you make it back to your car before the meter ran out?" she said.

"Barely. Look at them." Lauren nodded to the window above the sink. "I never met a man with such an affinity for kids as Andrew. It's time he had some of his own. We just have to get him married off first," she said brightly. Greer felt herself being watched but continued to stare into the yard.

In the spectral glow from outdoor spotlights, she saw Andrew and Bob climbing the rise to the house. Simonne sat on Andrew's shoulders, holding his ears and making whooping noises Greer could hear inside the kitchen. Every few steps, Andrew romped in a circle. Yes, he should have his own family—his own babies to watch grow up. If he didn't, it would be a waste.

"Has he told you much about his family?"

Greer felt remote, almost disoriented. Her thoughts, and the conversation, were becoming confused. "Not really," she said as she folded the dish towel, too carefully.

Lauren didn't seem to notice her discomfort and Greer didn't want to make a scene.

"He's the last Monthaven," Lauren announced. "They were landowners—farmers. A very old family that gradually dwindled until now there's only Andrew left. So it's up to him to make sure there are plenty of heirs to carry on the name, you see?" she said, pausing for effect. "That old house of his is an antiquated barn, but lovely in a curious sort of way. It would be sad if it ended up as a total museum. As long as there's a Monthaven or two around they'll have a right to live in it. Otherwise, it passes to the National Trust completely."

And you hope I'll be the one to provide a bevy of little Monthavens. "I'm sure that won't happen. That the house will...I mean..." Greer stumbled, wanting desperately to get away. Every word she spoke became unwittingly misleading.

"Are you and Andrew planning—something?" The pleasant glow on Lauren Wilson's face made her thoughts transparent. "Oh, Bob and I would be so happy. We've worried about Andrew being too solitary," she confided. "You'll be perfect together. Wait until Bob hears, if Andrew hasn't already told him. Those two have always been very close."

"Lauren. Please, wait," Greer said instinctively, grabbing Lauren's arm. Greer's fingers turned to ice. "There's nothing like that between Andrew and me," she said as firmly as possible. "We're friends, that's all. I didn't mean to give you any other impression."

In a short silence, the sputter of boiling water seemed deafening. "I'm sure you didn't try to give me any impression." Lauren's gaze was surprisingly penetrating. Greer dropped her hand as Lauren began bustling once again. "We'd better get these on the table if my mousse isn't going to fall," she said briskly. "Could you grab the rolls? I'll have to send Bob for the wine." Lauren picked up a tray of shrimp cocktails in smoky stemmed bowls and waited for Greer to open the door.

They met Bob and Andrew in the hall, where Simonne was bargaining for an extension on her bedtime. Greer gathered the child had already eaten.

"Go on up, kiddo," Andrew was saying. "And when we've finished dinner, I'll come and say good-night." He met Greer's eyes and his smile widened. "I'm sure Greer will, too."

These people had what he wanted. And there was no way she could give it to him. Each glance, whatever he did and didn't say, suggested he was beginning to cast her in the role Lauren had just been talking about. Greer lifted her chin. She couldn't let him hope for the impossible.

"All right," Simonne agreed, walking slowly upstairs, looking back at every step. "As soon as you finish, though."

Andrew and Bob laughed. Greer caught Lauren's appraisal and forced herself to chuckle.

Forget it. Get out of his life before it hurts too much—for both of us.

CHAPTER ELEVEN

"WON'T SHE BE asleep by now?" Greer said as she followed Andrew reluctantly from the Wilsons' dining room.

He stood back for her to pass him at the foot of the stairs. "Not this kid. She'll have propped her eyelids open with matchsticks if necessary."

The staircase rose to a second story at right angles to the living and dining rooms. Greer hadn't seen the rest of the ground floor but guessed there would be a study and, perhaps, a game or family room. Lauren had promised to give her a complete tour later.

"Which way?"

Andrew came behind her on the upper landing. "Left. All the way to the end. What do you think of the place so far?" he inquired.

"Interesting, if you go for ultracontemporary stuff. I prefer a softer feel to my surroundings," she said.

"I'm glad to hear you say so. I do, too."

Greer caught his smile and couldn't help giving one of her own. He was mentally pairing them, measuring their compatibility and finding the positive answers he wanted. She sensed it, but didn't know how to reverse the process or disillusion him. Later. Later there would be an obvious way.

Hall floors in the bedroom wing were glimmering oak. Probably Swedish-finished, Greer decided. Their heels clipped sharply to an open doorway where pinkish light cut a red swath over the dark wood.

Simonne, surrounded by a circle of stuffed animals, lay against plump pillows in a high brass bed. Bronzed lashes shaded her cheeks and her unbraided hair spread wide in shiny ridges. A hollow sensation twisted Greer's stomach.

Andrew put an arm around her shoulders. "I guess you were right. She's fast asleep."

He moved to sit with one thigh along the edge of the bed, a foot tucked behind the other knee. Without the jacket, Greer could see that his sweater fitted over his muscular torso like a second skin. Greer's spine tingled. She reached for a windup teddy bear and studied it closely.

"She's a neat kid," Andrew said. He leaned to kiss Simonne's forehead, then studied her with a slight smile.

Unconsciously Greer turned the metal key in the teddy bear's side.

"Brahms' Lullaby."

The child stirred and opened her eyes. "Hello, Uncle Andy. You came."

Andrew was staring at Greer and the smile had vanished from his eyes. "Right, Simonne. We came." He watched Greer and she vaguely noticed that his face seemed paler. "Time for sleep, young lady. I was going to see if you wanted to go out on Saturday. Maybe to Lyme. Does that sound good?"

"Mmm. If Greer comes."

He avoided Greer's eyes. "We'll have to ask her." He kissed the little girl again.

"I'm glad you're coming, Greer. Uncle Andy thinks you're great, doesn't he? So do I. Will you give me a kiss good-night, too?"

Greer hesitated, then bent to brush the soft fragrant cheek. "Good night, Simonne. Sleep tight," she whispered.

"That's enough, young lady." Andrew pulled the sheet and blankets up.

Another turn of the key in the bear's side increased the music's volume.

"I like that music, too," Simonne said sleepily. "Uncle Andy has a music box in his bedroom that plays the same thing."

"Does he?" Greer asked, but the child was asleep. Greer looked at Andrew through shimmering tears. When she tried to speak again, she couldn't.

"Greer. Oh, Greer," Andrew whispered as he rose from the bed.

"It still hurts you, dammit. And this probably doesn't help much," he said, nodding at the sleeping child. "I'm an insensitive idiot."

She set the stuffed animal on a chair. The lullaby's last notes faded into the night. *Help me say the right thing.*

He reached out to her tenderly. "I could never bring myself to get rid of the Hummel box," he said. "Would you like to have it now?"

Greer turned toward the door. "No, thank you. I don't think so."

His hands on her shoulders were so comforting she closed her eyes. Would he feel the same about her if she told him about the hysterectomy, or would he be disappointed? She wasn't ready to find out.

Gently he pulled her against his body. "The last thing I wanted was to upset you. For some reason Simonne reminds you of Colleen, doesn't she?" he asked very gently.

The name, on his lips, made the past rush around her like a suffocating blanket. "A little bit, but it's all right. Please stop worrying about me." At least he hadn't mentioned her having other children as he had done after Colleen died. She couldn't take that again.

He cupped her face and made small circles on her chin with his thumbs. "I can't help worrying. You matter to me."

The expression in his eyes warned Greer that he intended to kiss her. "Bob and Lauren will be wondering where we are," she said quickly. She took a step backward, breaking contact. "I'm supposed to have a house tour, and we shouldn't stay too late." She tried not to notice the hurt in Andrew's eyes.

They returned to the stairs in silence, just as Lauren started up from the bottom. "There you are," she said. "Andy, Bob's in the study. If Greer's game, I'm going to show her the illuminated parts of the grounds. It's a marvelous night."

"Sounds great," Greer said, with more enthusiasm than she felt.

Andrew helped Lauren into her coat, then held out Greer's jacket. He slid it up her arms and squeezed her shoulders briefly. "Watch your step out there. The paths are uneven in places."

"I'm not—" She rounded on him and stopped. "A cripple" would have ended her retort. But his concerned face told her she would be selfish to overreact to the simple kindness that came so naturally to him. "Thanks, Andrew. I'll be careful," she said instead.

Once outside, Greer raised her face to the stars and willed the velvet night to absorb her. Soft lights concealed in planting areas gave rocks and leafless shrubs an eerie glow.

"Isn't it super?" Lauren said as she overtook her. "I often come out here when it's dark. Bob's always talking about getting a telescope. We're so far from town we'd have a fairly good view of the sky. Very little artificial light to interfere."

Lauren Wilson wasn't the mental lightweight she seemed determined to project. "You're right," Greer said, following thoughtfully in the other woman's wake. Throughout dinner it had been obvious that her host and hostess cared deeply for each other, although Lauren consistently deferred to Bob, agreed wordlessly in a way that suggested she always left original idea and comment to him. Curious. But it seemed to satisfy them both.

"Come up here," Lauren said, scrambling over limestone outcrops to a ridge.

Greer cursed the high heels and used both hands to steady her on the way up. By the time she reached the top she was breathless.

"I'm sorry, Greer." Concern edged Lauren's voice. "Your shoes aren't meant for climbing. And I'd forgotten—"

"Don't worry. I'm fine." Greer didn't want to talk about her injury. Lauren was sure to have noticed the limp, but that didn't mean she knew of the accident. Andrew might have explained it to the Wilsons, but Greer doubted if he had, and there was no need for them to be told. "It looks like the dark side of the moon up here," Greer said, effectively bridging the awkward moment.

"Exactly what Bob and I call it." Lauren's voice rose. "See how the hills become rounded cones and the valleys are craters—with a bit of imagination?"

Greer laughed. "I think you must be a thwarted astrologist."

"Astronomer. But I do believe in following one's own star sometimes, don't you?"

Stupid mistake. The perfect excuse for another probe of your defenses, dummy. "I haven't given it much thought," she said vaguely.

"How long are you staying in England?"

Here it comes. "I'm not sure. Depends on how my business goes. My sister and I run a shop in Seattle. We deal in British goods and I'm here to look for new ideas." And a few other things she would never readily confess to Lauren Wilson.

"How interesting. I must hear all about it. Could we have lunch one day?"

"I'd love that." Greer responded automatically, then cringed inwardly. Lunch with Lauren probably would be fun. Another grilling session wouldn't.

"Where's Andrew taken you so far?"

Greer smiled despite herself. This woman wasn't at all dumb. "Nowhere, really. He just took me to the market to help me get my bearings. Wherever you decide we should go will be fine."

"Andrew's very dedicated, you know," Lauren said, skillfully directing the conversation.

"Yes." She already knew.

"Sometimes too much so. He forgets that a man needs to play as well as work."

Determined not to be led into dangerous waters again, Greer decided to take control.

"Maybe work is what makes him happiest," she said, turning carefully to study the house's dark outline. "We should start back."

"I've never seen him look at a woman the way he looks at you."

Please, don't. "Lauren, I understand how you and Bob feel about Andrew, and I agree he's a very special person. But as far as I know, Andrew's perfectly content. And so am I. We like each other—but that's all. We really should get back."

"Sometimes—Would you look at that child?"

"Where?" Greer stared at Lauren's upturned face, then at the house where the silhouette of a head showed above an upstairs windowsill. "Oh, dear," Greer said. "Simonne. She was asleep when we left her. Maybe she heard a noise."

"I'll have to get her back to bed. It must be almost ten and tomorrow's a school day."

"You go on, Lauren. I'll find Bob and Andrew."

Lauren moved ahead with surprising rapidity. Left alone, Greer went slowly. On the path, she took off her shoes to make walking easier and winced as the cold seeped up through her feet and legs. She was glad to get inside the warm hall.

She wiggled her toes for several seconds before stepping back into the pumps and going to hang her jacket in the closet once more. The rumble of men's voices filtered from the wing beneath the bedrooms.

Bob's baritone came to her clearly when she started along a corridor beside the stairs. "I'm asking you to reconsider, Andy. For your own sake."

In the short silence that followed, Greer reached a door that wasn't quite closed. She touched the handle, then froze.

"There's no question of turning back," Andrew said shortly. "And we're going to drop this, now. If I were likely to change my mind I'd have done it during one of the dozens of discussions we've already had on the subject. I'm totally sick of hashing and rehashing the thing with you. It's my problem, and my decision."

"Damn it all, Andrew. You're too hardheaded to know when you're flirting with disaster. Let it go, will you. The boy's dead. Trying to prove it was Coover's fault will only bring your life down around your ears. Believe me. Winston's got all the cards."

A sharp sound startled her.

"The hell he does," Andrew exploded. "Bob, you know I'm right. Why don't you get behind me. We all know that mistakes are made in medicine, just like they are in any other field. Mistakes are one thing—willful neglect of duty is another. Winston Coover was too busy entertaining cronies to go into the hospital and examine Michael. People don't die of a ruptured appendix these days. It just doesn't happen. Or it shouldn't."

"It does happen," Bob insisted. "And the only reason you're so all-fired worked up about this one is because you were in London at the time. This is your way of punishing yourself for daring to take a couple of days off. You're driven, Andy. Obsessed with duty. And you expect everyone else to be the same."

"Are you saying Coover didn't cause that boy's death?"

Greer wanted to retreat but she couldn't seem to move.

"I'm saying that it doesn't matter anymore. And it might have happened even with you on call."

Andrew made some derisive comment and this time Greer was sure she heard a glass being set down hard. He was drinking—they probably both were—and getting more and more enraged.

"Let's back up and take this slowly." Bob's attempt at reason sounded strained. "If you don't give up the hearing, Coover will use it as a weapon against you. The next step won't be what you want—his license revoked. Instead it'll be a disciplinary action brought against you and if *you* come out of it with *your* license, I'll be amazed. Please—don't—*do it*," Bob said emphatically.

"I don't believe this, friend." Andrew's tone dropped to an intense whisper. "You and I were going to set the world straight. Remember? No backing off. No compromises."

"That was a long time ago," Bob snapped. "We were kids then. This is life, Andy—the big time."

"And that means we bend our beliefs to keep the going smooth—the old bank account intact?"

"You sound like what you are. A man who never knew what it was to go without. I'm more realistic. I wasn't born with a silver spoon in my mouth, so I've had to keep both feet on the ground."

"You've changed. Standing up for what's right doesn't mean losing what matters to you, or it shouldn't."

What were they saying? Why was Bob trying to persuade Andrew to back down from something he believed in? Greer rolled against the wall, pressing both wet palms into its coolness.

"When I called you the other night, about Neil, did you understand what I was saying?" Bob's voice was low and she had to strain to hear him.

"I understood," Andrew shouted. "But I think you're cracked. What harm could Neil Jones possibly do me? I pity the poor bastard, that's all."

"Sometimes I think you missed a phase when you were growing up. You never learned that half the world doesn't give a damn about truth and honesty. The *poor bastard*, as you call him, can always use money. He moves on the fast track. He'll say anything if they make it worth his while.''

Several seconds passed. Greer's stomach lodged beneath her lungs. She yearned to be at Andrew's side. He was being threatened by something she didn't understand and her instinct was to protect him.

"What can he say, Bob? That we had lunch.''

Bob's expletive retort made Greer cringe, then she was coldly aware of every word. "Andrew, if your name is linked with that of a confirmed homosexual like Neil, your integrity will never recover. What parent would want you as a pediatrician? What examining board would run the risk of openly backing you, anyway?''

"It's not going to happen. Proving myself won't be difficult. Bob—drop it,'' Andrew said firmly.

But Bob had no intentions of dropping it.

"Proving yourself?'' he shouted. "Is that what this sudden infatuation with your glamorous American is all about?'' His voice was full of contempt. "Forget it,'' he said bluntly. "The convenient new girlfriend is just that—too convenient. She won't help and she could even work against you.'' There was a long pause during which Greer could hear their heavy breathing.

"Andrew.'' Bob said softly. "If you don't call off the hearing, Winston intends to prove you're an active homosexual.''

CHAPTER TWELVE

GREER FELT FAINT.

"Leave Greer out of this," Andrew said at the top of his voice. "How will Coover possibly prove I'm gay on the strength of my knowing Neil?"

"As long as you insist on remaining Neil's staunch buddy, that's all it'll take. Am I getting through to you?"

"I'm not the man's staunch buddy. Just an acquaintance who feels secure enough to be civil to him. This is mad. Michael Drake's death is the issue, nothing else." Andrew's voice was growing hoarse.

Hurrying footsteps jarred Greer's brain. "What on earth's going on in there?" Lauren said as she ran along the corridor, breathing heavily. "I could hear the yelling all the way upstairs."

"Just got here," Greer lied. "They're probably arguing about sports."

"Sports?" Lauren's expression was incredulous. "What do you mean?"

"I don't know." The problem was she knew too much.

Lauren swept open the door and marched into an austere room, paneled in ash. A billiard table dominated the center and floor-to-ceiling windows butted at a corner. The men faced each other, their erect postures exuding hostility.

"You two can probably be heard in London," Lauren said, barely managing to suppress her anger. "Simonne couldn't sleep and Greer's standing in the hall like a piece of fossilized wood. Care to tell us what's going on?"

Andrew's back was to Greer. He swiveled rapidly and frowned. "Just a difference of opinion," he said absently. "Nothing to worry about." His eyes met Greer's and held them.

"Good," Lauren sighed. "How about a liqueur and some music before you go home?"

"I don't think so," Andrew said as he looked at Bob who stared into an empty fireplace. "Greer and I ought to start for Weymouth."

"But..."

"It's late." Bob interrupted his wife brusquely. "We mustn't keep you."

"Thanks for everything, Lauren," Greer said awkwardly. "Dinner was lovely, and so were the grounds."

"Yes, Lauren. Thanks." Andrew echoed.

His blank expression confused Greer. She was whisked into her jacket and to the car with a sensation of being born along on a flash flood. Her last impressions of the Wilsons' house were of the open front door and Lauren's troubled face. Bob didn't join in the hasty goodbyes.

As the car door slammed, Lauren's faint, "I'll call you about lunch," faded away. Greer lifted a hand in acknowledgment but couldn't tell if it had been seen.

"Bloody rain again," was all Andrew said when he started the Mini and spun the steering wheel with a flattened palm. He didn't speak again while they jolted over the bridge and into the lane.

At first only a few large drops splattered the windshield, but soon the rain became torrential. Clouds obscured the moon. Thick darkness closed them inside the car with a sound like a million spoons hitting tin. Constant rocking of the tires into water-filled ruts sprayed high wings of mud.

She wasn't afraid—or upset. Greer assessed her feelings calmly and decided she was angry. Damn angry. A few more minutes and it would choke her. What happened back there? How could anyone dare to suggest Andrew was gay? And Andrew. Why did he sweep her from the Wilsons' house without clearing the air—or attempting to? And all he could say to her when they were alone was something inane about the weather. Okay, if he dropped her off in Weymouth without another word it would be just as well. A lot of explanations would be saved all around.

"You heard most of what was said, didn't you?"

Greer jumped and looked at Andrew. "Yes," she said feeling the blood drain from her face.

"Shocking I expect."

"Yes. I—"

"You don't have to say anything else." He cut her off. The faint glow from the dash etched deeper lines beside his eyes and mouth.

What on earth did he mean? "I want to say something else," Greer insisted. "I want to say a lot of things."

"I bet," Andrew said sarcastically. "How did it feel to hear yourself described as a convenient cover for a homosexual? If you can stand being with me, I'll get you home as quickly as this rotten squall will allow."

Anger turned to rage. Cheeks that had felt clammy, blazed. "Are you saying you think I believed Bob's crap?"

"It wasn't his," Andrew said harshly. "The esteemed Winston Coover is responsible for my new classification. If it is new. There's always a possibility my true colors are simply being exposed. Is that what you think, Greer?"

Greer could not believe her ears.

"How dare you?" she said in a low dangerous voice. "What kind of fool do you think I am? I know what you are, Andrew. You're gentle and sympathetic, because you can afford to be. You don't have to prove anything—to anyone." Her throat closed painfully and she smothered a cough. "I resent your implications. No one would believe such garbage, and even if you thought someone might, I should be about the last candidate."

Greer's voiced echoed in the long silence that followed. Just as she wondered what in the world Andrew must be thinking, he spoke.

"Thanks for the vote of confidence. It's nice of you."

Nice! Greer crossed her arms and went limp against the seat. She rolled her head toward the door, feeling the surge of adrenaline that had fueled her outburst ebb away. He didn't trust her. Instead of gratitude for the perfect excuse to exit from Andrew's life, she ached for his confidence.

Brambles scraped the windows. The lane was a black canyon augered by the car's yellow headlights.

"Greer," Andrew said quietly when they turned west.

She didn't look at him. "Yes."

"Would you come back to Ringstead with me? I think I need coffee—or a stiff drink. It would be good to have you with me. I'll understand if you don't want to."

She should end it now if she were smart.

"I'd love to," she answered. *Oh, Beckett.*

They didn't speak while Andrew negotiated the remaining rough terrain to Ringstead Hall's open gates and the tunnel of yews. Greer could feel their separate minds racing. She should have asked him to take her home, but his loneliness and hurt were so compelling they became her own. He needed her.

"We'll use the sitting room," he said, trying to restore normal conversation. "It's warmer. I don't have a kitchen upstairs so we'll have to brave the old one in the basement. You may even find it interesting."

He spoke in a rush, as if greatly relieved. Andrew hadn't wanted to be alone tonight, and she'd saved him from that for a while. "I saw the kitchen when I first visited the house," Greer said, following his lead. "It's super. What a kick to be there without fifty 'oohing and aahing' tourists. Do we have to light the wood range to boil water?"

Andrew laughed. "The microwave is carefully hidden on tour days. And I do have a percolator." He drove to the side entrance. "Wait for me to help you. It'll be muddy."

Without giving her time to protest, Andrew came around and scooped her into his arms. She vaguely heard his feet squelching in the mud. The feel of him, the scent, obliterated all other impressions until he set her down on the stone tiles inside the door.

"There. I wouldn't want you to ruin those tantalizing shoes," he teased.

He smiled into her upturned face and she saw him swallow, hard. There was nothing abnormal about Andrew Monthaven's instincts—or her own apparently. And this was all becoming more dangerous than she could handle.

"Lead me to the kitchen," she said with false lightness.

Surrounded by almost poignant evidence of what the great house had once been, Greer temporarily forgot Andrew and herself. He rummaged for the percolator, started coffee and began to assemble mugs on a tray.

Greer scraped a chair away from a scrubbed wooden table in the middle of the room and sat down. Banks of iron pots hung above the range and in an alcove used to store wood. Double sinks stood on exposed legs against one whitewashed wall, and she could see another sink in a small sunken room to the right. The scullery, she supposed.

Glass-fronted cabinets filled with china and utensils covered the walls. Counter tops were also of scrubbed wood, worn thin at the edges by years of use. Greer had a mental image of rotund women in floppy white caps and long cotton dresses laboring at their tasks. A meal appropriate for the formal dining room she'd seen on the tour must have taken many hands in the making.

"Hungry?"

Startled from her reverie, Greer looked at Andrew. "Oh, no," she said. "Not at all. But don't let me stop you from having something."

"I don't feel like anything, either. Coffee's ready if you are." Leaning against the counter and looking at her speculatively, he added, "You were miles away just now, weren't you."

She laughed self-consciously. "Years away would be more accurate. I was imagining this kitchen as it must have been during a big party when the whole house was in use."

"Most of that was over by my time," Andrew said without evident rancor. "Good thing, too. A lot of conspicuous consumption and empty posturing in many cases. I'm sure it would be fascinating to observe, but there's no excuse for that kind of waste anymore— never was really." Indicating for her to follow, he led the way out of the kitchen.

In Andrew's wing, they passed his study and entered a small room where pale umber walls were embossed with molded loops of laurel leaves beneath a carved plaster ceiling. He placed the tray on a mahogany writing table and went to set a match to the logs in an elaborate black fireplace.

Folding shutters stood open at a recessed casement where plump

pillows surrounded an enticing window seat. The drapes were floral
in shades of gold, dark blue and garnet, and when the fire caught,
rosy shadows leaped around the walls and over the well-worn furnishings.

"There." Andrew announced. "Choose your spot and I'll pour
the coffee. I'm going to put a shot of whiskey in mine. How about
you?"

"Fine." She turned toward an overstuffed couch and caught
sight of another room through double doors. A wide bed with a
simple cream bedspread. A chest of drawers. Oil paintings on the
walls. And books—everywhere. Andrew's bedroom. She swallowed hard and headed for the window seat.

He came to sit beside her. "This is my favorite place," he confided. "My window on the world. When I was a kid I came here
at any excuse. To think. To hide when I didn't want to be found.
To feel sorry for myself."

When he passed her a mug, their fingers brushed and she noticed
how cold his hands were despite the warm room. He was upset,
even if it didn't show. Greer craned her neck to peer out the leaded
glass windows. Treetops and outbuildings were hazy shapes below.
In daylight there must be a clear view of the ocean.

"I like it here, too. If I ever need to hide, I'll know where to
come," she said lightly.

"And I'll know just where to find you." His absent laugh told
Greer he was preoccupied.

Would he share his problems with her? Greer clenched her fists.
She yearned to touch him, to smooth the furrows between his
brows. He rested one ankle on his knee and leaned forward. Space
and silence gaped between them although only inches separated
their bodies.

"It might make it easier if you talked about what's happening
to you, Andrew," she said very softly. She held her breath, watching his shoulders hunch.

Andrew took a slow swallow of coffee, then held the mug up to
watch steam rise. "If I could talk to anyone it would be you. But
this stinks, Greer. You don't want any part of it," he answered
gruffly.

Impulsively she rubbed his back with long rhythmic strokes. "I do. I might even be able to help. Sometimes another point of view changes the perspective. When I go inside myself with a problem, it seems to swell until I can't think straight."

His eyes closed and she massaged the back of his neck. The vibrant dark hair was soft between her fingers. "You could try sharing whatever's going on," she repeated. The heavy heat was spreading through her limbs again. A slight move and she could lie against him, rest her cheek on his shoulder. She clamped her teeth together.

"I don't know where to start."

"You're asking for an investigation into that Dr. Coover's treatment of a patient, right?"

"Michael Drake was the patient. My patient. He was fifteen and he died because Coover couldn't be bothered to make a ten-minute drive and examine him."

Lithe muscle became rock hard under her hand. "Would the boy have lived for sure if he'd been seen earlier?" she wondered.

"You sure know the right questions to ask," Andrew said as he straightened. "Yes. As far as I'm concerned there was no excuse for what happened. And I intend to prove it."

"That's why people are trying to throw you off by threatening you with lies?"

"Winston Coover is the only one at the bottom of this attack on my reputation. He's the one who stands to lose if he can't find a way to stop me. So far he's got all the proper people in his pocket, but he's running scared. He knows I'm right and that I can probably prove it. His only hope is to head me off before there can ever be a hearing."

"He wanted to talk to you yesterday," Greer reminded him. "He said so. Have you confronted him with what Bob told you?"

He reached for her wrist and held it while he leaned against the cushions. "I don't have to confront him yet. That'll come later."

"If he's doing or saying what you think, it's blackmail. Winston Coover didn't seem the type to go in for blackmail and I don't see why you accept someone else's word for it that he is. All this might be..."

"By someone else, do you mean Bob Wilson?" Andrew's grip on her wrist tightened.

He was going to defend Bob, despite what she'd overheard. Suddenly, she was totally irritated. "Yes, I mean Bob Wilson," she said sharply. "If he were any kind of a friend he wouldn't allow things like that to be said about you. He was a human bulldozer tonight."

"I wouldn't say anymore, Greer," Andrew warned her. "Bob's been my friend as long as I can remember. He's worried about what may happen to me, that's all."

"You're blind, Andrew Monthaven," Greer insisted. "He may be your friend. But what he said to you this evening was indefensible. I could tell he knew your arguments were valid, but he wouldn't agree to support you." She slammed her mug on a small table and stood. Andrew's hold on her wrist was a vise now.

"Stop it," he demanded, pulling her close to his thigh. "You don't know what you're talking about."

Greer's breath came in little gasps. "I know what I heard. When he made that crack about me, he meant it. He was telling you that my sudden appearance on the scene wouldn't change anyone's opinion of your character—including his. He sounded as if he believed the stories about you, no matter who started them." Dammit, she was going to cry. "It makes me so angry."

With a jerk, Andrew brought her beside him. For a moment, the air sizzled around them. Without warning, his anger evaporated like scattering thunderclouds, to be replaced by compassion. Greer knew he had seen the tears in her eyes. "Shh. Shh. You're getting too upset," he said gently. "You'll make yourself ill."

"Don't patronize me," she answered. "I'm not an invalid."

"I didn't say you were." He trailed the back of one finger down her cheek.

"But you won't let me do anything for you and I want to. You helped me once—remember? I was alone and you tried to make it easier. Then I threw it back in your face and it must have hurt you. I'm sorry I did that. I've never stopped being sorry."

Andrew stroked her hair, the side of her face. "It's okay. Really. I just don't want you to misunderstand Bob. He almost lived here when he was a boy. He's like the brother I never had. And you're wrong when you say he believes the rumors that are circulating. His attack was intended to shock me out of doing something he thinks could spell my professional ruin. Bob cares about me. Accept that.''

''He'd better care about you,'' Greer said threateningly. ''A lot. Or I'll find a way to make him wish he did.''

Andrew moved swiftly, cupping her face to bring it within an inch of his own. ''Oh, my darling, darling lady.'' His eyes deeply probed her own before their lips met.

The kiss was different from those on the beach. He covered her mouth with barely restrained wildness that sent an electric thrill to her core. Nuzzling her head, he lifted her chin and pressed his lips into the hollow of her throat, from where he laid a swift map of kisses over her jaw, the soft skin in front of her ear, her temple and closed eyes. The edges of her mind became fuzzy, the center a spinning whirl of color. She slid her arms around him, felt the staccato rhythm of his heart answer her own. Would it be so wrong to just be with him; to take what he offered and give all she could in return? She knew the answer had already been decided. What she didn't know was if this was the right time and place.

Slowly, slowly, Andrew thought—don't rush her. He kissed her lashes, then smoothed his thumbs over her cheekbones. She cared about him. Her earlier defensive barrage and the way she responded to him physically proved that. But there was something else, natural shyness, perhaps. In time he'd figure it out.

''Let's sit on the couch,'' he said as he took her hand, pretending not to notice how she'd stiffened. ''We can see the fire better from there.''

When they were seated, he continued to hold her hand, but she put several inches between them and stared fixedly ahead. What was she afraid of? ''Would you like more coffee?'' The first mug was barely touched but he couldn't think of anything else to say.

''No, thank you,'' she answered politely. ''I should probably be thinking about leaving.''

''Not yet, Greer.'' He couldn't let her go yet. ''We have a lot of things to talk about. There may never be a better time or place.''

"You said you didn't want any more discussions," she hedged.

"About my current problems. It's all been said. But we've carefully avoided what happened to you, and to me, two years ago. I can feel it growing with every minute we avoid the subject."

"Me, too," she said, glancing at him. "When I decided to come back to England, one of the promises I made myself was to thank you—and to apologize for the way I treated you."

What would she do if she knew how badly he wanted her? "You already did, although there was no need. I understood perfectly at the time. But—Greer, I—" He must say it, for both of them. "I've never felt so helpless as I did that night. Guilty, too. I should have been able to save Colleen. You can't know how that haunts me. I don't blame you for hating me then—but I couldn't take it if you still did."

"I don't," she whispered. "Even when it happened, I wasn't really blaming you. Everything was too much. Losing Colin was like losing my heart. As long as Colleen was alive I hung on to her and tried to concentrate on our future. Then she was taken away, too, and you were the most convenient focus for all the anger and helplessness I felt. But it's gone now, Andrew. You must feel that."

She didn't draw away when he kissed the corner of her mouth. Sweet. The taste and scent of her tightened every muscle in his body. "I do," he assured her. "But I needed to hear you say it."

Greer turned to him and cautiously slid her arms around his neck.

"Have you ever considered that you may care too much about everyone else's troubles?" she said softly.

The sensation of her fingers in his hair made his insides shudder. "It has occurred to me," he admitted, smiling against her cheek. "Unfortunately I'm getting a bit old to change." Greer nipped his ear playfully and he knew he had to have more of her.

When he undid her vest buttons she sighed and arched her back slightly. Through the smooth silk shirt, he cupped her breast and felt the nipple crest. She found his mouth and strained against him, pitting her slight weight against his own bulk. His gut was afire. He tried to relax, allowed her to push him against the couch and open his mouth with her lips and tongue. Every instinct pressured him to respond as he wanted, to make love to her in all the ways he'd imagined for so long. A struggling speck of logic warned him that she might not be as ready as her beautiful body suggested.

Carefully he circled her sleek ribs beneath her shirt. "I love the way you feel," he murmured. "So soft." He wanted them both naked and fused together. The thought sent heat darting across his skin.

She pulled away and shed her vest and blouse. Andrew swallowed around a lump in his throat. *Oh, God.* Without looking at his face she tugged his sweater up and bent to kiss the sensitive flesh above his belt. Was the timing right? Every move she made said yes. But the expression on her face, the way she avoided meeting his eyes—She could be forcing herself, trying to prove something to them both.

Another second and he'd lose control. With her head bent, her lips pressed repeatedly to a hundred fiery spots on his chest and belly, her small body was a living aphrodisiac. Instead of a bra, she wore only a camisole of some gauzy pale blue stuff. It fell from the tops of her breasts, revealing thrusting nipples.

"Sweetheart, sweetheart," he whispered, pushing her gently away to pull the sweater over his head. "Now you." First he soothed her by stroking her soft flesh, molding her with his hands until she looked directly into his eyes. Then he lifted the camisole and she raised her arms for him to take it all the way off.

Gazing at the beauty before him, he felt whatever he said would be inadequate. But he had to try. "You're perfect. Absolutely perfect," he managed.

Her slacks fastened in front. Andrew eased the button free and slid the zipper down. Tiny waist but flaring hips.

She wrapped her arms around him so suddenly, so fiercely, he grabbed the couch to steady them. "Greer," he murmured into her hair. "Are you okay, my love?" He could hear the thud of his heart, feel hers. She didn't answer, only held on more tightly.

"What is it? Has something frightened you?" *Good God, she was petrified of actually making love.* "Please say something to me. Whatever's wrong, we can work it out."

"No." The word was muffled against his shoulder and the moisture on his skin told him she was crying. "I'm not the same as I was," she said brokenly.

"None of us is." Did she mean because she'd already been married? It couldn't be that.

"You don't understand," she insisted.

He didn't. But he would, if it took forever. "I will," he promised. "We'll understand each other perfectly if we just let it happen."

"There are things you don't know about me."

"We both have a lot to learn about each other."

Trembling overtook her and he crossed his arms over her back. There hadn't been another man since Colin Beckett. Andrew lifted his face, feeling first bemused at how long it had taken him to realize the truth, then incredibly, foolishly happy. Greer hadn't made love since her husband died and she was probably fighting two demons: loyalty she still held for him and insecurity about her ability to fully respond to another man.

"Hey," he said softly. He found her chin and raised her head. "You aren't ready for this, are you?"

Tears streaked her cheeks. She shook her head and he placed a soft kiss on her trembling lips.

"I'm not, either." If he wasn't careful, the happiness would show in his eyes. "And it's too cold for nudist activities," he said with an exaggerated shudder. "But don't get dressed. I'll find us a couple of robes and build up the fire."

A puzzled frown creased her brow. "Andrew. Aren't you angry with me? And shouldn't you drive me home?"

He tried not to look at her breasts, but failed. "I couldn't be angry with you, darling. I'll be right back."

The camisole was in place when he returned, but the blouse and vest had been neatly folded on top of his sweater. "Here. It'll wrap around three times but at least you'll be cozy." He helped her into a gray robe, turned her to face him and secured the belt. "Walk slowly, kid, or you'll fall over the hem."

"I must look like Sweetpea in 'Popeye.'" She laughed and Andrew felt as if the air became softer.

"Much more appealing. The coffee should still be lukewarm at least. Or would you like some brandy.'' He shrugged into his own robe and threw another log on the fire.

"Nothing—or yes. A little brandy does sound good.'' Her eyelashes were spiky from crying.

Somehow he was going to bring it off. His world had been steadily turned upside down in the past few weeks. But he wasn't going to lose this woman again. Just having her with him as often as possible would be enough until she could accept his lovemaking and return it fully.

He poured brandy into two goblets and came to kneel at Greer's feet where she sat on the couch. She took a glass and smiled at him over the rim. "To you, Andrew. You're unique.''

"Thank you. And to you.'' Clinking their glasses, they both sipped the golden liquor.

"It must be very late,'' Greer said at last. "I'm not wearing a watch.''

"Very, very late,'' he agreed.

He waited, then heard her clear her throat quietly. "I don't like asking you to go out again, but...''

"Then don't.''

Her eyes darkened and he moved to sit beside her. "Stay with me tonight. Lie in my arms, nothing more. I just want you with me. Will you stay?'' He was pleading but it didn't matter.

She tipped her head. "I never meant to tease you, Andrew. Frustrating a man is a new experience for me, and I don't want you to go through it again. You're wonderful.'' Her mouth came together tremulously for an instant. "But you're also human and I can't do this to you. You matter too much to me.''

It was happening. He almost whooped. "Come with me, lady,'' he said firmly. "You and I are going to help each other make it through this night. Sex isn't the only thing a man needs from the woman he cares for.''

Greer let Andrew lead her. Instinct told her she was totally safe with him. She used the toothbrush he found for her and stripped off her slacks and hose in the bathroom before swathing herself in the robe once more.

When they lay side by side beneath the quilt he reached for her hand and laced their fingers together. "Want to talk or just sleep?"

"Talk," she said, turning her face to his. "Do you know I'm English, too?"

He lifted his head. "You must have had too much brandy. What do you mean?"

She told him about her adoption out of a foster home in Weymouth, and about Ruby Timmons and Kurt. After minutes of totally one-sided talk she stopped awkwardly and tried to read his expression in the darkness. "So you see, I'm English, as well, in a way. And maybe I'm going to find my biological family. What do you think?" *Did he know how much his answer mattered to her?*

"That it's wonderful." He leaned to plant a kiss on her mouth. "Will you let me help track down your people?"

Greer's stomach felt odd and quivery. She didn't remember so much happiness since before Colin died. And she realized it without wanting to cry.

"I'd like that," she responded eagerly. "Ever since this afternoon I've been waiting to tell you. Yesterday, at the church, I was still too muddled to talk about it."

Andrew pulled her head into the hollow of his shoulder. "When I saw you sitting in the children's corner, I thought of Colleen. It brought back the day I went to her funeral."

A lengthy pause followed as the implications sank in.

"You—Thank you," Greer whispered as she rolled against his side and buried her face. "I wish I'd known. It always bothered me that no one was there."

"I couldn't bring myself to come and tell you afterward," he said, stroking her hair.

"No. And I don't blame you after the way I behaved. I don't suppose you know anything about the little white angel on the grave or the plants?"

"Don't suppose so."

"You had them put there. I know you did."

He rubbed his chin against her forehead. "It must be at least four. Can you sleep? I think I can as long as you're with me."

"Mmm." She snuggled closer, wrapping an arm around his

waist. Tears burned her eyes and throat but she didn't want him to know.

Andrew fell silent and soon she heard his regular breathing and felt the steady rise and fall of his chest beneath her ear. Cautiously she pushed up on an elbow until she could see his face. Faint light from the sitting-room fire penetrated the open doors and threw shadows across his features. She could see his dark, arched brows, the straight nose and high cheekbones—and the clear outline of his mouth. The urge to kiss him while he slept almost overpowered her. Moving smoothly, she curled against him once more.

She had come close to telling him about her sterility. Fate had caused him to interrupt and misunderstand, she was certain of it. Earlier, Andrew admitted he felt guilty over Colleen's death. Not his fault, anymore than Michael Drake's death was, but still the man berated himself. Feeling responsible was part of his makeup. A dear but potentially destructive part. If she told him of the hysterectomy he was likely to feel more guilt. Colleen had been the only child she would ever have. After what happened at the Wilsons', Greer was almost glad she hadn't managed to get her message across. Andrew had suffered enough for one night.

They had something incredible together. Perhaps he could help her through her reservations. As she'd told him, he was special. Lots of people found happiness when everything wasn't as perfect as they might have wished. But before her relationship with Andrew went any further, he must know about the surgery. He would have to come to terms with what she told him and decide if he still felt the same about her.

Greer's eyelids drooped. Slender gray lines painted the wall on each side of the drapes. Dawn. Night's end and another day's beginning.

CHAPTER THIRTEEN

HER NOSE TICKLED. Greer rubbed it with the back of a hand and turned over. She burrowed into the pillows, and smelled—Andrew's after-shave. *Andrew.* She sat up, pulling the quilt close to her neck and looked around. An old-fashioned travel alarm on a bedside table ticked loudly. Ten-ten. He must have left for the hospital. No, he wouldn't. She'd have no way of getting anywhere without him unless she walked.

"Morning, sleepyhead," Andrew greeted her as he scuffed barefoot into the room. He was wearing one towel draped around his waist while he dried her hair with another. "Sun's shining. It's going to be a beautiful day. But we already knew that, didn't we?" he added, giving her one of his devastating smiles.

"I guess so." Greer leaned back, wondering what to do next. She felt like taking a shower, too, even in Andrew's intimidating bathroom, but the idea of getting out of bed in front of him made her uncomfortable.

He obviously didn't share her reservations. He continued to vigorously towel his muscular shoulders and chest, moving to where the dark hair she remembered so well arrowed to a diminishing line at his navel.

"I'll go down and start breakfast while you get dressed," he offered. "Have you adjusted to English fare in the morning, or do you prefer something different? I don't think I can manage those pancakes you eat at home."

"I've converted," she said, laughing. "My ancestry is showing. I've got a thing for bacon and eggs—unless it's too much trouble," she finished hurriedly.

"Nothing's too much trouble." His hand went to his waist.

She managed to avert her eyes a second before the tug which would leave him naked. Greer studied a large landscape above the fireplace similar to the one in Andrew's sitting room. The painted shapes kept blurring together. Listening to the snap of fabric, a zipper, the swish of a belt passing through loops, was slow torture.

"You can look now," he said, unable to conceal his amusement.

"I wasn't..." She turned and caught the devilish glint in his eyes. "You enjoy making fun of me, don't you?"

"Ah, my dear," he said, approaching the bed with mock stealth. "You're so much fun to make fun of." His kiss was quick, but thorough before he left without a backward glance.

Greer pressed her fingers to her mouth. She still felt the burning imprint of his lips.

Half an hour later, her skin tingling from a lukewarm shower, she trotted downstairs in bare feet. Her damp hair curled mutinously and wet the shoulders of her vest and shirt. Applying lipstick to an otherwise clean-scrubbed face had seemed a waste of time. Andrew was about to see her as she really was. She hesitated, watching the sun send spiraling prisms through gem-colored stained glass above the front doors. When he'd first seen her she probably looked awful, frightening, yet it hadn't discouraged him. Her heart flipped. Andrew must have felt something for her even then or he wouldn't have spent so many off-duty hours on the surgical unit.

The last flight of steps to the basement was stone. Cold made her lift each foot quickly and she almost fell through the kitchen door at the bottom. Andrew, red-faced from standing over the crackling stove, turned with an iron skillet in one hand. He watched her hop to a chair and plop down.

"That'll teach you," he said, chuckling. "You could at least have borrowed a pair of my socks. Ouch!" The pan clattered on top of the range while he examined his palm.

Greer tried not to laugh. "Are you burned?" she inquired sweetly. "You could at least have used a pot holder."

Andrew glared at her, then went to run cold water on his skin. "I suppose you think that's funny, you sadist."

"Let me see what you've done," she said, trying to make amends. She walked to his side and looked at the reddened area. "Should I get something to put on it? Butter, maybe?"

"Oh my God," he said theatrically. "Preserve me from old

wives' tales.'' He circled her shoulders with one arm and brought his face close to hers. "I shall have to give you a crash course in basic first aid. Cold, my dear. Cold for burns. Ice if possible, otherwise water. Never, never any form of grease. It has a similar result to frying meat—sizzle, sizzle.'' His raised eyebrows made her mouth twitch.

"I'll remember that, doctor. And speaking of sizzle, sizzle, breakfast smells well-done.''

"Hell...'' Andrew swore, leaping for the stove.

They both swung around at the same moment as an elderly man in shirtsleeves, tie and pin-striped vest and slacks, came into the kitchen. "It's all right, sir.'' He crossed quickly to remove the smoking pan. "I've got it.''

"Thanks, Gibbs.'' Andrew said calmly, repositioning his arm across Greer's back. "I want you to meet Greer Beckett. Greer, this is John Gibbs, my forever friend, adviser and housekeeper. He could say—quite correctly—that he changed my diapers. Only he's too polite.''

Greer contained her surprise. She never remembered meeting a male housekeeper—or a housekeeper at all come to that. The man was taller than Andrew and cadaverously thin. His beaked nose and bushy white brows gave him a scholarly appearance. "How do you do, miss,'' he said with a movement around his wide mouth that was probably a smile, she decided. "Dr. Monthaven, sir—if you'd told me you were expecting a breakfast guest I'd have seen to this for you.''

While he spoke to Andrew, he looked at Greer with soft dark brown eyes.

She nodded and pressed her palms together.

"Nonsense, Gibbs. You've got more than enough to do and I like messing around in the kitchen, as you know.''

Gibbs opened his mouth, then shut it again firmly. Greer had a hunch he had been about to express surprise at Andrew's announcement. Again the deep-set eyes fastened on her face. John Gibbs was assessing her, but he seemed puzzled about something. *You're too sensitive, Greer,* she thought. Any strange woman in his boss's house—one who had obviously spent the night—was bound to raise interest.

She returned to her chair at the table. "You've known Andrew for a long time, Mr. Gibbs?" It seemed essential to say something, anything.

"Since he was born, miss." This accent was different from Andrew's. Less clipped, the *a*'s drawn out. Pleasant. She'd heard it wherever she went in Dorset.

While Gibbs deposited the blackened pan in the sink, Andrew took another and began cracking eggs against its side.

"Well, sir," Gibbs said. "If you're sure you can manage here, I'd better get to the packing. How many nights did you say you'd be gone?"

"Ah," Andrew glanced up, running a wrist over his brow. "Four. I'll be back on Wednesday afternoon."

The housekeeper gave Greer a last, penetrating stare and left. He didn't dislike her, she was almost sure—It wasn't important. But the prospect of Andrew being away for several days was. "You didn't mention that you were leaving," she said a little sharply. Immediately, she wished she hadn't spoken. What he did was none of her business.

"I would have," he replied easily, seeming not to have noticed her tone of voice. "We were caught up with so many other things, I forgot until Gibbs mentioned it. I'm giving a lecture series up north. Four days, four cities. It'll be grueling, but it's always worth the effort." He set two plates on the table and covered her folded hands. "I don't want to go, Greer. Not now."

So, stay, stay. "You'll soon be back." Did she sound convincingly cheerful? "And I have some work to get done, too. Maybe I'll have more news when I see you again."

"If I get back to my hotel in time each evening, I'll call."

ELEVEN WHITE LACE antimacassars. Greer counted the handmade cloths protecting Mrs. Findlay's lounge furniture for the third time. Wednesday morning. Andrew was due back in Dorset this afternoon and she hadn't heard a word from him.

Trusting innocent. Colin had called her that many times, and just as often his eyes and lips told her he loved her lack of sophistication. Apparently Andrew Monthaven hadn't felt the same way. He wanted, and needed, a normal woman with normal reactions. Not a shrinking violet who couldn't face consummating a relationship with the most desirable man ever likely to come her way. Damn. And she'd actually expected him to waste his time and money on long-distance telephone calls. But he'd said he would.

She tucked her feet beneath her on the couch and stared through the window at the spire of St. John's. The church partially obscured Greer's view of the Georgian buildings that fronted the ocean. When she craned her neck, Weymouth Bay was just visible to the west.

Her days since Friday had been busy. Even Sunday, when she visited the artist whose paintings dotted the walls at Bumble's tea shop. The man had agreed to sell her a small selection of his work immediately and supply more if it sold well in Seattle.

After battling with insecurity Greer had taken a train to Southampton the previous day and visited the Seamen's Union. And now she was really no further ahead than when she left the Reverend Colyer in Chaldon Herring. Kurt Timmons spent ten years at sea, from the age of sixteen, until he was twenty-six. His last voyage had been to South Africa, via the Canary Islands. The trail ended when he signed off in Southampton after the return journey. There was no mention in the Union records of his present whereabouts.

At the sound of the door opening Greer turned to see the man who, according to Mrs. Findlay, was "doing a paper on Roman stuff." The woman always referred to him in this way, as if she didn't know his name. He bobbed his head to push his glasses up and immediately dropped all but one of a pile of books he carried. "Sorry," he mumbled as his pale face flushed. "Didn't know anyone was here."

Greer went to help him retrieve the heavy volumes. "I was just leaving. Where shall I put these?"

"On the floor by the couch—if you don't mind."

She did as he asked and escaped the dusty room. Shy man. He plainly preferred Roman artifacts and books about them to people. Which might not be such an unsound idea.

In the hall she eyed the black pay phone. The contraption was positioned so that any conversation was bound to echo through the house like part of a theatrical production. Greer checked her watch. Casey should be at home now. It would be late, but she never went to bed early. Suddenly Greer needed desperately to speak to her sister. Finding enough coins was out of the question. The cost would have to be reversed.

Without giving herself time to reconsider, she placed the call, listening to the almost instant sound of lines popping open halfway around the world. Casey's voice was clear and calm when she answered, then excited when the operator asked if she'd accept the charges.

"Greer! Is that you?" she shouted.

Greer smiled, feeling happy and intensely lonely at the same time. "The same, sis. Thought I'd make sure you were behaving. How are things going?"

"Terrific," Casey enthused. "How are things going with you? Made any headway? Met a stupendously wealthy baron to marry, maybe?"

Same old Casey. "Loads of new ideas for the shop," Greer began. "They don't have too many barons in England. And I appear to have arrived at a dead end with the Timmons family. Things started to move, but my lead petered out yesterday, so I feel a bit glum."

There was a short silence.

"You still there, Case?"

"Listen to me, Greer," Casey responded. "Remember what dad used to say about setbacks being temporary pauses meant for catching your breath?"

"I remember."

"Right. This is one of those. Take a few deep ones and get back out there. If you made a start, then the answer's around somewhere. Start at the beginning and work through again," she said logically.

Irrepressible. Greer grinned wryly, wishing she had half her sister's optimism. "Yes, ma'am. But I can't stay away indefinitely. Don't you miss me?"

Another silence.

"Casey Wyatt. What's with you?" Greer demanded to know. "You're supposed to say you're pining away without your big sister."

"Of course I miss you," Casey said sincerely, but there was obviously something else on her mind. "Greer, something's happened—something wonderful. I don't know what you're going to think, but I've fallen madly in love and—"

"You've what?" Greer shouted. "Good grief. Who is he? Should I come right home?" Greer's mind turned upside down. *"Who is he?"*

"Do everything you set out to do in England, then I'll tell you," Casey insisted.

"Tell me *now*. I can't stand the suspense..." Suddenly, Greer was struck with a horrible thought. "Case, you wouldn't get married without me there, would you?" she asked nervously.

Casey's laughter shot across the wires. "No way. We're not tying the knot until June. I want the whole works. White dress, church, reception and...well, anyway, he says that's the way it's going to be. And I need you to help with everything—and give me away."

"Ooh, Case," Greer fumed. "You always were a tedious little pest. You're not going to tell me, are you?"

"No."

"Then I'm coming home."

"Greer." Casey's tone became serious. "Please don't until you've reconciled everything. When you do get back, we'll have a wonderful time. Okay?"

"I don't know—" She threaded the cord through her fingers. "Well, okay. But let me know if you decide to do anything rash."

"I will. Too bad you haven't found a baron though—would have done you good."

Greer stared at the phone for a long time after she hung up. She made a mental catalog of the men Casey knew and couldn't think of a likely marriage candidate.

It was more important than ever to finish what she'd set out to do and get home quickly. *Start from the beginning*, Casey had suggested. That's what Greer would do. This afternoon she'd return to Ferndale and ask more questions.

Greer practically jumped out of her skin when the phone rang. She glanced around, but Mrs. Findlay's door remained shut. Another ring came and she hesitantly lifted the receiver. "Hello," she said quietly.

"Greer?" Andrew's deep voice was unmistakable. "Thank goodness you answered. I was afraid I'd get Mrs. whatever her name is or one of the other boarders. How are you?"

Her brain blanked for an instant.

"Is something wrong?" he asked urgently.

"No." The word came out too loudly. "No, everything's just fine. How are you? How was the trip?" *And why didn't you call me?*

"Exhausting. I got back so late each night I didn't dare phone you. I had visions of waking the whole boardinghouse. Have dinner with me tonight—please. There're one or two things I've got to take care of this afternoon, then I could pick you up. Will you come?"

Will I come? "Yes. I'm going to take another run into Ferndale. I could be ready by seven," she offered.

The pause was slight, but it was there. "Greer, I've loathed the past four days. Sweetheart..."

She waited.

"I hate to wait until seven," he said, "but I'll see you then."

After Greer replaced the receiver, she covered her face with both hands.

Sweetheart.

"WHY ARE YOU looking at me like that?" Greer asked.

Andrew rested his chin on his fist. "I was trying to decide how I feel about the new hairdo."

Greer sipped her white wine. "Makes me look more sophisticated when I put it up," she said airly.

"Who says?"

"Me."

He grinned and wound a red curl around his index finger. "Then it must be true. And that dress is stunning," he added.

"Thank you." She toyed with the stem of her glass. Thank goodness he'd never know the classic Charmeuse outfit had been hastily bought during a change of buses in Dorchester only a few hours earlier. Or that she'd felt slightly dizzy when she converted the price-tag figure from pounds to dollars. "A little black nothing."

They both laughed. Andrew had brought her to an old pub a few miles outside Weymouth. The Elm Tree was hidden away among a warren of lanes and scattered cottages.

Their circular table and spindle-backed chairs were near a fire that glowed beneath a copper-trimmed hood. Pewter mugs and glittering horse brasses crowded a heavy oak mantelpiece, and Greer could have stood upright in the stone fireplace alcove. She breathed in the ambience. Occasional bursts of laughter punctuated a subdued hum of conversation. The place was perfect, she decided, unforgettable.

"Good," Andrew said, as the waitress approached the table. "Food. I didn't have time for lunch. How about you?"

Greer studied the huge slab of game pie the woman set in front of her. A slice of egg had been baked in the center and the flakey crust was golden brown. "I wish I hadn't eaten lunch," she said regretfully. "This looks marvelous."

"It is. Save room for a rum baba."

She raised her brows.

"Dessert. You'll see. Now, what else has happened since Friday?"

In the car she'd explained her disappointment in Southampton. But she'd insisted on waiting to share her latest news.

A bubble of nervous excitement rose in her throat. "You're not going to believe this," she said.

"Try me." Andrew watched her unblinkingly over the rim of his whiskey glass.

Greer colored. He made it difficult to concentrate. "I went to Ferndale this afternoon. I told you I was going to. My grandparents lived in a place called Marsh Cottage in Kelloway Lane. Something Casey—I spoke to her on the phone this morning—something she said made me decide to try retracing all my steps. Anyway, I went back there.''

"Kelloway Lane?'' He frowned. "That's where...''

"I know,'' Greer interrupted. She held his wrist. "John Gibbs lives there. Oh, Andrew. He looked at me so strangely in your house, I wondered if he liked me. I couldn't believe it when I walked all the way to the end of the row of cottages and saw him working in his garden.''

"I'll be damned,'' Andrew said, squeezing her hand. "Of course. Why didn't I think of Gibbs? But he's only lived in Ferndale eight or nine years. He used to have quarters at Ringstead until a couple of years after my father died.''

"I know, I know.'' Her hand was surrounded by both of Andrew's now. "But as soon as he saw me outside his fence he looked as if he'd had a visitation. It was funny. He's the nicest man,'' she confirmed.

"The best.'' He played his lips along her fingertips, always gazing into her eyes.

Greer tried to ignore a heated sensation in her thighs. "He said 'ahh' about three times and kept nodding. Then he asked me in and I sat on a step while he finished pruning back his roses. Andrew, Kurt was there a couple of years ago. *Kurt.*''

"Good Lord,'' he whispered. "Your brother.''

"Yes. Mr. Gibbs said a man who reminded him of me came by asking questions about a family who used to live in Ferndale. As soon as I mentioned Timmons, he remembered that had been the man's last name and the name of the people he was looking for. Kurt didn't ring a bell. But when I suggested Rusty, he was sure he recognized it. And do you know what else?''

Andrew inclined his head and turned her hand to kiss the palm.

She took a shaky swallow of wine. "If this is my Rusty Timmons, and I'm sure it is, he could be a hotel keeper in Bournemouth. Mr. Gibbs said he remembered Rusty telling him that. Andrew, I think I'm going to find him. How far away is Bournemouth?''

"About an hour by train. Go tomorrow,'' he urged her.

"I won't know where to look.''

"What's wrong with the telephone book?" he said, not giving her a chance to back out. "I'd come with you, but I've got a consultation in Salisbury and I'll be gone until the following day. You could wait for me, if you like."

This was something she intended to do alone. "I'll be fine," she assured him. "Then I can tell you about it afterward. I'm so darn muddled up, though. One minute I'm praying I find him and he tells me where my mother is. The next I'm in a cold sweat in case he does."

"You mean you're normal," Andrew needled her, kissing her jaw. "Eat up. I've got a few things to tell you, too. But they aren't as pleasant and I don't want to ruin either of our appetites."

Greer managed half of her pie and declined the rum-soaked cake Andrew had wanted her to try. On the return drive to Weymouth the pleasant effect of good wine and food were edged with apprehension. She made inconsequential comments about her purchases for the store, and some of the places she'd seen, certain that Andrew would tell her his own news when he was ready. But by the time they parked outside her boardinghouse a leaden weight had formed in her stomach.

"Feel up to a walk?" Andrew asked, as he opened her door.

Greer tilted her face to his. All trace of humor had disappeared. "Absolutely," she said. "I need to use up some of those calories."

They crossed the wide street in silence. A building on stilts pierced the perfect arc of the bay and Andrew helped her over a wide pebble bank to the hard-packed sand at the water's edge. "Let's head toward the town. Easier going," he said.

He threaded her arm through his. Though he strolled at a leisurely pace, Greer could feel the underlying tension in his posture.

"Look at the moon on the water," she sighed as she tugged them both to a halt. "It ripples up the beach with the tide."

Without warning, Andrew pulled her into his arms with crushing force. "I call it a moontide. It used to be the most beautiful thing the night had to offer, before you came along. Oh, Greer—I needed you with me tonight."

She pushed her hands beneath his jacket and clung to his sides.

"I'm here," she said intensely. "Something's gone wrong, hasn't it?"

He disentangled them gently but kept an arm firmly around her waist when they walked on. "I had a run-in with Bob this afternoon."

"Again?"

"Again. Only this one had a different twist. Evidently I'm not flamboyant enough with what little family fortune I have left."

Only the sharp line of his averted jaw was visible when she looked up. "Meaning?"

"Meaning I should buy a Rolls Silver Cloud and go in for mink-lined overcoats."

"I don't understand," she said.

"How could you?" His hard little laugh sent goose bumps across Greer's skin. "Bob says Coover has a new angle. Not instead, but in addition to the existing line of attack. This one suggests that because my home is open to the public, I'm short of money."

"But even if it were true, what could that possibly do to help Coover?"

"Give him a chance to suggest I want him out so I can have his job and the fat salary that goes with it."

"That's disgusting." Greer planted her feet and stuck both hands into her jacket pockets. She almost asked if Bob had tried to defend Andrew, but thought better of it.

"Yup," Andrew agreed as he turned to stare over the ocean. "But it makes me even more determined not to give up. Only a frightened man sinks so low. Friend Coover's days are numbered."

Tenderness swelled inside Greer. She moved close to Andrew's back, rubbed his shoulders, then wrapped her arms around his waist until her cheek rested on the smooth surface of his jacket. Andrew pulled her in front of him.

His eyes glinted in the moonlight and she saw a flicker of white as his lips parted. "Kiss me, Andrew," she whispered. She stood on tiptoe and brought his face down to hers.

For seconds he seemed to fight his own response, kissing her with a restraint that laid raw every nerve ending in her body. Then, his arms around her, he lifted her against him until her feet cleared the sand. The gentleness fell away and his mouth became forceful, his tongue making desperate forays past her teeth. Greer met his ardor, filling her fingers with his hair, forcing her aching breasts against him, rubbing, touching.

Their breath came in rasping gulps between kisses. Greer lifted her head and shuddered when Andrew repeatedly kissed her neck from the point of her chin to the low, loosely draped neckline of her dress. She took his hands and held them over her breasts. The night was alive with the sound of waves on the shore and another noise Greer realized only she heard—desire's steady thrum.

Abruptly he moved his hands behind her, pressed them into the firm flesh of her bottom until she was molded to him. "I love you," he said passionately, "I want you with me all the time."

Greer's heart bounded. She clutched his sleeves and felt his insistent erection against her belly. *Just admit you love him, too.* She bent her forehead to his chest.

"Greer." His breath moved her hair. "We both need more than this."

She must answer him. "I want to be with you, too," she assured him. "But it isn't clear-cut, Andrew." How was she going to tell him what he deserved to know, must know before he committed his life to her? And even if he accepted her physical limitation, there were other considerations. She couldn't get swept away too quickly.

Soft laughter penetrated her whirling thoughts. "You're embarrassed to say you need more time. Don't be, my love. As long as I know we'll be together in the end, I can wait." He took a step backward and gripped her shoulders. "But not if we don't slow this down. It's cold here, and could become public at any moment, and there's a danger that even my iron will's about to crack. I'm going to take you to your castle and get back to mine while I'm still sane."

His kiss when he left her felt as tremblingly vulnerable as Greer's heart.

CHAPTER FOURTEEN

FIRST DAY OF NOVEMBER. Greer sat on a bench and squinted through bare tree limbs at a blue-and-white sky. A lovely early winter day, a day that reminded her of Seattle at the same time of year.

She thought through her brief telephone conversation with Rusty Timmons. The silence after she first told him who she was had lasted so long she almost wondered if they'd been cut off. And he hadn't wanted her to come to his hotel. Tears burned her eyes and she blinked. He'd made a new life, just like the old vicar had said. Probably decided to forget his beginnings. A sister popping up from the past could be an embarrassment he'd rather avoid. Greer didn't want to do anything to hurt him.

A bus had brought her from Bournemouth station to a shopping square in the city's center. She'd called Rusty from a red telephone booth on a steep and busy street lined with shops. Even with the door shut, traffic noise had made it difficult to hear clearly. After several lengthy pauses he'd told her to go to the gardens in the middle of the square and wait by the river in the vicinity of a putting green. He'd be there as soon as he could. Yes, he thought they'd recognize each other.

Ducks bobbled in close groups on the shallow water, occasionally flurrying to shore after crumbs tossed by two toddlers crouching on the bank with their mother. An older boy, in short gray pants and a navy striped school blazer, poked at a toy sailboat with a long stick. His peaked cap was pushed back on his head and his pursed mouth clearly showed his displeasure at the lack of breeze to fill the miniature sails. Greer listened to the group talking. "Here comes another duck, mummy." "Yes, dear. But let him get a bit nearer." All so calm and uncomplicated.

"Hello, Greer."

She looked up sharply into a pair of eyes as blue as her own. "Hi," she said. Her chest ached.

"May I sit down?"

"Please."

They sat half-facing each other, separated by a giant barrier forged from twenty-four years, and two entirely different lives. Greer took a shaky breath before speaking. "I shouldn't have come," she blurted. Her throat was so dry it hurt.

"Don't say that." Rusty spoke with the soft accent she'd heard and liked in Dorset. He held out a hand and she shook it. "I told you we wouldn't have any difficulty finding each other."

The stinging moisture in Greer's eyes welled and spilled over. She wanted to hug this strange man, but knew she mustn't. "You've got the freckles, too." Inane. His face blurred when she tried to smile.

"And the red hair. Although yours is prettier," he added, crossing his arms and looking away. "I couldn't believe it when you said who you were. How did you manage to track me down?"

"By accident in the end," she said simply. "I reminded someone else of you."

Rusty turned back sharply. "Who?"

She *was* some sort of threat to him. "Just an old man who lives in Kelloway Lane, in—"

"Ferndale. I know where Kelloway Lane is."

One of the toddlers howled but Greer hardly heard him. "Did you ever find what you were looking for?"

"You mean, who, don't you?" Rusty corrected quietly.

A wave of nausea engulfed her. "Yes," she murmured. "Did you?"

He pushed off from the bench and stood with his back to her, watching the children. "I'm married now," he said. "We've got two sons and a steady little business. Nothing that's going to set the world on fire, but enough."

"I'm glad, Rusty," she answered sincerely.

"My wife knows that I was bounced around a bit as a kid. She had to know the rest, too, for the forms when we got married, but we don't talk about it. We'd both rather the boys never found out."

Greer shoved her hands deep in her jacket pockets. "And you're afraid I might tell them?" she guessed. "Don't be. I didn't even know you existed until a few days ago. Then I just wanted to see you—once, if that's what you prefer."

"It's too late for anything else between you and me." He squatted on his heels in front of her so that she looked down into his troubled eyes. "I don't know what made you decide to come digging around after so long," he said, shaking his head sadly. "The same thing that bit me a couple of years ago, I suppose. But forget it, Greer. Go home. I never saw you again after you went into the foster home as a baby, but someone told me you'd been adopted and taken to the States. I was glad. You were free—out of it. Stay out of it," he advised her.

"Of course," she said, standing abruptly. "We're strangers, nothing more. I'm sorry I've upset you."

A hand on her shoulder made her jump. Rusty stood beside her, a slender man, taller than she'd expected. "It isn't what you think," he said in a much gentler tone of voice. "I'm not hiding from my past for my own sake. But the kids are secure. As far as they're concerned, my parents are both dead. It seemed easier that way. How will I look to them now if they suddenly discover it's all a lie?"

"There's no reason for them to discover anything. Not from me." Greer studied his face intently, then dropped her eyes. She'd been unconsciously committing him to memory. "I'd like to meet my mother," she said softly, but firmly.

A long breath whistled past Rusty's teeth. "I can't help you."

"You never located her?"

He wouldn't meet her eyes. "I can't help you."

Greer touched the sleeve of his tan raincoat. "You did find her, didn't you? Why don't you want to tell me where she is?"

"Because some things are better left alone," he said loudly, then dropped his voice. "She's not every child's dream mom. No cottage with roses around the door. No smell of baking pies drifting through homey rooms. She didn't want us then, damn it. And she doesn't want us now."

The words jolted Greer. So did the tear her brother wiped angrily away. "I'm sorry," she said. "I can't seem to think of anything else to say, but I *am* sorry. And the last thing I intended was to bring back bad memories."

"I know that."

"But, Rusty, this is something I have to decide for myself. Will you tell me where she is?" She touched his hand for emphasis.

"You shouldn't go there. She's—she's got another life, too."

"Please let me have her address. I may never use it, but at least it'll make her seem more real."

Rusty reached slowly into the breast pocket of his shirt and brought out a folded paper. "I had a feeling you'd ask for this and that changing your mind would be impossible," he said. "At least I tried, and I can always hope you don't go."

Her fingers closed over the sheet and Rusty surrounded them, holding on. Desperation and sadness mingled in his expression.

"Don't worry," she said, managing a smile. "I'm a survivor, like you. Nothing's going to happen to me."

"Babies weren't my favorite things when you were born. I thought you were ugly and made too much noise. But our mother said you were the loveliest baby she'd ever seen—like an angel. She never meant to hurt us, but she was too young and poor to do much about it. Can't we just leave it at that?"

Tears pricked at her eyes again. "I don't know," she answered. "I just don't know yet."

Rusty checked his watch. "I'm due back. There's one thing I'd like to ask you."

"Anything." They'd never meet again.

"If you do decide to see our mother—her last name's Hawker now, by the way, married a London railroad engineer—" He reached for her hand again. "If you see Ruby, don't tell her where I am. I can't imagine she'd want to know, but I'd rather she didn't."

Greer nodded her head and impulsively reached to hug him. To her surprise, Rusty met her halfway.

"Goodbye, Rusty. Give your boys an extra hug and think of me."

He turned and ran. Greer watched while he crossed to the far side of the putting green and leaped a flight of steps in several bounds. At the top he looked back and raised a hand. She waved and pressed her fingers to her sore eyelids. When she removed her hands, Rusty was gone.

GREER PACED between her bed and the window. Not until tomorrow afternoon, Andrew had said when he called from Salisbury. They would be together then.

When she'd walked in, after taking a bus from the station, Mrs. Findlay had been about to hang up the phone. Andrew had found out the train schedule from Bournemouth and guessed, successfully, what time Greer might arrive home.

His main concern seemed to be their missed outing with Simonne, which he'd arranged to make up at the end of next week. There wasn't time before his afternoon consultation for deep discussion of Greer's day, and as soon as he had hung up, she felt resentful, then lonely. Tomorrow was too far away, she wanted him with her now.

She was being foolish. Mature women dealt with their own problems. What happened with Rusty should have been predictable. He'd been right. The arrival of a sister he had never mentioned to his family was a complication he didn't need.

Ruby Hawker's London address was pinned beneath a ceramic poodle on the windowsill. Greer pulled the slip of paper out and tucked it inside her wallet. Emotional tension had caught up with her. A nap and then a walk into town to eat dinner would clear her head. Eventually she'd know whether or not to complete the quest for her mother.

Greer had wrestled off one boot when she heard Mrs. Findlay's toiling footsteps on the stairs. "A Dr. Wilson to see you, Mrs. Beckett," she wheezed through the closed door. "Shall I send him up?"

"*No.*" Greer's mind ground to a halt for an instant.

"In the lounge, then?"

Why would Bob Wilson come to see her? "Yes. Ask him to wait and I'll be right down," she called through the door.

Clutching a chair back for balance, she tugged the boot on again and straightened the skirt of her camel suit. The train journey had left her feeling grimy. She ran a brush through her hair and quickly washed her hands. What was it about the thought of carrying on a conversation with Bob Wilson—alone—that reduced her insides to a Jell-O?

The lounge door was open. With a confident smile, Greer strode into the room, then stopped abruptly. Bob was seated on the edge of the couch, his head bent while both hands sagged between his knees.

She cleared her throat. "Hello, Bob. This is a surprise." *Original.*

When he lifted his face, purplish smudges beneath his eyes and the shadow of far more than a morning's growth of beard shocked her. He wore faded jeans and a dark blue turtleneck that bagged at the elbows.

"Surprise?" He stood as if every move were an effort. "Yes, I apologize for dropping in on you like this," he said. "But I thought it was time we got to know each other better."

Greer frowned. The man made no sense and he looked as if he hadn't slept for a week.

"Because Andy seems so fond of you, I mean," he added, his eyes sliding away. "Is there somewhere more private we can talk?" A jerky motion of his right hand took in the cramped little room.

Not if I can help it. "Oh, no, no. We won't be disturbed in here." She shut the door firmly and went to sit on a chair opposite the couch. Her heart thumped like a wild thing.

Bob's smile didn't reach his eyes. "I expect you're wondering why I came."

That was the understatement of the century. She studied her fingernails, searching for something to say.

The couch creaked as he slumped back into its hard upholstery. "You don't mind if I sit down?"

Greer shook her head. He was nervous—more nervous than she. "What's wrong, Bob? You didn't come here to make small talk," she said, hoping he would get to the point.

"Of course I didn't," he answered, his voice rising with each word. "Excuse me. I didn't mean to shout, but this is important and the past few days haven't been easy. Just hear me out. It won't take long. Then you can make up your own mind what to do.''

When she didn't answer, he turned sideways to anchor an elbow over the couch back. "I don't know how much Andy's told you about this thing with Coover. The hearing and so on. But you do matter to him and that may be the only thing that'll stop him from chucking his career away.''

Greer shivered, although she wasn't cold. "Go on," she said evenly.

Without warning Bob shoved his big body upright and started to pace. "A boy died—you know that already. Sad. But there isn't a damn thing anyone can do to bring him back. But Andy won't let it be. He's out for blood and revenge—honor and all that crap.'' He paused, running a hand through his ruffled hair. "I came here to ask you to help me stop Andy from destroying himself.''

"Bob." Greer was on her feet and beside him. "Andrew's told me all about the case. He believes he can win it. Why don't you support him?''

"Support him with *what*?'' he shouted, towering over her. His pale eyes pierced her heart. "There isn't one substantiated fact on his side and Coover's got *his* deck stacked. If Andy isn't stopped, in less than two weeks he's going to get nailed to the wall. And if he does, it's going to kill a part of me, too. Do you understand what I'm telling you?''

She'd been wrong about Bob Wilson. He did care about Andrew. He cared enough to be distraught. "Yes," Greer answered. She touched his arm, made long comforting strokes between shoulder and elbow. "I do understand. But I don't know what I can do about it. As you've said, Andrew's determined. He believes in what he's doing, and I'm not sure anyone can shake that kind of conviction.''

"But will you try?'' He grasped her hands and squeezed. "Will you?''

By the time she closed the front door behind Bob, Greer's temples throbbed. Yes, she would talk to Andrew, she'd agreed. No, she didn't know what she would say or how. And, above all, he'd never learn Bob had come to her.

She climbed the stairs slowly, her hip aching for the first time in days. What *was* driving Andrew to pursue the hearing? It had to be his sense of justice and a concern over the possibility of a tragedy similar to Michael Drake's death. Yet Bob knew the facts, and he was a principled man, too. Surely he'd be as worried as Andrew if he thought Coover was a potential threat.

After a restless night, plagued with muddled dreams, Greer could hardly wait to dress and go down to breakfast. Even the thought of seeing Mrs. Findlay's dour face was comforting.

Twenty minutes later, the sound of the phone ringing shattered her nerves and Greer watched the dining-room door with trepidation. She wasn't ready to speak to Andrew. Or was she? She waited, pushing toast crumbs around her plate. When the landlady launched into her latest list of complaints, Greer knew the phone call had not been for her.

The day dragged by and with each minute, her tension mounted. The only one who could sort this out was Andrew. Until she could see him she'd continue to feel like a pawn in a game she never agreed to play.

CHAPTER FIFTEEN

GREER HAMMERED on the side door of Ringstead Hall for the fourth time, then stepped back to stare up at Andrew's windows. No lights. But there wouldn't be at three in the afternoon.

The Mini, slewed at a haphazard angle near the garage, suggested its owner had arrived home. Where was he? She should have tried to telephone Andrew before paying a fortune for a taxi to bring and leave her here.

He could be in the shower. Impulsively she tried the door handle. It turned easily and she stepped into the passageway.

"Andrew!" Her voice bounced off the walls. "Andrew! Are you here?" Lonely place, she thought. Cold and silent.

Pressure built in her head and she gnawed at her lips. Too much. This last day had loaded her down with too many decisions and possibilities to consider.

She walked rapidly to the stairs, her pace increasing with every step until she half-ran into the private wing. "Andrew," she shouted along the corridor. His study, bathroom, sitting room and, finally, the bedroom. All doors gaping, all rooms empty.

"Where are you?" she muttered aloud. His medical bag and an overnight case stood at the bottom of the bed. She lifted the case— still full. But his raincoat and suit had been thrown over an easy chair in one corner, and dress shoes lay on their sides beside the open closet.

Greer picked up a striped silk tie that had slid to the floor and went to the window. The air had been oppressively still all day, as if there could be a thunderstorm. But with approaching dusk, a wind had picked up. The storm wouldn't come, she decided. Too bad. Everything around her seemed to be gathering momentum, with no promise of release.

Did Andrew feel tense, too? He must with the hearing looming ahead. And his feelings for her couldn't help. Good grief, he'd made them clear enough and he was plainly very human. Yesterday he'd promised to get in touch when he returned from Salisbury. Evidently something had changed his mind. Unwillingness to face more sexual frustration? She had no right to expect his endless patience. But she wasn't happy about their situation, either. They had to solve the mushrooming chaos surrounding them.

He must be outside. Greer tossed the tie on top of Andrew's suit. As she glanced up, the Hummel box caught her eye. Half hidden by a stack of books atop a small desk, its soft colors were unmistakable. She stopped, determined not to cry. Her chin quivered. He'd kept the wretched, sweet, music box. Despite Simonne's comment, Greer hadn't noticed it the night she stayed with Andrew. *Find him.* The uneven clipping of her heels echoed through the empty rooms as she made her way to the back of the house.

She'd never been through the grounds. Where would Andrew go out here? She surveyed the woods that topped a rise behind the house, and continued along the skyline to the east. Maybe there? Greer hurried up a flight of steps to a grassy plateau where tall, conical topiary edged a pool. The breeze sent ripples across the metallic-green water and shivers up her back. All still. An eerie setting from another age.

Trembling weakened her knees. Gray cloud banks slunk sullenly across the sky. Another hour and it would be dark. Greer turned along the path leading toward the ocean. The descent was steep and gravity pulled her forward at a trot. She should be thinking of a way to get back to Weymouth, not scurrying through empty acres, searching for a man who might have decided he never wanted to see her again.

The cliff, when she reached it, fell away as if a giant cleaver had severed land from sea. Below, a fluted band of pebbles bordered the tawny sand.

Her hair swirled across her eyes, and she wrestled it behind her ears. Then she saw Andrew. His dark hair and tall, lean body were unmistakable as he jogged along the water's edge. Even at a distance Greer could tell he was relaxed, not hurrying.

Damn him. While her insides threatened to explode, he enjoyed an afternoon run that was scarcely more than a saunter. She searched around and located a spot where a mountain goat, or someone very accustomed to the terrain, might get to the beach. Her nostrils flared. Anyone who was angry enough could make it down that steep, rubble pathway.

Small stones began to fly the instant she took her first tentative, downward step. With the second she slipped, landing with a bruising thump. *Damn, damn, damn.* She *would* get to him—and give him a piece of her mind.

Colored specks darted before her. As a kid, she and Casey had loved to run. Downhill meant fast and don't think. Greer scrambled, gathering speed. Her calves and the backs of her thighs pulled sharply, but she kept going. Twice she slithered, skinning the heels of both hands. She didn't look toward Andrew.

The bottom. She paused to breath deeply. Her lungs burned as if she'd been too long under water. The pebbles jabbed at her feet until she reached the sand bar. Andrew was a short distance ahead to her right. She caught up, then passed him, swerving closer to the ocean.

"Greer! Stop!"

A wild impulse engulfed her. Why should she stop? Because he said so? Surf swamped her shoes.

Andrew drew level. "For God's sake," he shouted. "Stop. What's the matter with you?"

"You should know." The words seared her throat. "You don't own this beach and I want to run."

"Your hip isn't strong enough," he insisted. "It should be, but it isn't."

She was openly crying now. So what? "Don't tell me what should and shouldn't be. Or what I can do," she shrieked.

"Stop this," Andrew said firmly. "Unless you want me to make you."

Greer winced at the pain in her hip, but kept on running. Ahead a spit of rocks jutted into the sea. Before she could reach it, Andrew ran to block her path. He faced her and halted, fists on hips.

"Get out of my way," she threatened him. She hobbled sideways to go around him and gasped as he snatched her arm.

"That's it, Greer," he yelled, shaking her angrily. "Enough."
He glared and abruptly released her. The force of his thrust caused
her heel to turn in the soft shingle and she started to fall.

"You little idiot," Andrew exploded as he attempted to grab
her, missed and overbalanced. "Oh, good Lord."

She took the full force of his crushing weight. His left forearm
slammed into her diaphragm, winding her and leaving incredible
pain in its wake. He shifted swiftly and Greer curled into a ball on
her side.

Instantly Andrew knelt over her, brushing back her hair, cradling
her head. "Sweetheart," he whispered. "Lie still. Where do you
hurt?"

"My stomach," she rasped.

Instantly she felt his probing fingers. "You're okay, thank God,"
he pronounced. "Just winded. But why the hell did you do this?"

"I'm angry."

"So you decided to come down here and run like a maniac?
What are you angry about? And it better be good."

Greer's wind was returning, plus her anger.

"When you called, all you could talk about was Simonne."

He rolled her into his arms and got to his feet carrying her.
"You're jealous of a little girl I happen to like? And this is my
punishment?"

"Put me down," she insisted. There was no escaping his tightened grip. "I'm not jealous of anyone. But everything's too much
for me and I can't go through another day of not knowing what to
do about it all."

"Fine." He started to walk. "I know how you feel. We'll get
your feet dry and talk about all our troubles. Yours, anyway."

She twisted angrily in his arms. "I'm not one more silly juvenile,
Andrew," she said. "You aren't going to pat me on the head to
make it all better. You're in as much emotional hell as I am and
we're going to start sorting your problems out by making love."

"Making—?" He almost dropped her. "I don't believe this,"
he said as if talking to himself. "Yes, I do on second thought."
Hiking her higher against his chest, he pushed her face into his
shoulder and marched on.

Greer tried to speak but the fabric of his black sweat shirt and his rapid progress over the pebbles made it impossible. She expected to be set down when he reached the cliff. Andrew only hitched her closer, wrapping one arm around her waist, the other across the backs of her thighs and buttocks, and climbed to the top without a pause.

Not until they reached his study did Andrew finally let loose of Greer. He dumped her in one of the leather wing chairs and yanked off her shoes.

"Andrew..." she began.

"Don't say anything."

Misery inched into the spaces where her anger had seeped away. She watched him leave the room and return in moments with a towel. "I'm sorry," she said automatically. He must think her mad. She thought herself mad. Temporarily unhinged at least.

His answer was to apply stinging friction to her feet with the towel.

She sighed audibly and slumped backward.

Andrew plopped down, cross-legged, still holding her feet. Now he rubbed them gently with his hands. "You scared the hell out of me down there, Greer. Then you made me *madder* than hell." Andrew paused to let that sink in. "But you're right about one thing," he added. "This can't go on. We've got to sort ourselves out—individually and jointly."

"Yes," was all she said.

"Ready to talk about it calmly?"

"Yes."

He lifted one foot. "Little feet." His lips grazed the instep. "You go first."

"Oh, Andrew." Blindly, she sought his warm strength, folding her arms around his neck and sinking to the floor until they knelt together, thighs touching.

"Tell me," he said hoarsely. "What's happened?"

It poured out. The meeting with Rusty. His attempt to stop her from seeing their mother. What it felt like to know her brother lived and breathed but she would probably never see him again. And all the time Andrew stroked her back, rocked her gently, until she punctuated her words with tears and tiny sniffling kisses along his jaw.

"I never even asked their names," she said miserably.

"Whose names?" Andrew prompted softly.

"The boys. Rusty's boys. My nephews. Or his wife. He must have had pictures, too. At least I could have seen what they look like."

"Some things are better left alone."

She pulled away abruptly and sat on the chair once more. "Everyone says that. But who decides, Andrew? Who decides what's best left alone? You?"

He frowned and tried to take her hand.

"No." Greer sat straighter. "Your life is rocking like an over-loaded teeter-totter, too."

"That's not something you have to worry about," he told her.

"It isn't? You think I don't care about what happens to you? I'm worried sick that you're going to get flattened at this stupid hearing. You love your work and if they say Winston Coover's right and you're wrong and he drags up a lot of lies that a bunch of his cronies may be only too happy to believe—" she said, drag-ging in a breath. "They could stop you from doing what means most to you and I couldn't stand that."

"Are you asking me not to go ahead?" His voice was as level as his golden eyes.

Greer tipped her head wearily to one side. "Of course not," she said slowly. "All I want is to be sure that when you do go into the ring, the fight isn't fixed." She found herself seized by panic. "An-drew," she said, leaning forward. "Is it going to be all right? Do you have enough evidence to prove your case? And *is* there any chance Coover can ruin your reputation?"

For agonizing moments he was silent. Then he pulled himself into the facing chair and rested his chin on his hands. "It's going to be all right," he said wearily. "I'm all the evidence I need to prove both my case and my reputation. And every step of the way I'll be thinking of a red-haired woman who—who's rooting for me." Andrew reached across the space to take her hands. "I can't tell you what to do about your mother any more than you can solve things for me,'' he continued. ''But I think you should give yourself plenty of time to decide, then follow your intuition. Rusty sounds like a nice guy. I'm glad you two met even if you don't see each other again—but he can't make your decisions, either. Does that sound sensible?''

''You always sound sensible,'' she said, grinning wryly.

''Great. Now try this on for size. Since I left you the other night I've been thinking about you and me.'' He stood and began to pace. ''On my way back from Salisbury I went to the Sealink ferry terminal in Weymouth and bought two round-trip tickets for Guernsey.''

Greer rubbed the bridge of her nose. ''One of the Channel Islands?'' she said.

''Right. About four and a half hours from here.''

''What are you really saying?''

''Greer. We're hemmed in on all sides by distractions. But there's one thing that overrides them all and we both know what it is. We want each other, and not just as sympathetic buddies. The way we feel—sexually—is there every second we're together. And when we're not together. You didn't include that in your list of frustrations, but the hysterical offer you made on the beach proves I'm not the only one being driven over the edge.''

She shifted to stare at the ashes in the fireplace. ''I wasn't hysterical,'' she answered.

''That's irrelevant.'' He stood over her. ''The tickets I bought are for the Tuesday-afternoon ferry. Come to Guernsey with me, Greer. It's beautiful there—and isolated. We need to be alone and completely separated from anything that distracts us from—''

''Taking me up on my hysterical offer,'' she blurted out, flushing. At the same time she felt the familiar throb of desire in her lower limbs. She knew he was right.

His fingers brushed her cheek. ''I was thinking more of—loving each other,'' he said tenderly.

''I do love you, Andrew,'' she whispered and closed her eyes.

She felt him move. His hand slid behind her neck, but she pulled away.

''Greer. Darling,'' Andrew said, clearly struggling for patience,

"I don't understand you. What's holding you back? It's not still Colin, is it?" he asked, as if he were afraid of her answer.

"No, damn it," was all she said. All she had to do was tell him, now—all of it—and let him decide how he felt. "Andrew."

"Yes." He kissed her temple.

"I'll come with you on Tuesday."

CHAPTER SIXTEEN

"IF IT WEREN'T so cold we could pretend it was a summer's evening," Andrew said, smiling. He hooked both elbows over the back of a slatted bench on the huge ferry's upper deck and half closed his eyes.

Greer squinted at a carmine horizon streaked with drifting lumps of miniature clouds. "Is there a name for formations like that?"

"Mmm," Andrew said as he considered the clouds. "Mackerel locally, I think. After the fish. I don't know why. Not my field. We'd better retrieve our bags."

"We can't be there yet."

He pointed over his shoulder. "That's Guernsey. We'll be docking in St. Peter Port shortly."

She twisted to see land and a harbor fronting clusters of buildings. Her stomach lurched. St. Peter Port, and the hotel where she and Andrew would stay. When he picked her up to come to the boat, it was the first time she'd seen him since the afternoon at Ringstead. They'd agreed to spend the intervening time apart, to gain perspective and get some work done. Greer had wandered through the two days devoid of inspiration for Britmania, thinking of little else but Andrew and, when she couldn't shut her out, Ruby Timmons Hawker.

"I half expected that landlady of yours to say you were out when I got there this afternoon," he said suddenly.

Greer turned to him. "If I'd changed my mind I'd have called," she told him. "Anyway, I made the hotel reservation, remember. I wouldn't have let you leave without a place to stay when you got here."

"You think I would have come without you?" He stood and hauled her to her feet. "Where are we staying? I still don't understand why you insisted finding digs was your territory."

She swallowed uncomfortably. "You already asked me that fifty times at least. And, like I told you before, it's a surprise." *To me, too, probably.* Choosing the most inexpensive listing on the travel agent's books might not have been such a good idea. But no way was Andrew going to pay more than half the bill and it was time to watch what she spent more closely. "I'm good at finding little-known gems in the hotel department," she hedged. "That's why I wanted to do it."

His expression suggested he was skeptical. "Like Belle Vista?" he challenged her.

"I like it there."

"Of course," he said, his eyes laughing at her. "You already told me that—must be getting forgetful. I'll put you in line to get off and collect our things."

Few of the passengers appeared to be tourists. Businessmen who might have been dressed for a day's work anywhere in the States, families whose lack of interest in their surroundings suggested they were returning home; only language and accents gave the small crowd a foreign flavor. Greer identified German, English spoken with a French accent and what sounded like a form of French— probably one of the Channel Island patois the guidebook had mentioned. The islands were now a part of Britain but had once been claimed by the Duchy of Normandy.

"What do you think?" Andrew said as he dropped their bags and leaned against the rail beside Greer. "It always seems more continental than English here to me."

She watched the gulls swoop overhead. "I've never been to the Continent. But the town looks like all those travel brochures for France or Spain. I like the way it comes right down to the ocean."

"Am I allowed to know where the hotel is? So I know what bus to catch from the terminal?"

"We're staying at Phelps in Smith Street," she said. He was close, his elbow touching her wrist. Fading sunlight cast shadows about the clear lines of his face. The salt scent of the air seemed a part of him. And they were going to be lovers on this green island in a cobalt sea. She stared silently at his profile until he faced her.

He reached to take her hands. "Relax, sweetheart. This is going to be a beautiful time for us. The start of the rest of our beautiful times together.''

"I hope so, Andrew," she whispered. Her lips parted to receive his soft kiss just as the ferry bumped against the dock. She clung to him, trembling inside, praying he didn't sense her clamoring turmoil.

Inquiry revealed Smith Street to be within walking distance of the jetty. Greer took in the scenery while Andrew carried both bags. Shops and cafés, each with a different and quaint facade, lined the narrow cobblestone streets. Could be somewhere in Brittany, she decided. All the photographs and paintings she'd seen of the northwest peninsula of France showed similar settings.

"This is super," Greer panted, concentrating on the rough pavement. "Slow down or we'll miss it all."

Andrew immediately dropped both bags. "Sit," he invited and pointed to his leather suitcase. "I happened to notice one or two drops of rain and it's rapidly feeling arctic. It's also dark. But don't let me rush you. I'll just use the time while you're sightseeing to catch my breath."

"Comedian," Greer quipped as she punched his ribs playfully. "I guess we can come back tomorrow—or maybe after we've checked in?"

His penetrating gaze seemed to probe every corner of her mind. "Tomorrow, for sure," he said. "I don't think we'll come out again tonight. It's almost six. Let's buy a bottle of wine and some bread and cheese and eat in the room later."

"Sounds terrific," she said, ignoring her racing heart. She lifted a bag but he took it from her.

At a stall heaped with fruit and vegetables, Andrew bought two apples and some grapes. A bakery yielded crusty French bread. Greer spotted the small grocery store where they picked out a box of Camembert, then passed over several fine white wines in favor of a bottle of very dry champagne. When Andrew added plastic glasses and knives to his purchase, the clerk looked amused. He grinned at Greer who promptly blushed.

"You should have seen yourself in there," Andrew said, laughing when they were back in the street. "You were beet red just because some stranger figured out we're going to have a picnic."

"That isn't what he was thinking."

Andrew bent to whisper in her ear. "He was thinking how lucky I am to have such a gorgeous woman to picnic with. And you're imagining things."

His breath tickled Greer's cheek. She arched a brow at him, quickened her pace and changed the subject immediately. "Pollet Street. Le Pollet. Why do they show each street name twice?" she inquired.

"To keep the French as well as the English tradition. I think this is our turn."

When Greer saw Phelps, she opened her mouth in horror, then snapped it shut again. Another Belle Vista, only less pristine. White paint peeled from brick facing below a sagging slate roof. A jutting sun porch at street level could have been attractive—if every window weren't securely covered by grayish lace curtains. Greer hugged the sacks of food miserably to her chest.

Andrew tipped his head, studying the building to its top story, and smiled at her benignly. "I'd have known this was it even if you hadn't told me," he claimed. "A true Greer *gem*. You certainly do have a flair for picking winners."

"Good grief," she breathed. "We could always look for someplace else. I really had no idea—"

"Wouldn't hear of it." The smirk on his lips curled her toes. "If you chose this, I know it'll be great."

The small foyer showed more promise. A copper vase filled with russet chrysanthemums glowed on a highly polished round table. The air was redolent with lemon oil. One ring on the desk bell produced a stout huffing lady who explained with pride that she was *the* Mrs. Phelps. She would take them upstairs herself.

Every few steps the woman stopped to glance at Andrew and Greer, her small black eyes shrewdly assessing them while she fired obsequious questions. "You're sure you won't be needing hot-water bottles—no? I'd be happy to turn down the bed if you'd let me know when you leave for dinner."

A few minutes after showing them their room, Mrs. Phelps returned with a daily paper, then, again, with a tray of tea and cookies. Each time she lingered to size up her guests and their belongings with avid interest. "You're sure there's nothing else I can do for you Mrs.—?"

"No. But thanks for the tea," Greer said, putting her hands behind her. Andrew hadn't noticed her wedding band was missing—Mrs. Phelps had. Without it her finger felt huge and naked. But she couldn't use Colin's ring as a mock symbol of respectability.

"Thanks very much, Mrs. Phelps," Andrew said as he backed the woman subtly toward the hall. "We'll certainly let you know if we need something."

Greer leaned against the closed door, listening to the landlady's retreating footsteps. "What do you think her next excuse will be?"

"Who knows? If she comes back again, we won't answer the door." Andrew rubbed his hands together and hunched his shoulders. "It's freezing in here," he complained.

"Maybe that's why she brought the tea. She knew we'd need warming up." Hot blood surged to Greer's cheeks. She studied the worn floral carpet, avoiding Andrew's eyes.

His arms were around her shoulders before she realized he'd moved. "What are you afraid of, Greer?" he asked her gently. "Me?" The fleeting kiss he brushed across her forehead made her already stretched nerves vibrate.

She wanted to say, "Me, Andrew. It's me I'm afraid of." Instead she touched his sides lightly and ducked beneath his left arm. "Don't be ridiculous," she told him. Her voice wavered, and she felt him watch her progress around the room as she pretended to inspect the furniture.

"So, what is it?"

"Nothing," Greer said, too quickly. "Just that this all feels like such a setup."

"A setup?" His short laugh was mirthless. "Does that mean you regret coming? That you feel I coerced you into this—trip?"

The watery sensation in Greer's legs spread throughout her body. "No, no. I want to be here with you," she assured him. "I even arranged the hotel, remember? If anyone's guilty of carefully planning an interlude, it's just as much me as you."

He went to the window and lifted a lace curtain to peer into the night through rain-splattered glass. "Speaking of which. What did make you choose this wonderful establishment?"

"Please, Andrew. Not now."

"Seriously," he insisted. "Why this one?"

"How can you switch topics like that?" she said, clamping her teeth shut to still the trembling in her jaw.

He wheeled around. "Humor me."

Greer sat on the edge of a chintz armchair beside the unlit gas fire. "It had one star in the book. Said it was clean with an ocean view." She brought her eyes to his, aware that he would see her defiance. "And even if you do need a telescope to see water, it's cheap," she snapped.

"That's good," he said objectively. "Now you're angry."

"You like me to be angry?"

"It's an excellent start. Sometimes we have to work our way through a pile of emotions before we can get where we want to be," he explained.

"I thought you were a pediatrician, not a psychiatrist."

"There's a repressed psychiatrist inside every doctor. The really good ones, anyway."

A sigh slipped past her lips. "One of the traits I admire most in a man is humility. And you are so humble."

His rumbly baritone laugh seemed to warm the room's cold air. "See," he teased her. "Anger to disgust. Moving right along. Work on feeling disgusted while I figure out how to light the fire. I thought this kind went out of use years ago. Do you have any matches?"

"What comes after disgust?" she asked dryly.

"Matches, I hope."

"I don't have any reason to carry matches. Maybe we should call Mrs. Phelps. She'd probably volunteer to come up and help us out."

Andrew crossed the room and knelt at Greer's feet. "Forget it. If necessary I'll break off a couple of chair legs and rub them together. I tried it a few times when I was a kid—with sticks, not chair legs."

"Did you manage to start a fire?"

"No. Not even a spark." He rested a forearm on her knees. "But we could forget the fire and see how much body heat the two of us could generate," he said suggestively. His head was bent, his face averted.

He was trying to take the tension out of the moment, but she couldn't laugh. Blue-black hair curled over the high neck of his cream sweater. The brown corduroy jacket he wore made his shoulders seem even broader. Greer stroked his hair tentatively, rubbing the skin behind his ear with the backs of her fingers. The shudder she felt pass through him was almost imperceptible. "I wanted us to be here, alone, so badly," she whispered.

"And now you're not sure it's what you want?" Andrew dropped his head farther forward.

She replaced her hand with her cheek, wrapping her arms around his shoulders. Slowly she nuzzled her face back and forth. "I've never been more sure of anything," she murmured. "But I don't want to disappoint you. You're so good, Andrew. You wouldn't say or do anything to embarrass me—including refusing to tolerate a skittish woman who puts you through hell every step of the way even though she wants to make love as much as you do," she confessed.

"What?" In a move that shocked her, he twisted around and caught her face between both of his hands. He studied her eyes, then her mouth. "Oh, darling lady," he told her. "You couldn't disappoint me. And if this is being put through hell, I hope it happens daily. You're something," he concluded, sealing his words with a brief but poignant kiss. "Just a minute," he said, leaping up and going to the tea tray the landlady had left. "Brain wave pays off. Matches on the tray. Don't move a muscle while I light this monster. Keep the thought patterns on hold, too—they have definite promise."

With a twist of a chrome key on the right side of the hearth, Andrew turned on the gas. He struck a match and the hissing settled to steady popping sounds as the flame immediately ignited. "There," he said, thoroughly pleased. "This place will warm up in no time." He tossed the matchbook on the mantel and faced her, elbows akimbo, his fine hands spread wide on slender hips beneath his jacket. "Now, where were we?"

"Already out of my depth, I think," she said nervously.

"Give me your coat."

"I'm still cold."

"No more excuses," he insisted. Andrew shrugged out of his jacket and held out a hand. "Up. I'll hang these in the wardrobe if that's what that thing is. Looks a bit like a Grecian casket on end." He tipped his head to one side, apparently concentrating furiously. "Possibly Roman—they were the ones into fruit."

Greer stood, laughing, and let him help her out of her raincoat. The heavy walnut closet was narrow and freestanding. Carved bunches of grapes encrusted the front. "I'm beginning to believe you really are very bright."

"Good," he replied. "I've been telling you as much all along. But what made you decide to agree at this particular moment?" He arranged their coats on hangers and reached to push them on the closet rail. The inch of taut flesh exposed at his waist sent a heavy spiral of heat into Greer's abdomen. She wanted this man. He awakened instincts she'd repressed too long.

She laced her fingers together to stop herself from touching him. "I read a book about types—of people," she explained.

"And?"

"It said that brilliance and a tendency to make irreverent connections often go together. So..."

"I know," Andrew said, cutting her off. He took their suitcases and pushed them beneath a high rickety table by the door. "I make Roman artifacts out of twentieth-century wardrobes, so I must be brilliant." His smile was lopsided and totally charming.

Suddenly Greer felt as if a million fluttering moths had been released inside. She was light, so light she might float away. Nothing was real but Andrew's supple body moving around her, capably performing insignificant tasks to fill gaps in their conversation. She squeezed her eyes shut and folded her arms tightly across her chest.

"Greer. Greer, what is it?" Andrew said in alarm.

When she lifted her lashes he was a few inches away, staring at her, his wonderful, golden eyes darkened with concern. The moths burst free, and with them the emotion she'd tried to suppress. "If you don't hold me, now, I'm going to break into little pieces," she told him urgently. "I need you. There's so much I want to tell you, but every time I try, I talk in circles about things that don't matter. Andrew, is there something wrong with me?"

He swiftly wrapped her in his arms. Her ear pressed hard over his heart and she heard its steady beat, a strong, calming rhythm that seemed to urge her own to slow down. "There's nothing wrong with you, my darling," he soothed her. "Nothing except that you've been alone too long, and now you're a bit frightened to allow yourself to feel again."

His chin rested atop her head while he made broad circles over her back. Their scents mingled, a mysterious and heady combination. Greer was aware of her own perfume, subtle, faintly reminiscent of sandalwood, but it was Andrew's after-shave, a hint of leather—so masculine—that wound threads of heat into her thighs. Heat and need, and longing. Greer stood on tiptoes to lock her wrists behind his neck. His jaw was tantalizingly rough from a day's growth of beard, and she followed its angular lines with a row of tiny nipping kisses.

Andrew lifted his chin to allow her to press her lips to his neck, but when she stretched to take his earlobe in her teeth, he twisted his head until he could capture her mouth. His kiss was gentle, an erotic movement with firm, barely parted lips. Then the tip of his tongue found a corner of her mouth and traced the line of her lower lip before he carefully drove deeper, skimming over smooth teeth to the sensitive inside of her cheeks. Greer sensed his conscious restraint. Andrew would never push her faster or farther than he thought she was ready to go.

"Sweetheart," he breathed against her mouth. "I'll take away the doubts, if you'll let me. It's okay to love again."

The uncertainty had gone. She wanted to tell him that, but buried her hands in his hair instead, pulling his face against her neck. "Andrew," was the only word she could form.

He moved away from her to pull the sweater over his head. Muscle and sinew flexed as he relaxed his arms, then threw the garment aside. When he looked at her, his hair was mussed, his eyes alight with a sensual glow that penetrated her heart, her soul.

As if she had no will to decide what she did, her fingers sought the textures of him. His skin was drawn tight over well-developed shoulders, rough where the dark hair on his chest narrowed downward over his flat belly to the low waist of his jeans. At his sides she found a smoothness that extended to his back. She held him, stroked him slowly and kissed a flat nipple. Nothing but Andrew mattered. With him she felt a new freedom and rightness she'd never dared hope for.

"I want to feel you against me, Greer." Passion thickened his voice.

Greer started to take off her sweater, but Andrew stopped her. He lifted her and carried her to the bed, setting her down like fragile china. Each contact produced an electric charge. When he removed her shoes the arches of her feet tingled, then tickled as he kissed each one. She wriggled and laughed, and their eyes met, gold with vivid blue. The laughter caught in her throat.

The lithe economy of his motions fascinated her. Under his deft fingers, her skirt zipper slid noiselessly down, followed by the skirt itself, her half-slip and panty hose.

At Greer's automatic attempt to hide her scars, Andrew shook his head. He captured her hands and carried them to his mouth. "Don't," he said. "You're beautiful. Absolutely beautiful."

"Thank you," she said brokenly. "So are you." Nerves in her cheeks quivered when she tried to smile.

Andrew kissed the tips of her fingers, then released them. Her green sweater was slipped over her head and discarded. Then he knelt before her and filled his hands with her hair. His kisses became a gentle storm that covered her face, her neck, her shoulders. He drew back to study the tender flesh above her low-cut bra. Almost reverently he stroked a line along the lace trim that barely covered her pulsing nipples.

Their sighs mingled as Andrew continued making his chart of kisses over her body. With both hands clasped around her ribs, the moist trail passed lingeringly from the tiny flower that joined her bra between her breasts down to her navel. Skimpy white bikinis couldn't shield her from the heat of his quest. When he found the soft insides of her thighs, his warm breath sent an erotic dart to her core and she reached to draw him to her.

"Lie with me, Andrew," she whispered. "Let me watch your face. I want to see it when we make love."

He stood, his movements suddenly fevered as he took off the rest of his clothes. But he didn't stop looking into her eyes. When he was naked, she feasted on the sight of him. His body was totally masculine, speaking of his need for her in a way that left her breathless.

"Darling," he said, so low she scarcely heard. "God, what you do to me."

Then he pulled her to her feet, flung down the bedcovers and lay her against the pillows. At his single urgent tug, her bra was undone and her aching breasts, already swollen with desire, burned under his circling palms. He slid the panties away and kissed her waiting body until every cell begged for release. His lips and teeth seduced her nipples to even tenser crests while the heel of one hand pressed into the softness between her legs. She arched against him, searching blindly to touch and hold.

"You are the loveliest woman I've ever known," he admitted. "What I feel with you almost scares me. I can't lose you again, Greer." He stared into her eyes as he spoke, then lowered his head to her belly and beyond. The molten spear his tongue created shot to her center, turning her mind blank, and although she heard her own strangled cry, she never knew what she said.

A second hung, suspended, throbbing, before Greer urged Andrew over her, parted her thighs and lifted her knees. "I want you Andrew," she breathed. "Now."

His face above hers was dark, the veins in his neck corded. Every feature was radiant and dear, the features, the expression of a lover. He entered her slowly, carefully. A tiny unexpected pain made her gasp and he paused until she moved against him, smiling, giving him her joy.

Their pace speeded, Greer reaching to meet each thrust, matching his passion, certain that his ecstasy equalled her own. And at their climax a sob broke from her throat, joining with Andrew's groan.

She looked at his face, as she tried to stem the explosion that threatened to tear her apart. Andrew's eyes were closed, his lips pulled back in a lover's grimace. *I love you*, her heart told him, but she didn't say it. Later she would tell him.

Andrew became still over her, his weight supported beside her head on his outstretched arms. Greer could see the pulse in his neck, the rapid beat of his heart.

"Hold me, please," she asked softly. "Need me. Let's stay like this forever."

Their damp limbs remained entwined when he slid beside her and folded her into his arms. "I'll always need you," Andrew said. "I love you. Oh, how I love you."

With a sigh he hoisted himself to one elbow and looked into her face. He wound a tendril of hair between his fingers. "Wouldn't it be something if you were already pregnant?" he said wistfully.

"What?" Her mind blanked, then came slowly into focus. He couldn't have suggested she might be pregnant. *No!*

Andrew smiled and nuzzled her neck. "It's supposed to only happen in the movies. But pregnancies do occur the first time a couple makes love. We can hope, can't we?" he asked tenderly.

Greer gripped him tight. He hadn't taken any precautions or asked if she intended to. It crossed her mind that it was something a doctor ought to think of. *Fate, you fool. Didn't you think it would catch up with you?* He must want children—his own children—at least as much as he wanted her.

"You aren't saying much, sweetheart," he said, caressing her neck. "I thought you'd like the idea as much as I do. It's time, my love. I've seen the way you look at children. You need another baby."

"Oh—Andrew." She cried and couldn't stop, didn't try. He would never guess that instead of joy she felt crushing pain and emptiness. The sudden tight pressure of his arms seemed to hold together the parts of her that threatened to fly apart. "I love you," she said, wanting to tell him there would be no child—ever—but unable to bear what his reaction might be. And she couldn't walk away from him, not now when they'd found such ecstasy in each other's arms.

ANDREW'S MIND fumbled through the day while he smiled and talked—and waited for Greer to admit the truth. In the evening they ate a late dinner at a small Italian restaurant near the harbor and returned to their room at Phelps for the last time. Only the irresistible power of their lovemaking temporarily blotted out his creeping anger and confusion.

Afterward he lay silent while she burrowed into the hollow of his shoulder. When her breathing slowed he knew she'd drifted asleep.

His head pounded. Did she think he'd ever guess about the hysterectomy? Why hadn't she told him? Damn it all, why hadn't he figured it out sooner?

Her reaction to his suggestion of pregnancy had clued him in. Desperation might sometimes be mistaken for happiness, but not this time. All day he'd tried to draw her out, tried to reach beyond the fixed smile and distant gaze that never quite met his eyes. The only definite reaction he'd gotten had come from his reminder of their date with Simonne on Saturday. At that, Greer had forgotten to smile for an instant. Her throat had moved convulsively as she swallowed. But then she'd smiled and chattered about where they would take the child.

He'd noticed the newer scar near the section site immediately. Secondary complications had occurred to him, possibly adhesions, but not hysterectomy. And that's what it was—he was sure of it now. Greer would never have another child and it destroyed her every time he mentioned the subject. He felt tears run hot to his temples and closed his eyes.

No children of their own. It hurt. How it hurt. But it completely tore him up that she hadn't trusted him enough to be honest. This was the only woman he wanted, would ever truly want again, but it wasn't up to him anymore. He couldn't make her confide in him, and unless she did they had no basis for a lifetime commitment.

SIMONNE'S FACE was wind burned. She backed down the beach, shovel in hand, making a trench. "This'll let water into the moat, Greer," she yelled.

Greer shivered inside her jacket. The wind made her eyes water.

Andrew would have to be called away on an emergency when they were due to take Simonne out. She bent to dig up several half-buried shells, then pressed them into the upper bastions of the sand castle she and Simonne had spent the past two hours making.

"Here," the child said, arriving back panting. "Scrape the trench a bit deeper so the tide can swoosh down harder when it comes."

"Yes, ma'am." Greer watched the spindly figure whirl away, arms flapping, as she revolved in circles. "Yes, little one," she whispered.

Her nails were crammed with sand and it stuck to the damp palms of her hands. She started to work at the dip Simonne intended the water to enter. The girl had already been with Andrew this morning when he picked Greer up in Weymouth. He ran them back to Ringstead, explaining he must visit the hospital before they went to Lyme. As soon as he left, Simonne talked her into clambering to the beach to build a castle.

She hunkered down and looked over her shoulder. The tide was coming closer—threatening to rush at her before she was ready. Like everything else in her life.

Simonne was sweet. It hadn't been so painful to hold her little hand coming down the steep cliff's path, or to rebraid a pigtail. Greer hugged her shins and rested a cheek on her knees. The tight knots she'd tied around the sensitive spots of her heart were gradually loosening. But would there be any way to hold on to what mattered most to her now—Andrew's love?

"That's perfect."

Wiry arms, wrapped around Greer's neck from behind, landed her on her rear with a thud. Simonne's cold face was pressed to her ear.

"It's going to be *stupendous*," the child announced noisily.

Greer held the wrists beneath her chin and laughed. Thin sun blinded her as she sensed another presence and looked up. "Andrew, is that you?" she said. His silhouette was unmistakable and when he didn't answer immediately, she shaded her eyes to make out his face. "We didn't hear you coming. What do you think of this palace?"

"Fantastic. The best." He smiled, but not before she saw his drawn, almost haggard expression. Every muscle in her body clenched. Despite all her efforts, her anxiety of the past forty-eight hours had been transmitted to Andrew. She'd suspected as much on the quiet boat ride back to Weymouth. He was trying to pretend, too, without even knowing why he should.

"We've had so much fun, Uncle Andy," Simonne chirped. "I wouldn't even mind if we didn't go to Lyme. We could watch the moat get filled up, then have tea in your kitchen."

"Sounds good to me," he told her. "How about you, Greer?"

She brushed at her jeans and went to stand in front of him. Simonne concentrated on the frothy water bubbling nearer her castle with each wave.

"Was she too much for you?" Andrew asked softly.

"I loved being with her. She's wonderful." Something caught in her throat and she tried to clear it. "I think I've decided to go to London tomorrow."

Andrew turned her toward him. "To see your mother?"

She nodded. "If I can. She may not be happy when I show up. She might even tell me to get lost, but at least I won't have avoided her," she said, hoping Andrew would say something encouraging.

He stared at the sky for a long time, then into Greer's eyes. "We can't avoid anything forever. We have to get the tough stuff out of the way if we're ever going to be happy."

CHAPTER SEVENTEEN

GREER KNEW Ruby was forty-eight. She looked older.

"Have you lived in Walthamstow long, Mrs. Hawker?"

Andrew's voice was polite, level, designed to help steady the woman's nerves. He shouldn't be here.

Ruby's hand shook as she lifted the cigarette to her mouth. "Eighteen years," she said. "Ever since I came to London." A nerve twitched beside her left eye.

A wooden clock on the sideboard chimed, startling Greer. "I'm in England on a visit," she said. "I thought it would be nice if we met."

"Yes." Ruby glanced over her shoulder at the door for the third time in as many minutes.

The room smelled faintly of cooked cabbage and seemed to get smaller and smaller. Greer's eyes flicked from ocher walls to a square dining table on bulbous-footed legs, to Andrew's gold brocade chair, the double of the one where she sat. Everything threadbare and faded—like this nervous, sullen woman who was her mother.

A train rumbled past behind the house. Greer had seen the elevated embankment from the street. "If this is a bad time I could come back," she suggested. "Perhaps you're expecting someone. I tried to call first, but there wasn't a listing."

The cigarette tip glowed red again and another thin line of smoke streamed upward. "My husband will be back from his club shortly," the woman answered enigmatically.

Damp silk stuck to Greer's back. "When would be a good time for us to talk?"

Ruby bent her head, rubbing a stained finger rapidly across her brow. Gray streaked her short red curls, but the hair was still vibrant.

"What—?" Greer began, before losing her train of thought. Had she been going to ask when to come or what she should call Ruby. It didn't matter.

Andrew leaned forward, tenting his fingertips. "Mrs. Hawker," he addressed her in a calm, clear voice. "I'm a good friend of Greer's and I know this is very hard on her. That's why I insisted on coming. You must be upset, too. Perhaps if you could both relax a little things would be easier."

Always in control, Greer thought, as dull heat flooded her cheeks. Dr. Monthaven playing the psychiatrist again. An interesting study in plebeian behavior, would probably be his conclusion. She glared at him. They were from different worlds—no common ground except the bedroom. The flush turned cold on her skin.

"Yes," Ruby was saying with a subservient edge to her voice. "But we shouldn't be long, see, because my husband's coming back and—well—there never was any reason for him to know about—her." Greer stared hard at Ruby's eyes. They were lighter than her own and deep set above wrinkled cheeks. This visit was another terrible mistake. All it could possibly achieve was more anguish for both of them. "We'll go," she said abruptly.

"No." Ruby waved Greer back into the chair. "No. You came a long way. It's just that Bill has one too many sometimes and I wouldn't want to upset him," she explained in a hurry. "There isn't a lot to say, but I don't mind talking about it. Did—? How did you find me?"

"I made some inquiries," Greer said promptly. Ruby had almost mentioned Rusty, she was sure of it. "Andrew and I came to London by train, then caught the underground out here to Walthamstow. I've been to Ferndale and seen Marsh Cottage. I also met the old vicar of St. Peters and he remembers your mother and father—and you as a little girl."

"And you saw Rusty, didn't you?" The pale eyes softened. "That's who gave you my address." The woman shook her head sadly. "I'm sorry, Greer. That's what I told him, too. I never meant to hurt anyone. If I could change it all I would, but they don't give you a second chance."

Greer's eyes stung and she pressed them with her fingers. "I didn't even know I had a brother until I went through the baptismal records at the church,'' she told her.

"He's your half-brother,'' Ruby clarified. "I named him after his father—Kurt Stevens. He was a sailor when I worked in Portsmouth. He went to Australia before Rusty was born. Never came back.'' Greer heard Ruby give an uneven sigh. "Said he would. We were going to get married after his trip.'' Greer waited as Ruby collected the memories she had tried so hard to forget. "I waited, but he wasn't on the ship when it came in and they all—the other men all said they didn't know where he was. We were kids, sixteen and seventeen. He was tall, like Rusty, with black hair and those dark blue eyes. You've got them, too, but I don't know—''

Who my father is—or was. "Are you happy, Ruby?'' She couldn't call her anything else.

"Yes!'' she answered without hesitation. "I've done very well, considering. Me and Jim never had any kids—We couldn't seem to, but we've got this house and he makes a steady wage.'' She sniffed suddenly, then coughed. "Everything's fine with you isn't it, Greer? You're happy? They've been good to you?''

"Of course.'' Greer heard her own voice crack. "They've been very good to me.''

"That's all right, then,'' Ruby said gratefully. "Rusty was too old—nobody wanted him. That's what I feel worst about. He got pushed around.''

"I'm sure he doesn't blame you for that anymore,'' Greer said instinctively. It was all so hopeless and pointless.

"He does,'' Ruby insisted. "He didn't say so, but I could feel it. When I saw him on the doorstep with my hair and Kurt's eyes—Kurt said he'd come back. We had plans. We used to dream.'' Ruby rubbed teary eyes. "Bunch of childish nonsense. I took too long to grow up, that's all. You're not married yet, then?''

Greer touched the back of her naked ring finger, trying to ignore Andrew's intake of breath, his sudden shift in the chair. "I was. My husband was killed,'' she said simply.

"I'm sorry. It's bad when you lose the one you love.''

"You get over it.''

Ruby's expression became distant. "Sometimes you do.'' She

winced as the cigarette burned down between her fingers. "Jim's bound to be back any minute."

Andrew stood immediately and offered Greer his hand. She hesitated, then took it.

"There isn't anything else to say," Ruby concluded. "You won't mind seeing yourselves out?" She sat rigidly in her cane-backed chair. "Good luck to you."

"Good luck," Greer echoed faintly.

The front door was open when she pulled away from Andrew and returned to the back room of the house. Ruby was staring straight ahead, her eyes dry. Lipstick had run into the little lines fanning out from her mouth.

Greer's nose felt stuffy and she opened her mouth while she fumbled for a tissue. "It's all right," she said, dropping to her knees. In an awkward motion, she hugged the woman quickly and kissed her papery cheek. "You did what was best, mom."

Ruby never moved.

On the way back to the underground station Greer rushed ahead of Andrew. The streets were grimy, some shop windows boarded. Newspaper rolled like tumbleweed along the sidewalks, curling into untidy cylinders in gutters and around lampposts. She hated it all. What she'd come from. What she really was. She was the lucky one who'd escaped and now the smart thing was to get out—go back to the States and forget all this. Ruby's dreams died with a young man, a boy, who'd sailed out of a harbor over thirty years ago and never returned. The woman she might have become disappeared with him, leaving her with nothing to give—to anyone.

Casey and Seattle. Greer pictured Britmania and the other store owners she'd come to know in Pioneer Square. There was nothing here for her, no future, certainly not with Andrew who couldn't possibly want her now he'd seen the background she sprang from. And it was all for the best. Time to go home.

On the tube-train, Greer avoided looking at Andrew. Steady and rattling vibration made conversation unnecessary, so she concentrated first on other passengers, then on advertisements pasted near the ceiling.

The cars hurtled repeatedly between tunnels and yellow-lighted stations until Andrew leaned close, pressing his shoulder to hers. "This is it," he said.

She moved mechanically to a platform before noticing the sign read Bond Street. "We're supposed to go to Waterloo," she told him. "We can't catch a train to Dorset from here, can we?"

"No. But we're not going back yet."

Greer watched the last train coach disappear into its inky burrow. An acrid blast of air shot back, driving grit into her eyes. "I want to leave, Andrew. And if we miss the seven-ten there's nothing else until early tomorrow morning," she complained.

He took her arm. "We're going to walk, and eat—and talk."

"I'm going to Weymouth."

"You're trying to hide from what happened out there. It's no good—"

"Save it for your patients," she snapped. Her face felt stiff. "I didn't ask you to come. And I'm not asking you to play shrink for me now."

The pressure behind her elbow was steady, propelling her through an archway to the escalator. "Playing the shrink, as you put it, is the last thing I want to do with you," he answered firmly. She couldn't help but feel badly for everything she'd put him through. "Don't shut me out, Greer," he continued. "You may not have asked me to come, but I'm glad I did. I can tell you feel like running for the closest foxhole right now, and you shouldn't be alone."

A steady drizzle peppered them when they climbed to the street. The sky was a slate backdrop to solid rows of buildings. Small shops at ground level were already closed.

"What time is it?" Greer said, yanking at her jacket sleeve for a look at her watch. "Seven? It can't be."

"We couldn't have made that train," Andrew said. "I know a little club off Berkeley Square. The food's good and later there'll be music. Do you like jazz?"

"Yes," Greer answered absently. "But I'm not dressed for a London club." She glanced down at her navy gabardine pants and flat shoes. "Why are we even discussing this? We've missed the train, Andrew. Is there a bus or something?"

He pushed a hand beneath the hair at her neck. "There's a warm club a few blocks away where you'll knock 'em dead in what you've got on. You would in anything."

Greer sighed audibly. "You aren't about to budge, are you?"

"Nope." He shook his head and wrapped an arm around her shoulders. "You're in my stomping grounds, so you might as well enjoy it. I'll make sure we get home."

The club proved to be an elegant room in the basement of an old hotel. Candlelight flickered over black-and-white ink sketches drawn directly on the wall. Chairs with wide curving backs turned circular tables into secluded islands. A soft buzz of conversation blended into the taped reggae music. A small dance floor, surrounded by mirrors, was empty, except for a cluster of draped instruments.

When they were seated and a waiter had taken their order, Andrew lifted her hand from her lap and pressed the palm against his cheek. "What did you expect to find in Walthamstow?" he asked softly.

She tried to pull away.

"Relax, darling. I only want you to be objective."

"I can't talk about it now," she replied firmly. The music's insistent beat made her temples throb.

"I'm glad you went, Greer," he insisted. "If you hadn't, you'd have spent the rest of your life wishing you had and wondering if you still should. It wasn't so bad, was it? She was honest, and—"

"Stop. Please, Andrew, stop."

He lifted her chin and waited until she finally looked at him. "We will talk about it—when you're ready," he added.

The waiter returned with fluffy crab mousse with asparagus sauce and Marfil Seco, a dry white wine from Spain that Andrew explained was rarely exported. Greer didn't feel like eating, but the wine tasted good. It warmed her veins and slowly melted the tension from her leaden muscles.

"Dance with me," Andrew said suddenly.

Greer started and looked uncomprehendingly at him.

He stroked a knuckle across her cheek. "We've never danced together." His mouth trembled slightly and her heart squeezed.

She fingered a spoon. "I don't—"

"You don't dance," he said cutting her off. "Likely story. Come on."

They were the only couple on the shadowy dance floor. Andrew folded Greer close, massaging her back, stroking her neck, until she softened and put her arms around his waist. She loved him. She always would. But there could be no mistake about the differences in their backgrounds or what they meant to their future. He behaved as if nothing had changed between them when he must think of her as part of a life-style he knew little about. He'd witnessed the sorry scene with Ruby. Heat flashed over Greer's neck and face. There were no family portraits to document her heritage.

Andrew danced smoothly, using his whole body to guide her around the floor. He held her against his length, turning them both with the rhythmic pressure of his hips and thighs.

"You know I've got a flat in London," Andrew whispered against her hair.

Greer frowned up into his face. "You never told me. How would I know?"

"I didn't think I'd mentioned it," he explained. "But I thought maybe Lauren said something at her house."

What would he say if she told him what Lauren had really said—and about Bob's visit to the boardinghouse? "Nobody told me. Where is it?" she asked reluctantly.

"About four blocks from here."

Greer's insides began a slow burn. He wanted to sleep with her tonight—to make love. Her nostrils flared and she closed her eyes. She imagined him around and inside her, and every female urge sprang to life. He'd planned it this way so why not go along with him? Memories would be her keepsakes and there would be too few of them.

She pushed her hands beneath his jacket and watched his eyes darken. "Kiss me, Andrew," she told him urgently. "Kiss me, then I want to go to your flat and make love." *For this one last time, my darling.*

He trembled, swung her back to the room and encircled her gently, gathered her to him until her toes barely touched the floor.

"I love you." The whispered words escaped through his teeth before his lips covered hers. When he lifted his head she was dizzy. Andrew buried his face in her neck, still swaying faintly to the music. Over his shoulder, Greer saw their bodies reflected in the mirrors like a single piece of sculpture. Tears sprang to her eyes. Every line, every texture and scent of him was dear. Would she ever smell a breeze off the ocean, hear a man's deep laugh, or see a pair of golden eyes and not think of Andrew? But Andrew must never suspect—especially not tonight.

"I want to go now," she said evenly. Blinking rapidly, she touched his cheek. "Take me home, please."

It wasn't nine, yet the streets were deserted. This was Mayfair, Andrew told her. The flat he owned had belonged to his father before him. John Monthaven had used it when he came up to town for plays and the horticultural shows he enjoyed. Now Andrew found it useful when he had a consultation or simply wanted to get away for a few days. The quiet elegance of the area spelled wealth and the remnants of a more graceful era to Greer.

"It's a mews flat," Andrew said, steering her into a quiet alley lit by old-fashioned streetlights shaped like carriage lanterns. "Years ago they were servants, quarters. There are garages on the lower floor that might have housed horses once. The rooms are upstairs," he explained.

The flat surprised Greer. Rather than the antique pieces she'd expected, it was furnished in Oriental style. A low, red lacquered table dominated the living room. The couch and chairs were deep blue splashed with giant Chinese peonies. An exquisite Oriental screen inlaid with gold and mother-of-pearl fanned across one corner and the deep-piled rug was the same dark blue as the furnishings.

"This is fabulous," Greer exclaimed. "You did all this?"

"It took a while," Andrew said dryly. "When dad had it, the place looked like something Sherlock Holmes would go for. Can I get you a drink?"

Greer went to the window, slipping off her coat. "No thanks. But don't let me stop you." Her breathing became suddenly shallow. "Looks a bit like Baker Street on a Sherlock Holmes night outside. Misty rain on slick cobblestones."

"And I thought I was the one with an overactive imagination. Do you want to listen to some music?"

"No."

His sigh was audible. "Will you come to bed with me?"

"Yes, Andrew."

She turned and he held out a hand. "I'm never going to get used to having you," he said. "I keep being afraid you'll disappear."

Greer felt as if she'd been kicked. Why would he say such a thing—now? As panic tried to invade her mind, Greer forced herself to think logically. He wasn't thinking past this moment and the desire that brought them here in the first place. She took his hand and they walked into the bedroom.

"I feel filthy, Andrew. Could I take a shower first?"

He spread his fingers over her collarbone on top of the white blouse, then looked at her breasts. "If I can come with you," he answered.

Carefully she stepped away and loosened the buttons at her wrists. Andrew's throat moved convulsively. Inch by inch, the blouse parted and she slipped it off, dropping it to the floor before kicking aside her shoes and unzipping the pants. Sweat had broken out on his brow. Greer kissed his jaw and dodged his reaching hand. Something primitive drove her on, made her want to excite him past the limit of his restraint. The slacks' silk lining swished past her thighs and calves to join her blouse. Panty hose followed and she stood in a white satin teddy fastened from neckline to navel by a row of minuscule buttons.

"Greer." Andrew's voice broke. "You're an enigma. Fire inside a fragile shell of shyness. You are so beautiful, my darling."

She came close. "I don't do very well with tiny buttons."

He looked into her eyes, then at the teddy. "You're driving me insane." With shaking fingers he pushed each satin bead through its hole until only ribbon straps and Greer's distended nipples kept the garment from dropping away.

"Take it off, Andrew," she whispered.

With finger and thumb he pulled down first one, then the other strap. His palms stroked the smooth fabric from her flesh, followed it over her ribs and waist, her hips, and let it rustle to her feet.

Andrew tore his own clothes off and lifted her into his arms. Cradled against his naked body, she turned to press her breasts to his chest while he carried her to the bathroom.

They washed each other, reverently, paying rapt attention to every millimeter of skin, touching, holding—following fingers with lips.

"I can't take this any longer," Andrew breathed against her belly. "I want you now."

Greer didn't answer. She dropped her head back, allowing water to beat down on her face and neck, and guided his mouth to a nipple. He shuddered, pressing the heel of one hand between her thighs until she cried out, then he lifted her and Greer wrapped her legs around his waist. Andrew entered her with a single thrust, wrenching sobs from her throat. In seconds her fingers were sinking into his shoulders for support. She bent her face to the side of his head and felt him fill her again and again, drawing raw breaths from her lungs. When their climax came they almost fell. Andrew clasped Greer in one arm, supported his weight against the wall with the other and slid her slowly down until they both stood beneath the cooling spray.

"Lady," he gasped at last. "We'd better lie down before we fall down. My God, woman—no wonder all I can think of anymore is you."

Greer hardly felt the towel on her skin or Andrew rubbing her hair. She dried him haphazardly, but wouldn't allow him to do it himself. They fell into bed and as she drifted asleep she wondered what the bedroom looked like, or the bathroom. Had she even seen them?

"SWEETHEART."

She began floating up from a great depth.

"Greer, darling. Wake up."

"Yes. I'm awake," Greer answered, sitting abruptly and looking around. Dawn was barely poking its fingers through tiny holes in rush blinds. "What is it?"

"I want to talk to you and I can't wait any longer," he told her.

Andrew's flat in London. She shook her head and shivered, then realized she was naked to the waist. Before she could pull up the sheet, he pressed her against the pillows and kissed her soundly. For an instant he raised his head to rake her body with his eyes, then rolled onto his back with her wrapped in his arms.

"Mmm." His fingers were buried in her hair. "You smell wonderful in my soap. We should always share showers."

Greer turned to nestle against his chest. "I doubt if either of our constitutions could take it for long," she murmured contentedly.

"Shall we give it a try?"

"You want to shower again—now?"

"No. But I thought we might consider taking lots of them together in future. *Will* you marry me, Greer?"

CHAPTER EIGHTEEN

SHE HELD HIM very tight, pressed her lips into the hair on his chest. If only—Greer rolled away, pulling up the sheet.

"Greer?" he said as he shook her gently. "What's wrong, darling?"

"Nothing." She splayed a hand across her face.

Agonizing moments passed before he leaned over her, sweeping back her tangled curls. "I asked if you'd marry me." He eased her fingers away. "Look at me, Greer—for God's sake."

Totally bereft of words, she lifted her face to his, knowing he'd see the tears.

"You will, won't you?" he said hopefully. Slowly he lowered his mouth to hers. His lips and tongue moved on Greer's, caressing, beginning their magic. She turned into his arms and filled her fingers with his hair.

When he propped himself on one elbow to look at her, Greer was breathless and throbbing.

"We don't have to wait," he began. "I'm not sure of the formalities with your being American, but I don't think they'll take long to deal with."

Greer took a deep breath. "I'm leaving for the States on Friday," she said bluntly, moving closer to the edge of the bed. "There are too many reasons why we can't go on."

"I don't get this," Andrew answered. "I just asked you to marry me."

She swallowed the lump that rose in her throat. Please, let her make it through this quickly and cleanly. "It's been something special, Andrew. Now it's time to call it quits and get on with our responsibilities. When's the hearing?"

"Tomorrow," he said mechanically.

Greer sat up. "Good timing." Her heart was running away, faster and faster. "I'm planning to spend the next few days finishing the arrangements for my trip home."

She swung her feet to the floor and immediately found herself flat on the bed with Andrew's strong fingers clamped over her shoulders. "Not good enough, Greer," he said, barely containing his fury. "You said you loved me."

Her insides clenched. His face was suffused with color, his eyes unnaturally bright. "Love?" She laughed, wishing her breasts weren't heaving with each painful breath. "Probably the most over-used word in the dictionary. I love ice cream. I love that dress. I love—"

"Enough." Andrew's brows knit together and he dropped his forehead for an instant. "You took off your wedding ring. Why?" he demanded.

"It was time," she said without expression.

"After two years it was suddenly time? And it just happened to coincide with—us?"

She'd never seen him so angry, but she must press on. "It didn't mean anything."

"I see." He released her and turned away. "It was time to take off your wedding ring and it had nothing to do with me. And saying you loved me meant nothing, either. You're purely hedonistic—is that what you want me to accept? A pleasure seeker, and a taker who doesn't like strings?"

Oh, Andrew, Andrew. "Let's not spoil what we've had," she answered with much more emotion than she should have.

"No," he said sourly as he clasped his shins. Muscles in his back stood out, rock hard. "Sex is an activity for you. Something not to be confused with feelings. That's what you're telling me?"

She was weary. "Passion shouldn't be confused with love. That's all I'm trying to explain. Tomorrow—next year—you'll be grateful we didn't get into something we'd both regret."

"Little liar," he said, as if the only way to get satisfaction was by provoking her. "There's something else. Why don't you give it a shot, Greer. Tell the truth for once," he challenged her.

"Okay," she snapped. "You want it, you can have it." In seconds she'd left the bed and gathered her twisted clothes into a pile.

"We have nothing in common other than sex. We turn each other on. And now I want to catch the first available train for Dorset. You should, too. There's a lot to do in the next few days." Greer thought the silence that ensued would drive her mad. When he spoke, his voice sent shivers down her spine.

"Tell me one thing," he said.

"Sure." There could be no tears yet.

"If you're a woman who can have a casual affair and walk away—someone who enjoys sex as a separate entity—why did it take you two years after your husband died to sleep with another man?"

Greer's hands felt like paws. The teddy gaped away from her breasts while she struggled with its buttons. Don't say any more, she ordered herself silently. Don't let your voice give you away.

"Convince me, Greer," he demanded. "Make me believe you mean all this crap. Why was I the first?"

He came to stand over her and she couldn't resist lifting her eyes to his lean face. Yes, she could have taken what he offered now— but how long would it have been before she became an embarrassment, before physical attraction wasn't enough?

"What makes you think you were the first?"

The deep hurt and disappointment in Andrew's eyes made her look away.

"I'm not a fool," he said finally. "Hurry up. I want out of here before I suffocate."

SOMEHOW GREER had dragged herself through the rest of the day and the longest night she remembered. On the train to Weymouth, Andrew's silence had hummed through her blood. He'd parked the Mini at the station while they were in London and, when they arrived, insisted with distant politeness on driving her to Belle Vista. Then she was alone with countless hours yawning ahead in which she could only try to cope with the beginning of her memories.

This morning the airline had confirmed a seat for Friday. She'd go to London on Thursday and stay overnight at the airport Holiday

Inn. That left today and tomorrow to firm up any outstanding contacts she'd made for Britmania.

At lunchtime she walked along the beach toward the town center. She wasn't hungry—hadn't been for days—but she stopped at the seafood hut and tried a little bowl of cockles. The orange-tailed shellfish were surprisingly pleasant, chewy and tart, sprinkled with vinegar and pepper.

Greer finished eating and trudged on, the heels of her boots sinking into wet sand. Fog billowed off the ocean, blanketing the traffic sounds on the promenade. She stopped and faced the fuzzy bay. Ever since Colin died and she'd lost Colleen she'd felt half-alive. For a little while, with Andrew, the dead parts of her had been resurrected. But what she had to offer him couldn't be enough for a lifetime. Fear of loving and losing was destructive in itself—she knew that now. But even if she could cope with the possibility of another personal disaster, she couldn't willingly bring one on Andrew. He'd never let her know when he began to feel cheated. In time their different backgrounds and her inability to have children would have become an issue, but Andrew wouldn't tell her outright. She'd simply know it because his feelings were something he couldn't totally hide.

In the town she visited a fishermen's supply store to finalize arrangements for a shipment of oiled wool sweaters. She'd seen them in Guernsey, the exclusive source, and been told they were available in Weymouth. They'd sell well—particularly to the younger set. Pottery from the Isle of Wight came next. Handmade by a couple, the smooth work reflected an African sojourn. Greer took a carefully packed box of samples with her. Later she'd send for more.

Nothing took long enough. By three she was in her room once more, too tired to pack, too afraid of her own imagination to lie down and think. She wandered downstairs to the lounge with a book. The preliminary hearing on the Michael Drake case would have started. How was Andrew doing? She bit her bottom lip, yearning to be with him.

Mrs. Findlay's door slammed and the woman came into the room rubbing her hands on a tea towel. "Made your arrangements, Mrs. Beckett?" she inquired.

Greer nodded. She didn't feel like talking.

"Did you call that Mr. Gibbs back? He sounded upset."

Gibbs? "I didn't know I'd had a call," Greer told her. "When— was there a message?"

"Just wanted you to get in touch with him. Said he'd be at Ringstead Hall and you had the number. I left a note on your bed," the woman explained.

"I didn't notice. Thanks, Mrs. Findlay."

Ten minutes later, Greer sat on the bottom step of the stairs, fighting down waves of panic. Gibbs had arrived for work this morning to find Andrew's bed untouched. The kitchen bore signs of his having eaten dinner, but Gibbs was certain he'd left shortly afterward, in a hurry. The clothes Andrew wore to London were thrown aside. And at the medical board they said he'd called the previous afternoon to postpone the hearing for a day. No one had seen him and Dr. Wilson didn't answer the phone.

Gibbs's agitation had worried Greer. He was an old man—too old for pressure like this. She'd tried to reassure him and told him to go home, promising she would let him know the instant Andrew showed up. And he would, she insisted, as much for her own sake as Gibbs's. This was her fault. Andrew had gone somewhere to lick the wounds she'd inflicted.

She should contact the Wilsons herself. There was no reply at their house and when she called the hospital the switchboard operator informed her Dr. Wilson was out of town for the day. An invisible hand squeezed her throat. Someone must have seen Andrew since he dropped her off at Belle Vista. She telephoned his number and let it ring fifteen times.

Greer took a taxi to Ringstead Hall and told the driver to wait. Gibbs would have locked the door. Without transportation she'd be stranded if Andrew weren't at home. She beat on his private door and waited, sweeping the grounds for a sign of him. At the front door, the bell jangled hollowly in the great hall and Greer didn't bother to try it again. Breathing raggedly, she ran to the cliffs and scoured the misty beach, knowing instinctively he wouldn't be there. He *wasn't* here. Her nose ran and she blew it on a crumpled tissue. *The car. Andrew's Mini.*

Her breath rasped through her clenched teeth while she rushed up the steps and across the lawn. At the back corner of the house she leaned on a drainpipe, peering through watery eyes. His car was gone. At least he wasn't lying somewhere in the house, unconscious, or—The only thing to do was try all the places he might be, then it would have to be the police. She instructed the taxi driver to take her back to Belle Vista. She'd make her calls from there.

At eight o'clock Greer gave up on getting help. There was still no reply at the Wilsons'. Andrew hadn't even called his service or the hospital, and the police clearly thought they were being asked to deal with the aftermath of a lovers' quarrel. A few more hours, the constable had calmly suggested. She should wait a while longer to see if the "gentleman" turned up. If he didn't, then she could ask for assistance. The police weren't authorized to act until the reportedly missing person had been gone twenty-four hours, anyway. And since the lady knew the subject had eaten dinner at his home the night before, wasn't she being a bit premature? Probably gone for a little drive to "calm things down a bit."

She would go back to Ringstead Hall and wait—all night if necessary. Sooner or later he'd have to show and his home was the logical place. The same taxi driver took her. When she got out of the cab she saw his quizzical expression. "There's someone home here now, miss?" he asked when she paid him off and said he could leave. "It's pitch-dark out here and the house looks dark, too."

"There's someone here," she said lightly, certain inside that she was wrong. "I'll be fine. Thank you."

She watched his taillights swing out of sight in the yew tunnel and turned to the house's oppressive hulk. Without a moon, its size was something she felt rather than saw.

Doggedly Greer went through the same motions as before, knocking and ringing and circling the building. She balked at ranging the grounds or approaching the cliffs, afraid of falling and of the gnawing apprehension growing with each second that passed.

The car was still missing. She sat on the step to the side door and bundled her jacket more tightly to her neck. Droplets of moisture in the fog wet her face and clung to her lashes. When the idea came, it was slowly, held back by her own unwillingness to consider it.

Treading carefully to avoid turning an ankle on the gravel path, Greer retraced her steps to the back of the house and opened the door of the outbuilding that doubled as Andrew's garage. She'd only seen him use the makeshift shelter that first day when he drove her home to Weymouth. He always left his car out.

But not this time. The Mini was pulled inside between stacks of garden tools.

Greer floundered in a paralyzing concoction of fear and confusion. Andrew had come home yesterday, eaten dinner sometime later and left. She rounded the vehicle and felt its hood. Cold. The engine was cold and there were no lights on in the house. Wherever he'd gone, she was certain it had been on foot. Her breathing speeded up, coming in shallow gasps from the tops of her lungs. Something had happened to him. She knew it.

She ran. Up to the glistening jet-black pool.

Sweat bathed her body. At the pool's edge she stared down into barely shifting nothingness. She shut out the thought of Andrew lying at the bottom and struck out for the woods at the top of the rise. If only she'd had enough sense to bring a flashlight.

As soon as the trees enveloped her she knew it was hopeless. Brambles scratched her face and hands and clawed at her hair. "Andrew," she called, and listened to her own voice ricochet between dense trunks. Her skin crawled, but she refused to cry.

She followed the tree line to an easterly ridge, stumbling every few paces on uneven ground. He'd come out here to walk and gotten hurt. The conviction grew and grew until it pounded in every brain cell. Would he go to the beach on a foggy afternoon? Her heart plummeted. Unless he'd gotten up early this morning and carefully made his bed, Andrew had been missing since last night. The moon glimmered through a slim break in the clouds and she peered at her watch. It was almost eleven—three hours since she'd left Weymouth for the second time.

Greer didn't have any idea how far the tide came in when it was high. She must find the way to the beach and search for him there. Forgetting caution, she took several running steps and pitched forward. Pain shot through her middle as the force of hard earth meeting her chest exploded the air from her body. She lay still, panting, until she could roll slowly onto her back. Every muscle and joint ached. Sharp pains seared her hip.

Far above, a blue glow came and went as the cloud layer wafted across the fickle moon. Water gathered in Greer's eyes. She did love him—so very much. And she'd hurt him, driven him out to wander over this deserted place. Lord, she prayed, just let him be safe. Tomorrow was something she could cope with when it came—as long as nothing had happened to Andrew.

Breathing was agony. Gingerly she got to her feet and started for the cliffs. She fell again when she drew near the house, tearing her slacks. Warm dampness seeped through at the knee. Blood.

Helpless sobs erupted from her raw throat. She sat huddled on the path, her cheek cradled in her elbow.

Then she saw a light.

CHAPTER NINETEEN

AT GROUND LEVEL a yellow sliver glimmered above a basement window shade. The kitchen? Greer stood, adrenaline pumping along every vein. There was a light on in the kitchen—probably had been all along, but she hadn't noticed it. Half-running, choking back tears, she scrambled to the side door and pummeled it with both fists.

She waited, her whole body shaking impatiently. Nothing. "Answer the door," she yelled, and pounded again. "Be here someone, please."

Abruptly, the door scraped open and Greer's mouth dropped. Andrew, dressed in faded jeans and a partially buttoned shirt, stared out at her. He swayed slightly on bare feet. "Hi," he said, and winced, rubbing his temple. "What do you want?"

Greer found her voice. "What do I want? Andrew." Her voice rose higher. "I've been searching for you for hours. I've been so afraid. Where have you been?"

He smiled sheepishly and rubbed his unshaven cheek. "Want to come in?"

She marched inside and slammed the door.

"Shh," Andrew whispered. "My head's coming apart."

"You've been drinking," Greer accused him. "I don't believe this. Gibbs is worried out of his mind. I'm running all over the countryside thinking you're dead. And you're holed up somewhere tying one on."

"There's coffee in the kitchen," he answered, turning away. Greer followed him numbly downstairs.

Under the kitchen's dim lights they faced each other and gasped simultaneously.

"You're a mess," Greer exclaimed, taking in his disheveled hair and almost two days' growth of beard.

"So are you," he answered. "You're bleeding right through your pant leg. Sit there and let me take a look."

"I'm fine. Your hands, Andrew. How did that happen to them?" His nails were ragged and his knuckles skinned.

He snorted. "I fell, too. Up the steps."

"Where have you been? When did you get back?" she demanded.

"At a club in Dorchester." He tried to straighten the wrongly buttoned denim shirt. "And I've been here for hours—several hours," he added.

"I rang the bell, and knocked—you didn't answer." A soft buzzing started in her ears. Her limbs trembled uncontrollably.

Andrew's eyes slid sheepishly away. "Must have fallen asleep," he mumbled.

"The hearing, Andrew. Gibbs said you postponed it." The buzzing swelled inside her head and she blinked to keep him in focus.

"I needed time, Greer. To get my act together."

Because of her. She felt sick. If the hearing never took place he'd always carry with him the frustration of missed justice. She did believe he should go through with the case. The insight shook her.

"Andrew." Her voice was far away. "I'm going to pass out." Her legs buckled before he could catch her and they both sank to the floor. Greer tried to bend forward, but he tipped her flat and pulled up her knees.

"It's all right, darling," he soothed. "Take deep breaths through your mouth." She felt his fingers on the pulse at her neck. "What's happened to you, Greer? You're scratched to pieces."

Oxygen flooded back into her brain. She opened her eyes and found Andrew's face scant inches away. "I searched for hours in the dark," she said. "I kept tripping over things. We have to call Mr. Gibbs and tell him you're safe. There wasn't anyone to help. Bob and Lauren aren't home and the police said it was too soon for them to do anything."

"Good grief. You called the police?"

She went limp while he eased her into a chair. "What should I have done? I was frantic. No one had seen you since yesterday."

Greer was amazed that Andrew had not considered the consequences of his actions. He was always so considerate. Now she knew how much she had upset him.

He rocked her, nuzzled his rough jaw against her temple. "I needed a few hours to think. I'm sorry I frightened you," he apologized.

Andrew made Greer sit still while he poured her some coffee and refilled his own, then he called John Gibbs.

The phone rang the instant it was hung up and Andrew put a hand over the receiver. "It's Bob," he said. "Says he's been trying to get me for hours."

Greer watched the play of expressions cross his face.

"It never came off—no—no, it's not canceled, just postponed until tomorrow. Where were you today? Ah. Look, I've had a hell of a day. We'll talk in the morning. Greer's with me now—" He smiled at her and raised his brows. "I don't think that's any of your business, Bob. 'Night." He let the receiver clatter into its cradle.

"He asked something about me, didn't he?" Greer probed.

"Only if you planned to spend the night." He interrupted her forming retort. "He and Lauren are dying to get the two of us permanently tucked up, so don't be mad. Let's take the coffee upstairs."

In the sitting room Andrew lit the fire and fetched Greer a robe from his bedroom.

"Here. Take off those slacks so I can get at your knee. I'd suggest a shower, but—"

"Andrew," she said before he could finish. "You may be bionic, I'm not. It's been a long time since I felt this lousy. All I want is to sleep for a few hours—and know you're safe." Her eyes met his and held them.

He touched her cheek, stroked a thumb over her bottom lip, then reached for the robe. When she'd slipped off the torn woolen pants, he wrapped her in warm terry cloth and left the room to return almost immediately with his medical bag.

Greer watched the top of his head while he worked. Deftly he cleaned the wound with medicated pads, then taped a gauze dressing firmly in position. "We'll give it a day or two, then leave it open." He moved his attention to her face and hands, swabbing at scratches while she winced. "These aren't deep. Need to be kept clean, though."

When he'd finished, Greer held his right wrist and flattened the hand across her thigh. She selected a pad like the ones he'd used and tore the wrapper open, sensing the effort it took to let her help him. "It's your turn, Andrew. You can't always be the crusader," she said more brusquely than she intended.

He grimaced. "Ouch!"

"You'll make it, doctor."

She concentrated on finishing her work on his hands. "I'll do this, then I must call a taxi," she told him.

"No you mustn't."

A shuddery breath slipped past her lips. "We can't start that again. Neither of us has the energy."

Andrew flexed his fingers, studying the knuckles. "No we don't," he agreed. "But since I am the doctor, I insist on keeping you under observation for the next few hours." He checked his watch. "Six to be exact. I need to leave at seven."

"It would be a mistake, Andrew. A reaction to stress. Please—"

"We're going to sleep, my love. Nothing more. In the morning I'll go my way and you'll go yours—for a while. No taxi's going to want to come out here at this hour of the morning anyway, so I'd have to drive you. And you wouldn't want to pressure a sick man," he teased her.

Greer was too exhausted to argue anymore. She drank a few more sips of lukewarm coffee and crawled between Andrew's sheets, falling asleep before he'd finished undressing.

The room was cool when she awoke, spread-eagled across the bed on her stomach. With a sleepy sigh she pulled a pillow beneath her chin and squinted. Music, softly played, came from the sitting room. Then Andrew's ancient travel alarm shrilled suddenly on the nightstand and she crammed the pillow over her head.

"Sorry."

Andrew's voice filtered through thick down and she gave up the pillow after a feeble struggle. "Rotten clock," she muttered. "Why'd you set it to go off after you got up?"

"I didn't," he said. "Unfortunately I can't shut down all mental systems the way you evidently can. I gave up on sleep an hour ago."

She sat on the edge of the bed and groaned at the pain in her knee. "I want to be with you today. If we could stop by Belle Vista—"

"No, Greer," he told her firmly, rubbing her chin. "You'd distract me, my sweet. And there may be some testimony I'd rather you didn't hear."

Greer opened her mouth to argue, but shut it again. What he said was right. He didn't need the added pressure of knowing she was watching and listening. She shunted against the headboard and sat cross-legged while he knotted his navy tie.

A devastatingly handsome man. Athletically lean in a pale blue shirt and a three-piece suit of silver-gray worsted, so fine it glistened faintly. He faced her again, finger-combing his blue-black hair and grinning. Totally masculine. Every clearly defined line of his body complemented by the perfect fit of his clothes.

"Do I pass inspection?"

"Mmm. How do you feel?"

"Better than I deserve." He bent to kiss her lips and she smelled warm sandalwood. Immediately heat suffused her limbs. Could she fight it forever? Did she really have to?

"Ciao," Andrew said cheerfully. "Why don't you rest a while longer. When Gibbs comes in he'll be happy to drive you to Weymouth for a change of clothes. Could you be here when I get back this afternoon?"

She should say no. "I'll be here, Andrew," she said instead. "Good luck."

For an instant he hesitated, his grazed knuckles whitening around the doorknob. "Later, then." His briefcase hit the wall as he left.

Greer tucked up her feet and hugged her knees. Somehow they had to work through the deterrents to their future together. Or at least give themselves a chance to try. She had to give them a chance. Her fears were throwing up the blocks. Fear of rejection.

Fear that their diverse backgrounds would eventually destroy whatever they tried to build. Andrew didn't even know what held her back. He did love her. Every look and touch proved it. Didn't she owe him honesty? Was it right for her to second-guess his reaction to her sterility? She could accept it now—he probably would, too. And they both knew she was a passionate woman. Though she had resisted making love, it was clearly evident how much she enjoyed it when they did.

A door slammed downstairs. Gibbs was early. Probably hadn't slept well, either. It was obvious the old man cared deeply for Andrew.

She straightened her sweater, slipped on the ruined slacks and went into the bathroom. In the age-spotted mirror she glowered at her puffy eyes. The brambles had designed a patchwork quilt on her forehead and a long scratch curved from temple to chin. *Mess* didn't come close. Cold water cleared her head and brought a hint of pink to her cheeks. There was a comb in her jacket pocket but she wasn't sure where she'd left it.

Humming in a monotone, she crossed the hall to the sitting room once more. The jacket lay on the couch. Greer reached into a pocket and stopped, an icy sensation climbing her spine one vertebra at a time.

"You might as well put that on, Mrs. Beckett."

Very slowly, she straightened, clutching the coat to her breast. There was no air in the room.

"It's all right. Keep quiet and nothing will happen to you," the strange voice assured her.

Greer turned around, her throat closing, and stared at the man who stood behind the door. He was nondescript, colorless. Average height, average build, thinning sandy hair, eyes not blue or brown. But his expressionless features struck mindless terror into Greer.

"Put on your coat please, Mrs. Beckett. We're going for an outing. You Americans enjoy our English countryside, I understand."

She sank to the edge of the couch. "Who are you? What do you want from me?" she said, stalling for time.

"Don't make this difficult," he answered calmly. "I already told you we're going for a drive. You don't need to know who I am. You'll never see me again after today.''

"I'm not going anywhere with you," Greer insisted. "And you'd better get out before Dr. Monthaven gets back."

"He just left and we both know he doesn't intend returning until this afternoon."

Her belly contracted. "Mr. Gibbs is due any minute."

"Not until ten. Let's go."

"Don't touch me," she croaked. "Stay away."

The man let out an exasperated sigh. "Violence isn't what I had in mind—not for you," he said enigmatically. "But if you don't do as I ask, Dr. Monthaven may not be so fortunate."

Greer wanted to scream. She was being used to exert some sort of pressure on Andrew. "Winston Coover put you up to this," she concluded.

"What you choose to believe is your business." He checked his watch. "We have to leave now."

She went. Securely belted and locked into a vintage, convertible Jaguar, Greer watched the hillsides as they passed, and the valleys, the farmhouses and clumps of trees. First north, then east, then north again. After what seemed like hours she lost her sense of direction and put all her energy into musing and trying to control her shaking arms and legs.

Her driver never spoke. He drove fast but skillfully, and Greer had no idea how far they'd gone when he pulled into a lane that was barely more than an animal track and wound for miles between stands of evergreen trees.

After they stopped he got out and went to the car trunk for a knobby bundle. Greer hung back when he opened her door, but one look into his eyes reminded her of what he'd said at Ringstead Hall. If she didn't do as she was told, Andrew might suffer.

Before she had time to consider her next action, he pulled her from the car, twisted her around and tied her hands. "No! Stop!" She kicked at him.

The blindfold came over her head in a flash. "Kick again and I'll tie your ankles," he warned her. He knotted the scarf securely around her eyes. "You shouldn't be too hard to carry. And I will if I have to," he added.

Greer stood still. For an instant she thought of screaming, then changed her mind. He'd probably gag her.

She felt marshy ground beneath her feet as the man appeared to zigzag endlessly, dragging her behind him. "This is it," he said at last.

"This is what?" Sweat soaked Greer's back.

Hands closed over her shoulders and she was forced to sit. "I brought food and water and extra sweaters. There's a blanket, too," he told her, as if she cared. "You'll get free, eventually. Then, if you're lucky, you may manage to find the track we came in on. Nothing comes up here. Making it to the highway would take you hours. By then it'll be dark." He paused to make certain she was listening. "Your best bet is to stay put until early tomorrow morning. You'll be fine here. When you do start out, take it easy and keep calm."

"Keep calm?" she shouted. "Don't leave me here—please."

She heard his retreating footsteps.

ANDREW SLAMMED through the corridor and down the basement stairs to the kitchen. "Gibbs," he yelled. "Gibbs. Where the hell are you?"

He smelled meat pie baking in the oven but there was no sign of John Gibbs. At a full run, Andrew dashed to the stairs and took them two at a time. "Greer—" Her name faded on his lips when he entered the empty sitting room.

"Hello, sir." Gibbs came from the bedroom carrying Andrew's dirty shirt and jeans. "You're early. I wasn't expecting you un-til—"

"Where is she?" Andrew cut him off. "Mrs. Beckett—Greer. You took her to Weymouth, didn't you? Why did she decide not to come back?"

The old man's forehead wrinkled. "Was I supposed to pick Mrs. Beckett up, sir? You never said."

Andrew ran his tongue over the roof of his dry mouth. "She wasn't here when you arrived?"

"No, sir. I spoke to the lady yesterday. She was most helpful. But she hasn't been here today."

His bones turned to putty. "Thanks, Gibbs. That's all I wanted to know."

As soon as the door closed, he pulled out the note: "If you want to know where Mrs. Beckett is—drop the case." Typed on a sheet of loose-leaf paper and enclosed in a white envelope, it had been put on his chair in the hearing chamber at the administration building during first recess. Andrew had set off for Ringstead immediately, leaving Bob to make some excuse.

He stuffed the envelope into his breast pocket and went to the phone. Mrs. Findlay's sniffs punctuated her replies to his questions. No, like she told the other man, Mrs. Beckett wasn't at Belle Vista. No, she hadn't been there today or called.

What other man called the boardinghouse? Andrew ripped off his tie.

Greer was gone. He went to the window seat and stared out at the tree tops. Between the time he had left for Dorchester and Gibbs' arrival someone came here—to his house—and took her away. Good God. She'd been abducted and the reason was so blatant it hurt. The note spelled it out. He was to be stopped from testifying in the Michael Drake case by whatever means necessary. And they'd found his weak point. Greer.

The one element that made no sense was Coover. The man wasn't a fool. And he was the first suspect anyone would zero in on. Coover would never risk a stunt like this.

Another idea took shape and Andrew ground a fist against his mouth. *Oh, no.* His eyelids felt stretched wide open. *It can't be that.*

He left the side door open when he left. The Mini spewed sprays of damp earth behind its rear wheels as he spun it around and peeled out of the gates. Driving west, he tried to put the pieces together calmly, but they kept overlapping, then blurring. His deduction couldn't be true, yet there was no other explanation.

Bob answered the door himself, dark circles around his sunken eyes. He was clean-shaven and still wearing suit pants and a white shirt with a tie pulled away from the collar. He stared into Andrew's face and turned to walk into the house. Andrew followed him silently to the game room.

His heart hammered against his ribs. This had to turn out to be a bad dream. "Where are Lauren and Simonne?"

"Away." Bob's voice was husky. "Visiting Lauren's folks."

"What did you say after I left the hearing?"

"That you had an emergency." Bob went to a bar by the wall. "Want a drink?"

"No, thanks," Andrew answered coldly.

Bob dropped ice cubes, one by one, into the glass, then paused. He looked quickly at Andrew, then stared through the window for an instant before splashing a huge measure of bourbon over the ice and adding a few drips of water from a jug.

Andrew's nerves threatened to snap. "We have to talk, Bob."

The straight back seemed to sag and Bob swung around. "You know, don't you," he said in a quaking voice. "Damn it all, Andy, you know. I can see it in your eyes. I never meant it to go this far. You've got to believe that. The last thing I wanted was to hurt you."

Iron fingers closed around Bob's windpipe. "The last thing you wanted was to hurt *yourself*," Andrew spat.

"No!" Bob insisted, struggling out of Andrew's grasp. He gulped greedily at the liquor. "You mattered most. Then Lauren and Simonne."

"Touching," Andrew said. "I guess the baby who's not even born is in there somewhere, too."

"I didn't want any of this to happen," Bob insisted.

"Why? Because you care so much about me." Andrew's mouth tasted sour. "So much you arranged to take Greer, then left that note in chambers."

The glass dangled from Bob's fingers. "What a bloody mess."

"Where's Greer?" Andrew demanded.

Bob shook his head slowly.

"Where is she, Bob? If you've done something to her I'll— Where is she, damn you?"

"Safe, Andy. You know me better than that."

"I don't know you at all," Andrew snapped. "That note was a

death threat. What are you afraid of? Your reputation? Do you think that if this hearing comes off—which it's going to—you'll be linked to me and ostracized because of it?''

"You don't understand," Bob answered wearily. The glass rattled on the rim of the pool table. "Andy, I wanted to tell you but I knew you'd walk away from me—for good. I couldn't take that.''

Andrew watched Bob's face crumple. He cried noiselessly, making no attempt to wipe away the tears. Panic crept over Andrew. "Where's Greer? Tell me.''

"I'll tell you, Andy," Bob assured him. "But first you have to know the rest. You love Lauren and Simonne—I know you do. For their sakes you've got to help me through this thing.''

"What? What thing? I want Greer," Andrew persisted.

"Look at me, Andy. Listen—hear me out to the end," Bob said, appealing to Andrew's sense of fairness. "I'm bisexual," he announced. "I've been bisexual since Cambridge.''

For seconds Andrew stared at his friend's drawn face. "My God," he said, dropping into a chair. "You can't mean that.''

"Neil was the first with me," Bob explained. "But there were others. I stopped when I met Lauren. I love her. You may find that hard to swallow, but it's true. And I love Simonne. I'd rather be dead than have this touch them," he said in obvious agony.

Andrew hid his face.

"For years everything went just fine," Bob rushed on. "Then I ran into Neil again about three years ago in London and everything started again. He didn't mean anything to me, just part of something I don't understand. But I couldn't help it," Bob finished, on the edge of fresh tears.

"Bob." Andrew looked up. "You poor stupid bastard. You could have come to me," he told him. "And there's counseling available. What have you done?''

"Only tried to stop the whole world from knowing what I am," Bob said miserably. "How could I have imagined—even in a nightmare—that one of Coover's boys would stumble on Neil and ask questions about you and me at Cambridge." Bob took a shaky breath and ran his fingers through his hair. "Neil blackmailed me. The guy hates me for running on both sides of the track. He played me off against Coover—threatened to tell him everything. I had no choice but to pay him—my reputation was at stake. It was the only way Neil would agree to help me stop the hearing,'' Bob said bitterly. "You see, even if Neil didn't testify, there was still a danger that Coover might have come up with someone else who would implicate me while he slandered you.''

"Someone else?''

"Neil said he had friends who might talk. My only safe bet was to make you call it off.''

"I can't cope with this.'' Andrew said as he stood and paced the room. "I'm going to ask this once more and if you don't answer I'm calling the police. *Where* is Greer?''

"Neil took her away,'' Bob finally admitted. "She's fine. Andy, are you going to blow the whistle on me?''

The muscles in Andrew's face hurt. He stopped in front of Bob and hooked two fingers over his tie knot. "Bob,'' he said quietly, and pulled him closer. "If Greer's okay, I'm going to drop this hearing. I can't destroy three more lives because Coover destroyed one.'' Andrew could not conceal his hostility. "I'll watch the guy every step of the way until he retires, if I have to,'' he continued. "And you'll take a leave of absence and get some counseling. You'll pull it all together, Bob. Maybe one day I'll even begin to forget what you did to me. But I want you to tell Lauren. It'll be hard on her, but she'll cope.''

"Andy. I'm sorry.'' Bob sobbed brokenly. "I'll make it. I *can* pull my life together. You'd better go after Greer,'' he told him. "Neil was going straight back to London once he left her.''

"Left her where?''

"Someplace north of Trowbridge. I've got a map. Neil used to go there with friends years ago.''

Andrew felt his breathing speed up. "A town near Trowbridge? About two hours or so from here—a bit more? Is she at a hotel?''

"Relax, Andy. She's safe.''

"*Don't*—say that again,'' Andrew seethed.

"Okay,'' Bob said, recognizing Andrew was on the edge. "The map's of a wilderness area. It's very detailed. Neil made sure she had food and water and extra clothing. I'm sure she'll have enough sense not to try to walk out before morning. I—''

"You son of a bitch. Give me the map. *Now!*''

CHAPTER TWENTY

THE FLASHLIGHT picked up fresh wheel tracks in the turnaround. Andrew spread the survey map on the hood of the Mini and followed Bob's red line with a forefinger.

Bundling the crackly paper together in one hand, he struck out. What kind of man left a woman alone in the dark—in the middle of nowhere? He frowned savagely. He knew the answer to that question.

On the chart the line ran almost straight in from the left side of the lane, but trees and tangled undergrowth made it impossible not to dodge this way and that. At least he'd had the foresight to borrow a compass from Bob. He gritted his teeth and checked it. Still the right heading.

A circle marked the clearing where Neil had supposedly left Greer. It couldn't be far now. Andrew broke into a run, immediately slapping into a bush that poked at his calves through his suit pants.

He moved on more slowly. Bob's confession came and went in snatches. It was unreal. They'd known each other all their lives. How could he have been so blind? Andrew thought of Lauren, then Simonne. That little girl wasn't going to suffer if he could help it. The hearing must be stopped—Greer would wonder about his reasons but at least for now he'd have to put her off. Later, when he was sure there could be no danger of a slip, he'd tell her. She'd understand then.

A clearing opened in front of him. "Greer," he yelled. "Greer." There was no sound and he pressed his lips together. However he approached she was bound to be shocked. How many shocks could one human being take in two days?

Treading lightly, he started forward and circled the spongy area. Nothing. Muscles in his thighs trembled. He shaded the flashlight beam to study the map again. This had to be the right spot. What if she'd tried to walk out and gotten lost? It could take hours to find her. He'd better save the battery.

An instant before he clicked the light off an irregular shape caught his eye. "Greer," he said softly, then he called more loudly, "Greer." When there was no reply he shone a full beam on the silhouette. A bundle of something. With fingers that tangled together, he loosened the string around the package. A jumble of sweaters and carelessly wrapped sandwiches spilled out to the ground. A bottle of water rolled against a rock and broke into a tinkling spray of shards and liquid that hung, glittering, before it fell. How far would she get without food and water?

Andrew picked up an old army blanket. "You did it, Greer," he muttered aloud. "You wandered away in this maze. My poor darling." Which way would he go first?

A tentative touch in the center of his back brought him spinning around.

"I hid," Greer whispered. "I heard someone coming—or something. I was afraid it might be an animal."

"Ahh—" Andrew dropped the blanket and grabbed her. "Oh, Greer. My sweet, my love. I've never been so scared in my life."

She hugged him, laughing and hiccuping. "Me, either," she admitted, tightening her hold beneath his suit jacket. "He tied my hands and blindfolded me," she explained. "When I finally got loose I kept trying to find the way out, but it was dark and I didn't dare get too far from this place. Andrew, I knew you'd come for me."

"It took me forever to find the lane. I overshot it twice and backtracked before I saw any kind of gap big enough for a car." He felt her soft body pressed to his and closed his eyes.

"How *did* you find it?" she asked. "How did you know where he took me?"

Andrew's mind went blank. Of course she'd ask that. "I got a note," he said slowly. "As soon as I arrived at the administration building. It was a warning not to go on with the hearing." He said nothing more.

"Thank goodness they told you where I was. I don't think I'd ever have gotten away from here on my own."

Andrew kissed the top of her head and gazed into the darkness. He hated lying to her, even by omission. But Greer was out of danger now and there were still others to be protected. "All I want is to get you home." It wasn't all he wanted. The thought shamed and amused him.

"Take me there, Andrew."

Her face was turned up to his. With infinite care he lowered his lips over hers, grazing leisurely back and forth until their tongues met. Her belly moved into his hips and the fire in his loins was immediate. "Time out, darling," he said, turning her away firmly, grateful in that instant for the gloom, although she'd probably felt the beginning of his arousal.

Greer leaned against Andrew's side. What she wanted was to stay in his strong arms forever and to be with him when they exposed Winston Coover. They trod cautiously, following the flashlight's beam.

Inside the Mini, Andrew produced a thermos of coffee and two plastic mugs. He added a measure of whiskey from a flask to Greer's. "Drink that," he told her. "Wrap your hands around the mug."

The smell of the liquor wrinkled her nose as she took a sip. "I memorized his license number," she said. "He drove an early model Jaguar—at least I think it was. Dark green with a black convertible roof. Shouldn't be hard to trace."

Andrew snapped on the ignition and shot the car into gear so abruptly her coffee spilled. "Forget it," he said bluntly.

Her head pressed against the seat. "You aren't serious?" she responded. "Some maniac drives me to the middle of nowhere, ties me up and blindfolds me, then leaves. Forget it? No way. This is going to win your case hands down," she insisted. "We get back, give the information to the police, and watch Winston Coover get nailed. He deserves it, Andrew. You said he did and you were right. The man's a criminal."

"It doesn't matter anymore."

Greer looked at Andrew's profile. His nostrils were flared. "Since when?" she breathed. "This morning nothing would ever stop you from seeing the investigation through. Now it doesn't matter? What happened?''

He drove too fast. "It'll be better for everyone if I let it go.''

"I don't understand,'' Greer persisted, unbelievably confused. "I was kidnapped to stop you from persecuting Coover. That means you're right. And I want the whole world to know it.''

The car skidded around the intersection of the highway. "It's not necessary,'' Andrew maintained. "Coover's got less than two years before retirement. I can watch him. Why risk a big flap?''

She took a long thoughtful swallow of coffee. She was beginning to understand. "Why not?'' she challenged. "Because of me, right? Andrew...they've won. You're backing off because you're afraid they'll try something else with me.''

"Not entirely,'' he said evasively.

"What then?'' Greer was not about to drop it.

"There are other elements to consider,'' he said, beginning to run out of patience. "Can we leave it at that?''

"No,'' she replied firmly. "We can't leave it at that. These other elements. Is your professional reputation one of them? And what people think of you personally? Has the possibility of scandal finally gotten to you?''

"I didn't say that,'' Andrew responded calmly.

Blood hammered in her ears. "Andrew, is it all right for you to be with me as long as no one finds out about Ruby? Would it embarrass you if we married and someone discovered I was a bastard?''

"Hell.'' He braked so violently they both slammed into their shoulders belts. "What made you say a thing like that?''

"Would it?'' Greer insisted.

"That doesn't mean a thing anymore,'' he told her. "And no one's going to find out.'' Instantly Andrew regretted his words.

Greer breathed deeply. "So it's all right—as long as it never comes out? But it could,'' she insisted.

The hand brake creaked on and he flipped off the ignition. "I don't see how,'' Andrew responded.

"Okay. At least you admit you've considered it and decided the prospect's unlikely. But Ruby could get down on her luck and come looking for me.'' Greer glanced over her shoulder. "We can't stay at the side of the road like this. It's dangerous.''

"She'd never find you.'' Andrew said, trying to reason with her.

"There's always a chance.''

"Stop this, Greer,'' he shouted, finally exploding. "I don't care who your mother is, or your father.'' Andrew lowered his voice when he glimpsed the shimmering tears in Greer's eyes. "My mother left us when I was sixteen,'' he told her. "The man of the moment was twenty years her junior. I never saw her again. She's probably still living it up somewhere in the south of France but I don't even think about it—it doesn't make me feel less than I am.''

"That's different.'' Greer bit her lip to stop it from quivering. "At least you were legitimate. But you might have told me when you knew how low I felt about Ruby, just in case it helped make me feel less of an untouchable.''

Andrew put a hand on her shoulder, but she scooted close to the door. "Tell me what you want me to say?'' he said.

"That you've woken up to the fact that you don't want to be a social outcast after all,'' Greer said flatly. "And that if I show up at the hearing to testify on your behalf, my undesirable past could come out. They'd be bound to ask questions about me.''

"This is absolutely insane, Greer,'' Andrew said, crossing his arms. "How long did it take you to come up with this gibberish?''

Greer rolled down the window and emptied the rest of her coffee. "I need to get to Weymouth,'' she answered. "My train for London leaves early in the morning and I haven't finished packing.''

She jumped when he threw open the car door, then slammed it behind him with enough force to vibrate the steering column. He'd left on the headlights and she watched him stride ahead and stand with his back to her. She wasn't being fair suggesting he was a snob, but it was the only excuse she could think of to separate them. Regardless of what he said, he *was* giving up his convictions out of concern for her. She was trouble to Andrew Monthaven and he deserved better. All she could offer him was sex. Not social support and not the children he desperately wanted. Leaving him would be her gift, and eventually he'd thank her for it. And she had a sister to consider, a business that couldn't be duplicated in

England. They had no common ground and she'd already hurt him enough. For his sake, she must make the break quick and clean.

She saw Andrew turn and heard gravel scrunch with each measured footstep. He got in and started the engine. "We're going to Ringstead and then you'll talk to me," he said without preamble. "If it takes the rest of the night and all of tomorrow, we'll end up understanding each other."

"I'm going to Weymouth," she insisted.

"I'm driving, lady. And you'll go where I take you."

In her agitation Greer caught his sleeve and the car swerved. "Sorry," she muttered. "Don't keep this up, Andrew. It won't get us anywhere."

He ignored her and drove on. When she tried to speak again, he turned on the radio and she slumped into the corner. He intended to make his pitch, whatever it cost them, so why fight? Once he gave up she'd leave as planned and work at forgetting. Angry tears smarted behind her eyelids. Again it was forget-and-get-on-with-it time.

Greer was surprised when the car stopped at Ringstead. She must have dozed.

"Wait for me to come around," Andrew said, opening his door. "I'll have to get some sort of light out here. You can't see a thing at night."

She rubbed her forehead wearily. He was going to pretend their last conversation never took place.

"Give me your hand."

Don't touch me—please. When she didn't move, Andrew took her fingers from her face and pulled her gently from the car.

With each step, pressure mounted in her head. Another confrontation—more accusations and denials, and for what? They didn't belong together, no matter how much she wanted to believe otherwise. She had her life thousands of miles away, and his was here. Andrew would be grateful for her decision one day. Why couldn't he see it now and let her go quietly?

He opened the door and led her inside. "Do you want something hot or a drink?" he asked amicably.

"Nothing, thank you." It was easier if she didn't look at him.

"We'll go straight up then." The airiness in his tone sounded false. "I'm going to have a double of whatever I pick up first." Sighing deeply, he continued. "What a day. What a couple of days—and nights. You must be exhausted. I know I am."

I'm sorry this has to be so hard on you. "Neither of us has slept much for the past two nights, Andrew. I really do need to get a good night's rest before tomorrow. Would you mind—?"

"I'd mind," he interrupted her. "I mind every second of this hell you've decided to put me through."

They walked into the sitting room and Greer stood awkwardly, just inside the door. Andrew went directly to a glass-fronted corner cabinet and took out a decanter and two glasses.

Greer's stomach seemed to flatten against her spine. "I don't want anything," she mumbled.

He set down the goblets and splashed each half-full with liquor. "Brandy," he said, ignoring her. "It'll warm us up. I'll start the fire."

"Please, Andrew," she insisted. "Don't bother for me. I have to leave."

"You don't have to do anything," he shouted, then ran a hand over his face. "I know what's happening here, but I won't let it. Do you hear me? I won't let it."

"Don't shout," she whispered. "You seem like a stranger when you sound that way."

"I'm sorry." He took a long, audible breath. "I feel like a stranger to myself. None of this makes any sense and I feel so helpless. There's nothing standing in our way now, Greer. Nothing."

If only he were right. But his vision was distorted by a dozen elements he wouldn't allow himself to face. "Andrew," she said quietly. "For a while I agreed with you—a future for us seemed possible. But that was only because I wanted to believe it. There *are* things standing in our way. I'm not the complacent, lady-of-the-manor type. I need the niche I've made for myself in Seattle and I can't recreate it here." Greer's voice faltered, but she was determined to go on. "In time you'll come to understand what I mean—about other things that wouldn't work, too. Let's simply accept that they exist and not try to hash each one through. It's too painful—for both of us. Go to bed and sleep. Tomorrow it'll all look different. I can find my own way back to Weymouth.''

Andrew watched her intently, his face gradually darkening. He lifted a glass and swallowed without taking his eyes off her. "So reasonable,'' he said as he came toward her. "Take two aspirins, drink plenty of fluids and go to bed. You'll feel better in the morning.'' The tone of his voice sent shivers of alarm down her spine. "Sounds like one of my lines. Only nothing is going to be better in the morning if you aren't with me.''

"I can't be.''

He caught her elbow as she turned away. "You can't? Or you won't stay with me? You're running away.''

"No!''

His laugh cut into her heart. "Direct hit, my love? You *are* running away. And we both know the real reason. Don't you think it's time you admitted it—particularly to me?''

She walked a few paces from him and stood, staring blindly at the wall. "You don't know the real reason. You couldn't.'' Suddenly Greer knew she had no choice but to tell the truth. "I can't have another child,'' she said simply.

He didn't answer. Had she spoken too quietly? "I had a hysterectomy several months ago. I'm sterile.''

Andrew's glass clattered on the coffee table. "I know,'' he answered. "I've known since we were in Guernsey.''

The sound of her own thundering heart was deafening. "How?'' she asked him. "You never said anything.''

"It wasn't up to me to say anything,'' he told her. "You had to trust me enough to be honest. I knew when you did, you'd be ready to tell me about the surgery.'' Instead of the anger Greer had anticipated, Andrew's voice was filled with sadness. "I'd wondered about the second scar on your abdomen,'' he continued. "It all came together when I mentioned pregnancy. You went to pieces. And you were always edgy around Simonne. At first I thought I'd imagined that, but then I knew I hadn't. Being near children hurts you. I'm so sorry, Greer. I wish Colleen—''

"Shh.'' She swung sharply to face him. "I'm getting used to

it," she assured him. "I already have. And it doesn't hurt me to be with Simonne—I enjoy her. There was nothing anyone could have done about Colleen. No one's to blame." Please, let him understand she didn't want him to feel guilty.

He pressed her hand. "Why didn't you tell me before?"

"You should have children of your own, Andrew. I never met a man more suited to being a father."

She saw the angles of his elbows as he put his hands on his hips. "Thank you. You didn't answer the question."

"I can't give you those children."

"You were an adopted child."

"Yes."

"Your parents loved you as if you were their own," he said, reasonably. "Why can't we do the same thing? I've loved dozens of children who passed through my life. I could certainly love a couple I was lucky enough to keep."

"You make it all sound so simple," she told him. "But it's not, Andrew. You deserve the best and I can't give it to you. We don't belong together."

"You're making excuses to escape, my love." His tone cut her to the quick. "What is it with you? The risk? Are you afraid to let go and risk another total commitment in case it doesn't last forever?"

"Stop it," Greer blurted. "It's not that. I'm over that." Suddenly she was desperate to make him understand. "All the things I set out to do, I've done," she said firmly. "I know I'm a complete woman in every way but one. And I've accepted it. Children don't make me curl up inside anymore. My family isn't the fairy-tale group I'd hoped for, but at least I found and faced them, and in time I'll reconcile myself to that, too. I'm not running away," she insisted.

"I don't believe you," Andrew said, grabbing her arm painfully. "What about the risk? Aren't you afraid to love in case you lose again? Isn't that why you're trying to walk out on me?" His angry face was inches from hers.

Greer twisted from his grip and slumped into a chair. "I *was* afraid to let go of my feelings again," she said heavily. "But that was a mistake and I realized it. Not to love is a loss in itself.'' In the silence that followed, Greer could hear Andrew's heavy breathing. ''But sometimes we think we've found something perfect and it turns out to be all wrong,'' she went on. ''We confuse what we want with love, what we need with love, and a dozen other physical responses with—love. And that's what we did. Leave it at that, Andrew—let me go without turning this into something ugly. We've had special times together and I want to remember them.'' She appealed to Andrew, but his back was turned toward her. She knew he was terribly hurt and angry.

''Not good enough,'' Andrew said, without turning around. ''If you've achieved all your admirable goals—and you'd like to believe we could be together—why are you leaving?''

Greer reached for the second goblet. The mouthful of brandy she took was too large and she coughed while it burned her throat. ''I've got to,'' she said. Tearing eyes distorted his image. ''I've got a life in the States, a business. That's where I belong.''

''Crap,'' he spat, spinning to face her. ''There's nothing there to stop you being with me. You're running, Greer. You're terrified of something. For God's sake, tell me what it is.'' As their eyes met and held, the anger seemed to drain away. Greer dropped her head and rubbed her eyes wearily.

Andrew came to sit on the edge of the table and tried to hold her hand. ''If it makes you feel better to think I'm scared—fine,'' she said. ''But let's stop this. I can't take any more.''

''I could go to the States, you know. I've been offered jobs. I even considered some of them,'' he admitted.

She looked at him sharply. ''But you didn't take any of them. Why?''

''I was established here,'' he answered. ''And there was no reason then to consider them for personal reasons, although I always thought the opportunities were good. I could consider them now.''

''You're established here,'' Greer repeated slowly. ''How long would it be before you regretted giving up what you've worked for—giving up the chance to have your own children—giving up all this?'' She waved a hand around the room. ''You're English, Andrew, to the core.''

He raked his hair. "I'm a man to the core, and human. I want to be with you."

"But I don't want to see the day when you look at me and remember all I've caused you to give up. I couldn't stand it."

"Damn." With a jerk, he stood and went to the window seat. "My window on the world. Hah. I wish I had a glass ball and I could see ahead to a time when all this would be resolved—happily. What do I have to say to convince you?"

Greer joined him and placed a hand on his forearm. "That you'll continue the hearing against Coover," she said softly. "That you don't intend to do anything differently from the way you'd have done it if you'd never met me again."

"That's not possible," he answered. "Nothing remains the same and we have to make changes sometimes. Even if they hurt."

Cold wound around Greer's insides. And changes *do* hurt, she thought. For now what Andrew felt for her would be enough, but it would be wrong and ultimately destructive to allow what he suggested.

"Andrew," she said. "If you give up the hearing and then decide to take a job in the States, who'll keep an eye on Winston Coover? Not quite two years to retirement, isn't that what you said? You can't leave and I can't stay. That's it. I'll always—care about you." *Too much to ruin your life.*

RAIN SLASHED the smoky windows of the terminal satellite at Seattle-Tacoma Airport. The Pan Am 747 made a slow arch and nosed toward the building. Greer peered at shadows moving beyond the tinted glass, but couldn't make out faces. Casey would be there—probably already crowding the passenger entry doors. For the first time since yesterday a small glow of happiness eased the stricture in her throat. She was home.

The solid thud of the loading arm against the plane's fuselage started passengers rummaging in overhead bins. Ahead, a shaft of light flooded in as the door opened, and Greer struggled to her feet, avoiding reaching elbows and crushing bodies. She straightened and joined the shuffling line. *Smile.* Casey had no idea what had happened since they were last together. Some of it Greer would explain—maybe all in time. For now she would hit only the high points. Andrew's face formed a clear picture in her mind, his amber eyes steady and questioning. Greer inched forward. Forget him, she'd told herself constantly since they parted. There would be no forgetting him—ever.

"Greer! Greer—here we are."

She looked up as she left customs and saw Casey's blond head bobbing above the crowd. "Hi," she mouthed, struggling to raise a hand weighted down by a plastic duty-free sack.

Josh Field, relaxed and younger looking than she remembered, hauled her hand baggage to a chair as soon as he could reach her. "We've missed you, Greer," he said. She didn't remember thinking of his smile as boyish, but it was now. "Let's have a look at you."

Casey swooped before Josh could stand back and assess her. Greer held her tall sister and blinked back tears of happiness—and gratitude. Close inspection might give away the misery she intended to hide. Masks took time to fix firmly in place and she hadn't had enough time, yet. Makeup camouflaged shadows, but the pain her eyes would show if she wasn't careful.

"Oh, Case. It's so good to see you," she said sincerely. "I guess you'll finally let loose of this dark secret of yours. I've been aching to find out who the mystery man is."

"Let's get you home first," Casey hedged. "We're parked in the lot. I'll get the car while Josh helps with your luggage." Casey lifted Greer's carryon. "Aren't you going to ask if the shop's bankrupt yet?"

"Whoa," Greer demanded. "I can spot evasion tactics when I see them. *Who* is the guy—Jack the Ripper?"

Casey set the bag back on the chair and held out her left hand. A square emerald flanked by diamond baguettes glittered on her ring finger.

"It's gorgeous, Case," Greer enthused. "Whoever the guy is, he's got great taste and he knows nothing suits green eyes like oversize emeralds. If you get tendonitis from the weight we can always put your arm in a sling," she teased.

"Greer," Casey shushed her, turning bright red.

"What's the matter?" Greer widened her eyes at Josh. "I'm glad because my sister finally stops dating deadbeats and finds herself a rich husband, and she doesn't want me to congratulate her."

Josh laughed. He put one arm around Casey's shoulders, the other around Greer's. "I don't think Casey likes you talking about her fiancé as if he weren't here," he joked.

Greer looked from her sister's pink face to Josh's amused gaze. "You two?" She opened and closed her mouth several times. "You stinkers. Why didn't you tell me? I always thought you'd make a fantastic pair, but I was afraid to hope."

"You don't mind?" Casey smiled slowly.

"Mind?" Greer nearly shouted. "It's the best piece of news I've had in—a long time."

They stood together, arms entwined, bodies held in a close triangle. Casey must have been afraid she would resent the engagement to Josh. Greer allowed tears to mingle with her laughter. There was only one man she'd ever want, one man she could never bear to see with another woman, and she'd had to give him up.

CHAPTER TWENTY-ONE

IN THE DISTANCE a burst of red lights blossomed like a gaudy dandelion puff. Greer watched it mushroom and fade, then locked her car while another firework crackled.

Casey would have a fit if she knew she was out alone in the middle of the night, but jostling groups celebrating the New Year made her feel safe, anonymous.

New Year's Eve. Six weeks since she'd left England. Once it would have seemed impossible she'd be thinking of them as the longest weeks of her life.... She covered her ears and laughed when a couple stopped to blow a noisemaker at her.

Josh and Casey were at a party. They'd both urged her to go along, but she'd begged off, pleading a migraine. Her headache hadn't been quite that severe, but she'd needed an unshakable excuse to make them leave her alone tonight.

Greer crossed Pioneer Square, passing a circle of revellers dressed in costume. They revolved, first one way, then the other, singing a discordant, but wildly enthusiastic chorus of "Auld Lang Syne." Detonators exploded on nearby railroad tracks and she broke into a run.

Past the laughing faces. Past grabbing hands that tried to pull her into the conga line they'd begun to form. She didn't stop until she'd stumbled headlong into Post Street and down the steps to Britmania's forecourt.

Breathing heavily, she dug in her purse for the keys and let herself in. For seconds she stood in the darkness, waiting for her racing heart to slow.

Why hadn't she gone with Casey and Josh instead of deliberately making an opportunity to wallow in self-pity? She tossed back her hair and marched around the store, switching on every light. In the storeroom she shed her jacket, started coffee brewing and flipped on a portable radio. Soft jazz—the kind she and Andrew liked. *Damn*. She took a deep, calming breath through her mouth. Tonight she wouldn't think about Andrew.

Bumping her toes with each backward shuffle, she dragged a box into the shop. It had arrived a week earlier, one of several from England she'd put off opening. This was postmarked Salisbury. It would contain the items she'd ordered from the city's Cathedral Guild.

Greer sat on her heels and fished a penknife from the pocket of her white slubbed silk pants. She shouldn't be working in this outfit. It had been outrageously expensive and designed to lift her spirits. An aqua shirt, worn blouson-style, was cinched at the waist by a wide metallic sash in shades of cerise, aqua and black. This evening she'd thought of Andrew while she dressed. He would have looked at her appreciatively and commented on the way her eyes picked up the color of the shirt....

Should she call him? Greer stared at the phone, the palms of her hands instantly damp. Did she dare? It was New Year's Eve, a time for well-wishing, particularly to those you—love. Casey knew something of what had happened in England and had nagged Greer to contact Andrew. Love had turned her younger sister into a starry-eyed romantic. She attacked the box, slitting tape and peeling back flaps with feverish haste. To hear his voice would be so sweet, and such torture. It would only make her cry and achieve nothing for either of them. *If* he'd even speak to her after the way they parted. Anyway, it was after midnight in Seattle, Andrew would already have been in bed and asleep for hours. Soon he'd be waking up to that old alarm of his.

Andrew in bed—asleep. Greer sat on the floor. In sleep he looked abandoned, his arms thrown wide, hair tousled. He'd always tossed until all the covers were on her side of the bed. Several times she'd watched him covertly, feasted on his lithe body, the broad shoulders and narrow hips, the strongly muscled legs and arms. The mental picture made her insides flutter, but it wasn't sexual fulfillment she yearned for now, it was the sight and sound—the simple presence of the man who was constantly in her thoughts.

She reached into the box and removed several potbellied objects.

At first she looked at them absentmindedly, then smiled, remembering their appeal. Church mice. Tiny pottery critters with bristle whiskers and overlarge ears, their pointed noses jutting upward. Inexpensive items a child might enjoy or anyone else come to that. Greer decided a cathedral mouse was exactly what she needed on her own kitchen counter.

Beneath the mice she found a layer of clock replicas. Salisbury Cathedral had boasted the earliest known clock. A thirteenth-century contraption with no face. She wasn't sure how it told time, but started to line up several of its miniature copies on a shelf. Later, she'd read the brochure that came with them.

From the storeroom came the distinctive wheeze the percolator made when it was ready. Greer hoisted herself up and went to pour a cup of coffee. When the street door slammed, she almost dropped both pot and cup.

She hadn't locked the door. *Good grief.*

For an instant she considered shutting herself inside the tiny stockroom. No good. There wasn't any way to stop someone from coming in after her. A crawling sensation made her skin tingle. How *could* she have been so careless?

"Greer—are you in here?"

She froze. Coffee sloshed from the mug as she set it down slowly on the packing crate and pushed open the door.

"Greer Beckett!"

No one else had a voice like that. She stepped into the shop, threading and unthreading her fingers. "I'm here, Andrew," she whispered.

He carried a suitcase in one hand and an overnighter slung across his shoulder. Greer took another step and stopped. His tan raincoat was creased and hung open over a navy turtleneck and gray slacks. Shadow darkened his beard area, accenting high cheekbones and the clear lines of his mouth. He looked marvelous and only the field of silent appraisal between them stopped her from rushing to hold him.

"What are you doing here?" she managed at last.

He grinned broadly. "You never sent the decals for my car, so I decided I'd better come and get them."

A laugh caught in her throat. "Funny man. Everyone loves a clown." She blushed. "But what did bring you six thousand miles?"

His tired golden eyes flickered over her. "Needing to look at you," he answered. "To make up for six lousy weeks of not being able to look at you." Without glancing away he jerked a thumb over his shoulder. "That door should have been locked, Greer. Some maniac could wander in here."

"I forgot." *Because all I can concentrate on anymore is you.* Greer brushed dust from her pants before shaking back her hair and meeting his eyes again. "There must have been something else you wanted, Andrew," she said, determined to remain calm.

He dropped the bag from his shoulder and covered the space between them before she could react. His embrace crushed the air from her lungs and her senses immediately registered the familiar scent of his sweater against her cheek.

Cupping her face, he tipped it up toward his. "I came for my wife," he said tenderly.

Everything inside Greer fell away. "I'm not your wife," she whispered.

"But you will be, won't you? You do love me?"

Greer's heart plunged. "I...yes, I love you," she told him. "But what I said in England hasn't changed. I can't be responsible for your dropping everything you believe in. And I don't want to make you anxious or ashamed—ever."

Andrew smiled and shrugged out of his coat. "I want to kiss you, sweetheart. But I'd better cool off a bit or I'm likely to ravish you right here on your shop floor." He backed into the only chair in the room and pulled her onto his lap.

Greer studied his finely chiseled mouth, the grooves beside it, and let her eyes wander over his features slowly, too slowly. This couldn't be happening. Any second he'd say something that would shatter this beautiful bubble in time.

"You look so wonderful," he said.

So do you, Greer thought. She touched silver strands in the blue-black hair at his temple and moaned when he brought their mouths violently together. He turned her, cradling her body with his elbows and forearms, locking her to him until the heavy heat of desire invaded her very soul. Lips grazed. Tongues reached, softened to tease, then thrust their hard, demanding message. Fingers threaded through hair in tender desperation. And their bodies pressed together with a primitive force neither could control.

When they drew back, still holding each other's trembling shoulders, Greer's mouth felt swollen and the pulsing in her breasts swept downward between her legs. She tugged free and stood, turning her back. The chemistry would always be there, but it wasn't enough. After a lengthy pause, Andrew cleared his throat and spoke.

"I couldn't get a direct flight to Seattle," he said. "Had to come via New York or I'd have gotten in this afternoon. I found your home number but there was no reply. Coming here was a last ditch effort to reach you tonight. I really thought you'd be at a party."

"Why would I be at—oh, New Year's Eve." She felt disoriented, foolish.

"Greer," Andrew said softly. "There are things I've got to tell you."

"You're tired, Andrew. You should sleep first." It was too soon. She needed time to regroup.

"Sleep?" he echoed. "Oh, I don't think so, my love. I don't intend to sleep again until I've said everything I came to say."

My love—my love. Greer spun to face him. "I just made coffee. And I need some if you don't."

She went to pour a second cup, pausing in the doorway before rejoining him. His eyes were closed, his head resting against the chair back. An invisible hand twisted her heart. "*My* love," she mouthed silently.

"Drink this," she said, sinking to the floor in front of him. She held up a mug.

"Thanks." Andrew sat straighter. "I'm going to get out all I have to say fast," he warned her. "The strain of keeping it in and feeling totally alone is more than I can stand any longer. And I'm not very proud of some of it," he added.

Greer raised her brow, but said nothing.

"Remember how I accused you of not trusting me?"

She nodded.

"Well. After you left I realized I'd done my own share of holding things back," he admitted. "If I'd trusted you enough and told you the whole story that night we parted, I could have saved us both a lot of heartache." Steam from the mug veiled his face briefly when he drank. "The hearing did go on in the end."

They both heard her intake of breath. Greer smiled up at him. "You decided to do it after all. Andrew, I'm so glad."

"It wasn't me," he told her. "It was Michael Drake's family who insisted on it. Isn't that something? You think decisions are in your hands—that you're in control—but it doesn't always work out that way. After what I'd said to Michael's parents, they decided to demand the case be heard. And Coover's negligence came out, his steady loss of interest in his work. They took away his license—not that it'll hurt anything but his inflated ego. The guy's filthy rich. The surgeon and pathologist got suspensions and an operating-room nurse was reprimanded—all for concealing evidence."

Greer dropped her forehead to her knees. "Thank God. But I don't see what that has to do with trust between us."

Andrew's fingers parted the hair at her nape and he rubbed slowly back and forth beneath her collar. "That's because I'm still skirting it." Pausing briefly, to kiss her neck, he went on. "I didn't want to go on with the hearing because of Bob. Or maybe more because of Lauren and Simonne." When she lifted her head, he smoothed the side of her face and hooked a knuckle beneath her chin. "The man who took you away was Bob's—friend, Neil Jones. It was Bob who was determined to stop that hearing."

"But why?" Greer frowned. "I don't understand. It always puzzled me that he didn't back you up, but I began to believe it was out of concern for you. He came to me, Andrew," she admitted. "He looked awful and begged me to stop you from ruining your career. Only I knew how much getting at the truth meant to you, and I couldn't bring myself to interfere."

Andrew gnawed his bottom lip and touched his forehead briefly to hers. "I should have told you."

"Told me what? Don't drag this out, Andrew," she said, moving away to see his face more clearly.

"Bob's bisexual," he said bluntly. When Greer tried to interrupt him with questions, he stopped her. "Please don't stop me until I get through all this." Taking a deep breath, he continued. "He confessed it to me after Jones took you from Ringstead. Neil and Bob were—damn it, I hate this. They were lovers at Cambridge. Bob straightened out and married, and everything went just fine until he ran into Neil again a couple of years ago. They've been seeing each other whenever Bob had an excuse to go to London. I never knew anything about it, but I did share a house with both of them while we were in college." Greer squeezed Andrew's hand in encouragement, and he raised it to his lips for a brief kiss.

"When Coover was looking for mud to sling at me—hoping to get me off his back—one of his henchmen stumbled across Neil and made a connection with me. I'd even seen Neil myself—in a restaurant a few months ago. They were going to make something out of that—or so Bob said. But what really had Bob running scared was the possibility that the truth about his private life would come out and ruin both him and his family. Neil played on that, threatened to incriminate Bob at the hearing if he didn't pay him off. Bob paid, but the hearing was still a threat and he tried to get at me through you, to stop the thing. That's it. I was afraid if the hearing took place and Neil was brought into it, Bob would be destroyed professionally, and Lauren and Simonne with him—and the baby they're expecting."

A pall of silence thickened in the tiny shop.

Tears sprang suddenly to Greer's eyes. "Lauren loves him," she said, thinking of her friend. "I don't understand how a man could do that to his family. And Simonne. Good Lord, Andrew—what will it do to them?"

He stood and hauled her to her feet. "They'll be all right," he assured her. "Bob's name never came up when the case was heard. Too many other people were scrambling to save themselves. It all sounds impossible when you first hear it, but Bob's a strong man."

She shook her head.

"He is, Greer. He's had a rough time, but he knows what he wants now."

"I don't see how they can work it out," she said miserably. "Hold me, please."

Andrew folded her close, rocking gently. "Bob's taken a leave of absence," he explained. "He's going to get counseling. All they know at the hospital is that he's exhausted and needs a complete rest."

"Lauren knows the truth?"

His fingertips traced her spine. "Yes. Bob told her. She's got guts, that lady. A lot of women would have been blown away, but not Lauren. As long as I've known her she's been Bob's shadow. Now she's the strong one. It'll work," he said with conviction.

"You didn't want me to go to the police about that man in case they found him and he told them about Bob," she said as she sought the rough skin along his jaw with her lips.

"Can you forgive me for not telling you at the time? I was so afraid of a slip and I'd promised Bob I'd make sure there wouldn't be one."

"I forgive you—I understand. It took me weeks to be open with you. Oh, Andrew." The insistent brushing of his thumbs on the sides of her breasts sent her against him, and she felt the slight rotation of his hips against her stomach.

Andrew's breathing quickened. "Leaving England and coming to you was the one way I could think of to prove how much I love you."

"Leaving England?" Greer leaned away. "What do you mean?"

"Just that, my darling. I told you I'd been offered jobs in the States before. When I contacted your children's hospital here they told me there was a position available if I wanted it. I said I did and started packing. My place in Dorchester has already been filled."

Greer stared at him. "You've given up everything you worked for?" she said, struggling to believe this was really happening. "It isn't fair. That's why I couldn't stay with you—you have too much to lose. And for what? I don't have enough to offer."

"Mmm." He inched the neck of her shirt aside and bent to kiss her softly swelling flesh. "You're wrong," he whispered. "*You* had too much to lose, and everything to offer: yourself. It wouldn't be

easy for you to start again in England. It *will* be easy for me here—
and exciting. Opportunities for research and really achieving something in my field exist here. They aren't so plentiful in England."
Andrew continued to explore the front of her shirt, pushing the
silken material aside as he went. "Can we talk about this more
later?" he said thickly.

"You intend to live here?" His mouth found her nipple and she
shuddered.

"Only if you'll let me."

She slid a hand around his neck. "What about children?"

"One step at a time," Andrew said, fondling her hair. "We don't
have to settle everything this instant."

"Darn," Greer laughed, then sniffed. "I'm going to cry."

"You're so beautiful when you cry, Greer," he said as he
straightened. The muscles beside his mouth trembled. "For the second or third or who knows how many times—will you *please* be
my wife?"

He closed his eyes and she stood on tiptoe to kiss each lid.
"Yes," she said. "Yes."

"I BEGAN TO WONDER if we'd ever be alone." Andrew crossed the
room and threw himself flat on the bed. "Come here, Mrs. Monthaven."

Greer poured champagne into two fluted glasses and handed one
to Andrew, evading his reaching fingers. "Not until I at least get
to put on the confection my sister bought me to wear on my wedding night," she said.

"Do it then," Andrew ordered, grinning wickedly. "But it's a
waste of time."

In the bathroom she unpinned the corsage of baby Hawaiian or-
chids from her mohair lace jacket. Carefully, she filled a water glass
and propped the flowers inside. The short jacket and floating chif-
fon dress were of palest ivory, and the only jewelry she wore was
a single strand of pearls and matching earrings—a gift from Josh.

The three weeks they'd spent clearing away formalities for this
day had seemed endless while they lasted. Tonight Greer hardly
remembered them. Finally she and Andrew were where they be-

longed. Together. She was glad they had chosen to remain in Seattle for their honeymoon. Andrew wanted to learn as much as possible about the area and there was still a lot he hadn't seen.

While she undressed she relived the simple wedding ceremony in a small church near the condominium she and Casey had shared. Andrew's face came to her clearly, the tender, almost tremulous expression in his eyes when he slid the ring on her finger and the tears of happiness he'd made no attempt to hide while she placed his.

Casey's gift was made of shimmering amethyst satin. Greer slid the gown over her head and let it fall sensuously over her body. Spaghetti straps, no thicker than threads, held the classically cut bodice in place—just. The fabric scintillated over every curve and indent, outlining her erect nipples, the dip at her navel, the mound between her legs. She ran her hands over the sleek surface and colored slightly. She wanted to excite him, to draw them both closer and higher than they'd ever been.

Andrew was no longer on the bed when she emerged. Sheer curtains billowed inward from the Edgewater hotel room's open windows. She picked up her glass and went out onto the veranda. He stood with his elbows on the railing, staring toward Elliott Bay.

"Hi," she said. "You'll freeze out here."

He turned to look at her. "Not with you looking like that. But you will." Quickly he draped his jacket around her shoulders and clinked his glass to hers. "To the moontide."

Greer pressed close and shuddered as his hand surrounded her breast beneath the gown. She couldn't think. He kissed her mouth while his fingers avidly caressed her yearning flesh.

"Drink," he ordered at last.

She took a sip and tried to remember his toast. "What are we drinking to?"

He moved behind her, wrapping an arm around her ribs. "See the way the moon makes a vivid blue path on the incoming tide," he whispered into her hair. "I've always thought of it as the moontide. I told you how I used to watch it do that on Ringstead Bay. The first time I saw you your eyes reminded me of my moontide."

"I'm glad we can go to your house whenever we want to," she said. "It wouldn't seem right if you'd given it up completely."

Andrew rested his chin atop her head. "Gibbs will keep the home fires burning. We'll go there regularly—if you want to."

"I'll want to." She smiled and wriggled to face him. "Let's go to bed."

"Anything you say." He led her inside and within seconds the ethereal gown was an iridescent puddle at Greer's feet. He shed his own clothes and settled her on the bed, stretching his length beside her while he stroked every inch of her waiting body.

Their lovemaking was languorous at first, then frenzied, its explosive climax leaving them spent and clinging, damp limbs entwined.

"Sweetheart," Andrew said when their hearts and breathing calmed. "When you left after Colleen died, there was no light in your eyes, only pain. I used to dream over and over again of finding a way to awaken the moontide in them."

"You found the way, darling—loving me."

Tyler Brides

It happened one weekend...

Quinn and Molly Spencer are delighted to accept three bookings for their newly opened B&B, Breakfast Inn Bed, located in America's favorite hometown, Tyler, Wisconsin.

But Gina Santori is anything but thrilled to discover her best friend has tricked her into sharing a room with the man who broke her heart eight years ago....

And Delia Mayhew can hardly believe that she's gotten herself locked in the Breakfast Inn Bed basement with the sexiest man in America.

Then there's Rebecca Salter. She's turned up at the Inn in her wedding gown. Minus her groom.

Come home to Tyler for three delightful novellas by three of your favorite authors: Kristine Rolofson, Heather MacAllister and Jacqueline Diamond.

HARLEQUIN®
Makes any time special ™

Visit us at www.eHarlequin.com   PHTB_T

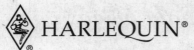

HARLEQUIN®

makes any time special—online...

eHARLEQUIN.com

your romantic
books

♥ Shop online! Visit Shop eHarlequin and discover a wide selection of new releases and classic favorites at great discounted prices.

♥ Read our daily and weekly Internet exclusive serials, and participate in our interactive novel in the reading room.

♥ Ever dreamed of being a writer? Enter your chapter for a chance to become a featured author in our Writing Round Robin novel.

• • • • • •

your romantic
life

♥ Check out our feature articles on dating, flirting and other important romance topics and get your daily love dose with tips on how to keep the romance alive every day.

• • • • • •

your
community

♥ Have a Heart-to-Heart with other members about the latest books and meet your favorite authors.

♥ Discuss your romantic dilemma in the Tales from the Heart message board.

your romantic
escapes

♥ Learn what the stars have in store for you with our daily Passionscopes and weekly Erotiscopes.

♥ Get the latest scoop on your favorite royals in Royal Romance.

HINTA1_TR

Spines will tingle...mysteries await...
and dangerous passion lurks in the night
as *Reader's Choice* presents

DREAM SCAPES!

Thrills and chills abound in these four romances
welcoming readers to the dark side of love.
Available January 2001 at your
favorite retail outlet:

THUNDER MOUNTAIN
by Rachel Lee

NIGHT MIST
by Helen R. Myers

DARK OBSESSION
by Amanda Stevens

HANGAR 13
by Lindsay McKenna